always forever

Also by Mark Chadbourn

The Kingdom of the Serpent:
Jack of Ravens

The Dark Age:
The Devil In Green
The Queen of Sinister
The Hounds of Avalon

The Age of Misrule:
World's End
Darkest Hour
Always Forever

Underground
Nocturne
The Eternal
Testimony
Scissorman

always forever

book three of
the age of misrule

MARK CHADBOURN

an imprint of Prometheus Books
Amherst, NY

Published 2009 by Pyr®, an imprint of Prometheus Books

Inquiries should be addressed to
Pyr
59 John Glenn Drive
Amherst, New York 14228–2119
VOICE: 716–691–0133, ext. 210
FAX: 716–691–0137
WWW.PYRSF.COM

13 12 11 10 09 5 4 3 2 1

Library of Congress Cataloging-in-Publication Data

Chadbourn, Mark.
Always forever / by Mark Chadbourn.
p. cm. — (The age of misrule ; bk. 3)
First published: London : Gollancz, an imprint of Orion Publishing Group, 2001.
ISBN 978–1–59102–741–6 (pbk. : alk. paper)
I. Title.

PR6053.H23A79 2009
823'.914—dc22

2009013236

Printed in the United States on acid-free paper

contents

all the news

by max michaels

We're a cynical race. With remarkable ease we manage to find the worst in everyone we meet. Charity workers selflessly slave amongst the poor in a disease-ridden quarter of some stinking tropical city. They get spotted kicking a dog or yelling at some unfortunate on a bad day that has somehow surpassed all the other bad days and instantly we're tearing them apart for being less than worthy. Where does that come from? Is it some kind of repressive religious thing slammed into us during schooling, where everyone is a sinner unless they're a saint? Look around—the world out there is a nightmare; the same as before, I suppose, only different. It's a struggle for anyone to get through it, but we carry on, trying to do the best we can under the circumstances. We're all deeply flawed—that's our nature. But if we fight to overcome those flaws, surely that's worth some praise, isn't it? The only time to make any judgment—and maybe not even then—is at the end of someone's life, when you can stand and look back, weighing all the good things and the bad things and the overwhelming majority of thoroughly mundane things, and decide whether it was a life well lived. Let me tell you now, you won't find many saints. I bet you won't find any at all. But you will find a preponderance of fundamentally good people striving to be the best they can. And isn't that the kind of thing we should be celebrating: not that someone is good, but that they're fighting to be better.

So let's talk about heroes.

The worst always brings out the best in people when they're pushed to the edge and find reserves they never realized existed in their day-to-day lives. And these are, indeed, the worst of times, so it's hardly surprising that in the midst of them we found the best of heroes. Just normal folk, like you and me, with the usual bundle of neuroses and weaknesses, but they've proved themselves to be champions. (Excuse the gushing language: it's not *modern*, and it's not *British*, and it's not *cynical*. But then, that's the point I'm making.) I'm writing this so the record of their deeds is preserved to inspire future generations. Is that a pretentious hope? I don't know, but it's important to me that I do it.

If you'd met them on the street in the time before the Big Change, you probably wouldn't have given them the time of day. Jack Churchill, Church to his friends, was moody and introspective, driven to the edge of despair by the suicide of his girlfriend, Marianne, two years earlier. That act had thrown his entire life off course. He'd been an archaeologist and a writer with massive potential, but he ended up going nowhere, losing his friends, his hope. Ruth Gallagher was a lawyer for some big-shot firm—sharply intelligent, as you would expect, but a little repressed, with a problem finding any relationship to match her exacting standards. Although she'd achieved a great deal for someone in her late twenties, she didn't feel fulfilled. She'd only taken on her career to please her beloved father, who'd died of a heart attack after learning his brother had been murdered in a bungled building society robbery. Laura DuSantiago was probably the most complex and misunderstood of all of them. By all counts, she was a sociopath and misanthrope with a past blighted by drugs and petty crime. Her acid tongue and sarcastic manner made it almost impossible to like her. At the same time she was brilliant with technology, and once you broke through the unpleasant exterior you found reasons for her attitude and the constant confusion that obscured her true nature: as a child she'd been to hell and back at the hands of a mother who used religious obsession to mask her growing psychoses; Laura's body and mind were left scarred in the process. And in a struggle with her mother in the family home she had woken from unconsciousness to find her mother dead, seemingly by Laura's hand.

Shavi—no one ever found out his full name—was certainly the most well balanced of the five. An Asian who grew up in a strictly Muslim family, he was eventually cut off by his father when he refused to accept his religion and traditional ways. A lifetime of searching followed, during which Shavi dabbled in every religion and explored every occult and New Age byway. It left him a deeply philosophical and spiritual man, and the solid moral core of the group. He was a neo-hippie, enjoying his mind-expanding drugs, espousing free love with men or women. Like the others, however, there was a darkness in his life. As he left a London gay club with his boyfriend, Lee, he was attacked by someone he couldn't identify in the dark. Lee was brutally murdered.

And then there was Ryan Veitch, a hard-bodied, hard-minded thug who grew up in a South London family of petty criminals. His childhood had been troubled by vivid dreams that he'd only been able to exorcise by having their images tattooed on his body. His mother died when he was young, leaving him and his brothers to make up for a father so traumatized by his wife's death he was unable to keep a job and barely able to hold the family together. It was hardly surprising that he viewed crime as the only option to survive. But then the young Veitches made the mistake of bungling a building society robbery. In the confusion Ryan fired his shotgun and an innocent man died—Ruth's uncle, one of the many *coincidences* that are thrown up in this new age. But, as we all know, there are no coincidences. Growing up under different circumstances, Ryan might have been a very different person. He showed great remorse for the murder, and from then on, every waking moment was spent trying to make up for his crimes, "to do the right thing" as he constantly told everyone. More than any of them he *wanted* to be a hero, to get the girl, the acclaim. To be good.

But that was their lives *before*. In the cauldron of hardship that came after the world changed they all found what their true characters really were. And in a way, that underlines the subtext of what I'm saying here: you should never judge a book by its cover, and although that's a bit of a cliché, it serves a point. You can't trust your perception at all; there's always something going on behind the scenes. So if you can't trust what you see, hear, smell, touch, taste, what should you do? Trust your heart, I say. Trust your heart. But I'm getting beyond myself. . . .

It started one cold, misty night beneath Albert Bridge on the banks of the Thames. Church and Ruth came across what at first sight was a mugging: a minor Ministry of Defence official, Maurice Gibbons, was being attacked by a giant of a man. Then the attacker's face appeared to melt. It changed into something monstrous, and Church and Ruth both blacked out at the sight. The incident turned their world on its head, though we all know what the creature was now—one of the unbelievably ancient race of shape-shifters that passed into Celtic myth as the misshapen, demonic Fomorii, things so alien to us our brain can barely give form to the signals it receives whenever we see them. Our mind fakes up the image the best it can, or it simply shuts down and buries the hideous experience in the subconscious, where it gnaws away like a maggot. Church and Ruth were so troubled by this process they were forced to delve into it further, eventually ending up at the studio of Kraicow, an artist who had seen the same kind of thing. He confirmed their worst suspicions.

The shock drove them on the road in search of Laura, whom Church had come across on the Internet and who seemed to have information which might help them; this was after Church glimpsed the ghost of Marianne outside the flat they used to share.

The Fomorii were on their tails immediately. The two of them were saved from certain death by Tom, on the surface a burnt-out hippie. It's hard to believe, but he was actually the mythic figure Thomas the Rhymer, hundreds of years old, gifted with the curse of second sight and The Tongue That Cannot Lie. The old stories said he was taken into the Land of Faerie, where time passes differently from here, by the Queen of Elfland. And like all the old stories, it captured the essence, if not the whole truth. He did spend time in that strange place, certainly, but no human could have come close to describing the extent of his experiences there. It was, by all accounts, a time of both pleasure and pain. He was "taken apart and rebuilt," suffering so incredibly his mind was scarred. It gave him his strange powers but left him completely detached from humanity; the loneliest man in the world, of neither here nor there.

While traveling west, the three companions were attacked by a flying, fire-breathing serpentine creature from the storybooks. This Fabulous Beast drove them to take refuge at Stonehenge, where that site's particular powers made them invisible to its attentions. And it was there Tom told them what was at first an unbelievable tale: of how myths and legends are the secret history of the world. Every creature that ever slithered through our dreams and nightmares into old stories actually existed, though perhaps not in forms we knew. And he told the oldest story of all, one that has become preserved in every culture: of a tremendous war between two opposing powers—the Fomorii, known as the Night Walkers, a force of entropy determined to drive all existence into darkness and chaos, and the Golden Ones, known by the Celts as the Tuatha Dé Danann, as hypnotically beautiful as the Fomorii were monstrous. Angels and demons, if you will. But the Tuatha Dé Danann were as alien to us as the Fomorii—unpredictable, unknowable, beyond all concepts of good and evil, and therefore just as dangerous.

The struggle between the Golden Ones and the Night Walkers almost devastated the world in antiquity, but at what the Celts called the second battle of Magh Tuireadh, the Fomorii were defeated. The postwar deal meant both sides vacated this planet for that strange place where the laws of physics don't seem to work—Faerie, Otherwords, T'ir n'a n'Og, Heaven and Hell, whatever name you prefer—and they took with them almost all the other creatures of myth. The deal was that they would never return. But some of them managed to sneak back for brief visits through the liminal zones, the lakes, the hilltops, the stone circles, where the division between our two worlds were thinnest, explaining all our history of supernatural phenomena from ghosts to UFOs to lake monsters.

The deal held reasonably well for millennia, until, through some process no one quite understands, the Fomorii broke through once again. They unleashed a tremendous force, the Wish-Hex, which trapped some members of the Tuatha Dé Danann in exile and brought some under Fomorii control; only a handful escaped.

But our own world was not without its own defences. Running through everything is a strange energy that manifests itself as a blue fire. The Chinese know it as *chi*; other cultures call it something different, but every race has an understanding of it. It's the lifeblood of the planet, the lifeblood of *us*, an overpowering spiritual force that heals and uplifts. The Fiery Network is in everything, but it is most evident at certain potent sites which have become sacred down the years—the places where our ancestors erected stone circles, or our greatest cathedrals. Over the years we lost touch with this force, and became the worse for it. In all but the most powerful places it grew dormant. The Fabulous Beasts, as the ancient Chinese knew, were both symbolic of the earth energy and guardians of it, following the lines across the land, living on the energy it gave off. These remarkable creatures had awakened with the return of the Fomorii, but the one which attacked Church, Ruth, and Tom had fallen, briefly, under the power of the Fomorii; it was too powerfully independent to be controlled for long, though.

And, too, there were human avatars of the Blue Fire, the Brothers and Sisters of Dragons, humans within whom the spiritual force burned most brightly. In ancient times they helped defend the world, and now, Tom said, they had been resurrected. There would be five in total, and Church and Ruth were two of them. The five were found by the Blue Fire and it was up to them to defend the world, however reluctant they felt about this task. But their job wasn't just defence; there was another side to it too. Prophecies linked to the old Arthurian legends spoke of a king awaking in Britain's darkest hour to save the land. Like so many other aspects of myth, this was a metaphor. The king was the spiritual force in the land and it was up to the Brothers and Sisters of Dragons to wake it from its slumber. Those tales of King Arthur actually proved a secret guide; sites linked to Arthur were places potent in the spirit power. The stories themselves told in their complex code how the earth energy and its champions defended the land and how it fell into dormancy, waiting to be called back again at a time of greatest need.

Understandably, Church and Ruth found it difficult to assimilate all this new information, especially when it went against the way they had been taught to see the world since childhood. But how could they deny the evidence of their eyes?

As they slept in Stonehenge that night, Church was visited by the spirit of Marianne once again, and this time she left him a gift: an unusual black rose, the *Roisin Dubh*. He took it, not realizing what it meant.

In Salisbury they encountered Laura for the first time. But they were also pursued by frightening aspects of the supernatural: the demonic black dog, Old Shuck, which acts as precursor to the Wild Hunt of legend, fabled for hunting down lost souls, as well as the Baobhan Sith, ghostly, bloodsucking creatures of the night. And Ruth had her first encounter with the goddess who would eventually become her patron, the mysterious triple nature deity that manifested as maiden, mother, and crone.

They also had what would prove to be a fateful encounter with a strange wanderer who called himself Callow. On first impression, he seemed merely eccentric, speaking in a theatrical manner, constantly trying to wheedle free drinks and food; harmless enough.

Laura took Church, Ruth, and Tom to a depot on an industrial estate where she had had a life-changing experience. The place looked mundane, but the depot was being run by the shape-shifting Fomorii for distribution of canisters filled with a foul black gunk. Church and Laura plunged through a hole in the air, finding themselves in the Watchtower, a structure suspended in space and time, somewhere between our world and the Otherworld. Here Church experienced several troubling, prophetic visions before encountering Niamh, one of the Tuatha Dé Danann who had escaped the Fomorii's Wish-Hex. Beautiful and enigmatic, Church felt he knew her instantly, which in a way he did. She had been visiting him at night throughout his childhood, preparing him for his role as a Brother of Dragons, although he had always thought her a dream. She told him everything about the Tuatha Dé Danann and what was expected of him: to find four mystical objects of power hidden for aeons. They were the sword, spear, stone, and cauldron—or Grail—which had played such a part in all our legends, and they were the only things that could free the exiled Tuatha Dé Danann. And *they* were the only ones who could repel the Fomorii; humanity stood no chance alone, she said. She gave him the Wayfinder, a magic lantern with a flame of the Blue Fire that would point him in the direction of the artifacts.

Church and Laura returned to Earth, only to find the depot in flames and Tom disappeared. They picked up Ruth and headed to the first location: Avebury. There they met the strange, old man known only as the Bone Inspector. He was caretaker of the country's ancient sites and the last in a very long line of wise men driven underground at the time of the Roman invasion. He led them beneath the stone circle to the main source of the Blue Fire in the south, and the home of the oldest Fabulous Beast. There Laura reclaimed the first of the artifacts, the Stone of Fal, rumoured to be able to recognize the true king of the land; it screamed when Church touched it, the first sign of his destiny.

Leaving the Bone Inspector behind, they headed east. They were halted by the inexplicable failures of technology that had been happening randomly since the change came over the world, stranded with their useless car just outside Bristol. After making camp, Church encountered a young girl named Marianne who gave him a cheap locket containing a picture of Princess Diana. Church felt a connection to the bright, optimistic child, not in the least because her name was the same as his dead girlfriend.

That night Ruth encountered the goddess again, who asked Ruth to look for the missing other half of the nature deity. Ruth fled in terror, but not before the goddess gifted her a *familiar* in the form of an owl.

The next day they were forced to rush the now-comatose Marianne to hospital. She had been living for months with a blood clot close to her brain. Before, it had been too dangerous to operate, but now only a touch-and-go op could save her. Not long after she went into the theatre, another technology failure struck and the hospital was plunged into darkness and chaos.

But then a remarkable thing happened. Somehow Marianne made her way from the operating theatre to cure an entire cancer ward with some power from within her. It manifested as a brilliant white luminescence, like a lightbulb burning itself out. She died immediately afterwards. It was almost as if she had wanted to commit some last act of goodness before moving on. This affected Church deeply. It showed that the change wasn't all bad; miraculous, wonderful things could happen too. He kept her locket as a reminder of that day.

They followed the lantern south until they came to an inn in the centre of Dartmoor where they planned to stay the night. But as they rested, the terrible, otherworldly Wild Hunt attacked. This shadowy troupe on horseback was led by the goblin-like Erl-King and was accompanied by a pack of devilish hounds. Many people at the inn were slaughtered by the Hunt's cruel weapons. Church fled across Dartmoor on a motorbike to try to draw the Hunt away, while Ruth and Laura drove off in the opposite direction, but Church hadn't gone far before he plunged into one of the abandoned mineshafts that dot the moor.

Not long after, Ruth and Laura encountered Shavi for the first time, and the three of them embarked on a desperate race across the countryside, with the Hunt in hot pursuit. They escaped only with the coming of the dawn, eventually winding up in Glastonbury.

Meanwhile, Church found himself imprisoned in a Fomorii den, deep beneath Dartmoor. His cellmate was Ryan Veitch, who had been captured earlier, and soon Tom was brought into the cells too; he had suffered greatly at the hands of the Fomorii since his capture in Salisbury. It wasn't long before Church met Calatin, the Fomorii half-breed and leader of one of the main factions, or tribes, in the Fomorii hierarchy. If you can attribute any human abstract to the Fomorii, it would be Evil, but Calatin was worse than the others, somehow. Perhaps it was just the fact he looked less twisted on the surface, so that whatever lay beneath was amplified. He put Church through appalling torture in search of information, but Church gave nothing away.

There seemed little hope for them until Niamh appeared in the cells, identifying herself firmly as Church's patron. She helped them to break out into a maze of tunnels with the Fomorii hot on their heels, and finally they made their way out across Dartmoor. Soon after, Church made the shocking discovery that his girlfriend, Marianne, had not committed suicide; she had been murdered. He vowed to find her killer.

Glastonbury turned out to be the location of another talisman, so Ruth, Laura, and Shavi continued the search. In the grounds of the Chalice Well, they encountered a man of the cloth named James, who doubled up his job with the Christian Church as a member of a secret society called Watchmen. The group had existed for centuries, perhaps millennia, with members drawn from various religious orders, generally operating independently of each other. Their role, I suppose, was as some kind of body to organize a defence against the supernatural powers represented by the Fomorii and the Tuatha Dé Danann, if they ever decided to return to our world. They were keepers of vital information that could be used in any coming fight, while at the same time overseeing important sites in the landscape, particularly areas where the Blue Fire was strongest; they all characterized that energy as their own religion's spiritual vitality. Perhaps it is.

James told them of the mysteries surrounding Glastonbury and of how the Grail was hidden beneath the Tor; not in an earthly space, but through some gateway into another place: T'ir n'a n'Og.

While this was happening, Church, Tom, and Veitch were trekking across Cornwall to Tintagel, the legendary home of King Arthur. There they found the mystical Sword Caledfwlch, but before they could get away, they were trapped on a cliff top by a Fomorii force led by Mollecht, the leader of another tribe. Mollecht was a sorcerer, but his experiments to gain greater power had done something terrible to him. His body had completely disappeared and the only thing preventing his life force from dissipating was a murder of crows constantly flying in a tight, ritual pattern around it. A figure made up of swirling crows must have been frightening enough, but then the crows parted to allow a burst of that awesome power. With no way to turn, Tom dragged the other two over the cliff into the churning sea below.

On top of Glastonbury Tor, Ruth, Laura, and Shavi were shocked to see Church and the others fall out of the sky, heaving up sea water at the highest point in the surrounding landscape. In a last desperate act, Tom had summoned up all his power and knowledge and moved the three of them along the lines of earth energy between two potent nodes, Tintagel and Glastonbury. It showed the potential of what they all could achieve if they learned to master the Blue Fire, but even Tom said he didn't know if he could repeat the act without the pressure of death at his back.

Introductions made, they opened the doorway and crossed over to T'ir n'a n'Og, where they recovered the cauldron—the Grail—from a mysterious structure.

Their next destination was South Wales, where they found the last of the artifacts, the Spear of Lugh. With all four talismans, victory was within their grasp, but they still had to face up to the awful threat of the Wild Hunt. After a terrifying confrontation on a storm-swept night, it was Ruth who saved the day, showing a depth of character she hadn't before exhibited. She plunged the Spear into the chest of the Erl-King, the two of them rolling down a hillside out of sight. There Ruth witnessed an astonishing transformation as the Erl-King became Cernunnos, another nature deity; this was the "other half" for which the triple Goddess had been searching. Like all of the gods, Cernunnos had different aspects, and he had been trapped as the Erl-King by the Wish-Hex, becoming a tool of the Fomorii. He thanked Ruth for freeing him by burning his brand into her hand and promising to aid her if she ever needed him.

With the Wild Hunt departed, everything was in place for the return of the exiled Tuatha Dé Danann and the defeat of the Fomorii. But the next morning, while Laura guarded the talismans, she was attacked by Callow, who had been secretly stalking them since Salisbury. He had thrown in his lot with the Fomorii for the promise of greater power. He took the artifacts, but not before leaving Laura at death's door, one side of her face carved up by his razor.

After getting her barely adequate hospital treatment, they raced across country in pursuit of Callow and the talismans, eventually ending up in the Lake District. Here Tom revealed himself as an unwitting Fomorii tool, giving the group up to Calatin and Callow. While in the Dartmoor cells, the Fomorii had inserted a Caraprix into his head, one of the small, shape-shifting, symbiotic creatures which all the Fomorii and Tuatha Dé Danann carry. The Caraprix allowed Tom to continue his normal actions while subtly bending him to the Fomorii will and preventing him from revealing the truth about what had happened to him.

Escaping capture, Ruth hid in the house of a woman who showed her the potential of the powers promised by the Mother-Maiden-Crone. Ruth led the way in freeing the others from the Fomorii, aided unconsciously by Mollecht, whose desire for supremacy in the Fomorii hierarchy led to conflict amongst the opposing powers. Callow was left behind to pay the price of his failure.

The Brothers and Sisters of Dragons made their way to Melrose in Scotland where they crossed over once again to T'ir n'a n'Og, seeking to save Laura's life and free Tom from the Caraprix. They were aided by Ogma, one of the Tuatha Dé Danann, at his immense library that contained all the secrets of existence. It was here that Church finally consummated his doomed relationship with Laura.

With time running out, they returned to our world and set off for Dunvegan Castle on the Isle of Skye, where the ritual to free the Tuatha Dé Danann had to take place. Naturally the Fomorii did everything they could to stop them: the Skye bridge was destroyed; the Kyle of Lochalsh was in flames, their dark forces massed on the island. But the companions commandeered a boat to sail to the castle, where Church and Veitch guarded the approach while the others carried out the ritual.

Church, however, was severely debilitated. The Roisin Dubh gifted him by the spirit of Marianne was actually a mystical Fomorii item called the Kiss of Frost. Its icy power crept into his veins.

In a grim battle with Calatin, Church was slain, but his sacrifice allowed the completion of the ritual and the missing Tuatha Dé Danann returned. The Fomorii, sensing potential defeat, fled the scene. Beseeched by Ruth and Tom, Nuada, one of the Golden Ones, allowed the cauldron to be used to bring Church back to life. And so he was reborn, like one of the heroes from legend, with the taint of the Fomorii and the power of the Tuatha Dé Danann coursing through his veins.

As before, the victory that was so firmly in their grasp was snatched away. They had achieved everything expected of them, but still the returned Tuatha Dé Danann refused to help them to drive out the Fomorii, even though the two groups of gods were bitter enemies. The reason: the Fomorii corruption within Church made him a lesser person in their eyes, too tainted to be an ally.

And then the Brothers and Sisters of Dragons were hit with the bitterest blow of all: since birth they had been manipulated by the Tuatha Dé Danann to achieve their potential, so they could aid the Golden Ones in just such an eventuality as the one that had transpired. The key to making the five companions true Brothers and Sisters of Dragons, with all the power that entailed, was the firsthand experience of death. And so the Tuatha Dé Danann had caused Veitch to fire at Ruth's uncle, had used an unidentified human agent to murder Lee, Shavi's boyfriend, Laura's mother, and Church's girlfriend, Marianne.

In all their dealings with the higher powers, the theme was constant manipulation. The Fomorii, too, had directed them like rats through a maze, allowing them to escape from the Dartmoor cells so the other talismans could be recovered; transforming Tom into an instrument to keep track of events; holding Callow in reserve to strike when their defences were lowered. At that moment, the five felt they had badly failed their calling as the champions of the land.

Devastated, they watched as the Tuatha Dé Danann rode away, knowing they had made the situation much, much worse: another alien force was loose in the land with little respect for the lives and values of humans. The season had turned; humanity's rule had passed to a higher power.

At this low point, the fibre of the five Brothers and Sisters of Dragons, and of Tom, their guiding light, came to the fore. Many would have given up in the face of such an overwhelming force, but the companions shouldered their responsibilities well; they decided to fight on. Church vowed to free the spirit of his dead girlfriend, Marianne, and to gain revenge on the Fomorii human agent who had made them all suffer so much. They knew their only option was some kind of guerrilla action, but time was short. The four ancient Celtic festivals—Imbolg, Beltane, Lughnasadh, and Samhain—marked periods in the great cycle of existence when the powers behind the gods were at their peak. Lughnasadh lay three months away, and that was the day that would mark the beginning of the end; what would become known as the End of Everything: for the Fomorii had set in motion their scheme to bring back the greatest danger humanity had ever faced, the ultimate urge to entropy. The Celts had characterized it in their myths as the Fomorii leader Balor, the one-eyed god of death, otherwise known as the Heart of Shadows, believed slain at the second battle of Magh Tuireadh when the Tuatha Dé Danann had driven the Fomorii from the land. But none of these gods ever truly died; they could never be described as truly living.

Somehow the five had to find a way to combat this tremendous power. Tom led them to a lonely spot on the west coast of Scotland, where they performed a ritual to summon the spirits of long-dead Celts, the original Brothers and Sisters of Dragons. The ghosts gave them guidance, but like all information offered by the dead it was couched in such vague terms it was easy to misinterpret. Yet three vital nuggets shone out: to prevent Balor's rebirth they should travel south to Edinburgh and the *Well of Fire*; to defeat the Fomorii they needed to find the *Luck of the Land*; and one of them was a traitor who would betray the rest.

Armed with this knowledge, they set off for Edinburgh, pausing at a small island in the middle of a loch to make an offering to Cernunnos, a likely ally in their struggle. In strange circumstances, Laura was given the mark of Cernunnos—the same one Ruth bore; the reason was never explained.

Back at the van they made a disturbing discovery: a severed finger was left as a warning to them.

They broke their journey in Callander. That night Niamh appeared to Church once more, and it was apparent her interest in him was much deeper than he had imagined; love lay there, certainly. All such considerations were driven away by a shocking discovery—Ruth was missing, and in her room was another severed finger: hers.

Laura had an inexplicable vision of Ruth being taken by an enormous wolf. Yet after a fruitless search, their only option was to continue to Edinburgh—but not before the local police put out an alert for them.

In Edinburgh, the source of the evil was unmistakable; the Old Town was shrouded in shadows that were almost alive. The Brothers and Sisters of Dragons made their base in the sunlit New Town and set out to investigate the ancient quarter that night. In a pub, they met a rogue member of the security services who suggested everything they had experienced was a great lie, masking the truth of a coup by dark forces in the Establishment. Drugs, psychological manipulation, and disinformation had served to present a picture of supernatural powers so the real social upheaval could continue unhindered. While discounting his story, it touched several deeply held fears that they could no longer trust their perception in any encounter with the gods.

Leaving the pub, they came face-to-face with the tremendous power the Fomorii had somehow managed to shackle to protect their plans in the Old Town. The *Cailleach Bheur*, or Blue Hag, was a nightmare out of ancient myths that carried around with it all the force of winter. The companions fled back to the New Town, realizing now the terrible extent of the struggle lying ahead.

It would be wrong of me to give the impression that this was simply a tale of tremendous forces; human emotions were just as important. Indeed, they set in motion events that would have powerful repercussions. Against the great backdrop, the Brothers and Sisters of Dragons were riven with loves and jealousies, petty dislikes and deceits.

Of them all, Laura was undoubtedly the most unstable. Her paranoia brought about an argument with Church that drove her to storm off. She attempted to lose herself in hedonism at some seedy nightclub, only to encounter the Cailleach Bheur. Reeling under the influence of some drug or other, she managed to escape only after a discovery that drove her to the edge. A minor wound bled green blood that had a life of its own, destroying the bars on a window so she could flee.

Desperate, she had no choice but to return to the others. However, her unreliable actions had convinced Veitch that she had something to do with Ruth's disappearance.

With the strain telling, they made plans to investigate the Well of Fire beneath Arthur's Seat, an extinct volcano overlooking the city. Tom told them it was once a tremendous source of the Blue Fire but over the years had grown dormant. Somehow they had to find a way to reignite the Well so the spiritual energy would spread out across that part of the land, weakening the grip of the Fomorii.

Once again they decided to consult the spirits. Shavi visited one of Edinburgh's most haunted locations, where the dead revealed Ruth was still alive, imprisoned beneath the castle where the Fomorii had made their den. Other answers were typically cryptic: the Well of Fire would not be enough to help them defeat the Fomorii. To halt the Cailleach Bheur they would need an extra power, something called the Good Son. There was also a price to pay for the answer—the dead sent the spirit of Shavi's murdered boyfriend, Lee, to haunt him.

Tom knew exactly who the mysterious Good Son was—the Tuatha Dé Danann god Maponus, missing for millennia. Tremendously powerful, he was the son of Dagda, the Allfather, yet the Golden Ones always refused to speak of what had happened to him. Tom, however, knew Maponus had been imprisoned at nearby Rosslyn Chapel, a mediaeval sacred site renowned for its Celtic and Masonic iconography.

Researching this new information at the Central Library, Church and Laura were attacked by whatever had been stalking them since Loch Maree. After a failed attempt to sever Church's finger, it fled before they had a chance to get sight of whatever it was.

During all this, Ruth was undergoing terrible torture in the secret Fomorii burrow beneath Edinburgh Castle, but while trapped in her cell, a strange thing was happening: her familiar manifested as a voice in her head, teaching her the great secret knowledge that was her heritage. Eventually, Calatin made her suffer the worst torture of all, forcing a large black pearl down her throat.

Finally it was time for the companions to go their separate ways: Church and Tom to find the Well of Fire, Laura and Shavi to seek out Maponus, and Veitch to launch a desperate attempt to rescue Ruth.

At Rosslyn Chapel, Shavi and Laura encountered another Watchman. The chapel's carvings pointed to something terrible hidden there, but although Laura was open to the warnings, Shavi appeared under the control of some spell, driving him onwards. The Bone Inspector was also drawn there by what they were attempting. He tried to prevent them, but they locked him outside the chapel so they could continue. While Shavi and the Watchmen dug into a secret chamber beneath the chapel, Laura listened to the Bone Inspector's warning.

He told her Maponus was struck down by the Fomorii as he attempted to cross over to our world from T'ir n'a n'Og. Whatever the Fomorii did to him drove him mad, so that when he arrived in our world he was an uncontrollable force, slaughtering hundreds and laying waste to many villages. Only a ritual enacted by the Culture, the Bone Inspector's people, could stop him, and then he was not destroyed, only bound in the sacred spot beneath the chapel that was raised up as both a marker and a warning. If he was freed, the Bone Inspector warned, devastation would be laid on the land once more.

Before Laura could act, Maponus was freed, slaying the Watchman on the spot. Laura and Shavi escaped as the mad god stalked out across the countryside. It appeared to be yet another of their great failures.

Back at Arthur's Seat, Tom helped Church through his first steps in learning how to perceive the Blue Fire in everything. The energy guided them through a magical doorway into Otherwordly tunnels beneath the volcano where the two were separated. In a massive cavern where time and space had no meaning, Church experienced visions of the past, present, and future. Reuniting with Tom, they came across an enormous hole plunging down into the bowels of the earth—the Well of Fire—ready to be reignited by what Tom called a leap of faith. Church decided to use the locket given to him by the young Marianne; he had always believed it was a powerful symbol.

Before he could act, Church glimpsed a giant wolf, the same Laura witnessed before Ruth was taken, the thing that had attacked him in the library. Tom told him it wasn't really a wolf; once the old gods had *tampered* with someone, the results confused the mind's perceptions; the real person lay somewhere behind the perceived image.

The two of them edged out around the abyss to hide, but their pursuer followed them. Church slipped into the well, dropping the locket into the depths. Somehow this created a tear in the fabric of reality. Blue fire licked out, the energy carrying Church, along with Tom, out to the foot of Arthur's Seat, where they could see Fabulous Beasts moving towards the Old Town.

Veitch, meanwhile, had entered the Old Town, where Maponus was already in conflict with the Cailleach Bheur. Making his way past the Fomorii defences into the burrows beneath the castle, he stumbled across a strange ritual where the Fomorii gathered before Calatin and a warrior, bigger and more frightening than all the others.

After rescuing Ruth, the two of them escaped the tunnels to discover the Fabulous Beasts destroying everything corrupted by the Fomorii evil, while the Blue Fire ran out from Arthur's Seat in a lattice of reinvigorating energy; the land was beginning to come alive. Maponus and the Cailleach Bheur were both forced to flee in the face of the Fabulous Beasts. And then, finally, the castle and the burrows beneath were destroyed in the conflagration.

The companions were finally reunited in Greyfriars Kirkyard, but their joy was short lived. The spirits of the dead rose to drive them out, saying they were "unclean." Weary but elated, they fled the city: not only had they rescued Ruth, they had also stopped the plan to bring back Balor.

That night, while they rested by the campfire, they met two minor members of the Tuatha Dé Danann pantheon who were wandering the land in search of experience. Cormorel and Baccharus told Church if he wished to remove the Fomorii corruption within him he should visit something called the Pool of Wishes in the Western Isles, a fabulous place in T'r n'a n'Og where the home of the Gods lay.

Heading south they came to a strangely quiet village—*my* village—where people refused to answer their doors after sunset. A few of us were gathered in the local pub and I remember how I felt the moment they wandered through the door. I was a rough and ready journalist. I'd met people from all walks of life, but I'd never met anyone like them before. They were apart from everyone else, as if they'd witnessed things none of us could ever dream of; which, of course, they had.

We rarely saw strange faces in that haunted place so I went over to introduce myself, and to tell them what kind of hell they'd wandered into. For weeks we'd been the prey of strange creatures we couldn't identify. They roamed the lonely fields during the day, but under cover of darkness they came into the village, looking like nothing more than sheets flapping in the wind—but one of our local farmers had seen them reduce a sheep to bloody chunks in seconds. Some people died before we learned they couldn't get into houses past locked doors. But even though we'd warned everyone to lock their doors at sunset, people were still getting killed in their homes. It was a mystery we couldn't understand. Naturally, those six brave people agreed to help us solve our problem.

After Shavi expressed his guilt at freeing Maponus, Church summoned Niamh, who agreed to marshall the Tuatha Dé Danann to bring back their errant god on one condition: that Church broke off his relationship with Laura so that he could learn to love her. Although it confirmed what Church had suspected about Niamh's feelings, it was still a shock. His relationship with Laura was in a state of flux, and he had no idea how he really felt about her, but to put her on one side seemed so callous. Yet the burden of responsibility proved too great. How could he set their petty emotions above the chance to prevent Maponus murdering more people? He agreed, reluctantly, and though he didn't recognise it at the time, his decision was swayed by that strange emotional power the Tuatha Dé Danann held over mortals.

Ruth was concerned that she had had no contact with her familiar since her imprisonment. She embarked on a tantric sex ritual with Veitch, during which the familiar came to her to tell her she was tainted—she must seek help or die. Tom obviously feared the worst; he told her she had to be examined by the Tuatha Dé Danann.

I drove Church, Tom, and Ruth to Richmond in Yorkshire, where a path was found beneath the castle to T'ir n'an n'Og and the Court of the Final Word. This was a disturbing place that claimed to be dedicated to healing but where much darker probings into the mystery of existence continued away in the shadows. Here they met the god the Celts called Dian Cecht, the master healer, who agreed to help them. I don't mind admitting he terrified me. He prepped

Ruth for an op and set his Caraprix free for an internal investigation of her head. It didn't last long. The Caraprix erupted out of her head like it had been fired out of a gun. "The Sister of Dragons has been corrupted beyond all meaning of the word," Dian Cecht said to us. "She is the medium for the return of the Heart of Shadows." It didn't sink in straightaway, but when it did, I felt like throwing up. The Black Pearl she'd swallowed back in Edinburgh had contained the essence of Balor. It had been distilled from all that black gunk Church and the others had found in Salisbury and beneath Dartmoor. Ruth was to be the receptacle that would allow its rebirth, but that doesn't begin to illuminate the true horror of the situation. In a matter of weeks, Balor would burst out of her, fully formed, killing her instantly. They'd obviously chosen her because she was powerful enough to cope with the rigours of what lay ahead. The pearl wasn't actually, truly, inside her, I don't think; I'm no good at getting my head around the physics of this.

Naturally, Dian Cecht refused to help her further. The Tuatha Dé Danann had a problem in dealing with anything corrupted by the Fomorii, and here was the corruption to end them all. So they threw us out, consigning Ruth to the worst fate of all. She took it well, under the circumstances, but it wouldn't be wrong to say we were all devastated. The others thought they'd done their bit to stop Balor being reborn, and all along they were doing the things that would make it actually happen. And there was the ultimate moral dilemma: could Church kill Ruth to prevent Balor from coming back into the world, even knowing she would die when the birth happened anyway?

On the way back from Richmond we encountered the terrifying Fomorii warrior Veitch had first seen beneath Edinburgh Castle. It was like a tank, enormous, unstoppable, ploughing through cars at a phenomenal speed. We escaped —just. The Fomorii had obviously unleashed it to retrieve Balor. That was the one bright spot for the companions, that the Fomorii must have been tearing themselves apart to know their supreme god was now in the hands of the enemy.

Meanwhile, Veitch, Shavi, and Laura continued to investigate the deaths in the village. It was Veitch who made the big discovery: the doors of the latest victims had been forced open, allowing the predators in. The trail led back to some of our supposedly friendly village's more well-heeled residents. They'd been sacrificing those they considered *undesirable* by breaking open their houses so the creatures could get in, leaving the rich free to carry on with their lives and businesses. Veitch dragged off the ringleader for summary punishment, much to the concern of Shavi and Laura.

I waved goodbye to them that day, not quite realizing how much they'd changed my life. For the first time I'd seen some hope in a world that had gone mad. Right then we desperately needed heroes, and I was determined to tell everyone who they were. That was *my* calling in life.

They continued south along the Pennines, with no idea what they were supposed to be doing anymore. Meanwhile, Ruth was growing sicker and sicker. Finally they sent out two missions to seek help for Ruth: one to Cernunnos and one to the Queen responsible for Tom's suffering. Church and Laura would stay to guard Ruth at Mam Tor in the Peaks, a place saturated in the earth energy which would blind the searching Fomorii to their presence.

Shavi went south towards Windsor Park where Cernunnos could be summoned, eventually hooking up with a group of travellers. But he woke one morning to find a woman murdered, her finger missing. Whatever had been pursuing them since Loch Maree was now after him alone.

Tom and Veitch headed north, through several adventures, including an encounter with a race of manwolves, the *Lupinari*, and the discovery that the Tuatha Dé Danann nature gods were reforesting the land. Finally they arrived at Inverness, where they were taken by the Queen's guard to the Court of the Yearning Heart.

The Queen proved an expert at manipulation. She focused her attention on Veitch, but Tom had already warned him to obey the rules of T'ir n'a n'Og: not to eat or drink anything there or he would become a prisoner of the Queen forever. She agreed to help if Veitch undertook one mission for her: to kill or capture the Questing Beast, a mysterious but fierce primaeval creature that had escaped from the Court into our world.

Veitch hunted the creature down, but he was almost killed in the process. As he was close to death, the Queen tended to his wounds, eventually tricking him into drinking a single droplet of water. He was forced to remain there, with the threat of undergoing the same terrible experiments that had so traumatized Tom.

On Mam Tor, Church, Ruth, and Laura discovered a deserted cottage where they could hide out. On one wall there was a mass of writing impossible to decipher. Church, who had continued his relationship with Laura, was confronted by a furious Niamh, who came close to slaying him for breaking his promise to her. Instead of helping capture Maponus, she had brought the mad god to the vicinity of the Tor, to wreak his vengeance upon Church.

In a moment of staggering revelation, Church deciphered the scrawling on the wall to read a message for him from his dead girlfriend, Marianne. He had no idea how she had managed to contact him, or why he was only aware of it at that moment, but it was a transcendental experience that gave him a glimpse of the meaning behind everything. Infused with this understanding at his lowest ebb, he found new strength to fight on.

With a half-formed plan in mind, Church crept through the Fomorii-infested countryside in search of Maponus. He found him—and the Bone Inspector, who had been tracking the insane god. Church explained his plan and the Bone Inspector agreed to help, but on his way back to the cottage, Church was finally brought face-to-face with the Fomorii warrior. The battle was short and brutal, and Church was left broken. But before the warrior could end his life, the beast was itself killed, by Mollecht, freed from his imprisonment at the hands of Calatin by the devastation in Edinburgh. Instead of slaying Church, he departed, leaving behind a mysterious black sword, obviously for Church's use. Church took it back to the cottage, attempting to recover from his wounds before the Fomorii's imminent attack.

In Windsor Park, Shavi summoned Cernunnos, who gave him a strange potion to help Ruth. The essence of Balor could not be destroyed, but it could be removed, Cernunnos told him; like everything connected with the gods, a price would have to be paid, a sacrifice made.

As Shavi made his way back, he was attacked by the pursuer they perceived as a giant wolf. It was Callow, hideously transformed by Calatin for his part in the débâcle that led to the freeing of the exiled Tuatha Dé Danann. His suffering had driven him insane and he had been stalking the Brothers and Sisters of Dragons as architects of his pain, cutting off fingers in a ritual that only he truly understood. He murdered Shavi with one blow of his knife, then loped away in pursuit of the others.

At Mam Tor, on the eve of Lughnasadh, the Fomorii attacked in force. Church sent Laura to stand guard over Ruth in the cottage while he faced up to Calatin in a mirror image of the confrontation on Skye that had led to his death. Although badly injured, this time Church had an advantage: the black sword bequeathed him by Mollecht. It had a life of its own, shaping his attack, then plunging into Calatin's heart of its own volition. Calatin was eradicated on the spot, a fate beyond imagining for a god unable to be completely destroyed. And then the sword revealed its true form: it was Mollecht's shape-shifting Caraprix.

Before the Fomorii could seek revenge, the Bone Inspector led Maponus into their midst, where the mad god wreaked vengeance for his suffering. When the carnage was finally over and the Fomorii fled, the Tuatha Dé Danann reclaimed their insane kinsman.

Then, in the middle of victory, there was only one last, terrible act for Church: to kill Ruth and prevent Balor from being reborn. As he approached the cottage with a heavy heart, Ruth stepped out, seemingly freed from the corruption of Balor. But nothing is ever that simple. Cernunnos had appeared during the battle and offered his potion to Laura, who accepted the sacrifice to save

Ruth. The essence of Balor was transferred from Ruth to Laura, an act of spiritual redemption that would mean her own death. As Ruth gradually came round, Mollecht and his loyal Fomorii broke in and took Laura; the crow-creature's supremacy in the Fomorii hierarchy was now assured.

Unable to come to terms with the act of sacrifice from a woman they had both considered beyond saving, Church and Ruth waited for Lughnasadh to dawn. There was no fire from heaven, nor instant destruction, just a sense of sadness in the air, a darkening of the sky and the smell of ashes in the wind. Somewhere distant, Balor had been reborn, and the last hope for the world had been extinguished.

But the one message the Brothers and Sisters of Dragons instilled in me was that there is always hope. It's a message I'm going to keep circulating to bring us through these dark times. A new dawn will come. We just have to believe.

Until next time.

chapter one
the end

Icy rain blasted across the deserted seafront like stones thrown by a petulant child. Jack Churchill and Ruth Gallagher kept their heads down, the hoods of their windcheaters up, as they spurred their horses out of the dark countryside. Despite the storm, the ever-present smell of burning was acrid on the back of their throats. Twilight lay heavy on the Cornish landscape, adding to the abiding atmosphere of failure; of a world winding down to die. The heavy clouds rolling across the sea where the lightning flashed in white sheets told them the storm would only grow worse as the night closed in.

Dead streetlamps lined the road, markers for the abandoned vehicles that were rusting monuments to the death of the twenty-first century. Occasionally they caught a glimpse of candles in windows or smelled smoke from fires in the houses that had hearths; beyond that, there was only the oppression of the growing gloom.

As they rounded a bend, a light burned brightly in the middle of the road. Surprised, they slowed their horses until they saw the illumination came from an old-fashioned lantern held aloft by a man wrapped in a sou'wester, struggling to keep himself upright in the face of the gale.

"Who goes there?" he said in a thick Cornish accent.

"Friends," Church replied, "who don't want to stay out in the night a moment longer than we have to."

The lantern was raised higher to bring them into its glare. It illuminated the face buried deep in the shadows of the hood: suntanned; grey, bushy beard. He eyed them suspiciously. "Where've you come from?" he yelled above the wind.

"A long way." Ruth fought to keep her lank hair from her face. "We started off in the Peak District. It's taken us days—"

"Aye, well, it would." He looked from one to the other, still unsure.

As the lantern shifted again, Church noticed a shotgun in the crook of his arm. "You haven't got anything to worry about—"

"You can't trust anyone these days." He nodded towards a pub that glimmered with candlelight a few yards away. "In there."

Church and Ruth dismounted and led their horses towards the inn. The man followed a few paces behind; Church could feel the shotgun pointed in his direction. But as they tied up their steeds in a makeshift shelter adjoining the pub, the guard relented a little. "Any news?" A pause. "What's the world like out there?"

Ruth shook the worst of the moisture off her hair. "As bad as you'd expect."

The guard's shoulders slumped. "Without the telly or the radio it's hard to tell. We hoped—"

"No," Ruth said bluntly.

It sounded unduly harsh. Church added sympathetically, "We followed the M5, then the main roads down here. We never ventured into any of the big towns or cities, but—"

"Nothing's working," the guard finished.

Church nodded.

"You better get in the pub," the man said with a sigh. "We haven't had any trouble here in town, but you never know. We've seen what's out there,"—he peered into the night—"and sooner or later they're going to get brave enough to come in."

"You're on watch all night?" Ruth asked.

"We do shifts. Everybody's involved. We're trying to keep things going. They'll tell you more in the pub."

Heads down, they ran from the shelter, but before they reached the door a crack of lightning burst over the sea. Church stopped to stare down the street.

"What is it?" Ruth blinked away the rain, following his eyes.

"I thought I saw something in the light."

"Probably another guard."

"It was on the rooftops, moving quickly. Looked like . . ." He paused. "Let's get inside."

A blazing log fire in the grate was the most welcoming sight they had seen in days. With the candles flickering in old wine bottles all around the room, it created a dreamy impression of another time. About thirty people were gathered around. A young mother with a baby watched some children playing near the hearth. Four old men played cribbage in one corner with the grim determination of a life-or-death struggle. Everyone looked up when they entered. In one instant Church took in curiosity, suspicion and fear.

He was distracted by a glimpse of himself in a mirror as he passed. His dark hair was now almost down to his shoulders, and his close-cropped goatee was a sign he'd given up fighting against predestination; he resembled the future-vision he'd had of himself in the Watchtower between the worlds, watching a city burn. His features fell into a naturally troubled expression that served to make him look older. But Ruth didn't look any different. Her long brown hair tumbled in ringlets around her shoulders while her face still looked as pretty and serene as the first time he had seen it. There was something new there, though: an enduring confidence that gave her bearing.

A burly man in his fifties hurried over, one large hand outstretched. His skin had the ruddiness of someone who spent a lot of time outdoors in all weathers. "Welcoming committee," he said in a loud, deep voice. They each shook his hand in turn. He was Malcolm, a local businessman. "What brings you to Mousehole? Don't get many tourists these days." Although he was friendly enough, the steely scent of fear was palpable in the atmosphere.

What's happening to us all? Church wondered.

"We're looking for a safe haven." Ruth's calmness was the perfect antidote; Church could see everyone warm to her instantly. "It's not very pleasant out there." Her understatement made them smile.

"Any idea what's happened?" Malcolm's eyes showed he was both hopeful and afraid of what her answer might be. "We thought . . . some kind of nuclear exchange . . . ?"

"No," Church said adamantly. "There's no sign of anything like that. Whatever's happened, it's not anything nuclear, chemical or biological—"

"Face up to it, Malcolm, it's the End of the World." A long-haired man in his thirties hung over his pint morosely. "You can't keep fooling yourself it's something *normal*. For Christ's sake, we've all seen the signs!"

Malcolm grimaced in a manner that suggested he didn't want to hear. "We're muddling on as best we can," he continued blithely. "Set up a local network of farms to keep the food supply going. With no communications, it's proving difficult. But we're pulling through."

"Boiling water," the morose man said to his beer. "Every day. Boil, boil, boil."

Malcolm glared at him. "Don't mind Richard. He's still working on his attitude."

"You're not alone," Ruth said. "We've travelled a long way over the last few days. Everywhere people are trying to keep things going."

That seemed to cheer him. "I've got to get back to the meeting—a lot of planning needs doing. You must be hungry—I'll get some food for you. We can't offer you much, but—"

"Thank you," Ruth said. "We appreciate your generosity."

"If this isn't a time to be generous, I don't know when is."

Malcolm left them to dry off at a table in one corner where the candlelight barely reached. "I feel guilty not telling them everything we know," Ruth whispered once they were sitting.

"They don't need to know how hopeless it all is."

Ruth's eyes narrowed. "You don't think it's hopeless. I can tell."

Church shrugged. "We're still walking."

"That's what I like about you." Ruth gave his hand a squeeze. "You're such a moron."

The exhausting journey from Mam Tor in the High Peaks had been conducted against a background of constant threat; although they saw nothing out of the ordinary, they were convinced they were about to be struck dead at any moment. Somewhere, Evil in its most concentrated form had been born back into the world: Balor, the one-eyed god of death, a force of unimaginable power dragging all of existence into chaos. Whatever it truly was, the Tuatha Dé Danann called it the End of Everything. They had expected fire in the sky and rivers of blood flowing across the land, but the reality had been more prosaic. At first there was simply a vague *feeling* that something was not quite right, then an *impression* of imminent disaster that kept them scanning the lonely landscape. There was a sour taste in the wind and occasional violent storms. The only true sign that the world had slipped further from the light was the complete failure of all things technological. No vehicles moved. Pylons no longer hummed. The night was darker than it had been for more than a hundred years.

The Bone Inspector had suggested Balor would not be at its peak until Samhain, one of the Celtic feast days marking an occasion when the great cycle of existence unleashed powerful forces. From a Christian perspective it was chillingly fitting: the Church had made Samhain into Hallowe'en, when the forces of evil were loosed on the earth. And there was no doubt the threat was gathering pace. The progression was like the darkness eating away at the edges of the vision of a dying man: each day was a little gloomier. Soon all hell *would* break loose.

There appeared little they could do; and just three months before the doors of Samhain opened: no time at all. But Church's experiences over the preceding months had left him with the belief that there was a meaning to everything; he refused to give in to fatalism, however dark things appeared. If the Tuatha Dé Danann could be convinced to help them, they stood the slimmest of chances.

To win over the Golden Ones, he had to expunge the Fomorii corruption from his body, an act he had been told could be achieved only in the mysterious Western Isles, the home of the gods somewhere in T'ir n'a n'Og. The journey to that place began at Mousehole on the Cornish coast, and a landmark called

Merlin's Rock where legend said it was possible to spy a fairy ship that travelled between this world and the next. But one thing in the myths disturbed him greatly: his destination had another name—the Islands of the Dead.

More than anything, Church was glad he had Ruth along with him. Her suffering at the hands of the Fomorii had been terrible, but she had survived to become a much stronger person, free from the fear and doubts that had consumed her before. Now when he looked into her eyes it was like looking into a dark river where deep waters moved silently. She maintained she had died in the last few minutes before Lughnasadh, when she had been close to giving birth to Balor; only Laura's monumental sacrifice had brought her spirit back to her body. Whether that was simply a hallucination on the verge of death or the truth of the matter, it had forged something strong inside her.

As their journey to the southwest progressed, she had been relieved by the reappearance of her owl familiar. But when Church saw it dipping and diving in the grey sky, all he could think of was its manifestation as a strange bird-man hybrid when it had warned him of Ruth's capture in Callender. Could something so alien be trusted, he wondered?

Yet the abilities it had bequeathed to Ruth were extraordinary. She had told him how it had whispered knowledge to her that wormed its way into her mind as if she had known it all her life. When Church fell ill with a stomach bug after drinking from a dirty stream, she knew just the plant for him to chew to restore his health within hours. When they were beaten down by an electrical storm with nowhere to shelter, she had wandered a few yards away from his gaze and minutes later the storm abated. It was amazing, yet also strangely worrying.

Across the roiling, grey sea, lightning twisted and turned in a maniac dance. There was too much of it to be natural: nature's last stab of defiance. Resting against the edge of the window in the bedroom that had been prepared for Ruth, Church let his thoughts drift in the fury of the storm, considering their options, praying the power of hope carried some kind of weight.

"I hope you've got a strong stomach for sailing."

Ruth's words pulled him from his reverie and he turned back to the pleasant, old room with its wooden floorboards and walls draped with nets and lanterns and other sailing memorabilia. He felt secure in its warm aroma of candle smoke, dust and fresh linen.

Ruth sat on the edge of the bed, finishing the cold lamb, mashed potatoes and gravy the locals had prepared for them. "I wish we could pay them back for this." She speared the last piece of meat. "They must be worried about maintaining their supplies, yet they offered to take us in without a moment's thought."

"Doing what we hope to do will be payment enough."

She made a face.

"I'm not giving in to hopelessness. Not any more. You know the band Prefab Sprout? They had a song which went, *If the dead could speak, I know what they would say—don't waste another day.* That's how I want to live my life. Whatever's left of it."

The candlelight cast a strange expression on Ruth's face, both curious and concerned. "You really think there's a chance?"

"Don't you?"

She shrugged. "I try not to think beyond the end of each day."

The window rattled noisily, emphasising the frailness of their shelter. "I think about the others. A lot."

Ruth drew a pattern in the gravy: two interlocking circles. It hypnotised both of them for a second. "They might still be alive," she said after a moment or two.

"I feel bad that they might be back at Mam Tor now, wondering where we've gone."

"If they're alive, I think they'll find us. That bond brought us all together in the first place. It could do it again."

"That's another thing." Church sat on the bed next to her, then flopped backwards, bouncing on the sagging mattress. "Everything we've heard spoke about the five Brothers and Sisters of Dragons being one. The five who are one. One spirit, one force. And now—"

"Laura's dead. No doubt about that one." Ruth shifted uncomfortably. "Where does that leave us?" The question hung in the air for a moment and then Ruth pushed away the rickety table and sat back. "No point thinking about it now."

"There's something else that strikes me."

His voice sounded odd enough for her to turn and look at him; one arm was thrown across his face, obscuring his eyes.

"Three months ago when Tom called back the spirits of the Celtic dead, they said one of us would be a traitor—"

"You know any help the dead give is always wrapped up in mischief." She waited for him to move his arm so she could read his mood, but he lay as still as if he were asleep. "It's not me, if that's what you're saying."

"I'm not saying anything. I was just mentioning—"

"Well, don't."

He mused quietly for a moment. "I hope I'm up to it."

"What?"

He gestured vaguely. "Everything. I do my best, like anyone would, but—"

"Not anyone. That's the difference."

"—I wonder sometimes how much is expected of me."

"I've never really been one to believe in Fate, but the more I've been through this, the more I've come to understand it's just a name for something else. We've been chosen, there's no denying it—"

"By God?" he said incredulously.

"By existence. Whatever. We have a part to play, that's all I'm saying."

He sighed. "I feel weary. Not physically. Spiritually. I don't know how much longer I can go on."

"You go on as long as you have to. This is all about a higher calling. It's about doing something important that's bigger than you and me. We can both rest when we're dead."

There was a long, uncomfortable silence until he said, "First light, then." He sat up and kissed her gently on the cheek. It was an act of friendship, but Ruth couldn't help the conflicting emotions she felt for him. "The two of us together, just like it was right at the start."

"You and me against the world, kid."

Voices echoed up from the bar as Church made his way along the dark landing to his own room: the locals, still trying to make head or tail of a life turned suddenly senseless. There was a twinge of sadness when he listened to their planning and rationalisations. Whatever they did, it would all amount to nothing.

He lay on his own bed for a while, staring into the shadows that clustered across the ceiling as his mind wound down towards sleep. A song by The Doors drifted in and out of his consciousness. Despite everything, he felt a deep peace at the very core of his being. He was focused in his intentions, ready to live or die as Fate decreed. Some of the debilitating emotions he had felt over the last few months were now alien to him: his despair after Marianne's suicide; the cold, bitter desire for revenge when he discovered she had really been killed. The knowledge that her spirit had survived death was a source of transcendental wonder that had lifted him from the shadows. He had known it from the first time her spirit had materialised to him outside his London flat, but in his misery, he had not realised what it truly meant. It was such an obvious thing, he still couldn't believe it had taken him so long to fully understand the monumental, life-shaking repercussions, but life was full of noise and the signal often got lost. The message that made sense of their suffering was plain, at least to him: live or die, there is always hope.

Gradually his thoughts turned to Laura. Amidst the sadness there was a twinge of guilt that he had misjudged her so badly. She had been selfish, cynical, bitter, cowardly, yet in the end she had sacrificed her own life to save another. He missed her. He had never come close to matching the intensity of her feelings for him, a love driven by desperation, loneliness and fear that burned too brightly, but he had certainly felt a deep affection for her. Given other circumstances, perhaps he could have loved her more; he wished he had been able to give her what she wanted.

Somewhere above him there was a loud clattering. The storm had plucked some slates from the roof, or torn down a chimney pot. The gale buffeted the building, wrapping itself around the frail structure, yet deep within the wind's raging he was sure he could hear other sounds. The slates sliding down into the gutter, he guessed. He strained to listen. Despite its violence, the storm was soothing, like womb sounds. Slowly, his eyelids started to close.

And then he was suddenly overcome with the strangest sensation: that he wasn't in a room in a pub on a storm-tossed coast in a world turned insane by ancient powers. That he was in a stark white laboratory with lights blazing into his eyes, strapped to some kind of bench, with shadowy figures moving all around. Somebody had a syringe waiting to inject into him.

And there was a voice echoing in his head, saying, "It all depends how we see the world."

Uneasiness started to knot his stomach. He wanted to shout out, but he couldn't move his lips. *You're daydreaming*, he told himself. Sleep came up on this image suddenly, but the words remained.

"It all depends how we see the world."

Of late Ruth didn't find sleep easy. Whenever she was on the cusp, her mind flashed back to lying in the cottage on Mam Tor on the brink of death, with the obscene sensations of Balor growing inside her: snakes writhing in her gut, slithering along her arteries and veins, her head resounding with the sensation of a thousand cockroaches nesting in her brain. But the worst was when the final date drew near and the thing had matured. One day she had become aware of alien thoughts crawling through her mind; then the awful feeling of another intelligence nestling at the back of her head, listening to her every secret, knowing her heart, slowly consuming her. It was like she was in a dark room with something monstrous standing permanently behind her shoulder.

She always woke with a start when she reached that point. It had been the ultimate violation, the scars so deep she was terrified she would never forget. And in her darkest moments, she feared much worse than that: that it hadn't gone away at all; that a permanent connection had been made.

Sleep finally came.

Ruth was dreaming, but some part of her sleeping mind recognised that it was not really a dream at all. Few details made sense, only abstract impressions adding shape to her thoughts. First was suspicion, until that gradually coloured into a growing apprehension. Then came the unmistakable sensation that something was *aware* of her. It was not simply unpleasant; she was overwhelmed with an all-consuming mortal dread; she felt she was going to choke and die on the spot.

Somewhere an eye was opening. Before she could drag herself away, the awful weight of its attention was turned fully on her, like a burning white light that made her brain fizz. And crackling through that contact was the intelligence she feared: a familiar, ugly hand reaching out to grip her. Her entire being recoiled. She wanted to flee, screaming, but it held her fast, probing continually, peeling back the layers of who she was.

She dreamed of a black cloud, as big as the world, and in the centre of it, the unflinching eye that watched her alone. It was the source of insanity and hatred and despair. It was the worst of existence. The End of Everything.

It had noticed her.

Balor, she thought, and snapped awake as the word burned through her mind.

Her eyes ranged around the room without seeing. Aspects of the contact still seared her mind. She remembered. . . . Black forces moving up around the edge of existence, starting to skin the world, pecking away at humanity, preparing to strip the carrion from the bones of all life.

She shivered at the thought of what lay ahead, but before she could begin to consider the depth of her fears, she half-caught a movement that snapped her out of her introspection.

Something was outside her window.

Church awoke, irritable and out-of-sorts, with a nagging in his subconscious. The storm still rampaged across the seafront, but there was another sound he knew had been the cause of his waking: an owl's shriek mingling with a high-pitched mewling that set his teeth on edge. He was out of bed in an instant, pounding along the landing towards Ruth, his mind flashing back to all the blood in her room in Callander.

At her door the mewling was so intense it made his stomach turn. Without a second's hesitation, he put his shoulder to the door.

Wind and rain gusted into his face through the windows hanging jaggedly in their frame. Shattered glass crunched underfoot. Outside, Ruth's owl emitted a hunting shriek. An impression of a grey wolf at bay formed in one corner, but then the image coalesced into something smaller, but just as frightening: a dark figure like a black spider. Even the quickest glance increased Church's queasiness. It was obviously a man, yet there was something sickeningly alien about it too.

When he turned to look at Ruth he saw her face was so cold and hard with brittle rage she was a different person. She was hunched back near the bed, her hair flailing around in the wind, one hand moving slowly before her as if she were waving to the intruder. Inches from her palm the air was gelatinous, moving out in a slow wave to batter her assailant with increasing pressure. Whatever she was doing, the creature's mewling turned into howls of agony. It clutched a hunting knife and looked torn between throwing itself forward to stab her and fleeing.

Ruth's concentration shifted slightly and her power flagged. The eyes of the creature took on a murderous glow as it attacked, screeching. Church was rooted in horror; Ruth didn't stand a chance.

Her brow knitted slightly, her hand made one insistent cutting action and the intruder collapsed in an unconscious heap.

Filled with questions, Church moved towards her, but when her head snapped in his direction a chill ran through him. She was still caught up in the intensity of the moment, fury locked in her face, so much that she barely recognised him. Her hand lifted, ready to strike out.

"Ruth!"

It took an uneasy second or two for recognition to seep into her coldly glittering eyes. "The bastard thought he could take me unawares again." Her voice was drained of energy.

Cautiously, Church approached until he was sure the Ruth he had seen earlier had departed. It wasn't the time to voice his doubts. Instead he asked, "What is it?"

She levered herself off the bed and crossed the room. "What is it?" she repeated bitterly. To Church's discomfort she launched a sharp kick at the prone figure. "He's the bastard that cut off my finger." She held up her hand to show him the mass of scar tissue that marked the missing digit. "The bastard that delivered me to the Fomorii and put me through weeks of hell." She used her foot to roll the intruder on to his back. "Callow."

Church started when he saw the figure's face for the first time. It was indeed Callow, but so transformed he was almost unrecognisable. The wild silver hair and dark, shabby suit were still there, but his skin was as dry and white as parchment across which the veins stood out in stark black. Although he was unconscious, his lidless eyes continued to stare; in his gaping mouth they could glimpse the dark of rotting teeth.

"My God, what have they done to him?" Church knelt down to inspect him, but the sour stench that came off the once-man made him pull back.

"Careful. He'll be awake soon."

They bound him tightly in the old fishing net that had hung on one wall, then waited for him to come to his senses. It was unnerving to watch his constantly staring eyes, not knowing if he was still unconscious or slyly watching them, but a slight tremor in his facial muscles gave away his waking.

"I ought to kill you," Ruth said.

"Do it. Put me out of my misery." He looked away. Tears had formed in the corner of his eyes, but unable to blink them away, he had to wait for them to break.

"Don't try to make us feel sympathy," Ruth sneered. "You drained the well dry a long time ago."

"I don't want sympathy, or pity, or any other pathetic emotion." It was the voice of a spoiled child. "I want you dead."

The curtains flew up like a flock of birds as another gust of wind and rain surged in. "We were very generous to you when we first met," Church said.

"I wouldn't look like this if not for you. I wouldn't be on my own, neither fish nor fowl. I can't move amongst people any more, and Calatin will no longer—"

"Calatin's been wiped from all existence by one of his own kind." Church watched the confused emotions range across Callow's face.

After a moment he began to cry again, slow, silent, juddering sobs that racked his body. "Then there's nowhere for me!"

Unmoved, Ruth turned to Church in irritation. "What are we going to do with him?"

The sobbing stopped suddenly. Callow was watching them intently. "Little pinkies!" He started to giggle at this. "Five fingers, and I'm taking them one at a time, to pay you back for raising your hand against me! I took your finger, did I not, girlie? Your life should have followed, but I can rectify that, given half a chance. And I have another finger in my collection, too."

It took a second or two for his meaning to register, and then Ruth flew across the room in fury. "What do you mean?"

The black veins tattooing his face shifted as his sly smile grew wider. "One little pinkie, one little life—"

Ruth cut his words short with a hefty blow to the side of his head. Church caught her wrist before she could repeat the assault.

"Temper, temper." Callow's overly theatrical voice was incongruous against his hideous appearance. Yet when he looked into Ruth's face his arrogance ebbed from him. He muttered something to himself, then stated, "The long-haired Asian boy, the one as pretty as a girl—"

"Shavi." The word became trapped in Ruth's throat.

Callow nodded soberly. "He's dead. Most definitely. I took his life, and his finger, in Windsor Park."

That last detail was the awful confirmation; Windsor Park had been Shavi's destination in his search for the solution to Ruth's predicament.

Ruth walked to the shattered window where she stood in the full force of the gale, looking out into the night, hugging her arms around her as if to protect her from her sadness. She was such a desolate figure Church wanted to take her in his own arms to comfort her. Instead, he turned his attention to Callow.

The twisted figure giggled again like a guilty schoolboy. Church's overwhelming sorrow began to transmute into a hardened rage. It would have been the easiest thing in the world to ease his emotions by striking out, but he controlled himself.

"I feel sorry for you," he said to the hunched figure.

That seemed to surprise Callow, who looked upset and then angry. "The first of five!" he raged. "You'll all follow!"

Church slipped his arm round Ruth's shoulders; she was as cold and rigid as a statue. The rain was just as icy and stung his eyes shut, but he remained there with her until she slowly moved closer to him.

"Poor Shavi," she said quietly.

Church recalled his friend's deep, spiritual calmness, his humour and love of life. Shavi had been a guiding light to all of them. "We mustn't let it drag us down," he whispered.

Ruth dropped her head on to his shoulder, but said nothing.

They rose at first light after a night in Church's bed, trying to come to terms with Shavi's death. Although they had known him for only a few months, he had affected them both deeply. They felt they had lost much more than a friend.

The seafront was awash with puddles and scattered with the debris deposited by the gales, but it was brighter and clearer than any morning they had experienced since Lughnasadh, with the sun rising in a powder-blue sky and not a cloud in sight. It felt strangely hopeful, despite everything.

Ruth's room, where they had bound and gagged Callow, was reassuringly silent as they passed. No one else was up at that time so they ventured hesitantly to the kitchen for breakfast. Aware of the shortage of food, they toasted a couple of slices of homemade bread each to take the edge off their hunger. While they ate around a heavily scarred wooden table, Church surveyed the jars of tea and coffee on the shelves.

"I wonder what's happening in the rest of the world," he mused.

"I thought about this." Ruth eyed the butter, but resisted the urge. "We get the analogues of Celtic gods because it's part of our heritage, our own mythology. Do you think they got Zeus in Greece, Jupiter in Italy, some Native American gods in America, Vishnu and Shiva or whatever in India? The same beings perceived through different cultural eyes?"

Church shrugged. "Possibly. What I can't figure out is why Britain is the battleground."

"With communication down, anything could be happening. The rest of the world might be devastated for all we know."

Church couldn't take his eyes off the coffee and tea, things taken for granted for centuries. "The global economy will have crashed. There'll be death on a massive scale—famine, disease. No international trade at all. Even here in the UK we've forgotten how to feed ourselves locally. What about in less-privileged areas?"

"Let's look on the bright side: at least all the bankers and moneylenders will be out of a job."

His laugh was polite and humourless.

"Best not to think about it." Ruth watched him from the corner of her eye while she chewed on her dry toast, trying to see any signs of the melancholy that had debilitated him too many times in the past. "Creeping death is the last thing we need to worry about. Everything could be over in the blink of an eye."

"You're right." He stood up and stretched.

"I always am. You should know that by now. It's my hobby." She finished her toast and tried to ignore the rumblings that still came from her belly. "We need to decide what we're going to do with Callow."

Church cursed under his breath. "I'd forgotten about that bastard."

"We could execute him." She appeared to be only half joking.

Church forced a smile that faded quickly. "We can't leave him here. These people have enough problems without a psycho like that around. And if Ryan and Tom are still alive he'll just go after them—"

"We can't take him with us!"

"We don't know we're going anywhere yet. If we do find the ship, we might be able to do some good for him. I'm going to try to get the Fomorii shit cleaned out of my system. Maybe we can do the same for him—"

"Do some good!" she said incredulously. "The bastard murdered Shavi! Almost killed Laura." She showed him the gap between her fingers.

"I know, I know." He waved her protestations away. "But still. Keep your friends close and your enemies closer, they say."

Ruth grunted in grudging agreement, but as she rose from the table she muttered, "I still think we should execute him."

"You sound more like Laura every day."

The morning was brittle, but filled with the warmth of a good summer. The air had the salty tang of seaweed and fish. In the daylight, Mousehole was quaint and comforting, hunkered up against the rugged Cornish coastline. Church and Ruth herded Callow along the deserted seafront, the half-man keeping his peeled-egg eyes away from the brilliant light of the sun. Church was disturbed how the creature had begun to grow into his new form; his manner of walking had become almost insectile in the way he skittered in and out of the gutter, a little too fast, a tad too angular.

"You make a bolt for it, I'll boil those freaky eyes out of your head," Ruth said calmly. "You know I can do it."

Church eyed her, not sure if it *was* within her new powers, which were as mysterious to him as the sea, a feeling she did nothing to dispel. Callow flashed her a brief glance that suggested he would kill her, given half a chance.

"What do we do when we get there?" Ruth asked.

"We call out for the ship to come to us." It sounded so stupid, he winced. He wished Tom were there. Despite the Rhymer's brusque and generally unpleasant manner, Church missed his wisdom and his knowledge about all the new, strange things that had found a place in the world.

The information they had found in the pub pointed them in the direction of Merlin's Rock. As Callow scuttled ahead of them, Church couldn't shake the ludicrous image of the world's most bizarre couple out walking their dog.

Ruth glanced at the white-rimmed waves before flashing a teasing smile at Church. "Better get calling, then."

"Your trouble, Ruth, is you're too straitlaced to let yourself go," he said wryly. "You should unbutton a little."

"I'll take that on board, Mr. Black Pot."

Callow started to edge away, sure the others couldn't see his subtle movements. Church grabbed the collar of his jacket and hauled him forward so he teetered on the edge over the choppy waves. "Enjoy the view. You might never see it again."

"You can't make me go!" Callow protested.

"I can't make you swim, either, but I can put you in a position where you have no choice."

"You don't understand! Those wretched golden-skinned creatures will detest everything about me. They'll make *me* pay for what the Night Walkers did to me, and it's not *my* fault!"

"They don't care too much for me either," Church replied. "Thankfully I don't give a toss what those inbred aristocrats think. They might believe they're better than us, but they're not, and given half a chance I'll bring that home to them."

"They'll hurt me!"

"Not while I'm there. You deserve some justice for what you've done, Callow, but not at their hands. You're one of us and if anyone's going to make you pay—"

Callow struggled frantically. He calmed instantly when Ruth rested a hand on his shoulder.

Church moved away from them and faced the horizon. The wind rustled his long hair with soothing fingers; a tingle ran down his spine. He thought of Frank Sinatra singing "Fly Me to the Moon," remembering the great times he'd had with that music playing in his head: kissing Marianne in the lounge of their flat in the early hours of New Year's Day, staggering through Covent Garden, drunk with all his friends, watching the dawn come up on a boat on the Thames. They were at the start of something big, a great journey, and there was still hope; he could feel it in every fibre of his being. The moment felt right.

"Come to us." The wind whipped the words from his mouth. He coughed; then spoke with greater firmness and clarity: "Come to us. Take us to the Western Isles." Once again his voice was caught by the wind, but this time it rolled out across the waves. The tingling in his spine increased a notch.

Cautiously he scanned the horizon. The weather was so clear he would see any ship miles away. He glanced back at Ruth, unsure.

"Be patient," she said firmly.

Once more he spoke loudly. "I beseech the Golden Ones to carry us, their humble servants, away to the wonders of the Western Isles." Behind him, Callow sniggered.

For several long minutes he waited, sure he was making a fool of himself, but gradually he began to sense slight changes in the atmosphere. The air grew more charged, until he could taste iron in his mouth, as if he were standing next to a generator. He looked back at Callow and Ruth and saw they could sense it too; Ruth was smiling, but Callow had an expression of growing anxiety. Church couldn't stop himself smiling either—almost laughing, in fact: a ball of gold had formed in his gut and was slowly unfolding along his arteries and veins. Everything around became more intense. The sea shimmered as if the waves were rimmed with diamonds, emeralds and sapphires and the sun's golden light suffused every molecule of the air. The scent of the ocean was powerfully evocative, summoning a thousand childhood memories. The wind caressed his skin until every nerve tingled.

This is the way to see the world, he thought.

Despite the glorious morning, a misty luminescence had gathered along the horizon like a heat haze over a summer road, igniting in him a feeling of delighted anticipation that he could barely contain.

"It's coming," he whispered.

It felt like the air itself was singing. Church realised he was kneading his hands in expectation and had to hold them tightly behind his back to control himself.

The white, misty light curled back on itself, suggesting a life of its own. There was a billow, another, and then something could be glimpsed forcing its way through the intangible barrier. His heart leapt.

A second later the ship was visible, ploughing through the waves towards him. It gleamed brilliantly in the sunlight, a water-borne star of gold, silver and ivory. At first it looked like a Phoenician galley he had seen during his university studies. Then it looked Greek, and then Roman, then like nothing he had ever come across before, its shape changing with each crash of white surf on its prow, although he knew it was his own perception that was altering. A white sail marked with a black rune on a red circle soared above it, but the ship didn't appear to be driven by the wind, nor were there any oars visible. Every aspect of it was finely, almost oppressively, detailed. Fantastic golden carvings rolled in undulating patterns along each side, culminating in an enormous splash of silver and white like streamlined swans' wings at the aft. The prow curled round into a statue with an awesome visage made of what appeared to be thousands of tiny, interlocking figures; the eyes glowed ruby red. There was something about the design of the face that spoke to Church on a deep level; it was as if it were an analogy for the ultimate secret made plain for all to see.

Ruth appeared at his side, eyes fixed on the approaching ship. Her arm brushed his and goosebumps rushed across his skin.

"It's magnificent," she said in a hushed voice.

Church turned, expecting Callow to be galloping away now Ruth had abandoned his side, but he remained just as fixated, although the wonder in his face was tempered by a steely streak of terror.

It took five minutes for the ship to reach them. Church attempted to scan the deck on its approach, but whatever was there remained hidden; his eyes couldn't focus on it at all and he was repeatedly forced to look away.

When it was only feet away, a jewelled anchor lowered into the water. Church was beginning to feel a touch of apprehension.

Once the ship was secure, they waited and waited. Ten minutes passed without a sign or sound. Before Church could decide on a course of action, there was a shimmer of movement on the deck, like light striking a mirror. A second later a booming voice rolled out over the water, the quality of it constantly changing across a wide scale so it sounded like it was rising from the deepest depths.

"Who calls?"

Electricity spiked Church's spine and he suddenly wished he were a thousand miles away.

chapter two
beyond the sea

The gangplank unfurled towards them as mysteriously as the ship had been propelled through the water. It was made of brass, and though there was a mechanical clattering, the motion was as smooth as if it were a carpet. Church released his breath only when it clicked perfectly into place. Everywhere was tranquil; waiting. It was still impossible to see what lay on deck.

When no one summoned them aboard, he put one tentative foot on the gangplank, although it didn't feel strong enough to take his weight. He threw out his arms to steady himself when it gave slightly, but it held firm. He glanced back at the others. Callow was shying away in fear, but Ruth placed her hand between his shoulder blades to propel him forward. He squealed and Church had to grab hold of his collar to prevent him plummeting into the waves; from his expression that would have been the better option.

Cautiously Church led the way. Beneath them, the water slopped against the sea wall in a straightforward wave pattern, as though the ship wasn't even there. Callow's whimpering grew more insistent the closer they got to the deck.

"Any last words?" Ruth said ironically.

"You wouldn't want to hear them." He took a deep breath and stepped on to the deck.

The moment his foot landed on board, everything became instantly visible. He caught his breath at the sight of numerous figures all around, watching him silently. The taste of iron filings filled his mouth.

"Ho, Brother of Dragons!" The voice made him start, but he recognised its rich, faintly mocking tones instantly.

"I didn't expect to find you here."

Cormorel was beaming in the same warm, welcoming way Church recalled from their talk around the campfire in the north country, but the darkness behind his expression was a little more obvious. In the sunlight his skin almost gleamed; his hair flowed like molten metal. "Our brief discussion of the Western Isles gave me a desire to see them again." Cormorel's smile grew tight as he looked to the shore. "Besides, the Fixed Lands have lost much of their appeal."

Church felt irritated at Cormorel's easy dismissal of a place he had professed to enjoy, but he knew by now the Tuatha Dé Danann cared for little. "You don't have the appetite to face up to Balor," he said, pointedly.

Cormorel answered dismissively, "There will come a time, perhaps. But for now the Night Walkers leave us alone, and we, in turn, have more enjoyable things to occupy us." Brightening, he made a theatrical sweep with his hand. "But I am forgetting myself! You are an honoured guest, Brother of Dragons. Welcome to Wave Sweeper."

Church followed his gesture, expecting to see only the Tuatha Dé Danann standing around the deck, but there were many who were obviously not of the Golden Ones, their forms strange and disturbing. Cormorel saw Church's confusion play out on his face. "Wave Sweeper has always accepted many travellers. The journey to the Western Isles is one of significance to many races, not just the Golden Ones."

"A pilgrimage?"

Cormorel didn't appear to understand the term. Church was also concerned that the god was talking about the ship as if it were alive. He looked more closely at the wooden deck and the unnervingly detailed fittings flourishing on every part of the structure.

Cormorel noticed Ruth for the first time. "Sister of Dragons, I greet you." But then his eyes fell on Callow and a tremor ran across his face. "What is this? Night Walker corruption, here on Wave Sweeper?" His gaze flickered accusingly to Church.

"He's a danger to others. We can't afford to leave him behind."

Cormorel weighed this, then reluctantly nodded. He motioned to two gods with the youthful, plastic, emotionless faces of male models. Callow shied away from them until they were herding him in the direction of an open oak door that led beneath deck.

"What are you going to do with him?" Church asked.

"We cannot allow something so tainted by the Night Walkers to move freely about Wave Sweeper. He will be constrained for the remainder of the journey."

"You won't hurt him?"

"He is beneath our notice." Cormorel turned, the matter already forgotten. "Come, let me show you the wonder that is Wave Sweeper before we set sail."

He led them from the gangplank across the deck, gritty with salt and damp from the spray. The crew and passengers watched them impassively for a moment before returning to their business, as strange and unnerving a group as Church could have expected. He felt overwhelmed at the presence of so many of the Tuatha Dé Danann in one place. The whole array were represented, from those like Cormorel, who appeared barely indistinguishable from humans, to what were little more than blazes of unfocused light he could barely bring himself to examine. Although he could tell Ruth was also disturbed, she maintained an air of confidence that kept Church at ease.

Cormorel was enjoying the attention the other Tuatha Dé Danann lavished on him. *Exhibiting his pets*, Church thought sourly.

"Firstly, we must introduce you to the Master of this ship." Cormorel directed them to a raised area bearing a wooden steering wheel with ivory and gold handles. Next to it stood a god whose presence took Church's breath away once the shifting perception had settled into a stable form. He stood more than seven feet tall, his long hair and beard a wild mane of silver and brown. His naked torso was heavily muscled and burnished. Gold jewellery wound around his arms from wrist to bicep, but beyond that all he wore was a broad belt and a brown leather kilt. Even from a distance Church could see his eyes were a piercing blue grey like the sea before a storm. With no sign of emotion, the god watched Cormorel, Church and Ruth approach, standing as still as a statue.

For once, Cormorel appeared humbled. "Here is the Master of Wave Sweeper, known to you in the ages of the tribes as Manannan Mac Lir, also known as Manawydan, son of Llyr, Barinthus, ferryman to the Fortunate Island, Lord of the Stars, Treader of the Waves, Nodons, Son of the Sea, known as Neptune by the journeyman, Lord of Emain Abhlach, the Island of Apple Trees, known also as the King Leir."

Church felt little respect for the Tuatha Dé Danann's willful disregard for humanity, but he feared their power and he knew, although he hated it, that they were needed if the day was to be won. He bowed politely. "Jack Churchill, Brother of Dragons. I am honoured to be in your presence." Ruth echoed his words.

Manannan nodded without taking his stern regard off them. "I welcome you to Wave Sweeper." His voice sounded like the surf breaking on a stony beach.

"It is auspicious that the Master greets you at the beginning of your journey," Cormorel said. "Who knows? Perhaps it bodes well for you achieving your stated aims."

"Which are what, Brother of Dragons?" Manannan showed slight curiosity.

"To travel to the Western Isles to cleanse myself of the corruption of the Night Walkers," Church began, "and then to beseech the Golden Ones for aid in driving the Night Walkers from the Fixed Lands."

Manannan was plainly intrigued by the suggestion. "Then I wish you well, Brother of Dragons, for that is an honourable aim." Manannan's attention crawled over them uncomfortably for a moment longer before Cormorel ushered them away.

Church and Ruth were gripped with the overwhelming strangeness of their situation, but they were distracted from discussing it by a tall, thin figure looming ahead of them. It appeared to be comprised of black rugs fluttering in the breeze beneath a tattered wide-brimmed hat. In the shadows that obscured the face, Church saw eyes gleaming like hot coals. It stretched out an arm towards Ruth, revealing a bony hand covered with papery white skin. "Watch your step," the figure said in a whispery voice like the wind over dry leaves. "There are things here that would drain your lifeblood—"

Before the dark figure could continue, Cormorel stepped between it and Ruth, brushing the arm aside. With one hand in the small of Ruth's back, Cormorel steered her away.

"What was it?" Ruth looked back, but the presence had already melted away amongst the busy crew. She felt as if a shadow lay across her, although the effect diminished within seconds of leaving the figure behind.

"The Walpurgis," Cormorel replied coldly.

"Yes, but what *was* it?"

"A memory of the world's darkest night. A disease of life. An unfortunate by-product of the Master's policy of admitting all comers is that occasionally we must play host to . . . unpleasant travellers." He eyed Ruth suspiciously. "You would do well to avoid the Walpurgis at all costs," he warned.

"Did you hear me calling?" Church asked when they stood in the shadow of the mast.

"We hear all who speak of us." Cormorel had sloughed off the mood that had gripped him after the encounter with the Walpurgis and his eyes were sparkling once again. "A muttered word, an unguarded aside—they shout out to us across the void." He surveyed them both as if he were weighing his thoughts, and then decided to speak. "You did not call the ship, the ship called you—as it did everyone who travels on board, myself included. Wave Sweeper offers up to us our destiny, revealed here in signs and whispers, symbols that crackle across the void. It is a great honour. For many who travel on Wave Sweeper, the journey *is* the destination."

The concept wasn't something Church wished to consider; he yearned for the old days of cause and effect, linear time, space that could be measured; when everything made sense.

Irritated by the salty sea breeze, Ruth took an elastic band from her pocket and fastened her hair back. It made her fine features even more fragile, and beautiful. "You don't mind us coming?"

"We accept all travellers on Wave Sweeper. They are a source of constant amusement to us."

"That's nice," Ruth said sourly. She looked out to the hazy horizon, aware of the shortening time. "How long will it take?"

Cormorel laughed at the ridiculousness of the question. "We will pass through the Far Lands, Sister of Dragons."

"We have to be back before Samhain. A long time before." She fixed him with a stare that would brook no dissent.

"You will be in place to face your destiny." There was something in Cormorel's smile that unnerved them both.

Before they could ask any further questions, they were hailed from the other end of the deck. Cormorel's companion Baccharus hurried to meet them, his ponytail flapping. Where Cormorel was overconfident, proud and arrogant, Baccharus was humble and almost shy, traits they had never seen in any of the gods before. If they could trust any of them, he was the one.

Ruth greeted him with a smile, Church with a bow, but if anything he was more pleased to see them. "We are honoured to have a Brother and Sister of Dragons on board the ship that sails the Night Seas," he said quietly; he even sounded as if he meant it.

Cormorel laid a hand on his friend's shoulder. "Baccharus will show you to your quarters. They have already been prepared for you—"

"You were expecting us?" Church asked.

Cormorel smiled in his irritatingly enigmatic way. "Food and drink will be sent to your rooms—" He caught the look in Church's eye and added, "It is given freely and without obligation. Wave Sweeper is a place that defies the rules that govern our existence. It is the Master's wish." He gave an exaggerated bow.

Baccharus led them to the door through which Callow had been herded. Behind it, creaking, irregular steps went down into the bowels of the ship. The torches that lit their path were set a little too far apart, so uncomfortable shadows were always clustering. Despite the flickering flames, there was little smoke and no charring on the wooden walls. Ruth steadied herself on the boards at one point, but the surface felt so much like skin she never tried again.

They came on to a corridor that twisted and turned so much it was impossible to see more than fifteen feet ahead or behind. It was oppressively claustrophobic, barely wide enough for one person, with the ceiling mere inches above Church's head; doors were on either side, each with a strange symbol burned into the wood that was not wood. Baccharus stopped outside two doors marked with the sign of a serpent eating its tail.

Or a dragon, Church thought. He let his fingers trace the symbol. It felt as if it had been branded into the wood years before. Not wanting to consider what that meant, he stepped into the room sharply once Baccharus opened the door.

The room unnervingly echoed their bedrooms in the pub, as if they were still on land, dreaming their encounters on Wave Sweeper. A fishing net hung on one side, while lanterns, billhooks and other implements of a seafaring life covered the walls. The bed was barely more than a bench covered with rough blankets beneath a window with bottle-glass panes that diffused the light in a dazzling display across the chamber; even so, shadows still clung to the corners. A connecting door gave access to Ruth's room, an exact replica of Church's.

Ruth summoned up the courage to touch the wooden walls once more. Something pulsed just beneath the surface, while her feet picked up faint vibrations, as if somewhere in the core of the vessel a mighty heart was beating. The notion left her feeling queasy and disorientated.

Baccharus watched her curiously, as if he could read her thoughts, and then warned, "The ship is large, with many wonders, but many dangers too. You are free to roam as you see fit, but take care in your investigations."

Once he had left, Church threw open the window and looked out across the waves. "This isn't going to be easy."

"Did you expect it any other way? From the moment we started on this road we've had trouble at every turn." Ruth examined the cupboards. They were generally empty and smelled of damp and dust.

"You can't trust any of the Tuatha Dé Danann, any of the other creatures. They've all got their own agendas, their own secret little rules and regulations—"

"Then we don't trust them. We trust each other." Ruth joined him at the window; the sea air was refreshingly tangy, but her face was troubled. "Last night I had a dream . . ." She chewed on a nail apprehensively. "No, it wasn't a dream at all. I felt Balor in my head." The gulls over the sea suddenly erupted in a crazed bout of squawking. "It knows what we're doing, Church."

A chill brushed slowly across his skin.

"It was so powerful." Her eyes were fixed on the horizon. "And it's growing stronger by the minute. I'm afraid of what the world's going to be like when we get back. And I'm afraid that Balor will be waiting for us."

The food was delivered about an hour later by one of the blank-faced gods: bread, dried meat, dried fruits, and a liquid that tasted like mead. They ate hungrily and then returned to the deck. Manannan was at the wheel, surveying the horizon, while the crew prepared the ship for departure.

"If we're going to back out, now's the time," Ruth said. "Once it sets sail, we'll be trapped with this collection of freaks until the bitter end." She thought for a moment, then revised her words. "Until we reach our destination."

They moved over to the rail to take one last look at Mousehole. People moved quietly along the front, oblivious to Wave Sweeper's presence. The sky was still blue, the sun bright on the rooftops, the wind fresh. Church scanned the length of the coastline, then closed his eyes and breathed deeply.

"I love it," he said.

"What?"

"Britain. The world. There's so much—" He broke off. "I never thought about it before. It was just there."

Ruth said nothing, caught in a moment of admiration for the untroubled innocence that still lay at the heart of him, despite all that was happening.

Twenty minutes later everything appeared to be in place. Manannan looked at various crew members scattered around the ship waiting for a nod of approval before raising his hand and slowly letting it drop. A wind appeared from nowhere, filling the sail with a creaking of canvas and a straining of rope. Almost imperceptibly at first, the ship began to move, turning slowly until it was facing the open sea in a tight manoeuvre that would have been impossible for any normal vessel.

Church allowed himself one last, yearning look back at the Cornish coast and then they were moving towards the horizon, picking up speed as they went.

Wave Sweeper skimmed the sea at an impressive rate. The activity continued on deck, but Church couldn't work out exactly what it was the crew were doing; at times their actions looked nonsensical, yet they were obviously affecting the ship's speed and direction. Overhead, the gulls screeched as they swooped around the sails. Manannan faced the horizon, eyes narrowed against the wind that whisked his mane of hair out behind him.

"Can you feel it?" Ruth asked.

Until then he hadn't, but her perceptions had become much sharper than his. It manifested as a burnt metal taste at the back of his mouth, a heat to his forehead that caused palpitations and faint nausea. A drifting sea haze appeared from nowhere and was gone just as quickly, and suddenly the world was a much better place: the sun brighter, the sky bluer, the sea so many shades of sapphire and emerald it dazzled the eyes. Even the scent of the air was richer.

The gods relaxed perceptibly and an aura of calm fell across the ship. Church went to the rail and watched the creamy wake spread out behind. "I wish I could understand how all this worked."

"I shouldn't trouble yourself." Ruth held her head back to feel the sun on her face. "For years all the rationalists and reductionists have been fooling themselves, building up this great edifice on best guesses and possibilities and maybes while ignoring anything that threatened the totality of the vision. It was a belief system like any religion. Fundamentalist. And now the foundations have been kicked away and it's all coming crashing down. Nobody knows anything. Nobody will ever know anything—we're never going to find out the big picture. Our perceptions just aren't big enough to take it all in."

Church agreed thoughtfully. "That doesn't mean we shouldn't keep trying to understand it, though."

"No, of course not. There are too many wonders in the universe, too much information. The best we can hope to do is build up our own, individual view of how it all fits together. Though most people can't be bothered to look beyond their lives—"

"That's not fair. When they're not held in check by authority, people can do—"

Ruth burst out laughing.

Church looked at her sharply. "What is it?"

"You sound like my dad! He was such a believer in the strength of the people."

"Everybody has to believe in something."

Their eyes held each other for a long moment while curious thoughts came to the surface, both surprising and a little unnerving. It was Ruth who broke away to look wistfully across the waves. "I miss him."

Church slipped a comforting arm around her waist. It was such a slight movement, but a big gesture; boundaries built up during the months they had known each other crumbled instantly. Ruth shifted slightly until she was leaning against him.

"Jack."

The voice made the hairs on the back of his neck stand alert. He snatched his arm away from Ruth like a guilty schoolboy. Niamh was standing a few feet away, her hands clasped behind her back. Her classical beauty still brought a skip to his heart, her features so fine, her hair a lustrous brown, her skin glowing with the inner golden light of the Tuatha Dé Danann. Church didn't know what to expect. Only days ago she had been dangling him off a cliff for his refusal to return her love in the manner she expected. The fury within her at that moment had terrified him.

"Hello, Niamh." He tried to see some sign in her face, but anything of note was locked far away.

Her eyes ranged across his features as if she were memorising them. He steeled himself as he felt a sudden surge of attraction for her. Proximity to the Tuatha Dé Danann set human emotions tumbling out of control. It wasn't manipulation, as he had at first thought, just a natural reaction to contact between two different species.

Ruth glanced from one to the other, then said diplomatically, "I'm heading back to my room for a rest. I'll see you later." She smiled at Niamh as she passed, but the god gave no sign that she was even there; Church was the only thing in her sphere that mattered. He couldn't begin to understand the depth of her feeling. They had shared barely more than a few moments, exchanged a smattering of words, the sketchiest of emotions, though Niamh had been with him all his life, watching him constantly from his birth, a whisper away during every great happiness and every moment of despair; even that couldn't explain the depth of her love, so pure and overwhelming it took his breath away.

"How are you, Jack?"

"As well as can be expected, given that my world is on the brink of being torn apart." He tried not to sound bitter; it wouldn't do any good. But he wanted to say: *considering you tried to murder me with a lunatic god who could boil the blood in my veins at a gesture*. Even as he thought it, contrition lit her face. "How is Maponus?" he asked.

"The Good Son is . . . as well as can be expected."

"Will he recover?"

She looked down. "We do what we can."

"I'm sorry."

"May we talk?" As she gently touched his hand, a spark of some indescribable energy crackled into his arm. She led him across the deck to the highest level beyond Manannan's vantage point. A table placed where one could admire the view was laid out with crystal goblets and a jug of water.

"The Master will not mind us sitting awhile. He knows I love the sea as much as he." Niamh filled two goblets, then watched the waves for several moments, a faint smile on her face.

"The Far Lands fill me with such joy," she said eventually. "In my worst times I feared them lost to me forever." She turned to him and added sadly, "As I fear I have lost you."

"What happened—"

"Fills me with the deepest regret. I was cruel and foolish in my hurt. I sought to punish you so you would feel some of my anguish."

"You tried to kill me—"

"No." She shook her head forcefully. "I would never harm you. Once I reflected on my actions, I sought to make amends. It was I who alerted my people to bring the Good Son back to the Far Lands. Yet I knew I could never take back what I had done, however much I desired to make things well between us again. And that was almost more than I could bear." She sipped at her water, the sun glinting off the glass in golden shards.

"I can't understand it. You're all so far beyond us, yet emotionally you're just as screwed up."

"Those of us who are close to Fragile Creatures still feel deeply. We have great passions. Yet it tears through us like fire in the mighty forest. It leaves us bereft. That is our curse until we move on to the next stage."

Church looked down at Manannan, who had his back to them, wondering what rules governed the evolution of the gods.

"My heart was torn apart at the thought that I had driven you away, Jack, the only thing I ever truly wanted. And so I came here, to Wave Sweeper, in the hope that I could wash away the pain with a visit to the Western Isles, where all balm lies, if one looks carefully enough."

"You've watched over me since I was a child—"

The note of sadness in her smile had a curious tone; almost too intense for what they were discussing. "I have known you for a very long time, Jack Churchill."

"All my life. That may be a long time for you. But I've only known you for a few months and then we've only been together for—what?—an hour or more? That's not enough time for me to fall in love with anyone. I don't believe in love at first—"

She turned her face from him so he couldn't see what lay there.

He hadn't the heart to finish. "I don't hold it against you, Niamh. What you did was wrong, but I wasn't fair to you either. I shouldn't have promised something I couldn't live up to."

She turned back to him in surprise, quickly checking that it was not a cruel joke before smiling shyly. "It seems that for all I know you, I do not know you."

"We've both got a lot to learn about each other."

"May we try to be friends?"

"Of course. But don't think about anything more than that. I don't know you, I don't really know myself any more, everything's in such upheaval. It would be wrong to expect anything to happen."

"I understand," she said seriously. "But to be friends—" Her smile lit up her face.

"It's all right to lose your heart, but never lose your head." The words popped into his head, from a lifetime away, a happier time, but oddly, he didn't feel despondent. Niamh looked at him curiously. "Just a line from an old song," he explained. "I'm glad we're going to get on fine. This could be a difficult journey for all of us." He took a long draught of the water, which tasted like no water

he had ever had before: vibrant, refreshing, infused with complex tastes. He savoured it for a moment, then said, "Tell me, the Golden Ones have a strange relationship with time. The past, the future . . . you don't see it how we see it. How are things going to work out? Not for me—I don't want to know that—but for the world, my world? Is all this for nothing?"

"Nothing is ever for nothing." The words had an odd resonance in her mouth. "There is meaning in even the most mundane act."

"The fall of a sparrow."

"Yes. The slightest act. A pebble dropped in water. Ripples run out, bounce back, and then out again. You might not be able to see the results from your perspective, but if your actions are taken with good heart, they will be magnified."

"I'm getting the feeling you're not going to answer my question."

"You Fragile Creatures have a limited view of the turning of the Great Plan. Until your abilities advance it would be unwise to provide you with a glimpse of our vista."

"That's patronising. You're saying we're not up to it."

"That is correct. You are not ready. It is the arrogance of all emerging species that they have an understanding of everything. True wisdom comes from accepting that nothing can be understood. All existence has a framework, but it is not clockwork, although at first glance it may look so. Consider this: from the clouds the coastline is a simple unbroken line. As you fall, you see the twists and turns, the tiny inlets, the craggy outcroppings that comprise its complex shape. You fall to the beach and you see a billion, billion grains of sand, and suddenly there is no shape at all, simply chaos making an illusion of a complex pattern."

"And so it continues. Yes, I understand that—"

"But the chaos is ordered." She smiled enigmatically. "You Fragile Creatures think you see the way everything works. You can measure the height and length and breadth of it, and in your arrogance—"

"Okay, okay, I get your point. We're just kids who haven't learnt how to draw pictures with perspective. So we have to learn to see before we can be shown the view. But—"

She shook her head.

He sighed. "I can see where Tom got it all from. Everything's just *too* complex to sum up with words."

"Yes," she said. "It is."

"So I just do my best, and be damned."

"Or not." She took his hand briefly, then pulled away, as if she had overstepped some invisible boundary. "Everything we need to know is encoded within. Everything. But you have to be strong to trust yourself. It is easier to be a child and let others tell you this and that. That is the key to all wisdom: listen to no one. Trust what your heart tells you."

For the next ten minutes they sat in silence while Church mulled over her words. She had made exactly the same point as Ruth. It might have been coincidence, but Tom had told him so many times that what he thought was coincidence was the universe contacting him. But what was he supposed to take from it?

High overhead the owl soared on the thermals rising from the waves. It had moved along effortlessly when the ship had slipped between the worlds, though now it looked bigger than Ruth recalled, and she was sure she could see its eyes glinting golden in the sun; more than an owl. But then it always had been. In Otherworld it was simply one step closer to its true nature, Ruth imagined. She shivered, despite the heat, recalling all the things it had whispered to her in the miserable dark when she had been a prisoner of the Fomorii: secret knowledge that had transformed her into something else, while at the same time terrifying her. She was afraid she was losing part of herself in the process; her innocence, certainly. Sometimes she even feared for her sanity.

As she crossed the deck, the whispering began in the back of her head, the secret code words that shaped existence bursting continuously in her mind like bubbles on a stagnant pond: the price she had to pay for her secret knowledge.

She ignored the sly glances from the crew that followed her and slipped through the door beneath deck. As she progressed along the oppressive corridor system she became convinced the layout had changed, although it was impossible to tell for sure. Confusion reigned everywhere on that vessel. Eventually she reached her room, but the moment with Church before Niamh had arrived had left her out-of-sorts and she didn't really feel like resting. Exploring was a good way to take her mind off things, so she ploughed on past her door into the heart of the ship.

She walked for what felt like an hour or more, until her legs ached and her throat was dry. From the seafront, the ship looked like it could have been traversed in ten minutes, but she had gone at least two or three miles and there was no sign of the boat ending.

The maze of claustrophobic corridors had soon changed in form. There were passages where the roof was lost to shadows high overhead and where a jumble of beams protruded at incongruous angles like an Escher sketch, or which were as wide as a Parisian boulevard, with carved stone columns and arches where gargoyles peered down ominously. Chambers led off, some as vast as banqueting halls, while others were as cramped as her own cabin. At one point she found what appeared to be a tree growing upwards through the floor and ceiling, its roots lost somewhere in the bowels of the ship. Strange scents floated everywhere, whisked on by phantom breezes: cinnamon and onions, candle smoke, something that had the tangy bite of fresh blood, the acrid odour of hot coals, fresh lemon and cooking fish. Disconcerting symbols appeared intermittently on the walls, as if they were sigils to ward off unquiet spirits; Ruth found she couldn't look at some of them.

The immensity of the vessel made no sense to her. After a while she became convinced that however much she walked, she would never reach the end of it. The surroundings, too, were growing more chaotic and unnerving and she was afraid of what she would find if she carried on. It felt like a good time to head back.

But when she turned, the corridor wasn't how she remembered. A brief spark of panic flared within her. She glanced back the way she had been going and saw faint lights dancing in the gloom. They dipped and dived in complex patterns, reminding Ruth of the tiny, gossamer-winged figures that could occasionally be glimpsed amongst the trees of an evening. Those creatures, which had inspired the dreams of generations in times past, represented much of the good that had swept in with the chaos that had descended on the land. The corridor behind had changed layout once again. She considered her options, then headed towards the phantom lights.

However fast she walked, she never managed to catch up with them, although she couldn't tell if they were fluttering beyond her reach, or if it were some trick of the warped perspectives in Wave Sweeper. After a while the dancing lights became almost hypnotic and she had the odd sensation she was being dragged along instead of pursuing of her own will.

It might have been minutes or an hour later when she became aware she was in an area devoid of torches; the gloom was so intense she was overwhelmed by the feeling of floating in space. Uneasily, she clutched on to a wall before her troubled senses made her pitch forward. She cursed herself for following the lights, unable to recall what had prompted her to do so in the first place.

When she had calmed, she noticed an odd animal smell, thick and musky; it rankled. She leaned against a wall, trying to decide what to do next, afraid she could be wandering for days, perhaps forever. Hoping for a sound to guide her, she listened intently. At first, she could make out only the distant womb-echoes of the waves against the ship, but then another noise drifted up to her like a stranger on padded feet. Sounding dimly like an anxious rumble a cat makes deep in its throat, it filled her with inexplicable dread. She pressed her back hard against the wall and began to slide away from the approaching noise. It could be nothing, she knew, but every fibre of her being told her it was a threat.

What's down there? she wondered.

If she ran, it was so dark she would either injure herself or stumble, so whatever was there would be on her in a second. The throaty growl grew louder, the shuffling of feet echoing along behind. There was more than one, she was sure of it: they were coming from different directions. Then: a ruby glint of an eye opening and closing, the smell growing stronger until she felt like choking.

The malignancy was palpable. *Be strong*, she thought.

Cautiously she crept away from the approaching figures, moving as fast as she could without making a sound. In motion, she couldn't hear what was behind, so after a while she stopped and listened again. Nothing. The gloom was undisturbed by movement, although the smell remained.

Satisfied whatever was there had taken an unseen branching corridor, she began to edge along the wall.

The growl was so close every hair on her neck stood erect at once. It brought up a primal fear of being hunted at night, so strong that, despite herself, she launched herself down the corridor. Now she *could* hear whatever was behind: low growls, padding feet, rough breathing filled with a hungry anticipation. Terror began to lick at her; the growls sounded so bestial, so predatory. She was blind, but instinctively she knew they could see. Unable to control herself, she ran faster.

It was madness. She clipped one wall, careered over to the other, stumbled, smashing her elbows and knees, so scared she scrambled to her feet in a second and was away again.

She hit another wall head-on, dazed herself. The pursuit was growing louder, closer, more eager.

Stumbling into a side corridor, she began to run again, this time trailing one hand against the wall in a feeble attempt to guide herself. It worked reasonably well; at least she didn't knock herself out, although she picked up several more bruises. Anxiety pain spread across her chest. And then, suddenly, she realised she could no longer hear anything behind. Gradually, she came to a halt. Had she lost them?

Out of the corner of her eye she glimpsed rapid motion and jerked herself to one side. Something that resembled a battle-axe, although oddly organic, crunched into the wall where her head had been. Splinters of wood showered over her. A roar nearby made her ears ache, and then shapes moved towards her, at first serpentine, then like a pig, and then covered in fur. The intensity of the stink made her retch. Her hypersensitive senses picked up more motion. This time she didn't wait for the jarring impact. She turned and ran as fast as she could, bouncing off the walls, somehow managing to keep her balance, her heart thundering wildly.

The sounds of pursuit were now deafening; there was a pack at her heels. The corridor turned sharply and in the distance she saw a flickering torch that provided enough light for her to increase her pace. She found a split second to look back, but all she could make out were leaping shadows, heavy and low, the burning sparks of eyes and the glimmer of weaponry.

She took another sharp turn into an area of more concentrated torchlight and then, midstep, a door to her left opened suddenly, arms reached out and she was dragged inside.

Behind the closed door, she dropped into a defensive posture, ready to claw at anything that came near her. But the only occupant of the tiny chamber was Baccharus, who pressed one finger to his lips, demanding silence. She calmed instantly, her breath folding into her throat as the frenzied pack approached, then passed without pausing. Once silence had returned, she relaxed her muscles and turned to her rescuer. "Thank you."

Baccharus nodded shyly. "You should not venture into this part of Wave Sweeper. The dangers down here are many and Fragile Creatures are easy prey."

"What were they?"

"The Malignos."

She stared at him blankly.

"Misshapen dwellers in the dark places, beneath the earth, or under bridges or within the barrows. The natural predator for Fragile Creatures. In your North Country one became known as Hedley Kow, another as Picktree Brag. On the Isle at the Hub off your west coast, another is still known in whispers as the Buggane. They haunt your race memory."

"I couldn't work out what they looked like."

"They are shapeshifters. In the old times they taunted their victims by appearing as gold or silver before adopting a form that could induce nightmares."

"They're like the Fomorii—"

Baccharus shook his head. "They share many qualities with the Night Walkers, but they are lowborn. They cannot transcend the Fixed Lands. Your world is their home."

Ruth slumped against the door, sucking in a deep breath as the adrenalin wore off. "I was following some lights—"

"The *Ignis Fatuus*."

Ruth started at the strange, tiny voice that was certainly not Baccharus's. She scanned the room twice before her eyes alighted on a figure barely half an inch high seated cross-legged on the floor next to the wall. She knelt down to get a closer look. It was a man, but although his body was young and lithe, his face was so wrinkled it looked ancient. His eyes gleamed with a bright energy that put Ruth instantly at ease.

"The Foolish Flame, your people used to call it, though it also went by the names of Spinkie, Pinket, Joan o' the Wad, Jack o' Lantern—"

"A Will o' the Wisp," Ruth added.

He nodded. "Very dangerous indeed. Another shapeshifter that used the form of gold to lure you avaricious creatures to your doom. It never allied itself with the Malignos, but here—"

"Here there are many strange bedfellows." Baccharus was still listening at the door. "Shared interests draw together. Races that would be at odds beyond these walls are forced to coexist in the confines; new alliances are drawn."

"It's not much of a luxury cruise," Ruth noted.

"All things dwell aboard Wave Sweeper. At one time, just two of each species, but now . . . There are many things long forgotten in these depths, some that have not seen the light of day since your world was new formed."

The tone in Baccharus's voice made Ruth grow cold. She turned quickly to the tiny figure and asked, "And what are you?"

"*What* is not a pleasant way of asking. *Who* would be more polite. And even then naming words should be proffered, not demanded." His eyes narrowed; Ruth thought she glimpsed sharp teeth as his mouth set.

"I'm sorry—"

"I will vouch for her, Marik Bocat," Baccharus interjected. "She is a Sister of Dragons."

"And thus above reproach," the little man said. "Then, to you I am Marik Bocat. To others my name is neither here nor there. And to answer the *what*, my people are the oldest species of the Fixed Lands, distant relatives to the People of Peace." He motioned towards Baccharus. "Though the Golden Ones have more wit and sophistication, we can stand our own in conversation." He smiled so pleasantly Ruth couldn't help smiling in turn. "Your people used to call us Portunes, thanks to one of your educated folk who first wrote of us and our *diet of roast frog*." He wrinkled his nose in irritation. "Damn his eyes. See how he likes roast frog."

Baccharus opened the door a crack to peer out into the shadowy corridor. "We should move back to the lighter areas before the Malignos return. They will be even hungrier after their exertions."

"Won't we meet them on the way back?" Ruth asked.

"Wave Sweeper's configuration will have altered many times by now. They should be a distance away."

"Or a room," Marik Bocat noted. "Speed is of the essence."

"Do you want me to carry you?" Ruth asked.

Marik Bocat looked insulted once again. "Perhaps my legs are invisible to you?" He motioned to what appeared to be a mousehole in the wainscot. "We have our own routes about the ship."

"I'm sorry." Ruth's head was spinning from everyone she had encountered, each with their own peculiar rules and regulations. "I seem to be saying that a lot."

"Never mind. You will have time to make up for your appalling manners." He smiled sweetly again, then bowed with a flourish before disappearing into the hole.

"A strange race," Ruth noted as she slipped out of the door behind Bacharus.

His voice floated back to her, strangely detached. "We are all strange. That is the wonder of existence."

She found Church watching the waves with Niamh at his side. There was an easiness to them, in their body language and the way they stood a little too close, that made her feel an outsider. She considered leaving them alone, but the tenacious part of her nature drove her forward.

Niamh smiled politely when she saw Ruth, but she didn't appear too happy with the intrusion. "I will leave the two of you alone," she said a little stiffly. "I am sure you have much planning to do if you are to achieve your aims."

Once she was out of earshot, Ruth said, "You seem like you're getting on."

Church's eyes narrowed; he knew her too well. "What does that mean?"

"Nothing. Just what I said."

"There's nothing going on." He turned his eyes back to the cream-topped surf. The sun was slipping towards the horizon, painting the waves golden and orange. "When it comes to romance I've been an idiot in the past. I was just trying to fill the gap left when Marianne died, and it was a big, big gap. But I couldn't see what I was doing. I can now. I'm not going to make any stupid mistakes again."

"Still, it's obvious she wants to get in your trousers."

"I don't think it's a physical thing. I don't know, maybe I'm wrong, but the Tuatha Dé Danann value emotions more than anything. Don't worry, I'm going to be careful, not lead her on. Especially after the last time." He flinched. "It's hard, though. The way they unconsciously manipulate emotions. It's overpowering."

"I can't understand why she's so full-on."

"What, you don't think I'm worth it?" He laughed as he leant on the rail to peer down the side of the boat.

"On second thoughts, go for it. You should take what you can get."

"Steady on, acid tongue."

She slipped an arm around his shoulders; it was something a friend would do, but, as earlier, the warmth was unmistakably stronger and they both drew comfort from it.

"I know lots of terrible things have happened, but when I think about everything that's been lost so far it's all the normal things I feel acutely about," he continued. "Never being able to go to a movie. No more *Big Sleep* or *Some Like It Hot*. No more electric guitars at some seedy gig. Sometimes I'm so shallow."

"What do you miss the most? The one thing above all else?"

He thought about this for a second, then gave an embarrassed laugh. "Never being able to hear a Sinatra song again. Stupid, isn't it?"

"No."

"It's not even about the music, it's what it means to me." He tried to pick apart the tangled emotions. "It means a love of life, abandon, not worrying—just enjoying."

"Does it remind you of Marianne?"

"No, it reminds me of what life used to be like before responsibility."

In the distance sea creatures resembling dolphins frolicked in the pluming water, their shiny skin reflecting the late afternoon light. There was a certain poetry to the image that wasn't lost on either of them.

"The quicker we get there, the quicker we can get back and do something positive," Ruth said.

"Maybe we shouldn't be in such a hurry to arrive."

"Why?"

"In all the old stories, the Western Isles are a metaphor. They're where the dead live."

"Heaven?"

"Or Purgatory, in some cases. So we're leaving life behind us and moving into death."

"Trust you to put a damper on things."

He forced a smile. "Let's hope we can make the return journey."

chapter three
on the wings of golden moths

After Ruth had related to Church her encounter with the Malignos, the Portune and Baccharus, they retired to their rooms for a brief rest. When the red sun was bisected by the horizon, Cormorel disturbed them with a sharp rap on the door.

"The Master requests your presence at his table for dinner," he said with his usual ironic smile.

They weren't about to argue; their stomachs were rumbling and the cooking aromas floating through the ship were mouthwatering. Spices, herbs and roast meat were prominent, but there were other, subtler scents they couldn't quite place. Cormorel led them across the deck to the raised section at the aft where Manannan's quarters obviously lay. A winding, wood-panelled staircase took them down to another corridor. Here torches roared furiously, as if fired by gas burners. At the end, Cormorel swung open two double doors to reveal a scene that took their breath away. Spread out before them was a banqueting hall so large it could have filled eight or nine ships the size of the Wave Sweeper they had seen from the seafront. They could barely think with the noise that echoed amongst the lofty rafters. Oak tables ranged in lines, around which sat a mesmerising array of strange creatures of all shapes and sizes, interspersed with the more sedate figures of the Tuatha Dé Danann. There was babbled, incomprehensible conversation, shouts and screeches; in a few places brawls rolled amongst the aisles.

"Do not worry," Cormorel said wearily, "you will get used to it."

The walls were an odd mix of stone and wood, hung with luxuriant drapes of the deepest scarlet. Log fires roared in enormous stone hearths at strategic points around the perimeter, yet the temperature remained pleasant; the flames cast dancing shadows over the army of diners, making them even more bizarre and terrifying. Some of them looked towards Ruth and Church with unpleasant stares that made the blood run cold.

"Is everyone here?" Ruth asked. "The Malignos?"

Cormorel raised an eyebrow. "Ah, you have met some of your fellow travellers, I see. No, not all dine here. Some have very, shall we say, individual tastes."

"Where do you find the food?" Church said.

Cormorel smiled. "Our kitchens are particularly well stocked."

He led them amongst the diners where the smell of sweat and animal musk was almost overpowering. The tables were laid out with what appeared to be pewter plates, knives and goblets, each section with an intricate centre-piece of feathers, flowers and crystal. Nothing had yet been served. Something reached out and tugged at Ruth's arm, but she shook it off without daring to turn around.

At the far end of the room was the long table of the Master, piled high with the most magnificent gold and silver plates and dishes. Manannan sat in the centre on a large chair carved with intertwining dolphins, fish and rolling waves, his face still a mask, his eyes unfathomable. On either side sat members of the Tuatha Dé Danann, obviously the more highborn members of the race; there were two whose forms were so alien they hurt Church's eyes and forced him to look away, but Niamh was there, at Manannan's right hand. Three spaces remained at the far end, next to where Baccharus sat patiently.

Manannan let his eyes wander over them when Cormorel presented them to him; they were unable to decipher his emotions. "Welcome to my table," he said in a voice like the cold depths. "It is good to dine once again with a Brother of Dragons."

Church gave a curt bow. "We are honoured."

"This sustenance is given freely and without obligation," Manannan continued. "Enjoy this repast, Fragile Creatures."

Cormorel led them to the empty chairs. "Good evening, Baccharus," he said a little tartly as he took the seat next to his friend. "I hope you have been passing your time well while I was engaged in the business of the Master."

"Well, indeed. I have met many of our travelling companions and investigated some of the wonders hidden in Wave Sweeper."

"You always were a sociable and inquisitive fellow," Cormorel noted dismissively. Church and Ruth sensed some kind of tension between the two. Cormorel clapped his hands once. Instantly some of the bland-featured Tuatha Dé Danann emerged from side rooms carrying platters of food and goblets of wine. Their perfect features, so devoid of even the hint of emotion, made Church and Ruth uncomfortable.

"Why are these young ones always servants?" Ruth asked.

"They are new. They must exist in servitude until they have learnt what it truly means to be a Golden One." Cormorel virtually ignored them.

"New?" Ruth persisted.

"Barely Golden Ones at all, but still not of the race of Adam. They have not settled into their greatness or understanding of the fluidity of it all. Fixed, if you will, like you and your world."

"So, the lowest of the low," Church noted acidly. "You can't escape hierarchy whichever way you turn."

"There is a structure to everything, Brother of Dragons. You should know that by now." Cormorel eyed him sardonically.

"Yes, that's always the argument. It must be nice to have such a full understanding of the rules and regulations of the Maker."

They were interrupted by the servants, who laid out the food and drink before them: roasted, spiced meat, a few vegetables, bread, and other things so strange they made their stomach turn. One platter contained something like a living squid, though it had fifteen legs, all of them writhing madly in the air. The food they could enjoy, however, tasted more sensational than anything they had experienced before; every complex flavour burst like a firework on their tongue. The wine was finer than the most celebrated earthly vintage and made them instantly heady.

Despite the wonders of the meal, it was hard to keep their attention on the food when so many strange sights were on view all around. The array of creatures and their confusing, chaotic mannerisms as they devoured the food was like staring into a grotesque parody of a child's fairybook. There were things Church half knew from the vague descriptions of folk tales, others that ignited recognition from some deeply submerged race memory; a few were completely unrecognisable. He was sure the echoing of archetypes dredged up from the corners of his mind would give him nightmares for the rest of his life.

Ruth recognised his thoughts from his expression. "The whole of our psychology was based on this," she said. "Our fears, our dreams. We're stripping back layers that shouldn't really be uncovered."

A half-man, half-sea creature moved down one of the aisles. It had fins and scales and bestial features, but it moved like a human being. Church leaned over to Cormorel. "What's that?"

Cormorel mused for a moment, then said, "I believe your race would know it as an *Afanc*. They once roamed the lakes and shores of your western lands, invoking terror with the fury of their attacks. Your people could not kill them by any means at the employ of Fragile Creatures."

The Afanc reared up, then rushed out of sight, but there were plenty more things to pique Church and Ruth's curiosity. Cormorel followed their gaze, smiling at the questions he saw in their faces. "If we had all night I would not be able to introduce you to the many, many races passing time on Wave Sweeper. But let me indicate some of the highlights." He appeared to enjoy the idea of playing host. With a theatrical gesture, he motioned towards a large, lumbering figure like an exaggerated circus strongman. He had his back to them, but when he half turned they saw a horn like a rhinoceros's protruding from his forehead. "The Baiste-na-scoghaigh. He stalks the mountains looking for prey in the island where you lost your life to the Night Walker Calatin." He smiled at Church; point scoring. On the far side of the room, large, misty shapes faded in and out of the light, occasionally appearing like mountain mist, at other times as solid as the other creatures in the room. When they became material their features were grotesque. "In the western land of moors, they were known as Spriggans, believed to be the ghosts of giants, a description that arose from their shape-shifting abilities, like many of our guests. The people of the Far Lands are always removed from the perception of those from the Fixed Lands. They could be found around the standing stones where the soul fire comforted their violent nature. They are the Guardians of Secrets."

"What kind of secrets?" Ruth asked curiously.

"The kind that can never be told." Cormorel was enjoying his games.

Church saw something that resembled mediaeval woodcarvings of a griffin, another that resembled accounts of a manticore.

Ruth stood up, suddenly spying something so hideous in the shadows on the edge of the room she could barely believe her eyes. "Is that a giant toad?" she asked disbelievingly. "With wings? And a tail?"

Cormorel laughed. "Ah, the Water-Leaper. The Llamhigyn Y Dwr. Feared by your fishermen, many of whom were dragged to their deaths after it seized their lines. The Water-Leaper rarely ventures up from the bilge tanks. I wonder why it is here tonight?"

Ruth shook her head in amazement. "God, I don't believe it. This place is insane."

"Oh, this is indeed a Ship of Fools, Dragon Sister. So many searching, looking for guidance, meaning, in their short, unhappy lives."

"But you don't need to search, Cormorel?" Church said.

"I am happy with my place in the great, unfolding scheme." Baccharus muttered something under his breath, eliciting a stony glare from Cormorel.

Before any further comment could be made, a group emerged from a door hidden behind curtains away to one side. There were five of them, all Tuatha Dé Danann, but of a branch on a par with Cormorel and Baccharus, carrying musical instruments: a pair of fiddles, a flute, something percussive that Church didn't recognise and another thing that looked completely unplayable. A muttering rippled through the diners; it appeared generally appreciative, though it was hard to be sure.

"Hey, they got a band," Ruth said in a bored, *faux*-Brooklyn accent.

But once the musicians began playing, both Church and Ruth were instantly entranced. Their music soared to the rafters, taking on a life of its own so it was impossible to tell which instrument was playing which section. Every bar evoked deep emotions within them: joy, sadness, wonder, passing in the blink of an eye, to be replaced by a new feeling. They could both understand the old stories of hapless mortals entranced by the fairy music, only to discover a hundred years had passed.

There were wild reels that set half the room dancing, a sight that was as terrifying as it was amazing; the crowd moved in perfect unison as if choreographed for some Busby Berkeley movie, yet they were as silent as the grave; it was eerie yet hypnotic. And then there were sad songs that made Ruth want to weep on the spot, yearning ballads that reminded her of her father, others that forced her to probe the feelings she had for Church. She fought the urge to hug him, though it brought tears to her eyes.

And Church was lost in thoughts of Marianne, of times frittered in the belief they could be picked up in the future, in thoughts of guilt at what he had done to Laura and Niamh; and then, once they had dissipated, at Ruth beside him. But before he had a chance to turn to her, the tempo increased and another emotion washed everything else away.

The food and drink came in a never-ending stream. Once they had eaten their fill, another dish materialised to tempt them, and when they certainly could eat no more, there was still wine, and more wine.

During a lull while the band members refreshed themselves with a drink, Ruth rose from her chair and hurried over to them. They drew in close around her as she spoke in low tones, their faces at first curious, then intrigued. When she retook her seat, Church asked, "What was that all about?" but she dismissed him with a wave.

He got his answer once the band started up again. Although the tone was oddly distorted, the song was unmistakable: "Fly Me to the Moon." Each note was filled with meaning, of his old life, certainly, but more importantly, and surprisingly, of the time at the pub on Dartmoor when he had performed karaoke with Ruth and Laura in a few moments of pure, unadulterated fun. He looked over to her, felt a surge of warmth at what he saw in her smile: she had remembered what he had said about never hearing Sinatra again.

"I hummed it to them," she whispered. "They picked it up straight away."

What he felt in that instant, he tried to blame on the drink or the music, but he knew he would not be able to deny it, even in the light of the next morning. He put his hand on the back of hers, but it didn't begin to express what he was feeling.

"You know," he said, mesmerised by the moment that felt like a lifetime, "these days everything is so much more vital." He was rambling, drunk. "This is what life should be. Meaning in everything. Importance in everything."

She smiled, said nothing; so much more assured. How could he not feel for her? He leaned forward, closed his eyes, savoured the anticipated moment as if he had already tasted it.

This is the time. This is everything. The words burst in his head unbidden, meaningless, yet filled with meaning. "It's like I'm on drugs." He could feel the bloom of her breath on his lips.

"I am the Messenger. The Message here is very clear." The voice was a blast of cold wind, freezing the moment. Church looked up at the tattered rag-figure Cormorel had called the Walpurgis, a sucking core of darkness, too much for one space. There was something so alien about it, Church's skin crawled; in the back of his head a worm of terror began to wriggle.

Cormorel had been involved in an intense, whispered conversation with Baccharus and the Walpurgis's arrival had taken him by surprise. He turned sharply, his face hard. Church hadn't seen that expression on any of the Tuatha Dé Danann before; he had the face of someone with something to hide.

"Away with you, Dark One." Cormorel waved his hand dismissively. "We have no time for your shadowy discourses."

The Walpurgis began to back away, until Church said, "Wait. Who are you?"

"I am the Messenger." The voice came from everywhere and nowhere.

"He is a dismal leech," Cormorel said. "Nothing more."

"A leech?" Ruth's brow had knitted; Church could tell she was sensing something too.

"The Walpurgis reaches into heads and pulls out dreams." Cormorel made a snapping motion with his fingers. "A distasteful trait, even by the low standards of his fellow travellers."

"You have a very contemptuous view of your fellow sentient beings, Cormorel," Church noted sardonically.

Cormorel eyed him, aloof. "All are beneath us." It was announced as a statement of fact, with no obvious arrogance.

Church was unable to pierce the gloom falling from the brim of the Walpurgis's hat; there were only those hot-coal eyes, unpleasant in their intensity. "You said you have a message?"

The Walpurgis nodded his head slowly. "But first there is something within you which should be examined."

"Within me?"

"A dream." A bony finger snaked towards Church's forehead. Instinctively Church drew back, his skin starting to crawl.

"You want to pull out my dream?"

"Did you know," Cormorel said icily, "the Walpurgis eats the souls of the dying?"

Church ignored him. There was something about the Walpurgis that made him feel queasy; it was so alien he couldn't begin to judge its trustworthiness. Perhaps this was how it preyed on its victims.

"All have dreams hidden away that could change the way they live their lives," the Walpurgis said in its rustling voice. "It is the nature of existence to obscure the important. A game it plays with us. The finding is often part of the lesson."

Church weighed this for a second. There was something repugnant about admitting so alien a being into his head, but he could see Cormorel did not want him to continue, and that was enough.

"Will it hurt?"

The Walpurgis said nothing.

"Okay. Do it."

Cormorel moved to stop him, then his pride made him turn back to his conversation with Baccharus, as if Church, Ruth and The Walpurgis no longer existed.

"You're sure?" Ruth asked.

Church presented his forehead to the Walpurgis. The creature reached out again with its skeletal hand. The fingertips brushed his skin like the touch of winter, but their advance did not stop there. Church was shocked to feel the coldness continuing into his skull. It had not been a metaphor: the fingers were literally moving through his head as if it were mist, reaching inside him. He gagged, shuddered involuntarily; a spasm made his fingers snap open and closed.

What's it doing to me? The thought fizzed like static on a TV; he was losing control of himself.

Panic rose within him, but just as he began to believe he had made a dreadfully wrong decision, the sickening sensations faded and he was suddenly jolted alert by a stream of intensely evocative images. The Walpurgis had tapped into the cable wire from his subconscious.

His mother and father, seen from the perspective of his cot. Niamh appearing at the end of his bed, strangely happy, yet tinged with sadness. Coming faster now: school, university, knee-deep in mud at an archaeological dig in North Yorkshire. And then Marianne. The shock of her face was like a punch; so clear, like she was really there, like he could reach out to touch her. His emotions welled up and threatened to overflow his body; everything felt so acute.

And then it was like the images were playing on a screen just in front of his eyes and he could see through them to the Walpurgis. His red eyes were growing brighter. "Near. So near." The words echoed so deep in his head he didn't know if the Walpurgis had spoken them aloud.

A rapid flicker of memories, the speed making him feel queasy. Making love to Marianne, slicked with sweat. Out drinking with Dean and his other buddies. Kissing Marianne under the stars. Watching a band. Drinking. Writing something. Eating . . . somewhere. A restaurant. Already gone, and two more as well. Brighton. And . . . and America. And back to South London. The pub with all the bric-a-brac in Clapham. Faster, and faster still. And then . . .

Oh God. No. Not that.

The images were slowing down as if the Walpurgis had been fast-forwarding through a video and was now getting closer to the point he was after. Flicker, flicker, click, click, click. The flat, the night he had been out drinking. The night Marianne died.

No. Please, no.

But how could he be remembering that? He hadn't been there. And then he realised he wasn't exactly remembering the night, he was recalling his experience in the vast cave beneath Arthur's Seat in Edinburgh, when time bent and he had been thrust into that awful moment.

The Walpurgis's eyes cut through the familiar image of his flat. "Here. Now."

"No!" Church said aloud.

The image coalesced. The empty flat, removed of the clutter of his maudlin bachelor years. And it was no longer just an image: he could hear and smell, feel the texture of the carpet through the soles of his shoes. In the background one of Marianne's acid jazz CDs played quietly, and she, just out of sight, was humming along. There was no sorrow, only cold, hard fear; he knew what was coming.

"Please." The Walpurgis ignored him, draining every sensation out of his head.

Marianne crossed to the bathroom. The sound of the cabinet opening, just as he recalled it from Arthur's Seat. But then he had broken the spell before the final, sickening moment, so what was the point of the Walpurgis's actions? He loosened up a little; of course he wouldn't see the worst thing.

And there it was: the faint click of the front door opening. Nearly there now. Through the moment, Church could feel his fingernails biting into the flesh of his hand. "Church? Is that you?" Her voice, almost unbearable. The shape, like a ghost, flitting across the hall. He hadn't concentrated before; it had all been too painful.

And then, oddly, the image rewound a few seconds and played again. Church's head spun. *What was going on?*

It reached the same point, then rewound again. And again. And again. And then Church realised: the Walpurgis was trying to show him something. This time he concentrated.

The shape, flitting across the hall. No, not the shape; that wasn't it at all. He was looking at the wrong thing. What was it? The image rewound and played again. And then he saw something: the shadow the shape cast on the wall as it passed. So brief, a fraction of a second, but Church knew he had seen its outline before. That wasn't all, though: a smell, wafting briefly in the air. A familiar smell. Vague, unsettling thoughts began to ripple up from the hidden depths of his mind. What were they? Piece them all together.

And then he had the first part of it. The realisation swept through him like the harshest winter. The shadow of the intruder, the one who had murdered Marianne, had been one of his recent companions: a Brother *or* Sister of Dragons. Every subtle indicator told him his instincts were right. At that stage he couldn't pin it down any more, but he knew if he watched the image a few more times he would have it.

His stomach was turning loops. Surely it couldn't be true. One of the people who had been closest to him over the last few months, someone he trusted more than life itself? Not Laura. Or Veitch. Surely not Shavi. Not Ruth. His stomach flipped again and he felt like he was going to vomit. It was so close, he could almost see the face. So close, so close.

"Here it is," the Walpurgis said sickeningly.

Church wanted to snap himself away. He didn't think he could bear the revelation, like discovering a loved member of your family had committed the ultimate perversion. It would destroy him, he was sure.

But he had to see. It was his responsibility. He concentrated and waited for the dismal tableau to begin once more.

But within seconds of it beginning again, the whole world went sideways. Electric fracturing lines lanced across his vision; pain crackled deep within his head. The Walpurgis was breaking contact. His stomach did another flip. When the bizarre TV screen effect disappeared and he saw the Walpurgis's fingers withdrawing from his forehead, he knew the revelation wasn't going to come.

"No!" he yelled. He reached out to drag the Walpurgis's arm back to him, but it was like a cartoon nightmare: though he stretched and stretched, the Walpurgis was receding in slow time. Church's stomach was continuing to move of its own accord. A sudden bout of vertigo made him reach for the table that was no longer there.

"Church!"

His thoughts rolled in a daze. The world was turning turtle.

"Church!" His shoulders were roughly dragged round. It was Ruth yelling at him, concern etched on her pale face. "We're going down!"

It took another second for her words to register and then he snapped completely back into the real world. The room was engulfed in chaos. Platters and cutlery were floating through the air, along with the occasional traveller. The floor was at an impossible angle.

"We're going down!" she screamed at him again, so close to his ears it made them ring. She pulled him to his feet, they clung for an instant before pitching across the floor.

Everywhere were screams and yells and clanging metal and splintering wood. Church was rolling as the floor rose to forty-five degrees. Violent vibrations thundered back and forth, at odds with the sucking, downward motion; it felt like Wave Sweeper was being shaken apart. Some enormous creature that smelled of burned rubber crashed against his back with such force he thought he had broken it. He had barely recovered when the gigantic top table began to slide, picking up speed until it was rushing towards his head. When it was inches from turning his skull to jelly, he propelled himself a few inches to one side so he passed between the hefty, carved legs.

He too started to slide backwards towards the mêlée of bodies thrashing near the far wall. He'd moved a few feet, spread-eagling his arms and legs as far as they would go to slow his fall, when his fingers found purchase in a crevice between two floorboards. Clutching on tightly, he searched for Ruth, but she was nowhere to be seen.

Something cut through the madness and left him feeling like he was floating in a soundless, slow-motion vacuum: Manannan moved eerily across the floor, perpendicular to it, oblivious to the force of gravity dragging everything else downwards. Bodies flashed past him, but he continued his gradual progress in such a languid manner it looked like he was actually floating an inch or two above the boards. And then, when he was halfway across the room, his head turned almost mechanically and his attention fixed on Church. It was only a second or two, but it made Church's blood run cold.

The ship tipped a degree more and Manannan was lost behind more flying bodies as he made his way to the main exit at the rear of the banqueting hall. Just as Church feared he couldn't hold on any longer, the boat pitched forward. The moment the keel hit the waves, Church was thrown six feet into the air before landing hard on the boards.

Instantly the ship began pitching from side to side. Creatures careered wildly around the room, throwing him to his knees every time he tried to stand upright. Finally he was attempting to run with them towards the exit, but the rippling floor made him stagger as if he were gallon drunk. In the end he clubbed aside anyone or thing which got in his path, anxious to find Ruth.

When he saw the heaps of broken, unmoving bodies he feared the worst until he caught sight of her in a space against the wall, dazed, half kneeling, a cut leaking blood on to her forehead. It looked like they would never get past the throng fighting to get out, but when the ship lurched crazily to one side they managed to hang on to a set of drapes while all the others near the exit were swept away.

The constrained space of the corridor made it easier for them to catch their breath. "What the hell's going on?" Church was still disoriented after the Walpurgis's intrusion.

Ruth pulled herself along the wall towards the deck. "I thought our progress was a little too smooth."

They emerged into madness. Black waves soared up, some passing completely over the boat before crashing on the other side. The ship rolled in the wild water so violently that first one rail almost touched the churning sea, and then the other. The night sky was cloud tossed and torn by lightning, with no sign of moon or stars. Church and Ruth had to grip on to the mast to prevent the howling wind hurling them into the turbulent ocean. Every time they inhaled they took in a mouthful of salty water; the very air was infused with it.

In a flash of lightning that froze the tableau in glaring white, they sensed movement above them. The next burst confirmed their fears. Something with the texture of black rubber gleamed in the light. It moved rapidly, but they recognised it was a tentacle, so large Church would not have been able to put his arms around it. Another lashed out of the water in an arc across the boat. The monster was trying to wrap itself around the entire ship to drag it down into the depths.

A further tentacle smashed into one of the crew, his body folding where no joints had been. Others skidded across the deck, fighting to keep control of the boat so it wasn't breached by the waves. And then, in another lightning burst, they caught sight of the bulk of the creature just off the port side, ten times as large as Wave Sweeper, something that was part octopus and part whale, with other, stranger inclusions too. It reminded Church of engravings he'd seen in old books about the mysteries of the deep.

"A G'a'naran." Baccharus was beside them, answering Church's unspoken question. He was almost white, trembling from the shock of the attack. "They breed on the ocean floor, grazing on the dreams of mortals. They rarely challenge ships, and never Wave Sweeper."

"Then why is it here?" Ruth yelled above the storm.

Baccharus was steadying himself with a rope around his wrist attached to a nearby spinnaker. "I fear it was summoned."

"By whom?" Church could tell from the god's face some vital information was not being passed on. Baccharus's gaze grew hollow.

"What's going on here, Baccharus?" Church pressed.

The god might have answered, but in that instant a tentacle swept along the length of the deck towards them. Baccharus ducked at the last moment, but the tip of it slapped Ruth away from the safety of the mast. She hit the deck hard, stunned. Church barely had time to register what had happened when a wave crashed over them and Ruth was propelled by the thick, foaming surf towards the rail. At the same time the ship began to roll on that side. In shock, Church realised she was going over the edge.

Without any consideration for his own safety, he threw himself forward, allowing the surge of water to give him speed. It was futile. He watched in horror as the waves flung Ruth over the rail.

At the last moment her jacket snagged on one of the hooks used to secure the rigging and she was jerked to a sudden halt. Church was already moving fast with the force of the water and it was difficult to direct himself. He prayed her jacket would hold until he reached her.

Somehow she managed to buy a little extra time by clutching on to the carved rail, and then he slammed into the side with such force it knocked all the wind from him.

"Hang on!" he yelled.

The boat dipped down even further. Church thought he was going to pitch over the rail too, while Ruth's feet were now dragging in the bubbling cauldron of ocean. He could see the panic in her face, though she tried to bury it; her strength gave him strength.

They were a pocket in a universe of water, where it was impossible to tell up from down; when he breathed, there was only brine. The rest of the world was invisible through the constant stream.

Somehow he found her arm. He tried to tug, but there was nowhere to get purchase. Ruth would have been dragged to her death if the boat had not then rolled sharply in the other direction. The sheer force of the reversal sent them both flying: Ruth's hand wrenched from the rail and they turned in the water-infused air before slamming into the deck. It stunned them both, but soon helping hands were dragging them to safety. Baccharus and a group of other Tuatha Dé Danann lashed ropes around their wrists to keep them steady. Despite the worsening situation, Church grabbed Ruth tightly, overcome with relief.

She fell into him for a second, before pushing him away. "I can help." She turned to Baccharus. "The storm is making things worse. If it stopped, can you do something about the monster?"

His answer was a gesture towards the poop deck where Manannan was floating a few inches above the boards, his hands making intricately complex gestures in the air, some so convoluted he must have disjointed his limbs to achieve them. Just beyond the cone of movement, starbursts flashed in the air, focusing and moving out in streams towards the dark bulk of the G'a'naran, where they exploded like arcing electricity, blue sparks showering into the water. "The Master is doing what he can," Baccharus said.

Ruth was already loosening the rope around her wrist.

Church grabbed her arm. "What are you doing?"

"I can do a lot of things." The look on her face scared him.

She heaved her way along the rolling deck, coughing out mouthfuls of seawater. Church lost her to the spray within seconds, but by then there were other things to occupy his mind. Tentacles lashed the boat with increasing ferocity, sweeping crew members into the boiling sea or crushing them against the deck. Church ducked the frenzied thrashing repeatedly, sometimes throwing himself flat on to the sodden boards.

The storm, too, was increasing in intensity. The lightning struck all around, freezing the conflict in bursts of white, the faces of those near him just skulls with black, terrified eyes. A tentacle swept by with the force of a boom. It narrowly missed crushing his head.

A cry drove through the howling wind. Baccharus had been pinned to the mast, the monstrous arm coiling gradually around him. Pain fanned out across his face as the pressure increased. Church was shocked to see the other Tuatha Dé Danann look on obliquely, then continue their tasks without any attempt to help; nor did Baccharus call out to them.

Church threw himself across the heaving deck, grappling the tentacle in an attempt to prise it free. The skin had the sickening consistency of decaying rubber, and it smelled like a compost heap with a few fish heads thrown in. But it was too strong for him to budge it even an inch.

Then the strangest thing happened: in the middle of the creeping pain, Baccharus's eyes locked on his. At first Church saw confusion in them, then curiosity and finally something he couldn't understand at all, but it appeared to drive the pain back. A second later a scurrying sensation moved over Church's waist and quickly up his chest. He jumped back in shock as Baccharus's Caraprix scuttled on to the tentacle and clung on with spider legs, the silver orb of its body glowing in the gloom.

"Take it," Baccharus yelled.

Church fought back his natural distaste and held out a hand towards the symbiotic creature. It instantly moved and changed, so quickly his stomach knotted in shock, slipping perfectly into his grip as it transformed into a cruel-bladed short sword, still brilliant silver. Church had seen the things' wild shapeshifting before, but it never failed to astound him.

At the moment before impact, the sword grew a row of serrated teeth that became a snapping jaw tearing into the rubbery flesh with remarkable ease. A shudder ran through the tentacle. Church struck again, this time with more force, then again and again until the air was filled with the flayed flesh of the G'a'naran. Finally the tentacle unfurled sharply, catching him in the chest. Winded, he slumped to the deck, but still found it within him to catch Baccharus as the god fell forward. Gratitude flooded his face.

"How are you?" Church asked.

"Not well, but well enough to recover. The Golden Ones are nothing if not resilient." He smiled, and once again Church was surprised to see none of the usual arrogance of the Tuatha Dé Danann.

At that moment Church became aware of a change in the atmosphere, subtle at first, but becoming more apparent. It took him a second or two to realise what it was: the storm was gradually moving away, the lightning flashes becoming less intense, the winds dying down, the thunder no longer hurting his ears. Subsequently, the waves dropped and the inches-deep water on the deck flowed away. Within a minute the storm had gone completely; the sea lay saucer flat, the night sky clear and sparkling with stars. The only wrenching motion came from the still-flailing tentacles of the G'a'naran.

Church peered along the deck to the aft where Ruth leaned against the rails, exhaustion hunching her shoulders. There was a faint nimbus of energy around her that disappeared so rapidly Church couldn't tell if it had truly been there or if it had been his imagination. He looked up at the clear skies, still not truly believing, but the rapidity with which the storm had receded had not been natural.

Baccharus levered himself up on his elbow. He was healing before Church's eyes, muscle and bone knitting, energy levels rising. "Look." He motioned towards the poop deck. "Your intervention has swayed the battle."

Manannan had doubled his attack, his attention no longer diverted by keeping the ship afloat in the face of the storm. There was a sound like silver foil rustling, then ripping. A smell of hot engines and baked potatoes. The air folded in, then ballooned out, a translucent rainbow rippling like oil in a roadside puddle. With a thunderous whip crack, the light ripped towards the G'a'naran. Church anticipated some coruscating display of energy, but there was only the noise of the G'a'naran's flesh rending as a furrow opened up across the rubbery side of the creature.

Church saw no mouth, and there was no real sound, but suddenly he was driven to his knees by a high-pitched noise stabbing into his ears. When he was finally able to raise his head, there was only a sucking section of the sea where the G'a'naran had plunged beneath the waves.

Church dragged himself to his feet, shaky, and then Ruth was at his side, smiling wearily.

"You did it," he said. He held out an arm and she slipped into it, coming to rest hard against his body.

"I wasn't sure I could, even at the last. But then when I opened myself up to it, it all came rushing out. It's like it's all battened down inside, things I've only half-heard but somehow fully formed. Fully remembered. Understood even." Her eyes had grown wide and wondrous. "The things I can do!" She caught herself, looked down modestly. "I think. I mean, I feel I have a lot of potential."

"What was it? A spell?"

She didn't seem quite sure herself. "Remember when we were talking about magic being the cheat code for reality? It was like that, like I could suddenly focus to peel a layer back and move things around behind the scenes."

Church kissed her on the forehead; that surprised them both. "Maybe you can conjure up sausage, bacon and eggs for breakfast."

They both felt the temperature drop a degree or two, and when they looked up Manannan was there. "Sister of Dragons," he said in his sea-tossed voice, "you are true to your heritage." He gave a little bow that, in his restrained manner, looked as if he was proclaiming her greatness to the heavens.

"Thank you," she said shyly.

"And you, Brother of Dragons," he continued to Church, "you aided this Golden One in his moment of need. Wave Sweeper is the better for your presence." He paused for a moment, then added, "We must talk about great things—"

Whatever he was about to say was snapped off by a cry of alarm from the other end of the boat. There was a note of terror to it that shocked them all into immediate action. Church and Ruth sprinted until they reached the raised area where Church had earlier sat with Niamh. At the top of the steps one of the younger Tuatha Dé Danann was rigid, his normally plastic features shifting like smoke. Church pushed past him to get a better look.

Cormorel was slumped half over the railings, his eyes staring, blank. His body appeared to be breaking up like a cracked mirror. Where the fracture lines spread out across him, a brilliant white light shone through, taking consistency, shape, becoming something like moths that fluttered wildly around the body before rising up and up to become lost in the night sky. Hunched over Cormorel was the shadowy form of the Walpurgis, his bony hands clutching at the god's shirt, his hot coal eyes growing brighter than ever. His mouth was stretched wide, the jaws distended inches away from the body so he could suck up some of the flapping moths. They swirled around frantically before disappearing into that black maw.

Church felt sick to his stomach. He knew exactly what the Walpurgis was doing; Cormorel himself had said it: *the Walpurgis eats the souls of the dying.*

Manannan and the other Tuatha Dé Danann surged up the stairs. Church moved aside, fearful of the transformation he saw come over them. Their bodies were like knives, like light, like a maelstrom of howling faces. And the sound they made was terrifying: a screech filled with desolation and elemental fury. As they rushed towards the Walpurgis, the creature broke off its feeding, looked around briefly like a cornered animal, then ran towards the rails. He vaulted over them to the lower deck, hanging briefly like a sheet billowing in the wind. Within seconds he had disappeared through the door that led down into the bowels of Wave Sweeper.

Instead of pursuing him, the Tuatha Dé Danann gathered around Cormorel, his body now little more than fragments in a pool of white light. Church and Ruth couldn't bear to hear their howling grief, if that was what it was, and hurried back down the stairs to the far side of the deck.

Ruth had a disturbed, queasy expression. "How could that thing kill him?" She looked around, grasping for understanding. "I thought they couldn't die."

Church shook his head, still trying to come to terms with what he had seen. He had witnessed Calatin's death and knew what a monumental thing it was; to all intents and purposes the gods went on forever, their vital energy unquenchable even if their forms were destroyed. It took something special to wipe them from existence.

"It doesn't make any sense," he said. "Why would the Walpurgis murder Cormorel? He would know he wouldn't get away with it."

"Maybe he couldn't control himself. Driven by hunger . . . ?"

He turned and rested on the rails, looking at the reflected starlight glittering on the waves, thinking how much it reminded him of that disappearing essence of Cormorel.

"How's this going to affect things?" he said. "At least we know we're going to die, even if we don't want to face up to it. It's no great shock. The Tuatha Dé Danann think they're going on forever. Seeing something like that, it's a blow we can't even begin to comprehend. What will it do to them?"

The question hung in the air, but after all they had been through it was too much to consider. Ruth stepped in next to him and again he slipped an arm around her shoulders. They both felt like they were huddling together for warmth in a world grown cold and dark.

chapter four
empty cisterns, exhausted wells

The noises echoing around the ship that night were terrifying to hear: shrieks and howls, grunts and roars; at times it was as if a pack of wild animals roamed the cramped corridors, things not even remotely human loose on board. Church and Ruth chose to stay together in the same room for security, but they did not feel safe, even with a huge chest pulled across the door.

Although the sounds were impossible to track, they knew the Tuatha Dé Danann were hunting the Walpurgis into the depths of Wave Sweeper. But Ruth knew how futile that exercise was, even if the gods understood the twisted confines of their ship. And so the questing continued into the small hours until it eventually died away. The silence was bitter and they knew the quarry had not been located.

They woke in a beam of sunlight breaking through the bottle-glass windows, entangled like lovers, although they had only held each other for comfort. Their position brought embarrassment and they quickly hurried to opposite ends of the bed. Eventually, though, in the warmth of the morning sun and their relief that all was calm without, their legs were soon draping over each other as they chatted lazily.

"You don't think he did it, then?" Ruth asked as she brushed with crooked fingers at the tangles in her hair.

Church threw open the windows so they could look out across the foam-topped waves. "There's something about it that's troubling me. When the Walpurgis was poking around in my head I got a sense of him. It wasn't quite a reciprocal thing—he had all my mind laid out before him—but I felt . . ." He fumbled for words. "I don't think he kills, however black Cormorel painted him. He certainly feeds on souls—"

"So you think he found Cormorel dying?"

"I don't know."

"Then who killed Cormorel? Who would have the *power* to kill him? What possible motivation could there be?"

Church held up his hand to stop her questions. "You've seen all the wild, freakish things travelling on this ship with us. God knows what's lurking down there in the darkest depths."

"The Malignos," Ruth mused.

"There was plenty of opportunity in all the chaos for something predatory to attack. Perhaps whatever did it thought we were going down and it had nothing to lose."

"I hope it's not going to deflect us from what we've got to achieve." Ruth leaned on the windowsill, filling her lungs with the salty air. "There's so much at risk, we can't afford any—"

"You don't have to tell me."

The dark tone in his voice made her look round. "What is it?"

"There's something else. When the Walpurgis was in my mind he pulled something out."

"That's right—he said he had a message." Her eyes narrowed as she scanned his face for clues. "Something bad?"

"He kept replaying the scene just before Marianne's murder in our flat, the one I stumbled across in that time-warping cavern under Arthur's Seat. The same thing over and over again. Someone entering the flat, a shadow on the wall. It wasn't just images—I could smell it too, hear, feel. He knew exactly what he wanted to show me, but I think he felt it was important I found it out for myself."

"More impact that way." She chewed on a knuckle apprehensively; Church watched, wondering. "So did you get it? I know how dense you can be," she asked.

He nodded. "Part of it anyway." He weighed his thoughts, not sure how much he should tell her, then hating himself for even thinking it. "One of us killed Marianne."

"One of *us*?"

"Laura, Shavi, Veitch—"

"Or me?"

"Everything went pear shaped before I had a chance to piece it all together. But I saw a shadow that I recognised. I smelled something—"

"What? Like perfume?" she said sharply.

"No. It was unusual. But familiar. Subtle. I don't know what it meant. Instinctively I was certain it was one of us. If I'd only had a few more minutes—"

"You're sure?"

He thought for a moment. "I'm sure."

She sucked on her lip. "So who do you think it is?"

"I don't know."

"Who do you *think*?"

"I don't know. Honestly."

"Do you think it was me?"

He looked her full in the eye. Her gaze was unwavering, confident, perhaps a little hurt. "I'm about as sure as I can be that it wasn't you."

That pleased her immensely. Her mouth crumpled into a smile before growing serious a moment later. "That ties in with what the Celtic dead told us about a traitor in the group. Whoever it was, they were there from the start."

"We mustn't start jumping to conclusions."

"No, but it makes sense."

And he had to admit that it did, but it was too upsetting to consider. The five of them had been friends through the hardest of times. They had saved each other's lives. He trusted them all implicitly, knew them all inside out, or thought he did. None of them had the capacity to be a traitor on the scale implied, he was sure of it. But if he could be fooled through such intimate contact, what did that mean? That the traitor was truly evil, and truly dangerous.

He could tell Ruth was thinking something similar; she rubbed her arms as if she were cold despite the warmth of the sun. "There's no point in guessing," she said eventually. "If we could piece it together from what we've seen we would have done it already."

"I know, but . . ."

"What is it?"

"It casts a shadow over everything. I know that sounds stupid with what's going down, but the fact is, the five of us . . . six, with Tom . . . we were the calm centre, something I could rely on to make everything else bearable."

"It's just the two of us now. *We're* the calm centre."

Any further discussion was curtailed by a sharp knock at the door. It was Baccharus carrying a tray filled with cold meats, fruit and bread. "I thought you might like to break your fast," he said quietly.

They ushered him in, then refused to let him leave while they hungrily ate everything on the tray. They questioned him about what was happening elsewhere on Wave Sweeper.

"The Master has called a meeting of all who travel upon Wave Sweeper, on deck shortly. There is a feeling for . . ." He chose his word carefully. ". . . retribution."

"Have you found the Walpurgis?" Church asked.

Baccharus shook his head. "There are many scouring the boat, even as we speak, but it is . . ." He made an expansive gesture.

"How serious is this?" Ruth said.

"How serious? To the Golden Ones it is a crime against existence. We dance amongst the worlds; stars pass beneath our feet. We are a part of everything, of the endless cycle. We are not meant to be eradicated—"

"But it is possible," Church said, remembering Calatin. "You know that."

"Anything is possible." Baccharus's voice had grown even quieter. "But there are some things that should not happen. One could imagine the whole of everything falling into the void before they came to pass. The eradication of a Golden One is one of those things. Cormorel may have appeared young to you. But he was enjoying his wild ways when your world was a steaming rock in the infinite dark. What you saw last night was something beyond your comprehension. A star exploding would not have matched one atom of its import."

"I'm sorry." Ruth rested a hand on his forearm. "I know Cormorel was your companion. We know what it is like to lose a dear friend." His expression brought her up sharp; it said she could never understand the slightest of what he—all the Tuatha Dé Danann—were experiencing.

"There are two issues here," Baccharus continued. "The Master is concerned that the Walpurgis had not only the power, but also the knowledge of how to use it to end Cormorel's days. And that he had the inclination."

"Do you believe it was the Walpurgis?" Church pressed.

Baccharus looked at him thoughtfully. "You saw as well as I—"

"I saw him drain Cormorel's soul. I didn't see him commit murder."

Baccharus shrugged. "The Master believes it to be the Walpurgis—"

"Isn't justice important?"

"Of course." Baccharus's voice grew cold for the first time since they had known him.

"Well, isn't it?" Church pressed.

"Justice is above us all."

An uncomfortable silence descended on the room until Ruth couldn't bear it. "That thing which attacked last night—"

"The G'a'naran." Baccharus was staring dismally across the waves.

"The G'a'naran. What was it?" She looked to Church. "It reminded me of old stories, mariners' tales—"

"More race memories, things that slip between the worlds."

"A sea monster?"

"The G'a'naran is unformed, from the age when all flowed freely, finding its shape," Baccharus said. "Its home is not beneath the waves, though sometimes it takes refuge there. It navigates amongst the stars—"

"Like you?"

Baccharus looked at Ruth. "No, not like us."

Church was troubled by Baccharus's description. "I don't understand why it attacked the ship if it's not some kind of mindless animal, which I presume it's not. Is it a predator?" He was surprised to see Baccharus was concerned too. "What is it?"

The god made to leave without answering, but Church dragged the reply from him. "The G'a'naran would not have attacked Wave Sweeper unless it was provoked. Or summoned."

"Summoned?" Church's head was thundering; connections were lining up, but not quite linking. "What's going on here?"

Before the matter could be pursued further, a long, low mournful sound reverberated throughout the ship. It drew an overwhelmingly dismal feeling from deep within them; Ruth found tears springing to her eyes involuntarily.

"The Master is summoning." Baccharus looked oddly distracted, almost dazed. When he realised they were still seated, he said, "You must come."

The sun was unbearably bright as they stepped out on to the deck, blinking. "Tell me," Church hissed to Baccharus in response to the silence that lay heavy over everything, "when you were in trouble on deck last night, why didn't anyone save you?"

On the surface Baccharus's face appeared emotionless, but Church could tell there were deep but unreadable emotions running beneath. "There is no recognition that we might not exist. Therefore there is no need to aid one in dire straits."

"I thought you lot always stuck together."

"You do not understand our ways." It was a cold statement; Church knew there was no point pursuing the matter. By that time they had arrived in the midst of a crowd filling every foot of the ship's boards, some of the freakish travellers even clambering up into the rigging. Others were arriving behind them. Amidst the reek of alien scents, the pressing of skin that felt like carbonised rubber or gelatine, Church fought to focus his attention on the tableau unfolding on the raised area preserved for the captain of the vessel.

His face like an ocean tempest, Manannan overlooked the crowd, hands behind his back, flanked by other members of the Tuatha Dé Danann. Niamh was close by his right arm, her beautiful face troubled too. She stared across the waves, lost to whatever dark scenarios were playing in her mind.

A low muttering had risen in the crowd like wind over the water, but when Manannan raised his left arm, everyone felt silent. His gaze slowly moved across the masses; even at that distance Church was sure his eyes were burning. His face held an odd quality too, as though it were about to become fluid, transform.

"A crime has been committed against the very fabric of existence." He appeared to be whispering, but his voice boomed over the throng, which grew visibly cowed. "Something more valuable than the stars above you, more important than the entire weight of all your races, from the beginning to the end, has been torn away. This will not go unpunished."

Church felt a pang of fear. Ruth's skin was unnaturally pale.

"The one who committed this atrocity is known to us, and though not yet within our grasp, know this: there is no escape from our unflinching eye. No hope. We will peel back the lies, strip away the moment and the mile, never rest, until we have it." He paused, letting his words fall like stones. "And know this also: our gaze will be turned on you, all of you, individually, even in your most private moments. And if we find any who have aided or abetted the committal of this monstrous crime, they will be punished." Another pause. "With the full weight of our wrath."

He surveyed the crowd one final time, with many flinching from his eyes, and then slowly descended to his quarters, the other members of the Tuatha Dé Danann trailing behind.

Even when they had all departed and the door had closed, no one on deck moved, no one spoke, there was not even a rustle of clothing. Church smelled fear in the air and more than that, an awful dread that events were rapidly deteriorating. There was darkness on the horizon and none of them knew which way the wind was blowing.

"He's in here?"

Baccharus motioned towards the heavy wooden door with the black sigil. It was two decks down, at the heart of the ship so no wall was next to the cool, green water. Church moved his palm gently a quarter-inch above the surface of the door, testing the sensitivity that had grown in him since Tom had introduced him to the Blue Fire. His skin prickled. Inside the room he felt an unpleasant coldness that was the antithesis of that spirit energy. He didn't know why he had asked Baccharus to take him there while Ruth rested—or hid—in her cabin, but the urge had been insistent. He pushed his palm forward and the door swung open at his touch.

The chamber was in complete darkness. It smelled of some zoo cage littered with dirty straw, reminding him uncomfortably of his imprisonment in the mine deep beneath Dartmoor. He couldn't help but think a cruelty was being inflicted, despite everything his rational mind told him of deserving punishment.

Baccharus stepped past him holding one of the torches from the corridor and lit an extinct one fixed to the wall close to the door. Unlike the torches without, it cast only a dull, ruddy glare, barely causing the shadows to retreat. Baccharus nodded to him curtly, then stepped out and closed the door behind him.

"So you've found it in your heart to visit another soldier of the road, now sadly down on his luck." The voice was infused with scorn.

At the far end of the room was an iron cage, barely large enough for a man to stretch out in. Straw was indeed scattered on the floor within, along with what resembled an animal's feeding trough. Callow squatted at the back of it, his peeled white eyes staring like sickly lamps. There was something about that unflinching gaze that made Church's stomach squirm: human yet not human. The parchment skin was a muddy red in the flickering glow of the torch, but the black veins still stood out starkly, a roadmap of hell.

"Don't get smart with me. You've brought everything on yourself."

"Well, that's a fine attitude for such a noble man to take. Filled with Christian values. Do I hear the sweet tinkling notes of forgiveness? The vibrato of salvation? The teasing choir of redemption? Or perhaps we truly are brothers of the byway. When the ditch is your billet, you see life with a different perspective, is that not true? Not so noble then, is it? *Means to an end* is the phrase on every good man's lips."

"Shut up, Callow. I haven't got the energy." Church eyed the heavy padlocks on the cage door. The Tuatha Dé Danann were taking no chances with him. Perhaps he should be more cautious.

"And how is the lovely *Miz* Gallagher?" Callow began oleaginously.

Church's glare stopped him dead; it left Callow in no doubt that here was a topic where he could never trespass. Callow scrabbled around in the straw for a distraction like he was looking for a stray piece of corn from his meal; a chicken waiting to be harvested. But then he looked up with a cold confidence and said, "Things have turned a little sour, have they not?" His thin lips peeled back from his blackened teeth in a sly smirk.

He knows why I've come, Church thought.

Callow's eyes were a vortex in the gloom. "You're here to beg for my help. Oh, Glory be! My time has truly come!"

"Your time has long gone, Callow. But you might still be able to rescue a thin chance of saving yourself if you start acting like you don't want to see the whole of humanity eradicated."

"Look after number one, my boy. You know that well."

The jibe hurt Church even though he had managed to put his own selfish interests to one side. "This is a new age, didn't you know? These days we look after each other." Callow looked away. "I may be wasting my time here in more ways than one," Church continued, "but I have to ignore my personal feelings if there's a chance everyone might benefit. And make no mistake, Callow, I loathe you. For what you did to Laura, and Ruth. For turning your back on the human race simply to achieve your own ends. You truly are a grotesque person. But it's still wrong the way the Tuatha Dé Danann are treating you like some animal."

"We are all animals to them."

"I know. They use us for their own ends, but this time we're using them." Church felt uncomfortable trying to play Callow. A streak of madness that ran through him made him impossible to predict; Church still didn't really know what the Fomorii had done to him inside. "I've got a feeling you know something that might help us. Where the Fomorii main nest is, where Balor is hidden, building up his strength. Some weakness—"

"Oh, you really are a prime example of hope over reality," Callow snapped bitterly. "I should give up my hard-won knowledge? For what? A chance to be seen as *good*?" He waggled his fingers to show the gap where he had sliced the one off himself. "You forget, my little pet, the only reason I would want to take your hand is to harvest your digits."

"So you don't know anything, then." Church made to go.

"I know a great many things that would shock and surprise you," Callow replied sharply, stung by the dismissal. "I know what makes your eyes light up. And where the Luck of the Land lies. And I know what happened on this Ship of Fools last night."

"How?"

"I can hear things through the walls. Through many walls."

"I know what happened last night. That's not important to me—"

"You would think, wouldn't you?" Callow smirked again; Church couldn't tell if it was more petty tormenting or if he truly did know something of import. "Now be off with you, and leave me to my peace and quiet," Callow snapped, "and don't return unless you have the key to release me from this foul den."

When he reached the door, Callow called out to him again, "Are you missing your friends? Do you feel lost without them? Too weak and inexperienced? What is it like to know they are all dead, dead, dead . . ."

Church stepped out and slammed the door hard so he wouldn't have to hear any more.

The first thought was like a candle in a room that had remained dark for an age. It flickered, dangerously close to extinction, but then caught. Slowly, the heat and the light returned.

For Laura, memories pieced together gradually and chaotically, sparing her the full horror of revelation in one devastating blow. Making love to Church. The joy she felt at finally finding someone to whom she could open up the dark chambers of her soul. Making love to Shavi, a friend who defied any insipid meaning she had given to the word in the past. Her hated mother, her pathetic father. Her friends. Her work: computer screens and mobile phones. One image returning in force: trees. The things she had fought for so many times with her environmental activism.

They gathered pace, memories clinging together, forming patterns in the chaos. The quest. The Quincunx, the five who are one. Brothers and Sisters of Dragons. Talismans and Blue Fire. Standing stones and old religion. Tuatha Dé Danann and Fomorii. And Balor.

And Balor.

Electricity jolted her body into convulsions. She recalled with crystal clarity the night on Mam Tor when she had taken the potion from Cernunnos and made the sacrifice that would end her life; for Ruth, for everyone. When she took Balor into her own body.

Another shock, dragging her from the recesses of her head. How could she still be alive, thinking? When Balor emerged from her it would have rended her body apart.

Gradually details of her surroundings broke through her confusion. She was lying on her back in a dark place; as her eyes adjusted she realised there was a thin light source filtering in from somewhere. The air was thick with the stench of decomposition. She choked, gagged, tried to breathe in small gasps that went straight to the back of her throat. She made the mistake of turning her head and looked into a pair of glassy eyes only inches from her. It was a woman, not much older than her. Beyond she could just make out irregular shapes heaped all around. They resembled bags of discarded clothing.

Closing her eyes, she took refuge once more in her head, but even there no safety lay. Her body was racked with pain. Slowly she let her hands move down her torso towards her belly, dreading the end of their journey. They were halted by sharpness and void almost before they had started.

Initially she couldn't work out what she was feeling, and then when she did, she refused to believe it. But there was no doubt. Her ribs were protruding on both sides like jagged teeth around the hollow from which Balor had erupted.

It couldn't be. She was dead. Dead and dreaming. Her arms collapsed to her side and her thoughts fragmented once more.

The next time she was aware, she let her hands investigate once more, praying it had been a hallucination. And this time there were no broken ribs and gaping wound, although her clothes around that area were shredded.

Her relief left her sobbing silently for several minutes.

Finally she found the strength to lever herself up on her elbows. From the air currents she could tell she was in some cavernous room, the ceiling and walls lost to the shadows. All around were corpses, piled in rolling dunes. Faces and hands and feet were pressing into her back and legs. So many dead. Hundreds. Thousands. Amidst the horror she was thankful for the small mercy that she was on the top and not drowning beneath the sea of bodies. And she was alive. Amazingly, astonishingly alive.

Then she cried some more.

In the Court of the Yearning Heart, laughter often sounds like the cries of the insane. The walls are never quite thick enough to prevent the noises coming through from adjoining rooms; whimpers of pleasure and pain, others a combination of both. Scents continually tease, each one subtle and complex so the passerby dwells on them for minutes, perhaps hours. Every surface has a pleasing texture; it is impossible to touch anything once without wanting immediately to touch it again. Addiction can spring from the merest taste of the food to the tongue.

In comparison, the chamber designated for Tom was almost unpleasantly ascetic. He had stripped everything from it to minimise the sensory overload so that his life was, if not acceptable, then bearable. At least he no longer had to worry about accepting the food or drink of Otherworld; there was little hope he would be leaving the Court any time in the near future. Prisoner by his own hand, or theirs, it made no matter.

He sat cross-legged in the centre of the room, smoking a joint to dull his searing emotions: wishing he could smoke enough to shut down his thoughts completely. Despite the clothes that had been offered to him by the Tuatha Dé Danann, he still resembled an ageing hippie: his greying hair was fastened into a ponytail with an elastic band, the wire-rimmed spectacles had been fashionable in the late sixties, his too-washed T-shirt and old army jacket: they all grounded him in the experiences of the world he had left behind. And for the first time he felt the hundreds of years piled high on his shoulders. He had thought himself immune to the rigours of passing time, but now it felt as raw as it had in the first century or so of his transformation.

They had taken Veitch four hours ago. How long before they spat him out of the inner recesses of the Court where the miracles and atrocities occurred, torn apart and rebuilt into *something else*? Decades, as it had been in Tom's own case? Or longer? He winced, unable to stop the razored parade of memories of his own early experiences at their hands. After so long, they were still just beneath the surface, torturing every second of his life. He had already shed tears for the suffering Veitch would face in the times ahead, and he did so again, briefly and silently. Would Veitch grow to love his tormentors even as he hated them, just as Tom had? He thought he probably would.

Then Tom, grown emotional through the drugs, battled a wave of damp emotion, this time for himself. For the first time he had found kindred spirits, friends even, although he had never told them that, and all he had done was witness their appalling suffering. Now he might never see any of them again, not even Veitch, who would no longer be Veitch when he returned, in the same way that he was no longer Thomas Learmont. Against all that, even the destruction about to be instigated by the Fomorii was meaningless.

He took a deep draught of the joint, trying to decide if that thought was selfishness or some deep psychological insight; not really caring.

The door was flung open some hours later and Veitch tumbled into the room. Dazed and winded, he came to rest in a heap against the far wall. It took Tom a second or two to realise what he was seeing; even then, he barely dared believe it.

"So soon?" he said, puzzled.

"Don't just sit there, you old hippie," Veitch snapped.

Tom scrambled over to help him to his feet. "You're fine?"

Veitch examined his hands, then stretched the kinks out of his arm muscles, unable to believe it himself. His long hair was lank with the sweat of fear, his tough, good-looking features drawn with apprehension.

"What happened?"

Veitch was surprised at the bald relief in the hippie's voice after weeks of his curt, dismissive manner. "I don't know what happened. When they took me from here I was brought before *Her Majesty*." There was a sneer in Veitch's voice, but Tom knew it was there only to mask the fear of the Queen of the Court of the Yearning Heart, architect of all desire and suffering. "She gave me some spiel about how I was setting off a *new phase of existence*. Didn't really know what she was talking about, to be honest." He examined his hands closely. "Wasn't really listening."

Tom remembered the same response: the fear of what lay ahead driving all rational thought down to its lowest level; not thinking, just reacting. He reached out a supportive hand; surprisingly, Veitch allowed it to rest briefly on his forearm; a small thing, but a sign of how deeply he had been affected.

"They took me through these red curtains into a room that was hung with tapestries. There was a wooden bench in the middle. They tied me to it. Up on the ceiling, there was something, a light of some kind. Only it wasn't a *real* light. It was like it had a life of its own, you know?" His description faltered under the limitations of his vocabulary and his unstructured thought processes, but Tom nodded in recognition. Veitch appeared relieved he wouldn't have to go into it further.

"And then whatever the light was, it made me black out. Next thing I knew

I was looking up at the Queen and she was . . ." He searched for the right word. "Furious."

A tremor crossed Tom's face.

"Her face sort of . . . changed. Kept changing. Like . . . like . . ."

"Like it wasn't fixed."

"Exactly. Like she was breaking up. Turning into something else. Lots of things. I dunno why. I mean, it wasn't like I'd done anything. I'd been out like a light. Next thing I know those jackboot bastards who always follow her around dragged me back here."

Tom dropped back on to the floor, slipping easily into his cross-legged stance, his face locked in an expression of deep rumination; it didn't make sense, whichever way it was examined. The Queen would not have given up the opportunity to spend decades tantalising and tormenting a mortal for anything. He eyed Veitch suspiciously. "Are you sure it wasn't some trick? Offering you the chance of hope, only to snatch it away. The pain is more acute that way." The note of bitter experience rang in his voice.

"No, you should have seen her, mate. It was real. Scared the shit out of me." Veitch grinned broadly, then cracked his knuckles. "Fuck it. Who cares? Maybe there's a chance we'll get out of here."

"The Queen will *never* let you go."

"Don't be so bleedin' negative. You didn't see them. They were all like . . ." He made a dismissive hand gesture. "Like I was something on the bottom of their shoe."

Before Tom could consider the matter further, the door rattled open. Melliflor and the Queen's Honour Guard stood without, dressed in the freakish golden armour that resembled a mix of sea shells and spiderwebs, offset by silk the colour of blood; armour worn only for the most important occasions. Recognising the signs, Tom struggled to his feet. Veitch stepped in front of him protectively, the tendons on his arms growing taut.

Devoid of its usual mockery, Melliflor's face was contemptuous, hacked from cold granite. "Our Lady of Light demands your presence."

Demands, Tom noted. Not *requests*. All pretence of politeness had been dropped; they were no longer favoured guests, nor even figures of fun. "How could we deny her?" Tom saw the dangerous glint in Melliflor's eye and knew he could afford not even the slightest mockery. He bowed his head and, with Veitch at his heel, followed the guard out of the room.

The Queen of Heart's Desire sat in the centre of a room where twenty braziers roared like blast furnaces. The air was unbearably thick with heat and smoke.

Despite the light from the flames, gloom still clung to the periphery, beyond the thick tapestries in scarlet and gold that swathed the stone walls. It was oppressively unpleasant, yet still seared with sensation.

The first time Veitch had seen the Queen, she had been the embodiment of sexual craving, sucking at every part of him that *needed*; naked, splayed, prostrate, for him alone, yet still somehow above him, still in control. Even though he knew she was manipulating every pump of his blood, he couldn't help wanting her; even though the rational part of him had only contempt for her, he would have given himself to her immediately, done anything asked of him.

Now, though, she was enveloped in a brocaded gown and cloak that covered her from neck to toes; a headdress left only the smallest heart of face visible, and that was glacial. She wouldn't even meet his eyes. Despite himself, he felt brokenhearted, unwanted. He looked at Tom and saw the Rhymer felt the same.

Tom bowed his head. "Have we offended you in some way, my Queen?"

She looked over their heads as if the voice had come from the shadowy corners. "Fragile Creatures are always offensive."

"What's wrong?" Veitch was shocked when the words emerged from his mouth, so rimmed with pathetic submission were they; he couldn't help himself, that was the worst thing.

"You are free to leave the Court of the Yearning Heart." She addressed Tom directly. "All compacts and contracts are rescinded. This is a gift given freely and without obligation."

Tom kept his head bowed. "We thank you for your hospitality, my Queen. And may I say—"

She raised her hand. Instantly Melliflor was at Tom's side, directing him towards the exit. The rapidity of their dismissal took them both by surprise, but Tom saw Veitch bristle before they had reached the door.

"Is that it?" Veitch hissed. Then: "What's up with her?" When Tom didn't answer, Veitch thought for a long moment and then said, "She just got bored, didn't she, like some fucking spoilt aristocrat." He tried not to sound too hurt. "She's found something else to interest her more. We're just . . . nothing."

"Hush!" Tom cautioned with blazing eyes. "If you want to get out of here alive—"

"True Thomas."

A look of horror crossed his face at her voice. He turned sharply. "My Queen?"

"The Quincunx are no more, True Thomas."

Veitch saw Tom blanch. "What's she on about?" he whispered.

"The shaman has moved on from the Fixed Lands." A cruel smile lay comfortably on her face.

Tom bowed his head, this time for himself. "And the other Brother and Sisters of Dragons, my Queen?"

She inclined her head thoughtfully. "One of them sleeps in a charnel pit. I hear the other two travel to the Western Isles, True Thomas. And you know what that means."

Veitch looked to Tom for explanation, although in his heart he understood the sense of the Queen's words. He stifled the rising panic, pretending he didn't believe them. Tom's face wouldn't allow him to wallow in the lie, and then Melliflor was once again steering them towards the door.

They emerged on to the summit of the Hill of Yews on an ethereal, late summer morning. Grey mist drifted amongst the gravestones and the clustering trees; the whole world was half-formed; fluid. It was cool and still, disturbed only by the occasional bird song and a wild fluttering in the treetops. They could hear no car nor plane nor boat on the nearby river. Their first thought was that they were the only ones left alive.

"Can you feel it?" Tom asked.

And Veitch did, though he was by far and away the least sensitive of them all: there was a sourness in the air.

"Balor is here," Tom said redundantly.

Like a child, Veitch still refused to accept. "Then why hasn't it all been wiped away?" His gesture took in the towering trees and the stones and the War monument and the glimpses of Inverness beyond.

"It can afford to take its time. Not that time has any meaning for it." Tom drew in a deep breath of air, surprised he was still alive, stunned by how much he was glad to be back; he had thought he couldn't feel anything so acutely any more. "It's waiting for Samhain, when its power is at a peak. But things are moving." He closed his eyes and gave himself up to the sensations. "Things are moving over the lip of reality, creeping here, eating away at the edges."

Veitch kicked at the wet grass. "That's why she threw us out. Suddenly she's got something more important to think about. She's like a spoilt brat who's been told she can't play with her toys because she'd got to do her homework."

"You could be right. It would be unwise for the Tuatha Dé Danann to ignore the threat of the Fomorii. The Queen may well have been entreated to face up to her obligations."

"Fuck it." Veitch furiously blinked away tears that had appeared from nowhere. "Shavi's dead."

Tom nodded slowly. "It appears so."

Veitch's shoulders slumped until a new revelation dawned on him. "But not Ruth!"

"Somehow she survived."

"But if Shavi died, and we failed, who saved her?" His eyes narrowed. "That bitch wasn't lying, was she?"

"No. She told us about Shavi to hurt us. If she could have hurt you more by telling you Ruth was dead, she would have done."

Veitch punched the air. "Yes! Jesus, yes!" Tom watched his emotions seesaw as he struggled to cope with Shavi's loss and Ruth's survival. "But Shavi . . ."

"You were close to him. I'm sorry." His sorrow was much deeper than his words suggested; without the five of them there was no hope. But that didn't make sense: he had seen the end, or part of it at least. That was the trouble with second sight: it never gave a true picture.

"I know he was a queen and all, but, you know, he was all right." Veitch, never one to express sensitive emotions, looked like he was about to tear himself apart trying to find words to maintain his pride, yet show his true feelings.

Tom spared him. "Come on. This isn't a place we want to tarry."

Inverness was a ghost town. It didn't take them long to discover that technology had finally given up its futile battle to maintain a foothold in the world. The people they met looked uniformly dazed, as if they were walking through a dream, waiting to wake. But as the day passed, those who were determined to maintain some degree of normality came out of the woodwork. They found a café near the river where the owner had sourced produce from local farmers, but her face had the perpetually troubled expression of someone who worried how much longer it could last. Cash was still accepted; things hadn't yet broken down that much. Veitch and Tom had only a few pounds left between them in crumpled notes and coins, and they decided to blow it all on a big breakfast. Nothing tasted as vibrant or heady as the food in Otherworld, but, surprisingly, it was more fulfilling. Three weeks had passed since Lughnasadh and Balor's return, nearly a month of so-far gentle winding down.

The breakfast passed in funereal silence. They should have been jubilant at their escape from Otherworld, but Shavi's death weighed so heavily on Veitch, nothing else felt important.

Over strong tea at the end of the heavy, fried meal, Veitch asked, "So what do we do now?"

Tom blew on his tea, but even before he spoke, Veitch could tell he had no answers. That disturbed him; the hippie had always acted like he knew everything. "Jack and Ruth are on their way to the Western Isles. There's nothing we can do until they return. *If* they return." He spent a moment floundering around for words, then looked Veitch squarely in the eye. "Everything has changed, Ryan. We cannot move ahead as we have in the past."

"So we didn't stop the biggest Bastard of all coming back. We've had setbacks before—"

"No. It's worse than you understand. I know you find it hard to see beneath the surface—that's not where your strengths lie. But I think you realise everything we see around isn't the picture at all. It's a shop window decoration, a lie designed with a particular aim in mind. Behind it is a complex pattern of powers and relationships. Things work differently there. A single muttered word can have unguessed repercussions. Symbols weave through that pattern, across time and space, wielding powers undreamed of. There are rules none of us know, Ryan, a language we can't begin to understand."

"What are you saying?"

"Five is one of those things that sends powerful ripples through all of existence, Ryan. Forget everything you know for a moment, if you can. Five is not a number. Let's give it another definition to point you in the right direction. Say, Five is a word we give to a nuclear generator, creating great energy that could transform the world, but also great destructive force." Tom stared into Veitch's eyes, waiting for that familiar glazing over, but Veitch's gaze remained true, if troubled. "There have to be five of you, Ryan. If not, the power isn't there. However much effort you expend, however clever you are, it will amount to nothing, because in the new language we're talking about, Three has a different meaning. It has to be Five. And it has to be the Five selected by whatever the unifying force is, whether you call it God or Goddess or the Voice of the Universe."

Veitch looked dazed. "You're saying it really is all over? I thought the message you were trying to drum into us all was that there's always hope? Because that's what I feel here." He thumped his heart. "So I know it's right. You taught us that, and I learned it well. So don't come here with your bleedin' mealy-mouthed talk of failure 'cause I'm not having any of it. Are you telling me we can't do anything?" He jabbed a finger at Tom's face. "Are you?"

Tom finished his tea thoughtfully. "I know things will come to a head. I know it will be a dark and disturbing time, but I have no idea if the resolution will be the one we all hope for. Perhaps we *can* do something." At that moment he felt the weight of his great age.

One of the other early diners leaned over them on his way out. He was an old man in a dark, faded overcoat and thinning snowy hair above a similarly bleached face. "Put a smile on your face," he said in his lyrical Highlands accent. "You'll be dead a long time. However bad it is now, think on that."

"See," Veitch said. "Even he can bleedin' well see it."

Rattling his cup in its saucer, Tom stood up and attempted to ease the strain from his limbs. The terrors of the Court of the Yearning Heart had shaken him to the core of his being; he needed time to find his true centre once more, his confidence. He truly didn't know which way to turn, but Ryan was relying on him, as they all had relied on him. He looked down at the childlike hope on Veitch's face and felt an abiding sadness.

"Come on, then," he said. "We'd better go and talk to the universe."

The clear night sky was awash with a thousand stars normally obscured by the mundane glow of sodium lights, while the moon shone its brilliant rays through the treetops. The air was warm from the heat of the day and filled with the aroma of pine. The only sounds were their footsteps on the deserted road and the lapping of the waves in the loch.

Veitch couldn't stop looking up at the sky, feeling a small part of something immense and wonderful. Even a country boy would have thought it was special, but to Veitch, raised in a city where the night sky was a mystery, it was unbelievable. Even the thick shadows that swamped the hillsides running to the loch took a friendly cast.

"It's a good night," Tom said, as if sensing his companion's thoughts.

"I've seen a lot of country over the last few weeks, but nothing like this."

"There's still magic out there. Even with all that's happening."

"Maybe it's become more powerful *because* of what's happening."

Tom was surprised at Veitch's insight; it was rarely given voice, but when it did it came in inspirational flashes. "You know what, I think you're right."

"Yeah, magic. Something for us to plug into." They walked in silence for a few yards and then Veitch added, "Shavi would have loved this."

Tom felt humbled by the aching loss he heard in Veitch's voice, but there was warmth there, too, of a kind Veitch had never before exhibited. During their journey north to the Court of the Yearning Heart Tom had learned to see his companion in a new light, more than just a caricature of muscles and South London *honour*; he was a good man, for all his faults, riven by neuroses, but with a decent heart. "He was developing into a fine shaman. I was surprised how quickly he took to his abilities, always pushing back the boundaries, striving to better himself."

"Yeah, that's it, innit? We all try to do the best we can, but it came natural to him. It's not fair he caught it first."

"How do you feel about it?"

"Like I've lost my best mate." Subconsciously he pushed himself a few paces ahead of Tom, head bowed, his hanging hair obscuring his face. "I miss his advice, y'know. He always knew the right thing to say. I've never known anybody . . . sensible before."

Tom was prepared to continue the conversation, but Veitch pushed on a little further, keen to be alone with his thoughts.

It had taken them most of the day to walk from Inverness, and even their hardened muscles were starting to ache. It would be just an hour or so more before they reached their final destination in Glen Urquhart, the valley running down to Loch Ness. For Veitch, the surroundings were still haunted by his memories of the hunt for the Questing Beast and the subsequent battle that had left him only a hairsbreadth from death.

They came up on the site Tom had identified on the map just before midnight; it was the place where Veitch had found the remains of one of the Questing Beast's victims, but the body was no longer there.

Corrimony was the home of a chambered cairn made of water-worn stone taken from the nearby river Enrick. It lay in green pasture at the foot of pine-covered hills, swathed in an atmosphere of abiding peace.

"Can you feel it?" Tom's voice was almost lost beneath the breeze.

Electricity buzzed in the soles of Veitch's feet, sending not-unpleasant crackles up to his knees. When he held up his hand, the faintest blue nimbus limned it against the dark of the landscape. "Bloody hell," he said in hushed awe.

"Since the Well of Fire at Edinburgh was ignited, this part of the land has come alive. At the right time, in the right atmosphere, it's quite potent." Tom squatted down and stretched out an arm. When his finger was an inch from the sward a blue spark jumped between them.

"What are you going to do?"

"What Shavi would have done if he'd been here, only not as well. I learnt bits and pieces from the Culture, but not enough. I'm not a natural like he was. The Pendragon Spirit is an unbroken chain linking Shavi to the ancient races that set up these things, the ones who preserved their knowledge in the land. He was a lightning rod, attracting it all to him." Tom dropped to his hands and knees and crawled into the claustrophobically low tunnel that led into the heart of the cairn. Veitch heard his voice float back, although the words were obviously not meant for him. "I'm not much good for anything, really."

Veitch followed until they were both sitting on the damp stone flags, backs against the rough rock walls, the stars scattered overhead.

"In times past you wouldn't have seen the night sky." Tom's voice echoed oddly against the stones. "There would have been a roof over us. Probably torn down by some stupid farmer to make his field boundaries. That brief journey through the tunnel into here is one of those symbols I spoke about earlier."

"The new language?" Veitch thought for a second. "The *true* language."

"It was a mark of distinction, between the real world without and the Otherworld here, a shadowy place where the outside rules didn't hold. It was supposed to symbolise death, too, and birth, or rebirth. Here, we are reborn into a new world of mystery and magic." He took out the tin in which he kept his hash. "*Here we are stoned, immaculate.*"

"I know that one," Veitch said. "The Doors."

Tom slowly rolled a joint, crumbling a portion of hash into the tobacco. "Then you had better prepare yourself for weird scenes inside the goldmine."

"A mate of mine used to smoke all the time. Off his face, morning, noon and night. Didn't mind the odd one myself, like, just to chill, but I couldn't do it like he could."

"Then he was a very stupid person. Would you buy a missile launcher and go out taking potshots? These drugs are sacramental. Those who use them for hedonism are like stupid children stealing the church wine."

"What do you mean?"

"Crowley had it right." Tom looked up from his task, saw the blank look on Veitch's face. "Aleister Crowley. A self-styled magician a few decades back. He was actually quite good, though I'd never have told the arrogant bastard to his face. I spent a weekend with him at Boleskin House, his place here on the shores of Loch Ness. He summoned up what he thought was the god Pan. I think it was Cernunnos playing games with him, but I digress. Crowley had no time for people who used drugs like a few pints down the local, because he knew the power of them; their capacity for touching the sacred. Throughout history ancient cultures have used psychoactive substances for breaking the barrier between the real world and the invisible world. That's why I use them, and why Shavi used them."

Veitch nodded thoughtfully. Tom thought how like a schoolboy he looked, taking a lesson from a stern master.

"So what's going to happen?"

"I don't know."

"Jesus!"

"I told you—I'm no expert. I'm just trying to do the best I can. This is the right spot, a powerful spot. The drug will condition our minds. Then we'll try to make contact with something that can help us."

Veitch cursed. "I wish you'd told me this before. I wouldn't be sitting here with you now."

"Why do you think I didn't tell you before?"

"You know what it sounds like to me? *The Deerhunter*. Bleedin' Russian roulette. All the things out there . . . Christ! You're saying we should call something in and take a chance it's something good. Shit!"

"If you put your faith in the universe, it often helps you out."

"What, if you jump off a bridge something will catch you?"

"Now you're being silly." He lit the joint, took a long draught, then passed it over to Veitch. "This is a ceremony—"

"No more Doors, all right? Get with the decade."

Tom slowly raised his eyes to the glittering stars. Beyond the cairn they could hear the wind shuffling through the trees. "Old stories."

"What?"

"Myths and legends are our way of glimpsing the true language of existence. In them we can see the archetypes. The real meaning of numbers and words and symbols. Those talismans you fought so hard for—they are not simply a Sword, a Spear, a Stone and a Cauldron. The Sword is the elemental power of air and represents intellect. The Spear is fire, the spirit. The Cauldron is water, compassion. The Stone is earth, existence. We just have to be clever. Ignore the worldview imposed on us by the Age of Reason. We have to go back to sensing the mystery at the heart of life. That is the only way forward."

"So we tell each other stories?"

"All of human society is based on stories, Ryan. They're not just words, they're alive; powerful. There's a theory about things called memes. In essence, they're ideas that act like viruses. You put an idea out into the world—tell it to a friend, get him to pass it on—and soon the idea filters out into society and everyone begins to alter their way of behaving to take the new idea on board. The idea—one person's idea—has actually changed the shape of society. That's the modern way of explaining it. Stories are memes, very powerful ones, because they speak directly to the subconscious using archetypes." He watched Veitch's face intently, still surprised the Londoner could maintain his concentration; perhaps he truly was changing. "Stories shape lives. People pick up little lessons from them, believe a certain way to act is the correct way, grow more like their heroes. If you have stories riddled with cynicism, the world will grow more like them, over time. Our myths today are Hollywood movies and TV. In America, in the eighties, there was a crime series called *Hill Street Blues*. The police who saw it started to mimic the way the characters acted, altered the way they went about their business on the streets. An entire culture was changed by one story. In ancient Sumeria the citizens took on board the worldview expressed by their archetypal hero Gilgamesh. He defined them."

Veitch coughed and spluttered as the smoke burned his lungs. "I get it. Down in Deptford I knew some villains—small-time wankers, you know—they saw that film *Lock, Stock and Two Smoking Barrels* and started dressing and talking like the geezers in it."

"Exactly. Stories are our dreams, Ryan, and we dream our society and our reality. If we dream hard enough, we can make it what we want. If we dream hard enough."

"Shavi said something to me like that."

"Oh?"

"Not the same, really. But like it. He said if I dreamed myself as a hero I would be. If I saw myself as a sad loser, that's the way I'd stay."

"Everything is fluid, Ryan. Nothing is fixed."

Veitch rubbed his eyes as Tom appeared to grow hazy; he didn't know if it was a trick of the drugs or if it was really happening. His attention moved to the dark rocks of the cairn walls. Occasionally ripples of blue light flickered amongst them. In that place it felt like anything could happen. He steeled himself. Tom's quiet, lilting voice was like a magical spell, weaving an atmosphere of change around him.

"I know what you're talking about," Veitch heard himself saying. "You want us to dream up some of those old stories to show us what to do. Arky—what?"

"Archetypes. Symbols that take the shape of something we can understand. Things that speak with power."

"Listen!" Veitch started. "Did you hear that?" It had sounded to him like a hunting horn, echoing mournfully along the glen.

Tom was watching him like a raptor. "What are you dreaming up, Ryan?" he asked softly.

"I don't know." Had he really heard it? An image of the Wild Hunt intruded roughly on his mind and he began to panic.

Tom placed a calming hand on his knee. "Something is rising from your subconscious—"

"Can this place do that?" The drug gave an edge of anxiety to Veitch's thoughts.

"The Blue Fire is the base stuff of everything, Ryan. It's there to be shaped and controlled, and this place was designed to focus that ability."

"Things are happening." Veitch chewed on a knuckle. He felt he could hear something moving through the deeply wooded slopes of the glen away near Loch Ness, although it was obviously too far for any sound to truly travel. "I was thinking of Robin Hood. When you were talking about stories. . . . It was something my dad read to me once . . ."

"The slightest thought, if focused enough, would be all it takes, Ryan."

"But Robin Hood, like . . . I remember what Ruth said. That was one of the names for—"

"Cernunnos, yes. The gods are archetypes given form, but the archetypes are bigger than them." He paused. "I'm not making any sense, am I?" He took another drag on the joint, as if determined to make it worse. "But perhaps that is the right archetype for this moment, Ryan. You may think the thought surfaced randomly, but there is no coincidence in this world."

"Robin Hood." Veitch's voice was heavy with anticipation; the atmosphere in the cairn was charged. The blue light had grown stronger, unwavering now, casting a sapphire tint over everything. He took the joint back and drew on it deeply. The sharpness of the rocks faded into the background and the light took on greater depth.

"Robin Hood," Tom mused. "The hunter in the deep, dark forest of the night. The rebellious force against the oppressive control of rigid authority. Wild creativity opposing the structured thought of the Age of Reason."

The words washed over Veitch, whatever meaning they held seeping into him on some level beyond hearing. Another blast of the hunting horn, not too far away. Now Veitch could tell it was different from the sound of the Wild Hunt's horn; not so menacing, almost hopeful.

"But be careful." Tom's warning sounded as if it came from the depths of a well. "If you lose control of the archetype, its power can overwhelm you, tear you apart."

"I wish you hadn't said that," Veitch snapped. "It's a bleedin' meme, isn't it? It's in my bleedin' head now."

"At least you were paying attention." Tom took several calming breaths; Veitch realised the hippie felt anxious too. "My warning will focus your mind. You won't lose control."

"Yeah. Keep telling me that."

Feet rattled the stones on the road beyond the gate of the cairn compound. Rhythmic breathing that could have been a man's but was more like an animal's filled the air.

"He's here," Tom said, redundantly.

Veitch felt his muscles clench with tension, barely able to believe it was something he had done, and with such little effort; but that tiny, out-of-the-way place felt so supercharged he was convinced he could do anything here.

"Speak to him," Tom whispered.

"Me?" More panic; that wasn't one of his strengths, but then he thought how well Shavi would have done in the situation and that gave him the courage to continue. "Hello." His voice sounded too fragile. He tried again, stronger this time.

The sound of scrabbling echoed as something moved up the side of the cairn, seeking footholds amongst the tightly packed stones. A silhouette appeared over the rim, looking down at them.

"Hello," he repeated once more.

The figure squatted on the roof's edge, watching them both sitting cross-legged on the stone flags. As it shifted, Veitch caught sight of a face filled with wisdom and kindliness, but also righteous defiance. There was certainly a beard, but while he saw the features, they were forgotten in an instant after his eyes lighted on them; this was all faces, all humanity boiled down. The indefinable, tight-fitting clothes were of the Lincoln Green he had anticipated from his storybook of old, but at times they appeared to be vegetation rather than fabric or leather; and growing out of the figure itself. Strapped across his back was a bow of gnarled wood that also seemed oddly organic.

"I heard your call." His voice, which came from everywhere at once, was comforting and fatherly; the tension eased in Veitch's shoulders immediately.

Instinctively, he knew how to talk to the visitor and what to say. "We're looking for help. Guidance." He was surprised to hear his own voice sounded disembodied too. "We've got this big job to do. A big *heroes'* job. Saving the world and all that. But things have gone pear shaped. We don't know what to do next."

The figure stood up gracefully and walked slowly widdershins around the precarious lip of what remained of the roof. Veitch watched his progress until he grew dizzy. Then, after what felt like an age, the figure spoke. "Every story is like a wave crashing against a beach, and there are as many stories as there are waves. There is the height when the sun sparkles on the white crest and the dark trough when shadow turns the water to slate. Each appears the end of something, but it is only when the surf runs over the sand that the equal importance of both can be seen in the journey to the shore." He turned on his heel and began his circular journey in the opposite direction. "In your story, times are unduly dark, but you maintain hope; I feel it shining from within you, and that is good for the heroes' work. I feel, too, your pain at the loss of one close to you."

A deep silence fell over the scene; waiting.

"We need five of us to continue," Veitch began. "There have to be five Brothers and Sisters of Dragons. You know, the Pendragon Spirit. One's dead now. What are we going to do?"

"There are no boundaries." The words echoed amongst the stones. "The emerald silence of the green wood stretches on to infinity. You pass through wooded acres and appear to move on, to a new place and new sights, but it is the same wood."

Veitch was struggling to understand, but he knew perfectly why the archetype was continually speaking in metaphors, the root of the true language.

The figure squatted down once more to look at them, as if invisible cycles had come into alignment, focusing its intent. "The shaman is gone, but he can be returned."

"Shavi?"

"You may fetch him back from the Grim Lands, the Grey Lands."

"How?" Tom interjected. "There is no return for our kind."

"Special circumstances have seen fit to forge a pathway. The link still remains between the shaman's corporeal form and his essence."

Veitch looked to Tom, puzzled but hopeful. The Rhymer pondered on this information briefly, then asked, "What special circumstances—"

"Your patron has chosen to preserve his form—"

"Cernunnos," Tom said.

"It resides in a bower, ready to be wakened." The archetype rose and looked towards the dark horizon as if something were calling it.

"Where?" Tom asked.

"On the Hill of Giants, where the Night Rider awaits his challenges. But time is short. The protection is diminishing and soon the link will be broken."

"How long have we got?" Veitch was afraid the information had come too late for them to act on it.

"Not long."

It was a vague answer, but it was obvious the archetype would not or could not elucidate. It began to ease back down the slope of the cairn. "Now—"

"Wait," Veitch said humbly. "Can I walk with you? Just for a while?"

The archetype paused, then held out a shadowy hand. It felt like velvet in Veitch's fingers. The archetype hauled him out effortlessly and they both slipped down to the ground. Veitch felt uplifted, sensing on some deep level the heroic essence. It felt more like energy crackling in the air than a person at his side, but when he cast a surreptitious glance, it was unmistakably Robin Hood. They moved across the road to the nature reserve beyond, keeping low like animals. Veitch was sure some of whatever constituted the archetype was rubbing off on him. His senses were sharpened, his spirit was soaring, as if he had consumed a quantity of drugs or was in the grip of some spiritual fervour.

When they had crossed a barbed wire fence into a field on the valley slopes, Veitch couldn't contain himself any longer. "Show me," he whispered like a child.

The archetype seemed to smile. In one fluid movement it took the bow from its back, fitted an oddly fashioned arrow and loosed it. Veitch heard the twang as the arrow neatly severed the top strand of barbed wire on the fence about thirty yards further down the field.

"'mazing." He *did* feel like a child again; a wizened memory of playing one of Robin Hood's Merrie Men in a Greenwich backstreet was given new flesh. It was the kind of feeling adults spent all their life searching for, but which he had convinced himself didn't exist anywhere in society. And perhaps it hadn't before; but now things were different.

The archetype appeared to read his thoughts. With an expansive gesture, it said, "This night is magic, alive with potential. Here you are connected to the infinite."

His feeling of exaltation grew stronger until every part of his body was tingling. He felt heady from the potency of the experience; it was truly religious, like he was about to turn towards the face of God. "What does this all mean?" he sighed.

"This is how existence should be." The archetype knelt on one knee to touch the grass gently. "Dreams start within, then grow bigger until one can live within them. There are no boundaries; anything can happen. Fluidity, hope, expression." He fixed a gaze on Veitch that was almost electric. "Mythologies were never intended to be only stories. Dream hard enough and you can exist within them: neither reality, nor fantasy: just one realm of infinite possibilities." He made another wide gesture. "Look. The stories live. All of this exists within the age of heroes, as it was intended."

When Veitch looked around, he noticed for the first time shadowy figures standing away on the field boundaries or amongst the nearby trees: old heroes, some he recognised, with shining swords and armour, crowns and shields, but many he did not; yet he *felt* he knew them all. The wonder washed over him in such force he was driven to his knees.

It was at least an hour later when Veitch made his way back to the cairn. A shooting star cut an arc across the sky. Tom was still inside, smoking the remnants of a joint while humming gently to himself.

"Weren't you worried about me?" Veitch said as he emerged from the tunnel, his face beatific.

"I knew you were in good hands. Did he give you an education?"

Veitch was unable to restrain his smile.

"Good," Tom said. "Make the most of your contact with the great beyond for tomorrow we have a life to save and choices to make which could wipe the smile from your face."

Veitch didn't hear him; he was looking up to the stars, for the first time in his life feeling he was a part of something enormous; feeling that there really was hope for him.

chapter five
in league with the stones of the field

Tom and Veitch stayed in the cool confines of the cairn until the sky turned gold and purple, and then a powder blue. It was going to be a fine day. Veitch's mood had remained ecstatic as he babbled through the final hours of darkness about what he had experienced with the archetype. Tom could see some long-neglected part of him had been touched by the encounter. He was loath to bring Veitch down with discussion of what lay ahead, but it had to be done; the archetype had stressed time was short.

After a brief, unappetising breakfast of roots, herbs and edible flowers Tom had foraged from the surrounding hedgerows and fields, the conversation turned to Shavi. Veitch was surprisingly confident, his usual strategic caution stifled by his joy that there was still hope he would see his friend again.

"You know where Shavi is?" Tom chose his words carefully as he gently prodded the small campfire that had taken the chill off the early morning air. "Not where his body is, but where *he* is."

"The Grim Lands. Or the Grey Lands."

"Two names to describe the same place. It's the Land of the Dead, Ryan."

Veitch shrugged.

"Doesn't that fill you with dread? It's been a source of nightmares for the human race since the dawn of our people, and with good cause."

"Don't start getting all negative." Veitch's body language showed he didn't want to hear any of Tom's cautionary tales. "Over the last few months I've seen and done things that would have had me screaming like a bleedin' idiot when I was just some chancer down in South London. Everything's a nightmare—that's the way it is these days. You just get on with it. So let's get on with it."

Tom cursed under his breath. "I knew it would be like this. You never listen to advice, do you? If you are not prepared before you go into the Grim Lands, they may never allow you to leave."

"*They?*" Veitch's brow furrowed. "Me?"

"Well, I'm not going in there. It's your responsibility, and besides, I don't have that wonderful Pendragon Spirit coursing through *my* system. And did you think the Dead would just allow some breathing, heart-pumping warm memory of lost times waltz amongst them and take away one they consider their own? The Dead have their own rules and regulations, their own beliefs, their own jealousies and hatreds. And the Grim Lands themselves are . . ." He looked down so Veitch could barely see his face. ". . . not a pleasant place for the living."

Veitch shuffled into a sitting position, annoyed that his good mood had been driven from him. "I'm sick of all this," he said obliquely.

"I'm sorry for having to say this, Ryan." Tom surprised himself at the sincerity in his voice. "You need to know. The archetype told us what you always believed: that there's still hope. But the outcome is never assured in these things. You need to understand that the danger of entering the Grim Lands would be, for many, insurmountable." He paused. "But if anyone can do it, you can."

Veitch brightened at the vote of confidence.

"But as I warned Shavi in Edinburgh, there is a great risk in allowing the Dead to notice you. A price might be demanded that could be too much for you to bear—"

Veitch waved a dismissive hand. "There's no point telling me that sort of stuff. You know I'm going to do it. I've got to go in for Shavi. How could I leave him there if there's a chance I could bring him out? That's what it's all about for me. Yeah, we might be able to do something to stop everything going belly up. But friendship, that's the important thing. You stand by your family, and you stand by your mates. Nothing comes up to that. Not even saving the world."

Though he didn't show it, Tom was impressed by Veitch's sense of right and wrong, and his understanding of obligation, traits he thought had long been abandoned since the nineteen-sixties, the decade he most loved. "As long as I know you're going into this with open eyes."

"So how do I get there? Don't tell me there's some big doorway in the graveyard."

"If only it were that easy. Firstly, we have to go to where Cernunnos has deposited Shavi's body for safekeeping."

Veitch began his regular morning routine of stretching to help prepare his muscles for the day ahead. "The Hill of Giants."

"That is one of its names, though it is more commonly known as the Gog Magog Hills, just outside Cambridge."

"Funny name."

"In the old tales, Gog and Magog were the last of an ancient race of giants. They are supposed to sleep under the hills, with a giant horse along the way, and a golden chariot beneath nearby Mutlow Hill."

Tom winced as Veitch cracked his knuckles, one after the other, oblivious to the Rhymer's displeasure. "So, just to prove I've been listening, all these old stories you keep going on about actually mean something, though not usually exactly what they say."

"They are an approximation, couched in metaphors."

"So, what does this one mean? No *real* giants, right?"

"That needn't trouble you for now. I merely tell you this to underline that we will be travelling to a place of great power and significance. The ancient races were drawn to the hills for that power, in much the same way they revered Mam Tor. On the windswept summit is Wandlebury Camp where Boudicca and the Iceni plotted their revenge against the invaders. The Romans themselves took over the site later."

"And that power's keeping Shavi's body safe?" A breeze blew along the floor of the glen, rustling the trees, making the phone wires sing.

"That and the fact that the hills have a guardian."

"Yeah?"

"The archetype mentioned him—the Night Rider. In the legends he was supposed to have ruled Wandlebury Camp ages ago, and no mortal could ever defeat him. Those brave enough would ride out to the camp on a moonlit night and call, 'Knight to knight, come forth!' He would ride out on his jet black stallion and happily accept the challenge. A further story from Norman times claimed a knight called Osbert went out to try to put the legend to rest. He managed to unseat the Night Rider and even took the black horse home to Cambridge, but was wounded in the thigh in the process. The horse disappeared at dawn, and on every anniversary of the battle his wound opened up and bled as if it were fresh."

"So what part of that load of old bollocks is true?"

Tom bristled at Veitch's typically irreverent reaction to the old myths and legends he held dear. "I'm sure you will soon find out," he replied tartly. "The Night Rider has rarely been seen throughout the centuries—the Gog Magog Hills is a particularly lonely spot—but all who speak of him talk of a great threat which is not explicit in the stories. There is danger there, make no mistake. If such a powerful place requires a guardian, it would be a fearsome guardian indeed."

"You expect me to be surprised?" Veitch kicked out the fire.

"I'm a little concerned that you're not taking this seriously—"

"I've had enough of taking things seriously. Since what happened to Ruth it's like that's all I've done. And if everything is going to end soon I don't want to end it like that."

"Fair enough. Then the next question is—"

"How the hell do we get there in a hurry? I mean, Cambridge!" Veitch paced around anxiously. "It's, what, five hundred miles away? No cars or planes or trains. That's crazy!"

"Horses," Tom suggested.

"Still take too long."

"A boat. We could sail up the Caledonian Canal, down the east coast to the fens—"

"No offence, mate, but I honestly don't fancy getting in a leaky old tub with you unless it's a last resort. I hate water." He sighed. "If it's the only option I'll do it, 'course I will, but it's still going to take too long."

"Well, what do you suggest?" Tom snapped. "We've gone back to the Middle Ages. A horse and a boat are top-of-the-range technology!"

Veitch chewed on his lip in thought. After a while he cast a sly glance towards Tom.

"What?" the Rhymer said sharply.

"Back at Tintagel when the crow man forced us over the edge of the cliff, you did something—"

"No," Tom said firmly.

Veitch squatted down next to him. "Yeah, you did, you did. You moved us all the way from Tintagel to Glastonbury. What's that? A hundred miles? Just like that!" He snapped his fingers.

"No."

"Stop saying *no* or I'll punch your head in."

Tom couldn't decide if he was joking. "What I did then was a one off. I'd been taught the principle, but I'd never been able to do it before. I don't have the ability. I *don't*."

"Then how did you do it?"

"The danger of the moment focused my mind. It was a subconscious act born of desperation. I couldn't repeat it if I wanted."

"Maybe I should stand with my crossbow next to your head. Focus your mind again."

Still Tom was unsure of Veitch's intention. His face was dangerously impenetrable, frightening in its coldness, with only the ever-present anger buzzing behind his eyes. "That wouldn't do any good. Too staged."

"Look, this is the answer, so we've got to make it work. Tell me about it. What makes it happen?" His eyes narrowed. "From the beginning, and make it simple. No talking over the top of my head or I really will do you. This is important."

"Make it simple, you say!" Tom cleaned his spectacles, an act of both irritation and preparation. "The Blue Fire is the essential force running through everything—the land, trees and animals, you and me. We are all part of the same thing. In ancient times it was fundamentally understood by all. The Blue Fire could be seen by everyone, and manipulated by many, particularly the adepts in a society, the shamen. Your society, certainly since the Industrial Revolution, has drifted away from the idea that man is a part of everything. Man is something special, *above* everything, is that not how it's seen?"

Veitch was concentrating on every word.

"The Blue Fire was forgotten. But it is as much about thought and belief as it is any subtle, flowing energy stream. Its source is in the imagination and the heart. It's a wish and a hope."

"So it sort of dried up."

"In your actions around the country over the past months you have been awakening the King of the World from his slumbers, but the task is not yet complete. The Fiery Network, it was called. Lines of the Blue Fire crisscrossing the country, the world, like the pulsing arteries in a body. The Chinese understood this perfectly. They called the force *chi* and mapped it out both on the land and in the body. In the latter it was controlled and refocused through acupuncture. On the land, the ancient sacred sites—the standing stones and first churches and cairns—did the job. But stones have been thrown down. In the last century, narrow-minded Christians who saw them as the work of the Devil rooted up whole circles. The Fiery Network fragmented; desiccated. If you imagine the land is a body, you would see some healthy arteries, an intermittent structure of veins and capillaries, and vast swathes of cold, dead skin."

"So, it's like a machine that keeps the world running smoothly."

"In a way." Tom was relieved at his breakthrough. "An ancient technology, if you will. A global machine that allows transportation across space, even across time, that allows one to jump dimensions. The manipulation of energy. That is the language of science, but this age's petty view of science doesn't even begin to encompass it."

Veitch began to pace once more, the thoughts coming thick and fast. "So, this is what you're saying, right? That you can move along these Blue Fire lines like roads, only, immediately, like a transporter beam on *Star Trek*."

"Correct. Well . . . some people could. Not everyone. Even when the ancient races had the necessary skills to manipulate the Blue Fire, becoming one with the flow of energy was always fraught with danger."

"Why?"

"Because it's possible to go in so deep you become lost. In effect, you give yourself up to the energy to which we all aspire. The Godhead. Our lives are spent trying to attain that, so why should we ever give it up when we have it in our hands? Imagine the troubles of life washing away as you become swathed in glory, in ecstasy."

"So it's like a drug?"

"In a way, though that sounds too negative. Those who are skilled can skim along the surface of the Blue Fire, taking from it what they need. Others get sucked beneath the waves and happily drown in its wonder, never to be seen again."

"And that's what you're scared of?"

"To go into the Blue Fire and never return would be a blessed release, indeed." He wouldn't meet Veitch's eyes. "To leave behind all this . . . shit." He waved a hand dismissively around. "No more struggle, no more tears and hatred and misery—"

Veitch looked around at the sweeping tree-swathed banks of the glen, listened to the bird song and the splashing of the river across the fields. "But no more of *this*."

Tom didn't appear to understand him.

"We've got a responsibility," Veitch continued, "to make things right for all those who can't go jumping into the Blue Fire."

"Yes, yes, I know that!" Tom snapped. "I'm simply saying I might not have the willpower to pull myself through it."

This time it was Veitch's turn to be puzzled. "You're not weak."

"Yes, I am. Every day is a struggle to keep going. I'm ready to give it all up."

Veitch mused on this a while as he looked out over the countryside. "Nah, I don't believe it. You've got a load of faults, same as us all, but I know you, you old hippie. You'll always come through in a crunch. You just don't know yourself well enough."

Tom was so surprised to hear this character assessment coming from Veitch's mouth, he was lost for words. Veitch laughed heartily. "Anyway, we have a responsibility—"

"Stop using that word! I know you've just added it to your vocabulary, but—"

"—to the others. Whatever the risks, we've got no choice but to try. You're telling me you could live with yourself if you knew you might have been able to bring Shavi back—"

"All right, all right! Lord, you do go on."

"You'll give it a shot?" Veitch didn't mask his surprise that he'd won the argument.

Tom snorted in irritation as he collected his haversack and stood up. "Yes, but if I have to spend the rest of infinity with you, that Blue Fire will seem like the flames of Hell."

The atmosphere on board Wave Sweeper was growing increasingly oppressive. The Tuatha Dé Danann had distanced themselves from the other travellers, retreating to a tight coterie around Manannan, who kept a firm grip on the running of the ship. The death of Cormorel had affected them even more than their aggressive response suggested; they were scared, Church could tell.

Many of the passengers confined themselves to the lower decks, taking food in their cabins or whatever shadowy area they inhabited. The ones who did rise to greet the sun kept their heads down and their eyes averted. Of the Walpurgis, there was still no sign, although the search parties departed daily at dawn, marching as far as they could into the infinite bowels of the boat before returning at dusk.

Baccharus, however, remained Church and Ruth's link with the Tuatha Dé Danann, repaying, perhaps, the kindness they had shown him since their first meeting. He spoke about his people's thoughts and their strategy without going into too much detail, and he stressed, on behalf of Manannan, that neither Church nor Ruth were under suspicion. They both knew that state of affairs could change instantly; the gods had loyalty only to themselves.

The ship skimmed the waves with great speed, even when the wind was low and the enormous sails scarcely billowed, but Ruth and Church were more concerned than ever that time was running away from them. It didn't help when Baccharus told them Wave Sweeper would continue to make its scheduled stops throughout the Western Isles before it reached its ultimate destination.

"I can't bear this," Church said one morning as they leaned on the rail and watched what could have been dolphins rolling in the waves, but which made cries that sounded like shrieking women. "Anything could be happening back at home."

Ruth shielded her eyes against the glare of the sun off the water. "It would be good to have a despatch from the front. Just to know we're not wasting our time."

Activity further along the deck caught their attention. A strange contraption with a seat fixed at the end of a long, jointed arm was being dragged towards the side by a group of the plastic-faced younger gods. Once it was in place, the arm was manipulated over the side until the seat hovered mere inches above the water. With remarkable agility, one of the gods skipped up on to the rail then manoeuvred his way down the arm until he was precariously balanced on the seat, with no straps to restrain him and only providence keeping him from a ducking in the blue-green waves. A spear made from an intricately carved piece of enormous bone with an attached rope was lowered to him. He weighed it in his right hand, then poised to strike, concentrating on the depths.

"Do you think this is our sole reason for existing?" Church waited for something to happen, but the fisherman remained stock-still. "The life we had in London, everything leading up to this point, it's like a dream sometimes. Not quite real at all. But the only thing that keeps me going through all this struggle is the thought that at some point, I'll be able to return to that life. If I thought this was all there was . . ."

"A lot of religions say we have one purpose in life. We just have to find it."

"That's my worry. I don't want to have a life of nothing but sacrifice. When I used to read stories of the saints, and Gandhi, and Mother Theresa, I never found them uplifting. They always filled me with something like despair, because they were missing out on all the great things life had to offer: you know, fun and friendship and love and all that."

Ruth brushed a strand of hair from her face. Oddly, she felt closest to him during his brooding moments, when all his attention was turned inward; a usually hidden fragility was revealed that made her want to protect him. "Some people have to give up their lives so everyone else can enjoy theirs. I'm sure it's tough for the person in question, but that seems to be the way it works. Anyway, you know what Tom and Shavi would say—we can't ever see the big picture, so it's a waste of time for us trying to put something like that into perspective. Perhaps the reward is in the next world."

"*This* is the next world," Church said dismally.

"You know what I mean. *There's always something higher*."

"Well, *I* want my life back when all this is over. I don't think that's too much to ask. I'll have met my obligations, done everything expected of me. I don't want to die an old man, still fighting this stupid, nightmarish battle."

"Hmm, considering old age—that's optimistic of you. Me, I'm happy if I make it through to tomorrow."

The water exploded upwards in a spout, followed by thrashing tentacles and the glinting of teeth. The fisherman struck hard with his spear, his face as calm as if he were lazing on the banks of a river, and then he struck again several times in rapid succession. A gush of black liquid soured the water. One of the tentacles lashed around his calf, and when it retracted, the flesh was scoured. More tentacles shot up, folding around his legs like steel cables. Church gripped the railing. It was obvious the fisherman was going to be dragged off the seat, yet none of the other gods who hung over the rail above him were in the slightest concerned.

"Dog eat dog." The words at his left ear made him start. Standing just behind him was Taranis, Manannan's right-hand man, who oversaw the mysterious star charts by which the crew navigated. The face Church had chosen for him had a faint touch of cruelty, thin and sharp, with piercing eyes and a tightly clipped goatee. His presence made Church feel queasy. "Fish eat fish," he continued, by way of explanation for the scene they were observing. "Bird eat worm, cat eat mouse, wolf eat rabbit."

Church returned his attention to the fisherman and the crazed splashing that surrounded him. He was on the verge of slipping beneath the waves, clutching on to the seat with one hand while hacking mercilessly with the spear with the other. At the point when Church thought he would have to go, the spear bit into some vital point and he managed to wriggle his legs free and lever himself back up on to the seat. A few more choice hacks and an indescribable black bulk bobbed to the surface where it floated, motionless.

"Dinner?" Ruth asked distastefully.

Taranis gave a thin-lipped smile at the outcome. "The way of existence," he said.

"I'm heading back to my cabin for a bit," Ruth said, before turning to Taranis. She motioned to the collapsible telescope made of ivory and inlaid sable and gold that hung from his belt. "May I borrow this for a while?"

Taranis seemed taken aback by her request, and Church, too, was surprised by her forwardness, but the god acceded with a curt nod. Ruth weighed it in her palms, nodded thoughtfully, and headed towards the door that led beneath the deck.

Without Ruth to talk to, and with Niamh distracted, Church felt out of sorts. The other occupants of the ship made his skin crawl, even the ones that most closely resembled humans. There was nothing to see across the water, nothing to do in his cabin, little anywhere to occupy his time. He was reminded of Samuel Johnson's quotation: *Going to sea is going to prison, with a chance of drowning besides.*

As he made his way along the corridor towards his cabin, his nose wrinkled at an incongruous, sulphurous odour; it was powerful enough to sting his eyes and make the back of his throat burn. It appeared to be emanating from a branching corridor he had never seen before. In the back of his head an insistent alarm was warning him not to venture down it, but if there were a fire on board the alarm would need to be raised. He vacillated for the briefest moment before turning down the offshoot.

The corridor followed a serpentine route that made no sense, even doubling back on itself before ending at a double arched door made from seasoned wood. The handles were big enough to take two hands, made from blackened cast-iron.

From behind it he could hear a thunderous pounding. The sulphurous stink was so potent now it almost made him choke.

Cautiously, he opened the door.

The room was stiflingly hot and the acrid smell hung heavily all around. His ears rebelled from the constant clashing of metal on metal, his teeth rang from the reverberations. It was almost impossible to tell the dimensions of the room, for it was as dark as night, with occasional pockets of brilliant light, ruddy and orange, or showering in golden stars. It was a foundry. On board a ship. Nothing in that vessel made sense at all.

The dull glow came from three separate furnaces. The sound of the bellows keeping them incandescent was like the turbulent breathing of a giant. He covered his mouth to keep out the fumes and prepared to back out, until his eyes grew accustomed to the dark and he realised he was not alone. Three huge figures worked insistently, pounding glowing shards of metal on anvils as big as a Shetland pony, plunging the worked piece into troughs of water, raising clouds of steam, moving hastily back to thrust tools into the red-hot coals.

Transfixed, he found himself trying to guess what strange implements were being constructed. He was woken from his concentration by a voice that sounded like the roar of another furnace. "Draw closer, Fragile Creature."

His heart thumped in shock, but it was too late to retreat. He moved forward until the glow from the furnace illuminated the shadowy form. It took a while for the figure to stabilise, marking out his position in the hierarchy of the Tuatha Dé Danann. Though none of it was real, Church smelled the stink of sweat, heavy with potent male hormones. The blacksmith had a rough-hewn face, marked with black stubble and framed by sweaty, lank black hair. He was naked to the waist, his torso and arms rippling with the biggest muscles Church had ever seen. His body gleamed, with sweat running in rivulets down to a wide golden belt girding his waist. In one hand he held a hammer as big as Church's upper body, poised midstrike; in the other he clutched a pair of tongs that gripped a glowing chunk of iron flattened on one edge. Without taking his eyes off Church, he lowered the iron into the trough at his side and was instantly obscured by the steam.

When it had cleared, he said gruffly, "We get few visitors here, in the workshop of the world."

"I smelled the furnace. Thought there was a fire."

The blacksmith's eyes narrowed. "Are you the Brother of Dragons I have been hearing about?" Church introduced himself. The blacksmith gave a nod, his movements slow and heavy. "*The cry goes out across the worlds, in death and black destruction, the child answers, full of fury, yet finds no absolution.*"

"What's that?"

"A memory." With a clatter, he dumped the tongs and the piece of iron on a workbench. "In the times when my workshop armed your world, your people called me Goibhniu, known too, as Govannon." He leaned forward and showed Church a ragged scar across his side. "See my wound." Church wondered why the god didn't lay down his hammer, but when he peered at it closely the edges of it rippled. Church couldn't tell if it were the heat haze from the furnace or if it were Goibhniu's Caraprix in the form that would help him the most. The god saw Church eyeing the tool and held it out before him. "Three strikes make perfection. I can work the stuff of existence, shape worlds or insects. With these hands, anything can be made in a single day, and anything can be destroyed."

Beyond him, in the shadows, Church could make out a tremendous armoury: swords and spears, things that looked like tanks in the form of beetles, and also enormous machines that served no purpose he could recognise.

"And weapons?" Church asked.

"Weapons from which none can recover. Weapons that can destroy the whole of existence."

The words caught in Church's mind. "Weapons that could destroy Balor?"

Goibhniu surveyed him for a long moment, then motioned towards the other figures, who had not paused in their work. "My brothers, as your people knew them: Creidhne and Luchtaine, known as Luchtar, who works wood and metal, as well as the stuff of everything."

Luchtaine had paused from his work at the anvil to shape an unusual piece of wood on a lathe that whirred like a bug. Creidhne was fashioning what appeared to be rivets made of gold. They both looked at Church with eyes filled with flame and smoke.

"Why are you here, on board this ship?" Church felt uneasy, as if he was missing something important and terrible in the scene.

Goibhniu's eyes narrowed; an atmosphere of incipient threat descended on them all. "The Western Isles beckon. These are difficult times."

"Difficult times? You mean the murder of Cormorel?"

Church shrank back as Goibhniu advanced with his hammer before him. Light glimmered off the head and shone like a torchbeam into the depths of the room; Church was shocked to see the beam of light appeared to stretch for miles. And it was packed with weapons as far as he could see. Near to the foundries was some hulking piece of machinery that dwarfed all others, but it was unfinished; waves of menace washed off it. The angle of light changed and the view was lost, but it had been enough.

Goibhniu continued to advance until Church's back was pressed against the door. Fumbling behind him, he found the door handle and flipped it open, almost tumbling out into the corridor. The last thing he heard before Goibhniu slammed the door shut was the god saying forcefully, "Stay away from here, Fragile Creature. We have work to do."

The sweat trickled into the small of Ruth's back as the full force of the noon-time sun blazed through the open windows into the cabin, even though she was sitting naked on the floor. Her visit to the kitchen stores had been a success. It was a vaulted hall that went on forever, its air laden with the aroma of spices, fruits, cooking meats and steamed fish, and it was apparent from the demeanour of the dour-faced god in charge that she could find *anything* she wanted there. Even so, she was surprised to locate so easily such rare items, and ones that were not used in any dishes she knew; but then, who could guess the tastes of the other travellers on Wave Sweeper?

With a borrowed mortar and pestle, she had prepared the ointment in just the right way and now she was filled with a wonderful anticipation; it had been too long.

Soon after came the familiar sensation of separation from her body. There was rushing, like a jet taking off, and then she was out of the window and soaring up into the clear, blue sky. Once her mind had found its equilibrium, she looked down at Wave Sweeper ploughing a white furrow through the green-blue sea far below. The sails billowed, the deck was golden in the sunlight, the crew moving about like ants.

The exhilaration filled her as deeply as the first time she had experienced the spirit flight in the Lake District, her limbs divested of earthly stresses, her mind glowing with a connection to the godhead. It would have been wonderful just to stay there, floating amongst the occasional wisp of clouds, but she had a job to do. "Are you there?" she asked the sky.

In response came a beating of wings that was much more powerful than she had anticipated. When she turned to greet the arrival she was even more shocked: her owl familiar was a bird no more. It resembled a man, though with an avian cast to the features: too-large eyes with golden irises, a spiny ridge along its forehead, and its torso and limbs a mix of leathery brown skin like rhino hide and dark feathers. It beat through the air towards her on batlike wings.

The breath caught in her throat. When she had just considered it an owl, albeit with a demonic intelligence, it had not been too threatening, but now it was patently menacing; she felt instinctively that if she did not treat it right, it would tear her apart.

"Is that your true form?" she asked hesitantly.

He smiled contemptuously. "As if there is such a thing!" He could have left it there, but he took pity on her. "It is the way I appear to you, in this place, at this time."

She turned to look at the dim horizon. "I need to return to my world, to see what's happening. Is that possible?"

"All things are possible when the right will is imposed. I told you that."

She recalled their conversations in the cells beneath Edinburgh Castle when he had been a disembodied voice, passing on the information vital to her development in the craft. "I can't believe I've learnt so much, so quickly."

"Others would find it harder. You have been chosen for your abilities."

"I still wonder how much I can actually do."

"You will find your answer, in time." There was a disconcerting note to his voice.

She allowed herself to drift on the air currents, overcome with apprehension. "I'm worried I won't be able to get back here quickly enough." Nina's warning of what would happen if the spirit did not return to the body within a reasonable time weighed heavy on her. "It's so far—"

"Then you should waste no more time." He moved ahead of her, heading higher, towards the sun, then dipped down and made a strange movement with his left hand that stretched his ligaments to their limits. By the time he had finished, a patch of air had taken on a glassy quality; Ruth had the odd impression that it was a pool of water, floating vertically. He flashed a piercing glance that charged her to follow him and then he plunged into the pool and disappeared. She hesitated for only a second before diving.

A sensation like icy rain rushed across her skin and then she was high off the coast of Mousehole, as if, for all their travels on Wave Sweeper, they had not gone anywhere at all. Everything seemed so much duller after her time in T'ir n'a n'Og, the quality of light, the sea smell, the greens of the landscape beyond the shore. Her companion had once again reverted to his owl form, keeping apace with her with broad, powerful wing strokes.

As she moved inland across the late summer fields, her apprehension became more intense. On some rarefied level she was sensing danger ahead.

Increasing her speed, she swooped over the landscape, uncomfortably eyeing the deserted roads and tiny villages that appeared devoid of life. And faster; Dartmoor passed in a brooding, purple-brown blur with memories of the Wild Hunt and senseless slaughter. In Exeter a fire was raging out of control. The grey ribbon of the M5 was a string of abandoned vehicles. And on through Devon, acutely aware how much the land had changed. No more comforting mundanity, supermarket shopping and boring commutes to work, daytime radio and bank managers and accountants. Even with the cursory glance she was giving the rolling greenery below, she could see it had become wilder, a land of mythology where humans were at the mercy of competing species with much greater powers. A place where anything could happen.

Over Wiltshire and Hampshire, closer to the source of the danger. Some towns and villages were wrecked and burning, others reclaimed by strangely wild vegetation. But there were still signs that people were there, either in shock or in hiding: cows, obviously milked and fed, here, clothes hanging on a washing line there. Little markers of hope; it was something. The faint, insistent tugging dragged her eastwards.

The owl had been keeping pace with her, beyond the ability of any true bird, but the beat of its wings began to grow slower until it had dropped back a way, dipping and diving with obvious caution. The reason was clear. On the horizon, London brooded. Although the sun shone down on its sprawling mass, Ruth had a definite sense that it hung in darkness. Her heartbeat speeded and anxiety began to gnaw at the back of her head; an aura of menace was rolling out across the Thames Valley.

It had to have been London, where it all started. The circle had closed.

Yet from that distance, nothing appeared out of the ordinary, apart from the stillness that lay over the approaching M4. She dropped back until she was beside her familiar, adopting its cautious approach. She listened: nothing, but not a serene silence: no birdsong at all. She sniffed the wind and caught the faintest hint of acrid smoke. As the suburban tower blocks and estates fell into view, that ringing sense of menace became almost unbearable, hanging like a thick cloud of poisonous gas over the capital. It was moving out across the land, barely perceptible in its slowness, but inexorable.

"Dare I go closer?" she asked the owl. When there was no reply she took it on herself to advance. She still needed something substantial to tell Church.

She knew she could be seen by the Fomorii in that form—they had spotted her as she watched their black tower being constructed in the Lake District—so she soared higher, desperately wishing for some cloud cover. And with that thought came the realisation that, if she wanted it, she could make it. Under her breath, she mumbled the words the familiar had taught her, making the hand gestures that activated the primal language: words of power in both sound and movement.

The wind changed direction within seconds and soon a few fluffy white clouds were sweeping in from the north. Not too many—she didn't want to draw attention to the sudden change in the weather pattern—but enough to provide a hiding place.

With a slight effort she sent them billowing towards the capital and slipped in amongst them. The air became filled with pins and needles; her heart was pounding so hard she thought she was having a coronary. "It *feels* bad," she said to her familiar, although she was really talking to herself, "but it doesn't *look* too bad."

And then the clouds cleared.

She was still beyond the suburbs, but from her vantage point she had a clear view deep into the heart of the city. At first it looked like the outlines of the buildings were rippling as if they weren't fixed. She wondered if it had somehow slipped into T'ir n'a n'Og, where things regularly looked that way. But as she drew closer, she could see it wasn't the outline of the buildings that were changing; something was moving across them.

A wave of revulsion swept through her. London was swarming. It looked like an enormous jarful of spiders had been emptied out on to the buildings and streets. The Fomorii scurried everywhere, at times as though millions upon millions of long-legged insects were racing chaotically over everything, then as if one beast lay across the capital, flowing like oil. Many or one, it didn't matter; London was subsumed. And at the heart of it, an abiding darkness pulsated: Balor, replete in its lair, growing stronger after the strain of rebirth, sucking in energy ready to consume the planet. Beating like a giant heart. Thump-thump. Thump-thump. She couldn't truly see it, had no real idea of its form, but it was there on a spiritual level, tendrils creeping out from the cold sore. She gagged, despite the fact her corporeal body was a world away.

What made her flesh creep the most was the way that vibrating black mass was pushing out from the centre, reaching into the suburbs, moving out across the country. Nothing could have stood in its path.

"All those people," she gasped. The realisation of what must have happened made her head spin: an atrocity on a grand scale; perhaps millions dead, and more to come.

"We have to get back," she said to the owl. "We can't afford to waste any more time."

But as she turned to depart, brutal reverberations crashed inside her skull and her body doubled up with pain. Looking back she saw, rising up above the skyscrapers of the City, an area of infinite darkness, blacker even than deepest space, cold and sucking. It was impossible to tell if it was truly happening in the real world or if it was a metaphor imprinted on a higher level of consciousness, but it filled her with utmost dread. It was alive, and it had an intelligence so vile her mind screamed at even the slightest brush with it.

Balor. The name tolled like a funereal bell deep in her head.

And it rose up and up, bigger than the city, bigger than all existence. *How can we beat something like that?* she thought with the bitter sting of despair. And still it rose, and washing off it came waves of malignancy. And then, as it had in the dream that was not a dream in Mousehole, an eye opened in that black cloud, an eye that was not an eye, though she characterised it as such. And it focused its attention on her and she thought she was about to go mad with fear.

It could see her there, hidden in the clouds, miles away. It could see her anywhere. But worse than that, it *recognised* her.

The shock dislocated her thoughts; it was already in motion before she registered it was coming for her.

A wide flailing disrupted the air currents next to her. Her familiar was thrashing and screaming, an owl, a ball of feathers, then the owl man, and then something infinitely worse, moving rapidly backwards and forwards across the spectrum of its appearance in a terrible panic.

In terror, she attempted to flee, only to realise she couldn't move. The evil had her in some invisible grip, holding her steady like a fish on a line. Until it reached her.

Her consciousness finally burst from whatever spell it was under, and suddenly she was thinking at lightning speed. "Help me!" she yelled, but the owl was already moving away from her, every wing beat a flurry of desperation.

She tried to flee once more, but it was as if her limbs, or her mind, was pinned; no amount of effort could move her. Behind her, the monstrous gravity of the thing grew more powerful.

"Come back!" she screamed. "You were supposed to help me!" The familiar was lost in the glare of the sun.

A freezing shadow had fallen across her, reaching through her physical body to the depths of her soul. It was creeping up her spine, deadening the chakras as it passed, crawling towards her brain. Incomprehensible whispers began to lick at her mind. In that contact she sensed the sickening presence of Balor, and she knew it was the reason why fear had been implanted in the human consciousness. The Celts had given it a name to try to contain it, but it could not be contained; it was bigger than everything.

Her vision started to close in, until there was only a tunnel of light towards the sun. A strain was being placed on the invisible cord that connected her with her body. One snap and she would be lost to the endless void forever. And then, slowly but relentlessly, the thing started to drag her back.

Just as she thought the darkness was about to engulf her completely, she caught sight of faint movement in that tunnel of light. Nothing. It was nothing. She slipped back further.

She was startled from her panic by the owl erupting from nowhere close to her face. Its bristling feathers obscured the whole of that tunnel of light, and for a second she was sure she had gone blind. But then it moved back slightly, changing shape back and forth as it had done at the height of its desperation. She could still feel its fear, but now behind it was determination and obligation.

The air pressure increased, iron filled her mouth and a weight built behind her eyes until she was convinced they were going to be driven from her head. Slowly, she started to move forward.

She felt like she was trying to push a truck up a hill; every agonising inch she moved was a triumph. Yet although the grip of the darkness didn't relinquish in the slightest, gradually her strength increased and she began to make slight progress. It was nowhere near fast enough, though; the tension zinged through her arteries.

With determination, she drove herself on until she reached a point where her speed began to build. Finally it felt like she had crossed some invisible barrier, and with a burst of relief she was soaring out over the golden-tinged clouds. The coldness left her head, skidding down her back to her thighs. Later she wondered if she had imagined it, but she thought she heard a howl of fury that was at once the movement of tectonic plates, the boom of cold water shifting in the depths of the Marianas Trench.

And faster still; hope soared in her heart at the same time as tears of fear stung her eyes. *She would never be so stupid again.* If she got back. A pain in her solar plexus told her time was running out. She had been away from her body for too long, and the flimsy spiritual bond was close to being broken.

The shadowy cold was still on her legs. Stupidly, she glanced back and thought her heart would stop. The entire sky was black, boiling like storm clouds, but not natural—sentient—and pursuing her with venom.

Fire filled her belly. Focusing all her attention on the flight, she propelled herself forward with a speed that made Dorset flash by in the blink of an eye.

Still the darkness didn't give up. She knew it would *never* give up now it had recognised her. She put the thought out of her head. Faster, faster, thinking of Church, giving meaning to her struggle; if not for her, for him.

Soon they were over the choppy sea and the owl was ahead of her, already turning itself inside out. The sky and sea swapped place, turned blood red. And then they were soaring over Wave Sweeper and the darkness was nowhere to be seen.

She plummeted towards the ship as the connecting strand grew thinner by the second. It was just the width of a hair when she finally slid into her body, exhausted. Amongst the receding terror, one thing stayed with her: at the last, she had looked into her familiar's eyes. What she saw was a definite impression that *she* was now in *its* debt.

She recovered in her cabin for an hour or more, listening to the soothing wash of the waves beyond the open window. She couldn't believe how stupid she had been to venture so close, but until then she had not truly grasped the enormity of what they faced.

Once she had calmed herself, she made her way back to the deck, though she kept her shaking hands hidden from view. Taranis was at the rail, scanning the horizon. She handed him his telescope with a sly smile.

"How curious." He turned it over in his hands. "It is so very warm."

"Hmm," Ruth replied. "I wonder why that is?"

Church had spent the time on deck, watching the crew go about their puzzling tasks. Few of the passengers ventured up from the depths in their attempt to keep a distance from the grim Tuatha Dé Danann, so that the ship had the dismal, empty appearance of a seaside resort in off season. The atmosphere was so intense he had felt it politic to stay away from the gods himself, nestling in a heap of oily tarpaulins and thick ropes where he could watch without drawing attention to himself.

He had never seen the Tuatha Dé Danann so strained. Irritation gripped them because they had not managed to track down the Walpurgis, a failure that only added to their pain at Cormorel's death. Their aloof nature had always made them appear dangerous in a haphazard, detached way; now they were a constant threat, ready to take out their fury on anyone who crossed their path.

If the gods could not find the Walpurgis with all the heightened abilities at their disposal, there was little chance Church would be able to locate the creature he had increasingly convinced himself was not the murderer. Yet he felt a growing imperative to do so, for he was sure the Walpurgis had information of vital importance.

His thoughts were disrupted by a cry from one of the crew perched in the crow's nest. Everyone on deck stopped moving. Church couldn't tell if it was because of hope, or apprehension—or fear.

Across the pea-green sea he could just make out a purple and brown smudge on the horizon. *Here it is*, he thought, suddenly concerned himself. *The Islands of the Dead.*

chapter six
islands of the dead

The waters were unnaturally calm as Wave Sweeper sailed in, leaving barely a ripple in its passing. Insects skimmed the surface of the ocean in the heavy heat, buzzing noisily. An unpleasant smell of stagnancy hung over everything, but it was the stillness that unnerved everyone the most. There was a feeling of death in the air.

As Wave Sweeper closed on the land, Church was surprised to see it was not one single mass, but an archipelago, the strangest one he had ever seen. Numerous small islands protruded from the sea like fingers pointing at the sky, rising precipitously to dizzying summits, many looking like they could barely support their own weight. They were gnarled with rocky outcroppings and fledged with twisted trees and tenacious bushes. Stone buildings perched on the top of the island towers, occasionally obscured by drifting plumes of cloud. However, on the loftiest, most twisted, most precarious island stood a grand castle of bronze and glass, the walls afire in the dazzling sunlight. Its enormous bulk atop the slim column was in direct opposition to any natural laws on Earth. But this was Otherworld.

Manannan's order to drop anchor drew the crew out of their trance. Church noticed Ruth had appeared beside Taranis, who was observing the peaks of the island through his telescope, his face as hard as the stone of the cliffs.

"What's wrong?" Church slipped in quietly beside them.

Taranis looked at him as if an insect had chirped in his ear. "There has been no greeting," he said distractedly, returning his attention to his telescope.

Church eyed Ruth, her face uncommonly tired and drawn, but she shrugged noncommittally. "Who were you expecting to greet you?" Church pressed.

Taranis sighed. "In the Fixed Lands she was known as Hellawes. She foolishly grew too close to Fragile Creatures during her travels and became afflicted with the weariness of existence. She retired here, to her island home, though whether she truly recovered, none know. Still, she provided a welcome for travellers. It was the Master's wish to dine at her table."

Church followed the angle of the telescope to the castle that appeared to be floating on the clouds that drifted beneath it. "Maybe she doesn't know we're here."

Taranis snorted; it was obvious he was not going to give them any more of his time. Ruth caught Church's arm and led him away, eager to tell him what she knew of home.

"The Fomorii are already moving out across the country?"

"It won't be long before they're everywhere." Ruth shivered at the memory of what she had seen.

Church's shoulders were knotted with tension. He watched the crew preparing the landing boat. It had an oddly shaped prow that curled up and over the rowers. "Being here makes you feel detached from it all, even when it's buzzing away at the back of your head. I needed a slap like that to focus my mind."

"I wish we could just get to where we're going." She hugged herself, despite the heat.

He saw Baccharus and Niamh lining up to join the small band ready to go ashore. "Maybe we can gee them along."

He led her over to the boat as it was hoisted up above the level of the rail ready for the crew to climb aboard. Church pulled Baccharus to one side. "We'd like to join you. All of this is new to us. We want to experience—"

"Of course."

Church was taken aback by the speed of Baccharus's agreement, but he wasn't about to question it. He quickly climbed aboard, with Ruth behind him. Niamh was already seated at the aft. She gave him a warm, secret smile, hidden from the crew who silently filled the seats. Church was curious to see that they all wore the gold and ivory armour of the warrior caste.

Ruth echoed his thoughts. "They're expecting trouble," she whispered.

Even though her words were barely audible, Baccharus picked up on them. "The greeting is always issued," he said ominously, his darkly golden eyes flickering towards the lofty castle.

The oarsmen propelled them across the flat sea with powerful, seasoned strokes. Church had the oddest impression they were skimming the surface of a mirror, so disturbingly smooth was the water. Even around the base of the rocky islands there was only the slightest swell and no breakers. It was as if the ocean itself was holding its breath.

Ruth was driven to cover her mouth to block out the choking stagnant odours. Church passed the time swatting away the alien insects, some of which were like meat flies that had grown as big as his fist, others like minute, jewelled dragonflies, sparkling as they whizzed by.

At the base of the island was a tiny jetty. Once the boat had been made secure with a thick rope, they clambered out. There was barely room for them all to stand, so they progressed one at a time along an uneven path that wound upwards around the island. It was just wide enough for one person and dangerously precarious the higher they climbed. On the outer edge it was badly eroded by the elements; one wrong foot would have sent them plummeting into the waves or on to the protruding rocks. Church and Ruth held their breath as they fixed their gaze on the next step, but Baccharus and the other Tuatha Dé Danann climbed nonchalantly, oblivious to the drop.

The higher they rose above the flat, green sea, the harder it became to avoid feelings of vertigo. For distraction, Church found himself focusing on the wiry grass and diminutive yellow and white flowers that thrived in pockets on the rock face. His fingers gripped the stone until the joints hurt; behind him he could hear Ruth's laboured breath.

They climbed for almost an hour, until their thigh and calf muscles were fiery. Near the top, the buffeting wind threatened to snatch them off their uneasy perch so that even the Tuatha Dé Danann had to face the rock and edge around the path.

Finally they passed through cloud to reach the flat summit and an area the size of a tennis court leading to the castle's imposing gates. That close it was even harder to understand how the place had come to be built in that almost inaccessible position; how it continued to survive there. The bronze and opaque glass walls rose up high above their heads, too bright to look at in the seething sunlight. Windows looked out on every vista, but they were all too dark to see within. It was unpleasantly quiet.

"Maybe she's not in," Ruth muttered.

"The mistress of this place never leaves its walls." Baccharus looked up to the battlements, as impassive as ever, but troubled.

At the castle gate they considered their actions. "A knock," Church suggested.

Baccharus agreed. "Cover your ears," he said to Church and Ruth. They looked at each other curiously. "Sound has power. Mere words, or the sound they make, can alter existence. You know that?" He read their faces, then nodded in approval before continuing; Church and Ruth both felt like children being guided by a knowledgeable parent. "The reverberations from the striking of this door will send all Fragile Creatures into a deep sleep, for—" he struggled with the mortal concept "—a long time."

"How many *Fragile Creatures* do you get up here?" Ruth asked.

Baccharus returned his attention to the door. "It is the way it is."

Church and Ruth covered their ears, but even through their hands they could feel the strange vibrations of the struck door driving like needles into their heads, making them queasy at first, then drowsy. Baccharus shook them both roughly to keep them awake.

They waited for long minutes after they had announced their arrival, but all they could hear was the wind blowing around the castle walls, sounding at times like plaintive human voices.

Niamh, who had the position of superiority in the group, stepped forwards. "We enter."

Two of the guards put their shoulders to the gates, but they swung open easily, as if they could have been moved with the touch of only a finger. Beyond was a breathtaking hall soaring up to a glass roof that made the interior as bright and hot as a greenhouse. Within, they were assailed by numerous sensations. The breeze moved the most melodic chimes hanging in enormous trees that grew mysteriously out of the tiled floor, their tops almost brushing the roof. A white waterfall gushed down from an opening halfway up one wall, splashing in a cool pool that emptied out through a culvert in the floor. The smells were as complex and heady as any they had experienced in T'ir n'a n'Og. Church picked up lime, honeysuckle, rose and cinnamon before he gave up.

"It's beautiful." Ruth was overcome by the sheer wonder after the air of threat without.

"It is the mistress's palace. Her sanctuary," Niamh noted. "She loved the Fixed Lands and wished to bring her memories of that place to life here." She paused thoughtfully before adding, "She loved a Fragile Creature—"

"Well, there's no future in that, is there?" Ruth ignored Niamh's pointed stare.

"And she retired here to nurse her broken heart?" Church asked. Niamh replied with a sad smile.

They pressed on through the hall into a maze of rooms decorated in different earthly styles: mediaeval, Celtic, Mexican, Japanese, Native American. Yet each felt as if an unpleasant presence had been in it only moments before, although there was no visible sign of recent occupation. Even the usually stoic Tuatha Dé Danann appeared uneasy.

Occasionally Church and Ruth glimpsed flitting grey shapes on the edge of their field of vision, accompanied by barely audible but insistent whispering, and a growing anxiety. Sometimes they caught sight of faces, most of them unknown, but one or two that were almost recognisable.

"Can you see them?" Ruth hissed after they had passed through a room where the shapes swarmed at their backs, disappearing the moment they turned round.

"They are the spirits of the dead," Baccharus interjected. "You will encounter them throughout the Western Isles."

"Ghosts?" Church moved his head sharply to try to bring one of the figures to the centre of his vision, without much luck. "Real ghosts?"

"Some of the dead are drawn here, Fragile Creatures with a yearning nature, unsettled, troubled. It has always been that way. The Western Isles are a destination for those of a questing nature." The figures kept well away from Baccharus as he spoke.

"Are they dangerous?" Ruth asked.

Baccharus chose his words carefully. "They can be. The dead bring their dark emotions with them. Many are fuelled by bitterness, resentful of those still living. Beware of them and their whispered words. They will wish to lure you to your doom."

A chill turned Church's skin to gooseflesh. Another face he half thought he knew. Ruth gripped his hand in hers, fixing her attention on the path ahead.

The layout of the castle was incomprehensible; they trailed from room to room without encountering anyone, constantly sensing a passing presence, always one step ahead.

"Maybe we should head back to the ship," Ruth said. "She's obviously not here."

"But she *should* be here," Baccharus said. "She may be in need of assistance."

"I thought you Golden Ones rarely helped each other," Church said.

"We are not all the same." It was a passing comment, but Church caught the briefest glimpse of something in Baccharus's face that gave him pause.

Before he had time to consider it further, one of the guards said curtly, "In the next chamber," although it was impossible to tell how he could know when the door was closed.

As one, the guards drew long golden swords from hidden pockets in their armour. They approached the door cautiously. Church's blood was pulsing loudly in his head; now he could also sense something, and although he couldn't pinpoint it, it set his nerves on edge. *In the room.* He saw Ruth could feel it too. Her warning hand fell on his forearm, urging him back.

Niamh made a sign to the captain and the door was thrust open. The guards surged through, with Church so close behind, he ran into them when they came to a premature halt. They were so still Church first thought they were the victims of some enchantment until he realised they were staring at the corner of the room. He eased his way through until he had a better view.

The remains of a woman were slumped over a divan, her body breaking up just as Cormorel's had done on the point of death. Her body had been torn apart from neck to crotch. There was nothing anyone could do for her: the flight of golden moths had dwindled to a handful fluttering up intermittently to the ceiling, where they passed through it like wisps of light. Church guessed it was Hellawes.

Niamh thrust past him and dropped to her knees in front of the divan, an unnerving keening sound of grief emanating from her. She kneaded her hands together, dipped and raised her head, barely able to comprehend what she was seeing. Baccharus looked away, sickened.

"Cormorel's murderer—" Church began.

"No." Baccharus eyed him forcefully. "This crime was not committed by the same."

"Who would want to kill a woman who lived like a hermit?" Ruth said.

The guards slowly moved backwards until they had formed a circle, swords ready to repel an attack from any direction.

"Remember: the mistress of this place was a Golden One," Baccharus cautioned. "To do this to her takes tremendous power, or specific knowledge." The words caught in his throat and he raised the back of his hand to his mouth in disgust, unable to hide his feelings any longer.

"Who committed this crime?" Niamh wailed.

The nerves along Church's spine suddenly sparked. "Something's coming," he said hoarsely, feeling it acutely as he spoke.

Ruth looked up at him curiously. "I don't sense anything."

His left arm began to tremble uncontrollably. He gripped it at the wrist to steady himself. "You haven't got a cocktail of alien shit in your blood," he said hoarsely. He half stumbled; Ruth caught him. "Fomorii," he wheezed. The taint of the Kiss of Frost was responding to the presence nearby.

The guards glanced at him, concerned, then at Niamh for guidance. "Listen to him," she ordered. "He is a Brother of Dragons. He understands the Night Walkers." She hurried behind their line of swords as the group began to back out the way they had come.

Before they were halfway across the next room, a guard's head split open. The blow had come so quickly no one had seen it. The Fomorii were all around them. To Church, they appeared to rise from the floor and drop from the ceiling, oil black and filled with malevolence, armed with the cruel serrated swords. His stomach knotted at the waves of evil washing off them. The air was filled with an animal stink, the walls ringing with the echoes of their shrieks and grunts. He still couldn't bear to look them in the face, so all he got were fleeting impressions: darkness and shadows, moving fast, shapes continually changing, horns and bony plates, sharp teeth, ridges and staring eyes. But most of all, power.

The Tuatha Dé Danann responded with force. Their swords were a whirling golden blur, and while they had appeared delicate before, now they carved easily through any Formor who came close enough. The ferocity of the attack had obviously shocked the gods; more, the simple fact that the Fomorii had attacked at all. In their arrogance they had presumed the Fomorii would leave them alone out of fear. Now their very existence was at risk.

"What the hell are they doing *here*?" Church wished he had some kind of weapon to join in the fray, but the guards had formed an impenetrable wall between him and the Fomorii.

"It doesn't make sense." Ruth was preoccupied, trying to find a space to concentrate so she could use some aspect of her craft, but in the mêlée it was impossible.

Another guard fell, split almost in two. Church saw none of the golden moths, so he couldn't tell if the victim was dead or not; there were still so many unknowns about the Tuatha Dé Danann, but there was no time to dwell on the puzzle. The Fomorii surged all around, black water shifting and changing, striking with venom, desperate to prevent the gods leaving the building. Church couldn't tell how many there were—a handful; a raiding party—but there were enough.

As they inched backwards through the next room, it became clear the Tuatha Dé Danann were prepared to respond with equal ferocity. Church had always seen the Fomorii as bestial and the Golden Ones as aloof and refined, but the guards hacked and slashed with a brutality that matched their historic enemies.

The Fomorii had one thing in their favour: a complete lack of self-preservation. Insectlike, they swarmed forward, attempting to overcome the guards with the sheer weight of their bodies. The floor was slick with the foul, acidic grue that spilled from the dead Fomorii. The guards slipped, then righted themselves, tripped over severed limbs, fought as hard to keep their balance as they did to repel the enemy; and still the Fomorii drove on.

The Tuatha Dé Danann paused at the threshold of the next door, blocking the Fomorii from circling behind them. The guards were an impenetrable wall, shoulder to shoulder as they lashed out, but the captain found a second or two to shout back, "We shall hold them off. Go with speed."

Niamh gave a faint, deferential bow. "Your sacrifice will not go unmarked."

Baccharus stepped through the door into the next chamber with Niamh close behind. She had gone only a few steps when she checked behind to ensure Church was following. "Come," she mouthed.

"Don't wait for us," Church yelled above the rising cacophony as the Fomorii saw what was happening.

Baccharus and Niamh were astonishingly fleet—another ability they shared with the Fomorii—and soon they had outpaced Church and Ruth.

"What are the Fomorii doing here?" Ruth gasped as they sprinted through chamber upon chamber, trying to piece together their route back to the entrance hall. The grey shapes that dogged their route had grown frantic, shrieking silently on the periphery of their vision.

"It doesn't make sense. They should be preoccupied with our world before getting mired in a potential war with the Tuatha Dé Danann."

They paused at a junction of corridors, peering up and down in desperation. From behind came an eruption of noise: the Fomorii had broken through the guards and were in pursuit. Church swore under his breath, selected a path and set off.

It wasn't long before they realised it had been the wrong choice. They were soon passing through chambers and corridors they didn't recognise, swathed in dark colours, deep carpets, black wood, purple drapes. The noises of pursuit were drawing closer; it was as if all the cages of a zoo had been opened at once.

"We're getting nowhere! They'll be on us in a second!" Ruth snapped, exhausted.

Church skidded to a halt next to a window crisscrossed with lead flashing. The glass was of a type that let light in while preventing any view out. When the catch wouldn't open, he searched around anxiously until he found a small stool, which he heaved through it. Smashing away the remaining shards with his elbow, he leaned out. They were about twenty feet above the main gate.

The animal noises were about two chambers away. With an effort he tore down one of the luxurious drapes and threw one end out of the window. "Climb down," he barked, bracing himself against the wall.

"What about you?"

"I'll be able to hang, then drop after you. If you get a bloody move on!"

She reflected for only a second and then clambered out of the window, lowering herself as quickly as she could down the heavy cloth. Church grunted as he took her weight. She dropped the final few feet to the ground, then beckoned anxiously for him to follow.

The cold hit him in a wave, frosting his skin with tracings of white. He sucked in a deep breath of air and his lungs were seared. Winter had stormed into the chamber. Shaking so much he could barely control his limbs, he turned to look towards the doorway. The Fomorii were surging through the next room, a black river sprouting limbs and fangs. One had separated from the mass and was gesturing towards him with strange movements that occasionally vibrated so fast he couldn't see them. More cold hit him with the force of a truck. His fingers contorted into talons; there was ice in his hair. He knew some of the Fomorii had control over temperature, but he had never experienced it himself. It was unbearable; his body was telling him to sink to the floor and seek respite in sleep. That was where warmth lay. Another shiver made his teeth rattle.

"Church!" Ruth's plaintive cry shocked him alert. A wave of darkness was sweeping towards him, rising up, ready to strike. No time to climb out; his limbs could scarcely respond anyway. Somehow he found the strength to shift his body weight, and then he was toppling out of the window, the air rushing past him, the cold dissipating as quickly as it had come.

He heard Ruth scream and then he hit the ground hard. There was a sickening crack and pain shot through his leg into the pit of his stomach. It was too much; he blacked out.

He came round only moments later to find Ruth shaking him, her eyes filled with tears. Pain filled his body. He looked down to where the worst of it writhed like a nest of snakes and saw a white bloody bone bursting from midway down his shin; another joint where one had not existed before. The sight almost made him black out again.

Ruth shook him harder. "Church! You can't stay here!"

Above him he saw insectile swarming at the window. There was some kind of disturbance; he guessed the last of the Tuatha Dé Danann were making a final stand. At least it would hold up the Fomorii for a little longer. "You'll have to help me." Every word was like a hot coal in his throat.

He didn't know how he got on to his good leg, but then he was hopping like crazy, one arm round Ruth's shoulders, trying to stay conscious when spikes were being rammed through his body. With his head spinning and the sea and sky becoming one, they reached the top of the vertiginous stairs. He felt Ruth's tension through her arm, knew exactly what she was thinking: they would never make it down the stairs together, there wasn't enough room, they had to go one at a time.

"You go first," he gasped.

"Don't talk so beered up." She tried to ease him ahead of her, but he grabbed her and shoved her down the first few steps. She cursed, then said, "I'll help you. Give me your hand."

"No. I can do it. Go on. Go on!" He could hear the Fomorii at the gate, only seconds away. He clung to the rock face and began to hop down a step at a time. It was easier going down, until he made the mistake of steadying himself with his broken leg and felt pain like he had never before experienced. Somehow he kept going. He found a rhythm that kept him moving quickly, focusing on Ruth's pale, concerned face so that he didn't overbalance. How he did it, he had no idea; it was all down to his subconscious.

Through the pain he could hear the Fomorii just a few steps behind him. At least the path was so narrow they were also forced to advance cautiously, but he couldn't afford to slow up for even a second.

"Not far now, Church," Ruth shouted encouragingly. "Halfway down. More than halfway."

His lungs and muscles burned from the exertion. He glimpsed the sky, brilliant blue through the clouds, the sea, a queasy green; spinning, merging.

"Church! Keep going! Concentrate!"

He looked back, saw something black snaking around the rock face towards him, attempted to push himself away from it, realised that with his damaged leg he had no sense of balance whatsoever. And then he was moving away from the rock, reaching out frantically for the dry grass, feeling it burn through his fingers. And then he was toppling backwards, over the edge, scrabbling for purchase, but he had only one good heel and that was not enough. Ruth was screaming and the air was thick with beast smell and jubilant shrieking. And he was falling.

The world rushed by. He hit the water hard, gulping in a massive mouthful of salty, sickeningly pungent liquid that felt more like oil. His precarious consciousness fled once again, but the cold shocked him awake when he was several feet beneath the surface, wrapped in bubbles, feeling the sea flood his nose and ears. Panic washed him in its wake and he tried to strike out for the surface, but he was hampered by his leg, and anyway, he couldn't tell which way was up. The Otherworld sensations were too potent, the smell of the water too strong, the feel too greasy. His mind fizzed in protest. He was drowning, sweeping down towards the dark water below. And that wasn't all. Whatever thinking part of him remained alert had caught sight of movement in the water, heading towards him. Something as big as a car, with fins and trailing tentacles, undulating with the speed of a torpedo, a large black maw opening and closing in hungry anticipation. Beyond it, other terrible shapes darted in the green depths, smelling blood, sensing food.

Strength returned to his arms enough to make a few feeble strokes in what he hoped was the right direction, but the predator bore down on him relentlessly.

Just as he anticipated those enormous jaws crunching down on his legs, rending and tearing and dragging him down into the dark depths, his collar was gripped and he was hauled out of the water. Face down on wet boards, he felt the boat rock violently as the creature passed just beneath. Then Ruth was at his side, caring for him as he coughed up seawater, and, as he looked up, he saw Niamh watching him worriedly.

Baccharus was beside him, his sleeve wet where he had rescued Church. "Quickly, now. You must help me row. The Night Walkers are close."

Barely conscious, Church let Ruth help him into a seat where he clutched an oar feebly. Ruth and Niamh both joined them and soon the boat was moving slowly away from the island.

"I don't understand why they aren't following us," Ruth said, glancing over her shoulder.

"They know we can be seen from Wave Sweeper. Any further pursuit would be futile." Baccharus turned to Church. We will find treatment for you on Wave Sweeper, Brother of Dragons," he said with surprising tenderness.

"Thanks for saving me."

"I could not let such an honourable being die, Jack Churchill." His words and tone were unlike any Church had heard from the Tuatha Dé Danann before. Closing his eyes, he leaned across the oar and reflected on what it meant as they drifted back towards safety.

Church woke in his cabin, the window thrown open to reveal the last sunlight of the day, mellow gold in a pastel blue sky, coolness on the wind. His leg ached with a rude heat beneath the rough blanket, but there was none of the agony that had consumed his body immediately after the break. Cautiously, he peeked under the sheet.

"It's still there."

Ruth was sitting just out of his line of vision, keeping watch over him. "Yes, but will I still be able to play in the Cup Final?"

"I'm glad you've retained your sense of humour. I lost mine when I saw that bone jutting out. Almost lost my lunch too." She sat on the edge of the bed.

There was a splint fastened hard around his lower leg; it bit sharply into his too-taut flesh as he shuffled up into a sitting position. "When I saw it I was convinced it was an amputation job. Luckily I didn't have much opportunity to think about it after that."

"You were luckier than you think. Most ships of this kind have some old sawbones. But this being the gods and all, you get operated on by some self-proclaimed deity. Geltin, I think his name was. And did he work miracles! His hands disappeared into your leg like it was water, popping the bone together and fusing it. He slapped some poultice on and Bob's your uncle. With that and the Pendragon Spirit you'll be back to normal in a day or two. Even beats BUPA." She took his hand. "I was worried."

He gave her fingers a squeeze.

She leaned over and kissed him gently on the forehead, lingering a moment, her lips cool and moist. When she withdrew she hastily changed the subject, as if embarrassed by her actions. "They've been in conference ever since you went under. This murder, coming so hard on Cormorel's, has really shaken them up. I think they thought they were inviolate before. Now it's like any old enemy can knock one of them off whenever he feels like it."

"And now they know how the rest of us feel." Church instantly felt guilty for the harshness in his voice. "I know it must be hard for them—"

"No, you're right. It's hard to feel sympathy when they have such little regard for other living creatures. It has really shaken them up, though. And just as much because this murder was committed by the Fomorii."

Church tried to choose his words carefully, but after a moment gave up. "I know this might sound coldhearted, but this could really work in our favour. It's not just a murder. With the history between the Fomorii and the Tuatha Dé Danann, it's an act of war."

"You'd think, but I could tell from some of the comments flying around the deck that they weren't exactly breaking a neck to retaliate."

Through the window, Church watched a gull skimming the surface of the sea; the other islands must be nearby. "I don't understand."

"Neither do I. Who knows how their minds work?"

Church tried to shift into a more comfortable position, then gave up. "Why would the Fomorii risk committing such a senseless act? The Tuatha Dé Danann, their arch enemies, were giving them free rein to wipe out our world."

Ruth examined her palm for a while, then said, "I think it might be me."

"What do you mean?"

"When I did the spirit flight to London, that awful thing I told you about . . . Balor, I suppose . . . followed me back, at least across our world. Maybe it saw us as a threat, sent out a killing party to wipe us out."

"They'd have had to move quickly."

"You know time means nothing to these freaks."

Church grabbed her wrist and pulled her down on to the bed next to him so he could slip his arm around her shoulders. "It's too confusing to try to work it out sitting here. Who knows what's going on? The important thing is I need to be up and about to lobby our case if I have to."

She leaned down beside the bed and emerged with a cane, carved in the shape of a dragon. "Voilà."

"That's very fitting."

"Yes, and they seemed to have it waiting for you." Another mystery, but he had long since given up trying to comprehend.

There was movement in the corridor without, and a second later the door rattled open without warning. Church was about to castigate the visitors for not knocking until he saw their faces. Three members of the Tuatha Dé Danann cadre who always accompanied Manannan entered, but they were subtly changed. Their faces, which before had been impassive and waxy, now had a cunning and malicious cast at the edges of the mouth and in the eyes, barely perceptible in direct glance, but on another level, quite striking.

"The Master requires your presence," the leader of the group said. His hand rested on the pommel of a sword Church had not seen in his possession before.

"The worms have turned," Church muttered so only Ruth could hear.

They silently followed the guards, Church hobbling as best he could. On deck there was no sign of any of the other travellers, only small groups of the Tuatha Dé Danann, watching their passage with dark, brooding expressions.

In his expansive cabin, as large as a mediaeval banqueting hall, Manannan sat behind a desk of gold, carved with figures that appeared to move of their own accord a split second after his attention left them. Other high-ranking members of the Golden Ones were scattered around the room. Church spied Niamh behind a couple of thin, cruel-faced aristocrats, but she would not meet his eyes. The strained, icy atmosphere told him things were about to get much worse.

Manannan rose once they stood before him and clasped his oversized hands loosely together in front of him. His face, too, was changed, though not as unpleasant as those of his guards; but it was harsher, certainly. "Another of our number has been driven on." His voice was as cold and hard as a swordblade. "The circling stars have been shaken, not once but twice." The message was repeated almost for his own sake, as if he could barely believe it. "Two times, in the fleeting memory of Fragile Creatures. Two abominations in the face of existence." Fury flared in his eyes, but his voice dropped to a whisper. "Monstrous."

Church didn't dare say anything for fear of retribution.

Manannan raised a hand to point an accusing finger at them. "You Fragile Creatures brought this upon us."

Ruth stirred angrily; Church fumbled for her wrist to restrain her, but she took a step to one side. "The Fomorii—"

"—were brought to the Western Isles in search of you. Were driven to acts of vengeance by you. The Night Walkers are rough beasts, once prompted, rarely stopped. You must be accountable for this."

"You're surely not blaming us for Cormorel?" Ruth held up her face defiantly.

Manannan did not answer.

"Scapegoats, then."

The disrespect in her voice was a step too far. Manannan's face shifted furiously before settling into its original form. "We have no interest in your feeble concerns."

"The Night Walkers will attack you as soon as they've finished with us," Ruth said, unbowed.

"And when they do we shall eradicate them as we did before. Until then, they are beneath our notice, as all creatures are."

Manannan's tone and the mood of the other Tuatha Dé Danann filled Church with apprehension. The situation was worse than he had imagined.

"The time has come. It has been proposed that you Brother and Sister of Dragons are a threat to the good running of Wave Sweeper and should be wiped from existence before any further troubles arise."

Ruth blanched. Church couldn't believe what he was hearing. "You're going to execute us?"

"No." Niamh's voice was filled with passion. She pushed her way past the other gods to stand before Manannan, her skin flushed to a golden sheen.

Manannan fixed his emotionless gaze on her. "You speak in defence of these Fragile Creatures?"

"I do."

"What worth have they?" one of the cruelly aristocratic gods said.

"You know their worth," Niamh said directly to Manannan. Her words were strangely weighted.

Manannan nodded. "Still, there is a need for discipline."

"Do not be swayed by the voices of the dissenters." Niamh bowed her head slightly so her hair fell around her beautiful face. "In your heart you know—"

"Do you question the word of the Master?" The aristocratic god stepped forward, a dim fury flaring behind his eyes.

Curiously, Church watched. For so long they had pretended to be detached from most human emotions—truly gods. But they weren't gods at all, however much they pretended. His concern grew when he saw the flickers of fear cross Niamh's face; it was obviously a great transgression to question Manannan's thoughts.

"I do not question—" Niamh began, but Manannan held up his hand to silence her.

"I will listen to our sister, who speaks for the Fragile Creatures," Manannan said to the assembled Tuatha Dé Danann before turning to Church and Ruth. "You are fortunate to have such a powerful advocate."

Church's relief was mingled with surprise that Niamh's voice carried such weight; he suspected Manannan was hoping to be convinced to change his opinion.

"Be warned," Manannan continued, "the eyes of the Golden Ones will be upon you from now on. Accept your role in existence, Fragile Creatures, and bring no more pain to this place."

His attention was gone from them in the snap of a finger. The sneering guards—now strangely less malicious and cunning—herded Church and Ruth to the door. Niamh flashed Church an affectionate smile before she joined the others who were milling around in obvious annoyance at the outcome.

Outside, Ruth's eyes blazed. "Those bastards!"

Church was taken aback by the vehemence in her voice. "They're losing control. Looking for scapegoats. They can't believe they're not as all-round wonderful as they think they are."

"And what was that witch doing?"

"Defending us—"

"Trying to get into your pants, more like. She never gives up, does she?"

She took a deep breath of the refreshing sea air, but her temper didn't diminish. "What's wrong with you?" Church said. "We were about to get summarily executed, but she got us off."

Ruth turned to him, defiant. "You know, when it comes to women, you've got a real problem."

"What are you talking about?"

"The witch still thinks she's got a chance with you. Maybe she has got a chance, I don't know. But you just keep diving into all these relationships, stirring up a whole load of emotional mess, without once thinking about the repercussions."

"I know I've made mistakes—"

"Well, sort yourself out."

"I can't believe the world is falling apart and we're talking about this!"

"Oh, come on. You know this is the important thing. The rest of it is just stuff that happens."

Church was lost for words.

"Do you want her?" she pressed.

"Niamh?" Ruth's gaze held him tight. He could finally read in her eyes all the truth that he had secretly known all along. "No."

"Are you sure?"

"Yes, I'm sure. I just get the feeling there's something else going on there, but I can't put my finger on it. Her feelings are so intense, they don't have any connection with how long I've known her. Everything feels completely out of balance." He watched the gulls swooping around the masts. "I don't like to hurt people's feelings, especially good people. And she does seem good."

"Sometimes you have to be firm." Her voice softened a little. "You need to talk to her—"

"I've tried."

"—be honest with her. She might be upset at first, but if she knows there's no point she can adjust. And then if you close all that down you can focus on your own future." Her voice remained calm and detached, but there was a tremendous weight to her words.

"I just wish I understood her better—"

"Oh, for God's sake!"

She made to go, but he caught her arm. "Let's not screw this up."

Her eyes moved slowly across his face, reading every thought in his head. Eventually she nodded; the tension between them evaporated, leaving another tension beneath.

A universe away, the emotions that had been crushing Laura for so long had finally started to dissipate. The dislocation when she awakened in the charnel pit had brought shock, despair, horror, futility and a debilitating fear that had left her unable to move.

Eventually all that was left was an emptiness gradually filling with a near-religious relief at her survival. With an effort she pulled herself into a squatting position, squirming as the soft corpses gave beneath her or when she brushed against cold skin. The only way she could cope was by not thinking about it. Instead, she fixed on the faint light filtering in on the other side of wherever she had been dumped.

The journey across the bodies was sickening. At the far side of the room was a flight of brick stairs leading up to a partly broken door. Beyond it she could see grey sky.

Refusing to look back, she scampered up the steps and tried the door, which swung open at her touch. She was in a street running amongst dilapidated Victorian warehouses that rose up high overhead. It was eerily still and quiet. The damp vegetation smell of open water hung in the air, but there was nothing to give her any clue where she was.

But as she stepped out of the shadows of the building a detail caught her eye that shocked her. The skin of her right hand and forearm had a greenish tinge. It was only faint, but unnatural enough to worry her. Anxiously she checked the other arm and then her legs; it was the same all over.

Finding a window with an unbroken pane, she examined her face closely: another shock, this one uplifting. The scars that Callow had carved into her face were gone, the skin as smooth and clear as a baby's. There wasn't even the vaguest trace of the wounds. It made no sense to her, but her overwhelming joy wiped out any worries. Hastily fluffing her short blonde hair into spikes, she wiped some of the smeared dirt and blood from her face and then set off to investigate her surroundings.

The warehouses had been in use recently. In one there was the strong smell of cinnamon; others had been fitted with modern security systems. Ominously, several had open doorways leading down to cellars, from which familiar unpleasant odours rose.

One side street led down to a broad, grey river. It took her only a second or two of scanning the riverside properties to realise it was the Thames; she was back in London. Heading along a road overlooking the water to the edge of the area of warehouses, she began to make out dim sounds of activity.

Just as she was about to emerge from the cover of the final warehouse she was suddenly grabbed from behind and dragged backwards, a hand clamped over her mouth. She fought furiously, but her attacker was too strong.

Only when her assailant had pulled her into the warehouse and flung her unceremoniously on to an oily concrete floor did she see who it was. "What are you doing?" she raged.

The Bone Inspector levelled his staff at her, as if to frighten her into silence. His piercing blue eyes gave him a menacing quality, emphasised by the unkempt grey-black hair hanging lankly around his shoulders. He wore the same dirty cheesecloth shirt, baggy trousers and sandals Laura had seen him in the first time she met him at Avebury.

"Keep silent if you want to keep living," he growled.

Laura dusted herself down as she flashed him a contemptuous look. "I bet you get all your women this way. Let's face it, they're never going to compliment you on your dress sense."

He grabbed her wrist roughly and dragged her over to a window, wiping away the dirt so she could peer out. Fomorii ranged as far as the eye could see, some carrying human bodies, others moving intently about some activity she couldn't discern.

"God." Her throat had almost closed up.

"The whole city is their stinking pit now."

Her fear was so strong Laura couldn't mask it; she stared at the Bone Inspector with wide eyes. "So this is their base?" Then: "They've killed everyone?"

The Bone Inspector took pity on her. He let go of her wrist and led her gently to a pallet where they sat side by side. "It's a shock, I know."

"You know what? Let's forget trying to describe things, because there just aren't the words." She buried her head in her hands, shaking as all the repressed tension came out in a rush. When it had eased, she looked up at him suspiciously. "What are *you* doing here?"

"Looking for you."

This made her even more suspicious. "How would you—"

"So I don't have to sit here answering stupid questions all day, I'll tell you. I came looking for your body. You made a sacrifice. It wasn't right that you were just dumped, forgotten." He looked away to minimise the impact of what lay behind his words. "Thought I'd take your bones back to somewhere fitting—"

"You're just a sentimental—"

He waved a threatening finger in her face. "It's my job. I'm a guardian of the old places because I'm a priest of the land, if you will. I tend to the people who fight for it." His eyes narrowed. "But I don't have to like them, understand?"

"Well, God forbid you should show some sensitivity."

"The earth energy's strong in you and your travelling troupe of hopeless cases. I can feel it even more now the changes you've wrought have started to wake the land."

"So you followed your nose." She looked back towards the window uncomfortably. "But how did you get past all that?"

"It wasn't so bad when I came in. They were spreading out across a different part of the city, doing whatever foul business they do, and the eastern approach was pretty open. Even so, I had to move under cover. Took time." He shrugged. "Can't see how we're going to get back out, though." He eyed her askance. "So how come you're not a pile of blood and guts and bone? And why do you look like you've been sleeping in a compost heap?"

"You really know how to chat up a girl."

"Well?"

"How should I know? I've given up trying to work anything out any more."

They sat alone with their thoughts for a while until Laura said, "Did it work?"

He knew exactly what she meant. "You saved her life. Who knows, you might even have saved much more than that. I pointed her and that miserable leader in the direction of the Western Isles to try to get the Golden Ones on our side. They might even do it, if they can put a lifetime of failure behind them."

"The others?"

"Don't know."

There was another long silence before she asked the question they'd both been avoiding. "So I've escaped a particularly horrible death to spend the rest of my life in a stinking warehouse with someone who doesn't know what soap is. Or do you have anything approaching a plan?"

He stared blankly at the dirty floor. "No. No plans."

Church and Ruth stayed in the cabin until night had fallen. The air was tinged with the fading warmth of the day and the scent of burning oil as the flickering lantern in the corner sent shadows shivering across the wooden walls.

All their attempts at making head or tail of the eddies of mystery and intrigue swirling around them had come to nothing, but so much was at stake they couldn't afford to just sit back any longer.

"We have to find the Walpurgis—he's the key," Church said eventually. "There's something very strange going on here, on this ship. These days I trust my instinct more than anything, and sometimes it's almost like I can feel deep, powerful currents moving just beneath my feet. I don't know if the death of Hellawes has anything to do with it, but Cormorel's murder *is* right at the heart. I don't understand why the gods in the furnace are stockpiling weapons, what the meaning is of all the strange looks and half-heard comments the other gods are making. Whatever it is, I *know* it's going to affect us, even if it's only that we're definitely not going to get any help from the Tuatha Dé Danann until the suspicion has been taken off us."

"How do you expect to find the Walpurgis if Manannan's massed ranks can't?"

"I don't know, but I know I've got to try. He's down there somewhere."

"I don't know." She shook her head worriedly. "The Malignos are still roaming around. You cross them, you won't be coming back up again." She sucked on her lip thoughtfully. "I'd better come with you."

"No," he replied forcefully. "I'm not being chivalrous, it's just good tactics. If I don't come back, at least there'll be one of us left to try to hold it all together." The shadows had pooled in her eyes so he couldn't read her expression. "You still think it's going to end in tears?"

"Oh yeah."

They were interrupted by a cry from the deck, strangely lonely in the still of the night. Church got up and peered out of the window. "Another island." A couple of lights glimmered in the sea of darkness. A rumbling ran through the walls as the crew prepared to drop anchor.

"More delays," Ruth said with irritation.

Church watched the lights for a moment longer, then said, "I think we should try to get on the landing party again. Any information we can pick up is going to help us."

"Do you really think they're going to let us after the last one?"

"We can get Baccharus to help—he seems to like our company."

"Or Niamh."

Church agreed uncomfortably, "Or Niamh."

Ruth looked away.

"We have to—"

"I know." Curling up on the bed, she rested her head in the crook of her arm and tucked her knees up to her chest. "We have to do what we can to make things right, however unpleasant. It's war."

The rocking of the ship changed its tempo as Wave Sweeper came to a gradual halt. Chains rumbled and clanked dimly, followed by a splash as the anchor hit the water. Then there was only a gentle swaying as the boat bobbed at its tether.

Church left the window and returned to the bed, sitting in the small space at the end that Ruth's long limbs weren't occupying. Her feet touched his thigh; she didn't move them away. "Do you remember, just after Beltane, sitting by the campfire?" She shifted slightly, put her feet on top of his legs. "That was a funny time. We'd already been through so much, had this massive blow, yet we felt—"

"So close."

"Exactly. This year hasn't been like anything else in my life. I know that's stating the obvious, but I mean on an emotional level. It's been so . . . potent. I've never felt more alive." He cupped the top of her pale foot in his hand. It felt so cool, the skin as smooth as vellum. "And it makes me feel guilty."

"What, we'd be better off moping around?" She stretched lazily. "There was a lot missing from the life everyone led before. Nobody was *living* at all."

"Now people are living, but they're dying too. That's not right." He moved his hand up her leg to stroke the gentle curve of her calf through her jeans.

"We'd forgotten how to feel anything. We were wasting our lives, and it must be one of the great ironies of the moment that when there was a chance we all might lose everything, we finally started to appreciate things."

"You don't know what you've got until you're in danger of losing it." His hand moved over her knee to her thigh; she didn't flinch, or make any attempt to push it away.

"Let's face it: this is the place where memories are made. How many people can say that?"

"Is that enough?"

"'Course it is." She smiled, put her hand on the back of his. But instead of pushing it off her leg, she pulled it towards her, over her hip, on to her side, and up, until he was overbalanced and falling on top of her. She manoeuvred herself until she was on her back, looking into his face. Her smile was open and honest and for an instant he was back in those early days, just after Albert Bridge, when they had spent their time piecing together the first clues about the unfolding nightmare. And with that remembrance came a blinding revelation: he had felt strongly about her from almost the moment he had seen her, as if they were of one kind, one heart. But in his despairing mood after Marianne's death any emotion had been muffled. Even when that had finally cleared, his feelings had been in such chaos that nothing made sense. But now he saw it clearly.

He loved her.

And he could see in the opal shimmer of her eyes that she loved him too; secretly he'd always known it. But the difference now was that she could see his feelings as well.

She pulled his head down and kissed him gently on the lips; she tasted faintly of lemon, her skin smelled clean, her dark hair felt silky in his fingers. And her smile was strong, with so much in it; it was all so heady. She was right; the end of the world didn't matter, the conflicts and power games of other people, all the petty concerns of the outside world. Inside was all that mattered; inside their heads, inside their relationships. The places where memories were made.

Ruth felt like crying, she felt like laughing. She'd managed to convince herself it was a package of sensations she'd never ever appreciate, except by proxy, in books and films and the wilting, easily discounted conversations of friends: that ocean swell of the senses, filling her throat, her head. She'd told herself that failure to feel wouldn't be so bad; there were always things to do and see. And now she could see how ridiculous that had been. A life touched by this could never be filled by anything ever again; except more of it, and more, and more, and more. She could keep the fear at bay now; not a fear of being alone, in a holding hands in the park way; she was too strong and confident to need someone to fill her time. But of being alone in the human race; we weren't made that way, she thought.

And here it was. If the world fell apart, and the stars rained into the void, it was all right. It was all all right.

They stripped the clothes from each other with a sensuality that was slow and measured; unfocused passion would let it all slip through their fingers too quickly. It was something to be savoured, not just by the body but by the mind, and that was how they knew it was exactly right. Church wondered how he had never known that before.

They knew each other's shape from embraces, but the fiery skin beneath the clothes made it all new and different. They were each surprised at how hard their bodies were, freed of the fat of lazy living by their punishing existence on the road. As he penetrated her, they kissed deeply, filling each other with soft darkness illuminated by purple flashes that reminded Church of the view across space from the Watchtower. He moved slowly at first, then harder as she enveloped him with her legs, and her arms, and her kisses, and her thoughts. His mind had one brief instant of complete awareness and then it switched off so there was only everything he felt, wrapped tightly in the moment; as timeless as Otherworld.

They lay together in silence while the sweat and semen dried on their bodies, listening to their breathing subside, their hearts slow down. Their thoughts were like the movement of luminescent fish in the deepest, darkest fathoms, slow yet graceful under the gargantuan pressure, struggling with the immensity of what they had felt. After a while, Ruth fumbled for Church's hand and he took it. Two, as one, passing through time.

A movement somewhere in the shadows of the cabin roused them from their introspection; a mouse, they both thought. But then something that at first sight was a large spider scurried into the flickering circle of lantern light. It was a human figure barely half an inch tall. Ruth recognised Marik Bocat, the Portune she had encountered after escaping the Malignos.

She rolled over to cover herself. "How long have you been there?"

"I have more to do than watch you make the beast with two backs," he said sharply. He sprinted to the edge of the bed where he looked up at Church's bemused face. "Ho, Simple Jack! Heave me up and mind how you do it!"

Church leaned down so Marik Bocat could clamber on to his palm. Once the tiny man was level with their eyes it was obvious concern lay heavy on his brown, wizened face.

"What is it?" Ruth asked.

"I come out of respect for fellow denizens of the Fixed Lands, and, of course, in respect for your exalted roles as champions of our home." He raised one minuscule finger. "A warning, then. Danger is abroad and your lives may be at risk. The door lies open, the cage is empty." He paused while he looked from one face to the other. "Callow is gone. The Malignos have freed him."

Away across the water, the Islands of the Dead breathed steadily and silently and the night was filled with the terrible chill of their exhalation.

chapter seven
peine forte et dure

Marik Bocat told them little, although they were both convinced he knew more than he was saying. His people had the run of the ship, he explained, and witnessed many things: secrets and slanders, matters of great importance and minor betrayals. The freeing of Callow had been the latest example of their surveillance at work.

"The Portunes will, of course, maintain their vigilance, and if information regarding this situation comes to light I will relate it to you," he said in an oddly formal manner.

"Why are you helping us?" Ruth asked.

"Horses and teeth," he cautioned, before half turning from them and motioning to be put back down on the floor. But as Church lowered him, his voice floated back: "We are all fellows of the flesh in the Great Village."

Church limped off the end of the bed and dressed, surprised at how quickly his leg was healing. He could already walk without the aid of a stick. "That bastard will be coming for us when we least expect it, so we have to expect it all the time."

"Like we haven't got anything else to do."

A thought came to Church as he ransacked a chest in the corner where he had come across a number of seafaring implements, including a bill-hook and a short dagger used for cutting rope, which he stuffed into his belt. "Can you help me find the Walpurgis?" he said turning back to Marik Bocat.

"Now why would you be looking for that bundle of rags?" Church could tell from the suspicion in his voice that the Portune had some information.

"He can help us. He *was* helping us before he ran away."

"I'll ask around." He eyed Church askance.

"You *can* trust me."

"So it seems."

Church dug down to the bottom of the chest, but there remained only oily rags, sand and dried seaweed. When he turned back to prompt Marik Bocat further he discovered the Portune had already departed.

Ruth dressed quickly and a little nervously. Their bonding had been truncated and there was still so much they had to discuss.

Now was not the time, Church thought. "We really need to find the Walpurgis," he said redundantly.

Ruth easily accepted the rearrangement of priorities. "Marik Bocat will probably be back once he's had a think about us. He's a suspicious sort." She threw open the windows to let some cool night air into the stifling room, which was still filled with the scents of their lovemaking. The sparse lights of the island twinkled over the waves. "I think he will come back," she stressed. "We need him to, really. It's even more dangerous to venture below decks now, with Callow on the loose as well as the Malignos. I've been down there, and believe me, when you get to the lower levels you can't tell what's a few feet ahead or behind you."

"If I have to—"

She silenced him with a flap of her hand. The silence was broken by a dragging noise on deck. "They're readying a boat," she said. "Looks like they're off to the island."

"What, now? In the dark?"

"Hey, they're the Golden Ones. They don't jump at shadows," she mocked.

Church said, "We ought to go, you know. There might be something important out there."

He looked reluctantly at the dishevelled bed and she laughed quietly. "There'll be time enough for that. Come on."

A cool breeze moved effortlessly across the deck, teasing out the heat of the day, bringing a hint of lush vegetation to the familiar aroma of salty water. The night was filled with the slap and rustle of the flaps hanging from the furled sails and the rusty hinge creaking of the rigging. Up on the mast, Ruth's owl glowed like a ghost, watching ominously. Although lanterns hung at regular intervals, there were still too many dangerous shadows lapping across the deck. Church and Ruth moved as quickly as they could to the small group of figures preparing for the landing party. Taranis was overseeing the activity as the crew prepared to lower the boat into the water, while Niamh and Baccharus hung back ready to board.

Taranis eyed Church and Ruth with cold suspicion, but Church ignored his gaze. Instead, he spoke directly to Baccharus and Niamh. "We'd like to come with you."

"You may accompany us, Brother of Dragons," Baccharus said as Taranis opened his mouth to speak.

Surprisingly, Niamh looked unsure. "There may be danger abroad," she cautioned. "The arrival of Wave Sweeper is always heralded by the denizens of the Western Isles."

"And you've heard nothing," Church noted. "It could be the Fomorii again. Have you considered this is their first strike in a war against you, catching you off guard as they work their way towards your most sacred lands?"

There wasn't the slightest flicker across the faces of the assembled Tuatha Dé Danann, but for the first time Church felt that unease was gestating deep inside them.

Wave Sweeper floated in silence as the landing boat was lowered to the waves. There was no sign of Manannan, or any of the thousands of strange creatures who occupied the lower levels. Taranis watched them impassively from the rail until he was swallowed up by the night, and then there was only the gentle lapping of the waves against the side.

As they neared land, Church was surprised to feel the air grow substantially warmer, as if each island had its own microclimate. Here it was almost subtropical, the heat lying heavy on his lungs as his T-shirt grew steadily damp from the spiralling humidity. Their destination was more familiar than their last port of call; it reminded Church of one of the smaller Caribbean islands. From a rocky base where the spectral surf splashed, it rose up sharply through thick vegetation to a mountaintop lost in the dark. It smelled heavily of steaming jungles, rich and evocative, but tainted by an underlying corruption.

A small beach came into sight, at which point the crew had to fight to keep the boat steady against the heavy currents that swirled just off the shore. Church spied the tip of cruel rocks breaking the surface on either side and realised a delicate path was being picked; one miscalculation and they would have been dashed in an instant. As the currents grew more intense, the boat became a stomach-churning rollercoaster ride. Church and Ruth gripped the sides tightly, but the crew were in complete control at all times.

Eventually the shore came up fast and the rowers jumped out into the shallows to haul the boat up on to the white sand. A minute later they were all standing on the beach, allowing the adrenalin to drop while Church and Ruth surveyed the dazzling array of stars overhead. There, with the night sounds of the jungle at their back and the waves crashing before them, there was an exhilarating sense of paradise that outshone any South Pacific dream.

"Do you notice how each of these islands has a different feel?" Church whispered to Ruth.

"The last one was edgy," she agreed. "This one makes me want to kick off my shoes and run across the sand like some moron in a Bounty ad. So relaxing."

"Come," Baccharus interjected. "We have a long walk, and it is dark beneath the trees. We must stay close together."

"Who are we visiting this time?" Church asked.

"This is the Isle of Lost Lament," Baccharus said, as if that explained it all. But then he added, "Six dwell here. Kepta, Quillot . . ." He waved his hand dismissively instead of listing the remaining names. There was a strange undercurrent in his manner, but Church couldn't quite put his finger on it.

Once Niamh had given the word, the leader of the guards motioned them to move out, his men taking up positions behind and on either side. They quickly passed the tide line on to the dry sand beyond and then into the impenetrable darkness beneath the trees.

It was claustrophobic under the cover of foliage in the hot, steamy atmosphere. The trees were clustered quite tightly in areas, their trunks oddly twisted, with branches resembling arthritic claws. They vaguely reminded Church of ones he had seen in the mangrove swamps of the southeastern United States on a holiday with Marianne, only these trees had thick, fan-like leaves of a shiny green that served to keep the light out and the heat and moisture battened down against the ground. Vines as thick as Ruth's forearm trailed from the upper branches, clinging to their flesh with some unpleasant sticky substance when they brushed past. They weren't the only obstacle: scattered all around were thick bushes covered in thorns like razors; with only the slightest pressure, one drove through Church's jacket and shirt and into the soft flesh just above his waist. Away in the dark they occasionally saw colours glowing, dull scarlets and fuschias and sapphires, which they eventually discovered were disturbingly alien blooms, like orchids, only much larger; their perfume was cloying and sickly. They appeared to be straining for the faint moonlight that occasionally made its way through the vegetation.

When they had first crossed the forest boundary they had expected silence, but the jungle was alive with movement and sound. Their feet crunched noisily on the carpet of twigs and branches, sending things scurrying for cover ahead of them: the sinuous motion of snakes, and the creepily rapid and erratic motion of large lizards. Church saw one of them nearby; it resembled an iguana, but when it half turned away in the trees he thought he glimpsed a human face on its scaly body. Spiders as big as his hand dropped from the branches and scuttled across their path, their corpulent bodies coloured rouge and cream.

The screech of night birds, again distressingly human, echoed amongst the treetops. On several occasions, Church and Ruth thought they heard voices whispering comments, but when they looked round they saw only grey shapes fading in the strands of mist that floated around the boles; the dead were restless.

After twenty minutes of hard hacking, with the point men slashing a path through the thickest flora, Niamh dropped back until she was standing beside Church. Despite herself, Ruth tensed.

"You must promise me you will take care of yourself, Jack." Niamh kept her head slightly bowed so her hair fell forward, obscuring her face. "There is great risk here."

"I always take care of myself, Niamh."

Ruth was convinced she heard tenderness in his words, though he had managed to keep his face impassive. Despite everything he said, she knew Church still found his emotions as unknowable as the Tuatha Dé Danann; he could react to them on a superficial level, but he had no idea what was moving far beneath the surface. Ruth could see he felt affection for Niamh, against all his protestations. What was happening here? As Church said, they *had* experienced little contact, certainly no intimacy, yet sometimes, in little movements or looks, it was as if they had known each other for a lifetime. Now she had found Church, after all those years of looking and knowing *exactly* what she wanted without even coming close to finding it, she was not about to give him up. She would fight if she had to.

Church and Niamh were engrossed in a conversation about the jungle plants when they were shocked into silence by the sound of something enormous crashing through the trees about half a mile away. The loud splintering was followed by a wail like a crying baby; the effect made them feel sick to the pit of their stomachs.

"What's that?" Church asked anxiously.

Niamh looked puzzled. Ruth thought she spied a glimmer of fear.

The leader of the guards came back to hurry them along the path they were carving ahead. Church and Ruth tried several times to peer through the darkness in the direction of the sounds, but only once did they see movement, and that faded away in an instant.

"Large predators," Church said to Ruth, one eyebrow raised comically.

"There's always something bigger." She tried to lighten the mood, but whatever it was had upset them immensely.

Conversation dried up for the next fifteen minutes. It might have been their imagination, but since they had heard the creature, the atmosphere had grown steadily more oppressive, until they were starting at every crack of wood or bird's cry.

Then, so sharply that Ruth broke out in goosebumps, they entered an area of complete silence: no birdcall, no rustling in the undergrowth. Even the trees appeared to be holding their breath.

Ruth shivered. "What is it?" Her voice was a whisper, but it sounded like a shout in the stillness.

Ahead, the lead guard raised his hand to bring them to a halt. Although he couldn't see the reason for their stop, Church felt his throat close up. The same anxiety was clear in Ruth's face. She looked at him, said nothing.

A change in the mood of the Tuatha Dé Danann rippled back from the front, like the first tremors before an earthquake. Anxiously, Church pushed his way through the group until he reached the head.

It was the stench that assailed him first, so rich with fruity corruption it made him gag. Across the path lay the carcass of some animal, a cross between a zebra and a warthog. Yet the beast had not been killed by a predator. The body was covered with deep, suppurating sores and a thick, creamy foam frosted its mouth and eyes. Around the belly, the groin and the neck, the tissue had liquefied into an oily black goo.

Church backed away until he found Baccharus. "What's wrong?"

"The creature is diseased." There was more to it than that, but however much Church pressed, he would say nothing more. Neither would Niamh make any comment, but there was evident concern in her face.

"I don't know what's going on here, but they've certainly got the jitters," Church whispered to Ruth. "Watch your back."

After a few moments' reflection away from Church and Ruth, the guards decided to cut a path around the carcass, but even when they were several feet away, the stench still followed them. Not long after that they came across another creature, this time a deer, small, with sharp, furry ridges on its back. It had the same marks of awful illness. The two discoveries in such close proximity only confirmed the worst fears of the Tuatha Dé Danann. The guards were in two minds whether to press on, but Niamh ordered them to continue.

"Whatever it is, it's not affecting the lizards or birds," Church hissed.

"As long as we don't catch it." Ruth kept her head down, watching Baccharus's heels.

"I don't think the Tuatha Dé Danann would be carrying on if there were any danger."

"I'm glad you're confident."

The incline increased sharply until they were slipping on the crumbly, peaty soil that quickly turned to mud in the humidity. Breathing was difficult and both Church and Ruth were sleeked in sweat, but at least the arduous progress kept their minds off the disease-ridden animals.

Cresting the slope, they came on to a broad, thickly forested plateau, and were hit by a sudden choking stink worse than anything they had experienced so far. Trees had been smashed down to create a wide clearing, their jagged stumps protruding from the ground like broken teeth. In the centre of the space lay a mound of decomposing flesh: the bodies of a score or more of the jungle's mammals, a range of species, all of them ravaged by disease and leaking the obscene black liquid that puddled and ran off down the slope.

Ruth took in the sight, then picked up trails on the ground. "My God, they've been *dragged* here."

"Maybe the local residents were clearing up to burn the carcasses. You don't want rotting animals all around your home," Church suggested unconvincingly.

"Baccharus, you know what's doing this," Ruth said sharply. "Please tell us."

He shook his head slowly, but kept his eyes fixed in the depths of the jungle. "It is not the time. Or the place."

The stench was so thick they couldn't stay there a moment longer. Covering their mouths, they bypassed the site as quickly as they could and continued on their upward path. In the eerie silence, the tension was almost unbearable. The lights hadn't been visible since they left the beach so they had no idea how much further they had to travel. The guards had grown particularly jumpy, and when the sounds started up close by, they formed a defensive posture.

"Keep moving," Niamh pressed, but even in motion they were half turned towards the source of the sound—breaking branches, snapping trunks, the noise of a large bulk moving through the vegetation. When the sickening wailing baby cry echoed loudly, they all knew they had not left the mysterious fearsome beast behind.

"Is it coming this way?" Grimacing from the sound, Ruth cocked an ear to hear the rise and fall of the cry, cut off for a moment, then appearing again suddenly. Her realisation dawned at the same time as the rest of the group. "It's coming after us!"

The crashing in the trees grew louder, unmistakably surging towards them. "What the hell is it?" Church asked hoarsely.

They were all frozen to the spot for a moment. It was impossible to tell from which direction the chilling noise was coming; distorting echoes bounced amongst the trees so that it appeared to be approaching them from every direction at once.

Baccharus was the first to move. "Come, quickly!" Surprisingly, it was to Church and Ruth that he turned his attention, grabbing their wrists and dragging them on. "The court is not far ahead—we can take refuge there!"

They moved swiftly, the guards taking up the rear, but before they had progressed far a terrible screeching erupted in the treetops above them. Suddenly the air was alive with frantic movement. Flashes of deepest black crossed

Church's vision. A hard form swatted the side of his head. It left him seeing stars, and when he drew the back of his hand across the aching spot, a trail of blood was left behind. The sight of that scarlet line stunned him; he hadn't been hit that hard. Then he saw what was happening: winged creatures whirled amongst the trees, lashing out with claws and sharp teeth. Another one slammed against his head, his chest, his arm. He ducked and ran forward, trying to wave the attackers away. They were moving so quickly it was hard to see what they were; although he had an impression of bats with leathery wings, their faces were lizardlike.

He caught up with Ruth, her pale face also splattered with blood. The guards were on every side, slashing with their swords. The flying things plummeted from the sky in their tens, hacked in half. There was too much blood, like rusty rain, as if their bodies were bloated with the stuff.

Ducking and diving, now feeling the pain from many cuts, Church and Ruth managed to spy a tree with low, thick branch cover. They dived beneath where they could watch the scene. The bat creatures were an airborne maelstrom of fur and teeth, but the Tuatha Dé Danann stood their ground, their golden skin now an apocalpytic red, striking furiously, though their faces still registered no emotion. The bodies piled high around their feet.

It was soon apparent the bat creatures had simply been disturbed during a period of heightened tension. Eventually those on the fringes began to flap away until only a few fluttered overhead, to be swiftly dispatched by the guards' swords.

Church crawled out into the bloody mire, Ruth close behind. "What the bloody hell was—"

The screeching baby noise was so close, the words caught in his throat and his stomach did a flip. Trees crashed; they felt the tremor of the fall through the soles of their boots.

The guards hurried Niamh away through the trees. Baccharus ran over to collect Church and Ruth. "If you stay here, you will join the beasts on the pile," he said.

They ran with him, slipping on the slick, churned-up ground. Church had to haul Ruth up from her hands and knees, all her clothes now sopping with mud and the blood of the bat creatures. Another baby cry wailed close behind. It instilled in both of them a deep urge to vomit.

"It is slow," Baccharus noted as he ran. "If we move quickly we can evade it. For now."

Church didn't like the sound of his final words, but before he could question him further they had broken out of the trees on to an area of clipped, green lawns, rising up gently to an imposing edifice of white marble built partly into the mountainside. Towers and minarets and columns formed strict lines of grace and power, like some odd mix of Greek and Middle Eastern architecture. Lights burned brightly within, welcoming after the seething darkness of the jungle.

They sprinted across the lawns, relieved that they had found sanctuary from the many terrors of the preternatural forest, grateful for the cool breeze sweeping in from the sea after the suffocating heat. But when they reached the building their relief evaporated. The front was a mass of glass windows offering panoramic views over the island beneath; all were shattered and the white muslin curtains billowed out into the night. The Tuatha Dé Danann slowed their run until they were once again advancing cautiously, swords raised. Niamh glanced at Baccharus, but said nothing.

The cry of their pursuer from just beyond the tree line prompted them into action once more and they hurried through the broken windows into an interior which glowed white with the light from scores of lanterns, torches and candles, like some Byzantine impression of heaven.

The leader of the guards made several chopping motions with his hand and within seconds his men were in action. They dragged enormous stone tables and heavy wooden furniture to block up the windows, continuing ceaselessly until the blockade was several feet thick.

"Will that work?" Ruth asked.

"No," Baccharus replied curtly.

"Now," Church stressed, "you've got to tell us. What's out there?"

"The Plague-Bringer." Baccharus peered at the thin gap between the pile of furniture and the top of the window. "Known in your land as the Nuckelavee."

"It carries the plague with it, infecting all higher creatures in its path," Niamh interjected. The baby cry rose up again just beyond the wall; Church and Ruth started, then gagged; every aspect of the creature assailed the senses.

"Even you?" Ruth added once she had recovered.

Niamh looked away, but Baccharus answered for her. "There are some who think the Golden Ones unassailable, the highest of the high in all of existence. That is not be my belief." Niamh flashed him a curious stare and he changed tack. "We have seen two Golden Ones eradicated. There is no doubt an ending can come to our race, though it is blasphemous to admit it. And it is told that that creature, the Nuckelavee, is one of the few things that can bring about that ending."

The baby cry again; Ruth covered her ears. There was a rough sound as if the Plague-Bringer was dragging itself along the foot of the wall.

"And it lives on this island? Near this court?"

Baccharus shook his head. "Like all the Western Isles, this is a safe place for the Golden Ones. It was brought here."

"By the Fomorii," Ruth interjected. "Specifically to kill your people. It *is* war."

Baccharus nodded slowly.

They were interrupted by a cry of alarm raised by one of the guards. There was activity at one of the large arched doorways that led to the inner chambers. The guards were backing away hastily, half holding up their swords, yet somehow unsure. At first Church could pick out only a long shadow cast along the floor, moving in an odd manner. A few seconds later a figure appeared in the archway.

It was unmistakably one of the Tuatha Dé Danann; the male's skin had the familiar golden tinge and he was wearing what Church perceived to be a white toga held by a gold shoulder clasp. Yet he was lurching from side to side, his legs buckling every now and then, until he caught himself at the last. The smell reached them a moment later. As he closed in, Church could see the terrible ravages of whatever disease the Nuckelavee carried: part of his face had been eaten away, revealing what should have been a cheekbone and part of his jaw, but instead there was only a golden light. An unsightly black stain scarred the front of his pristine toga and left a trail as he passed. He had one arm outstretched, in greeting or pleading, Church couldn't tell, and although he opened his mouth to speak to them, the only thing that came out was a stream of shimmering moths, drifting up to the ceiling.

Niamh's jaw dropped in horror; the guards looked to her for direction. Baccharus stepped forward and said firmly, "Do not let him near."

"But he's still alive!" Church protested. "Surely you can do something to help him."

Baccharus turned and there was a shocking emotion alive in his face. "There is nothing I would like to do more," he said in a cracked voice. "He is a kinsman; we are all brothers of the same village. But if he comes near he will infect us all, and what is the good in that?"

Church watched the pitiful figure advance slowly, with a very human air of desperation. "Definitely not gods," he whispered.

"Hold him back," Baccharus ordered. "He is not long for this existence."

Ruth was about to protest that Baccharus was acting too harshly when his face grew suddenly sorrowful. He ran forward until he stood as close as he could to the diseased god. "Know this, brother. We are all *people*, all joined. I am filled with the great sorrow of the Golden Ones for your plight. Not because it is a crime against existence, but because of you. My brother. But, know this and forgive: I cannot let you near. You will take us all with you."

The diseased god appeared to hear this, for he paused in his relentless forward motion. The weight of the decision Baccharus had been forced to make was heavy on his face, but he could only hold out his arms impotently as the guards stepped forward to drive the ailing god back. They herded him through the archway and then Church heard the slam of a heavy door and the piling up of more furniture.

When Baccharus trailed back to them, his face a lie of composure, Church laid a friendly hand on his shoulder. "I'm sorry you were forced to do that," he said.

Baccharus looked honestly touched by this gesture, and a warm smile briefly overrode the air of sadness. It was just one of many little incidents he had witnessed in Baccharus over the previous few days: cracks in the arrogant composure of the Tuatha Dé Danann that suggested something approaching humanity within, if that was not a contradiction. Perhaps he had been wrong in judging all the gods so harshly.

His thoughts were driven away as the bile rose in his throat at another bout of wailing just beyond the blockade. This time the heap of furniture rattled and a heavy oak chair rolled off the top and splintered on the marble floor.

"Can it force its way through?" Ruth asked anxiously.

"Seems like it's got some muscle. I'm going to take a look at it." Church ran forward and began to climb the unsteady mound, Ruth's shrill warnings echoing behind him. It probably would have been safer to have kept his distance from the barricade, but if he knew what it looked like he thought he would be more able to contain his fears, and maybe even find a way to strike back.

But the moment he crested the rocking pile of furniture and wriggled forward on his stomach to peer over the edge, he wished he hadn't. His gorge rose as he peered down at the Nuckelavee moving backwards and forwards at the base of the wall, not knowing if his disgust was at what he saw or what he felt coming off the beast. It was as big as three cars in a row, with a barrel-shaped body and a snakelike head that lolled sickeningly from side to side, as if its neck were broken. It had no legs, instead dragging its slug body along on stubby, multi-jointed arms that looked too thin to support its bulk. Most foul of all was that it had no skin; there was only a thin membrane covering its body so the blood could be seen pumping through the network of veins as its muscles slithered and stretched like an obscene anatomy textbook.

Church allowed himself only a few seconds to take it all in before he turned his eyes away in relief. He retreated cautiously down the blockade and returned to the others, his pale expression telling Ruth everything she wanted to know.

"Is there another way out of here?" Church asked. Niamh and Baccharus were almost paralysed by what they had found on the island.

"No." In the white light that flooded the room, Niamh's face was uncommonly pale. "Perhaps the Master will send others to fetch us back."

Baccharus eyed her with a curious expression. "Or perhaps he will listen to the whispered words and sail away at dawn."

A table flipped off the top of the barricade, forcing them to move aside hastily as it crashed into the floor. "I don't think we have the luxury of waiting," Ruth noted.

"We cannot run," Niamh said. "Nor can we confront the Plague-Bringer, or we will all be destroyed. What do you suggest?"

There was a brief, hanging moment of confusion until a shiver ran through Church: the gods were looking to him and Ruth for a solution. How could they have faith in *Fragile Creatures*? He turned to face the rocking barricade, feeling the cold weight of responsibility. They were saying there was nothing they could do; they were elevating him to a height beyond his capabilities.

Beyond the barricade, the baby cry began again, but this time it didn't sound like it was going to stop: it rose higher and higher until his ears rang and his teeth were set on edge; mingled in it somewhere he was sure he heard a note of triumph.

In T'ir n'a n'Og, time moved fast, or slow, or stood still with no rhyme or reason, but in the Fixed Lands life crept on at its solemn, relentless pace. Veitch and Tom could not be frozen between moments or see the days and weeks flash by like the view from a train, but they both felt it was moving quicker than they could handle.

They had spent twenty minutes with their own thoughts, preparing for the trial that lay ahead, watching the birds or the swaying branches of the trees, but never straying too far from the cairn at Corrimony. It felt like sanctuary: the Blue Fire that could be tapped so easily there was both protector and energiser, filling them up and giving them purpose.

Veitch was still enthused with all the energies his encounter with the archetype had instilled in him; to him, he *had* met Robin Hood, a hero of Britain whose good deeds transcended time. Veitch barely dared admit to himself how much that excited him; and how much he wanted something similar. He wouldn't even mind dying if he could become a hero people would remember, wiping out in an instant the petty, twisted parts of his nature, the waste he'd made of his life.

For the first time in many years, Tom was feeling bewildered, and it wasn't from the two joints he'd smoked in quick succession as he ambled around the cairn, fascinated by the shape of the stones, their colour in the sun. He'd lived for hundreds of years. His memory was a vast library stretching into deep, subterranean chambers, but his own character he knew with weary boredom. Or thought he did. But Veitch, rough, uneducated, shallow, had made several sharp comments during the course of the night that suggested he didn't know himself very well at all. In his own eyes, he was compromised by the complexity of an age when things could no longer be seen in black and white. To Veitch, he was a hero, a conclusion born from observation, for not so long ago the Londoner had railed against his *mythological* status. What had Veitch seen that he couldn't see himself? It troubled him, yet excited him a little too. But it was a *frisson* nonetheless, and for anything that stirred his blood after such a long life he was eternally grateful.

When he finished his last joint, he peered over the top of the cairn and shouted, "It's time."

"You know you're not supposed to drive on that stuff," Veitch said as he wandered over. "I'm not so sure I want you in charge when we're throwing ourselves into the Universal Transporter."

"Oh, shut up. We had a name for you back in the sixties."

"I have a name for you right now. Get on with it."

They crawled on their bellies through the symbolic tunnel until they were sitting cross-legged inside the cairn. After the previous night, when the stones had been alive with the crackling blue energy, the place looked flat and dead, but they both could feel the vitality deep down in the earth, waiting to be brought out.

"You're sure you're ready for this?" Tom said.

Veitch peered up into the blue September sky. "It's for a mate. I'm ready."

"As long as you know what you're letting yourself in for. Don't forget—this isn't a test. No trial runs."

"In life or anything else. Just get on with it."

At first Tom was annoyed that Veitch hadn't grasped the true dangers of what they were attempting, but as he watched the Londoner's face he saw that wasn't right; Veitch simply didn't care. The dangers paled into insignificance compared to what they might achieve: bringing a trusted, much-loved friend back from the other side of death.

"So what do we have to do?" Veitch asked blithely.

"We rip out our souls and throw them to the four winds."

Veitch shrugged.

Tom shook his head wearily before taking in a deep breath to clear his head. The drug lifted him one step beyond day-to-day existence. Closing his eyes, he said in a dreamy, hypnotic voice, "Stone has strange properties. It vibrates, did you know that? It collects and responds to the energies at the heart of everything. That's why so many ghosts are seen in places made of stone—castles and old houses and monasteries. The power affects the brain, raises the consciousness. Lets you see the Invisible World." He took another deep, calming breath. "These old, sacred places, these circles and cairns, were constructed out of stone for that reason, not simply because that was the only material at hand. The peculiar qualities of stone made it easier to release the stored energy our ancestors needed to *transcend*. All they had to do was make the stones vibrate. Do you know how they did it?"

Veitch was gripped by Tom's mesmerising voice weaving a spell around him.

"Sound. All these places are designed for auditory effect. Consider the fougous in Cornwall. The great chambered cairns. They have the sonic qualities of the best musical halls. The perfect pitch, the exact timbre. All are achieved within their confines. Yet they look so rough, just thrown together." To illustrate his point, he made one low note, which bounced around the walls without losing any of its sharpness. "When this place was complete, with a roof of stone to contain the sound, it would have been even more effective. Primitive woodwind instruments, carved from bone or wood, rhythmic chanting, the tools of the shaman the world over. Sound has power. Music has power—even on a mundane level. Yes, sound releases the energy in the stone, but it shifts something in our brain too, making us more receptive to the transcendent experience. That's why hymns are sung in church. The music provides direct access to the god centre, helping us to see the wonder that is around us all the time."

He waited for Veitch to make some deflating comment, but his companion was rapt. Tom hadn't expected that. He was only really using the rhythm of his words, the rise and fall of the sound levels, to make Veitch more receptive to the kind of sonic manipulation he was describing. And there he was, actually *listening*.

"So, it's like pop songs . . ." Veitch winced. "Tell me if I'm being stupid, all right? But it's like some crappy little pop record. You hear it on the radio or somethin', and suddenly that moment that you heard it is . . . locked in. It's, like, more real than all the moments around it. Brighter, you can remember what things smelled like and sounded like, all the detail, even years after, when you've forgotten every other moment that got you to that point."

"You have it." Tom restrained a smile of deep affection. "Now, say no more. Prepare yourself. Don't see or smell or touch. Hear."

Veitch closed his eyes, surprised at how centred he felt. Even the anger that in recent times had become a constant background buzz had faded away.

Tom took another deep breath and when he released it, he made a low, rumbling sound deep in his throat, sustaining it until every part of the breath had been expelled from his lungs. *Soooooooooooooooo*. Another breath, and then he repeated the sound. This routine continued, building up a mantra that filled the whole of the cairn. After a while Veitch felt confident enough to introduce his own chant into the breaks when Tom gathered his breath. It created a constant wall of sound swirling around the walls in ripples and eddies.

The first thing Veitch noticed was a tingling in his fingertips. Gradually that sensitivity progressed along his arms, while a similar force rose up from his spine, like a snake sinuously progressing round the bony stem, a sensation he recognised from the time Ruth had practised her sex magic on him. Flares burst at different points as the snake passed on its journey towards the back of his brain.

All around, the sharp edges of the stones were limned with the now-familiar blue glow. And it wasn't just in the stones, but in the ground, and in Tom, and in him, everything linked.

The snake passed his shoulder blades, wriggled its way up to his neck, ready to make that final leap. Veitch prepared himself for the rocket ride he had experienced previously.

Only this time it was different. At the final moment, he heard, or thought he did, Tom utter a word, one that he couldn't remember a second later, but which was filled with a tremendous weight of power, and then he felt like he was slipping into a warm bath. The tension was stripped from him in an instant; the tingling transferred to his groin; he felt as light as a leaf caught in the wind.

A tremendous sense of well-being washed over him. No problem was important, no financial worries, no argument with his friends or his family, no doubts about his own abilities; not even death. He was consumed with *perspective*, of being part of something enormous, that crossed the boundaries of time and space, life and death. From that vista, everything dragging him down was meaningless. The true meaning was all around.

He wanted to communicate this enlightenment to Tom, but when he opened his eyes again all he saw was blue. It wasn't a flat colour, more like a diffuse light, a glow, a liquid, warm and enriching, but he wasn't drowning or choking. Out of curiosity he tried to call Tom's name, but either his vocal chords wouldn't respond or sound wouldn't travel in that medium.

Where was he? he thought without any panic. *Floating . . . drifting . . . happy . . . content . . .*

There wasn't any sense of real motion. It reminded him of lying in the sun in the back garden as a teenager, floating in a ring at the lido on a Saturday afternoon. Cocooning. No need to worry about anything at all, ever again. In fact, all negativity had been thoroughly expunged from his thoughts; he couldn't think of anything unpleasant even if he tried. He found himself dwelling on the truly good things in his life: the moment he first saw the mermaid swimming next to the boat on the way to Caldey Island, his friends, particularly Church, his role model whom he admired more than anything; and then Ruth, whom he loved in a way he had never thought possible, so acute it was almost physically painful not to be with her.

And that thought did trigger something unpleasant in his head, just the faint tremor in the deepest reaches, but it was there. What was it? Why wouldn't it go away and let him enjoy the experience of floating?

What was it?

Something . . . something about Tom. No, something Tom had said. His head was stuffed with candy floss, in consistency and sweetness; dredging up any kind of rational thought progress was a struggle. Ruth. Tom. Ruth.

And then he had it. Tom had warned him of the dangers of getting lost in the blue fire, of its seductive qualities that would make him not want to return to the real world. It *was* seductive, but if he didn't go back he would never see Ruth again; all the joys of the Blue Fire paled next to that.

The thought that he might already be trapped brought a bubble of panic, but the moment it surfaced he was moving. The blue sheen in front of his eyes still looked the same, but he could feel motion; he was shifting, faster and faster, until he felt he was speeding at a hundred miles an hour.

Before he could consider any further action, he sensed a presence beside him, Tom, although he could see nothing but blue when he looked around. More, he could sense his companion's mind, and what he saw there left him with a potent, bittersweet sensation. Laid bare was Tom's affection for all the travelling companions, which was both a shock, and humbling. But lying behind it all was a powerful self-loathing triggered by Tom's fear of what the Tuatha Dé Danann had truly done to him. He felt like an outsider, filled with a loneliness Veitch could not even begin to imagine; the only thing that gave his life meaning was the Brothers and Sisters of Dragons and the success of their mission.

Then he was moving again, only this time Tom was directing him. Soon he was whizzing faster even than he had before. A burst like TV interference crackled across his mind; another; and another; and then he was overcome with a monumental anticipation.

Another burst of static, and images began to flash across his mind so fast he could barely keep track. Some, though, were important enough to stick: Ruth, standing on the deck of a storm-tossed ship as black tentacles lashed through the air; Church, standing at a pool as the grim spectre of a woman rose out of the waters; Church and Ruth, sitting close beside each other on a cabin bed; the vampiric Baobhan Sith, grey and merciless, rising from the dusty ground; Laura, sitting in a damp warehouse, her skin an odd tinge of green, and a figure with white, papery skin scarred with inky-black veins looming over Church.

The images and the pure blue of the energy vanished with the feeling of passing through a membranous wall. For a brief moment an unending whiteness filled both his vision and his thoughts, and then he was thrust roughly into sensation: the wind and sun on his skin, the sight of trees and sky, the smell of fresh vegetation, made all the more powerful by their brief absence. It was followed by the realisation that he was several feet above the ground. He had no chance to prepare himself—he hit hard, winding himself. There was a crunch a split second later as Tom landed beside him.

"Can't you do anything about re-entry?" Veitch sat up, irritatedly rubbing his bruised ribs. His annoyance was less to do with the pain of the landing than the fading memories of his overwhelmingly joyous experience in the Blue Fire; it had left him hollow and dissolute. He controlled his rumbling temper when he saw Tom was undergoing the same separation pangs.

The Rhymer struggled to his feet, obviously in some discomfort, plucking his spectacles from a bush where they had landed in the fall. They were on a gently sloping hillside in the deep shadow cast by heavy tree cover, although the sun burned brightly on a grassy path cutting through the wood nearby. There, the last Brimstone butterflies of summer fluttered amongst the burdock flowers. Bees buzzed lazily round the boles while midges danced in a sunbeam. The chattering of birds was everywhere. The air smelled dank and peaty from the leaf mould that covered the wood floor, obscured in areas by patches of bramble and nettles and the occasional pile of coppiced wood.

"I saw things. Just before we got here." Some of the images lay heavily on Veitch's mind, pregnant with meaning he couldn't discern. "Church. And Ruth . . ."

"I noticed that the last time." Tom grumpily checked his faded haversack to ensure nothing had fallen out. "When you are about to exit the energy stream you pass through an area where you can see through time and space. Neither of those things are fixed anyway, except in your limited perceptions."

Veitch checked his watch. Barely a second had passed since they had been in the cairn at Corrimony.

"You were right." He stood up to see if he could discern their next direction. "That was some smart bleedin' place. It was—"

"Heavenly."

"Right. I didn't want to leave. But you know what? It didn't feel like that before when we went from Cornwall to Glastonbury."

"Then you were panicking in the sea, blacking out, trapped in the mundane so you couldn't perceive the ultimate." Tom readjusted his ponytail, then strode up the slope.

"You know where we're going?"

"Yes, out of the trees so I can get my bearings."

Tom had retreated into his usual state of ill-tempered reticence, but Veitch wanted to talk about the many confusing thoughts the experience had engendered. "That was amazing," he said quietly as they walked.

"And dangerous."

"You know what? I don't think it is. I reckon I've got it figured out."

"My. Aren't you the smart one?"

"It's only really dangerous if you've given up on living."

This struck Tom sharply. "What do you mean?"

"You're all right as long as you've got something to hold on to in the real world. If you haven't got anything here, you give up, float away. If you have unfinished business, something important, you drag yourself back. You don't really mind leaving 'cause you know that sooner or later you're going to end up back there. You can wait."

Tom thought about this for a long moment. "And you had something to bring you back?"

"That's right. I've got stuff still to do here. But when it's all over, you know, when my number's up, I wouldn't mind going back there. Just knowing it's there changes the way you look at life, y'know?"

"Yes. I know."

They emerged on the sunlit path and followed it up to a tarmac-covered route where an information board showed a tourist map of Wandlebury Camp.

"We made it, then. We could have ended up anywhere in that stuff, but we came to exactly the right place. We *thought* ourselves here, didn't we?"

Tom read the sign's notes on the historical background to the camp, then estimated their position from the noon sun. He pointed back down the slope. "That way, but later. First we need to see if Shavi's body is here."

Veitch shifted uncomfortably. "What if something's got at him? Some animal?"

"Do you really think Cernunnos would allow that to happen?"

He set out along the path that curled around the eastern side of the low hill. A thick bank of trees obscured the top. The path drew tightly past a small nature reserve settled on a pond that was thick with rushes where jewelled dragonflies dipped and dived. Beyond, it took a sudden turn, cresting a slight rise to present them with a view of a magnificent mansion house, its grand eighteenth-century architecture oddly out of place on the flat-topped summit. The house looked out on to gardens given up to lawns where a flock of sheep nibbled aimlessly. A large, old-brick wall marked the boundary, beyond which thick trees rose up imposingly. There was stillness to the place, odd, though not unpleasant.

Veitch sauntered over to another tourist sign. "Gog Magog House. Used to be a big place for horse racing, breeding and all that. Funny old spot to do horse racing, on a bleedin' hill."

"People are instinctively drawn to these places of power." Tom cleaned his glasses to get a better look at the ornate clock on the cupola mounting the stable block. A gold weathervane stirred slightly in the breeze.

From the corner of his eye, Veitch caught the faintest movement, but it was enough to lock his muscles and still the breath in his lungs. Tom continued ambling around, surveying the scenery. Just to be sure, Veitch waited and watched, and when he picked it up again, he launched into action. Tom whirled in shock, but Veitch had already hurdled a low fence and was sprinting towards the stable block. A figure lurked at the base of the wall, too slow to take evasive action before Veitch was upon him.

It was a man, short and plump, with a ruddy, wind-blasted face. He wore a checked flat cap pulled low on his brow and a gaberdine mackintosh fastened tightly over his broad belly. "Don't hit me! You can have everything!"

"Chill out, mate." Taken aback by the response, Veitch adopted an easy-going posture. "You can't be too careful these days."

The man composed himself, but still looked wary. "You're lucky you caught me without my shotgun."

"You live here?" Veitch scanned the courtyard and windows for any other sign of life.

"What's it to you?" The man backed off a few paces as Tom wandered up. He appeared to be considering whether he could make a break for it.

"We're not looking for trouble." The edge of Veitch's voice suggested that trouble could, however, be on hand if necessary. "We've got some business in these parts. We're not going to rob you or nothin' like that."

"We're here to collect the body of a friend." Tom held out a hand as he introduced himself.

The man took it, intrigued; his name was Robertson. "A body, you say." His eyes flickered towards the lawned area.

"Is that where it is?" Tom followed his gaze, but could see nothing.

Robertson rubbed his chin thoughtfully, then beckoned for them to follow him. He crossed the courtyard and entered the mansion. From the lonely air of emptiness, it appeared Robertson was the sole occupant. The wind blew through a broken window that hadn't been fixed and there was tracked mud across the tiled floor. Despite the grandness of the building, Robertson only lived in a couple of adjoining rooms that had a makeshift appearance, with furniture obviously dragged from other parts of the house. The first thing that caught their eye as he led them into his quarters was the strange array of items hanging around the door. Over the top was a large, ornate cross. Beside it were horseshoes, another cross made out of twigs of rowan, the old symbol for protection from witchcraft and fairies, the withered remnants of a mistletoe sprig for protection from thunder, lightning and evil, a bunch of St. John's wort to ward off spirits, a roughly carved wooden swallow for insurance against fire, and many more.

Robertson caught Tom's inspection. "Like your friend said, you can't be too careful."

Once safely inside his room, he crossed himself and touched wood before offering them chairs next to the unlit fire. "I'd make you some tea, but with the way things are I've got to conserve. Even water," Robertson said. "I hope they get the bloody thing sorted out soon. We can't go on like this much longer. Bloody government."

"Do you work here?" Veitch asked.

"Nobody works anywhere any more, do they? Not in the old sense," Robertson replied. He settled into a comfortable armchair within easy reach of the shotgun resting against the wall. "I used to have a business down in Cambridge. Got out of there when the riots started."

"What riots?" Veitch looked puzzled.

"What riots?" Robertson replied incredulously. "I don't know where you come from, but round these parts it seems that's all there's been. When they brought in the fuel rationing. When the supermarkets stopped filling their shelves. Then when everything stopped working . . ." Suppressed emotions briefly turned his face into that of a child and he covered it with his hand until he had composed himself. "I left the city when my Susie died. She was a diabetic, couldn't get her insulin."

"I'm sorry." Tom was honestly sympathetic.

"This place was abandoned so I moved in," Robertson continued. "I soon found out why they'd left. Still, at least there's no riots, and it's not too bad as long as you don't go out at night." His eyes narrowed suspiciously. "Strange things happen round here," he said, obviously not wanting to go into detail. "Never used to believe in those things, but now . . ." He nodded to the charms on the door. "I don't know what's happened to the world. Do you find it's like a dream, where none of the rules apply? Where you can run as fast as you can but never get anywhere, and rooms are bigger inside than out? Sometimes I wonder if it's ever going to be right again."

He sounded on the edge of a breakdown. Stress had brought twitches to his hands and a tic to a muscle beneath his eye.

"The body?" Tom prompted.

He nodded a few times too often. "In the lawns out there, there's a large hollow. You can see it easily if you stand by the stable block. It's a dew pond, manmade, dates back to the Stone Age or something, according to the signs. If you go down there at certain times—sunset, sunrise—you can see it. Only not, which sounds a queer way of putting it, but that's how it is. The first time I saw it, it scared the living daylights out of me, but when I realised it came back regular as clockwork, just lying there, there was no point getting worked up about it. There are worse things." He looked down at his hands, which he quickly clasped together.

"What do you mean, there only not there?" Tom leaned forward so he could read Robertson's face.

"How can I describe it? It's like it's half there and half not. If you stand at the right point, so the light's coming in just so, it almost looks solid. Take one step to the left or right and it disappears."

"Can you see who it is?" Veitch asked.

"Looks like some Indian or something. Hard to tell. He's lying on his back, hands across his chest."

Veitch looked at Tom excitedly, but the Rhymer kept his face emotionless. "Can you show us?" Tom said.

"I can. But you won't see anything at this time. Sunset's probably the best time, but you won't be getting me out there then."

"So what *is* out there?" Veitch asked.

Robertson rose quickly, suddenly uncomfortable. "Well, I don't rightly know. And even if I did, I wouldn't want to be talking about it. They can hear everything that's said, you know. Take their name in vain, they'll make you pay." He crossed himself, then once more for luck. "You want to be careful what you say."

"We don't bow our heads to anything undeserving," Tom said curtly.

Robertson looked on them pityingly before leading them out, stopping briefly to touch all the charms around the door.

The September sun was warm on the backs of their necks as they wandered across the lawns to the dew pond. Robertson was right; there was nothing to be seen. The ground was hard baked from the summer sun, the grass clipped close by the sheep.

Robertson looked up cautiously to check the sky. "Two days ago there was a rain of frogs. A carpet of them all around here, hopping like mad. Do you think it was a sign?"

"Yeah, it was a sign we're all going to croak." Veitch knelt down, brushing his fingers across the grass as he surveyed the area; it was too open. If they returned at sunset they would be easy targets. "So what do we do now?"

"Now," Tom said, "we go to talk to the giant."

chapter eight
the sickness at the heart

The night was hot and humid, filled with the distant cries of alien birds. Beyond the barricade, the Nuckelavee roamed relentlessly, testing its strength with repeated attacks that sent furniture rolling off the top. Time and again the Tuatha Dé Danann guards clambered up to replace them, but it was a futile act. Sooner or later the Plague-Bringer was going to break through.

Church had led Ruth and Baccharus on a tour of the building to try to find something they could use to escape, but had given up after an hour. The rooms went on forever, filled with insane bric-a-brac and useless objets d'art. When they tried to retrace their steps the layout of the house had changed, just like Wave Sweeper, but after a while they passed through the chamber where the dying god had been imprisoned. All it held now was a noxious black stain on the floor to mark his passing.

When they finally made it back to the main area, the baby cry was rising and falling until Ruth wanted to tear at her ears. She dragged Church to one side. "What are we going to do?" Before he could protest, she added, "You're the leader."

"Don't worry, I know my responsibility." He scrubbed his hand roughly through his long hair; he had only one option. "We need a diversion. Someone to pull that thing over to one side so the rest of us can get out, get back, or—"

"Attack it."

"You've got an idea?"

"I can do some stuff." She tapped her head. "It's all locked up here."

"You've been trying it out?"

"Little things. Here and there. Just to get a feel for it." For some reason she looked guilty, wouldn't meet his eyes.

"How much can you do?"

There was a long pause before she said, "I honestly don't know. But it's like I've been made the receptacle for all the knowledge that exists about the Craft. It's like being supercharged." Still not meeting his eyes, she added, "Sometimes I feel like I can do anything."

Church rested a hand on her shoulder, played with her hair. He was worried about how distant and troubled she appeared. Most of the time she had a blasé attitude to her new-found abilities, but it was obvious that behind it lay a deep-seated concern. "What are you planning on pulling out of the bag this time?"

She peered at the thin gap of dark sky above the blockade. "I have a couple of ideas."

Church gave the back of her neck a squeeze before heading over to Niamh and Baccharus, who had been waiting patiently. "I hate to ask this," he said, "but I need a volunteer to draw that thing's attention. There's not much chance of getting off alive. One of the guards—"

"I shall do it," Baccharus said confidently.

"No!" Niamh's face crumpled with worry. "There is no need—"

"There is every need. How could I ask another being to take such a risk if I would not do it myself?"

"Your abilities are needed. You have responsibilities." Niamh's voice rose a notch.

Baccharus took her hand with surprising tenderness, the mark of deep friends. "I have to shed my burden."

Niamh nodded reluctantly. Baccharus turned back to Church. "What do you request?"

"We need to move most of the blockade from the far end. When the Plague-Bringer moves up the other end, we kick over the last of it, and you make a break for the tree line." He paused. "How close does it have to be to infect you?"

Baccharus gave a faint smile, said nothing.

Church spent the next half hour fashioning a spear with a length of wood and one of the guards' swords. It was a paltry weapon compared to what roamed beyond the walls, but there was nothing else to hand that he could use. He longed for the mystical sword he had rescued from its hiding place underneath Tintagel; he had responded to whatever power it held, understood how it had been responsible for the coded legends of Excalibur. He had never seen himself as much of a fighter, but with that sword he had felt capable of anything.

Ruth spent the time meditating quietly in one corner. Church watched her serious face as the arcane knowledge gradually emerged from its secret chambers. Some of it brought a smile of surprise to her lips, others left her brow furrowed in concern.

When they were nearly ready, he knelt next to her, caressing the back of her neck. "Are you fit?" he asked softly.

She flashed him an unsure smile. "As fit as I ever will be. The way this thing seems to work is that I have to act on instinct as much as possible. That means I can't plan. And if the instinct fails, I have no idea what I'm going to do."

"You could always run."

"That doesn't help Baccharus. Or you." Her smiled faded. "I'm not going to let you down."

"I never for a minute thought you would." He leaned over and gave her a gentle kiss.

"We can't afford to lose this, you know," she whispered.

There was nothing he could say to that.

As he stood up, he realised Niamh was watching them from the other side of the room, her face impossible to read. She turned away when she saw him looking at her.

By the time they were ready, the Nuckelavee was rattling the blockade so hard it was rocking wildly, nearly toppling over. Church marshalled the guards, who obeyed him reluctantly, their eyes flickering in the direction of Niamh and Baccharus. When the beast reached one end of the row, Church dropped his hand and the guards hastily dismantled the barricade at the other end where Baccharus waited.

There was a moment of intense tension and then Church gave the nod; Baccharus silently slipped out into the hot night. The response was instantaneous. The cry rose up several notches, followed by the thunder of sturdy arms hitting the ground and the obscene slithering as it dragged its body behind it. The speed of the movement shocked them all. Church wondered briefly if his plan was already doomed; at the rate it was moving, it would reach Baccharus and be back on them before anyone reached the tree line.

Once the Nuckelavee was far enough away, Church gave the signal and the guards demolished the barricade at the other end of the room. They were hurrying out into the moist dark before the last item of furniture was rolling away. Ruth blanched when she laid eyes on the Nuckelavee for the first time—there was something sickening about it beyond mere appearance—but then she caught herself and set off in pursuit with Church beside her while the guards hurried Niamh towards the trees.

"Why us, eh?" Ruth said with a tight smile.

"Cannon fodder. We know our place in life." Church shouldered the spear, ready to throw.

Baccharus moved across the lawns like a shimmer of light cast by numerous mirrors, his form growing hard to perceive, but he was not fast enough for the Nuckelavee, which had surprising speed for its bulk and awkwardness. Church could see every bunch of its muscles, every pulse of its blood with each minor exertion.

At the tree line, Baccharus came to a halt. Church had given him strict instructions not to take the creature into the jungle, where it would be hard for them to attack it in the dense undergrowth, but it was bearing down on him so quickly it was impossible for him to run in any other direction. He sensed this, for he brought himself round to face the Nuckelavee and drew himself up ready to meet his fate. There was something so noble about the way he stood—head slightly bowed, accepting the worst kind of death; even worse for the Tuatha Dé Danann, who thought they would never die—Church felt compelled to succeed. He hurled the makeshift spear as hard as he could, even though his plan had optimistically called for it to be used for the deathblow once Ruth had made her attack.

In the split second before Church launched the spear, the Nuckelavee drew itself up and threw its grotesque head back, before making a silent belching motion. A barely visible exhalation rushed from the creature's mouth. It had little substance—Church could see the jungle and dappling stars through it—but Baccharus's face darkened as it raced towards him, and at the last moment he threw himself to one side. The cloud continued into the trees, where there was a sudden crash as an ape-like beast fell from the branches in violent death throes.

The sword spear embedded in the Nuckelavee at the base of its skull; a fountain of dark-red blood gushed out. The creature went into paroxysms, the baby cry turning into a shriek of agony. Near to it, it smelled like an old rubber boot that had been left in the rain.

The size, speed and hideous appearance of the beast were hypnotic. Church found himself rooted as it curled around on its slug-like body to examine him, the spear waving on its back with every violent tremor that ran through the torso. He took a step back and then became rooted once more when he looked into the Nuckelavee's pink-rimmed black eyes; what he saw there was cruel and alien, but undoubtedly intelligent.

"Church! Back off!" Ruth yelled.

He heard her words, but all he could do was consider the Nuckelavee's swirling gaze; it drowned out all his senses until the only thing in his world was the creature. Deep in his head came a skittering, like cockroach feet on the surface of his brain: the Nuckelavee's thoughts, reaching out to his own. The part of him that held the Fomorii taint *understood*, and somehow that was worse than anything.

Ruth saw Church freeze in the grip of the Nuckelavee's mesmerising eyes. It brought itself round, its mouth thrown wide to emit those stomach-churning cries, the disproportionately powerful arms dragging the body in lumbering jerks. It gave the illusion of slow, methodical progress, but Ruth had seen how quickly it had pursued the now-forgotten Baccharus, and the lightning-fast reactions when the spear had struck.

His life lay in her hands, and that was the fear that had gripped her from the moment he outlined his plan. She would never reach him in time. Even if she could knock him out of the way, they would be too close to the Nuckelavee to evade it. She wouldn't be able to utilise her Craft quickly enough.

But she *had* to do it or she would never be able to live with herself. She had to do it or nothing else would matter in her life ever again.

Seconds, that was all. Seconds.

She closed her eyes in an attempt to shut out all extraneous sensation: the cries that sounded like a war zone orphanage, the stink that made her nostrils flare and her throat close up, the wind in her hair, the sweat on her back, the nausea in her gut, the thunder of her heart. She closed it down like she was pulling shutters in her head. She was surprised how quickly it worked; accessing the Craft was predicated on *need* and at that point she needed it more than ever before. It came up like whispers from a deep, dark well. And as the images and sounds that shaped reality began to coalesce in her mind, she felt the power ignite.

And then she opened her eyes. Church was still rooted, the Nuckelavee rising above him, opening its mouth, ready to release the infection. Her concentration fragmented as desperation intruded.

She fought to get her focus back, her eyes fixed on Church, knowing he was about to die, knowing it was her fault, her stupid weakness, the shame and the guilt making it even harder to reach that quiet part of her.

Just as the knowledge began to rise again, there was movement like a flash of light on the periphery of her vision. It hit Church in a shimmer of gold and an instant later he was gone, just as the Nuckelavee's corrupting breath washed through the spot where he had been.

He reappeared several yards away, dragged by Niamh; and then was gone again. It wasn't as if the goddess was running, more that she was dropping in and out of reality, becoming, in the process, not human, something that was almost composed of light. They finally settled into her perception across the other side of the lawns, in safety. And then her shame was coloured by other, darker feelings: self-loathing, jealousy, irritation, then anger.

The rush inside took her by surprise, petrol on the bonfire of her emotions, more potent even than the exhilarating explosion of her abilities at the end of her tantric bout with Veitch. Fire filled her belly, her limbs, her head, until the world without didn't exist at all, only flame, blue, blue flame, and the feeling that she wanted to jump out of her skin and explode.

Shining across her mind with a blinding light were words her rational mind found incomprehensible, but which she instinctively understood. They leapt to her lips unbidden; she felt her mouth forming them as if it were someone else's. Her will became a spear, plucking the words and launching them into the night sky.

And then, spent, the fire cleared and she was overcome with a calmness that kept all sound from her ears. In the eerily silent scene, the Nuckelavee was rising up over her, veins throbbing, muscles glistening, eyes glowing. And beyond it, the stars were being eaten. Thick, black clouds rushed in from the north. Unnatural winds alive with rage tore through the trees. The Nuckelavee was buffeted back and forth, but Ruth stood calm in the eye; untouched.

The gale drew strength, flexed. Baccharus had lashed himself around a tree, the others were unseen. The Nuckelavee slid forwards against its volition, was driven down on to its bony elbows. The mouth still opened and closed, emitting the baby cry that Ruth could no longer hear, too distracted to unleash its infection. Now bowed before her, Ruth thought she glimpsed a cast to its eyes, not of fear but of incomprehension. It was time.

More words in her mind, but this time they were surrounded by the coldness of deep space. She spoke, and whatever sound she made cut through the heart of the gale, reached up directly to the clouds that swirled overhead. Briefly they appeared to spin faster, a whirlpool of grey, until at the heart of them a hole formed through which she could not see the night sky, could see nothing at all. Lightning erupted from it, filled with a force beyond the control of nature. In the time between seconds it scorched through the air to strike the Nuckelavee squarely. There was a burst of brilliant light, a shockwave that split and folded around Ruth before moving on to blast the nearest trees, a smell of charged air that became the sickening stench of a butcher's shop on fire.

And when it cleared a moment later, there was only a circle of blackened grass where chunks of flash-fried flesh smoked or were limned with dancing, blue will o' the wisps.

Ruth was filled with an emptiness that made her feel weepy for something vital that had been lost. But when that faded, there was at first regret, then fear, and then horror at what she had done without even realising. For the first time she had a glimmer of what she was capable, of dark paths that lay ahead if she so chose, and she knew she must never let her anger get the better of her again.

Weakly, she staggered around, almost blank to her surroundings until she felt strong hands on her shoulders. Church pulled her close and kissed her. "I knew you could do it," he said in a whisper, tinged with relief, but also coloured by something that sounded like dismay. She saw Niamh sitting alone on the lawns, the guards gathered in a huddle far away, not wishing to approach her.

"The thing caught her," Church said. "She's been infected."

Ruth couldn't begin to describe her emotions, although she knew she wouldn't be proud of them. Already aware of the situation, Baccharus rushed over. "We are all in danger. We may already have been infected." He looked coldly at the sullen guards and then, without a moment's thought, walked over to Niamh. She tried to wave him away, then fend him off as he dropped down next to her, eventually giving in and allowing her head to drop dismally on to his shoulder. Ruth was suddenly consumed with guilt.

"You must not come near me," Niamh said directly to Church and Ruth. "The Fixed Lands need you. All of existence needs you. You must leave me here."

Church turned to Ruth and asked in an anxious, low voice, "Can you help her?"

Ruth tried to read his face, wondering if she could be so evil that her choices would actually be decided by what she saw there, then feeling disconcerted by what she did see.

"Perhaps," she replied, trying not to give her thoughts away. She knelt down next to Niamh, who looked up at her with an honest, open face that made her feel even worse. She wished she had seen bitterness there, or jealousy, or incipient rage, something that would blight the goddess's inherent goodness, or make her as distant and contemptuous as most of the other Tuatha Dé Danann. "Lie down," Ruth said a little too sharply; "let me examine you."

Niamh had obviously not caught the full force of the Nuckelavee's infection, but it was certainly there in nascent form; the golden skin of her forearm was mottled with faint blue rings that were spreading up to her armpit. Her body hadn't yet started breaking up, but Ruth knew it was only a matter of time. "Alien viruses," she muttered wearily. "As above, so below. This whole place is a nightmare."

She turned to Baccharus. "I need you to send one of the guards back to the ship for supplies. You seem to stock everything there. I need some dainty weed ground ivy and wild celery to help with muscle cramps and vervain for an analgesic. That should help combat the side effects of the virus. Then I'll need some rowan berries, mugwort and mallow to fight off any enchantment, as I suppose this thing doesn't act like any ailment we've come across on earth."

"Will that do it?" Church asked hopefully.

Ruth looked up at him wilfully. "No," she said. "Then it's down to me."

Baccharus and Church carried Niamh back to the house, where they made her comfortable on a large divan piled high with sumptuous cushions. She was already growing weak. Once she was settled, Church brushed the hair from her pale face. "Thanks for saving my life," he said gently.

She smiled faintly.

"Why did you put yourself at risk for a *Fragile Creature*?"

"You know why, Jack."

"You're not like others of your kind."

"We are not all alike." She paused. "My kind have more differences than you could know."

"But you gods see yourself as infinite, as much a part of existence as the stars in the sky."

"More so."

Church's expression grew more puzzled. "You believe your continued survival is paramount in the rules of nature. I know what the concept of death means to you—a hundred times worse than it even means to us. I don't—"

She shushed him with a wave of her hand.

"But—"

"A small sacrifice."

He smiled again, though it was a troubled one, and withdrew slowly until Ruth caught his arm on the other side of the room. "Why don't you give her a big kiss?" she said and regretted it instantly. She'd always prided herself on her maturity and here she was acting like a stupid, jealous teenager.

The puzzlement on Church's face became comical until his expression darkened. "Don't be an idiot."

"Don't call me an idiot."

"Well, stop acting like one. I'm not going to start mooning for her like some stupid kid just because she saved my life."

"It looked like mooning to me." She tried to bite her tongue; why couldn't she help herself?

"Look, she showed some nobility there." His voice was low, filled with both hurt and annoyance. "She was ready to sacrifice her life for another being, whatever her motivations. It's not about stupid relationship issues—"

"Relationships are stupid, are they?"

"I didn't say that."

She marched away, regretting that Church would see it as some argumentative point-scoring ploy, but she only did it to save herself from saying anything further that would damn her. She was supposed to be smart, educated, and emotions had made her a moron in seconds.

She had planned to walk out of the room to get some calming night air, but to do that she had to go past Niamh's divan; the goddess motioned to her to come over. Reluctantly she perched on the end.

"I want to thank you for trying to help me, Ruth. I know my kind appear aloof to Fragile Creatures. But I hope you will accept I am very grateful."

"Don't worry. I would have done it for anyone."

"And that is why you are honourable and good. One of the best of your race."

"No, I'm not. I'm typical, not good or bad, not stupid or smart. Just . . . just human."

"You do yourself a disservice." Niamh waved this part of the conversation away with a gesture and began, "I know you are concerned about Church and me—"

Ruth stood up sharply and made to go.

"Please hear me out."

"I don't want to talk about that."

"Please—"

"I'm not used to having my emotions in this much upheaval." *I've never been in love before*, she could have said. "I don't want to say anything I might regret."

Niamh continued to plead silently until Ruth felt she couldn't walk away. She sat down heavily and stared into the middle distance. "I hold nothing against you, Ruth, for your feelings for Jack. I can understand them completely. He has a good, good heart."

Ruth listened, but didn't respond.

"We are not rivals, Ruth. We are not fighting. There is nothing *we* can do. Jack will decide the direction of his own heart. The tragedy is that only one of us can benefit. That should cause sadness for both of us, not anger or jealousy."

"When someone has a relationship, however new," Ruth began, "it's not considered very decent to try to break it up."

"You do not know the whole story, Ruth."

"Then tell me." Ruth's eyes flashed; she was sick of being patronised by the gods.

Niamh chose her words carefully, which made Ruth instantly suspicious; there was something the goddess was trying to hide. "You think my emotional response to Jack is some fleeting thing. After all, we have seen each other little, spoken to each other less. But that is simply your perception." Ruth flinched visibly; Niamh noticed and caught herself. "You should know by now, Ruth, that there is more than one way of seeing existence, and the way of the Fragile Creatures is the least apt. My love for Jack is not new and ill formed."

"I know you watched his development from when he was a child without interacting with him, but if you'll forgive me for being so forward," she said tartly, "that's both a little sick and a little pathetic. Love from afar, without any interaction, is worthless."

Niamh's face remained calm, despite the sharpness of Ruth's words. "I have loved Jack for longer than that, Ruth."

Ruth snorted derisively. "How can that be?"

Niamh ignored her. "My feelings grew stronger as I understood his true nobility. He has a good heart. He is confused, directionless, has little confidence in his own abilities, but at his core he is good."

Listening to Niamh, something struck Ruth sharply. "Sometimes you don't even sound like your own kind. You sound like one of us."

Niamh smiled, a little sadly. "I have had a good tutor."

Ruth watched her carefully, but Niamh wasn't giving anything away.

"Ruth, I will speak honestly to you. This is a vital time for my relationship with Jack." Ruth wanted to yell: *You have no relationship!* "If I cannot convince Jack to love me before the festival you know as Samhain then my love will never be returned. Therein lies my desperation, and my tragedy. Such a small window to convince a Fragile Creature to match the feelings of a god. If I lost Jack now it would be forever."

Niamh had grown oddly introspective; the gods never usually appeared to have any real inner life. "There will be no peace for him, Ruth," she said quietly. "That is not the path that existence has mapped out for him. Jack will have a life of struggle and strife, but that only makes love and comfort so much more valuable to him. He will have to seize it where he can, and cherish it, for it will be transitory."

"What path *is* mapped out for him?"

"The same path all you Brothers and Sisters of Dragons must walk. You have been chosen to be champions of the vitality that runs through everything. That is a responsibility that dwarfs all. You must suffer for the sake of everyone else, everything else."

"Well, isn't that wonderful," Ruth said sourly, trying to ignore the panic flaring inside her.

"But is that not always the way? A few must redeem the many. If those with ability do not act, the darkness will win. There are few rules of existence open even to we Golden Ones, but that is one of them."

"Yes, but why *me*? Why *us*?"

"Simply? Because you have what it takes." A wave of exhaustion crossed Niamh's face; the disease was starting to bite.

"Take it easy," Ruth said. "The guard will be back with the supplies any minute and then we can get to work."

Niamh smiled and took Ruth's wrist with her long, cool fingers. "You have a good heart too."

Once Ruth had the flowers and herbs she administered them to Niamh, although she had no idea how they would work on her constitution. The ones that worked magically appeared more effective than the simple medicinal ones, but it was still only a stopgap measure. She had Niamh moved into a chamber where the lights could be darkened until only one candle flame cast a dim light across the proceedings. The others were driven from the room so the atmosphere was calm and reflective.

The mottled blue rings had spread across the right side of Niamh's body and in places had grown black. In some areas the skin was fracturing.

"What are you planning to do?" Niamh asked weakly.

Ruth raised a chalice of water and kissed it gently. "I'm planning on approaching a higher authority."

"Higher?"

"When I met Ogma in his library, or court, or whatever you want to call it, I asked him if you really were gods. He said, there is always something higher. And now I have the knowledge gifted to me by my owl friend I can see that's true. I have no idea what it really is, but I like to think it has a feminine aspect, like the triple goddess that first led me down this path. Whatever it is, I feel close to it, because it's the source of the Blue Fire. And I, as you pointed out, am the champion of the Blue Fire."

Niamh nodded thoughtfully. "It is as I thought. Can you reach that power?"

Ruth's laugh came across as faintly bitter, to mask her inability to answer that question. "Keep your fingers crossed."

If she were honest with herself, she would really have preferred leaving the ritual to another day. Every time she utilised the knowledge of the Craft it took a great deal out of her, as if she was pushing herself beyond the limits of endurance, or psychologically beyond what her body had been created to do. But with Niamh's deterioration, there was no chance of delay. She would have to press on and deal with the repercussions later.

Baccharus had found some incense in another part of the house; Ruth burned it in a small brazier next to the divan on which Niamh was lying. Like everything in Otherworld, it had an unexpected potency, filling the room with heady aromas. But it was soothing and aided the concentration that her growing exhaustion made increasingly difficult. She closed her eyes and took a deep breath as the fragrant, sweet fumes enveloped her.

She began slow, rhythmic breathing, giving herself up to the shussh-boom of air, matching it with her heartbeat until it filled her consciousness, until she began to drift . . .

In T'ir n'a n'Og, Ruth could achieve things that would have been impossible at home, but it was still a struggle for her to break through the barrier. After a while, she moved outside time, so that her whole world was only the beat of her heart and the rhythm of her breath and the smell of the incense. Eventually, though, something appeared to crack in her mind, a hairline fracture running through a rock. She exerted pressure and the rift grew wider, and suddenly she was inside the protected area, and just as quickly rushing out, through her head, passing through the chamber where she could see Niamh lying sickly, through the ceiling and the upper rooms of the house and out into the night sky. And still upwards, until the green island lay like an emerald in a sea of ink, and up. And then through the sky itself . . .

What happened next came back to Ruth only in vague, fleeting impressions later. She knew she had entered some kind of blue, blue world, for the colour haunted her for days after, but of any other detail of the place—if it were a place—there was nothing. She sensed a tremendous presence, a sentience, so big it dwarfed the entire universe; even so, it appeared to recognise her. But the most striking impressions were abstracts: contentment so powerful everything else disappeared; connection; losing all her fears and worries in an instant. She didn't recall uttering a sound, never mind begging for what she required, knew instinctively she didn't have to.

And one other thing: an odd, fractured remembrance of Veitch and Tom, so quick it could easily have been a memory leaking through from another time.

She came out of what felt like a deep slumber with Church's hands on her shoulders, feeling more refreshed than she had done in months. She took his hand and smiled beatifically; whatever he saw in her face appeared to shock him briefly. Then he said, "I was worried when there was no sound so I took a peek in. I saw you slumped on the floor here, thought something bad had happened. Did I screw up?"

She turned to Niamh who was sitting up, rubbing her arms, looking faintly dazed, yet also slightly transcendent. The blue-black mottling on her arms was fading before their eyes, the strength returning to her limbs with amazing speed.

"You have changed the course of existence, Ruth," Niamh said with deference. "The alterations to the fabric spinning off from this point will be startling."

Through her bliss, Ruth wasn't wholly sure she liked the sound of that.

Back on Wave Sweeper, an account of what Ruth had achieved passed swiftly through the crew and passengers. Ruth and Church barely had time to put their feet on the deck before they were ushered into Manannan's cabin. He stood next to his table, hands clasped behind his back.

"You have achieved a great thing, Brother and Sister of Dragons." His voice appeared to come from all parts of the room at once. "The gratitude of the Golden Ones is with you." He moved around the table, still aloof, barely looking at them, but Church thought there was a surprising warmth somewhere far beneath it all. "More than gratitude. You prevented another of our kind being stripped from existence. You have helped maintain one of the vital props of the way things are."

"We see all life as equal," Ruth said pointedly. "That's why we helped."

He nodded thoughtfully, as if, for once, he was actually listening, then fixed a curious gaze on them. "This is indeed an argument that has raged amongst my own kind. I have never held strong views, allowing my opinions to be swayed by the voices of one side or the other, dependent on who was speaking. Now, I feel, I have made my choice." He went to a crystal decanter filled with an unusual golden liquid. He poured three glasses and brought one each for Church and Ruth.

"Is it given freely and without obligation?" Church asked.

"Of course. Everything on my ship is given freely and without obligation. That is my way. And it is especially true for Brothers and Sisters of Dragons."

He raised his glass and drained it in one draught. Church and Ruth followed suit, and were stunned by the immediate effect of whatever the drink was. The aroma was flowers and spices. The instant the drink touched their tastebuds, it created an explosion across all five of their senses, a bizarre synesthaesia, and as it passed down their throat it filled them with a warmth and light as golden as the liquid itself, infusing them with a transcendent feeling of wonder and excitement. Once it settled into their system their vision sparkled around the edges. Objects in the room took on a strange cast, as if the very essence of them was visible. Manannan appeared to be made of light, and when Church and Ruth looked at each other they saw the same illusion—if that was what it was—although the light was of a slightly different shade.

"What is this?" Church asked in awe.

"The drink of gods. The distillation of all there is."

Church looked at Ruth again; they felt like they could read each other's thoughts; in one moment they could see the connections that bound them, something it often took couples a lifetime to discover. They would have embraced there and then, committed themselves to each other for all time, if Manannan's foreboding presence had not stopped them.

"Fragile Creatures have rarely tasted this liquid," Manannan continued. "Some of my kind consider it too rarefied for your tastes, that you are too rough to appreciate it and so should be denied it." He took the glasses from them and returned them to the table. "It can make you see like gods." His voice drifted back to them, disembodied, yet filled with meaning they couldn't discern.

When he came back he took Ruth's hand and pointed to the mark left by Cernunnos. "My brother, I see, has already come to his decision. Know this, then: you have an ally here too. I will take my stand with the Fragile Creatures."

"Thank you." Church made a slight bow. "And can we count on your arguments to influence the minds of your brothers when we reach our destination?"

"I will do what I can."

His mood changed abruptly as his attention focused on a number of charts unfurled on his desk, and it was obvious the audience was over. They thanked him, but he was already engrossed in new business.

Outside, they rested against the rail, pleased that the hot, humid microclimate of the island was no longer with them. The anchor had been raised while they were in Manannan's room and they were already speeding out into open water.

"You know what?" Church said curiously. "I had a feeling there was a lot going on behind that conversation, stuff that wasn't said."

"It's like he was talking about something important without telling us exactly what it was."

"Maybe he thought we already knew."

"These gods don't give anything away unless they have to, even when they're supposedly being friendly."

Church pulled Ruth close, draping an arm across her shoulders; he still felt warm and fuzzy from Manannan's drink. "I think it's time we stepped up our investigations." She rested her head on his shoulder, enjoying the comfort of contact after the stress of the day. "There's something very strange and disturbing going on here. We've been moving through it, seeing and hearing little parts of it. I think it takes in Cormorel's murder, and . . . lots of things."

"Would you like to elaborate, or are you going to keep talking vaguely just for the hell of it?"

"I don't know what else to say. It's a gut instinct." In his arms, she felt soft and hard and warm and cold all at the same time. "I think if we don't find out what's going on, we're going to lose everything."

"What do you suggest? An inquisition? You know they won't tell us anything."

"I suggest it's time to go searching for the Walpurgis. Tomorrow. Just after dawn."

An hour before first light they came upon the third of the Western Isles. Taranis summoned Manannan from his cabin and together they surveyed the rocky outcropping. A thick column of smoke rose from the island and settled in a pall across the area, the underside of it a dull ruddy brown from the fires that raged there.

Manannan did not even bother dropping anchor. Taranis moved to mobilise the crew. The itinerary was dropped instantly and they set a course for the island they called the Green Meadows of Enchantment, with the certain knowledge that the vile corruption of the Heart of Shadows had extended to the very walls of their home.

"There weren't really giants," Veitch said as they wandered down the hill from Gog Magog House.

"There were so." Tom's face had grown sterner as the day passed. He had been quite rude to Robertson, who had refused to come with them to an area he claimed was cursed. "Even in my time, before the Queen got her hands on me, there were still a handful of giants scattered around the island. Some died off, some wandered through to T'ir n'a n'Og. But they're not the kind of giants we're interested in right now."

"So . . . what? These are short giants?"

Tom snorted with irritation, even though he knew Veitch was only trying to provoke him. "*There are giants in the earth*," he muttered to himself. "How little they knew."

They crossed the path and made their way alongside a defunct electric fence that once kept sheep from the nature preservation area. The early afternoon sun was hot. Flies and wasps buzzed along the tree line, while darting mosquitoes made brief forays from the pond. Under the trees the atmosphere had grown sweaty and oppressive. Tom picked his way amongst the brambles, scrambling over fallen trees and amongst the thorny bushes, with Veitch following easily behind.

"So, is it going to be a surprise, then?" Veitch continued to gibe. "Like always. Blowing up in my face at the last minute. Like in the Queen's court?"

"You were warned about that."

"Well, you didn't do a very good job of it, did you?"

"Sorry. I underestimated your stupidity."

Veitch said something obscene, but Tom had already picked up his step until he arrived at an area where the topsoil had been cleared to reveal mysterious patterns on the ground.

With a puzzled face, Veitch attempted to make head and tail of them. "Looks like one of those ink blots they show you when they think you're crazy."

"The Rorschach Test," Tom noted. "That's quite fitting. Everyone who comes here sees in these patterns what they want to believe."

"Not what's actually there?"

"Nothing is *actually* there, anywhere. You've not learned anything in all this, have you?"

Veitch stared at him for a long moment, then said, "I've learned you're a—"

"Archaeologists have been digging around here for decades, ever since the famous antiquarian T. C. Lethbridge excavated this site on the south side of the ring in late 1955 and 1956." Tom rested his hands on his knees so he could lean forward to get a better look. "He pumped metal rods in the ground, claiming he found different depths, bumps, shapes underneath the surface which marked out this. He christened this the Gog Magog figure. All told, he claimed he'd discovered a sun goddess, two other male figures and a chariot."

"You're talking like it isn't true."

"Not in the eyes of archaeologists who came after him. All of Lethbridge's work here is steeped in controversy. Academics and the usual amateur historical sleuths who want to be seen as professional claim there is absolutely no evidence for Lethbridge's claim. All this is a figment of his fevered imagination. But if there's one thing we've learned, it's not to trust the establishment. Is that not so?"

"Too bleedin' right."

"The occult groups always backed Lethbridge because they knew truth does not always come in facts and figures, quantifiable evidence."

"You've lost me again." Veitch's attention was drifting amongst the trees, searching for any signs of threat. For a while he had been aware of a deep level of unease that he couldn't quite understand. He was good at sensing obvious danger near at hand, or even more subtle signs of peril, but this was different; it was almost like the threat was there but not there, buried very deeply or watching from such a distant place it could barely be called a threat. But he felt it nonetheless.

"Whatever they say, there were certainly some hill figures carved on this site," Tom continued. "There are many antiquarian sources which confirm that. And with these hills bearing the name Gog Magog, and the house on the summit, it doesn't take a great detective to know who this sacred site was dedicated to."

"Giants?"

Tom sighed, clambering on to the rough pattern and kneeling down so he could sweep it with his fingers. "You should know by now, no one knows anything about the past. Every historian and archaeologist has *theories*, and yes, they can make convincing arguments. The ones who shout loudest set the agenda. But the clever man ignores their voices and looks closely at the evidence. And once he realises all of it is conflicting, he understands: Nobody. Knows. Anything."

"But you know it all, right?" Veitch took the opportunity to check his weapons: the crossbow slung across his back, the sword secreted in his jacket, the dagger strapped to his leg. All in place, all ready for action.

"Who is Gog Magog? Who are *they*? They are there in the Bible, in Jewish and Christian apocalyptic literature. In one account, Gog and Magog are two hostile forces, in another Gog comes from the country of Magog. But the Bible is adamant they or he is a force for evil in the final battle between God and Satan. The Battle of Armageddon."

"So they're evil?" Veitch had the blank expression that always irritated Tom.

"The Bible is a *book*, Ryan. The Church likes to pretend it's the word of God, but as we *all* know, it's the word of God as edited by men, by councils of the religion's great and the good for hundreds of years after Jesus lived. Many of *God's words* were thrown out to present a more cohesive *story*. And man is flawed, so the Bible tells us. Ergo, the Bible is flawed and cannot be wholly trusted."

Veitch chuckled. "They'd have you dragged out and stoned for that in some places."

"Then they would be morons," Tom said sourly, "mistaking intellectual questioning for blasphemy. It's all a matter of intent." He stood up and stretched his old limbs. "In the Guildhall in London are two wooden effigies of Gog and Magog, supposedly the last of a race of giants. And that itself is a mistake of history, for in ancient times they were statues of Gogmagog, a twelve foot Goliath, and Corineus, the Trojan general who threw him to his death. Or perhaps we listen to another story that says Gog and Magog are two mythical London heroes. Or Geoffrey of Monmouth, the mediaeval historian, who said Gogmagog was a giant chieftain of Cornwall. Or are we, indeed, talking about the giant oak trees at Glastonbury, sole survivors of an ancient Druid grove and ceremonial path? No one knows anything."

"So is this the time for your catch phrase? Mythology is—"

"—the secret history of the land. Exactly. We read between the lines. We look for common threads. We search for the metaphors that all the old stories are reaching for. Giants in the earth, Ryan. A sacred site since the earliest times of man, their bodies buried far beneath our feet, along with a horse, the familiar metaphor for wild energy, for fertility, and the chariot of spiritual transcendence. People believed in this enough to keep the myth alive for thousands of years. Isn't that astonishing? Doesn't that shout out about the power that resides here?"

Veitch surveyed the light through the trees. "Okay, enough talk. Get on with what you've got to do."

"That's easier said than done." Tom wandered around the pattern left by Lethbridge's excavations, swatting away the wasps that assailed him continually. Although to Veitch his meanderings looked random, Tom was actually following the tracings of Blue Fire in the land that Veitch had not yet learnt to see. The camp was a potent source of the earth energy, scything in sapphire strands across the grass, pumping through arteries as wide as a gushing stream, reaching through capillaries into the roots of trees and bushes. The Blue Fire added new shape and meaning to the barely discernible pattern Lethbridge had uncovered. The archaeologist had instinctively uncovered a figure that was spiritual in nature, rather than an exact outline on the hillside: a true representation of an ancient figure of worship, carved through ritual and prayer by the ancient people who first inhabited Wandlebury Camp, kept in focus by the Celts who followed.

But it wasn't just a figure. It was a mandala for reflection, allowing direct access to the spiritual realm, as well as one of the ancient people's landscape markers for a defence against incursions from Otherworld—and also a doorway. Near the top of the outline, at the large circle Lethbridge had identified as the head of the figure, the Blue Fire flowed back and forth between this world and the next. Tom knelt down, steeled himself, then thrust his hand into the current of flames.

"My body is the key," he whispered.

From Veitch's perspective Tom's hand disappeared up to the wrist in the soil. For long minutes nothing happened, until soft vibrations began, growing into a deep rumbling and a shaking in the ground that made his knees buckle. A large section opened upwards like a trapdoor, trailing soil and pebbles. Beyond the mass of hanging roots, Veitch could see a dark tunnel disappearing down into the depths.

He made to duck into the opening, but Tom waved him back. "This is for me," he said. "You must stay here to prepare yourself for what is to come. I will attempt to be back with the information we need by sunset. But if not, flee this place until the sun rises on the morrow. Do you hear me? Do not stay during the night."

Veitch agreed silently. Tom nodded goodbye before diving into the hole like the White Rabbit. It closed at his heels with a thunderous shaking, leaving Veitch alone with a growing sense of apprehension.

chapter nine
gods and horses

A deep shiver ran through Tom as the ground closed behind him. He was far more fearful than when he had entered the Court of the Yearning Heart; another scare on the top of so many others. He had been afraid of losing himself in the Blue Fire, witnessing the deaths of the people he had grown to call friends, seeing the End of Everything. At times he felt fear was taking over.

Yet it was also uplifting, if it was not contradictory to view fear in that way. For so many centuries he hadn't been truly afraid of anything, hadn't *felt* anything at all, except for a brief period of enlightenment in the sixties. To know he *could* still feel was almost a price worth paying.

The tunnel drove directly into the heart of the hill, although he knew it was not a tunnel at all. The air was filled with aromas that soothed his heart: hashish, reminding him of warm California nights, red wine plunging him into a memory of a shared bottle with a pretty woman in a hippie dress at the side of the road in Haight-Ashbury, soft rain on vegetation, bringing him back to that first morning at Woodstock.

In the same way that it wasn't a tunnel, none of those pleasant fragrances were truly there; it was the reality, welcoming him with cherished memories, making him feel good.

So why was he afraid? Not because of some incipient threat, certainly, but because of immensity. What lay ahead was the infinite, the source of all meaning. And who could look on the face of God and not be destroyed?

Veitch sat on the trunk of a fallen tree, tapping his foot anxiously. Doing nothing felt like needles being driven into his body. He would rather fight one of the Fomorii than sit quietly; if he admitted it to himself, he actually enjoyed that pastime. While the others were talking their usual intellectual rubbish, he often reflected on the time beneath Edinburgh Castle when he had hacked one of the creatures into bloody chunks. He recalled the super-heated haze that fell across his mind, the adrenalin driving his limbs, the smell of the gore, the uplifting weariness that followed the exertion.

The fading image left an emptiness that disturbed him. Had he always been that way? Surely there had been a time when he could appreciate peace.

His thoughts were disturbed by movement in the branches overhead. Golden flitterings shifted quickly amongst the pattern of light and shade that made up the green canopy. At first he thought they were butterflies searching for the last nectar of summer, but there were too many of them and the activity was too localised. He counted twenty? Thirty?

It was the gossamer-winged tiny people he had seen before in tranquil places. The perfectly formed little men and women moved through the treetops with grace, like sunlight reflected off a belt buckle.

Searching for a position that allowed him to view the soaring creatures more easily, Veitch slipped from the trunk so he was lying on the ground with his head resting against it. Their flight, the wild shifts of light they engendered, was hypnotic. There was a definite calmness about them, but he was dismayed to find he was only aware of it in a detached way; he couldn't *feel* it, and at that moment it was all he wanted in the world.

"Come to me," he whispered.

There was no way they could have heard his words, but they altered their flight patterns, some of them hanging in midair, as if listening, or musing. Veitch caught his breath, waited, but after a few seconds they returned to their rapid dipping and diving. Sadly, he closed his eyes, thinking of Ruth to cheer him, remembering when they had made love, the smell of her hair, the look of intelligence and sensitivity in her eyes. He loved her more than he had loved anything in his life. If he could have her, his life could be just as he had dreamed as a boy, when he had pictured himself as the storybook hero. A random tear crept out under his eyelashes, surprising him. He blinked it away hastily, not really knowing from where it had come.

When he opened his eyes one of the tiny golden creatures was hovering just above his belly, observing him with a curious expression. The fragility of it was profound, something that went beyond the construction of its body to the very depths of its spirit. He felt that if he touched it, its body would break apart and its soul would disappear into the afternoon breeze. Its eyes were large and dark and it blinked slowly, like a baby observing its parents. Its cheeks were high and refined, its hair long and flowing, like some nineteen forties movie star. The skin, golden from a distance, now looked like the glittering Milky Way.

"You're made of stars," he whispered in awe.

The faintest smile crept across the creature's face. Here was ultimate innocence, supreme peace, a being not troubled by hate or anger or lust or desire for revenge. It held out a hand, fingers so delicate it was hard to imagine how they were formed, and as it moved the air shimmered around it. Slowly, so as not to scare it away, Veitch reached out one long, calloused finger until it was almost touching the creature's hand. He didn't go the final millimetre for fear of overstepping some unknown boundary, but the little figure merely smiled again and reached out the extra distance. When they touched, it felt like honey was flowing into his limbs. Suddenly tears were streaming down his cheeks, soaking into his shirt, and he had no idea where they came from either; there were so many it seemed as if they would never stop.

When they did finally dry up, the creature touched his finger once more and then, with a movement that might well have been a parting wave, rose up to its companions, casting regular backwards glances at Veitch's prostrate form.

Veitch watched them for the better part of an hour, his face beatific, but no thoughts that he recognised crossed his mind. And then, with the sun dappling his skin, he drifted into the first peaceful sleep he had had for years.

While he slept, the Woodborn stirred in their silent, leafy homes all around; knowing in his sleep they could not be discovered, they looked down on the still form, frail and insubstantial next to their mighty trunks. And, being spirits, they felt deep currents and saw more than eyes could ever see. After a while a soft shower of leaves fell from their branches all around the sleeping figure, like tears.

Tom thought of Van Morrison singing about "Summertime in England," about Cream in "White Room," the Stones doing "Sympathy for the Devil" and The Doors cranking up "Five to One." *Old man's music*, Laura would have called it, before rattling off a list of percussive-heavy songs that had been released in the past week. She missed the point. Music was the great communicator. It had nothing to do with fashion; it was part of the central nervous system, linking old memories and sensations and new ideas, joining everything of human experience up into one whole, a single bar releasing it in a torrent. Old music, new music, Gregorian chants, country and western tearjerkers or opera, it didn't matter; it was all power.

Right then, it was a barrier, blocking out all thoughts of what lay ahead. The best songs from his internal jukebox, the soundtrack to his life.

The tunnel curved down and up, and down again. Its serpentine progress reminded him of the tunnels beneath Arthur's Seat in Edinburgh and the Fabulous Beast that slumbered there. Like that site, it was a direct access to the force that bounded everything, but unlike Arthur's Seat this place had—or at least he expected it would have—*presence*; intelligence; whatever it was that the Blue Fire encompassed. The Godhead, he supposed.

"Giants in the earth, you see," he muttered, disturbed at how his words rattled off the walls with a force that changed their tone.

During his time with the wise men of the Culture, he had heard talk of the giants—the metaphor giants, not the real ones that existed in times past. The Culture had understood the power of stories for communicating vital, instructive information, and how metaphors imprinted on the subconscious much better than bald facts. And this metaphor was quite transparent to the trained eye: something like men, only greater, stronger, more vital, something to provide awe and wonder, and a little fear too, responsible for great feats of creation, now sleeping beneath the earth.

How could he explain something so monumental to a man like Veitch, who thought deeply about nothing? Veitch hadn't even grasped the enormity of what was being planned. Crossing over to the land of the dead was not some weekend jaunt; humanity had been barred from it for a reason. And only a higher power could grant access.

"Thomas the Rhymer." The voice shocked him, and not because it used the name by which he had moved from humanity to legend, now rarely heard. It was American, barely above a whisper and faintly mocking; and it was familiar.

The empty tunnel ahead filled with a faint, drifting luminescence, like autumn mist caught on a breeze, and when it cleared a figure was leaning against the wall, a bottle of Jack Daniels clutched in one hand.

"Jim?" For a second, Tom forgot where he was. The face, angelic, thick-lipped, framed by a lion's mane of hair, transported him back to the Whiskey on Sunset, when his bored wanderings had begun to show him a little meaning for the first time in centuries.

"They were good times, right, Scotty? Good times for poets. Peace, love and understanding. Not bread and brutality." Morrison wandered forward shakily, his stoned smile unable to hide that troubling edge to his character. He tried to focus on Tom, but the cannabis laziness of his left eye kept hindering him. It was the charismatic Morrison Tom remembered from their long, rambling discourse about life and the universe and politics, not the one who had died bloated and bearded in a Parisian bathtub.

The sight was initially disorienting until Tom's razor-sharp mind cut through the shock. "A memory," he said dismissively.

"More than that, Tommy." He proffered the bottle; Tom waved it away.

"A memory given shape."

"You could be on the right road there. The road to excess." He chuckled. "Leads to the palace of wisdom, Tommy. But you still haven't hit that nail on the head." Morrison lurched beside Tom and slipped a friendly arm round his shoulders.

Morrison's body had substance, and smelled of whiskey, smoke and sweat, just like the real Morrison had.

"I'm your . . ." He drifted for a moment while the drug thoughts played across his face. "Not a guide, exactly. Not a muse. I'm an angel to you, Tommy. Yeah, an angel in leather."

Glancing at him askance, Tom caught sight of a blue light limning his wild hair, a halo, not golden like the ones the mediaeval Christian artists painted believing it more fitting for a sun king, but its true colour. "You're the voice of the Godhead. A form which my mind can communicate with."

"Godhead? Yeah, well . . . whatever you say, Tommy. But I've gotta tell you, there's some serious shit a little way ahead. Blow your mind, Tommy. Better to turn back now. You sure you don't wanna drink?"

"I have to go on. I need information . . . more than that . . . a blessing."

"It's your head, Tommy. I'll walk with you aways. You remember, you can turn back any time."

"I need to speak to the giant." There was a potency to the air—the effect of the Blue Fire, Tom knew—that made him almost delirious.

"No giants here, Tommy. But . . . yeah, maybe we can do that. Come on, let's go to the bar."

There was a subtle shift in the air, as if paper scenery had been torn away in the blink of an eye. Suddenly Tom was standing in the Whiskey a Go Go, breathing in the familiar odours of stale beer and old smoke, thick with the LA streetlife of 1966. Krieger, Densmore and Manzarek were perched on stools at the end of the bar, chatting lazily with Elmer Valentine, the ex-vice cop who co-owned the joint. Tom looked around, dazed. The stage was all ready for the first set of the night—at that point in their career, The Doors were the house band, yet to record their first album. "Incredible," he muttered. It was just as he remembered, only more so. How could it have been plucked from his mind when he was seeing detail he was convinced he had never noticed before: the woman with the bright red hair and headband marked out with astrological symbols, the bikers near the stage, like barrels with arms of oak, blue from tattoos.

"This was the start of things," Morrison said, quietly; his voice rarely rose above a whisper. "For you, for me, for a way of life. The last time of innocence, Tommy. When this innocence died, the last chance of the world went with it. After that, everything was just livin' on borrowed time. There had to be a change."

Tom nodded. "There did."

Morrison ordered two shots of Jack. Tom eyed his suspiciously before knocking it back with one swift movement. He didn't know what he expected—a taste like fluffy clouds—but it burned the back of his throat and made him cough. "Real." He held the glass up to the light. "I suppose I should have been prepared. I've wittered on about the impermanence of so-called reality often enough."

"That's right, Tommy. You wish hard enough, you can live in any world you want. Nothing is fixed. It's like . . ." He went druggy-dreamy, his hand floating through the air. ". . . smoke. You see shapes in it. A face. A dog. You look away, look back, see something different."

"Christ," Tom sighed. "I hope I don't sound like this when I'm off my face."

"You know, you got all these people whinin' about how the world is a pile of shit," Morrison continued. "Well, it's their own fault. They want it different, they should do something about it. You can't trust your eyes, you can't trust anything, and a big wish can change it all. *I am the Lizard King*, Tommy. *I can do anything*."

Tom had to drag himself out of the seductive reality that had been presented to make him feel more comfortable. It was easy to slip into it, but wasn't that the point the Morrison thing was making? People settle for the reality shown to them when there could be a better one just a thought away. With an effort, he managed to retreat from his surroundings to gain perspective, and then things did begin to make more sense: he was in a place that allowed direct access to the force that lay behind the Blue Fire and it was communicating with him. He couldn't allow himself to be distracted, or this fake reality to take over.

"I want to talk about that, Jim." He called the barman for another shot, but this time he sipped it slowly. "All this . . ." He gestured widely. ". . . it reminds me of the last true happy time in my life, perhaps the only really happy time, when I thought there were values that mattered all around. There was an alignment between the things I held dear to me and the world without. I was always a hippie," he smiled ruefully, "even when I was a mediaeval spy." His face hardened. "But now . . . now there is something worth fighting for. A world to change. That's why I'm here, to appeal for the rules to be . . . not broken, bent slightly. For a good cause. For something worth believing in." The illusion that was not an illusion closed in around him again. He eyed Morrison, who was staring into the coloured lights above the stage where the roadies fiddled with the settings on the amps. "You always were a spiritual man, Jim. When you weren't being a drunken oaf and a bastard to women."

"I was a product of my times, Tommy. Hell, you remember the fifties! But we're all flawed, aren't we? Even the greatest. There are no saints in this world. You just have to make sure the balance tips on the side of the angels, that's all. With our nature, that's the best you can hope. No saints, no heroes, just people who try their best most of the time, and fuck up the rest."

"And you think you did that?"

He stared into his shot glass for a long moment, then grinned broadly at Tom, downed the drink and ordered another. "At least I can say I was trying."

Morrison's voice had taken on such an odd quality Tom was drawn to stare deep into his eyes. He was mesmerised by what he saw: stars, whole galaxies, swirling in their depths. "You're very good at making things real."

Morrison's smile was oddly serious. "There are no Fixed Lands, Tommy. Everything is spirit, you know that."

"I suspected it."

"It's all a matter of perception. You see things a certain way to make you feel comfortable, but there is no space and there is no time." Morrison was altering before his eyes, although it was in such a subtle way—the cadence of his voice, a change of expression—Tom couldn't quite put his finger on it. He fixed Tom with a deep, unwavering stare that had the weight of the universe behind it. "I told you, Tommy. You can wish things the way you want them to be if you know how. Is that predestination?"

Tom couldn't bear the weight of his gaze, broke it to stare at the optics behind the bar.

"We are all gods, Tommy."

Tom's head began to spin. The words were delivered simply, but there was something hidden deep in them that suggested here was the most important message of all. His heart started to pound as he attempted to peel the true meaning from the heart of the comment, but before he could ask any further questions, Morrison held up his hand to silence him. He shook his head slowly, his eyes told Tom there would be no further discussion on that subject.

Tom was overcome with the drugged atmosphere; his thoughts ebbed and flowed and he was drawn continually to detail in the surroundings, instead of the heaviness that was building up in his thoughts.

"Tell me," he asked hurriedly, "the gods . . . the ones who call themselves gods . . . the Tuatha Dé Danann . . . do they speak for you? Are they part of you?"

Morrison smiled mockingly. "Me?"

"You know what I mean."

He thought about this for a while, his eyes glinting in the flashing coloured stage-lights. "The gods reflect aspects of what lies beyond," he began in his whispery voice. "Some reflect it more than others, some better than others. But that light shines through all living creatures, Tommy. Even the smallest is a part of something bigger. It's all linked."

Once more the grip of the illusion loosened slightly, as if he was caught in the ebb and flow of a supernatural tide. "I'm running out of time, Jim. I can't afford these diversions. You must help me to stay on the path."

Morrison nodded slowly. "You want help."

"I need to talk to the giant, Jim. The physical representation of the source. You must take me to it."

"You know what you're getting into?"

"I know my mind might not be able to cope with it. It's a risk I'm prepared to take."

"Yeah? But you know what you're getting into with the big shit back home. You know what I'm getting at?"

"Yes. I'm aware of it."

"But do you *know*?" His eyes went hazy, focusing through the walls of the club, across Sunset and LA, across worlds. "There are things moving out there that haven't been seen in your place for a long, long time, man. It's like when you move a rock and all these spiders come running out. They were born way out, and I mean *way out*. Right on the edge of the universe, where there's no light. They don't like the light. They're worse than your worst nightmare, man. You can't even *dream* these things."

"My friends and I have no choice, Jim." But a chill ran through him nonetheless.

"Just so you know, though." He fumbled in his pocket and pulled out a small blotter with little pictures of Mickey Mouse and offered one to Tom. The Rhymer declined. Morrison swallowed one and washed it down with the Jack. "I wouldn't be doing my job properly if I didn't do the warning thing. These are bad times, Tommy. It's the End of Everything. Some people would be running and hiding—"

"It may well be the End of Everything—"

"Don't listen to me, listen to them." He motioned over Tom's shoulder. The Rhymer turned round to see The Doors, the roadies, the barflies had all disappeared. In their place were a mass of people Tom instantly recognised as Celts. Long-haired and dark of eye, some had distinctive sweeping moustaches. Others were prepared for war, their manes matted with a bleaching lime mixture that made it stick out in spikes like latter-day punks. "I called them to announce sadness," Morrison said with a faint smile.

One of them moved forward. He had a face of unbearable seriousness, framed by long hair, eyes limpid with emotion. Beside him were two women, sisters, skin like porcelain, hair shining black. Tom saw pride in all their faces, and strength. "In the days before days they washed across the land like a giant wave from the cold, black sea." The man's voice appeared from nowhere although his lips were not moving. "We fought, and died, and fought again. And died. Many, many of us driven to the Land of Always Summer."

"See?" Morrison said, tapping Tom firmly on the chest.

The Celt shook his head slowly from side to side. It moved jerkily, like an old movie rattling through a worn projector. There was the faintest smile on his face, despite the darkness of his words. Tom watched it curiously until he realised he was seeing defiance and self-belief and righteousness.

"The hand of bones comes for all," the Celt began. He pointed at Tom. "Fear is right, but fear must not rule. Death means the same to all, however they might die. But life has value. How you live, with fear at your back. What choices you make. Do you turn your back and live? Or do you face the threat and die? Which has more value? Which has more meaning?"

Tom looked at Morrison. "You're not very good at presenting an argument." Morrison smiled, unabashed.

"Know this," the Celt continued, "you know no fear like the fear you will know in times to come. Your death will be the worst death imaginable. But you will not die enfeebled. You will go as you should have lived, with the blood in your head and a song in your heart."

Tom turned back to the bar and finished his mysteriously full glass. "You're wasting your time. I'm under no illusions. Apart from this one. Remember, I can see the future. Not all of it, granted, but snapshots. Once you have that *gift* you stop worrying so much about what's to come."

Morrison made a clicking song in his cheek and raised Tom's eyeline with a finger. On the periphery of Tom's vision, the bar was warping. The row of optics stretched into infinity, the lights above the low stage were running like treacle. The whole of it swelled, then receded as if it were scenery painted on the rubbery skin of a giant balloon.

"Is everybody in?" Morrison leaned in close to Tom and whispered in his ear, "The ceremony is about to begin."

Tom turned slowly on his stool, but the bar was already gone. Instead he was standing on a grassy area next to a wooden roundhouse with a turf roof in a night torn by lightning of such ferocity he bowed his head. There were other houses around, half hidden in the unnatural gloom. A cacophony of frightened animal noises filled the air—pigs, sheep, cattle and horses. The boom of thunder sounded like cannon and there was a cruel wind making him stagger from side to side. But there was no rain, not even the slightest hint of it.

Morrison's eyes were lost to the acid. "You see the future, you say, but you don't see everything."

"Where are we?"

"The last time your world faced the End of Everything."

The Celt who had spoken to Tom in the Whiskey staggered from the bar clutching a spear, naked and ready for battle. Others followed him, defiant, moving quickly. The quality of the lightning changed slightly, until it was more like flashes of gold, raging against the encroaching night.

"They called this in their legends the Second Battle of Magh Tuireadh." Morrison was still whispering, but somehow his voice carried above the wind.

"The night of victory," Tom said in awe. "When Balor was slain."

"One way of seeing it, Tommy. Or you could say it was a night of ultimate suffering. When the hills and dales ran red with blood and bodies clogged the rivers. This is why the Celts left their coded warnings hidden in the landscape, Tommy. This is when humanity looked into the face of the storm and almost became extinct."

The atmosphere was loaded with tension. Tom felt his teeth go on edge, his stomach start to knot.

"You think you know everything, Tommy." Morrison's smile had an unpleasant edge to it which Tom couldn't quite read. He raised his hand and pointed slowly to the roundhouse. "Do you know what's in the hut? Do you want to look in there?"

Tom stared at the gaping door of the house, and felt what might have been dread, but wasn't quite; like fate come calling. Something he didn't want to see lurked just beyond the shadowy entrance. A part of him wanted to go in there, to see what was on the edge of his mind, but tantalisingly just out of reach. Another part of him knew it would break him to see it. Defeat in victory, he knew, and victory in defeat.

"Why are you trying to frighten me away?" he said to Morrison.

"Because you can't come in here and ask for the world without showing you really want it." Morrison's smile was easier now. He clapped an arm around Tom's shoulder and shook him roughly, amicably.

"I wish you'd just tell me about Texas Radio and the Big Beat," Tom sighed. "Take me to GogMagog."

The Celtic village had been replaced by the tunnels once more, although Tom still quietly yearned for the Whiskey; one more drink would have been nice, a time to rest. Morrison had not made the journey.

After about half an hour he noticed the quality of light was growing brighter, richer. At the same time the tunnel dropped into a steep incline, where he had to clutch on to the rocky walls to prevent himself sliding down into the unknown. The temperature rose rapidly; sweat soaked his shirt and dripped from his brow; the heated air choked his lungs.

Finally, he came out into a large cavern so bright at first he had to shield his eyes. In the centre was an enormous lake of bubbling, popping lava, occasionally shooting up in miniature geysers. The heat radiated off it, but there was none of the sulphurous stink that should have poisoned the air.

Covering his mouth with his shirt to prevent his lungs searing, he eased forward until he stood at the edge of the red lake. The air pulsed.

Tom wondered if madness were only seconds away. He knew it would be best not to be there, but how could he turn back? The others had put him to shame with their continued risk taking, like he was a child, not the mentor. It was time to face up to his responsibility.

"I plead for help!" he said in a commanding voice, while at the same time bowing his head to show deference. It also helped to hide the fear in his face.

The pressure in the air ratcheted up a notch and he had to swallow to make his ears pop.

"I know that to look upon you could mean the end of me . . . I know that I'm not supposed to be here. But I have to. So much is at risk."

Would it come? Or was he wasting his time?

"I'm prepared to sacrifice myself if that's what it takes. That the world should survive is more important than me."

The pressure finally burst and a cooling wind rushed across his face, bringing with it a deep apprehension. His words had touched a chord. Something was coming.

The lava in the centre of the lake erupted, showering burning coals all around, although, miraculously, none of them touched him. Tom threw himself back in shock, dropping to his knees, one arm across his mouth. The lava bubbled up higher in a fountain of fire and smoke, up and up, gaining weight and consistency. And when it appeared it would finally come crashing down on him in a tidal wave, it stopped, hanging silently. It stayed that way for just a moment and then the lava shifted until shape came out of its globular form: an oval, indentations folding out of it, two slits halfway up, an elongated one running vertically and a horizontal slash below. Within seconds a rough-hewn face had grown from the glutinous lava, appearing remarkably like one of the statues that looked to the endless horizon on Easter Island.

Tom climbed to his feet, but a deafening roar burst forth from the lava thing, knocking him back to his knees, his ears ringing. This time he stayed there.

For a long moment he didn't dare speak. The cavern was filled with ebbing sound, dull and reverberate, as if the thing was breathing.

"Are you the Godhead?" Tom whispered. His voice carried with remarkable clarity. "The source?"

"I am GogMagog." The voice was the eruption of a volcano, an earthquake turning the ground to fluid. Tom knew he wasn't *really* hearing it; it was something else prepared for his limited perception. And he also knew this wasn't the Godhead either; he had been presented with another intermediary, albeit a much more powerful one. He felt both relieved and disappointed at the same time. "You have been judged," the force continued.

"But I haven't made my case yet," Tom protested. "Please—"

"We see through you. Your shell, to the essence inside. We see it all. Saw it as soon as you crossed over."

Tom's spirits plummeted. It saw through him, just like that; picked the worthlessness from his soul, the cowardice, the indecision, the hopelessness, all the things he had tried so hard to hide. He had failed.

"You shine. A star in miniature." The voice became richer, less elemental. Tom looked up curiously; the face could almost have been smiling. "Stand tall, little light. You do good work, as do your companions. You do the work of existence."

"I do?" Tom felt befuddled. "I expected to be presented to the Godhead."

"Do you really wish that, little light?" The lava glowed brighter. "There is no going back from that. Only forward, only forward."

"I hoped—"

"Your mission has been recognised. You need to return to the world."

A part of Tom still yearned for the bliss of giving himself up to the spiritual source, and he accepted that some of what drove him to follow the path underground was akin to a death wish. But what lay beyond had saved him from himself by interposing GogMagog at the last moment. That affirmation was both surprising and affecting; he could feel it warming the cold, dark parts of him.

"The path you have chosen is fraught with danger," GogMagog said, "but it is the most important path. Many things hang in the balance, both now and in the years to come. In the great cycle, a change has taken place. There will be no peace until the period of transformation has passed and the new order has been established."

"I understand."

"No. You do not. The Adversary awaits on the edge of everything. Choosing his time carefully. Preparing for the ultimate battle."

"Balor?" Tom asked. "But he—"

"That is but one small part of the Adversary. A fragment of shadow within the greater shadow."

"There's something else?" Tom's heart fell. "Something worse?"

"There is always something more. Your kind must always be on its guard. There is no peaceful home on this side of the inviolate boundary." The lava rose, then receded.

"When?" Tom asked. There was no reply. After a while, Tom put the matter to the back of his mind to concentrate on the issue at hand. "A friend must cross into the Grim Lands to bring back someone vitally important to ridding the world of the evil now occupying it. This friend is not dead, nor is he alive, but his spirit is trapped in the Grim Lands. That itself is a transgression of the rules. I ask that you allow my agent to cross over. And to return with our friend."

There was a long silence, filled only with the sighing of the heated air currents in the cavern. The more time passed, the more Tom feared rejection. But then GogMagog spoke: "The inviolate boundary may be traversed. Your agent can make the voyage from which your kind may not return."

"Is he given safe passage?"

"He is."

"And for the return?"

"Yes. But know this: your agent faces great peril. He may cross the inviolate boundary as the rules say."

Tom thought about this for a second, until realisation suddenly dawned with a cold chill. "He might die?"

Another silence, the shush-boom of the lava breathing. "Night is drawing in. The beast is preparing to snap at his heels."

Tom cursed quietly; had Veitch not obeyed his order to vacate the camp at nightfall? "Then I must return to help him."

"Also, beware: when he crosses the inviolate boundary, the dead will be waiting. You know what that means?"

Dismally, Tom nodded. "How can the doorway be opened?"

"Here, I will give you knowledge." A tendril of lava extended from the lake just below the swaying head, slowly covering the gulf between them. The superheated smell of it was powerful; his skin bloomed when it wavered in front of his face. Like a snake, it started, striking the centre of his forehead. He yelped in pain and recoiled as the flesh sizzled, but in that moment the information he required was transmitted.

"Know this also: you have seen more than any of your kind in an age. Carry this memory with you, but never return. There are boundaries that must not be crossed, and information that must never be learned, until your transformation . . ."

The last word was drawn out like toffee as the cavern receded at great speed. Tom's head spun with the sudden warping effect, and then he was lifted on a blast of super-hot air, flying backwards out of the cavern and up the tunnel so fast the breath was crushed from his lungs. He hurtled through the Whiskey, with Morrison smiling at him mockingly, through the Celtic village, and then the pain in his lungs became unbearable and the dark folded around him sharply.

Veitch emerged from a deep sleep, disoriented and aching; some hidden branch had been digging in his back and his thighs felt like they'd been stoned. A string of drool soaked his cheek. It was not a sudden awakening; his dream still had its talons in him—an upsetting scenario of Ruth telling him something he couldn't bear to hear—leaving him feeling irritated and out of sorts. As he came to his senses, he was aware of a chill in his limbs. The patches of warming sunlight had departed, taking the tiny flying creatures with them. Colour was slowly leeching from the vegetation as twilight took hold.

"Shit, how long have I been out?" He dragged himself awkwardly to his feet, shaking his arms to get the blood flow moving.

In the half light, the woods appeared less idyllic. Unease scurried under rustling nettles and made branches sway wildly when there was no breeze. Shadows crept along the ground menacingly from the boles of trees, clustered under bushes, waiting. Rubbing his wrists, Veitch wandered down the slope a little way to a path. From there he could see the sun so low on the horizon it was really just a glow of red and gold.

Tom's warning came back to him, but he had never given it serious consideration—he had faced too many bad things to run at the first sign of trouble. Even if he did heed it, where would he go? And what if Tom returned from wherever he was, only to find himself alone, at night, in a place he considered dangerous? He might be a miserable git at times, but he deserved better than that.

Weighing his options, Veitch decided to return to the mansion to sit with Robertson while the superstitious squatter rubbed his mojos till dawn. He strode out through the forest, the chill in the air telling him the deceptively warm season was slipping out quietly. Unsure of his direction, he paused at the system of paths leading from the car park around the hill. Everywhere looked different in the growing gloom. He still hadn't adjusted to the dramatic change the night brought to a land free from electric lights: deep, still darkness heavy on the countryside and the stars so bright overhead it was as if he had never seen them before. The last few midges drifted away to wherever they spent the night, pursued by the flitting shape of a bat darting from the trees across the open areas. The jarring screech of an owl echoed away in the woods. All the night creatures were coming out to hunt.

At a fork in the path, Veitch took the one he thought he remembered, but it was soon apparent he'd taken a wrong turning. The Tarmac gave way to stones and then hard-packed soil as the path became a thin trail amongst the bushes.

Ahead of him he could see the outline of the house silhouetted against the night sky; it didn't appear too far away.

The path bore down steeply until Veitch found himself in a strange, broad ditch that looked as if it ran around the circumference of the hill. He vaguely recalled Tom muttering something about the fortifications of the old Iron Age fort, but, as usual, he hadn't been paying much attention. The bottom of the ditch was flat, some six to eight feet wide, and obviously used regularly as a footpath from the hardness of the soil. On either side the banks rose up steeply. Clustering firs formed a natural roof that only added to the gloom. As his eyes adjusted he made out festooning ivy, chest-high nettles and thick banks of bramble that made the sides of the ditch impenetrable. On the house side there was also some kind of high wall or fence at the top of the bank.

Sooner or later there would be a path up to the truncated summit, he guessed, so he set off clockwise round the fortification. The low level of the ditch and its flat bottom against the steep banks reminded him of a racetrack, and he briefly fantasised about scrambling round on a motorcycle; just another thing he missed with the passing of technology.

At intermittent points, crumbling flint walls protruded like ghostly fingers from the bank, while gnarled roots snaked out of the ground, threatening to trip him. He kept his eyes down, his ears alert and walked slowly; the last thing he needed was a broken ankle.

The first sign that something was wrong was a wall of cold wind that came from nowhere, raising goosebumps on his arms before continuing along the ditch behind him. It was starkly unnatural the way it clung to the bottom of the trough; the vegetation on either side never moved and the trees that hung overhead were still. Even when he could hear its whispering disappearing far behind him, the goosebumps remained. It felt like a sign delineating a change, as if something profound had shifted in nature itself; the old time had gone, the new time was near.

He found it disconcertingly eerie there in the darkness of the ditch, where the banks were so steep his only way of escape was forward or back. The place was intensely still and each footstep sounded like the crack of a whip. Perhaps it was the odd acoustics of the place, but no sound came from outside the ditch, not even the cries of owls. An unpleasant loneliness hung over all.

Veitch started having second thoughts about his choice of route, but it was too late to go back. His bravery took a further knock when he heard a long, low noise; he couldn't tell if it came from ahead or behind, nor what kind of animal had made it. After the heavy silence, it was deeply unnerving. It rolled along the bottom of the ditch as the wind had done, suggesting something akin to the whinnying snort of a horse, but different enough to raise the hairs on the back of his neck.

He turned slowly, full circle, trying to pinpoint the location, while his mind raced to plan a course of action.

Just a horse, he told himself. The place used to be famous for horse breeding and racing; that was the rational explanation. But he couldn't forget the story Tom had told him about the Night Rider.

It's coming. The words jumped into his mind unprompted.

Just ahead of him, the left bank was cut through with a path that ran down the slope of the hill. Hurrying up it to get a better view, Veitch saw only thick vegetation and open fields ahead; nowhere to hide if he was pursued. His best bet was still to get to the house and bar the door; suddenly Robertson's superstitions made a lot more sense.

Back on the floor of the ditch, the silence had returned, now weighted with anticipation. The familiar pressure drop that always accompanied some unnatural event left his ears humming, and he could taste iron at the back of his mouth. Almost loping, he moved forward, trying to avoid any twig or stone that might give his location away.

A hard, clicking sound brought him up sharp: hoofbeats, slow and measured; just a few and then silence, as if whatever was out there was also advancing and listening. It was still impossible to identify the location. The *clack-clack-clack* appeared to circle him, loud and crystal clear in the stillness. Cautiously, Veitch withdrew his crossbow and carefully fitted a bolt. The dark would make it hard to get a clear shot, but he felt more comfortable being able to launch an attack from afar.

Clack-clack-clack. This time he was sure it was behind him. Veitch peered into the gloom, waiting for the sound to stop. Only this time it didn't. The horse was coming towards him at a measured but relentless pace. Now he was convinced it was ahead of him. He turned back, raising the crossbow until it was lined up for anything advancing along the ditch.

Clack-clack-clack-clack-clack.

He continued to wait for the dark to peel back, until, with a sudden *frisson*, he realised the sound wasn't ahead of him at all. He spun round to see a creamy cloud filled with sparkling stars twisting and turning as it hurtled along the path right at him. A buzzing like a swarm of angry bees filled the air, setting his teeth on edge.

Expecting a horse, the sight caught him unawares. The cloud rushed towards him at great speed, then, just as he decided to loose a bolt, it winked out; the disembodied hoofbeats continued thunderously.

Veitch paused for a split second before his instinct kicked in, then he was sprinting along the bottom of the ditch, not sure if he could outrun it, knowing there was no other way out.

Twisted roots threatened to trip him before retreating back into the shadows, but his reactions were electric fast. Behind him the storm clatter of hooves grew louder and louder, matching the beats of his heart. Twenty feet away, then ten, then at his heels.

From out of the dark, an obstacle rushed at him: a pile of hard earth forming a bridge path between the two banks piled as high as his head. He went up it with what felt like snorts of fire burning the back of his neck, threw himself down the other side and rolled into a ball. A large form tore over his head and landed with a heavy crash before pounding on for several yards. Looking up, he saw a shimmering in the air like malleable glass rein itself to a halt, then whirl round, catching the light with pools and glints. The limning of moonlight indeed suggested a horse with a bulky figure on its back before it was lost to the dark. The hooves began to pound once more, building up speed.

Veitch waited until the last moment before throwing himself back over the bridge path to perform the same manoeuvre. Again his pursuer passed overhead. This time he launched himself to gain a few vital yards before the Night Rider could round.

As the horse rattled down on him, he whirled and rolled, loosing a bolt in the same motion. A second later a tear of fire appeared in thin air, followed by a cry like a metal crate being dragged on a concrete floor.

He had no time to discover how much damage he had wrought, for the sound continued to bear down on him. He threw himself to one side at the last moment, but it was not quite far enough. His jacket and shirt tore open, his flesh mysteriously burst as a raw red line rushed up towards his neck. He just had time to jerk his head before the invisible blade could rip through his jugular, and then he was rolling backwards against the bank, his shirt growing hot and wet.

The pain sharpened his thoughts. When he moved, the rest of the world felt like it was frozen; he was scrambling to one side, rolling, ignoring the pain, reloading the crossbow, readjusting the balance of his body like a machine.

He landed on the balls of his feet, poised to attack, but though his eyes and ears were charged to pick up even the slightest sound of his attacker, there was nothing. The bottom of the ditch was still; even the faintest hoofbeat would have sounded out loud. Not even a hint of movement, the barest shift in air currents.

His blood thundered in his head. Where had it gone? He turned slowly, but the thing really had disappeared. Perhaps the bolt *had* caused some damage.

He waited for a few seconds longer, just to be sure, and then set off at a slow lope around the ditch. He was under no illusion that the Night Rider had gone for good, but its absence might just provide him with the time to find a route to the house.

His feet padded on the hard-packed mud as he ran, his breath ragged; the night air was chill and fragrant. Every sensation was heightened. The enveloping trees that made the ditch feel like a tunnel instilled an oppressive claustrophobia in him; he was trapped, like an animal. The thought brought a burst of adrenalin and he threw himself up the side of the ditch, feeling the thorns of the brambles tear at his flesh, the nettles stabbing with their poison needles. Somehow he made it to the top, but the trees there were impenetrable, and beyond them the brick garden wall was too tall to climb. He still tried to force his way through, but the trees acted as if they were alive, forcing him back until he was slipping down the slope to land on his back at the bottom of the ditch once more.

As he lay there while his breath subsided, tremors ran through the ground into his bones: rhythmic, powerful. He was up in an instant, running once more. This time, when he actually heard the hoofbeats, it was almost hallucinogenic; they faded in and out of his hearing, the rider here, then not here. And then they disappeared completely again, leaving only silence.

A moment of clarity overwhelmed him. Tom had spoken of *liminal zones* where the boundaries between this world and T'ir n'a n'Og were blurred. The camp must be such a place, he realised, and the Rider was shifting in and out of the worlds as it pursued him.

Veitch whirled, crossbow at the ready. His nerve endings prickled as he slowly surveyed the scene. His pursuer could be anywhere. How did it make itself invisible? Or was that its natural state? Yet he knew now what he had to do: attack at the moment it was fully in this world, when—he hoped—it would be most vulnerable.

Another low whinny drifted along the ditch. It sounded unimaginably distant, but it brought back the gooseflesh. And then, as it wound its way through the undergrowth on the ditch banks, it began to change; slowly at first, but definitely, losing its equine characteristics. The sound became shorter, broke up into linked sounds; became words.

That eerie noise made the snake around Veitch's spine pull the coils in tighter. "What the *hell* is that?" he hissed.

He was already moving when the words rattled around him like pebbles on a frozen lake, devoid of emotion, but threatening. "Run fast, run fast, at your back."

They were barely audible, could almost have been the distant echoes of hoofbeats, but the chill they brought to his blood drove him on. Faster and faster still, with the rumble of pursuit building behind him. He glanced over his shoulder as he hurdled a twisted mass of root: nothing yet. The words were all around him, some indecipherable, hidden in the snort of a horse, others barely registering on his consciousness, but disturbing him nonetheless.

As he rounded the curve of the ditch, running faster than he ever had in his life, an arching shape loomed up out of the night. The mass of trees had thinned out and the light of the moon revealed a brick bridge across the ditch. He was sure he would be able to scramble up the side to get to it and then it would be only a short sprint to the house. With the thunder of hooves almost at his heels, the sight gave him enough of a filip to drive himself that little bit harder.

But just as he thought he would make it, his foot caught one of the roots that had threatened to trip him ever since he had ventured down there. He hit the ground so hard all the air was driven out of his lungs; the pain in his chest felt like someone had swung a hammer there. At first he was stunned, but then his mind scrambled in panic. It was too late.

He looked back and was briefly hypnotised by the strangest thing: little flames, like will o' the wisps, alighted at ground level, drawing towards him. It took him a second to realise what it was: invisible hooves striking the flints that were scattered across the ditch.

The moment locked. He wondered what it would be like to be trampled to death; wondered if anyone would mourn him.

And then he was transfixed by something else. As the little flames closed on him, the air above shimmered and began to peel back. It looked to him like the Night Rider was shedding his skin: at first there was nothing, then the translucent glassy substance, until that slipped away to reveal the true form of his pursuer, or as true a form as his perceptions would allow. The first shock was that the picture he had created in his head was so wrong: this was no mediaeval knight with a broadsword or a lance on a black charger. There wasn't even a man and a horse. What bore down on him in a rage of clattering hooves was both man *and* horse, the two forms constantly flowing together, never staying the same for too long. A head that had the flowing hair of an Iron Age warrior, becoming a wild mane, the face growing longer, nostrils flaring, blasting clouds of steam in the chill night; two legs, then four, then two again. It wasn't like a classical centaur, but was half formed, or still forming, or never quite forming; continually halfway between the two in the same way that the sounds had appeared to be coming halfway between here and there.

The intoxicating shock was riven out by a burst of blood in Veitch's brain. Suddenly he was ready to move. He tried to fling himself to one side, but even as he was moving, the futility of it was strangling his thoughts. The Night Rider was on him, rising up, iron-shod hooves glinting in the moonlight. One of them caught Veitch on the temple, knocking him back to the ground where stars flew briefly.

When they cleared, all he could see was the creature's terrible face framed against the night sky. It was filled with all the fury of the animal kingdom, wild and unfocused, the eyes ruddy and smoky as they branded him. Its musk was thick and choking, blanking out all his senses, yet behind it all Veitch sensed something resolutely human; once a man, and now greater than a man.

"I ride the courses between the worlds." Those stony words again; Veitch wanted to cover his ears at the unbearable force of them. Everything about the thing was so *vital*. "I am the power and the fecundity of the stallion, the speed and the strength. Worlds are dashed beneath my feet."

Veitch snatched his head away as the Night Rider brought a hoof down sharply. It slammed the ground an inch from his ear, jolting his head upwards so powerfully he knew his skull would have been crushed if contact had been made. With the next blow, sparks burned his cheek. He was trapped beneath the body of the creature, with no way of wriggling free.

"This sacred place belongs to the Machan who made me. Totem of Rig Antona, our Great High Queen, who made the sky and the stars and the green grass on which we run." The words reminded Veitch of a recorded announcement programmed to be delivered to intruders in the earliest of days. "In this place, where the barrier is thin, the wild, untamed spirits of the horse gallop to the Grey Lands and back."

Another hoof came down in punctuation, this time clipping Veitch's shoulder; a bolt of pain shot down his arm.

"No one but the Machan may ride here betwixt sunset and sunrise. That is the law." The horse had human features, but the Night Rider's face was now wholly that of a demonic horse with blazing red eyes, an alien conqueror who would brook no trespass on his domain. Veitch felt swallowed up by that scarlet glow, forced to accept his place in the scheme of things. *You are nothing*, it said. *Insignificant in the face of a higher power. You will obey, and you will die.*

It meant nothing to Veitch. As the Night Rider rose up high, its hooves tearing at the air ready for the killing blow, Veitch brought the crossbow up and loosed a bolt directly into the creature's belly. That unmistakable metal-on-concrete roar erupted from its wildly shifting face as it threw itself into a furious downward drive at Veitch's head.

But the bolt had unbalanced it. In a sinuous movement, Veitch pulled out the short sword from his belt and drove it upwards at the same time as he kicked himself backwards. The sword ripped into the belly and tore upwards. "Nothing scares me any more," Veitch growled defiantly.

He was too busy doing a backward roll to see the results of his attack, but he could hear the Night Rider's hideous cries. And then he was sprinting for the bridge, scrambling up the bank at the side of it, his feet slipping on the weeds, but gaining enough purchase to propel himself to the top.

Only when he was on the bridge did he allow himself a glance back. There was neither blood nor intestines, but the Rider was lurching from side to side in obvious discomfort, his head held back, roaring his pain to the night. Once his gaze fell on Veitch, the face changed once more to the demonic horse's head and, with the eyes shining like red lanterns, the Rider overcame his agony to spur himself into pursuit.

Veitch paused to give him the finger, then flipped over the wall of the bridge and landed on the Tarmac path that curved around the trees into the flat summit of the hill. *Nearly there*, he thought breathlessly, energised by his escape and his defiance. For a moment he felt indestructible, until he heard the Night Rider thunder effortlessly up the side of the ditch and the hooves clatter on the Tarmac surface.

Veitch weighed up the prospects of loosing some more bolts, but he estimated the effect would be negligible. It was now all down to his fitness and his energy reserves. He followed the curve of the path until he saw the lawns laid out before him, silver-grey in the moonlight with the dry dew pond at the centre. Before him the dark bulk of the house loomed up. The comforting golden glow of candlelight illuminated a square on the courtyard from the window of Robertson's quarters.

Behind, the rumble of hooves came on like a runaway train.

I can make it, Veitch told himself.

He ran as if caught by the north wind, hurdling the small fence and pounding across the courtyard. The hooves grew closer, only yards now. He couldn't outrun a horse, but the house was close enough to reach before it got to him. Past the stable block with its silent ghosts of horses past. Their energy was everywhere, he thought.

Now he could hear the beast's breath, explosive bursts punctuated by the gnashing of its teeth. He waited for the hot bloom of it on the back of his neck.

He slammed into the door, sending the panes ringing in their frames. Fumbling around, he caught the handle and yanked. Locked.

"Robertson!" His throat was torn by the yell.

Robertson appeared at the window, his face pale and desperate. Veitch was already reading the signs, recalling the man's nature. "Come *on*, you bastard," he said under his breath. The sound of hooves was deafening; Veitch forced himself not to look. As Robertson took in the situation in a glance, an expression of revelation crossed his face; and the revelation was that the world was the hell he had always imagined, where reason didn't exist and superstition crushed lives at random. He backed away rapidly, waving his hands in front of him.

From behind, there was a hiss like escaping steam, loaded with a note of triumph.

Veitch cursed under his breath and turned, the house heavy at his back, the enclosing walls of the courtyard too oppressive; nowhere to run.

The Night Rider had slowed his speed, revelling in the cornering of his prey. In the candlelight, Veitch could make out more details of his pursuer. The rider's legs went directly into the body of the horse, not just fused there, but utilising the same muscular and vascular system. The rider's arms disappeared into the mane, the horse hair wrapping round, becoming part of the human flesh; and still the features on both the heads were hideously changing places.

Nowhere to run.

The rider came to a halt. Slowly one hoof dragged along the ground, raising sparks. The head at the front lowered, the rider leaned forward.

Still a chance to move, Veitch told himself optimistically. *Don't give up. Never give up.*

Before he could break away from the door, a voice boomed across the courtyard. The tone and volume made Veitch jump in shock. It was in a language he didn't comprehend, but the words—if that was what they were—made his ears hurt just by hearing them.

It had an effect on the Rider too; he paused as he prepared for the charge, cantered round, backed off. Veitch noted the mutating appearance had speeded up; the features were now just a blur, suggesting uneasiness.

For a time the whole of the world hung in abeyance. With his heart in his mouth, Veitch saw movement in the shadows surrounding the stable block. Whatever had spoken was there. Veitch wanted to flee to a secure hiding place immediately, but the figure was now emerging from the gloom. The Night Rider, too, appeared to be waiting with something like apprehension.

When the figure stepped into the moonlight, Veitch was shocked to see it was Tom. He was staggering a little, as if exhausted, but the most curious detail was that he was smoking, as if he had been singed by a blaze. The Rider focused all his attention on the slight figure. When Tom was ten feet away he made a strange hand movement which appeared to involve another set of joints in the wrist. It was followed by another word; Tom whispered it, but it crashed like the peal of cathedral bells.

The Rider responded as if chastened by a whip. The front of the horse bowed down, bending its front legs until its head was almost on the ground. The Rider followed suit with a similar act of deference. Then it rose back up and, without a second glance at Veitch, calmly cantered off.

Veitch remained tense for a few seconds, barely believing what he was seeing, but then his shoulders relaxed and he turned to Tom with a broad grin. "You old bastard! Like the bleedin' cavalry!"

Tom marched over and stabbed a finger into Veitch's face. "I thought I told you to get off the hill at nightfall!"

Veitch's expression soured. "Since when did I do what you say, you senile old bastard?" The adrenalin still pumped deliriously around his system. "Hang on a minute." He turned and launched a hefty kick at the door, which burst off its hinges, shattering all the panes at once.

Tom recognised the expression on Veitch's face, the consuming rage that he carried with him at all times. "Now, steady on—"

Veitch had already marched inside. There was a loud crashing within and a moment later he emerged, dragging a writhing Robertson behind him. The squatter was almost insane with fear, his eyes rolling, his jaw sagging.

"Ryan! He's scared!"

"Yeah? Well, here's something to be scared of." He thumped Robertson so hard on the side of the head, Tom was afraid his neck had snapped. He slumped to the ground in a stupor.

It took fifteen minutes before Veitch had calmed enough to have a reasonable conversation with Tom. Robertson had scurried back indoors, barricading the doorway with furniture. Even then Veitch couldn't sit and spent the time pacing in circles around Tom, who sat cross-legged, drawing on a joint, unable to hide the shake in his hands.

"What was that thing?" Veitch asked.

"This place has been linked to horses much longer than the racing fraternity realised. Back in the earliest times, it was dedicated to Epona. Her name derives from the Celtic word for horse and she was one of the greatest goddesses of the Celts. All riders—warriors, travellers, whoever—bowed their head to Epona. In Wales, she was known as Rhiannon, in Ireland Etain or Macha." Tom let the smoke drift into the wind. "She was the patron of journeys, particularly the most important journey of all: from this life to the next. She was usually pictured carrying a key that unlocked the door to Otherworld."

"Yeah? Then it ties into this place. The doorway to the Land of the Dead, and all that."

"Yes. Amazing how it all fits together." Veitch didn't appear to notice the sarcasm in Tom's voice; he was lost in his own childlike amazement. "The Night Rider was her avatar. Once he was probably a man like you or me, perhaps a man who even lived at this site. But at some point he became infused with the essence of Epona, became, in a way, the totem he worshipped. And so he eternally guards this sacred spot were she canters back and forth between the worlds."

"Horses." Veitch kicked a stray stone across the yard. "Don't see the bleedin' attraction. Smelly animals."

"Horse worship persisted from the earliest times of the nomadic people in this land. To them, the horse was a symbol of fertility, energy and power." Dreamily, Tom nodded his head to some inner soundtrack. "Worshipping is wishing by any other name, and if you wish hard enough you can create something from nothing." Words from another world came back to him.

"What's that, then? You're saying all those folk gave her the powers. Made her. She's one of the Danann bastards, right?"

"Yes and yes and yes, and no and no and no."

"Oh, shut the fuck up. I'm not going to talk to you any more when you're smoking." He marched irritatedly into Robertson's apartment.

The chill before dawn brought a deep ache to their bones. They sat on a bench, watching the moon scud across the heavens, the sky slowly turn from midnight blue to pink and gold, the grass growing from grey to green. An affecting peace lay over everything. When the birds came alive in the trees that ringed the lawned area, Veitch turned to Tom and smiled. "It'll be all right, you know."

Tom nodded noncommittally.

"What happened? You know, when you met the giant?"

Tom considered how to put the experience into words, then simply shook his head. "That's a story for another time. All you need to know now is you've got the necessary permission to bring Shavi back."

The sun came up soon after. The diffuse golden light glimmered through the branches, eventually making its way across the lawn until it reached the dew pond. At first nothing happened, but when the light was just right they could make out a shimmering image of Shavi's body lying in a flower-bedecked bower. It was insubstantial, fading in and out like a poor hologram. He appeared to be sleeping; only the stark paleness of his skin gave a clue to his true state.

Tom thought he saw the glint of tears in Veitch's eyes, but the Londoner looked away before he could be sure.

"We better do it," Veitch said solemnly.

"Are you sure? This is your last chance to back out."

"Yes."

"You understand where you're going? What lies ahead? What it could do to your mind? You know you might not be coming back?"

Veitch fixed a cold eye on him. "Just get on with it."

A pang of guilt clutched at Tom's heart. He *knew* what lay ahead, and he knew Veitch could not even begin to guess the extent of the horrors that lurked in the Grim Lands. How could he send the man to face that? But even as he thought it, he knew he had no choice; only Veitch stood a chance of bringing Shavi back. And therein lay the tragedy.

On the edge of the dew pond, Tom knelt down and kissed the damp grass. When he stood back up, he had composed himself. "Are you ready?"

"Bring it on," Veitch replied in a cod-American accent.

Tom closed his eyes and attempted to access the knowledge GogMagog had implanted there. He had already used the secret words of power to dismiss the guardian. Now there was one remaining: the key to the door. He couldn't reach it in his memory by normal means. He simply made a space, and then it leapt into it. He didn't remember speaking, but when he opened his eyes, Veitch was clutching his ears and grimacing.

There was a sound like a jammed door being wrenched open and the air over the dew pond peeled back. Through it Tom could see thick grey fog, swirling in the wind.

Veitch made to say something, but couldn't find the words. Instead, he grinned, winked and then launched himself through the hole in the air. The wrenching noise echoed again as the door closed, leaving Tom alone to stare at the fading visage of Shavi.

chapter ten
below

"It's time." Church tried to sound more confident than he felt, but Ruth was not about to be fooled.

"I still think I should come with you."

He shook his head firmly. "I'm not trying to protect you like some big macho idiot. You'd be the first person I'd want alongside me in a fight. But I told you, one of us has to be here to see things through."

"You're not being very consistent. You made a big thing about how you felt all five Brothers and Sisters of Dragons had to be together to get a result. Now you're saying I can do it on my own—"

"I hate having smart people around me. Okay, I'll be back. Did that sound like Arnie Schwarzenegger? Sorry, I wasted the eighties at the movies."

"You're so lowbrow." She put her arms around him and pulled him to her, planting a wet kiss on his lips. "Be back soon. We have a lot of lost time to make up for."

In the constantly changing corridors where the flickering torches never cast enough light, the kiss brought an ache to his heart. More than anything, he wanted to stay with Ruth, secure in their newfound world, but he knew that was an illusion. He had to journey down into the deep, dark bowels of the ship where there was no security, no softness. He drew his jacket around him, resting one hand on the cold short sword that hung at his belt.

"Life's good as long as you don't weaken," he muttered, repeating the credo he had once only half-jokingly spoken aloud. "Please don't weaken."

The ship grew icier and smelled danker the more he progressed, as if he were journeying beneath the earth itself. He had adjusted to the constant gentle rocking, but the creak of the timbers was like the background chatter of a hundred voices, obscuring other subtle sounds that might come as a warning. The hiss of the torches brought sweetly perfumed smoke to his nose, but the underlying odour of dampness could never be hidden.

After a while he started cautiously trying the doors on either side. Most were locked, some rooms were empty, but in one something that was a mass of tentacles and snapping jaws rushed towards him squealing insanely. He slammed the door and hurried on, vowing not to open any more.

The ship went on forever. More than anything, Church feared getting lost down there, spending the rest of his life wandering around in the dark, living on rats (although he had not seen any vermin—perhaps something else was already feeding on them), slowly turning pale and mad. But he had a gut instinct that the ship was sentient in some way he couldn't explain, and that while the corridors behind him might close and move, when he returned, they would lead him back to the upper decks by one route or another.

At that point he began to wonder if he was really on a ship at all; if the spy he had encountered in Edinburgh had been right and all this was a warped perception brought on by some outside force using drugs or deep hypnotism, for whatever reason. As this thought entered his head, he was convinced he heard the throb of machines and the hubbub of men's voices through one of the doors; it troubled him inexplicably and he chose to hurry on.

Further on, the corridors took on a different appearance, so that it was no longer obvious he was on board a ship. It might have happened so gradually he didn't notice it, or in the blink of an eye, but suddenly the walls were in part limestone, in others, rough-hewn timbers, peppered with holes of varying sizes. It smelled differently, too. The saltiness that had permeated everything had been replaced by a faintly sulphurous odour of dust. The heavy echoes of his tread had taken the place of the constant creaking, nor was he even aware of the ship's rocking. Other sounds were more prevalent now, through the walls or further along the corridor: movement, fast and light like the scurrying of vermin, or slow and laboured as if enormous creatures were shifting slowly.

He was startled at one point by the sound of small feet near to his ear. He turned sharply to see a blur passing quickly across a hole in the wall at head height. One of the Portunes, he guessed, spying on him. The little people were everywhere, the eyes and ears of the ship. But why were they always watching? What did it benefit them?

As the atmosphere became less like that onboard ship, the more the air of tension rose; it was enough to warn Church he had moved into an area of more immediate danger, rather than the general background threat of the upper decks. There was a quality to it that made him queasy. His palms grew slick around the handle of the sword, his knuckles aching from holding it.

His eyes, by now well accustomed to the gloom, felt sore from continually probing the shadows ahead; so much that at first he thought the flickering shapes he occasionally glimpsed were just the tremors of an over-worked eye muscle. But gradually he came to realise there were things moving just beyond the light of the now-intermittent torches, darting around corners at the last moment. He was sure they weren't the Malignos; as Ruth had described them, they would not be so restrained. It could, of course, be Callow, playing some sneaky little game, waiting for just the right moment to attack. But still—

Church almost jumped out of his skin when a hand protruded from an unnoticed branching corridor to his left, reaching for his arm. It was just a glimpse out of the corner of his eye, but he was whirling instantly, lashing out with the sword. His reactions were perfect, but the hand became a blur of golden lightning. Before Church had time to launch another attack, Baccharus stepped out sharply, motioning for Church to remain silent.

Church's angry face passed on all the fury of the curses he wanted to yell out at Baccharus's unthinking approach, but Baccharus, as usual, was oblivious. They hurried several yards along the branching corridor until Baccharus turned and said bluntly, "You must turn back."

"I'm starting to worry about you, Baccharus," Church snapped. "Do you spend all your time hanging around down here? You know, is it the Tuatha Dé Danann equivalent of the street corner where the furtively smoking teenagers hang out? Or do you just wait in the shadows until Ruth or I come along?"

Baccharus gave several long, slow blinks while staring into Church's eyes. Eventually he said, "You must—"

"Yes, yes, I know. Turn back. I know it's not a saunter through Covent Garden—"

"You do not realise the extent of the danger."

Church sighed, running his fingers through his long hair. "Baccharus, I really do appreciate you looking out for me. It's such a rare trait in your kind I'd be a fool not to recognise it. But this is something I have to do. There's so much at stake here for all . . . all the Fragile Creatures. And at the moment only Ruth and I can do something about it. I wish someone else was having to do the business, but that's not the way it is."

Baccharus's stare was still intense. "How does your journey here, in the depths, bear upon your mission?"

The question was curious, the fact that Baccharus was asking it more so. "How did you know I'd be here anyway? Have you been spying on me?"

Baccharus appeared a little taken aback by the question, but not hurt or irritated; the emotions of the Tuatha Dé Danann were so difficult to read he might simply have had no idea what Church was talking about.

Church thought a moment. "The Portunes. Running through the walls. That one was with you when you saved Ruth. So why are you particularly interested in us?"

Baccharus, in his usual honest manner, did not attempt to bat it away. "A long story."

"And when we get back topside you're going to tell me. But right now—"

"You must not continue. The danger is out of control. The Malignos are preparing for something unpleasant. Your fellow Fragile Creature, the one tainted by the Night Walkers—"

"Callow."

"—he has whispered secrets to them, given them guidance. My associates are searching for them now, but they can wrap the night around them."

Something was jangling deep in Church's head. "*Your* associates? Why isn't Manannan doing something about this if it's such a threat?"

Baccharus didn't answer.

"What's going on here, Baccharus? The five of us, the Brothers and Sisters of Dragons, we've been run like rats and had our lives ruined by your people. I'm not having any more of it. I feel like some massive thing has been going on all the time we've been on this ship, but Ruth and I have seen only a tiny part of it. Used when your people feel it suits their needs. Ignored or barely tolerated the rest of the time."

"No." Baccharus's voice was firm. "If you knew the truth, you would not say that."

Church searched his face; something sharply human hung there, something few of the other Golden Ones carried. A faint sound echoed nearby. Church glanced over his shoulder. "This isn't the time. I have to find the Walpurgis."

"I will take you to him."

Church's attention snapped back. "You know where he is?"

"If it will prevent you blundering into the areas of greatest peril, I will accede to your request." He strode out along the branching corridor, then turned right down another branch that Church hadn't noticed. Church was rooted for a second, but then he skipped into step behind the hurrying god.

Church lost track of how many junctions they came up on, and the constant branching made his head spin. When he had set off below deck, the corridor had stretched on and on with no other side route, but Baccharus found a myriad, lurking in shadows, or disguised as hanging drapes. At first Church fired numerous questions, but when the god refused to answer any of them, Church fell into a steady silence, trying to make some sense of his topsy-turvy thoughts.

Eventually Baccharus came to a halt before a stretch of corridor that was lit more brightly than most of the others. The wall in this area was of wooden timbers, uneven and nondescript. He rested one hand on it, fingers splayed, bowed his head and muttered something under his breath. The wall became like the running water of a waterfall. Baccharus strode through it. Church jumped behind him, expecting to get soaked, but it felt like the overhead hot air heaters some shops treat their customers to on a wet winter's day.

On the other side was a large chamber, comfortably fitted out with thick rugs, heavy tapestries on the polished wood walls, chairs and tables bearing a few half-filled goblets and trays of dried fruit and nuts. Several figures were scattered around. They broke off from what appeared to be intense conversation to stare at him. There were a few members of the Tuatha Dé Danann Church recognised by sight, but whose names he didn't know, a smattering of Portunes scurrying around like mice, and one or two of the odd figures he had glimpsed at the banquet. At his gaze, these moved back into the shadows where the torches did not reach.

"What's going on here?" he asked suspiciously. His hand moved towards his sword as the half thought entered his head that Baccharus might have led him into a trap.

"We are all friends here." Marik Bocat squatted on the back of a chair, shouting, although his voice sounded barely more than a whisper.

"Then why are you hiding away?"

"The situation is complex," Baccharus said. "Perhaps it is time to unveil it to you." He turned to the others. "This is Jack, Brother of Dragons." All those who had not been introduced to Church before bowed their heads.

"Maybe later." Church walked to the centre of the room and looked around. "First, I want to talk to the Walpurgis."

A fluttering bundle of rags emerged from the gloom at the back of the chamber. Beneath the broad-brimmed hat, the hot coal eyes glowed as intensely as Church recalled. "I am here." His voice was a chill wind over a graveyard.

Church put the confusing scenario to the back of his mind. There were more important subjects. But first he had to know if he was right. "Did you kill Cormorel?"

"He did not," Baccharus interjected.

"I want to hear it from him."

"I do not kill."

Church nodded thoughtfully. "You said you were a Messenger. With a message for me. A message that was very clear." The Walpurgis stared, said nothing. "What is the message?"

"Do you not want your dream examined?"

The Walpurgis was talking about the hidden memory of who had really killed Marianne; the identity of the traitor amongst them. "Yes. More than anything. But first, this."

The Walpurgis came forward, pushing cold air before him that raised the goosebumps on Church's arms. When he was only a few feet away, the tattered creature intoned gravely, "You will find no peace in this world. For some, that is the way it must be."

Church's heart fell. The Walpurgis's words were like a death knell, tolling out his deepest fears.

"But you must not lose hope." The Walpurgis reached out a papery hand. "You must never lose hope. You are part of something much larger than what lies around you. Many will benefit from your sacrifice."

"Do you think that's enough?" The bitterness in Church's voice shocked even himself. He looked around the gathered faces and was unnerved by how they were hanging on his every word. "All the pain I've already had. My girlfriend . . . my love . . . the love of my life . . . murdered. All the grief that followed, beating myself up because I thought she'd committed suicide, that I was *responsible*. Laura . . . the young Marianne . . . all the other ones I've seen die." Ruth's face flashed into his mind, followed by a sharp pang of regret that was almost painful. "And now I can see a way out, some kind of good life ahead for a change, and you're telling me it's not going to happen? No fucking way."

The Walpurgis took another pace with his outstretched hand, oddly comforting now, but Church waved it away.

"I don't want to hear it."

"These things are written, Jack." Baccharus's voice was sympathetic too.

"What do you know about it?"

"You are a Brother of Dragons—"

"Yes, I know my responsibility and I've accepted it. But once I've done all I can do, that's it. No more Fabulous Beasts, no more *waking the sleeping king* and all that Arthurian shit, no more Blue Fire. I'm getting my life back."

"Then you think you can actually do something? In the face of such overwhelming odds? That *a life* still awaits you?" Baccharus's words, as always, were calm and measured.

Church turned back to the Walpurgis. "Now. I want to know who killed Marianne."

"There is always something bigger, Jack." Baccharus's voice sounded closer and more intense, although he had not taken a step. "Bigger powers. Bigger plans."

"Show me," Church said harshly to the Walpurgis.

The Walpurgis began to move. Church felt butterflies in his stomach. This was it: the final, bitter revelation. He put his head back, closed his eyes and waited for the Walpurgis to push his fingers into Church's mind.

Something was nagging at him as he waited. Not the silence in the room, so heavy he could almost feel currents flowing through it. Not the way the hairs on the back of his neck were prickling, the way his gut was knotting in dread at what he would discover. He felt his nostrils flaring and that triggered recognition; smell, the least developed of all his senses, the reason why he had not been able to pinpoint Marianne's killer. Smell.

An odour was shifting gently through the room, caught on the subtle movements of air caused by the heat from the torches. The primal part of his brain kicked into gear, generating memories before he had even identified the source: the adrenalin, wild, wild action and then the rush of terror that was so all consuming it could only come from one source. The stinking, zoo-cage smell of them.

"Fomorii." The word was on his lips before the thought had found purchase in his head. It appeared to be a word of power, for in the instant that followed, very many things happened at once: there was a rushing through the chamber like a mighty wind; the smell grew suddenly choking; his eyes snapped open to reveal faces frozen in disbelief; and movement, all around, so rapid his eyes at first couldn't focus on it, like the shadows in the room were breathing.

The Walpurgis was framed in his field of vision, hanging in that single moment like everything else in the room. Church took in the seething red eyes, which glowed brighter, as if fanned by the breeze, the wide-brimmed hat, the tattered black rags of his body. And in the next instant they started to come apart. Scarlet lines were being drawn across the figure. A section across the arm here, across the torso there, underlining the head, pointing up the waist. Spaces appeared between the segments; a hallucinogenic moment filled with fascination. The Walpurgis was falling apart.

He snapped from the moment as if someone had punched him in the face. The room was in turmoil. The occupants dashed here and there searching for an exit as dark shapes moved lethally amongst them. For only the briefest time, Church focused on the remains of the Walpurgis scattered across the floor before him, consumed by the immensity of what had been snatched away from him; wondering how his future life had been changed by that one moment.

And then he was moving instinctively, just as some heavy object whistled past his ear. One of his fellow passengers with tentacles where his face should be lay in chunks under his feet. He skidded on the remains before finding his balance, propelling himself toward the place where he had entered the secret chamber.

The Fomorii were all around, moving so quickly it was impossible for him to estimate how many of them there were.

His thoughts were cut short by a heavy axe that splintered into the wooden wall next to his head. Thinking would be the end of him; he gave himself wholly over to instinct. The chaos of fighting bodies, flashing weapons and striking limbs became a series of frozen instants through which he could dart and dive. All his reactions had improved immeasurably in recent times, more than just learning from experience; it was the Blue Fire, or Destiny, or whatever he wanted to call it. He was changing.

He dodged another Fomorii attack that increasingly appeared to be directed towards him. The Tuatha Dé Danann were fighting back ferociously. Church slid towards the entrance through a stinking, poisonous grue washing across the floor. But it was a solid wall, and he had no idea what Baccharus had done to make it accessible.

The stink and shadow overwhelmed him before he glimpsed any hint of movement; then he realised an axe was swinging down with such force it would likely cleave him in two. Reacting instantly, his hand was on his sword, whipping it up sharply. The blade just caught the handle of the axe at such an angle that it managed to deflect the strike slightly, but the impact jarred his bones so much he thought his teeth were coming out of his head. He went down on one knee. The Fomor was already raising the axe for the killing blow.

A flashing motion crossed the beast's throat and its thick, stinging blood came gushing out. Church threw himself out of the way at the last moment, watching as it sizzled into the wooden floor.

Baccharus stepped forward as the creature slumped down, wiping a small, sharp blade. "Now, quickly." He made a hand motion and muttered, and the wall became like water.

Church was just about to dive through when a figure burst out of the shimmering wall, knocking him to the ground. Others followed, and in a second he and Baccharus were surrounded. They were not Fomorii, but they were misshapen, lithe and reptilian, with scales and slit eyes. *The Malignos*, Church guessed. As they huddled around, bending over him with forked tongues darting, he felt so destabilised the only thought in his head was that they smelled like wet grass.

He saw a glint of teeth, sharp talons, and then the circle of them parted and in stepped a maliciously gleeful figure.

"Now we shall find a balance for old wrongs," Callow said sardonically.

The voice sounded like the rustle of brown paper just beyond the window, where only the sea spray lived. Ruth had been dozing intermittently on the bunk, but she woke sharply when the familiar tones insidiously infected her drifting mind with memories of cells and chains and torture. Throwing open the windows to the crashing waves of a burgeoning storm, she frightened the owl, which fluttered upward towards the deck like the ghost of a bird in the gloomy night. Yet its words stayed in her head like a bad taste: "The war has begun."

A tremor ran through her; a premonition, perhaps. She riffled in the chest and came up with a long, thin dagger, ideal for poisonous court intrigue, but little use in any fair fight. But it was easy to secrete upon herself, and she had other weapons for confrontation, locked away in her brain. An insurance policy, nothing else.

Her familiar's warning could have meant nothing at that time, but she thought she ought to discuss it with Baccharus at least. Yet as she made her way to the door she heard an unidentifiable sound without that brought a shiver to her spine. She rocked briefly on the balls of her feet, then hurried back to the bunk, glancing round for somewhere to hide. Not so long ago she would have dismissed her instinct as stupid and childish; now she trusted it implicitly. She realised there was no worthwhile hiding place in the cramped chamber. She flung open the windows again. Beneath her the waves crashed crazily, topped with white surf. The boat dipped and rose sharply. Lightning crackled along the horizon as the storm rushed towards them.

A slim wooden spur ran around the boat, slightly below the level of the window. It was slick with spray, barely wide enough to get a toehold, but an oily rope stretched above from which members of the crew could hang if they needed to make repairs.

Don't be stupid! the rational side of her brain yelled at her. The ship rolled from side to side. *You'll be off there in a second.* And if she fell into the tossing sea, she would be lost in a moment. No one would even know she was overboard.

She looked back at the door. The strange noises, both rumbling and slithering at the same time, were closing on it. Steeling herself, she launched a leg out of the window, clutching at the rope and swung on to the ledge. With her other foot, she kicked the windows shut.

This is insanity. You really have lost it. But the warnings sounded like the faint, dying voice of the old Ruth, who had been supplanted by someone smarter, braver, more in control.

Outside the comfort of the cabin, the full fury of the night assailed her. The spray lashed against her like ice bullets, while the ship bucked on waves that appeared to grow fiercer the instant she stepped outside. Bracing her feet against the spur, she hung on as if she were about to rappel down the side. Self-preservation took over all thought processes; nothing concerned her beyond the strength of her arms and the intensity of her grip, on which her whole life depended.

Through the smeared panes, she could just make out the golden-suffused interior of the cabin. It looked warm and comforting, and safe.

She leaned over to get a better look and had to fight to prevent herself sliding off the rail. Steadying herself with one hand on the sopping boards, she tried again, just as the door eased open. Through it came a shadow with substance that still made her gorge rise however many times she saw it. The Fomorii were onboard.

After the shock, her initial thought was for Church. She prayed that however the Fomorii had got on, they had focused their attentions on the upper decks where the Tuatha Dé Danann were, and not surprised Church in the dark below.

The Fomorii swept into the cabin and turned everything over. The smashing and rending should have alerted someone, but when no one came after a full five minutes of destruction, Ruth feared the worst.

Suddenly she thought that they might see her through the window. She pushed herself back a little too animatedly, throwing her careful balance awry; both feet slipped off the rail. For an instant she was like a cartoon character, frantically scrambling for purchase on the side of the boat, her feet kicking over the drop into the waves that clamoured for her.

Her toes slid and slid, and then she dropped. The arm that clung on to the rope took the full force of her weight, jerking her like a puppet. Fiery pain shot through her tendons and muscles into her armpit. Her fingers felt like they were going to snap; they slipped around the rope, barely holding. Wildly, she lurched out with the hand that had been leaning against the boards, missed, tried again, missed.

All she could see was wet wood and spray and the hungry waves below. Her fingers slipped a little more, barely holding on now. An unbearable heat was burning in her knuckles.

Finally her free hand caught hold, but she was still hanging tight against the boards, slamming into them with every roll of the ship. Any second now, she would be knocked off.

Four months ago, it would have been too much of an effort to save herself: too much pain, not enough desire. She would have hung there until her knuckles finally gave way, feeling the skin strip from her fingers as they slid down the rope, and then the long drop into the hard, cold, suffocating depths.

But she *was* a different person; her suffering at the hands of the Fomorii had seen to that. Somehow, for all the agony, it had brought out the best of her, given her a reason to live beyond all else; a dichotomy too great for her to ponder.

With tremendous willpower, she clamped her fingers tight on the rope. Flexing her muscles, she rocked back and forth, bouncing off the boat, but with a bigger and bigger space between her and the wood until she could bring her feet up to plant them on the side. Then it was only a matter of inching up slowly until she found the rail again.

Finally she could peer through the window to see the cabin was empty. Shaking from the shock, she managed to hook the window open with her foot before swinging in on the rope to land hard on the bunk. It winded her, but she felt exhilarated at her victory over death.

It faded too quickly, to be replaced by that familiar unease. Cautiously, she approached the door. No sound came from beyond except the usual creak of the timbers. How many Fomorii were there on board? And where were they now?

After a moment's reflection, she gripped the dagger tightly, eased open the door and slipped out into the dark corridor.

The mists had a disturbingly cloying texture that felt like wet cotton wool slowly being drawn across the skin. For Veitch, that wasn't the worst thing, although it was unnerving enough. Nor was it the chill that reached deep into his bones, even though the air itself was not particularly cold. It wasn't even the way the mists occasionally cleared to reveal brief glimpses of a terrifying scene, different every time it happened, too quick to ever settle on any detail, but enough for the subconscious mind to know it was shocking. It was the feeling of someone constantly at his shoulder, about to draw icy fingers down his neck, but whenever he turned round, there was nothing but the subdued echoes of his footsteps.

His destabilisation began the moment he stepped into the Grim Lands and discovered the door through which he had passed was no longer there. How would he ever find his way back?

But there were many things to do before he even had to think about getting back, and it was possible he might not have to worry about it at all, so, true to his nature, he simply put it out of his mind.

Occasionally the mists cleared enough to provide a view of the lowering gunmetal sky. Oppressive enough, he also glimpsed black shapes sweeping across it; birds, he guessed, but of a size that made him think of pterodactyls. Perhaps it was their unnerving silence, but there was something immensely threatening about them, although he never saw them in enough detail to decide if they were raptors. But that gave him pause. If he was in the land of the dead, were they dead too? Or did the Grim Lands have its own life? Dead life.

Thinking about it made his head hurt. He wished Tom had given some directions. A *Rough Guide of the Grim Lands*, with a nice tourist map. Avoid this place, especially after dark. You'll get a good welcome here. And here you'll find Shavi.

But he was on his own, as always. He went for the simplest option: keep walking and something would turn up; then adjust your path accordingly. He just wished that terrible feeling of something at his heels would go away.

The uneven terrain alternated between hard rock and shale. What he could make out of the landscape was featureless, with no markers for his journey there or back. Nor was there anything to judge the passage of time, so it was impossible to tell how soon after he entered the Grim Lands that he heard the noises. At first it was like scratching, as if a dog were trying to claw something out from beneath the shale. This came and went for a while, continuously matching his progress, and then, gradually, it mutated into the sound of footsteps, echoing near at hand, then far away, then disappearing completely. He had to accept there was something out there and it was tracking him.

His hand went to his sword for comfort, though he knew it would be useless in that place. He tried not to get distracted; head down, keep going, a mantra he repeated over and over.

And then, as if they had been commanded, the mists parted and a figure emerged from them. It was a woman, her face blank, her skin a pallid grey, clad in an ankle-length, colourless dress of some harsh material. Long blonde hair hung limply around her face. Her head was held uncomfortably towards one shoulder and she moved awkwardly, as if her limbs were not used to any activity. She paused a few feet away from Veitch, swaying slightly.

"Hello?" he said tentatively. A beat had started to pulse deep in his brain.

Instead of turning her head, she inched her whole body round until she was facing him. He expected to see some kind of terror, some severe intelligence in her eyes, but they were cold and dead and that was even worse. Slowly, she beckoned for him to follow her.

For a second or two, Veitch hesitated as Tom's words briefly tapped a warning: the dead hate the living. They were jealous and bitter. Yet he could see no threat in her, and following her was preferable to wandering aimlessly; any presence, however strange, was a respite from the awful sense of foreboding gathering all around.

"I'm looking for someone." His voice, so vibrant and full of life, sounded jarringly out of place. He modulated it so it sounded less expressive. "A friend."

She turned towards him with those eyes that showed no glimmer of thought, gave nothing away, then shuffled back round silently and continued slowly on her way.

"So, are you ignoring me? Or can you talk? Who knows what the bleedin' rules are in this place?" He eased a little as the minutes passed without event and slowly he warmed to the sound of his voice, like a flame in the deep, dark night. "I hope this isn't a wild goose chase. For all I know, you've got no sense left at all. You're just a shape or something. And I'm acting like a right twat talking to you. No change there, then." He smiled to himself. "This isn't as bad as I thought. The old bastard built it up into some big, bleedin' fright. Thought I'd be fighting for my life the moment I crossed over here. And look at us. Having a nice stroll. Shame about the scenery." He paused thoughtfully. "Still better than Greenwich, though." His chuckle rolled out through the mists, eventually coming back to him distorted into the growl of a wild beast.

They continued until the ground sloped downwards and became littered at first with stones, and then with large boulders. Veitch had to pick his way through them carefully, but the woman moved effortlessly, almost oblivious to the obstacles.

"You really better not be taking me for a ride." He clambered over a rock with lethal-looking fractured edges, as sharp as razors.

Beyond the rocks, passage became even steeper and it was necessary to take a winding route down to avoid careering out of control. Veitch was disturbed to realise his journey was like a distorted analogue of the landscape he had left behind in the real world: the flat summit, the thickly forested rim, the sweeping hillside; instead of lush vegetation there were only dead land and dead people. He wasn't taken with many thoughts of reasoning or perception, but at that moment one came to him that excited him with its novelty. Perhaps all the words—T'ir n'a n'Og, the Grim Lands, and whatever lay beyond—were just like his own world in layout, only altered to fit whatever rules of the place abided. It was a big notion, and there were too many questions building up behind it to consider it for too long, but he felt a remarkable sense of achievement that he had thought it in the first place.

As he made his way down the hillside, the mist cleared a little. What he saw wasn't as disturbing as on the summit, but it still brought troubling questions. At one juncture, he seemed to be looking out over London, only it was transformed by shadows shifting along the streets with a life of their own. Later he saw a Spitfire sweeping across the sky, and then a tribe of fierce men and women in furs and leather.

And in one particularly upsetting moment, he even saw himself, or thought he did, but it was so fleeting he couldn't be sure. Yet in that half moment, he was overcome with a consuming horror. The expression he saw on his face had the look of a man who had peered into the depths of Hell and saw it was even worse than he could possibly imagine; broken, filled with despair, and more, an almost inhuman self-loathing. It made him sick to his stomach at the thought of what that vision meant, but try as he might, he couldn't put it out of his head.

It troubled him enough to lose his common sense briefly. Suddenly overcome by doubt that his guide was taking him no closer to Shavi, he hurried forward and grabbed her arm. He regretted it instantly. The flesh felt as dry and lifeless as sandpaper. At his touch, a tremor ran through the woman and she turned once again to fix that blank gaze on him. Once more he tried to see some meaning in those implacable eyes, but there was only a defiant idiocy there. He retreated quickly and didn't speak to her again for the next half hour.

By then his thoughts had started to move on to more questions about his surroundings. Did all the dead stay in that place? If so, why was it so empty after the long spread of human existence? Or was it like a waiting room before the departed moved on to somewhere else?

"Maybe this is it, just you and me, and everyone else has already passed on," he mused. "The only living boy in the Grim Lands and his dead girlfriend."

"Oh, there are more." He jerked in shock at the sound of her voice, like a file on metal.

"You *can* talk." All his carefully constructed conceptions were shifting under his feet. His mind raced to get back on track; he was thinking, *If she can talk, what else can she do?* but by then it was too late.

The remaining mist swept away, although he could not feel any breeze. It was an eerie sight, billowing across the bleak landscape like a reversed film. As it did so, she was turning to face him once again, only this time she was fundamentally changed. Her posture had become more upright, but it was most evident in her eyes, no longer dead, no longer stupid.

He thought: *She tricked me.*

The tinge of a cruel smile appeared. "Welcome to the Grey Lands. May you never leave."

She made an expansive gesture. Hesitantly, he turned to look, although every fibre of him was screaming that he didn't want to see.

They were behind him. Dead people, as far as the eye could see, line upon line, column upon column, stretched across the grey stone land beneath the grey sky. Figures leeched of colour, of expression, of body language, bereft of life in all its signifiers. But not bereft of emotion. Although their faces were impassive, he could see it in their hateful eyes. A thousand, thousand unblinking stares radiating darkness, silently roaring that they wanted to tear him limb from limb; to punish him for the crime of living. The planetary weight of their gaze made him feel sick.

As he scanned them slowly, he began to understand. Here were the ones who had not yet moved on, but also the ones who *could not* move on; those trapped by hatred or fear or shock. He came across the face of Ruth's uncle, whom he had shot down in cold blood, and felt a terrible, crushing guilt. To understand the awful repercussions of the murder had been traumatic enough, but to be faced with the cold, accusing eyes of his victim was infinitely worse. He quickly looked away, knowing he would never forget what he had seen in that face. But there were others he had seen slain during the long, hard days of his youth, when he first started to move with the wrong kind. The ones nearest were unknown to him, but he could still read the harshness of their existence in the lines on their faces, the sour turn of their mouths.

It was a strange, hanging moment of complete silence; he was looking up at a tidal wave the instant before it crashed down. And then they moved.

Veitch launched himself across the rocky ground as the wave broke. In the instant of his turning he had glimpsed them all shifting as one, a single grey beast of hatred and retribution bearing down on him with outstretched arms, wide, staring eyes and silently screaming mouths. A million dead, hunting. If he survived, he knew it was a sight that would haunt him for as long as he lived.

As he passed the treacherous spirit that had guided him to that spot, she spat like a wildcat and lashed out with sharp nails that raked open the side of his face. Without breaking his stride, he cursed and returned the blow with his sword. Her bloodless arm fell to the ground.

The fear and adrenalin took conscious thought from his head. Instinctively he recognised his only hope was to run faster and longer. But could the dead tire? And he had already been pushed to his limits by the Night Rider.

The ground passed in a blur beneath his feet, the featureless, rocky landscape streamed on either side; he was locked into the beat of his heart, the surge of his blood, the pump of his muscles. Through it all he could feel the weight of them pressing at his back, just a hand's-width from him, constantly reaching. One wrong step and they would have him.

And he ran.

The silence was the worst thing. His ears told him there was nothing there, seductively teasing him to stop, but the primal part of him sensed them, responded to them as his ancestors would have done. He had reached the foot of the hill, crossed the first two miles of a flat plain that reached to the horizon. But he was starting to tire. The constant pounding on the hard rock sent spikes of pain from his knees into his groin and a knot had formed in his gut. Fire was creeping out in a web across his lungs.

He slowed, almost imperceptibly, but it was enough. Some fluttering thing brushed the back of his jacket. He propelled himself forward to escape it, but he didn't have the energy to maintain the spurt. When he slowed this time, the touch on his jacket was as sharp as a knife. He pressed forward again. Stars burst across his vision. Winding down, nearly over. A pinching sensation seared his shoulder like red hot pokers. The hairs on the back of his neck were prickling from nearly contact.

He would never give up. Death or glory.

The rock fell away beneath his feet. For one frightening moment he was pedalling thin air, and then he reconnected with the ground hard, skidding on his heels down a pebbled scree slope, windmilling his arms to maintain his balance. Dark walls rushed up around him and shadows clustered far below. A fissure of some kind, invisible until he was upon it.

Gravity dragged him faster, barely able to keep his balance. A boulder leapt out of nowhere, but he had no control of his momentum to avoid it. He clipped it and did a forward roll in the air, crashing down on to the stones and shale, twenty knives in his back, ripping his flesh. Faster and faster, the shadows looming up, impossible to tell what dangers they hid. His head slammed against the rocks and he lost consciousness for the briefest instant. He awakened to realise the sucking shadows were close at hand. The force propelled him over a rock ledge into the heart of them.

He awoke in so much pain he was convinced something bad was broken. Blood slicked his clothes from a deep gash on his head and numerous other cuts across his body. He wiped a puddle from his eye and loosed the splatter with a flick of his wrist. Cautiously, he tested his limbs. Apart from a searing pain in his ribs, he appeared in one piece; he guessed that was probably bad bruising rather than a break.

After the initial stupefaction, he came to awareness sharply, jumping to his feet to flee his pursuers. He was alone on a flat stone floor. High overhead he could see a sliver of grey sky and, as his eyes adjusted to the gloom, the shapes of the dead moving down the walls of the fissure towards him.

Exhausted and brittle from the pain, he headed along the floor of the fissure into the dark.

It continued much further than he imagined. At the far end he found stone that had definitely been worked into blocks. It formed a doorway around a black hole leading into the ground. With the relentless grey shapes drawing in on him, he had no choice: he dived in.

Inside he was surprised to find more worked stone lining the walls, floor and ceiling. He had no idea who was responsible—surely not the dead—but it gave him hope it might lead to a way out. Fumbling for the matches he always carried in his pocket, he struck one and saw the walls were covered with primitive paintings, inexplicable in design but which resonated uneasily with him. The match also illuminated a dead torch. It was dry as a bone and lit quickly.

Glancing back, he could just make out hints of movement at the other end of the fissure. There was no time to proceed with caution. His footsteps bounced off the walls of the tunnel as he ran.

After five minutes the tunnel led into an enormous room that must have been carved from the bedrock and then lined with stone blocks. The ceiling was lost in the shadows far beyond the reach of his torch. The effort that must have gone into its construction stunned him: the wall paintings were now the size of three men, and there were carved effigies all around, squat, misshapen figures with no human characteristics, and tall, spindly forms that loomed over him like grotesque children's doodles. He couldn't help slowing to a walk to mask the echoes of his feet; suddenly he didn't want to make any sound that would bring attention to him. The scale of the place suggested no human sensibilities, nor did the jarring lines of the alien and unsettling architecture. It reminded him of a temple. Did the dead have their own gods? Did they pray for relief from the bitterness of their grey reality?

The grey shapes were again visible where he had entered the cavernous chamber. He hurried on, hoping he hadn't taken himself into a cul-de-sac.

But the more he progressed into that place, the more he felt an oppressive dread, even worse than the feeling when he had first entered the Grim Lands. Something was out there, lurking in the shadows, perhaps, or even further afield: just beyond the spiderweb veil that separated the worlds. Close enough to reach out and swallow him whole.

Do the dead have their own gods?

He couldn't shake the question from his head.

Before he could consider skirting the perimeter in search of an exit, he found himself at a slightly raised area. At the centre of it was a short column on which stood a foot-high egg, its surface swirling with shades of sapphire and emerald. The moment he laid eyes on it, a part of him told him to avoid it, keep moving by. But there was something hypnotic about the thing that sapped his natural caution. He took a step on to the dais and realised obliquely it was even more than that: the egg was actively blanketing his fears to draw him in; he could feel it tinkering on the edge of his consciousness. The time when he could have ignored it had already past, and so he found himself approaching the column with trepidation.

Three feet from the egg he passed through some invisible boundary. The air wavered briefly and then he was inside a bubble where everything was green-tinged, the chamber beyond unreal, all sounds muffled. The egg was pulsing slightly, although it was certainly not alive in any true meaning of that word.

Tentatively, he reached out. The air itself gathered a charge, humming like an electricity pylon. A second later he felt a dull jolt and the bubble transformed. He was in the centre of a three-dimensional view, so real he might as well have been amongst the ruins of Urquhart Castle on the banks of Loch Ness, looking down at himself being charged by the Questing Beast. The detail left no doubt that it was a true view, across time and space. Had it been plucked from his mind, he wondered? And if so, why that moment? He had a vague answer to that: it was the moment when he felt he had really, truly failed, not only everyone else, but also himself.

The repercussions of what he was seeing began to worm its way through his mind. On a hunch, he thought of Ruth and what she was doing at that moment. The 3-D view shifted and he was on the rolling deck of a boat in the middle of a nighttime storm. The rain was flying horizontally, the sails flapping so wildly it was almost deafening. A figure crept in the shadow of the raised cover to the hold, its long hair flattened to its head and back. As he watched, Ruth looked around, her face grimly determined. The first thing Veitch noticed was how much her features had changed in the short time they had been apart. A hardness made her appear, if not a little older, then certainly more mature; some of the innocence that softened her features had gone.

Seeing her brought a damp wave of emotion inside him, but in an odd way it invigorated him too; here was all the motivation he needed. Focusing his mind, he pushed Ruth out of it and thought of Shavi.

There was only the briefest period of transition before the image around him showed a strange, hopeless landscape of yellowing grass and twisted, leafless trees. Shavi sat on a stone box of some kind, staring deeply towards the horizon. Veitch couldn't tell if there was anything wrong with him or if he was simply lost in thought.

"That's a start," he muttered. "Now show me how I get to him."

He was now looking down on himself standing at the egg, only the shadows all around had cleared to reveal several tunnels leading off. The angle of his view highlighted one directly ahead.

Cautiously he walked backwards until he stepped out of the bubble with a faint pop. Away from the magical cocoon, he felt suddenly exposed and hurried towards the tunnel, pausing at the threshold to look back. Curiously, the dead did not appear to have pursued him; he would have expected some of them to have arrived by that time. Something else was in the chamber, though far away. He could hear the dim echoes of the movement of an enormous shape. With an involuntary shudder, he hurried along the tunnel.

Laura lit a small fire in the corner of the warehouse while the Bone Inspector foraged for food. The last time he came back with cans for just the one meal. She berated him enough that he wouldn't make the mistake again, stressing that a choice between meatballs resembling glutinous chunks of mud and fatty steak pie filling was really no choice at all.

In the cavernous warehouse, the fire provided little warmth, particularly at night when the chill radiated up out of the concrete floor. For some reason she felt the cold more than she ever had.

She pulled the packing crate closer so she was almost on top of the flames and rubbed her hands together. She found it amazing she still hadn't given in to despair. The Fomorii now appeared to be everywhere in the city. They'd climbed up into the roof of the building to peer through broken slates across the capital. There were swarming black shapes as far as the eye could see. The sheer volume was sickening, drawing on the basic human revulsion for anything insectile. At times they would disappear to some lair, possibly beneath the ground, in an eerie, silent exodus. The Bone Inspector had suggested fleeing through the deserted streets at that time, but the beasts were never gone for long and the thought of being trapped as they swarmed out of the sewers filled Laura with dread.

In the firelight, her skin looked even greener. Earlier she had cut her wrist on a rusty nail. The blood—green blood—had flowed freely for a second before performing a startling u-turn on the back of her hand, returning to the wound, where it proceeded to seal it as if it had never been there.

The Bone Inspector had stared in amazement, but nothing shocked her any more. She'd died and come back; after that anything paled into insignificance.

She was a freak in a world that no longer made any sense. What was the point in considering it for even an instant? Instead, her thoughts were for the others: Church, of course, Shavi, Ruth, Tom, even Veitch. She missed them in a way she never thought she'd miss anyone. More than anything, she wanted to be sitting round a roaring campfire in the cold night, laughing, teasing, mocking; the company of good friends made life right.

The army of Fomorii on every side told her it would probably never happen. Samhain was coming up hard, the world was going to hell, and they were scattered God knows where.

She wondered what was to become of her; what was to become of all of them.

The rope bit roughly into Church's wrists and his joints ached from having his arms dragged so tightly behind him. He'd been in this position before, looking up at a sneering Callow pacing maniacally and triumphantly back and forth, and it had made him sick to his stomach then; of course, on that occasion Callow hadn't looked like someone had injected printer's ink into his veins. Now his nightmarish appearance made the situation even worse, as if Church had found his way into a Goya painting.

The Malignos kept to the shadows—they'd extinguished several torches to feel more comfortable—and the Fomorii were now nowhere to be seen. Baccharus was next to him, bound just as tightly, but the rest of the room's occupants had been dragged somewhere else, out of sight, possibly out of the chamber.

It was obvious what his own eventual fate would be, but Callow was determined to get some kind of payback for the suffering that had been heaped upon him; agonies which he blamed on Church and the others, but which had come only from his own will.

"These are the ways we live our life," Callow was saying, not making much sense any more. "In fear of this and in fear of that, never quite knowing the wherewithal and the whywithal. It makes us broken, like dogs in the yard. But you wouldn't know about that, would you?" He turned and spat in Church's direction, the lamps of his lidless eyes bright and terrible.

"Take a stress pill, Callow." It was childish, but Church couldn't resist it, even knowing the reaction he would get.

Callow hovered for a long moment, then threw himself forward wildly to swing a vicious kick into Church's gut, as if he were planting a football the length of the pitch. Church snapped shut, retching, before two of the Malignos ran forward to haul him back up. The pain was so acute he cursed his stupidity, fearing something had ruptured and his stomach was now filling up with blood.

"Violence is unnecessary," Baccharus interjected gently. "You fail to see we have a common enemy."

"Oh, you're *so* superior," Callow mocked in a pathetic singsong voice. "I have no friends, I have no enemies. That makes it easy to understand how things work. No surprises." He bent down until his face was inches from Church's, the rotten-meat reek of his breath blooming, his features hideously distorted by the tear blur in Church's eyes. "You and your filthy little followers destroyed everything. I had plans for my life. I had a way out of the misery of my existence. Unlike you and your favoured brood, there have been no opportunities in my life. No pleasant acts of chance that lead me on to the sunlit uplands. It has been hard toil and suffering. And when I found a way out of that, you spoiled it for me."

"Quisling," Church said through gritted teeth. "You tried to sell out all of humanity just to get some grubby little advantage for yourself."

"You say that like it's a bad thing." Callow jumped back, his eyes rolling like a madman. "Life is brutal and short and we need to take what we can to make ourselves comfortable before the jaws of night close around us forever."

"Fine. As long as no one else gets hurt in the process."

"Oh, why qualify it? Will it matter you made a few people cry when the worms are crawling in and the worms are crawling out?"

"Look at yourself, Callow. Where's your self-analysis?" The sharp pain had turned to a dull throbbing. "Has that philosophy worked for you? At all?"

"There is only hope," Baccharus interjected, "if you look beyond your petty concerns, to the needs of your fellow Fragile Creatures, to the needs of all things of existence. Everything is—"

"*You* should not preach goodwill to your fellow man." Callow danced around him, but couldn't bring himself to strike out.

"So you've teemed up with those things now?" Church nodded towards the Malignos. "Are they the only ones left who'll have you?"

"The Malignos recognise the opportunities for personal gain in any situation. They always loved their hoards of gold. And their human flesh, of course."

"But you're helping the Fomorii again, after all they've done to you!"

"I may not be able to forgive, dear boy, but I am incisive enough not to antagonise the eventual winners."

Church snorted bitter laughter. "You think they're going to take over like any other invader? They're going to wipe out everything, you mad bastard! They're not interested in gold, or any other creature comforts." He laughed again at the stupid pun. "They're driven by the need to eradicate all of existence. They're a force of nature. A hurricane—"

"Oh, well, you've won me over. Of course I'll help you," Callow mocked.

He wandered over to converse with the Malignos. Church seized the opportunity to talk to Baccharus. "How did the Fomorii manage to get on board the ship without anyone knowing? I thought it was completely under Manannan's control?"

"The power of the Heart of Shadows is growing. The Night Walkers can achieve things they never would have been able to do before."

"Do you think this might actually motivate your people to do something about it?" Church asked acidly.

"It may already be too late for that."

"What do you mean?"

"If the Night Walkers can strike at the heart of Wave Sweeper, they can strike anywhere. They might have already launched their assault on the Court of High Regard."

"If only you'd done something before." Church caught the negativity before it spread. "The first thing we have to do is get out of here." He looked over at Callow, who was performing a mad little dance around the Malignos. "Before that bastard slits my throat. Or worse."

"Then you are fortunate to have friends in low places."

The voice was barely audible, but Church recognised it instantly. It felt as if a mouse was scurrying around his hands. Marik Bocat was hard at work severing his bonds with a tiny implement that occasionally pricked his flesh. A surge of hope rose in his chest, but he kept it from reaching his face.

After a few moments, Callow returned, loping like a wolf. "The arrangements have been made." His eyes slithered from side to side while he rubbed his hands oleaginously. "Once this filthy little skiff has fallen, then it's the turn of your happy little palace of dreams."

Church felt Baccharus stiffen beside him at the news that the Fomorii had not yet moved on the High Court of the Tuatha Dé Danann. Still hope. Always hope. "What now, Callow?" he said. "Is this where you get your kicks?"

Callow slipped his hand into his threadbare jacket and pulled out a knife whose blade was smeared with dried, brown blood. Church tried not to look at it, but he knew it was the blood of his friends. Callow weighed it in his hand, smiled.

His bonds gave suddenly. He kept his face emotionless, his arm muscles taut. *Pace yourself*, he thought. *Wait until he bends forward*. His eyes flickered towards the Malignos; they were too far away to stop him if he was quick enough.

Callow struck like a snake. Church didn't even see the blow, but he felt his forehead rip open and hot blood bubble down into his eyes. He cursed, threw his head back, but Callow, in his crazed state, was sweeping in with eager blows. Church dodged one, but another took his cheek open. The next one might hit his jugular.

He threw himself forward at the same time as did Baccharus, whose own bonds had been sliced. They piled into Callow, who folded up like a sheet on a line, and then their impetus carried him with them as they drove towards the door. The Malignos exploded into a frenzied activity of snapping jaws and flashing limbs. One of their talons caught Church's other cheek and it burst open as cleanly as if it had been sliced with Callow's knife. Their speed was frightening. With reptilian sinuousness they had swept round to attack Church's and Baccharus's exposed backs, but by that time the two of them had reached the door. Baccharus shouted a word, twisted his left hand and the wall shimmered into the waterfall.

They rolled into the corridor with Callow screaming before them, his face contorted with rage. Church silenced him with a sharp headbutt; not wholly necessary, but it made him feel good. Then he grabbed Callow by the collar and hurled him into the path of the approaching Malignos. They fell backwards in time for Baccharus to seal the door.

"That will not keep them for long," he said.

"Doesn't matter." Church fingered the sword that Callow, in his arrogance had failed to remove. "We need to raise the alarm—"

The words died in his throat as the ship came to a sudden, lurching stop. Baccharus's expression told him all he needed to know. The Fomorii had seized control.

chapter eleven
grim lands, grey hearts

It was a graveyard, though why there should be a graveyard in the land of the dead made no sense to Veitch at all. It stretched as far as the eye could see: stone crosses, gleaming white like fresh-picked bones, or chipped and mildewed, some standing proud, others bowed and broken as if they had been forced from the earth; single standing stones and ancient cairns; mausoleums styled with fine carvings of angels; rough built stone tombs. Mist drifted languorously at knee height. The sheer weight of the monuments brought an air of severe melancholy.

As he emerged from the tunnel into the city of the dead, the view triggered all his primal fear of death. His more immediate fears were more prosaic: what if each of those graves and tombs and mausoleums contained one of the dead, ready to rise up the moment he walked amongst them? His heart beat faster.

There was no alternative. He placed a foot next to the first grave and waited for a hand to grab his ankle. Nothing. He proceeded to the next one.

After several minutes the tension was starting to tell. It felt like walking through a minefield. He couldn't let his concentration slide for a moment; if the dead were present, they would choose the moment he least expected to strike, when he was in the midst of the graves with nowhere to turn. He looked around slowly; there *was* nowhere to run. A million graves, packed so tight he could barely move amongst them.

The direction he had chosen—from the view presented to him by the egg—proceeded past one of the largest mausoleums in the vicinity. It haunted the edges of his vision and he found himself drawn back to it continually. Its size made it out of place in the surroundings, but there was another aspect that did not feel *right*. As he approached it, his gaze snapped back, and back again, on the heavy, marbled door, waiting for a crack to appear, on the way the mist appeared to be drawn towards it. A few feet away he was convinced he could hear something dimly scrabbling within, like an animal, but not.

When he was parallel with it, a small droplet of sweat trickled down his back, like water off a glacier. Even when he had passed by, his anxiety did not diminish, and he could feel it on his back for many moments after.

Eventually, his attention was drawn by what appeared to be a giant crow, sitting on a low, stone box. Shavi had his eyes fixed on the horizon, as Veitch had seen him in the vision presented by the egg. It didn't seem right that he was so still. He wanted to call out to his friend, but the thought of his voice, loud and hard in that place of whispers, filled him with dread.

And so he hurried on, his heart beginning to soar, hardly daring to raise his expectations. His mate, his pal, his buddy, his best friend; alive.

As he neared the unmoving form, he finally found the courage to speak. Shavi's name drifted across the final feet between them, as dry and insubstantial as the spindly trees that poked up amongst the graves. At first there was no response. Veitch's heart started to beat faster: it was all another stupid game, dangle the prize, then snatch it away at the last minute, laughing at how foolish the *Fragile Creatures* were.

But then a shiver ran through the hunched, dark form, as subtle as wind on long grass.

"Shavi?" Veitch repeated hopefully.

Another tremor. Slowly Shavi's head began to turn. Veitch caught his breath. Would he see something terrible in that face? The eyes of someone driven insane by the experience of dying?

Shavi's limbs moved with the gradual adjustment of a man waking from a deep sleep, and when he did look round, Veitch was relieved to see his old friend as he had always looked. Shavi blinked long and slowly, squinting slightly as he focused on Veitch.

"I was having the strangest dream." His voice was strained, as if he hadn't spoken for a long time.

Veitch ran forward, beating down his surging emotions, and awkwardly put a celebratory arm round Shavi's shoulders before quickly pulling back. "You're all right, mate. It's all going to be all right now."

Shavi smiled faintly, brushed a lock of hair from Veitch's forehead. Veitch didn't flinch. As his waking became sharper, his attention was drawn to his surroundings. "Where are we?"

"Don't worry about it," Veitch said hastily. "I know it looks like the biggest bleedin' graveyard you've ever seen, but you're not dead, all right?"

Shavi's brow furrowed. "A graveyard? Is that what you are seeing?"

Now it was Veitch's turn to be puzzled. "Don't you?"

Shavi covered his eyes, then slowly ran his fingers through his long, black hair before letting them drop cautiously to his chest. He tentatively probed the area around his heart. "Callow. He stabbed me." He examined his fingers for any sign of blood. "The pain was . . . intense. Like needles being forced through my veins." He looked up at Veitch with panic flaring in his eyes. "He killed me."

"Calm down, mate—"

"Lee was here." He looked around wildly. "He brought me into the land of the dead—"

Veitch took his shoulders roughly. "Pull yourself together, pal. You're not dead. One of the freaks—the big, horny-headed bastard—he saved you. Well, not quite, but he kept you sort of half alive and half dead. I'm here to take you back."

"This is not still a dream?"

"I'm here. Hit me if you want. But I'll hit you back, you dim bastard."

Shavi smiled, calmed. "Just a different kind of dream, then."

"You can't wait to start talking bollocks, can you?" He helped Shavi to his feet. "We've got to get you back to your body—" Shavi stiffened. "Your body's not here."

Shavi thought about this for a moment, then nodded in understanding. "My essence has created this form to house it. There is so much to assimilate. You need to rejoin my essence to my body."

"We don't know how much longer you can carry on like this before you really do peg out."

Shavi took a few shaky steps, his legs quickly regaining their poise. "The others?"

"Tom's with me. Don't know where the others are exactly. I think they're fine."

"Ruth?"

"She's okay."

They looked at each other for a moment, then broke out in broad grins, the telepathy of old friends replacing the need for talk.

"Then," Shavi mused, "the question is, how do we return?"

Unsure, Veitch surveyed the cluttered landscape of cold stone. "I reckon we head back to the place where I came in, if we can find it. We'll find it," he added positively.

They had to walk single file to pick their way amongst the grave markers, but Veitch could still tell Shavi was distracted. "What's wrong?" he asked.

"I was thinking about Lee."

"Your boyfriend."

"When he died that night in Clapham, I thought I had seen the last of him. My heart was broken, but also I was consumed with guilt because I was sure I could have done something to save his life. When the spirits in Edinburgh sent him back to haunt me as the price I had to pay for gaining their secret knowledge . . . I was almost pleased." Veitch turned to stare at him, surprised by this new information. "It was terrible—psychologically, emotionally—but I felt I deserved it. And even at the point of my death, he was there, ushering me across the boundary for more suffering."

"So where is he now?"

"That is exactly what I was thinking. I do not really know what happened to me in the period that followed my death, but I do know that in some way I have come to terms with Lee's death, and my involvement in it. And now he is not here. It is almost as if the way I felt about myself turned *him* sour." He paused thoughtfully. "We make our own Hell, Ryan. In many ways, many times a day."

Veitch continued his measured pace. "You just be thankful you're shot of him."

The hand closed round his ankle with the speed of a striking snake. It took him a second or two to realise what was happening, his gaze running up and down the pale limb protruding from the rough, pebbly soil of the grave, and by then movement had erupted all around.

"Shavi!" he yelled, but the word choked in his throat at the shock of what he was seeing.

The ground was opening up in a million small upheavals, mini volcanoes of showering earth and stone. Across the vast graveyard, bodies were thrusting out on locked elbows, alien trees growing in time-lapse photography. Veitch, as brave as any man alive, felt his blood run cold.

In sickening silence they surged from every side. Hands clutched his arms, his hair, pulled at his jaw, slipped into his mouth. Odourless, stiff and dry, they dragged him down to the hard ground. He tried to see Shavi, but his friend had already been washed away in the tidal wave of bodies.

Even that thought was eradicated when he saw where they were dragging him: to the mausoleum that had haunted him from the moment he saw it.

It loomed up among the mists, only now its door hung agape and the interior was darker than anything he had ever seen before.

Tom smoked a joint as he watched the sun come up over Wandlebury Camp, but even the drugs couldn't take the edge off his anxiety. Veitch was sharp, a strategist, a warrior: there was no one else he could have despatched into the Grim Lands. Yet the decision was still a crushing weight on his heart. Despite his constant ferocity, Veitch was, to all intents and purposes, a child and the Grim Lands was the worst battlefield in the worst war in the history of the world. Tom winced at how he had fooled himself that his protégé was operating under free will. Veitch had no capacity to make a rational choice.

Some people have to see the big picture. Tom had utilised that mantra many times during his long life and it had kept the beast locked up on most occasions. But increasingly his guilt was getting out of the cage. He'd been around the Brothers and Sisters of Dragons too long. Why did they have to humanise him? How could he be a general sending the innocents off to war if he felt every death, every scratch?

Some people have to see the big picture. All of existence is at stake. Against that, no individual matters.

He sucked on the joint, then let out the draught without inhaling, spat and tamped out the hot end. He had taken on the role of teacher, an archetype demanded by the universe, but he didn't feel up to it at all. The others might see him as all-knowing, but in his heart he was the same romantic fool who had fallen asleep under the hawthorn tree in the Eildon Hills. Whenever anyone described him as a mythic hero, he felt faintly sick. A man. Weak and pathetic like all men, crippled by insecurities, guilts and fears. Not up to the task at all. But like all men he put on a brave face and pretended to the world he was the one for the job; it was a man thing, as old as time, and it involved pretending to yourself as much as everyone else.

But still, in his quiet moments, when he dared look into his heart, he knew. Not up to the job, Thomas. Not up to it at all. Smoke some more hashish.

He stood up just as Robertson was approaching fearfully from the shade of the house. A bruise marred his cheek from Veitch's attack. He glanced at the sun now beating down on the lawns before he dared speak, "Your friend—"

"I haven't got time for that now," Tom snapped. "Show me the stable block. I need some horse dung, some straw where a mare has slept, and then I need you to leave me alone for the next hour."

Robertson stared at him blankly.

"Don't ask any questions." Tom pushed by him. "Or I'll do to you what my good friend did."

Veitch was fighting like a berserker within seconds of being swamped by the wave of dead, a few limbs lopped off here, a skull or two split there. By the time the sword was knocked away from him, he was already aware how worthless it was.

He tried to yell Shavi's name to check his friend was okay, but dead fingers drove into his mouth like sticks blown off an old tree. Sandpapery hands crushed tight around his wrists and his legs, pulled at his head until he feared they were going to rip it off. He choked, saw stars, but still fought like a wild animal.

And the gaping black mouth of the mausoleum drew closer.

Dead hands passed Shavi from one to the other across the angry sea. It was impossible to get his bearings, or even to call out, and any retaliation was quickly stifled. From his occasional glimpses of Veitch he knew the dead were not treating him as roughly as his friend. Perhaps they considered him one of their own.

Veitch was thrown roughly into the mausoleum first. Shavi was pitched at head height into the dark after him. He skidded across the floor, knocking over Veitch, who was clambering to his feet in a daze.

Before he could say anything, Shavi noticed his pale hand was slowly turning grey. At the entrance only a thin crack of white mist and grey sky remained. As he threw himself forward, the door slammed shut with a resounding clang.

"Are you okay?" Veitch whispered.

Shavi felt a searching arm grab his sleeve, hauling the two of them together. "Bruised."

"Bastards." A pause. "Is this the best they can do? We'll be out of here in no time."

"How?"

A long silence. "How solid can this thing be?" Another pause. "It's not like it's meant to keep things *in*. We could jemmy the door—"

"Wait."

"What?"

"We are not in here alone."

"What do you mean?"

"Hush."

There came the sound of a large, slow-moving bulk dragging itself at the far end of the mausoleum.

"What the hell's *that*?" Unease strained Veitch's voice.

Shavi felt the hand leave his sleeve as Veitch scurried in the direction of the door. Several moments of scrabbling and grunting followed before he crawled back, panting and cursing.

Whatever else was in there was shifting towards them. Shavi had an image of something with only arms, dragging what remained of its body across the floor. He couldn't help but think it was hungry, probably hadn't been fed for a long time.

"I've still got my crossbow." The note of futility in Veitch's voice suggested he wasn't about to use it. "I thought this was just the land of the bleedin' dead."

"Ryan. Hush."

After several minutes, the dragging noise died away. From the echoes, Shavi estimated it had halted about fifteen feet away. All that remained was the sound of breathing, slow, rhythmic and rough. Although there wasn't even the faintest glimmer of light, he couldn't shake the feeling it was watching them with a contemptuous, heavy gaze; sizing them up, dissecting them.

At his side, Veitch's body was taut. Neither of them knew what to do next.

"The rules of this place were formed long before your kind emerged from the long night." The voice sounded like bones rattling across stone. Its bass notes vibrated deep in Shavi's chest; he felt instantly queasy, not just from the tone of the voice, but from the very *feel* of whatever squatted away in the gloom. "No warm bodies, no beating hearts, no words or thoughts or ideas."

"No. There's a deal. I was allowed to come here," Veitch protested cautiously.

"You were allowed to *cross over*, but the rules of this place can never be transgressed. The living are not wanted. The dead rule here. And they will have no warm bodies spoiling the cold days of this land. They will have punishment."

Shavi waited for it to attack, but there was only silence. He pictured it savouring its taunting before the inevitable. Here was not only intelligence, but also cruelty, and hatred.

"What are you?" Shavi asked. The hairs on the back of his neck had snapped alert.

"This is a place without hope for those who do not leave. Where behind is too terrible to consider, and ahead is an unwanted distraction. This is desolation, and despair. Misery and pain."

"A land for those who prey on those things," Shavi said.

"Here, the dead have their own existence, their own rules and rhythms, their own hierarchies and mythologies, fears and desires."

The dark was so all-encompassing Shavi was beginning to hallucinate trails of white sparks and flashes of geometric patterns. The atmosphere of dread grew more oppressive.

"What are you?" There was no bravado in Veitch's voice. Shavi really wished he hadn't asked the question again; he was afraid the answer would be too terrible for them to bear.

"I am the end of you."

Those simple words made his stomach clench. They were flatly stated, yet filled with such finality, hinting at a fate much worse than death.

Slowly it began to drag itself forward, an inch at a time.

"Wait," Veitch said sharply. "I *was* allowed to come here—you can't get away from that. And Shavi here, he's not dead—"

"He will be." A blast of cold air.

"But he's not now. He shouldn't be here. What I'm doing . . . yeah, it might go against your rules—but against the bigger rules I'm doing the right thing. I'm taking him back. I'm making everything all right again."

For a long period the mausoleum appeared to be filled with the soughing of an icy wind. Then: "There is the matter of trespass."

"What do you mean?"

"The dead want no reminder of the living. It makes them aware of what they have lost and what they have yet to gain. To remember makes their suffering even greater."

Veitch sensed a chink in the seemingly inviolate position. "So they want some kind of payback," he said, warming to his argument. "We can do that. Then you let us go, and everybody's sweet."

"No!" Shavi gripped Veitch's wrist; the memory of the price he had paid for the deal with the dead of Mary King's Close was still too raw. "You never know to what you are agreeing. Words are twisted so easily."

Veitch shook him off. "We have to cut a deal—it's the only way. There's too much at stake."

"Ryan! You must listen to me—"

But Veitch had scrambled off in the dark. "Go on then." His disembodied voice filled Shavi with ice. "What's the deal?"

There was silence from the brooding presence. Shavi couldn't work out what that meant, but he felt like it was swelling in size to fill all the shadows.

After a moment or two, Veitch repeated, "What's the deal?"

"A hand," the rumbling voice replied.

"Ryan, please do not do this. We can find another way."

"A hand?" Veitch's voice was suddenly querulous. "Cut off my hand?"

"A small price to pay for your friend's life."

The price is too high! Shavi wanted to cry out, but he knew his voice would only tighten his friend's resolve. The sense of threat in that confined space felt like strong arms crushing his chest. They both knew their lives were hanging by a thread.

In the silence that followed, he could almost hear the turning of Veitch's thought processes as he considered the mutilation, what the absence of his hand would mean in his life, what the absence of Shavi would mean. There was an awful weight to Veitch's deliberations as he desperately tried to reach the place where he could do the right thing, whatever the cost to himself. *Do not agree, Ryan*, Shavi pleaded silently.

"Okay." The word sounded like a tolling bell.

Shavi tried to throw himself between Veitch and the dark presence, but he misjudged his leap in the dark and crashed into the wall.

"Don't worry, mate. Really," Veitch said. "I know you'd do the same for me. Whatever you say, I know that. We've got bigger things to think about. That's what Church always said. I can do this. For everybody else."

Shavi bit sharply on his knuckle to restrain his emotions. All he could do was make his friend feel good about his choice. "You are a true hero, Ryan." Shavi knew it was what Veitch wanted to hear, what he had wanted from the moment he had got involved with them.

Veitch didn't reply, but Shavi could almost feel his pride. "Get it over with," the Londoner said.

Veitch was trembling, despite the bravado he was trying to drive through his system. He still couldn't quite believe what he had agreed to, but from his position the lines appeared clear cut: Shavi was the better man; the world couldn't afford to lose *him*. What did his own suffering mean against that? Once they were back in the world, he'd take it all out on the Bastards. Bring on an army of them.

He threw off the shakes, set his jaw, and extended his left arm.

The first sensation made him shiver with disgust. Hot air on his hand, rushing up his forearm, then something wet tickling the tips of his fingers, brushing his skin as it enclosed his hand. The flicker of something that felt like a cold slug on his knuckles.

He closed his eyes, despite the dark.

The sharpness of needles encircled his wrist. The pain increased rapidly until the sound of crunching bones brought nausea surging up from his stomach. The noises that followed were even worse, but by then he had already blacked out.

He lost consciousness for only a few seconds, and when he came round there was heat in his wrist and the sickening smell of cauterised flesh. His left arm felt too light. Amidst the shock and the nausea, thoughts flitted across his head without settling.

And then he did capture one, shining more brightly than all the others: he had saved Shavi. Through his sacrifice, he alone.

"That's my part." He didn't recognise the ragged voice as his own. "Now you've got to let Shavi go."

The wet, smacking sound churned his stomach even further, but he wouldn't allow himself to accept what was happening. When it had died away, the rattling bones voice returned, flat, almost matter-of-fact: "Then he may go."

A wave of relief cut through the shakes that convulsed him.

"But you must stay."

Veitch couldn't grasp the meaning of the words. Shavi was yelling something, trying to grab at his arms, getting knocked away by a figure, more than one figure; not the monstrous presence, which was dragging itself back into the depths of the mausoleum.

He drifted in and out, his left arm by his side, trying to move his fingers.

Movement all around. Shavi was being dragged away. He fought himself back to clarity, knowing it was vitally important, but he still felt wrapped in gauze. At some point he realised he could see, although he couldn't guess the light source; the illumination was thin and grey, like winter twilight.

The dead had come back in. Shavi was against the open door, hands clamped across his mouth, head and arms. Veitch could just make out what appeared to be a large rough box, the lid open, next to a gaping hole. His shock-addled brain couldn't put the information into any coherent shape.

Then the dry-wood fingers of the dead were in his clothes, pulling him forward. He had no strength to resist. They bundled him into the box, which was just big enough for him, and then the lid swung shut with a bang. That jarred his mind into life: with a surge of panic he realised what they were planning.

"No!" In the dark again. He punched the lid with his remaining hand; the splintered wood grated into his knuckles.

The box was lifted into the air. Yelling his protests, he threw himself from side to side, but it didn't overbalance. A brief moment of weightlessness, then a crash that jarred his head so sharply he lost consciousness again.

The next thing he heard was a rattling on the wood. Smell pebbles. The slush of gritty soil falling on the lid, kicked or thrown in. Then the occasional slumps turning into an insistent fall. He screamed and shouted, hammered on the lid and box walls, but there was no room to get any purchase, barely any air to breathe. The stones and earth fell faster, but grew more and more distant.

Finally he couldn't hear anything at all, apart from the sound of his own hoarse voice, growing weaker by the moment.

With the dead gripping him tight, Shavi watched Veitch buried alive. His empathy made him feel acutely the choking claustrophobia and rising hysteria; horror, almost as much as he could bear. As soon as the hole was filled in, he was released, but the dead formed an impenetrable wall between him and the grave; they were not going to allow him to save his friend.

"This is not fair!" he raged to the shadows at the back of the mausoleum, but although they pulsed slightly, there was no reply.

Flailing around, Shavi wandered out into the thin grey light. The area that Veitch had seen as a graveyard, but which he saw as a battlefield spanning the entire history of human existence—trenches and barbed wire, iron age earth defences and mediaeval fields of sucking mud—was deserted. With retribution achieved, the army of the dead had returned to wherever their homes lay.

He couldn't leave Veitch, but what could he do? Sacrifice himself to save his friend? Perhaps that was what the dead truly wanted: a neverending cycle of sacrifice and suffering, the best punishment of all for being alive.

As he paced back and forth in distress, he noticed a figure about fifty feet away, almost hidden in the cotton-wool mists. A chill ran through him as he instantly recognised the body language: Lee, back to haunt him.

His first thought was to ignore the spirit of his dead boyfriend; at that moment it was too much to bear. But then he changed his mind and hurried over until he was a few feet away. The mists folded around Lee, providing only the briefest glimpses of him.

"I need you now," Shavi said. The words hung in the damp, misty air. "I have paid my dues to the dead of Mary King's Close." He caught his breath. "I carried a burden of guilt for what happened to you, Lee . . . that I could have done more to save your life. But the truth is, I could not do anything. I remember you in life. I loved you, I think. I loved your values, your beliefs, your gentleness. You were never a man who would want to see anyone suffer." He let the words flow from his heart without any interference from his mind. "The pain you caused me over the last few weeks, I think . . . I am sure . . . that was not through any desire of your own. It might have been the Edinburgh dead, but I believe it was probably me, punishing myself. Whatever the cause, that lies behind us now. Now I want your help."

The coffin had grown unbearably hot from Veitch's rising body temperature. It was also becoming increasingly harder to breathe. His chest felt like rocks had been placed upon it, and there was a prickling sensation in his arms, regularly obscured by waves of pain washing up from his missing hand. He tried to suck in some of the air tainted with the odour of rock dust and soil, but there wasn't enough to fill his throat.

After the swinging emotions that surrounded his sacrifice, the adrenalin had died down and panic had started to set in. He recalled how terrible it had been trapped in the tiny tunnel beneath Edinburgh Castle, and knew that if he gave in he would go crazy, tearing futilely at the wooden lid until his fingernails were broken and bloody.

He rolled round as much as he could to test the lid with his shoulder. It wouldn't budge. Trapped; powerless. Another wave of panic. His throat almost closed up. Flashes of light crossed his eyes.

Dying.

Trust in the others. He tried to focus on something Church had told him. *Have faith. It's out of your hands now.*

The dark closed in around him and the panic rushed up through his chest into his head and then he was yelling until his throat was raw.

The blood trickled from Tom's nose into the corner of his mouth. The ritual had been an awful strain; he felt as if his life had been sucked out of him, and part of it probably had, but he felt good about himself, for the first time in a long while.

Robertson had fled back into the house and buried himself beneath a pile of furniture once he saw what was happening. The stable block door had been torn from its hinges. Intermittent smoking pitholes marked a trail across the courtyard to the sweeping lawns, where another route of churned mud continued to the dew pond.

Tom hoped he had done enough. More, he prayed he had not made things worse.

The stillness was like the moment after the final exhalation of breath. Shavi thought that place had been that way for as long as time, and would probably remain in that state of suspension until the end of existence. So when the ground shook and the sky cracked with thunder, it really did feel like everything was coming to an end.

Shavi spun round, his heart pounding. The thunder was tearing towards him through the thickening mist. The vibrations drove nails into the soles of his feet.

Was it some kin to the thing that lurked in the mausoleum, sucking up the despair of the dead? The notion chilled him.

He knew there was no point in running. As he waited for it to present itself to him, he became aware of a prickling on the back of his neck, a familiar sign of warning from his supercharged subconscious. When he turned, the sight was so shocking he couldn't help an exclamation. From nowhere the dead had appeared in force, a silent army of thousands forming a grey barrier around the mausoleum. All their eerily staring eyes were turned towards the direction from which the thunderous noise was approaching.

The vibrations were now so powerful the nails had reached Shavi's knees. There was a rhythm to it; not thunder at all. The sound of hoofbeats. All other thoughts were lost as he turned to stare alongside the dead.

The mist usually drifted with a life of its own, but now it was sweeping away rapidly. Unconsciously he cupped his hands over his ears against the deafening noise. The dead remained impassive.

Shavi was buffeted with a warm wind filled with the stink of stables and the musk of sweating, over-worked horses. When the intruder appeared, he was instantly overcome with the swirling destabilisation of perception that always accompanied the most powerful of the Tuatha Dé Danann. This was worse than anything he had experienced before; his mind revolted at the image his eyes were attempting to present to it. After a few seconds, the sensation eased slightly, to be replaced by a succession of rapidly changing forms: a beast that looked more serpent than animal with gleaming black scales and a pointed, lashing tail, a voluptuous woman oozing sexuality, a pregnant mother, blissful in her fertility.

The uneasy flickering eventually settled on one form that his mind found acceptable. A woman, naked apart from a silver breastplate and a short skirt of leather thongs, long, chestnut hair flowing in the wind behind her, riding a stallion of inordinate vitality. Her beautiful face was filled with pride and joy, power and defiance. In her raised right hand she carried a wooden spear tipped with a silver head, while in her other hand she held aloft a gleaming silver shield. Shavi thought of Boudicca, of the power of womanhood, strength and sexuality so potent he could almost taste it.

"Epona," he said beneath his breath.

Her terrible gaze snapped towards him as if she had heard him, and the sheer force of what he saw there made him look away. Here was a power he had never experienced before, one of the oldest gods, the most primal and powerful, not far removed from the archetypes. Her form had resonated in the belief system of mankind from the earliest time.

The horse reared up before the ranks of the dead, its hooves striking the air. She let that withering gaze move slowly across the army of the dead. It was apparent they were not going to allow her through.

From the way she was directing herself towards the mausoleum, Shavi guessed she was there for Veitch, although he had no idea why. She took her charger back and forth across the frontline of the dead in search of access.

At one point she paused to address the dead in a language Shavi had never heard: wild shrieks that disappeared off the register, interspersed with the snortings of horses. Whatever she suggested, it had no effect.

Why can she not force her way through them? Shavi wondered. But from what he remembered from the stories Tom had told him of the Tuatha Dé Danann, one of her obligations had been the Grim Lands, or at least where it bordered with the world of the living. Perhaps she served them as much as she dominated them, in the way that Cernunnos had a similar dual relationship with the *Fragile Creatures*?

The delay cranked up his anxiety. How long could Veitch survive in the shallow grave with the air running out? What terrible things would be going through his mind?

No air was left in the coffin. Veitch wheezed like an asthmatic old man. The weight on his chest was crushing him. There was blood under his fingernails and his head swam with shifting lights and the sensation of tumbling down a never-ending well. No one was coming for him. It was the end; life was being sucked out of him, one breath at a time.

"Lee! I need you! You must help me!" Shavi turned towards the spirit of his boyfriend once again, but the place where Lee had stood was empty, and in the vast crowd of the dead there was no hope of finding him.

Perhaps he could force a way through so Epona could follow. He started to push through the stiff, unmoving bodies towards the frontline, but before he was halfway there he noticed movement not far from Epona. The army of the dead was parting like grey waters before the power of God.

Shavi used his elbows to drive his way towards the path. Epona had already started to trot down it towards the mausoleum. He slipped in behind her before the dead closed ranks.

As Epona moved before the mausoleum door, Shavi caught sight of the reason for the dead's change of heart. Lee waited in the shadow of the stone building, and for the first time that day Shavi saw his face. It was not terrible and frightening and filled with the horrors of death as it had been during the long days and nights following his return in Edinburgh. It was the Lee he remembered: gentle, thoughtful, smiling. For one fleeting moment, things passed between them: acknowledgement, gratitude, friendship, love. And then Lee was moving away towards the grey horizon; not walking, but simply appearing further and further back, as if there were shifts in Shavi's perception. For one instant he appeared to glow like a star, and then he was gone.

Shavi's eyes filled with tears. Lee had achieved his own salvation; he would never have to walk in the Grim Lands again.

He barely had time to think what that meant before he was jolted by a resounding crash as the flinty hooves of Epona's mount broke down the mausoleum door. Although she had appeared too tall to pass through the doorway, a second later she was inside. Shavi ran in behind her.

Close to Epona he felt faintly queasy, his teeth on edge as if he were standing in an electrical field. The goddess moved beyond the rough grave and faced the shadows that still pulsed at the rear of the chamber. From the outside, the Mausoleum appeared twenty feet long, but peering into the gloom, Shavi had the unnerving feeling that it continued forever.

He didn't wait to see what the goddess was doing. Throwing himself on top of the grave, he tore at the shards of rock, the pebbles and soil, with his bare hands. Within seconds the blood streamed down his fingers until his palms were covered with a brown sludge of rock dust and grue.

"Ryan!" he yelled. "Hold on!"

From the corner of his eye, he could see movement in the shadows. Epona's horse reared up to face it; the goddess issued a warning in that half-shrieking, half-equine cry.

The response was not in that deathly voice Shavi had heard before, but an incomprehensible bass rumble filling him with dread. It was followed by the dragging sound of the huge bulk moving across the stone floor. The shadows swelled forward.

Shavi threw the contents of the grave wildly in all directions. It was loosely packed and easy to move, but it was still taking too long.

"Ryan!" he shouted again. "Ryan!"

This time he heard a muffled response that spurred him on.

On the edges of his vision he realised Epona was glowing with a faint blue light that lit up their end of the mausoleum, but made no inroads into the advancing shadow. The rumbling sound emanated once again from the dark. This time Epona altered in shape, becoming almost opaque, then something that Shavi didn't recognise. Crackling blue energy washed off her up the mausoleum walls. The shadow stopped sharply before responding with what at first appeared to be a black lightning bolt, or could have been an arm, or a tentacle, lashing out furiously. Epona fended it off with the silver shield, but the force of it drove her back a pace.

No one else would have been able to hold back that thing, Shavi knew. Whatever reason she was there, it had given him the only chance he might have had of saving his friend. He could no longer feel his swollen hands as he tore through the rubble, but eventually the sound of his scraping changed and he realised he had reached wood. Frantically he ripped out the remaining stones while Epona and the unseen presence conducted a ferocious dance in the background. Blue light and black shadows flashed wildly around the mausoleum.

Thrusting his tattered nails under the lid, he wrenched it free. Veitch shot upwards, gulping air, clawing at Shavi's shirt with his one good hand. Shavi was sickened to see the charred black stump that flailed behind.

Even when his lungs were full, Veitch continued to choke. Shavi grabbed his shoulders and held him tightly, stroking his hair until the panic subsided. "You have survived," he whispered. "You are the stronger for it."

The battle in the background came to a sudden halt. The dark throbbed around whatever it contained. After a moment the bass rumble began, at first so loud it hurt Shavi's ears, but then it changed to words in the chilling, boneyard voice they remembered. "You have broken the pact. Transgressed the rules of this place. In times to come you will discover you cannot evade your punishment, and it will be inflicted not only upon you, but upon your world."

"Our world is already suffering," Shavi muttered.

"There are worse things than the Night Walkers. Worse than the Heart of Darkness. Beyond the edge of existence, the void is stirring. Soon you will fall beneath its unflinching eye. And then it will move towards you."

Shavi levered himself to his feet, still holding Veitch to his chest. "We will face it as we have faced everything else. With dignity and hope and faith."

The shadows began to drag towards him, but the pulsing light around Epona flared and it withdrew. Shavi stared at it defiantly, then turned and helped Veitch out into the thin, grey light.

Epona led the way across the blasted, grey land to the slope on which Veitch had first appeared. She kept a way ahead of them, sometimes disappearing in the mist, but they were always aware of her presence. Now that the conflict was over, there was something eminently soothing about her that raised even Veitch's spirits. They found bread and fruit in her path, which they devoured hungrily; it quickly made them replete and relaxed and imposed a warm sensation of abiding safety that for some reason reminded Shavi of his mother.

The goddess slipped into a state of flux now that the warrior side had been put away. Sometimes when Shavi glimpsed her, she was a young girl on a pony, then a plump mother on a mare, and finally an old, old woman with streaming white hair, on a similarly ancient white charger. Shavi recognised the sign instantly: the triple goddess, mother-maiden-crone, one of the most powerful of feminine symbols. Just like the goddess who had manifested to Ruth.

The more he considered this, the more it gave him pause. He couldn't understand why some of the Tuatha Dé Danann were so close to humanity, both sources of worship and symbols of all that was good, while others had provided the template for the mischievous and malicious sprites and fairies who held humanity in contempt if not hatred. It didn't make sense.

When they reached the summit, Epona cantered round it clockwise three times and the doorway appeared, shimmering in the mist. The goddess turned and briefly acknowledged the two of them, with something akin to the respect of a wise matron. Then, proud and aloof once more, she drove her horse through the doorway and was gone.

Tom was waiting for them when they crossed over. As Veitch emerged, the bier bearing Shavi's body fell into stark relief. Tom's face crumpled in a broad beam as he clapped eyes on Shavi sitting up in a daze. It was the greatest joy they had ever seen him exhibit, but then he noticed Veitch's stump and his jubilation was replaced by an equally intense horror.

"Epona?" Shavi asked.

Tom couldn't take his eyes off Veitch's mutilation. "I called her to help you."

"How long was I over there?" Veitch's weak, gravelly voice was on the edge of delirium.

"Two hours."

Veitch bowed his head. "It seemed longer."

Shavi explained to Tom what had happened in the Grim Lands as they both helped Veitch back to the house to recover. He was particularly troubled by the loss of Veitch's hand.

Eventually he brightened enough to say, "We must not lose sight of the great thing we have achieved this day. You have been brought back from the edge of death, a victory over some of the most powerful rules of existence. That is symbolic of the great power, and hope, invested in the Brothers and Sisters of Dragons."

"Hooray," Veitch croaked.

"Now we must find the others and prepare for the battle that all your lives have been leading towards." He nodded thoughtfully. "Five once more. Amazing. Perhaps we can carry ourselves with a little more hope than the situation would suggest."

chapter twelve
infected

Church and Baccharus hurried along dark, twisting corridors with the expectation of an attack at any moment. They had left the vicinity of the Walpurgis's secret hideaway rapidly, and Callow and the Malignos had so far failed to catch up with them. At some point they had expected to come across the Fomorii occupying force, but the lower decks were strangely free of them. Wave Sweeper was still stranded in the same spot, tossing and turning on waves that were obviously being whipped up by the growing storm. Church wondered what that meant for Manannan, whose will alone appeared to power the ship.

At his cabin, he darted inside and then into the wreck of Ruth's room, but there was no sign of her. He threw off the first bolt of despair: Ruth was resilient; she would survive, he told himself.

As they reached the steps up to the deck, they realised how presumptuous they had been. Through the open door, framed against the night sky, they could see the swarming silhouettes of the Fomorii. From their perspective it was impossible to tell how many of the Night Walkers were loose on deck, but it was obvious they had control of Wave Sweeper, and Manannan, if still alive, was probably a prisoner in his cabin. A little guilt crept up on Church as he secretly relished how the Tuatha Dé Danann would feel at being the prisoners of beings they considered less than bacteria.

Cautiously they retreated along the corridor until they had reached a point where they would not be overheard. Baccharus watched him silently, until Church realised the god was waiting for him to decide a course of action. "What?" he said uncomfortably.

"You are a Brother of Dragons," Baccharus replied, as if that answered everything.

Church shook his head disbelievingly. "Okay, okay." He fidgeted with the sword at his side, then said, "We've got to move soon. Callow and the Malignos could be upon us at any moment. Callow's got a bastard's tenacity; he won't give up until he feels he's paid me back for ruining his life. But we can't go forward. There's no way we'd ever get past all those Fomorii on deck. They'd cut us down before we made one step out there, like . . . like Butch Cassidy and the Sundance Kid or something." Baccharus continued to wait on his words. Church pedalled furiously. "So . . . so . . ."

"We have to find another course of action."

"Exactly." And then he had it. "The first time I was down here I was searching around and I came across another secret room . . . at least I think it was secret. And there were three Golden Ones in there—Goibhniu—"

"Creidhne and Luchtaine, as they were known in the Fixed Lands. The room *was* secret, but it would have opened itself to you because of your heritage."

Church felt too weary to question what this meant. "They were making weapons," he said instead. "What was that all about?"

"That must wait until later, when there is time."

"If the room is still there, if the weapons are still there, if Goibhniu and the others are still there—"

Baccharus was already moving along the corridor. Church kept up with him, still amazed to see branching corridors appear as if from nowhere. Five minutes later they passed through the door into the foundry, with its familiar smell of sulphur and smoke. The furnaces were cold, the room silent. Hammers lay where they had fallen. Iron remained partly worked on the anvil. In the gloom beyond, Church could see the mysterious weapons stacked in heaps, untouched.

Baccharus traced his slim fingers along the edge of the furnace. "I do not think the Night Walkers found this place. The three smiths would have gone to the aid of the Master once the interlopers were discovered."

"So it's still just us." Church investigated the first pile of weapons. The uses of most of them were impossible to divine. "Do you know how to use these?"

"Some. I am not a warrior."

Church picked up a sword with twin parallel blades. It was extraordinarily light, made of gold and silver, useless in battle. A blue gem was imbedded at the top of the handle between the blades. Casually, Church brushed the jewel with his thumb and was instantly shocked by a sucking sensation deep within him that rapidly grew stronger until it felt like his innards were being pulled out. The sword jumped like a living thing in his hand, so powerful he could barely control it. Before he could fling it down, he noticed coruscating blue energy crackling between the blades near the base, slowly rising up towards the tip as it grew stronger.

Baccharus stepped in quickly and touched his thumb to the gem. The energy died away and Church's jolted body returned to normal, although he could still feel faint vibrations running through his skeleton. "A Wish-Sword," Baccharus said. "To be used with caution."

"You're telling me." Church placed it back on the pile, wary of touching anything else. "Is there anything a little less apocalyptic?"

Baccharus mused for a moment before pulling out a leather thong with what appeared to be a Japanese throwing star tucked in a fold. The star had six points in the shape of extended teardrops, cruelly tipped with barbs, and was made of the same silvery metal that was a constituent for most of the weapons.

Baccharus weighed the weapon in his hand a moment, then slowly began to whirl the thong around his head. Unnerved, Church took refuge behind one of the furnaces where he could just see Baccharus building up speed. When the weapon was a blur, Baccharus snapped his wrist and the star went flying out of the thong. It ripped in an arc through the air; a primitive if effective weapon, Church thought. But then Baccharus nodded his head towards a heap of unformed metal and the star jumped unnaturally in the air to follow the direction of his gaze. It tore through the metal like it was made of sand. Baccharus moved his head sharply two more times and the star obeyed him exactly, making two more cuts through the pile, which fell with a resounding clatter. The star spun back to Baccharus, slowing and hovering slightly so he could pluck it out of the air with his thumb and forefinger.

"That's amazing." Church snatched the star and examined it closely. There was nothing to show why it should act in such a manner. "Can anyone use it like that?"

"Anyone with a will." Baccharus smiled.

"It's still not going to help us if we have to face the massed ranks of them, but it's a start."

"What do you suggest?"

Church shifted uncomfortably. There was one avenue he had been resisting, but he didn't see how he could ignore it any longer, however detestable it was to him. "The Fomorii corruption your people all sense in me," he began, "has a side effect. The taint was left after the Kiss of Frost almost took me over, and soon after my life was saved by the liquid I drank from the Cauldron of Dagda. Whatever it was gave me some essence of your people too, so inside me I've got Fomorii and Tuatha Dé Danann fighting it out. The result is that sometimes, when I really try, I can sense what's going on in the Fomorii mind. It's not like I can read thoughts—at least I don't think it's like that. I don't even know if the Fomorii *have* thoughts. It's more a vague impression. But if I really concentrate on it, I'm convinced I can get right inside their heads to work out what's happening. I have to be in close proximity, though." He winced. "It feels like my head is filled with spiders. But that's not the worst of it." He paused as he tried to find the words to express his fears.

"What is it?" Baccharus obviously saw something in Church's face for he rested a steadying hand on his friend's shoulder.

"I'm afraid I could get lost in there. Somehow . . . it's like their minds are all linked. Lots of different bodies, but one being. I've only had the briefest hint of what's inside them, but even then it felt like a rushing river. Of oil, black and so cold. It was tugging at me even then."

Baccharus nodded. "I understand. You must do what you feel you have to do. No one will judge you."

Somehow that made things even worse for Church. "I've got to stop being such a wimp. What would Tom say?" He grinned defiantly. "Come on, then. Let's get us a guinea pig."

They crept back to the foot of the stairs that led to the deck, constantly checking for any sound of Callow and the Malignos. A cold, heavy wind buffeted them and through the doorway they could see swirling clouds occasionally lit up by flashes of white lightning. In the storm, the ship pitched so much that Church had to clutch at the wall to remain upright. At least the pounding thunder would hide any noise they made, Church thought.

The view through the doorway was occasionally obscured by a large shape lumbering slowly by. A guard, Church guessed, to prevent any of Wave Sweeper's passengers interfering with whatever was happening on deck. Even though they had discussed the plan—and it was a simple one—tension still tugged at his neck muscles. One mistake and they would bring the whole of the Fomorii force down on them.

"Are you ready?" he whispered.

"Yes." Baccharus's voice was characteristically cool.

Church held the throwing star gently, keeping his fingers well away from the razor-sharp barbs. "You sure you wouldn't be better off using this?"

"You have the ability. And I am faster than you."

"Okay," Church said. "I'm set. Go carefully."

Baccharus smiled shyly, then loped towards the stairs. Church backed off along the corridor and round a bend. His breath was fast, his heart beating hard. With nervous hands he loaded the star in the thong and held it at his side, rolling on the balls of his feet, ready to move in an instant. Despite Baccharus's vote of confidence, he still doubted his ability, even though he'd had several practice attempts with the star. It responded to his thoughts remarkably easily, almost as if it were a part of him, but the Fomorii were fast when they had to be. Were his reactions sharp enough to build up the velocity and release the star before the beast was on him? Before it could raise the alarm?

Don't think, he told himself. *Just act*.

In his mind's eye, he saw Baccharus sneaking to the foot of the stairs, sliding up them sinuously on his belly, waiting for the guard to pass to the furthest reaches of his path, hoping there were no other Fomorii anywhere near. Tossing one of the coals from the furnace so it rattled on the wet boards just beyond the doorway. Sliding quickly back down the stairs and retreating to the shadows while the guard investigated the sound easily discerned by its magnified perceptions.

Church held his breath and listened: nothing but the wind.

And now Baccharus would be hurling another coal to the foot of the stairs and retreating again. This time Church thought he heard the rattle of the coal. The guard would be advancing down the stairs like the onset of a winter night.

Church couldn't breathe. He shifted from foot to foot as the adrenalin made his body shake with repressed anxiety. Slowly he began to twirl the thong around him, taking care not to clatter the weapon against the walls. Swish. Swish. A gentle breeze.

Another coal tossed from the security of the shadows. This one rolling almost to the guard's feet. Now it had a suspicion of what was happening. But it was not scared. It created fear, it did not know it.

Events happened like a house of cards collapsing. Baccharus appeared round the corner, a blur of gold, not slowing as he approached Church, ducking beneath the whirl of the weapon in one fluid moment. Church suddenly spinning like an Olympic discus thrower, faster and faster until he feared his vision would be too blurred to see the Fomorii approaching. The star singing to him, a plaintive tune. And then the shadows at the bend becoming filled with something even darker than shadows; that sickening stink, the roar of a jet taking off punctuated by a monkey shriek. Something so huge it filled the entire corridor, moving with the speed of a racehorse; a shape that had tentacles, then teeth, then silver knives, fur then scales, then nothing but an absence of everything.

Church whirled one final time, then snapped his wrist to release the star. The weapon was like a glimmering light in the void as it tore through the air. It ripped through where the creature's arm should have been and something heavy fell to the floor. The monkey shriek grew more high pitched.

Church's mind was clear of everything but the star. Back and forth, up and down, he chased the pin-prick of light, tearing the beast apart. Things fell; the floor grew sticky beneath his feet. The smell was unbearable, part of it the odour of his boots being corroded by the thing's essence. His heart zinged as relief flooded in; he was actually doing it. But he had to be careful. Not too good. He had to keep the thing alive, at least long enough for him to get into its head. A pang of guilt hit him at the suffering he was inflicting on another living thing.

The shrieks were cut off and the beast crashed to the floor. This was the most dangerous moment. It was still alive, but he didn't want it so alive it could still kill him with its dying blow.

Baccharus brought up a torch so he had a better view of the sickening havoc he had wreaked on the body. He tried to avert his eyes, but it was all around.

"It is time." Baccharus's words gave him a gentle push, but were at the same time supportive. He steeled himself and stepped forward.

His sizzling boots slid in the grue. A tendril flapped wildly before curling around his legs. In a moment of panic he kicked out wildly. The tendril flew off and continued to judder aimlessly.

He had no choice but to climb on the body, which was sickeningly resilient beneath his feet. His boot slipped into a hole that felt like a sucking bog. He withdrew it with an unpleasant slurping sound.

Finally he reached the point where he guessed its head would be. There was certainly a raised area with what appeared like eyes rolling back and forward in its dying spasms, but they were as black as oil, glinting with an inner light which was inexplicably black too, but of a different quality. Fighting the nausea, he bent down and brushed his fingers against the skin. Although he couldn't begin to describe the texture, it felt so unpleasant his stomach rolled and he truly thought he was about to be sick. When the queasiness had passed, he placed his hands near those shivering eyes, closed his own lids, and concentrated.

He was caught aback by the speed and severity of the reaction. One second he was fighting back his disgust at his surroundings, the next he was sucked violently into a surging river of crude oil, immersed in a vile stench that was part chemical, part excrement, feeling revulsion in every fibre of his being at what his senses told him. It was such a totally overwhelming experience he felt he was living it; the corridor, the Night Walker, Baccharus, all disappeared from his mind.

He was swept along in the black stream, choking, not from a lack of oxygen, but from the sensation that his body was being suffused with such Evil his very spirit recoiled. The abstract was given form by his mind as a complex mix of feelings, strangulation, a feeling that something vile, like human brains, was being forced into his mouth, that his skin was being touched by the innards of a loved one's corpse. The rush was amphetamine-fast, pulled this way and that so dramatically he didn't have a second to think. He was fighting, for his life, for his sanity, sure he would never get out again.

And then he felt the full force of what had only been hinted at before: the awful, alien intelligence that linked the Fomorii. Spiders burrowed deep in his brain. There were no words, no images that made any sense to him, but there was an intense *impression* of that thing's thoughts. He was swamped with a soul-shattering despair as it cruelly disseminated the point of view that there was no meaning to anything, no reason for anything to exist, that it would be better if nothing existed at all.

He saw through multifaceted eyes London cast in negative: bodies piled in the streets and the Thames running thickly, white shadows reaching into buildings and hearts. He glimpsed the world from a hundred thousand eyes, and more, the Lake District, the Welsh borders, the South Coast, the Midlands, moving out with the tramp of an infinite marching army ringing all around.

Even more sickening was that the longer he was in it, the more he could control, picking eyes here, then there. And eventually he saw through eyes that looked out over Wave Sweeper and soaked up the oily impression of intent.

His body prickled with cold sweat. He *was* Fomorii, and it would never, ever let him go. The vibrations that convulsed him grew stronger and stronger, until he thought he was beginning to shake apart . . .

He hit the floor hard, driving the wind from his lungs. It took a second or two for the black oil to drain from his mind, but daemonic voices still rang in his ears, even when he saw Baccharus's face above him.

"Jesus." He choked; a mouthful of bile splattered on the sizzling ooze that ran from the now-dead Fomor.

"Find peace, Brother of Dragons."

"I was one of them . . . I couldn't get away . . ."

"Your face told me what was happening. I thought I would never be able to break the spell."

Church took several deep breaths, then put his head between his knees, but he couldn't shake the squirming in his brain.

"I know what they're going to do," he gasped.

Baccharus helped him to his feet. "You saw?"

"Saw . . . felt . . . whatever." He heaved in another breath, trying to keep the nausea at bay. "Are they really a part of me? Is that it? For the rest of my life?"

"We are all a part of everything, and everything is a part of us."

"That doesn't sound like one of the Tuatha Dé Danann." He rested on Baccharus as the god led him away from the corpse. "I saw something . . . a structure . . . a geometrical shape that seemed to disappear into other dimensions . . . glowing ruby, then emerald."

"The Wish-Hex." Baccharus's voice was suddenly so dismal, Church snapped alert.

"But it wasn't just that," Church continued. "I got a hint of something about disease . . . a plague . . ."

Baccharus turned away so Church couldn't see his face.

"What is it?"

"The Wish-Hex is a construct of unimaginable power. The Night Walkers used it to break the pact and sever the bonds that chained them to the Far Lands. It decimated my people. Some were contaminated by the essence of the Night Walkers, some—"

". . . were driven into exile and some fled. I know the story."

"The Night Walkers must have sacrificed much to focus it again." He bowed his head and put a hand to his temple. "But to bind one of the great plagues into the matrix . . ."

"That's even worse?"

He looked up at Church with liquid eyes. "My people will not be exiled. They will be destroyed, in the worst way imaginable. Eaten away from within."

"They're going to convince Manannan to take them to your high court, and then they'll unleash it there."

Baccharus shook his head. Church thought he was going to break down in tears.

"It's not done yet, Baccharus. The ship is still stationary. They haven't broken Manannan."

They were both disturbed by a scuttling across the wooden floor behind them. They whirled to see a silver spider disappearing into the shadows: a Caraprix, one of the symbiotic creatures shared by the Fomorii and the Tuatha Dé Danann. It had vacated the cooling body.

"Quick!" Baccharus said.

Church whirled the thong and loosed the star, but it simply raised a shower of splinters from the floor. The Caraprix was already en route to the deck. They both chased around the corner to see it disappearing out into the night.

Baccharus grabbed Church's arm forcibly. "We must flee. The alarm will already have been raised. They will be on us in moments."

As if in answer to his words, a shocking outcry of animal noises tore through the night. It was followed an instant later by the thunder of forms rushing to the lower decks.

Church and Baccharus turned as one and sprinted away along the endless corridors.

The cacophony of pursuit dogged them for fifteen minutes, but Baccharus took them down hidden tunnels which, from the cobwebs that festooned them, appeared not to have been used for years. After a while, the silence lay heavy again and they could both rest against the wall to catch their breath.

"Now they've found their dead comrade they'll be fanning out across the ship," Church noted. "There's no element of surprise any more."

"We cannot hide forever." Baccharus was unusually anxious.

"We're not going to be hiding."

"Then what do you suggest? Two of us, against an army . . ."

"There're more than two of us, Baccharus." Church smiled at the god's curious expression. "You seem to know the ship well."

"Very well."

"Good. Then there are some places I want you to take me."

Liquid echoes and dancing splashes of light reflected off the oily water below. The stink of rotten fish and seaweed choked the air. Church and Baccharus hurried through the gloom along a wooden walkway that hung shakily over the black, slopping contents of the bilge tanks. They were vast and deep, filled not only with the buoyant seawater, but also the runoff from the kitchens. This was only one of many, but Baccharus had convinced Church it was the correct one.

It was also one of the most rundown sections of the ship. The walkway was creaking and bowing, and in some areas vital planks were missing so they had to jump gaps, or edge along a strut with their backs to the wall.

Two Fomorii who had pursued them down there entered the tank when Church and Baccharus were about a hundred and fifty yards along the walkway. Church felt the chill rippling out from them long before he looked back to see the looming shadows. "This better work."

The Fomorii closed the gap quickly. Baccharus could move faster, but he was holding back to stay with Church. Church was feeling the strain of the exertion; his chest hurt and his legs occasionally felt like jelly. A bout of weakness overcame him just as he was jumping one of the gaps in the walkway; his toes caught the edge, but began to slip back on the slick, broken boards.

"Bacch—" was all he had time to shout before he slid off the edge and plummeted through the gap. At the last moment he jammed out his elbows and wedged himself between the two supporting struts. Peering down, he could see his boots were dangling only two feet above the water. The Fomorii were coming up like a train, now only thirty yards away.

Suddenly there was a frantic splashing in the water sweeping towards him. A second later golden fish with enormous jaws and twin rows of razor-sharp teeth were leaping from the bilge, snapping at his feet. One came within half an inch of his toes; if those monstrous jaws closed on him, the thick leather of his boot would amount to nothing.

He kicked out wildly, but before any more of the fish had a chance to go for him, Baccharus's iron hands closed on his shoulders and hauled him effortlessly out of the gap. Lacking the breath even to gasp thanks, Church drove himself on. He did not have to run far. The walkway came up against the end of the bilge tank with no sign of any other exit.

Church and Baccharus turned to face the approaching Night Walkers, who slowed as they realised their prey was cornered. The walkway creaked beneath their bulk. In their shadows, Church could see armoured plates and bony spikes, constantly shifting. They carried the cruel serrated swords favoured by Fomorii warriors, rusted and bloodstained.

"No way out now," Church said. He didn't take his eyes off the approaching warriors.

Baccharus dipped into his pocket and pulled out a lump of clinker from the furnace, which he tossed over the side. It splashed loudly in the dark waters, sending out ripples and wild echoes.

The Fomorii paid no attention. Church watched as their centre of gravity shifted, ready to strike.

The water beneath them began to boil. Big white bubbles, rainbow-streaked, burst on the surface. Church would have been forgiven for thinking it was more of the razor-toothed fish, but it was soon obvious whatever was rising was much, much bigger.

The Fomorii gave it only a cursory glance. They realised the mistake they had made when they saw the grin break across Church's face. An instant later, a long, rubbery object lashed out of the water at lightning speed, smashing through the walkway between the Night Walkers and Church and Baccharus. The Fomorii teetered on the edge, but before they could regain their balance, the enormous bulk of the Llamigan-y-dur burst from the water on its batlike wings and smashed into them. One of the warriors was clamped in the jaws of the grotesque toad-creature, while the other toppled into the tank where there was the sudden white water of a feeding frenzy.

Church had a brief glimpse of the first warrior being ripped apart by the Water-Leaper, named by Cormorel at the banquet before his death, and then the toad disappeared back beneath the waters. The fish finished their meal soon after, and then there was stillness once more.

"How did you know it wouldn't go for us?" Church said, eyeing Baccharus suspiciously.

Baccharus smiled. "It is not only the Golden Ones who detest the Night Walkers. Low beasts like the Malignos may walk the same path, but most denizens of the Far Lands despise those foul creatures."

Church leapt the gap in the walkway before pausing to look back at the oily waters. "A giant toad. With wings. And a tail. Yes, the Age of Reason is well and truly dead."

They spent the next hour probing the darker recesses of the lower decks. As a member of the Tuatha Dé Danann, Baccharus commanded a respect amongst the other travellers that Church would never have had alone. Arrangements were made. Some refused; many agreed.

The kitchens were a relief after the stink of the bilge tanks, rich with the aromas of spices and herbs, the smells of cooking meats and roasting fish drifting. The room stretched the size of four football pitches; Baccharus told Church it was only one of several. Clouds of steam rose from abandoned pots bubbling on the iron ranges that crackled and spat from the well-stoked fires roaring in each one. Bunches of dried herbs hung from the ceiling, releasing scents as they brushed against them, mingling with the wood smoke from the fires. Pots and pans gleamed brightly in the light of scores of torches. The most unnerving thing about the spacious room was the way it magnified even the smallest echo as they crept down the aisles.

They knew it was only a matter of time before the Fomorii found them there, and sure enough, three entered at the same time, two through one door, another on the opposite side of the room. The Night Walkers made no attempt to approach cautiously. They launched into a charge, smashing over bins of vegetables, sending pans and cooking implements flying; the sound of crashing metal was deafening. They didn't waste time following the aisles, instead jumping on to the ranges, filling the air with the stink of their searing flesh.

It was a terrifying sight, but Church stood his ground coolly. He loaded the star in the thong, whirled it round three times and loosed it, taking out one of the pair in a shower of black rain. It was too late to reload for the others who bore down on them with swords raised.

The Afanc rose up from where it had hidden itself in one of the aisles. The half-sea beast had mistimed its entrance so it was too close to one of the attacking Night Walkers. The beast swung its sword in an arc, slashing the Afanc's chest to the bone. It should have been a killing blow, but as quickly as it appeared, the wound closed. Cormorel had been right: the Afanc could not be killed by normal means.

The Night Walker paused in surprise at this revelation. The Afanc grinned, although it was more like a grimace on its extended face. It brought up the strange, twisted spear it had been carrying low and with its powerful arms thrust it right through the Fomor's body, from the gut to the top of the spine.

The Afanc backed off quickly while the Night Walker yanked at the spear. Although it looked mundane, it was another item from the secret weapons store. There was a soundless burst of blue light and the spear clattered to the floor as burning chunks of Fomor rained across the room.

Church and Baccharus ducked the smoking missiles as the last Night Walker launched its assault. It leapt on to the range and swung its sword at Church. There was no time to use the star; the Afanc was too far away.

Baccharus grasped a large clay jug from the side and hurled its contents at the warrior. The golden oil sprayed the Night Walker from head to toe, splashing on to the range where the flames licked through the hole in the top. A second later the beast was burning with a furious heat. It fell backwards off the range, then blundered clumsily around as it feebly attempted to damp the conflagration. Before long, it crumpled into the aisle, filling the kitchens with an oily black smoke and an unbearable stench. Church and Baccharus hurried for the nearest door, covering their mouths.

"There are weapons," Baccharus said brightly, "and there are weapons."

"Smokin'," Church added in his best Jim Carrey impression. "You do realise I've got a humorous saying for every eventuality? That won't be very irritating, will it?"

The wine and beer store was cool and musty, long and thin and low-ceilinged, with enormous oak barrels in lines on opposing walls. The floor was stained with a million wassails; it smelled sour and sweet at the same time, reeking of happier times. There were too many deep shadows, too many places to hide. It was perfect.

Church and Baccharus made no attempt to disguise their entry from the three pursuing Fomorii. As they sprinted between the barrels, the echoes of their footsteps took on a strange deadened tone, like nails being driven into hard wood. Halfway along the store, they loitered briefly in a puddle of light from one of the few flickering torches, just to make sure they were seen. Once they had slipped into the encroaching folds of darkness, they dropped to their knees and crawled under the barrels, scraping their hands and face on the rough wood, drinking in the even more potent aroma. As the Fomorii thundered over the boards, they wriggled like snakes under the next few barrels until they reached a point where they could clamber up the back and lie on top of one for a better view.

The Fomorii hadn't seen them. The Night Walkers knocked the taps on several casks as they passed so the beer and wine foamed out into the gulleys. When the two leaders were about twenty feet from Church and Baccharus's hiding place, there was a sigh and a faint breeze. The two Fomorii continued, only now they were missing the top third of their heads. It took them several more feet before they realised this important fact and then they crashed down hard in the aisle, sizzling like cooking bacon where their blood met the beer and wine.

Church was stunned. When Baccharus had described the Whisper-Line's abilities, he couldn't quite grasp how something as thin as cotton could cut through any object. Even the demonstration—remote-triggered from what appeared to be a yo-yo to whisk out and slice an anvil in two—hadn't wholly convinced him. But here it was.

The Night Walker who was a little behind came to a halt when he saw his fellows drop. Slowly it sniffed the air currents, its rough breathing like the rumble of an old engine. Church was convinced the thing knew exactly where they were.

He needn't have worried. The cry that echoed along the store was enough to jar even the Fomor. Part bird, part animal, part human, Church realised the dread it must have invoked when it had been heard echoing amongst the lonely hills of Skye.

From out of the shadows at the other end of the store emerged a large, lumbering, human figure, the torso heavily muscled, the arms like the branches of an oak. Bloody furs of goat and sheep hung from its waist where they were bound by something that Church didn't want to examine, but had definitely started out as human. The smell was as vile as the first time he and Baccharus had spoken to it.

Roaring, the Fomor launched an attack. Unconcerned, the Baiste-na-scoghaigh stepped into the light; the lethal-looking horn protruding from its forehead cast strange shadows. It waited, yellow eyes glowering. At the last moment it ducked down beneath the cleaving sword, drove forward like a bull and buried the horn deep in the spot where Church presumed the Night Walker's belly to be.

The battle was furious, the noise of roars and squeals and shrieks deafening. Barrels were smashed, drink flooded everywhere. The Baiste-na-scoghaigh took several nasty wounds to its arms and chest before it smashed the sword in two, but they didn't seem to bother it. The Fomor then proceeded to change shape in the unnerving manner that always reminded Church of stop-go animation, adopting razor-sharp thorns, snapping jaws and at one point what appeared to be giant lobster claws. But the Baiste-na-scoghaigh was so ferocious it simply powered through every offence, tearing with its horn, its enormous fists coming down unceasingly with the force of jackhammers. The Fomor was soon trailing most of its innards, but still fighting on, even when it collapsed. The Baiste-na-scoghaigh didn't relent, not even when the Night Walker was unmoving: it proceeded to pound every last inch of its prey into a thick paste.

Church and Baccharus left it there, slamming its fists over and over again into the floor.

Church and Baccharus had considered playing a part in the map room and library, but there didn't seem much point. Instead, they secreted themselves behind some enormous volumes heaped on the floor where they could watch the proceedings unobserved.

Hundreds of torches and lamps lined the walls or sat in the middle of the reading desks, but even the smell of oil and smoke couldn't stifle the warm aroma of old, dry paper and papyrus. After the gloom of the store and the bilge tanks, it was refreshingly light and airy.

The room was oddly detached from the storm that raged without. There had been so many of them in recent times; certainly the Fomorii had something to do with it. Windows along one wall allowed a vista on waves rising up higher than the ship. Lightning filled every corner of the room with brilliant illumination while the rain slammed in a constant, violent rhythm.

Yet the charts and books covering every table, desk, chair, shelf and most of the floor were not thrown around. It was almost as if they were watching the storm from some distant place, which Church suspected was probably true.

The Fomorii came in about ten minutes later. They acted unnerved by the light, wandering around the room with uncharacteristic caution, prodding potential hiding places with their swords. Church was surprised to see that in the glare of the torches they looked diminished; quite literally. They were smaller, their gleaming sable forms no longer holding so many surprises: two legs, two arms, a head.

As one of them passed a bookshelf packed with maps, it didn't notice a column of mist, fading in and out of the light. The haze curled around the Fomor, then moved away as if it had been caught on a breeze. For a second or two the beast froze. Then slowly it threw its head back and released a terrible cry that was immediately and surprisingly recognisable as despair. The Night Walker lashed out wildly, demolishing the bookcase with one blow, then began to run backwards and forwards in a frenzy, tearing at its eyes and ears. Black gunk splashed on to the pristine white of the charts.

"What's happening?" Church whispered.

Baccharus shrugged slightly. "The Spriggan has whispered a secret."

"Christ, what kind of secret?"

"One that can drive anything insane."

What this could possibly be disturbed Church so deeply he decided not to consider it further.

The other Fomorii grew as animated as monkeys in the jungle at their fellow's demise by its own hands, but they didn't back off. Opting for a tight defensive formation, they moved cautiously through the vast room in search of the invisible enemy. Church couldn't identify the Spriggans either, and he had suggested areas where they could secrete themselves. He knew of the legends surrounding them long before Cormorel had pointed them out. The ghosts of giants, supposedly, haunting the standing stones of Cornwall, but in actuality they had the shapeshifting abilities of many denizens of T'ir n'a n'Og. Often they appeared as insubstantial as morning mist, but when they took on substance they were even more grotesque than the Fomorii.

Despite their fearsome reputation, they respected Church for his links with the Blue Fire, which apparently calmed their violent natures.

The Fomorii were growing irritated with their inability to locate the enemy and had taken to hacking randomly at shelving and piles of books. But as they passed near heavy purple drapes flapping in the breeze from one open window, there was sudden movement. The drapes folded back and out of them—out of the air itself—came the Spriggans, now solid, and monstrous in their rage. They descended on the Fomorii like frenzied birds, intermittently fading so the Night Walkers could never get a handle on them.

If there had been fewer than the eight Spriggans Church counted, the Fomorii might have stood a chance; as it was the Night Walkers managed to bring down one with a lucky blow while he was solid. But the white-hot rage of the Spriggans drove them on relentlessly. Soon the torn bodies of the Fomorii lay heaped in the centre of the room.

In the light of what he had seen, Church was wary of emerging from his hiding place, but Baccharus was quickly out to thank the Spriggans with a taut bow. They were shifting anxiously around the corpses, as if they were considering feasting. Rather than see what transpired, Church thanked them from a distance and quickly exited.

For the next hour and a half, the attacks proceeded relentlessly. Here the tearing claws of the thing that resembled a griffin, there the ferocity of the Manticore analogue. Losses amongst the ship's passengers were relatively few—a couple of Portunes crushed by a falling Fomor, something that had a body covered with sharp thorns, like a human porcupine—but the Night Walkers were decimated. Once Church and Baccharus had convinced themselves no others roamed the corridors, they moved speedily towards the deck.

They emerged into the face of a gale as sharp as knives. The rain was horizontal, bullet hard, and mixed with sheeting salt water. Lightning tore the sky ragged with barely a break between strikes. Below deck, they had been aware of the ship's movements on the waves, but had somehow been protected from it. There in the open they faced the full force of the wild pitching that almost tipped Wave Sweeper from end to end. Even shouting, they could not be heard above the explosive force of the thunder. Purchase on the streaming boards was almost impossible to find. They skidded from side to side, clutching on to rigging or railing to prevent themselves being thrown overboard. At one point, Church was hanging on by only his arms, his legs dangling out at near right angles to the deck. Strangely unaffected by the yawing, Baccharus hooked a hand in Church's jacket to keep him anchored until the boat began to turn the other way, and then they hurried to the next safe point.

After fifteen minutes, the door to Manannan's quarters loomed agonisingly close. Church clung to a spinnaker, ready to make the final dash. Just as he was about to put a foot forward, lightning painted the deck a brilliant white and from the corner of his eye he caught sight of an incongruous shadow. He whirled and dodged with a second to spare. Talons like metal spikes turned wood to splinters where his head had been.

Another flash brought a face into stark relief only inches from his own: slit pupils turning to a black sliver in the glare, reptilian scales, a flickering tongue, flaring nostrils steaming in the storm's chill, the bone structure of the skull ridged and hard.

Church thrust hard and the Maligna flew on to its back and rolled down the deck. But he was not alone. The lightning flashes created an odd strobe effect, freezing then releasing, before freezing again, as the rest of the Malignos attacked. It was a surreal scenario, the creatures leaping like lizards from railing to rigging, caught in the light, untroubled by the wild swings of the ship. And at the back, clutching the jamb of the door that led below deck, was Callow, his face as furious as the storm.

The Malignos were flitting shadows until the lightning caught them, and then it was apparent why they were so feared. Their bodies were lithe yet packed with muscle, efficient machines with only one brutal purpose in mind. The speed with which they moved made it impossible for any prey to avoid them in open pursuit, while their reputation as flesh eaters made them even more fearsome.

Church was caught between running for cover and standing and fighting his ground, but in the violently tossing ship it was impossible to do either; the most he could do was hang on to the spinnaker for grim life.

There must have been six or seven of the Malignos, but it was impossible to pin down the exact number because of the speed of their movement and the force of the storm. They were coming at him from both sides, but shifting around rapidly to confuse him like a pack of hunting wolves.

Baccharus was yelling something, but Church couldn't hear above the wind. In that instant, the Malignos struck. A ball of flailing, wiry limbs slammed into Church head-on. He lost his grip on the spinnaker and went down hard. Another Maligna flashed by just close enough to rake him with its talons. Warm blood seeped out through the tears on his jacket. The first one planted itself astride him, raising up one arm ready to tear out his throat. Church frantically tried to throw him off, but the creature was too strong. The talons curled; the arm came down.

Baccharus caught the Maligna with the back of his hand, a blow of such force Church felt the vibrations in his bones. The beast flew down the deck. Baccharus managed to get Church to his feet. The god was still trying to tell Church something, but before Church could decipher it, another Maligna crashed into his back. The deck tipped, his feet left the boards and he was flying down the length of the ship, careening off the rigging, bouncing off the railing, inches from going overboard into the savage sea. He slammed into the wall next to the door leading below deck, and for a second lost consciousness.

When he came to, Callow was over him, a rusty razor blade clutched between thumb and forefinger, ready to slice into Church's jugular. His hideous face glowed white in the lightning, the black veins standing out in stark relief. Church suddenly flashed to Callow's attack on Laura in the back of the van, to what he had done to Ruth in Callendar, and he was overcome with fury.

Church came up sharp, catching Callow on the jaw with the top of his head. Callow stumbled back; the razor blade was washed away. Spinning round, Church faced the Malignos and knew what Baccharus had been telling him to do. From his side, he pulled up the Wish-Sword that he had been saving for the final assault on Manannan's captors; Baccharus had warned him the effect it had on his spirit would mean he could only use it once in a day, but there was no other option. He thumbed the gem in the handle and waited as the blue fire crackled between the twin blades, building from the handle towards the tip.

The Malignos were almost upon him. They leapt as one from different directions, but they were a second too late. The energy leapt from the blade in a sapphire flash; lightning brought down to earth, it jumped from one Maligna to the other, seizing them in a coruscating field so bright Church had to look away. When his eyes cleared, all of the attackers were gone, with not even the slightest remains to indicate they had ever existed.

Weary, Church slumped back against the wall. He felt as if a vital part of him had been lost, but Baccharus had told him the debilitating sensation would pass.

Nearby, Callow was shakily making his way to his feet. Church didn't know if he would have the energy to repel another attack.

When Callow saw Baccharus approaching, his expression grew sly and he pointed accusingly, mouthing something over and over. The insistence in his face suggested the importance of his unheard words, but they were snatched from his lips the moment they were born. Church was drawn magnetically to the shaping of that mouth, divining the syllables. Again. And again. He almost had it . . .

The wave must have been twenty feet high, the water as grey and hard as stone. It came down with the force of an angry god swatting flies. Church grabbed hold of the door jamb the moment he saw it rushing towards him, screwing his eyes and mouth shut tight. For a brief moment a new universe closed around him and he was convinced his arms were going to be torn from his sockets. He held fast while his fingers felt like they were breaking, and when the rush passed and he opened his eyes, Callow was gone.

There was little point searching overboard; even if Church could spot him in the turbulent waters he would have had no way of getting him back on to the ship. He didn't feel any sense of victory at the loss; he didn't feel anything at all. The weariness that had afflicted him since using the Wish-Sword reached into his very bones and although it had eased slightly in the passing moments, he wondered if he had any reserves left to face what lay ahead.

They paused at the door to Manannan's quarters briefly before stepping inside. There was no guard waiting for them; the remaining Fomorii still expected their forces to be swarming on deck.

A moment later they stood outside Manannan's private room. Through the thick wood came the muffled growls of the Fomorii, but there was no other recognisable voice. Church wondered if Manannan was still alive, and Niamh too, but his real thoughts were for Ruth.

"Give me the Wish-Sword," Baccharus whispered, pulling Church a few paces back from the door.

"What am I going to do?"

"Rest, and watch my back. What I can provide the Wish-Sword will not be as powerful as you, but it should suffice."

"So, what? We just barge in there?"

"An act of surprise may win the day."

They exchanged a look that underlined their mutual respect and trust, paused to gather their thoughts, and then rushed the door.

The scene inside the vast cabin was shocking enough to take the edge off their charge the moment they crossed the threshold. The Tuatha Dé Danann had been herded to one end of the room, where they were guarded by several prowling Fomorii. The Golden Ones were on their knees, humbled, eyes fixed dead ahead. The scene reminded Church of old pictures from the Second World War, of Nazis guarding brutalised POWs. Niamh was at the front, pale and worried, but there was no sign of Ruth.

The attention of the gods was fixed on Manannan—at least Church presumed it was Manannan—and at the glowing geometric shape he had seen when he had probed the mind of the Night Walker. Three Fomorii had Wave Sweeper's Master bound across the enormous desk, where several monstrous implements appeared to have been used to torture him. It was impossible to tell the exact use of the instruments, which resembled bear traps and hand drills, but they had obviously had a profound effect on the Master. He had lost his familiar shape. The body was blurred and pulsing, leaking light in dazzling beams, and the face was like a running mixture of oil and water.

Church couldn't believe the Fomorii had overwhelmed Manannan, one of the most powerful of the gods. The only explanation was that he had been forced to succumb because of the Wish-Hex; yet he had still patently resisted attempts to coerce him to take Wave Sweeper to the Court of High Regard.

Even to glance at the Wish-Hex made Church feel queasy. It looked like a system of interlocking cubes and triangles and pentagons made of light, hovering in midair, but at some point all the elements seemed to disappear into a different dimension.

By the time he took this in, the Fomorii were aware of their presence. Five of the Night Walkers rushed at once, the others preparing to follow.

Church looked to Baccharus to use the Wish-Sword. To his horror, he saw the god's thumb wavering over the gem. *Why is he holding back?* Church thought until a shocking thought ripped through him. Perhaps Baccharus was a traitor. In the pay of the Fomorii. He was going to give Church up to the enemy. Was that what Callow had been trying to tell him?

At the last moment, Baccharus did thumb the trigger. The blue fire built quicker than it had with Church, but it did not burn so brightly. It surged through the Fomorii, creating a chain of blue balls of light where it passed through the Night Walkers' chests. Four, five, six, all writhing in the brilliant arc light. But with each one it possessed, the light grew a little dimmer, and then Church realised Baccharus's strategy: he had been waiting for the Fomorii to get close enough for the force to strike them all. Eight, nine, ten. The light dying now.

Come on, Church prayed silently. *Only five more.*

Twelve, thirteen. But after it had passed through the fourteenth, the light faltered, then died. The corpses of the Fomorii fell to the ground, crumbling into a black dust.

The single surviving Night Walker was already moving. He reached the Wish-Hex before anyone in the room could react.

Niamh dashed over to Manannan and loosed the shackles. As she helped him up, his body and features gradually returned to the form Church knew, but his body was still leaking too much light. He didn't have the strength to help.

The Night Walker positioned himself with one arm on either side of the Wish-Hex. Church removed his sword and weakly moved forward, hoping he didn't look as impotent as he felt.

"Hold." Baccharus waved Church back frantically. "The foul beast will trigger the Wish-Hex if you approach."

"It can't hope to get anything. What's it going to do? Commit suicide?"

"It will destroy us all, and itself, in the blink of an eye. But it does not want to waste the Wish-Hex. The Fomorii will not be able to create another one in the near future."

"A standoff."

"We will never take this foul beast to the Green Isles of Enchantment." Niamh was speaking with pride. "We will see ourselves wiped from the face of existence first."

The Night Walker appeared to understand her words, for he brought his hands closer to the Wish-Hex. It began to throb; the light turned scarlet, then black. A faint tremor ran across Niamh's face, but she did not back down.

The Wish-Hex glowed brighter and brighter. The unease it radiated became more intense, turning Church's stomach, making him inexplicably want to cry. *This is the end?* he thought in disbelief.

And then the strangest thing happened. The Night Walker tripped backwards. The light surrounding the Wish-Hex began to die. The Fomor fought to get back to the weapon, but it stumbled, and then it propelled itself in the direction of Church.

In that moment, the empty space where the Night Walker had been was suddenly occupied. Astonishingly, Church realised he was looking at Ruth, her face anxious, fearful, but with a rising note of triumph.

The Night Walker turned at speed to rush back to the Wish-Hex. Church didn't even think. He drove his sword into the base of its skull, cleaving the beast's head in two. And then when it hit the floor, he waited for a second before splattering the Caraprix the moment it left the corpse.

A cry rose up from the assembled Tuatha Dé Danann—not just triumph, but also gratitude, directed at him, and Ruth. Directed at *Fragile Creatures*.

He threw his steaming sword to one side and rushed over to Ruth, throwing his arm around her waist.

"Well, aren't you Mr. Testosterone." She held her head back from him, grinning. "See, even the sensitive ones can't wait to let it out."

"What was that all about? How did you do that? Where did you come from?"

"I am a woman of many talents and great fortitude and you are very, very lucky to have me."

While the Tuatha Dé Danann tended to Manannan's wounds, feeding him the strange drink Ruth and Church had sampled earlier, the two of them sat next to the window where they could watch the storm.

"It was something the familiar taught me," she said as she cupped his hand loosely between hers. "*To avoid being seen in plain sight*. But you can't keep it up for long, and it doesn't really work if anyone is actively looking for you, but—"

"How much more have you got in your bag of tricks?"

"I don't really know." She fixed an eye on him. "What's the matter? Scared?"

"Should I be?"

"*I'm* scared."

"That's understandable—it's powerful stuff. But Cernunnos and his partner wouldn't have invested it in you if they didn't trust you to do a good job with it."

This comforted her a little. "We're all *becoming* something, aren't we?"

"I think we're achieving the potential we always had. I think everybody has great potential, but necessity is the greatest motivator for discovering it."

"Stop it. You're starting to sound like an optimist." She smiled shyly. "I was worried about you."

He gave her hand a squeeze. "It's made things worse."

"What do you mean?"

"Before, I had only myself to worry about, and let's face it, I didn't worry too much. Now I can't stop worrying about you. All the time."

"You're saying that's too much of a price to pay?"

"No. I'm saying it's given me even more of an impetus to find some way out of this mess so we can get back to our lives." He felt a deep yearning for the normality he had once taken for granted. "I want to lie in bed on Sunday morning with you, wander out for a lazy lunch. I want to feel what it's like just to do nothing with someone you love."

She looked surprised. "Do you love me?"

"Yes." And he realised in that moment, for the first time, that he truly did, and that it was a feeling as potent as he had had for Marianne.

"Brother and Sister of Dragons." The interruption came from Baccharus, who was bowing formally. "The Master requests your presence."

"Oh, we're back to *requests*, are we?" Ruth said under her breath. From the colour of her cheeks and the brightness in her eyes, Church could tell he had touched her deeply.

Baccharus led them to Manannan who rested in a large, high-backed chair. The light no longer broke out of his form, but his face had a weary cast. Even so, he brightened perceptibly when he laid eyes on Church and Ruth. It was strange to see any emotion on that normally impassive face, never mind something as subtle and human as gratitude.

"Brother and Sister of Dragons, you have my thanks for the part you have played this day. Amongst the Golden Ones there is a hard-held belief that we are the pinnacle of creation, a part of the fundament of existence. And with that belief is the certain knowledge that all other creatures lie beneath us. Some would argue this is reason enough to treat all other races with contempt. They are beasts of the field, and we are shepherds. But you have shown this day that Fragile Creatures are not so fragile, that you have the facility to climb the ladder of existence, even to rub shoulders with the Golden Ones. The signs are true. No more the centre path. This is my belief. And I mark it with this." Manannan beckoned them forward, then gently took their hands in turn. His fingers felt like cold light; insubstantial, ghostly. There were faint sounds of surprise from some of the gathered gods, but when Manannan levelled his heavy gaze slowly around the room, the murmurings died away sharply.

"You will have my support in your undertaking, Brother and Sister of Dragons. My voice carries weight. The Golden Ones shall heed your call. This is the day the seasons have turned once more. This is the time. The Night Walkers shall be cleansed from existence."

He spoke with such authority, Church almost believed him.

chapter thirteen
all stars

"This is crazy! We can't sit here forever!" Laura hurled the empty baked beans tin across the warehouse.

The Bone Inspector winced at the clattering echoes bouncing around the vast, empty space. "What do you suggest, then? Going out there and asking them nicely if you can go home?" He snorted contemptuously, wiping the bean juice from his mouth with the back of his hand.

Laura paced around the embers of the fire, her irritation turning to curiosity at the unfamiliar emotions growing inside her. For months she had been arguing with the others about running away from their obligations; now she couldn't do it even if she wanted. "The responsibility's on us to find a way out," she said firmly. She realised the Bone Inspector was watching her with a strange expression. "What?"

"Nothing." He slurped some more beans. "I always thought you were the weak link who'd bring everything down."

"You and me both." She wandered over to one of the dirty windows. Smearing a patch clear, she watched the Fomorii scurrying along the banks of the Thames as they went about their mysterious tasks. The view was sickening, but strangely hypnotic. In another moment or two, though, another notion began to creep in. She turned to the Bone Inspector with a confident smile and said, "Okay, here's the plan."

The river had the dank, sour smell of rotting vegetation. Under the night sky, the water looked almost black as it lapped languidly against the creaking wharves. A hint of frost sparkled all around; it was the coldest night so far. Laura lay on the sodden boards and held out a hand so the Bone Inspector could steady himself. It had taken them three hours to find something they could use. The boat was holed and filled with a couple of inches of water; it looked like it had been abandoned for months. But it was big enough for them to lie in the bottom while it drifted in the strong currents out of the city and towards the sea.

After ten minutes of splashing and cursing, the Bone Inspector finished plugging the hole with the oily rags they had brought from the warehouse.

"Do you think it'll hold? I don't fancy swimming in this weather."

"How should I know?" he snapped. "I'm not a shipwright."

"No. What you are is—"

"Just get in the boat."

She lowered herself down to the tiny pebbly beach where plastic bottles and old ropes formed a trail along the water line. She was still amazed they had managed to avoid the Fomorii. They had encountered several large groups of them moving silently through the dark streets, but had always had time to find cover. She hoped it was a sign luck was on their side.

Once they had baled out as much as they could, they pushed the boat out into the freezing shallows, then jumped aboard. Water had already started to trickle into the bottom.

"We should stay near the banks," the Bone Inspector said.

"There'll be too much chance of being seen."

"This river has powerful currents. If we go down in the middle of it, we won't stand a chance."

"All right. But if we get caught, I'm blaming you."

They guided the boat into the current with a broken plank and then lay down in the bottom, watching the stars pass overhead.

Manannan recovered quickly enough to take back control of Wave Sweeper and soon they were speeding on their way. By the time dawn was breaking the sea was calm, the sky poised to turn a brilliant blue, free of even the smallest cloud. Soon the gulls were clustering around the mast and a cry was rising up from the watcher in the crow's nest. The Green Fields of Enchantment came up quickly on the horizon, a sunlit haven of rolling, emerald downs dotted with crystal streams and cool woods.

From his position at the prow, Church watched in growing wonder. There was something breathtaking about the place that went far beyond its appearance; it was in the air, in some too-subtle signs that only his oldest senses could perceive, but it left his nerves singing and his stomach filled with tremors of excitement. Some deep-seated part of his mind was registering recognition of one of the oldest archetypes: a place of miracles and peace. Heaven.

Wave Sweeper sailed into a small harbour built of gleaming white marble. There were no other ships in sight and the dockside was deserted, apart from two of the younger gods manning the jetty. They took the ropes Taranis's men threw out and fastened them to iron spurs, but Church had the feeling Wave Sweeper would have waited there like a faithful dog anyway.

The Tuatha Dé Danann were allowed to disembark first, while the other strange travellers congregated below deck ready to begin their search for some meaning in their lives. Church and Ruth, however, were given pride of place at the front of the column with Manannan and Niamh.

They marched along a dusty road, baking in the heat, which wound briefly along the golden beach where the blue sea broke in white-topped waves before ending amongst the soothing shadows of the trees. Flowers bloomed in clusters of blue, red and gold. It reminded Church of Andalucia, or Umbria, an unspoiled rural climate designed for dreaming.

Manannan was borne on a gold chair carried sedan-style by four young gods. He was still weak, but he cocked his attention to Church and Ruth often enough for them to know they lay heavily on his mind. Niamh watched Church surreptitiously from beneath long lashes; it was impossible to tell what she was thinking, though her praise in the aftermath of the rescue had been fulsome, for both Church and Ruth.

The Court of High Regard lay in a shallow valley beyond the wall of soaring black pines, surrounded by pleasant grassed slopes where the breeze moved back and forth soothingly. If the first sight of the island had taken Church's breath away, the Court of High Regard was a hundred times more affecting. Tears of sheer awe stung his eyes; it was in the very fibre of the place, majesty in every atom.

Unlike the Court of the Final Word, it was more of a town—if not a city—than a court. The buildings were all white stone, so that the whole was almost impossible to view in the sun. In the architecture, Church glimpsed touches of the Middle East, of ancient Greece and Rome, Japan and the heavy Gothic stylings of mediaeval France. There were domes and towers, cupolas and obelisks, Doric columns and piazzas and sweeping boulevards where fountains tinkled pleasantly. Clusters of cultivated trees provided shade to talk and think.

"It's beautiful." Ruth blinked away her own tears. "Now I know why the stories said visitors never wanted to leave."

They entered through gates of ivory and glass. Once within, the Tuatha Dé Danann dispersed into small groups conversing quietly but intently.

Church and Ruth were left alone next to a statue that resembled the god Pan, but every time Church looked at it, it had a different face. "Now what?" Ruth said.

After ten minutes Baccharus returned with a tall, thin god with flowing black hair and sculpted bone structure who resembled an aristocrat in his late twenties. "The Master has already announced your presence to the court," Baccharus said. "A decision will be announced soon on when you may make your case. In the meantime, I have discussed your needs with Callaitus, Provarum of the sector of Trust and Hope, who will make the arrangements for your stay."

Church took his hand and shook it. "Thank you for everything you've done for us, Baccharus."

Surprisingly, Baccharus appeared humbled by this. "I will be along shortly. There are other matters—"

"I understand," Church said knowingly. "We'll talk later."

Callaitus took them to a light and airy chamber, far removed from the cramped quarters of Wave Sweeper. At the window, the most delicate linen blew gently in the breeze. There was a large bed covered with sumptuous cushions and deep, soft blankets. A small wooden table held a bowl of fruit and a crystal decanter filled with sparkling water.

"Married quarters," Ruth said, looking round at the furniture and space.

"What?"

"On the ship they put us in adjoining cabins. Here we've got a room together. How very presumptuous of them," she added with mock affront.

"They're good at looking beneath the surface."

She eyed him studiously, remembering his words on Wave Sweeper, saying nothing.

"I wonder where I'll find the Pool of Wishes." He threw himself on the bed and slipped his hands behind his head. The soothing atmosphere made him feel instantly sleepy.

"I wonder what you'll find there." A dark note rang clearly in her voice.

"What are you inferring?"

"You know how these things work. Everything comes with a price. You want to get rid of something big. That's got to be balanced out."

He threw an arm across his eyes. "I don't think I can take any more sacrifice."

"Let's have none of that." He felt the bed give as she climbed on. There was a rustle of clothing, more movement, and then she straddled him. He looked up to see her naked to the waist. She laughed silently at his expression. "Remember your mantra: *Life's good as long as you don't weaken*. So stop thinking about all the sacrifice and suffering. Focus on the good stuff. That's a rule for living, Churchill." She slowly ground her hips on his groin, smiling now, gently teasing.

Sleep was going to have to wait.

When he woke, dark had fallen. It was still warm, and fragrant with woodsmoke and the heady perfume of night blooms. There was a sense of magic in the air. He eased his arm out from under Ruth, who stirred and muttered, but didn't rouse, then dressed lazily before stepping out. The evening was alight with flickering torches gleaming off the white buildings. Faint, melodic music drifted across the jumbled rooftops, and somewhere he could make out the excited chattering of many voices. He leaned against the doorjamb and breathed deeply, enjoying the peace.

Across the piazza, a shadow stirred, then separated from the surrounding shadows. Baccharus made his way over from the bench where he had been sitting patiently.

"You needed to rest," he said by way of greeting.

"Have you been waiting long?"

"It is not waiting if you are engaged in something important, and I was enjoying my time here in the Court of High Regard. I could have sat there until light."

"You missed this place?"

"It is where I feel comfortable." He placed a hand on Church's shoulder. "Come, there is much we need to discuss, and this is not the best place."

The streets wound round and back on themselves, diverged, became vast boulevards, then a network of interlocking alleys; briefly Church felt like he was back on Wave Sweeper in the endless corridors. He mentioned this to Baccharus, and for a second or two he had the odd impression he was lying on his back looking up into a brilliant, phosphorescent light. It faded into a gentler luminescence that flickered over a studded oak door. Baccharus pushed open the door and beckoned for Church to step through.

It was an inn, low ceilinged, straw on the floor, lots of tables and stools nestling in the comfortable shadows of nooks and crannies. A large fire roared in the grate despite the summery warmth, yet the temperature remained agreeable. The drinkers were a mixed group. Church recognised many of the travellers he had seen on Wave Sweeper—some of them even nodded to him as if they were old friends—but there were many strangers.

"None of your people?" Church said.

"This place is for the benefit of others. The many who come to visit us, seeking the gratitude of the gods, seeking direction or redemption."

There was a raucous group of muscular men with red beards, so they headed to a quiet table under the overhang of a staircase. It was pleasantly dark and secluded. Baccharus returned from the bar with two pewter mugs filled with ale that frothed over the edges.

"Given freely and without obligation?"

"This is a place for visitors," Baccharus replied. "Everything here is given freely and without obligation."

Church took a sip. It felt like light and colours were streaming down his throat; a faint buzz of exhilaration filled his veins. "You're trying to get me drunk before you tell me what you have to say?"

"No. This is the drink of welcome, to put you in a receptive frame of mind."

"That's what I said." Church took a long draught, then looked Baccharus directly in his deep, golden eyes. "What's the true story?"

"That is unanswerable. You strip away one story and another lies behind, and another, and another. You will never find the true story that lies behind it all, for there lies the truth of life. All is illusion, each illusion as valid as any other, until you reach that final level, and to find that is to know how everything works. To know the mind of . . ." His words trailed off and he ended his thought with a gesture suggesting something too big to comprehend.

"You're as bad as Tom. Ask a simple question and you get a philosophy lecture."

"The Rhymer is a good man."

"That's not the point. In *this* story"—his sweeping arm took in the whole of the bar—"there are a lot of illusions, and now it's time for the truth. Like why you murdered Cormorel."

Church expected some kind of surprise from Baccharus, or guilt perhaps, or even anger that he had been uncovered, but there was nothing. "I pay a price every day for that act."

"You were *friends*."

"More than that. To lose Cormorel was like losing part of myself. My existence is forever tainted."

"Then, why?"

"How long have you known?"

"Don't change the subject." He softened slightly when he saw Baccharus was telling the truth about his hurt. "It came to me just before we disembarked. No blinding revelation. Just a gentle understanding that that was what must have happened. You were arguing at the banquet just before he died—"

"Cormorel and I held contrary positions of a kind that you would find hard to grasp unless you were a Golden One."

"Try me."

Baccharus finished his beer, then signalled for the barman to bring over two more. "Then I will tell you of the things I brought you here to understand. Of truth, of a kind. Consider: the view held by the Golden Ones of Fragile Creatures."

"That we're the lowest of the low."

"There are many of my kind who would disagree."

Church was taken aback by this. "I know some of you are closer to us than others, but I thought all of you at least vaguely held the same view. Veitch defined it: you're like aristocrats looking down on what you consider the lesser-born. Some of you despise us, some of you hold us in contempt, some of you mock us, and even the ones of you who think we're okay still think we're way beneath you."

"I can understand how you might think that, for that is the view of some, but not all. No, some of us believe the Fragile Creatures are in an exalted position; even above the Golden Ones in the structure of existence, for in their arrogance the Golden Ones have embraced stagnancy, while you Fragile Creatures continue to rise and advance. Within your kind lies tremendous potential. The Golden Ones no longer have potential. This view, as you might expect, is tantamount to blasphemy in some quarters. Indeed, the Golden Ones are riven. But for those of us who are concerned with the great sweep of existence rather than the narrow perspective of our kind, the future of the Fragile Creatures is very important indeed."

At the bar, the red-bearded men had started to punch each other hard, while laughing heartily. Some of the other drinkers were moving away hesitantly. "That would be quite a turnaround. Riven, you say. Like a civil war situation?"

"It is very close to that. The Golden Ones have always seen our position as unassailable. Yet to suggest we are not all-knowing, all-powerful, would weaken our position and allow us to be supplanted. A contradiction that gives the lie to the former. I think the latter is not only inevitable—for it is the way of existence—but also to be desired, again, in terms of existence."

"I remember the first time we met you and Cormorel at the campfire," Church mused. "The two of you had a disagreement about whether humanity could ever evolve into gods."

"At that time, Cormorel did not know the extent of my beliefs, although he was aware of the fractures forming amongst my people. I was influenced by others who have had more contact with the Fragile Creatures across the turning of the ages."

"Niamh?"

"And the one you know as Cernunnos, and his partner. Ogma. And many more."

"The three smiths on Wave Sweeper? Were they preparing weapons for a civil war?"

"Perhaps." Baccharus was uncomfortable. "Or for a war against the Night Walkers. We would have launched one independently, if necessary. It was, as you pointed out, inevitable. To pretend otherwise was the height of arrogance."

"Goibhniu wasn't very pleasant to me."

"He is new to our beliefs, brought round by Niamh, who knew he would be an important asset to our side. He accepts the way things are, but he finds it hard to break from past feelings for Fragile Creatures."

Church stared into the dark depths of his beer. "Tom knows about all this?" Comments Tom had made, which at the time had been cryptic or just plain strange, suddenly fell into a new perspective; Baccharus nodded. "So this isn't just about saving humanity from a big threat, it's about preserving the future of life, everything?"

"True Thomas knew the Golden Ones would have to be resisted as much as the Night Walkers if you Fragile Creatures were to prosper. He is an adept at politics." Baccharus smiled. "I like him immensely."

What had been a quiet conversation about Baccharus's motivation for murder had suddenly taken on a terrible significance that he couldn't absorb all at once. "What are you saying exactly?"

"I am saying you are all stars. Each Fragile Creature bursting with the potential of a god. Given the right situation, that potential could easily blossom, and from what I have seen of you and the other Brothers and Sisters of Dragons, you could far surpass the Golden Ones. You could all become greater than everything that ever existed. For you love and cry, you are tender, and caring—"

"—and hateful and murderous."

Baccharus shrugged. "It is there within you. The light burns very brightly. Brighter than my own."

"You're talking about a long period of time—"

Baccharus lowered his head so shadows pooled in his eyes; a skull in the play of light and shade. "These events you find yourselves in are a catalyst that could propel you—all of your kind—into the next phase of development. My people know this—some will deny it, but they know it somewhere within themselves—and they seek to prevent you achieving your destiny. You will have to fight for your future."

"That makes a change." Church pushed his stool back on two legs and rocked, tipsy now. "So, trickery and deceit right the way down the line. Situation normal."

"There are manipulations ahead," Baccharus continued. "You need to know what is at stake so you can act accordingly; when lies are told to you, when seemingly simple choices are asked of you. Do not allow anyone to make you believe you are lesser, unimportant."

"I never did."

Baccharus smiled. "I always admired your confidence, Brother of Dragons."

"I saw some of the splits on Wave Sweeper. Many were angered that Manannan offered us his support."

"The Master had always steered a calm path between the troubled waters. I felt his sympathies lay with you and your kind, but with his position amongst the Golden Ones, to openly endorse our stance would have caused too much upheaval."

"But now he's going to do it?"

Baccharus nodded slowly.

"This must be the first time that gods are servant to the people who worshipped them."

"All should be in servitude to others, and all should be free."

"But this split amongst your people . . . is it really so bad?"

Baccharus gave a thin-lipped smile. "If there is to be war amongst the Golden Ones, you will find many fighting for the future of the Fragile Creatures."

"You'd do that? Against your own people?"

"This concerns much more than one severely limited perspective, even if that vista belongs to the Golden Ones. We are all servants of existence, and we must do what we can to ensure the best possible state for all."

"So let me get this straight—humans have the potential to become gods—"

Baccharus winced at the description, waved it away with a lazy hand.

"—greater, then. Than we are now. To achieve the massive potential—"

"—encoded in your very make-up." Baccharus nodded emphatically. "You were made with the powers of stars inside you. All sentient creatures are formed to rise and advance. That is the reason for all this." He made an expansive gesture.

"The Golden Ones have stopped advancing, for whatever reason. Some fatal flaw. But they don't want to be supplanted by Fragile Creatures and so they will do everything they can to keep us down. To prevent us achieving our destiny." Church looked dreamily towards the bar where the red-headed men were still punching each other, though their laughter was now more forced.

Baccharus smiled proudly at Church's expert summing up of the complex matters he had raised. He raised a finger. "One more thing: the lie is given to my people's assertions of superiority by the mere existence of the Court of the Final Word."

Church grew cold at the mention of the Tuatha Dé Danann court supposedly devoted to healing, but where more sinister things happened in its deepest recesses. "What do you mean?"

"For many generations of your people the Court of the Final Word has been *investigating* mortal children." Baccharus pronounced the word carefully. "My people wish to know what innate part of Fragile Creatures is the key to their advancement."

"So they can steal it for themselves!" Church grew rigid at the repercussions that spun out of Baccharus's comment. "That's why Tom's Queen was so adept at taking him apart and putting him back together!"

"Oh, my people know every component part of Fragile Creatures. They know how every molecule interlocks with every other molecule. But they have still not found the source of your potential." His eyes sparkled. "And they never will."

"This is too much for me to take in right now." Church held up the beer. "This doesn't help. But you're right—it puts me in the correct frame of mind. I thought I'd get everything laid out in my mind about what we were fighting for. Now it's even bigger stakes. Not just survival, but our . . . evolution? Crazy."

"These are monumental times."

"You're telling me. Wait till Ruth hears about this." He leaned forward once more and peered back into his beer. "Now tell me about Cormorel," he said quietly.

Baccharus stared at one of the flickering torches for a long time. "It is said my people feel nothing like you Fragile Creatures feel. But I loved Cormorel. I think, once we see things from your perspective, we learn to be how we perhaps once were."

"Then how could you kill him?"

"It was not my intention at the time, but in the instant before I acted, I knew it had to be done. Cormorel had discovered there was a conspiracy afoot. That is his word. Conspiracy. Niamh, myself, certain others, had taken the decision to confound those who attempted to block the chances which might come the way of the Fragile Creatures on their path to enlightenment. Niamh and I had formed an alliance with some of the other creatures on Wave Sweeper—"

"The Portunes."

"And others. And in the eyes of my people, associating with such lowly creatures against our own kind was the ultimate crime. Cormorel was preparing to expose us. The Portunes and all the others would have been eradicated. Niamh would have been despatched to the Court of the Final Word, where she would have suffered. Immeasurably." He bowed his head even further. "I pursued Cormorel on to the deck during the upheaval of the attack—"

"That was the Fomorii's first strike, right? Not you?"

He nodded. "I was pleading with him. He would have none of it. In fact, he took great pleasure in the pain he saw he was causing me. For all that he considered himself above the emotions of Fragile Creatures, he was filled with cruelty."

"How did you do it?"

"There is a manner known only to my people." Church wouldn't have dreamed of asking, but Baccharus added, "It cannot be revealed to any outsider."

"And the Walpurgis was caught with his hand in the biscuit tin, having a final meal."

"Destroying the evidence. If he had succeeded, my people would have believed Cormorel was simply washed overboard during the attack and would have turned up sooner or later."

The weight that lay on Baccharus's shoulders was palpable. Church rested a supportive hand on his forearm. "You did the right thing. Under the circumstances. There was too much at stake."

"But that does not diminish the pain I feel, for I committed a crime against existence itself. While striking a blow for existence. I have wrestled with the conundrum every hour since then and still made no sense of it. Did I do the right thing? Can an act of such terrible negativity create something worthwhile?"

The questions were not rhetorical; the weight of emotion in Baccharus's voice showed he was asking for guidance. The fact that he felt Church somehow had the wisdom was shocking; how could Baccharus possibly perceive him as someone who had a grasp of such things? "Time will give you the answer to that, Baccharus." He hoped it didn't sound like too much of a platitude.

They were disturbed by a blast of warm air as the door swung open. Ruth walked in, looking around curiously. Church called her over.

"Typical. First chance you get, you men are straight down the pub," she said in a faux-chiding voice.

"How did you find us?"

"A little bird told me." She wrinkled her nose as she looked round at the raucous activity at the bar. "So let me guess. I've got a choice of beer, beer or beer."

"I'll see if I can get you a lady's glass." Church dodged away before she could hit him. She turned to Baccharus. "So what were you two talking about so seriously?"

"Death. Conspiracy. The rising and advancing of the spirit."

She rolled her eyes. "Oh, how we laughed."

"It could have been worse." Veitch huddled closer to the fire. In his weakened state, the chill October night bit deep into his bones.

"In what way could it have been worse? The Grim Lands were a particularly unpleasant experience." Shavi took a sip of the bright green absinthe they'd picked up in a deserted off-licence before passing the bottle on to Tom.

"I could have had to give you the kiss of life."

"And how would that have been worse?"

"Because you'd still be lying there!" Veitch chuckled.

"Well, you seem to be getting better." Shavi eyed his friend warmly. He had been worried Veitch was going to crack under the shock of losing his hand—certainly the first few hours after their return from the Grim Lands had been very hard—but since then he had regained much of his equilibrium. However, there were still too many worrying signs for Shavi to relax: a wildness in the eyes, exaggerated movements, overreactions. He hoped the Blue Fire would work its magic before things started to fall apart.

Veitch took the absinthe from Tom.

"You know you're not supposed to drink it neat," Tom said, with a little too much contempt. "You mix it with water, a spoon of caramelised sugar. They say you'd have to have half a brain to take it without watering it down."

Veitch grinned, waving the bottle in front of Tom's face before taking another slug.

Tom gave him a sour stare. "It's got hallucinogenic properties, you know. The active ingredient from cannabis."

"Oh yes . . . you're right." Veitch pretended to waver. "I can see things! It's amazing! You look . . . almost human!"

Tom snorted and waved him away.

Veitch let his chuckles die away before rubbing his hand thoughtfully over his three-day stubble. He looked over at Shavi curiously.

"What?"

"How you doin'?"

Shavi gave a questioning shrug.

"You died, or nearest thing to it. That must have done your head in. How do you come back from something like that?"

"So you do care."

"Just checking you're not going to go psycho with an axe in the middle of the night." His smile gave the lie to his words. He threw another log on the fire; it cracked and spattered, sending sparks shooting up with the smoke.

"I actually feel better than I did before I died." Shavi pulled the blanket tight around his shoulders, his breath white. Winter was not far away. "You may find that hard to believe. But I have made my peace with Lee. I have seen the other side of death and returned to talk about it. I have been reborn, bright and new in the world. It was a redemptive experience, highly spiritual, uplifting."

"Yeah, but can you still get a stiffy?" Veitch leaned back against his rucksack, laughing drunkenly.

"Don't be talking to him," Tom said sternly. "You won't be getting any sense out of him tonight."

"You are implying I get sense out of him at any time." Shavi didn't see the boot coming; it hit him on the side of the head.

"Yessss! One-nil!"

They had embarked on a meandering route west after leaving Wandlebury Camp, careful to keep a good distance from London. The darkness in the south was growing with each hour, like night eating the day. The cinders in the breeze were more pronounced, and there was an overall sense of despair hanging in the increasingly cold wind. The world was winding down.

With Samhain approaching rapidly, a deep anxiety had gripped them, amplified by the certain knowledge that there was nothing they could do alone. They needed Church to succeed in his mission. They needed Ruth and Laura too. Sometimes it was almost too hard to hope, and that was when the depression set in.

But their abiding friendship, forged through hard times, kept them going and ensured the evenings around the campfire were filled with light talk and humour, lifting spirits dampened by the day's sights of deserted villages, frightened people hiding in their homes, or children and old people begging for food.

It wasn't as if they had any plan except to find Church and Ruth and Laura. That lack of direction left Veitch feeling strained and irritable. He was not a person who coped well with inactivity, particularly with time running out, when there was so much that *needed* to be done.

Shavi, however, guessed Tom knew more than he was saying.

"Do you think we'll find them?" Shavi said, breaking the rule of keeping the conversation light. Next to him, Veitch snored loudly in a drunken sleep.

"I think there is always hope." Tom enjoyed a joint as he stared into the fire.

"But you are True Thomas. You can see the future. You must know something."

"I try not to look. What will be, will be."

Perhaps it was the drugs or the drink affecting him, but for the first time Tom's cool exterior was not impervious. Shavi caught a glimpse in the Rhymer's face of all the things Tom was not saying, and he was uncomfortable with what he saw.

"What if you really did see everything?" Shavi suggested. "What if you knew exactly what was going to happen, bar a few minor hiccups here and there. What if you knew who lived and who died?"

Tom raised his head sharply to fix a stare that was so cold Shavi felt a chill in his bones. "Then," Tom said, "my life would be damned."

At the heart of the Court of High Regard stood an enormous tree with a trunk as far around as an office block and a top lost high overhead. All around it spread an area of distortion that left Church continually disoriented; buildings were never quite the same each time he looked at them. Some were substantially altered, one moment a sweeping dome like St. Paul's, the next a thrusting tower of Middle Eastern design. At times Church would glimpse rapid movement from the corner of his eye, the hint of crystal birds flapping across the sky, but when he looked there was nothing. People came and went as they crossed a piazza, or appeared in a haze on a corner, while the dead appeared to be everywhere, dazed, beatific, unthreatening.

"This is where our heart beats, the closest to the fabled home of our deepest memory." Niamh's voice trembled with awe. Church was struck by how young and girlish she appeared, not alien at all. Now Baccharus had explained the distinction amongst the Tuatha Dé Danann, Church was amazed he hadn't seen it before. It was as simple as those who felt and those who didn't.

"Have you always been like this?"

She looked at him curiously with her large, innocent eyes. "No," she said after a moment's thought, "once I was a true daughter of the Golden Ones, one of the confirmed rulers of all existence, above all else."

"Then why did you change? When you hold such a position, it must take something phenomenal to turn you around."

"I was taught, over what your people would consider a long period of time."

"Who taught you?"

She smiled a little sadly, but did not answer.

They continued their tour in silence for a while, until Church broke the restrained mood by asking about the enormous tree.

"It is the World-Tree," Niamh said, looking up into the distant branches. "It is at the heart of all worlds. Its roots go down, its branches reach up."

"Linking Heaven and Earth. This is an amazing place." And it was. Wonder brought every nerve alive, just breathing air, looking round at the fluid scenery. It was filled with magic, the thing his life had always lacked.

"Once the Fixed Lands had the same power. Everything was alive, constantly changing. But your brethren stopped believing, or believed in the wrong things. You wished your world to be something lesser."

Church examined a fountain where the water turned into tiny diamonds. "I keep hearing that phrase, about wishing the world a certain way."

"Nothing is truly fixed. The Fixed Lands are only such because they are sleeping. All is illusion, and all illusion is fluid. Belief is a powerful tool. Creatures great and small—life—is at the centre of everything, and they can shape things as they see fit. Nothing has to be accepted."

"If you just wish hard enough," he mused. "I was never happy with how things were in my world. There was always something lacking. And it was getting worse. The people I didn't like, the ones interested in money over everything, and personal power, they seemed to be driving things their way. It wasn't a world for people like me."

"You gave up your responsibility, Jack."

"What do you mean?"

"The people you despised were wishing harder, setting the world the way they wanted. They are the Night Walkers, whichever form they take. People like you, Jack, people who truly believe, have a responsibility to take a stand and wish the world the way it should be. To wake the land, to dream it real. Belief is stronger than anything the Night Walkers have."

The crystal birds were still flying around the edges of his vision and there was faint music on the wind, still powerful enough to make his emotions soar. What Niamh was saying echoed deeply inside him. He realised she was staring at him intently, and when he turned to her he was shocked to see tears in her eyes.

"I have made my peace with the way things are, Jack."

He took her hand, concerned. "Don't cry. What's wrong?"

"The Golden Ones have always used their power without responsibility. They have achieved their ends by force. I would never do that, for I have learned it would be valueless, and the thing I strive for has too much value to be wasted. I see now we will never achieve the love that has filled my thoughts since the darkest days of the Fragile Creatures." She gazed into the middle distance, her eyes full. "I had hoped, once it came to this time, your heart would have opened to me, as mine did to yours so long ago. But I see clearly now your love for the Sister of Dragons is true; that indeed it is worthy of a love that transcends all time."

Church felt truly sorry for what he saw in her face. "We can still be friends, Niamh."

She smiled wanly. "And that enriches my existence, but if you only knew what lay before this point . . ." Her words drifted away.

"What do you mean?"

Her smile became a little brighter, to hide her thoughts. "I will always love you, Jack, and in time you will understand where that love comes from." She cupped his hand in hers. "I have always had your best interests at heart, but from this moment on I dedicate myself to helping you achieve your aims, whatever it may cost me."

He gave her hand a warm squeeze, overwhelmed by the level of emotion that was being expressed. "You're a good woman, Niamh."

"Now, come, I have many sights to show you. Wonders beyond your imagining." She brushed her tears away, her smile gleaming. "These days will stay with you always."

The tour was indeed as amazing as Niamh had predicted. Some of the sights were so startling his mind could barely cope within them, and within the hour the reality of them began to fade until they took on the warmly comforting but intangible quality of dreams that would haunt him forever.

But even though time meant nothing in that place, he was acutely aware of events running away from him. The real world seemed so far gone, but what he might find when he returned filled him with dread. Each moment wasted could mean another death, another life filled with suffering. And it felt like he had been gone so long.

But when he returned to his chamber, Baccharus informed him that approval to enter the Pool of Wishes had been granted by some higher authority. It was finally time to act.

As twilight fell across the Court, thousands of torches sprang into life like summer fireflies. Baccharus, Niamh and Ruth gathered in the main piazza with four horses. The beasts were powerful, snorting and stamping loudly on the shimmering marble; at first glance they appeared normal to Ruth, then she noticed the hint of Otherworld in their eyes where a disturbing intelligence burned.

Church had spent the previous hour in his room preparing himself; he had enjoyed the tranquillity after spending so long with Ruth discussing the shocking repercussions of what Baccharus had told him in the inn. Baccharus had also warned him that the Pool of Wishes was not something to be taken lightly, as if anything in that realm was. He would be forced to journey deep inside himself to locate the taint of the Fomorii, Baccharus said, and if he was not at ease with himself, the experience would drive him mad.

And so he spent the time thinking of his life, of Dale and his friends in London—where were they now?—of Marianne and his love for her, of the terrible grief he had felt at her death, of his parents, and his studies, his dreams and fears, of Laura and Niamh and Ruth, and at the end of it, it still didn't make any sense.

Finally he was ready. The other three were already mounted when he took the long walk across the piazza, his footsteps echoing solemnly. Their greeting was just as serious, a simple nod, a faint smile, and then they were away through the labyrinthine streets of the Court towards the green countryside beyond.

Baccharus led the way, with Church behind, then Ruth, and Niamh taking up the rear. As they passed, Church glimpsed strange faces watching him from the darkened windows, some of them golden and alien, some of them terrible and dark. The buildings grew more solid as they approached the outskirts, jumbling tight up against themselves like the oppressive weight of ancient habitation that lay crushed within Jerusalem's walls.

Once the Court was behind them, green fields lined by thick, old hedges rolled out. They passed intermittent copses and trickling brooks that made their way through culverts under the rough road. But then the country became wilder, the trees taller and darker, pressing hard against the roadside, forming a roof above their heads. Baccharus held up a lantern as they rode and they were all grateful for the flickering golden light that flooded ahead.

Church occasionally heard movement, although in the thick shadow it was impossible to discern what was amongst the trees; some seemed too large for any animal he knew, others were small and fast, some came far too close to the circle of light, which increasingly felt insignificant. Eventually the road all but disappeared and the trees came up so hard they could have reached out and touched them on either side if they had so wished. Church spent so much time attempting to probe the woods on either side, he nearly ran his mount into Baccharus on more than one occasion. The undergrowth was thick with bramble and bracken, which would have made the going hard if they had strayed from the path.

To Church's relief, as the going became steeper the wood eventually gave way. When they finally emerged from the trees, he realised they were on the foothills leading up to snow-capped mountains, although he couldn't recall seeing them from the ship as they approached the island.

"Are we going right to the top?" Church asked.

Baccharus put a silencing finger to his lips. "There are things around here that appreciate silence," he whispered.

The road—now barely more than a track—became rocky and the horses had to step slowly. Boulders piled up on either side, cracked and patchworked with moss. The air was much cooler. Church pulled his jacket around him, oddly wondering what the weather was like back home.

After a little while longer, Baccharus reined in his horse and nodded towards a group of pine trees separated from a thickly forested slope by a rocky outcropping on three sides. A distinct path wound its way into the centre of the copse.

"In there?" Church asked quietly.

Baccharus nodded once more.

Church jumped down and advanced several paces before he realised the others were not behind him. "From here your journey must be alone," Niamh whispered in reply to his quizzical expression. That brought a sharp chill to his spine.

In the trees, it was even cooler, but the air was beautifully scented with pine and the tang of the mountain snows. Overheard, a stunning full moon glowed white and misty butterscotch, framed by icy, glittering stars. His breath bloomed; a shiver ran through him. Thankfully Baccharus had allowed him to bring the lantern to keep the shadows at bay, although his movement made them jump and recede as if they were alive. Pine needles crunched underfoot, but beneath them the path was oddly well made, with large flagstones worn by age.

The first thing he noticed when he entered the copse was the soothing sound of tinkling water. The path opened out on to a broad, still pool, black and reflective, with trees all around it. On the opposite side was a jutting rock, face down, over which white water cascaded, churning the pool just beneath but obviously carried away by some underground stream before it sent waves lashing out across the surface. The air was heavy with a feeling of deep tranquillity, but as Church stood and drank in the atmosphere, it changed slightly until he sensed something jarring uneasily just beneath it. As he gave in to his instincts he could feel a dim electricity in the air, waiting to be awakened. This was the place.

He played the lantern back and forth and noticed the stone flags disappeared around the back of the waterfall. With anxiety tight in his throat, he stepped cautiously around the edge of the pool, half expecting something to leap out and drag him in. He paused briefly next to the waterfall before darting behind.

It was like crossing over into a place completely detached from the other world. It was a grotto, with barely formed stalagmites and glistening walls where the lantern made a million sparkles dance, and reds, greens and yellows shimmered in the wet brown of the rock. It was small, barely a couple of car lengths across, and within lay another pool, a mirror image of the one without, only without the waterfall the water was even darker. The flagstones gave out to a small, rocky path that ran around the edge, at some points barely wide enough to walk around. Echoes of gently lapping water rolled off the walls, distorting but peaceful. He set down the lantern and kneeled to peer into the depths.

He expected to see the pebbled bottom of the pool easily, at least around the edges near the lantern, but the black water appeared to go down forever. He didn't really know what to do next. Baccharus had told him simply to wait, stressing that "the pool would see" and know what was needed. Yet the surroundings felt so normal it felt silly sitting back waiting.

There was a certain odd oiliness to the quality of the water, so he reached out a hand to stroke his fingers across the surface. At the last moment he withdrew; something was sending alarm bells ringing in his head. He slumped back against the wall, hugged his knees and waited.

It was less than a minute later when he perceived—or thought he did—some activity deep below. Now on all fours, he pressed his face close to the water's surface to get a better look. Something was swimming. The perspective it gave him was shocking, for the pool went down more than twenty or thirty feet, and even then he couldn't see the bottom. Whatever was there was striking out for the surface. The lantern light brought reflected glints from its skin, at times silvery, at times flesh tone. It was certainly a trick of the distorting effect of the water, but it gave him the impression that the pool's inhabitant kept changing back and forth from a fish to a human. Or was somehow both at the same time.

And still it rose, until it was obvious it was human, long arms reaching out, feet kicking, but the face was still obscured by shadows. It covered the last few feet very quickly, but stopped short of coming completely out of the water. Instead, it hovered patiently, looking up at him, only an inch or two beneath the surface, and in that instant he was overcome by a deep dread. The face he was looking into was his own, his long hair drifting in the currents, only it was changed very slightly, in the way the features were held or in some sour experience that had left its mark, so that it was darker in essence.

For long seconds they were locked in that connecting stare, and then there was a flurry of rapid movement in the water. The Other-Church's arms shot out of the pool, clamped on Church's shoulders, and before he could resist, dragged him under.

In the shock, he didn't have time to grab a breath of air. The cold water rushed into his mouth and up his nose before he clamped his lips shut and struggled frantically to push his head up above the surface. But though he fought wildly, turning the pool into a maelstrom, his other self was far too strong. Further down it hauled him, and down even more, until the light from the lantern was too dim to illuminate the water and his lungs seared from the strain. He struck out futilely a few more times, the blows so weak they barely registered, and then his mouth jerked open and the water flooded in, filling his throat, his lungs. Fractured thoughts flared briefly in his mind, but the abiding sense was that it wasn't supposed to be like that.

Except that one minute later, he realised he was still breathing; inexplicably. His brain fizzed and sparked, somehow found a state of grace that allowed his thoughts to grow ordered once more. He wasn't dead; he was breathing water.

The Other-Church released his grip, although his face still had that mean cast; Church thought how much older and unattractive a state of mind could make him look. He signed for the Other to tell him what was happening, but it gave an expression of slight contempt before turning and swimming away. Church had no choice but to follow.

The experience had the distorting feeling of a hallucination. Briefly he wondered if he was dead and this was some final, random activity in his dying brain, but then he noticed a strange sheen across the whole of the pool that resembled the skin of a bubble. The Other swam into it, and through it; Church couldn't see anything on the other side. He hesitated, then followed suit.

The bubble gave slightly as he touched it, then eased over his body, finally accepting him with a slight give. Emerging on the other side, he was shocked to realise there was no water at all; he was in midair and it was dark. Suddenly he was falling, the water shooting out of his lungs. The sensation lasted for only a few seconds until he found himself standing on a broad plain covered in stubby grass, beneath a star-studded night sky and ringed by black mountains. Before him was a pile of rocks fused into a pillar that rose three feet above his head. The Other-Church stood on the far side of the pillar, the same distance from it as he was.

"What is happening here?" His voice resonated strangely in the wide-open spaces. As he spoke, the Other-Church mimicked him silently.

The pillar of stones began to hum with a low, bass note. Church couldn't take his eyes off it; the atmosphere was heavy with anticipation. As the Other-Church continued to glower at him, movement became visible within the pillar and gradually a figure stepped out of the solid rock.

Church's stomach flipped. Marianne looked exactly as she had when she was alive, not the gaunt, spectral figure sent by the Fomorii to torment him. His shoulders sagged; conflicting emotions tore through him: doubt, terrible sadness, a touch of joy. "Marianne."

She smiled at him weakly.

"You're another hallucination of this place." He rubbed a hand across his face, but when he looked back up she was still there.

"I'm here, Church. At least, a part of me, a part they couldn't get to. An echo."

Tears flooded his eyes. "Really?"

"Really."

He made to move forward, arms outstretched, but she held up a sudden hand to warn him back. She shook her head strongly. "We can't."

"Why not?" Almost a plea.

"There are rules, Church. Things going on that you can't imagine, beyond what you see here, or there, or anywhere. I can't tell you . . . can't explain. I'm not allowed."

"Not allowed by whom?" Her face grew still. She took a step back towards the pillar. "No! Okay, I won't ask any more about that!"

She smiled, brighter this time. "It's good to see you, Church."

For a brief while, he couldn't see for the tears. "Thank you," he choked as a delaying tactic, "for the contact you made in the house . . . on Mam Tor . . . The writing . . ."

"I had to do something, Church. I couldn't bear to see you so broken."

"You could see me?" No answer. "Okay . . . the part of you the Fomorii have—"

Her face darkened; she hugged her arms around her, a mannerism he recalled her doing when she was distraught; when she was alive. "It feels like it's tearing my heart out."

His voice grew rough and fractured. "I'm going to save you, Marianne."

Her expression was, if not quite patronising, then certainly pitying.

"I am." Reassuring at first, then defiantly: "I am."

His emotions felt they would break him in two. He wanted to ask her about her death, about who had killed her, how bad it had been, whether she had really suffered as he always imagined, but looking into her face where the Marianne he loved still resided, he couldn't bring himself to do it. There were a thousand questions, but his overwhelming desire was for the one thing every bereaved person wished for above all else, but could never, ever achieve: to tell her how he truly felt.

As he was about to speak, she silenced him with a raised finger. "I know how you feel, Church, and I always felt the same about you. You were the only person I ever loved."

He covered his eyes.

"I know your thoughts now, Church. I know your hopes. And that's a good thing, truly. In the days that follow, remember that. And I know about Ruth, and that's okay. She's a remarkable person. You've made a lot of silly mistakes since I died, but she was the right one. You stick with her, she'll stick with you."

A sob choked in his throat. "I miss you."

"I know. But you should have learned a lot of things by now. That nothing is truly fixed in the Fixed Lands." Her use of words he had heard before brought him up sharp. He blinked away his tears and started to listen. "You see things from your own perspective, but in the broad sweep of existence, things look very different. When you know the rules, everything changes. Things are switched right around when they're put in context: what seems a bad experience becomes good, good, bad. I can't explain better than that at the moment, but you can't judge now, Church. Just accept things, and know there's something more."

"I know, I do."

"But sometimes it's hard."

He nodded.

"Feel it, don't think it. The Age of Reason is long gone."

"I feel so tired, Marianne. I want a rest from all this."

Her smile grew sad. "There won't be any rest, Church."

"I heard that before."

"It's true. No rest. But there'll be a balance. You'll know why there's no rest, and though it'll be hard, it'll make you feel good to know that what you do is valuable."

"Life's good as long as you don't weaken."

She laughed, and he was surprised at how wonderful it sounded, even in that place. "That's the kind of person you are, Church. A good person. Someone for people to look up to—"

"You haven't been watching very closely over the last few months, have you?" Church moved around the circle a few paces to get away from the glowering stare of the Other-Church, but it matched him pace for pace.

"—you shoulder your burden and still focus on what's important in life. It won't grind you down. Life's too good."

He shrugged. His surroundings had started to intrude and so he asked, although he didn't want to, "What are you doing here, Marianne?"

"You called me."

"No, I didn't."

"Yes, you just don't know you did."

He turned his thoughts over rapidly, trying to make sense. "I'm here to get rid of the Fomorii corruption that's eaten its way into me from the Kiss of Frost that you—that Calatin made you—give me. That's why I'm here. At least, I think that's why. Nothing makes sense any more. Nothing ever has."

There was movement in the shadowy distance, high above the mountains, against the sky. At first he thought it was clouds, but it looked briefly like a Caraprix, only enormous, hundreds of feet larger than the tiny creatures the Tuatha Dé Danann and the Fomorii carried with them. It was gone so quickly he could easily have dismissed it as a bizarre hallucination, except that he was convinced it had been there. The part of his back brain that always attempted to make sense of what was happening told him he had glimpsed something of a much larger truth, although what it was, and why the Caraprix *felt* so at home in that place, was beyond him.

"Church." Marianne called his attention back. "The symbolism is bigger than the reality. In the wider sweep of existence, symbols tell the truth. I'm the cause of all your misery, Church. I'm what's holding you back from achieving your destiny. The stain of the Night Walkers is minor compared to that, and it wouldn't even be there if I wasn't holding it in place."

"What do you mean?"

"Do you want to talk like smart people?" Her expression was teasing. "Or shall we carry on as we always have done?" He motioned for her to continue. "Thanatos, the death urge. When I died, you were consumed by it. That's what infected you. It made your days black, your thoughts worse. You couldn't see life, you couldn't see yourself. You've pulled away from the worst part of it, but it's still there, a little black cancer of the soul. A mess on that Fiery Network that makes up the real you, stopping the true flow. Making something so vital and powerful grow dormant. You have to wake the sleeping king if you want to save the world."

"All that Arthurian stuff is a metaphor. For waking the Blue Fire in the land. Nothing to do with me."

"As without, so within. This whole business is about celebrating life in all its forms, Church. Seeing death as part of a cycle: life, death, rebirth. You've been through the damn thing yourself, as have most of your merry little group. Haven't you got the picture yet?"

"I have to let go of you, is that what you're saying?"

"You don't have to *forget* me. Just remember the good parts. Don't let death rule your life."

The Other-Church's expression was even darker now, murderous. "Am I really seeing you?" Church asked. "Or is this some hallucination, some part of my subconscious speaking to me?"

"You should know better than to ask questions like that by now."

"Then what do I have to do? It's one thing saying I won't obsess about death, but it's a subconscious thing—"

"Just wish, Church. Wish so hard it changes you from inside out. Kids know best how existence works. We unlearn as we go through all those things the Age of Reason saw fit to throw at us during our formative years. The Celts never had that, all those ancient people who shaped the world. You know I'm not some stupid, anti-progress Luddite. But the truth is, we took a wrong turn and now it's time to get back to how things should really be. A time to *feel*. The world's been waiting for this for a long time."

"For all the death and suffering?"

"No, of course not. It's your job to minimise that. But it's not your job to take things back to the way they were. You've got a bigger destiny than you ever thought, Church. It's all down to you to make things better."

His lips attempted to form words, but nothing would come.

"Just wish, Church." A whisper. "Just wish."

He closed his eyes. And wished; not with a thought, but with every fibre of his being, and he found power was given to that wishing from somewhere else, either deep within himself, or without, in the distance where strange things moved against the sky.

And when he opened his eyes, Marianne was smiling. "If you could only see yourself as I see you. We're all stars, Church. All stars." She drifted back towards the pillar of stones.

"Is that it? Have I done enough?" His question was answered by the Other-Church, who began to fade, slipping back into the shadows that had gathered around the area until he was no longer there.

"From here it gets hard. Harder than anything you've been through so far. Pain and death and suffering and sacrifice and misery. It'll be a trial, Church, but you always knew that." Parts of her became misty, merging with the rock. "If you stay true, you'll see it through. Have faith, Church, like I have faith in you."

The tears were flooding down his face now; he had never cried so much since he was a child. "Thank you." His voice, autumnal. "For this, and for everything else you gave me. I'll never forget you."

"Until we meet again." The smile again, filled with long, beautiful days, fading as she was fading. And then she was gone.

It was like a rope tied around his waist had suddenly been attached to a speeding truck. He shot straight up into the air, that strange place disappearing in the blink of an eye, the sky and the stars whizzing by, rocketing so hard he blacked out.

And when he woke, he was sitting on the edge of the Pool of Wishes.

He made his way back along the worn path in a daze, trying to separate reality from hallucination and to make sense of the true weight of what he had learned.

When he reached the others, Ruth said curiously, "What's wrong?"

"What do you mean?"

"You've only been gone about five minutes. Isn't there anything there?"

His smile gave nothing away. He climbed on his horse and spurred it back down the slope, feeling brighter and less burdened than at any time before in his life.

The Palace of High Regard lay at the centre of a confusing geometric design of streets, laden with symbolism. Church and Ruth's winding progress along the route was an intricately designed ritual, affecting their minds as well as their hearts; it was an odd sensation when simply turning a corner resulted in a flash of long-lost memory or insight, a fugitive aroma or barely heard sound. By the time they reached the enormous doors of ivory and silver, it had worked its magic on their deep subconscious so their heads felt charged with a disorienting energy, as if they were about to embark on a drug trip.

Baccharus was waiting to admit them. He carried a long staff carved from black volcanic rock. When Church and Ruth paused ten feet away, as they had been instructed, he tapped the doors gently with the staff. The resultant echoes were so loud Ruth put her hands to her ears.

The doors swung open of their own accord. Within was a hallway flooded with sunlight from a glass dome a hundred feet above. There were columns and carvings, niches filled with statues and braziers smouldering with incense. The floor had an inner path of black and white tiles, but on the edge was a pattern Ruth remembered from the floor tile at Glastonbury, with its hidden message that had pointed them towards T'ir n'a n'Og.

They waited for an age at the second set of doors, eventually being admitted to a room so large it took their breath away. It resembled the Coliseum in size and layout: rising tiers of seats in a circle around a vast floor area that made them feel insignificant. There was enough distortion of perception around the edges that Church wondered what it really looked like. The power of the Tuatha Dé Danann was focused there in all its unknowable, fearful glory. Ahead of them, the highest tier of gods was obviously seated, but the golden light that came off them was so forceful Church couldn't look at it. At the centre was the being the Celts had called Dagda, the Allfather, and around him others of the oldest and most powerful branch of the Golden Ones. On the perimeter he could just make out the ones the Celts had characterised as Lugh, and Nuada, whom he had first met on Skye when he had been brought back from the dead.

The air was crushing down on his shoulders and deep vibrations ran through him. It made him feel queasy, and he didn't know how long he would be able to endure it; it was apparent Fragile Creatures were not meant to be in that place, or to spend time in close proximity to those potent gods.

They waited, uncomfortable beneath the oppressive attention of the Golden Ones; the weight of all those fearsome intellects focused upon them was almost palpable. The debate started soon after. Nuada rose to deliver a speech to the assembled mass, although they couldn't understand a word he was saying; it sounded like a song caught in the wind, lilting and beautiful, with occasional threatening notes. Others spoke: some from the rank of the highest, many from the lower levels. Back and forth the discourse ranged. It felt odd to be under the scrutiny of such powerful beings, having hopes dissected with the very fate of the world hanging in the balance, but Church refused to be cowed by it. He held his head high and looked every speaker in the face.

Eventually Manannan rose, but instead of making his speech from the tier of the highest, he descended to the floor and stood beside Church and Ruth. He spoke with a passion and belief not previously visible in his reticent nature. Standing next to him, his ringing, incomprehensible voice resonating in the cavities of their bodies, they had an even deeper sense of the power around them.

Though Manannan never acknowledged their presence in the slightest, they knew he was arguing their case powerfully. The Tuatha Dé Danann hung on his every word, and when he finished speaking, a ripple of obvious disagreement ran around the arena. The tension in some of the comments that followed suggested that even Manannan's involvement might not swing the Golden Ones' support behind humanity.

But when the notes of dissent threatened to become a tumult, a hush suddenly fell across the arena. It was eerie the way it went from noise to silence in the merest moment. Church turned, searching for the source, and saw a large shadow fall across the arena. Cernunnos strode forward, his partner at his side. As she moved, her shape changed from that of a young, innocent girl, to a round-cheeked, middle-aged woman to a wizened crone and back again.

They stopped beside Manannan, and when Cernunnos spoke in a clear, booming voice it was in words Church could understand. "No more. The seasons have turned. The days of holding on to faint beliefs have long since passed. Some of us have been wiped from existence for all time. Is this not a sign that it is time to act? How many more Golden Ones must lose the shining light before a reckoning comes? You have heard my brother speak of many things, of the warp and weft of existence, of reasons and truth and change, of the rising and advancing of spirits. Yet at the last, it must come down to this: do we sit proud and true and wait for the Night Walkers to bring their foul corruption to our door—even to this hallowed place itself—or do we fight as we have done in the past, for what is ours and for our place in the scheme of things? We aid these Fragile Creatures in their task, and thereby aid ourselves. The greater questions that trouble you need not be considered at this time. This is about the Golden Ones, and the Night Walkers, and the age-old history of lies and treachery and destruction that lie between us."

He paused as his voice continued to echo around the vast chamber. There was no other sound; every god was listening intently to what he had to say. A swell of hope filled Church's heart.

"The Golden Ones have always been fair-minded, and we have always come to the aid of those who have aided us," Cernunnos continued. "These Brothers and Sisters of Dragons freed us from the privations of the Wish-Hex, and they prevented an even more heinous crime being inflicted, one that might well have wiped *all* of us from existence." Mutterings of disbelief ran round the hall. "They acted freely, and without obligation, and the Golden Ones should repay that debt. There is no longer the taint of the Night Walkers upon this champion. We are free to act at his behest." He paused once more and looked slowly round. Briefly his appearance wavered and instead of the creature that Church saw as half animal, half vegetation, there was something almost angelic, but it was gone in an instant.

"I stand here with my brother, the two of us shoulder-to-shoulder. We say the old ways of noninvolvement must end now. Risen and proud, the Golden Ones were always a force to be feared. The time is right."

Complete silence followed his plea. Church's heart fell; his words had not stirred them at all. He looked around frantically, wondering if he should speak himself, but before he could decide, Baccharus had gripped his arm and was leading him and Ruth out of the hall. "The case has been made," he whispered.

They were deposited in an annex where a crystal fountain gently tinkled. Baccharus refused to answer any of their questions, but they had only to look in each other's faces to confirm their private thoughts: they had failed.

Baccharus returned to them an hour later. At first they couldn't read his face, but when he was close it broke into a broad and unlikely grin. "They will ride with you. The Night Walkers have been designated a true threat, and the feeling is that an agreement of cohabitation is not enough. It is time to eradicate them completely."

Church jumped to his feet and hugged Ruth. "We did it!"

"We need to thank Cernunnos and Manannan," Ruth said.

"There will be time enough for that later," Baccharus replied. "The decision has been reached. The Golden Ones will act swiftly and we must be away at dawn. But first there is a ceremony to be enacted."

"What ceremony?"

Baccharus ignored Church and motioned to the door. In the chamber, Cernunnos and Manannan waited patiently on the floor, but around them were gathered some of the highest of the gods, with only Dagda and those whose form was most fluid still remaining in their old place.

"Your hearts are true, Brother and Sister of Dragons," Cernunnos said. "An agreement has been reached that rings across existence. Not since the most ancient times of your people has the like been seen."

He raised his right hand and the crowd parted to admit Lugh, leading four of the younger gods. Each carried one of the ancient artefacts Church, Ruth and the others had located to free the Tuatha Dé Danann from exile: the Stone of Fal, the Cauldron of Dagda, the Spear of Lugh and the Sword of Nuada Airgetlámh. Lugh himself carried the Wayfinder, the lantern with the flickering blue flame that had pointed them in the direction of the mystical objects.

"The Quadrillax," Cernunnos intoned, "are yours once more. Use them well and wisely."

Church could barely believe what he was seeing. The four objects were so powerful, such a part of the traditions of the Tuatha Dé Danann, that he could never imagine an occasion when they would have freely given them up. But he could tell from the way the other gods looked to Cernunnos and Manannan that he knew who to thank.

He bowed. "The Brothers and Sisters of Dragons thank you. And we shall use them well and wisely."

Barely able to contain himself, he walked over to the sword that was resting on a cushion of strange, shimmering material. He had once seen it as a rusty, crumbling artefact. Now it gleamed as if it were made of silver and gold, and looked as sharp and strong as if it had just been forged. A shiver of anticipation made him pause before his fingers closed on it. But then it was in his hand and once again the power rushed through him; it felt warm and alive, comforting, against his skin. "Now we'll see some justice," he said in hushed tones.

Church sheathed the sword in a leather scabbard presented to him by Baccharus, while Ruth took the spear that she had used to such good advantage when freeing Cernunnos from Fomorii control in South Wales. The other artefacts were placed in a golden box that the young gods would hold until directed by Church.

Once they were on their own in their room, Church dragged Ruth on to the bed and hugged her tightly. "A result," he grinned, "on every front."

"So where's that familiar pessimism? Come on, you're the man who manages to drag misery from every victory."

"I'm still pragmatic—I know it's still going to be near impossible. But at least we have the two things we need: the support of the Tuatha Dé Danann and the Quadrillax. That's a chance, and I'm going to seize it with both hands."

"Oh, get away from me. You're not the real Church. You've been possessed in that mysterious pool." She playfully attempted to push him away, before relaxing so he could fold into her. "Go on, there's got to be *something* on your mind." The flicker across his face gave her answer. "Spit it out."

"Okay, there's one thing that worries me, and it's a big thing." He rolled over so he was lying next to her, staring at the ceiling. "Everything was tidied up nicely on the ship, except for one thing. You've seen the Tuatha Dé Danann. You know what they're capable of. And now they have the Wish-Hex."

chapter fourteen
like a serpent play'd before them

Water began to flood in around Laura as she shivered in the cold beneath the insipid dawn light. The Bone Inspector attempted to force the rag back into the hole, but it only made matters worse. "We're going to go down like a brick," he hissed.

"I can get a bit further if I throw you overboard." She leaned up just enough to peek over the rim. They hadn't even made it as far as the Dartford river crossing. Nearby, gleaming mudflats lined the bank. There was no movement anywhere, nor was there any sound, not even birdsong. The stillness was unnatural.

"If we drag it over to the side, we might have a better chance of plugging it up again," she hissed.

The Bone Inspector grunted before rolling over the side into the waist-deep water; he appeared oblivious to the cold. Laura allowed him to drag the boat close to the flats before she jumped out to help it across the last few feet.

Once they'd beached it, the water drained out and the Bone Inspector could attempt the repairs a little easier. But it was soon apparent why the previous owner had abandoned the craft. As the Bone Inspector worked the rag in tightly, his hand went right through the bottom, taking out a chunk of rotten wood about a foot square.

"You ham-fisted git!" Laura slapped a shaking hand over her eyes. "Now what do we do?"

The Bone Inspector ignored her attempts at blame. Quickly surveying the area, he pointed toward some streetlights beyond an expanse of waste ground. "The Fomorii may not have spread this far out of the city. If we proceed cautiously, it would be quicker to use the road to put the city behind us."

Laura wrapped her sopping arms around her. "All right. But you go first."

The wasteland had been used as a dump. Burst dustbin bags lay around amidst broken bottles, empty milk crates, a burnt-out car and decaying furniture. It smelled of chemicals and excrement. The road beyond was deserted, apart from a jackknifed petrol tanker.

"Looks safe," Laura mused after ten minutes in the shadows of the hedgerow. "Shall we chance it?"

"No choice." The Bone Inspector sniffed the air, then stepped out on to the pavement.

They'd gone only a few yards down the road when Laura experienced a prickling sensation. Looking back quickly towards the city, all she could see were a few birds swooping in the grey sky. She attempted to dismiss the nagging feeling, but if anything it was growing stronger. She took a few more paces and only then realised that since she had woken in the charnel house she had not seen any birds at all. With a shiver of dread, she turned back.

The dark smudges had moved much closer in the seconds between looks, and now she could see they were far too big for birds. Their uncanny speed held her rapt for a few seconds and by then she could see they were winged Fomorii. "Shit. I didn't know some of them could fly."

The Bone Inspector turned at her strained voice, before grabbing her arm to propel her back the way they had come.

"Away from them!" she yelled.

"There's no cover." His voice was remarkably calm, although his body had dropped into a low, loping posture that reminded her of a hunting wolf.

He was right; their only chance was to attempt to hide and hope the Fomorii couldn't see where they were going, but there was hardly anywhere in the flat open landscape.

The only place in view was the jackknifed tanker. It offered little protection, but if they could crawl beneath it they might be able to scurry into the ditch beyond where the Fomorii would have trouble reaching them. In the heat of the moment Laura didn't have time to consider how sickeningly short-termist that was.

The Fomorii had the terrifying speed of jet fighters. The tanker was still yards away when the wash of driven air buffeted Laura and the Bone Inspector. There was a smell like rotting meat and what sounded like a power drill. Their peripheral vision was filled with constantly changing horrors; a deep, arctic shadow fell across them. The Bone Inspector knocked Laura to the ground and threw himself across her.

They both felt the breeze as the Fomorii tore through the space where they had been. Despite his advancing years, the Bone Inspector was on his feet in an instant, hauling Laura up behind him as if she weighed nothing.

Amidst the frantic activity and danger, Laura was surprised to find an area of deep serenity in which she could step back to observe herself. What she saw surprised her: just weeks ago she would have been paralysed by fear. Instead she felt calm and focused and, if it hadn't sounded so incongruous, brave.

She was thrown out of the moment by a hard impact to her right shoulder. Relieved that the Fomorii had missed clubbing her to the ground she continued a pace before an object came flying past her to skid across the road. It was an arm. Her arm.

The shock of the sight brought her to a halt. Her vision wavered a second; impressions rushed towards the front of her mind, but didn't coalesce. She was dimly aware of several shapes converging on her.

The Bone Inspector was in her frame of vision, yelling something she couldn't hear. A second later she was being lifted across his back as he ran the final few yards. They dived beneath the tanker as the road erupted at their heels.

Laura came out of her daze, aware of a dull ache at her shoulder. She didn't look at all. Shards of metal clattered across the road as the Fomorii tore frenziedly at the side of the tanker to get at them. "Keep moving," she croaked. "I'm fine."

The Bone Inspector cast a searching eye across her face, and then scurried into the ditch. Laura followed, keeping low, feeling brambles tear at her face and hair, not really caring.

The Fomorii continued to attack the tanker. "Stupid bastards," Laura said under her breath.

The two of them had managed to crawl three hundred yards away when the inevitable happened. The tanker went up in a massive explosion that rained burning debris all around them. They had just crawled in a culvert that ran beneath the road as the hedgerow disappeared in a blur of flame; trees turned to charcoal and the field beyond disappeared in red and yellow smoke. For a second or two, Laura couldn't breathe, until fresh air rushed in to fill the vacuum. Her ears rang from the blast.

She slumped back against the culvert, suddenly convulsed in tremors. The Bone Inspector was at her side in an instant, ready to bandage her shoulder with his shirt. When he paused suddenly, she gasped, "I know. Green blood."

"And not much of it." He pressed the shirt against the protruding socket joint and torn arteries. Despite his comment, it quickly grew wet.

"It had to be the right one," she said miserably. "Now I'll never beat Veitch at darts." Her attempt at humour sounded pathetic. She let her chin slump on to her chest, listening to the roar of the inferno.

"We'll rest here for a while," the Bone Inspector said. "We'll start moving again when the fire dies down."

"Good idea," Laura murmured. "I feel so tired." She closed her eyes and drifted away.

"I'm just saying it's bad strategy, that's all." Veitch finished up the last of his plate of rabbit stew hungrily and eyed the black pan on the old range with a measure of hope. Through Tom's judicious herbal treatments, he had recovered from the shock of the amputation and appeared back to his old irascible self; a piece of white cloth he washed obsessively was tied around his stump.

"Ryan *is* our strategist, after all." After his dinner of steamed vegetables, Shavi gnawed on a raw carrot, his dessert, much to Veitch's disgust.

Tom furiously dunked his homemade bread in the last dregs of gravy. Before he could launch into a bad-tempered tirade, Davenport, the farmer who had taken them in earlier that day, poked his head round the door. He was wearing a dirty, shapeless hat and old coat, protection against the evening chill as he finished up the last of the jobs around the farm. "Everything all right, lads?"

"It was a very enjoyable meal, Mr. Davenport," Shavi said. "Our compliments to your wife. And we offer you our thanks for feeding us, when we have nothing to offer in return. We know there are shortages—"

Embarrassed, Davenport waved him quiet. "We've got enough to go round. I'd be worrying if I was one of the big boys. They won't know what to do now they can't get hold of their pesticides and chemical fertilisers. But I've been organic for a few years now, so, cross fingers, we should be all right for a while."

His wife, Rowena, pushed in next to him. She was in her late thirties, attractive, though weary looking. "Go on, Philip," she said, nudging her husband in the ribs, "ask them."

"I'm not going to ask them." Davenport shifted uncomfortably.

"If you don't, I will."

He sighed with irritation. "The wife wants to know if you're the heroes—"

She slapped him on the arm. "Don't say it like that!"

He wiped his nose with the back of his hand. "If you're—"

"Oh, get out of the way!" She pushed past him. "People are talking about a group of men and women going round the country trying to put right this awful thing that's happened. The farmers have been talking about it for weeks. They keep saying how some of these people helped out a farmer down in the West Country who'd got one of those spooks or goblins or whatever in his house. That's the story, anyway. But then we heard it from somebody else . . . a woman in the village. She's part of this parish pump news grapevine that's being set up to let everyone know what's going on. And one of the stories passed down the wire was about this group up in the north somewhere who fought against all those horrible things and saved an entire village. And they were doing all sorts of other . . ." Her voice faded away as she realised she was starting to ramble. She looked at her husband and added, "And yes, they did call them heroes. Said they could do things no other people could do. Said they were special."

Veitch tried to appear nonchalant, but he was fighting against pride. The woman noticed his fidgeting. "It is you, isn't it?"

"We are not special," Shavi said. "Not really. We are simply trying to do the best we can in a very difficult situation—"

"I told you they were the heroes," the woman said to her husband. She turned back to them excitedly. "What are you—"

Her husband pushed her out with undue roughness. "They don't want to be bothered by us!" He shuffled around uncomfortably. "We'll leave you alone now, lads. I know you'll have important stuff to talk about. But if you've got a moment before you take your leave—"

"We'll fill you in, mate." Once he'd gone, Veitch said conspiratorially, "Can you believe that? They're talking about us!"

"One should never believe one's own publicity, Ryan," Shavi said wryly. He eased back in his chair and sipped on his boiled water.

"Yes, control your ego before your head explodes." Tom collected the plates together and put them in the sink. "It's not important—"

"It's important to me. Nobody's ever called me a hero before."

"And this lot wouldn't either, if they knew you," Tom snapped. "To get back to the matter at hand—"

"Your strategy's all wrong."

Tom picked up his chair and banged it down in irritation. "So you said. Then what do you suggest?"

"You're the big bleedin' psychic. Shav here can talk to the birds. Can't you find out where the others are—exactly—so we can link up with them? We haven't got the time to keep wandering around. I want to be there the moment they roll up, ready to ride on London."

"And do what? Shake your stump at them?" Tom recognised it was a cheap shot the instant the words had left his lips but he refused to be contrite, although he wouldn't meet Veitch's eyes.

Veitch wasn't upset. He leaned forward, resting his elbows on the table so he wouldn't look so combative. "You know I'm talking sense here. We need a plan. There's only a matter of days until Hallowe'en . . . Samhain . . . that's all. There's not even a guarantee Church and the others are coming back."

"Then we're lost," Tom said sharply. "Separately, we are nothing."

"Sometimes you're so bleedin' pathetic."

"They will be back," Shavi said. "I have faith."

"Then we can get down to the fighting." Veitch adjusted the cloth around what remained of his wrist.

"You all appear to be forgetting something vitally important." Tom spun the chair around so he could lean on the back. He looked at Veitch accusingly. "Church will not have forgotten."

"What?" Veitch looked from Tom to Shavi.

"The land," Shavi said.

"Exactly." Tom took out his tin and made a roll-up with his dwindling supply of tobacco. "Wake the land. The primary mission, encoded for generations in myth and legend. There will be no defeating the Fomorii, no future for Britain—or the world for that matter—unless the land is woken from its long sleep."

"Like Church did in Edinburgh," Veitch said, "when the Fire helped blow those Bastards in their lair to kingdom come. But, yeah, it *helped*. Why's it so important?"

"The Tuatha Dé Danann would not have beaten the Fomorii before if the power in the land had not been vibrant."

"I do not remember you telling us that before," Shavi said suspiciously.

Tom sucked on the roll-up a few times to get it alight. "The power in the land, at its height, weakens the Fomorii. The Blue Fire—and what it represents—is the antithesis of the Night Walkers, and what they represent."

"So it's everywhere—" Veitch began.

Tom had no patience left. "It is powered by belief and faith and hope, by humanity and nature in conjunction. By all that is good in us. And for generations it has been slowly growing dormant. Several hundred years ago humanity took a wrong path. We gave up all that was most important for the promise of shiny things, home comforts, *products*. There was a time we could have had both, to a degree. But the ones who shape our thoughts, in politics and business, and the fools who invested their faith in science alone, convinced us to trade one off for the other. And without the belief of the people, the energy slowly withered, like a stream in a drought. Not gone for ever, just sleeping."

"But you know how it can be woken," Shavi said. "You have always known."

Veitch watched Shavi's face and then turned his narrowing eyes to Tom. "Another thing you've kept from us. You can't be trusted at all, can you, you old bastard? We could have done it weeks ago and saved us all a load of trouble."

"The time was not right then. Church was not right. The Fomorii corruption in him would have brought failure. And to fail once would have meant failing for all time."

Shavi watched Tom carefully. "What else do you know?"

"More things than you could ever dream." Tom was unbowed. "Some have to be learned through hardship and ritual—they can't be imparted over a quiet cup of tea. Others, well, the telling of them could alter the outcome of what is being told. I ask you to trust me, as I always have."

"We do trust you," Veitch said irritably. "That doesn't mean you don't get on our tits half the time."

"At least we have some common ground," Tom said acidly. The strain of events was eating away at all of them.

"Then what needs to be done?" Shavi asked. "And can it be done in the time that remains?"

Tom sucked on the roll-up thoughtfully; they couldn't quite divine his mood: dismal or hopeful? "The energy in the earth crisscrosses the globe, interlinking like the lines of latitude and longitude, only not so uniform. The Fire is not a straight line thing. It splits and winds in two strands around a central point, so that from above it resembles the double helix, the map of life, or perhaps the caduceus, the age-old symbol of two serpents coiled around a staff. Imagine, if you will, powerpoints where the energy rushes in, or is refocused and driven out into the network. The Well of Fire at Edinburgh was one, and Stonehenge and Avebury and Glastonbury Tor. The last three are important for they all fall on the divining line for Britain."

"The St. Michael Line," Shavi noted. "A ley running from Carn Les Boel at Land's End to St. Margaret's Church at Hopton on the east coast in Norfolk."

"Along that line are many of those powerpoints. They feed the whole network. For the land to come alive with the earth energy, the St. Michael Line must be vibrant and powerful. But it is fractured in part, sluggish in others, a trickle in many places."

"And to wake it?" Shavi asked.

"On the tip of Cornwall there is an ancient and mysterious place known as St. Michael's Mount. It is the lynchpin of the entire line. I have spoken in the past about the Celts and the other ancient races encoding great secrets in the earth itself. At St. Michael's Mount is the greatest secret of all. Locked under that place, Church—and Church alone—will uncover the key to bringing the line, and the land, back to life. Or he will find death."

Veitch tapped out a monotonous beat on the kitchen table with a teaspoon. "They'll have the place well defended," he said, staring into space. "Those tricks and traps they lined up to guard the spear, sword and the rest of it were bad enough. If this is their biggest secret—"

"Exactly," Tom said.

"Then," Shavi said, "we need to get Church to St. Michael's Mount as soon as we can."

In a quiet orchard at the back of the farmhouse, with the yellowing, autumn leaves glowing spectrally in the moonlight, Shavi sat cross-legged and listened to the sound of the night. Amongst the surrounding vegetation, eyes glittered—a fox, a rabbit, a badger, several stray cats—all of whom had come to see the shaman at work. The ritual, his first since leaving the Grim Lands, had been wearying, necessitating some of the tricks of concentration he thought he had become too experienced to need. But it had worked.

A few feet above the ground, the air was boiling as what appeared to be liquid metal bubbled out and drifted down; it was accompanied by the familiar smell of burnt iron. Behind it came one of the bone-white, featureless creatures Shavi had summoned before, a human-shaped construct used by one of the denizens of the Invisible World. It pulled itself forward and hung half in and half out of the hole in space.

"Who brings me to this place?" Its voice was like the wind on a winter sea.

"It is I, Brother of Dragons."

"I know you, Brother of Dragons. Have you not learned your lesson, of reaching out to the worlds beyond your own?"

"I know my place, and I know yours. I seek guidance."

"You did not heed our words before." The creature put its head on one side in a faintly mocking style.

Shavi recalled the prophetic message one of these creatures had given him about his murder at Callow's hands, but it had been couched in such cryptic terms he had not realised its meaning until it was too late to do anything about it. "I chose my path. And I am here to hear your words again."

"There is a price."

Shavi ran a thumb over the rough pad of his left hand, now crisscrossed with a score of tiny scars, chose a spot, then slit it with a knife. The blood dripped on to the damp grass.

"You give freely of your essence, Brother of Dragons." An underlying note of warning.

"Another Brother of Dragons, our leader, known as Church, is currently abroad in the Far Lands. Firstly, how does he fare?"

"He fares well. You have achieved all that you desire, but what you desire may do more harm than good."

Shavi noted this subtle warning, knowing there was no point attempting to get the construct to elucidate. "Then he will be back shortly. My second question: where will he arrive?"

"He will return to the Fixed Lands at the point from which he departed, where Merlin's Rock marks a doorway between worlds."

Shavi didn't recognise the name, but he guessed Tom probably would. "Then I thank you for your guidance. Return safely to the Invisible World." He paused. "No final words of warning?"

Although the construct had no features, Shavi was convinced it was smiling. "No warning would ever do justice to what lies ahead for you and your Brothers and Sisters."

And then it was gone.

Tom and Veitch sat around the range in the candlelight, drinking homemade beer. They were used to Shavi's ragged appearance after making contact with the Invisible World, but were eager to discover what he had learned. As he had expected, Tom knew the location instantly.

"Mousehole," the Rhymer said gruffly. "Then he joined Manannan's sick crew."

"Where's that, then?" Veitch swilled the beer down rapidly; six large mugs in a quarter of an hour.

"Cornwall." Tom stared at the red coals in the open door of the range. "In the furthest tip. The part of the country where the Celts buried their greatest secrets, and subsequently the most spiritual part of the land."

"Bloody hell, it's going to take us ages to get down there." Veitch took another swig, then looked up suddenly. "You could make another jump."

Tom waved him silent, his eyes still fixed on the fire, deep in thought. Shavi asked what Veitch meant and the Londoner spent the next five minutes attempting to explain how they had slipped into the energy flow between Scotland and Wandlebury Camp. Shavi was enthused by the entire concept and excitedly questioned Tom about it.

"Didn't you hear me say the St. Michael Line is fractured?" he snapped. "If we attempt to travel along it and hit a dead spot we will be unceremoniously spewed out into the world. Perhaps over a gorge or a cliff face or above a river in torrent. Now what good will that do?"

Veitch examined the deep lines of Tom's face, the fix of his eyes, until Tom could no longer pretend he hadn't seen him. "What?"

"You're thinking about it."

"No, I'm not."

"Yes, you are. I can see it in your face, you old bastard. And I know exactly what you're thinking. You're thinking it's too much of a risk for all three of us, but one of us needs to try it because we're running out of time."

Tom was particularly irritated at Veitch's sudden insight.

"I'm right, aren't I?"

"Oh, shut up." Tom rose from his chair and went over to the window to peer out into the dark. "It has to be me because only I can give Church the guidance he needs. Only I can point him towards St. Michael's Mount." A few beats of silence. "And the two of you are too valuable to risk. Five of you are needed to put this square. Any less . . . if any of you don't make it through the next two weeks . . ." He made a dismissive gesture.

"Then what should we do?" Shavi asked.

Tom was already gathering his things together in his haversack. "You must make your way to a meeting place, somewhere just beyond the reach of the Fomorii influence on the outskirts of London. I would suggest the west—"

The door crashed open and Davenport lurched in, his face pale and drawn. Shavi helped the farmer to a chair. Veitch's eyes went instantly to the door and window; the farmhouse was sprawling, impossible to defend.

"Down at the pub," Davenport gasped between juddering breaths. "I was talking to some bloke about you lot. Never seen him before. He was asking a lot of questions. I thought he'd just heard the stories, like the rest of us—"

"What happened?" Veitch gripped Davenport's shoulders and had to be prised off by Shavi.

"After I told him you were up here, his face started to change . . . melt . . . I thought I was going mad. Then I thought I was going to black out. One of the other blokes down there was sharp. Chucked a pint glass at him. I got away, still thought I was going to puke my guts up."

"Fomorii," Shavi snapped.

"There were more of them," Davenport continued. "I saw as I ran up here. They were following me—"

His sentence was cut off by a crashing at the front door.

"No time," Tom said. "We will find each other in the west, along the M4 between Reading and London." He nodded to them all, then darted through the back door where he snatched Davenport's bicycle from its resting place against the wall.

"Hide," Shavi said to the farmer. "They are after us. They will leave you alone." He saw Veitch's fixed expression and knew he was considering a fight. "This is not the time. We cannot afford to fail now."

Veitch backed down, and then they were both out of the door, running across the orchard and into the fields beyond.

His joints aching, Tom pedalled as fast as he could. The evening was alive with monkey shrieks, dark shapes flitting across the fields towards the farmhouse, the candlelit rooms surprisingly bright in the sea of night. He desperately hoped

Veitch and Shavi would escape—if anyone could, they could—but he had his doubts for Davenport and his wife.

That the Fomorii were still looking for them had taken him by surprise. He had thought that in the aftermath of their great success at bringing back Balor, the Night Walkers would have little time for failed insurrectionists.

He narrowed his eyes and concentrated until the thin tracings of Blue Fire rose from the shadowy background, like silver filigree glinting off the blades of grass in the fields. It was not strong in that area, but he could still pick out the ebb and flow. Driving himself on as fast as he could, he searched for a confluence on the St. Michael's Line.

An hour later he found himself in the Hertfordshire town of Royston, at a point where the ancient Royal Roads of Britain, the Icknield Way and Ermine Street, crossed. The town was still, although candles glowed in many windows. The moment he saw the town name, he knew where he was heading. The old stories enshrined the mythic power of certain locations so they would never be forgotten by the adepts, however much locals became inured to their mystery.

A grating in the pavement showed his destination, but it took him a while longer to raise one of the residents to point him in the direction of an old wooden door. Taking a candle, he made his way along a tunnel to a thirty-foot-high, bell-shaped chamber cut into the solid chalk lying just beneath the street. He remembered how one of the Culture had told him of its rediscovery in the eighteenth century when a group of workmen digging a hole found a millstone sunk in the earth; beneath it was a shaft that led into the cave.

Tom held up the candle and the walls came alive; carved pictures swelled and receded in the flickering light. Here *Sheela-na-Gig*, one of the old fertility goddesses, there Christian images of the crucifixion, and then a mix of the two, with St. Catherine holding the symbolic eight-spoked wheel of the sun disc. It had the same resonances as Rosslyn Chapel, where Shavi and Laura had freed the mad god Maponus, and like that place, it had also been a haunt of the Knights Templar, the old guardians of secret mysteries and the last people to truly understand the earth energy.

Cautiously he set down the candle and sat cross-legged in the centre of the chill cave, allowing its symbolism to work its magic on his subconscious. The shape of an inverted womb and the female images on the wall showed it was a place where the Earth Goddess was honoured by the ancients; more, it was a place where the life-giving power of the earth was celebrated.

The atmosphere was already crackling, setting the hairs alive across his arms and neck. He closed his eyes, breathed deeply, and prepared for his trip.

The deep dark of predawn clustered along the coastline as Wave Sweeper sailed in to the sleeping land. The waves crashed in bursts of white along the rocky coast and the salty scent of seaweed filled the air. Church stood at the rail, filled with excitement at the prospect of returning home after too long in the strangest of strange lands. Behind it, though, was apprehension at what lay ahead.

Ruth gave the back of his hand a squeeze with a reassuring smile. Her hair had been tied back, but the force of the wind still lashed it around. "Ready for the final act?"

"I don't like the way that sounds." He slipped an arm round her shoulders, comforted by her warmth.

All around them the deck milled with the Tuatha Dé Danann readying the ship for landing. The decks below were crammed with even more of the force: horses, and strange, gleaming chariots with spiked wheels, an entire deck of armaments prepared by Goibhniu and his brothers, plus tents and supplies and all the other minutiae needed by an army on the move.

"I wonder if we'll see the others?" he mused.

"When. It's only a matter of time. We were drawn together in the first place, and it'll happen again." Her thoughts turned to Veitch; she quickly drove them out.

"It's funny that it's going to end in London." The spray flew up around him. "We've come full circle."

"The Universe speaks to us in symbols, that's what Tom would say. I still can't get over how much we've all changed. If the stakes weren't so high, that would be . . . an achievement in itself."

"You feel better for it all?" He gently touched the space where her finger had been.

She only had to think for an instant. "As stupid as it seems, I do. Between this and the rest of my days stretching out in a safe but mundane legal world, there's no contest. It's such an obvious thing, but we never, ever grasp it: life's short, so why spend it bumping along in a secure existence that stops you feeling anything? Life should be about snatching as many great experiences as you can before you die, trading them in for wisdom. But if you want that, you've got to take the risk of great lows as well. Any sane person would say there's no contest, but we keep doing it."

"It's society. Conditioning. That's what we all need to break."

She laughed. "Life in the Age of Reason isn't all the brochures say."

"Reminds me of an old song."

"One nobody else has heard of, I suppose."

"I guess." As they neared the coast, he picked out a few lights in Mousehole; either early risers or the night watch.

Ruth watched the shadow of thoughts play on his face. "What's wrong?"

"Just wishing the Walpurgis hadn't died before he could tell me what he knew."

"About the one of us who's going to sell all the others down the river?" She kept her eyes fixed on the shoreline.

"I just hope that wasn't a turning point, the one moment when we could have saved everything, only to lose out by a hair's breadth. And Callow's treachery."

"No point worrying about it now." Her face was dark, unreadable. "We've just got to play the cards as they fall. That, and other clichés."

If the residents of Mousehole knew an alien ship was disgorging some of the most powerful beings of all existence in their midst, they never showed it. Doors and windows remained resolutely closed, despite the clatter of metal and the grind of wheels on stone and the whinnying of horses that looked like any other until one saw the unnaturally intelligent gleam in their eye.

Yet there was one figure, waiting near the pub where they had stayed on their arrival. He was wrapped in a voluminous, extreme-weather anorak, the snorkel hood pulled far forward against the chill so his features were lost to shadow. Even so, Church recognised him in an instant from the stance, at once relaxed, yet, conversely, taut.

He ran across the road and threw his arms around the figure. "Tom!"

The Rhymer pulled back his hood to reveal a face worn by exhaustion, the edge taken off it by the flicker of a smile. "If you knew the trouble I'd had to get here—"

"We wondered if you were dead!"

"If only." He blushed as Ruth bowled up and planted a large kiss on his cheek before throwing her arms around him. "Enough of that." He tried to recapture his grizzly demeanour, but they could both see his true feelings. "We have serious business ahead."

He filled them in quickly before motioning towards three horses he had tied up at the side of the pub. "We can be at St. Michael's Mount soon after dawn, if we hurry."

"And what do I get to do while Mr. Hero goes off and does all his testosterone business?" Despite her tone, Church knew Ruth wasn't offended that she had to sit it out; she was afraid for him and wanted to help.

"It'll be okay," he said. "I have to do it alone. It's a destiny thing. You know, like the old stories. Except this time they've got me instead of King Arthur. Bummer, eh?"

Baccharus sauntered over when he saw the three of them conversing. "Greetings, True Thomas. I knew you would not let hardship come between us meeting again."

"Baccharus. So your people have finally decided to stir themselves into action, I see."

"The Golden Ones like to conserve their energy so they are more effective when the time is ripe."

Tom tried to read his face, but the god gave nothing away. "You better watch yourself, Baccharus. Humour? What's next: laughter, tears and broken hearts? They'll be drumming you out of the Arrogance Club for good behaviour."

"Oh, I can still be arrogant, True Thomas. When one is highborn, one does not lose that trait."

Tom shook his head, stifling a grin. They told Baccharus that they would have to take their leave, without giving him details of their mission, in case news leaked out to those of the Tuatha Dé Danann not sympathetic to humanity.

Baccharus shook their hands in turn. "Then I wish you all well, for you have been the best of companions. We shall meet again before battle is joined."

As the three horses left the mêlée behind, Church felt sad. Baccharus had proved both a good comrade-in-arms and a friend, despite his difficulty in expressing emotion. But soon the night closed in around them and all thoughts turned to the dangers that lurked beyond the black hedgerows.

The village of Marazion was peaceful in the pale, early morning sunlight. Tom, who had amassed several lifetimes of knowledge, gave them a potted history of the oldest chartered town in Cornwall, its great age marked by the twisty-turny thirteenth-century streets running down to the wide stretch of sandy beach.

Ahead of them, St. Michael's Mount rose up majestically, a throne of stone in the bay bearing the crumbling castle and ancient chapel silhouetted against the sky; it had been the source of dreams for generations. Legends clustered hard around the bulky island, hazy in the morning mist; stories of giants and angels, lovers and redeemers.

Ruth reined in her horse, closed her eyes and put her face up to the sun as she took a deep breath of the cool, soothing air. She wrinkled her nose thoughtfully. "It's weird. It's only been a matter of weeks, but already it smells different . . . sweeter."

Church knew what she meant: no traffic fumes, no faint aroma of burning plastics, no hint of the modern world that made all the senses recoil, but that everyone had simply grown to accept. He followed the sweep of golden sands to the break of surf on the edge of the blue sea. "We've got everything here that makes life worth living. So tell me again why we need to go back?"

Tom slid off his mount and tied it to a tree. "Leave the horses. From here, we go on foot. Like pilgrims."

He led them across the dunes to a rough stone causeway. The tide was out so they could walk easily to the Mount. Despite the time of year and the salty sea breeze, it was peculiarly warm, reminding Ruth of the same unseasonal weather she had appreciated at Glastonbury. "I feel safe here," she said.

As they walked, Tom spoke in a dreamy monotone, describing the history and symbolism of the place that now towered over them. The beat and tone of his words made it almost a ritualistic chant, lulling them into deep thoughts born in the dark subconscious.

"In the old Cornish language this place was called Carreg Luz en Kuz, translated as the Hoar Rock in the Wood. In the ancient Celtic language, hoar often refers to a standing stone. There is no standing stone now, but who knows? You now know what the stones mark . . ." His words were caught by the wind, disappeared. When they picked up his monologue again, he had changed tack. "Once this place was known as Dinsul, or Citadel of the Sun. This is where the wise men of the Celts called up their god of light. There is a very clear tradition of sun worship at this site. Then the cult of St. Michael grew up in the Middle Ages after a vision of the saint filled with light appeared atop the Mount. So the old ways were passed on through the Christian religion where the site became dedicated to St. Michael, a saint who became a symbol associated with light. In the language of symbols, there is no differentiation between the old religion and the new. The same source, different names."

Tom's words had begun to nag at the back of Church's mind; it wasn't just travelogue. "Why are you telling us this?"

Tom ignored him. "Christ, too, another symbol of light, in legend is believed to have landed with his uncle Joseph of Arimathea at St. Michael's Mount before making his way to Glastonbury. He began to sing softly, "'And did those feet, in ancient times . . .'"

Church glanced at him uneasily. "I said, why are you telling *me* this?"

"St. Michael—some writers once described him as the Spirit of Revelation, and that is a fair description," Tom said. "For if he stands for anything, it is this: there are mysteries heaped on mysteries and nothing should be taken at face value. Religions, all religions, are ninety percent politics and ten percent belief. The belief continues eternally, only shaped by the politics to appear this, or that, but it always is as it was. One thing; one belief." Tom took a deep breath. "Old stories," he said with pride; he thought of the Mount's legends of giants in the earth, as there had been at Wandlebury Camp.

"In Cornwall," Tom continued, "there's a legend that St. Michael sleeps beneath the land, waiting to be woken."

Church felt a shiver down his spine as the threads of disparate ancient stories drew together to reveal a pattern behind the chaos. There were similar threads drawing together different religions, all leading back to the same source, though he was sure many worshippers of those faiths would refuse to see the connections. Yet it was all there for anyone who chose to see it. What did it mean, that was the question? Possibly the most important question he would ever have to consider in his life: a pattern behind everything. That was the message that had underpinned every step of his journey around the country since that cold night beneath Albert Bridge.

They reached the end of the causeway. A steep path wound upwards in the shadow of the mount. By the time they were halfway up, they were sweating in the morning heat.

"All these secrets hidden in the earth, buried in old stories, it makes me feel queasy," Ruth said.

"That's because you are being spoken to in the true language of symbols, the ur-language, but you are not yet educated enough to understand it." Tom rested briefly to catch his breath. "Yet your subconscious hears and it grasps the importance, if not the meaning. The signals it sounds out to your forebrain causes conflict, upsetting your equilibrium. Secrets and mysteries—hints at the true universe that lies behind the one you see."

They fell silent, meditating on his words, until they reached the summit and the ancient buildings. Church suddenly felt heady and had to reach out for a wall to support himself.

"You can feel it?" Tom asked.

He could: a tremendous surge of the earth energy, running through every stone, as if the place were an enormous battery. His flesh tingled and there was a corresponding tightness across his chest that eventually eased, to be replaced by euphoria.

"What a rush." Church laughed; he could see Ruth was experiencing it too.

"This is why people take drugs," Tom said, "to attempt to reach this state that they only have a vague race memory of, from the days when their ancestors could manipulate the subtle energies at the ancient sites. But nothing earthly can ever come close to it."

They moved slowly in the long shadows of the castle until they came to an ancient stone cross rising out of the ground. At first glance it was nothing special, but once they drew closer they saw a double swirl of the Blue Fire continually flowing all around it.

"This is where the lines all draw together," Church said. It was so potent he almost felt like kneeling before it.

The mood was broken when, from the corner of his eye, he caught sight of a dark figure away to his left. He whirled, half drawing the sword, only to see a man dozing in the sun on a low wall, his dog collar just visible beneath a lightweight blue cagoule. He was in his late sixties, his face sun-browned and lined, his hair a shock of white. He stirred, as if Church's gaze had disturbed him, and then jumped to his feet, straightening his clothes with a mixture of embarrassment and anticipation.

Once he had calmed he looked penetratingly into their faces in turn. "Is this it?" he asked with a note of excitement. "Is this the time?"

"It is the time," Tom said, stepping forward. Church and Ruth looked at him curiously.

"That's a relief, you know. After all that waiting and waiting. Of course, when I saw the signs . . . the failure of technology and all that . . . I supposed it *must* be the time. But when the message has been lying around for hundreds of years . . . longer, of course . . . it's difficult to believe it's actually going to happen in *your* lifetime." His cheeks coloured at the realisation that he was rambling. He held out a cautious hand and greeted them in turn. "I'm Michael." He smiled at what some would have considered a coincidence. "Watchman of St. Michael's Mount." He paused. "Chief Watchman, of this time, and this land. There. That seems so odd to say, after thirty years of never being able to say it to anybody. When the obligation was first passed to me, it felt such an honour . . . the mysteries that were opened to me! . . . and I can honestly say that has never diminished with time." He stared into Church's face so deeply Church felt uncomfortable. "Is this the one?"

"It is," Tom replied.

"Yes. I can see it. In his eyes, always in the eyes. The one good man." He cupped Church's right hand in both of his. "May God go with you, my boy." Then he did the most curious thing: he dropped to his knee and gently kissed Church's hand.

Ruth, who had been watching the scenario intently, inexplicably grew angry. "What's going on here?" she snapped.

Church looked around puzzled. "That's a very good question."

"It's time, Jack." There was a strange cast to Tom's face that Church had not seen before, and it took him a second or two to realise what it was: Tom's features were unguarded; completely open.

Church was a little disturbed by this out-of-character intensity. "What do you mean?"

"Time to tell you something I've been keeping a secret ever since I've known you. A big secret."

Church thought of the Celtic dead talking of the traitor in their midst and his hand instinctively went to the sword.

Tom smiled and shook his head, as if he knew exactly what Church was thinking. "A big secret, Jack," he said softly. "So big you might not be able to take it all in. From the very beginning, this has all been about you, more than anything. You're on a journey to enlightenment. You think you've been doing one thing, but instead you've been doing this." He took a deep breath; there was a faint tremor in his voice. "You need to gain illumination for what lies ahead, to prepare you for the next step. The biggest step of all. There will be a long period of trial, but after that . . ."

"So what are you saying? That he's some kind of Messiah?" Fury waiting to burst forth was buried in Ruth's voice.

"That's a particularly *stupid* way of putting it," Tom said sharply.

"But it's essentially true." There were tears in her eyes. *What is she thinking?* Church wondered.

Tom dismissed Ruth with a curt wave of his hand and turned to Church. "Jack, you have died and been reborn. You have the essence of the gods in your veins. *You* are the next step."

Church felt sick; his head was spinning and he couldn't breathe as the full weight of what Tom was saying finally crushed down on him.

"What you are about to embark on is the final stage of your transformation." Tom's words were droning like flies. "This is what the old alchemists were talking about. You, Jack. The transformation of lead into gold was a metaphor for what you are undergoing."

"This was all about *me*?"

"The future of humanity, the rising and advancing of our race towards the next stage, depends on you. The prophecy has been with us since the earliest times. *In Britain's Darkest Hour, a hero shall arise.* You will arise, Jack. You will awaken the land, and through your tribulations you will make the next step of spiritual evolution that will lead humanity from the shadows to—"

"Godhood?"

"Perhaps. The Watchmen were established to help defend the land against incursions by the old gods, but they were also brought together to see this through. To find the one on whom the whole of the future rested, and to help shape him."

"I've been manipulated by the Tuatha Dé Danann, the Fomorii and now humanity?" Church felt like he was going to be sick. It was too much, both of comprehension and responsibility. And it was stupid! So many people had called him a hero, but he knew what he was like inside: flawed, unsure, conflicted. And now they were trying to thrust all of humanity's future on to his shoulders. Who could cope with that?

"Not manipulated. You had a choice every step of the way. You still have a choice. No one would blame you for turning away from this. But you need to know what rests on your decision."

"Am I going to change?"

"Physically? No, it's much more subtle than that—the great leaps forward always are, at the time. But inside, you will change, and you will wish that change in all humanity. It will move through people like a virus, altering their thought processes, making them look up from the gutters to the stars—"

"It's not fair!" The hurt in Ruth's voice was almost painful. "How can he turn away? Who could throw down that responsibility for selfish reasons?"

She was right. He tried to comfort her, but she was having none of it.

"We just wanted to be together, to appreciate what we've got now, to appreciate life, if we ever sort out this mess we're in. That was always the slim hope that kept us going, but now what you're saying means there's never going to be any rest! Not for Church, who deserves it the most. Not for me."

"Some things are more important—"

"Don't give me that!" Her eyes blazed, and away on the mainland a wind rushed wildly through the trees. Church stealthily signalled to Tom not to anger her further.

"We've all sacrificed so much! We deserve a break!"

He tried to take her in his arms, but she fended him off. "Ruth, it's okay—"

"It's not, Church. It's not okay, and it's never going to be okay. This is like some stupid, sad old story where the heroes go through hardship and end up sacrificing themselves so everybody else can have a good life. It's just not fair!"

Her tears were flowing freely now. She couldn't bear to look at any of them. She wandered away and faced the sea, her head bowed as if she had been struck.

"Why couldn't you tell me all this before?" Church said to Tom.

"You wouldn't have reacted the same way in your trials if you knew they were trials. All your achievements are wholly your own. Your choices were made by your own sense of goodness."

Church rubbed his eyes, overcome by what he had been told. "Baccharus told me the gods were afraid humanity would come up and take their place."

Tom rested a friendly hand on Church's shoulder. "They know. Thousands of years have led to this one point. Millions of variables falling into line. No coincidences, Church. Make no mistake, there are no coincidences. The gods may not have known you were the one, but they knew the whole game was coming to a head—"

"It isn't a game!" His voice broke.

"I'm sorry, that was the wrong word." As Tom shifted, the sun fell behind him so Church could not see his features in the dazzle of light. "But I knew you were the one, Church, from the very first moment I met you. As Michael said, you can see it in the eyes. I knew you were the one, good man."

The note of respect and friendship in his voice brought a swell of emotion in Church. He looked over to Ruth, frail against the rugged surroundings, and he felt both love and sadness at the same time. More than anything he wanted to spend the rest of his days with her, but the obligation was too much. He had no choice. He never had a choice from the moment he was born.

"Ruth."

She ignored him, wrapped her arms a little tighter around herself.

Standing behind her, he hesitated briefly before putting his hands on her waist. "Don't do this."

"Why not? You're going to do it."

"Of course I'm going to do it."

"That's typical of you. No doubt at all." Her voice trembled. "You're throwing us away."

"I'm not going to do that. You're more important to me than anything."

A long pause. "You never said that before."

"There are a lot of things I've not said. I'm not very good at expressing my emotions in words. But I do love you, Ruth."

Another pause, and then she turned slowly and rested her head on his shoulder. "This thing isn't like anything else. It's too big. Christ, the responsibility for leading humanity into the Promised Land!"

"You're mixing your Biblical stories."

She took a deep breath to regain her equilibrium, then cuffed him gently on the shoulder to break the mood. "They'll never let you back after this. It's like the Mafia. You're a Made Man. You don't get out alive."

"I believe things have a way of working themselves out."

"That's a very childish and naïve view of existence."

"Sure. What's wrong with that?"

She hugged him tighter, her fingernails biting through his clothes.

"I'll do whatever it takes to make sure I'm with you when all this blows over."

"Cross mighty oceans?"

"Yes."

"Climb the highest mountain?"

"Yes."

"Travel the length of time and scour the universe?"

"Yes and yes."

"You're a lying git, but I love you too." He could feel her tears soaking through his T-shirt. She gave him another playful hit on the arm and then stepped back. "Go on with you, then. Just make sure you're back for lunch."

Tom was sighing loudly and shifting from foot to foot when Church returned to him. He made to speak, but Church silenced him with a jabbed finger. "Don't say a word."

Michael stepped in and motioned towards the chapel. "It's this way."

Church could feel the lines of force buzzing through the soles of his boots; he could have found his way to the destination blindfold.

Outside the chapel door, Michael paused. He looked both unsure and ecstatic. "This is it, then?"

Tom took Michael's hand and shook it firmly. "Well done. You've discharged your duty well. The long watch is over."

"Well, I don't quite know what I'll do with my time."

"Be patient. And pray to your God for success."

Tom slapped him on the shoulder to send him on his way back to Ruth before stepping into the chapel with Church at his heel. Inside it was cool and dark, filled with the ages-old smell of damp stone.

"What am I going to find?" Church asked.

"You'll know when you get there."

"You're a great bloody help, aren't you?"

The very air was charged with the earth energy; from the corner of his eye, Church could see blue sparks, like stardust.

"There are realities upon realities," Tom said. "You can't rely on anything you see, hear, smell, touch, taste. But that's always been the way. The only thing that matters is what's in here." He levelled his fist at Church's heart.

"Nothing is fixed in the Fixed Lands," Church said, repeating the words that had haunted his thoughts.

"Exactly. There are realities that may not be to your taste." He was looking at Church in such a strange way it was troubling; Church tried to make sense of the unease he saw behind Tom's eyes, but it wouldn't come; something else the Rhymer wasn't telling him. "Sour realities. Pinched and mean. Places where there are none of the values that make life worth living—friendship, love, honour and dignity. Where there is only power and greed and money. You don't have to accept them, Jack. Wish the world better. Everything is illusion. You just have to wish hard enough to shape it."

He looked as if he was about to hug Church, but he caught himself at the last. In the end he stepped aside and pointed to a small stone stairway not far from the altar.

"What's down there?"

"A tomb about nine foot square cut out of the rock. In 1275 the monks here came across the bones of a man eight feet tall. A giant."

"Who was he?"

"Not important."

"The place is important?"

He nodded.

"Are you coming with me?"

"No. This is something you have to do alone."

Church sighed, tried to force a smile but it wouldn't come. Without another word, he put his foot on the first step.

chapter fifteen
war is declared and battle come down

Blood thundered in Church's head as he made his way down the steps to the chill interior of the tomb. Trepidation filled every part of him, but it was tinged with relief that finally there would be some kind of revelation after so many mysteries.

Inside the bare tomb was a powerful sense of *presence*. Narrowing his eyes, Church allowed his deep perception to take over until the walls, floor and ceiling came alive with a vascular system of Blue Fire, interlocking at pulse points, drawing together at one section where the depth of blue glowed in the shape of a hand. He steeled himself, then placed his own palm down hard on the spot. There was an instant of hanging before the wall juddered apart to reveal a dark tunnel beyond. Church slipped through quickly and the rock closed behind him with a resounding clash.

The tunnel reminded him of so many others he had experienced in the dark, secret places beneath the earth, although he knew that description was not wholly correct. The Celts and the people who came before them understood perfectly the symbolism of the routes they had established; indeed, it was probably the main reason for their location. He was entering the womb, going back to the primal state.

After a few minutes, the tunnel opened on to a wide corridor filled with different coloured light filtering through a gently drifting mist; near the roof it was golden, near the ground the rich, sapphire tones of the Blue Fire, and in between were flickers of red and green and purple. The mist gave the place an ethereal quality that was deeply soothing. The air smelled like dry ice.

For a while he hovered anxiously, concerned that it was impossible to see what lay ahead. Knowing he had no choice, he strode out, feeling the unnatural sensation of feathers on his skin as he entered the mist. If it resembled the other secret places he had visited, somewhere ahead would lie a puzzle with a particularly lethal sting; if Tom's description of the place was correct, this one would be worst of all.

Within the mist, he lost all his bearing. After a while, a dark smudge appeared in the drifting white, quickly forming into a figure. The Sword was in Church's hand in an instant, electric against his skin. It was a man, dressed in the armour and white silk of a Knight Templar, the red cross on his chest glowing eerily. His face was drawn, his eyes hooded above a drooping white moustache. He rested on the long sword the Templars favoured.

Church waited for him to adopt a fighting posture, but the Knight simply motioned for Church to continue along the corridor. There was an air of deference about him, but his face was dark and threatening. Inexplicably, Church shuddered as he passed.

Further on, other figures emerged from the mist. These were Celts ready for battle, naked and tattooed, their hair matted, spiked and bleached with a lime mixture. They stood against the walls on either side, watching him with baleful eyes. Some broke away, loping past him in the direction from which he had come. Again he felt the same old mixture of wariness and reverence, but his fear of a sudden attack had started to wane.

As he progressed, representatives of the races that preceded the Celts floated in and out of the mist, but most of them were swallowed up again before he got good sight of them. At some point, a troubling noise had started up, so faint at first he hadn't noticed it, but it built until it was pulsing through the walls with steady, rhythmic bass notes that resonated in the pit of his stomach. It sounded like war drums, or the beating of an enormous heart.

And then, suddenly, the mist cleared and he was looking at something so incongruous it was at first hard to take: a large window, and beyond it people in modern dress stared back at him with hard, uncompromising expressions. Before he could see any more, the mist closed in once again. There had been something dismal and threatening about the scene, although he couldn't quite put his finger on what it was. He hurried on and didn't look back.

Finally he was out of the mist. The corridor was even wider at this point—enough for ten men to lie across—but the most curious thing was that the floor was a mass of intricate patterns carved into the hard bedrock. There were the familiar spirals and cup holes he had seen at prehistoric sites during his days as a working archaeologist, but also the detailed interweaving designs of the Celts. The patterns of hundreds, if not thousands, of years were portrayed there.

The swirls and fine detail were almost hallucinogenic, but there was no time to waste examining the inconography. He put one foot on the edge of the pattern.

A spike burst from the ground, through the sole of his boot and into the leather uppers. A bolt of red agony filled his leg and he howled, wrenching his foot off the iron nail with a sickening sucking sound. The spike disappeared back into the design the moment he was free of it. Feeling sick from the shock and the pain, he crumpled down hard on the cold stone, tearing off his boot. The spike had torn the flesh off the insides of his big toe and his second toe, but luckily, had done no further damage.

As he laced the boot back up, he surveyed the floor pattern: a trap. The spikes were obviously buried along the length of the design: step on the correct place, you were fine; make the wrong move and you were impaled. The pattern stretched out in delirious confusion. How was he supposed to divine the path through it?

He retreated a few paces to see if the change in perspective offered any clues, then moved in close; it was a miasma. From a distance, it was a mess, meaningless; near to, the design hinted at great meaning, but none of it made any sense in any context he understood. Sighing, he sat back, trying to ignore the pain stabbing in his foot. He took comfort from the knowledge that all the previous puzzles they had encountered had been soluble if seen from the cultural or philosophical perspective of the Celts and the earlier people who had originated them. His university studies helped him a little in understanding their worldview, but he had never studied in depth the group that seventeenth-century romantics had designated a unique people. He knew the Celts were a fragmented collection of tribes, originally rising from a broad area centred on India, but common threads tied them together, of which their view of life and spirituality were probably the strongest.

He thought back over the previous puzzles and their odd mix of threat and spiritual instruction: the one at Tintagel, where sacrifice was the key, or the clues at Glastonbury that demanded Shavi, Ruth and Laura search for the "signal hidden in the noise," the truth buried in the confusion, a metaphor for life. There it was. Quickly, he crawled forward to the edge of the pattern. The Celtic design showed serpents—or, he thought excitedly, dragons—flowing in a spiral pattern that progressed from side to side along the floor. And the Spiral Path had been the Celtic metaphor for both the journey through life and a ritual procession that allowed access to the Otherworld, like the spiral path carved into the slopes of Glastonbury Tor.

Was that it? He had no way of knowing for sure until his foot was on the design, so in the end it came down to an act of faith; in himself and his own abilities.

He cracked his knuckles, then took a deep breath. It was time to embark on the Spiral Dance and move from this life to the next.

With the air leaden in his lungs, he stepped on to the stylised Celtic serpents. Every muscle hardened. When he realised nothing had happened, he relaxed a little, but the path was barely wider than a curb, a tightrope winding its way through a sea of danger. What happened if he slipped? A spike ripping through his sole, sprawling across the design, spikes punching into his body wherever he landed. With the blood thundering in his ears, he took his second step.

The path took him from wall to wall, forwards then backwards, in slow progress along the length of the corridor. Sweat soaked through his shirt, ran in rivulets into the nape of his back. His head hurt from staring at the tiny pattern in the half-light. Follow the serpent in the earth to enlightenment. As the ancient Celtic inventors had undoubtedly intended, his stark concentration brought a deep meditation on what he was undertaking; the metaphor of walking a thin path through constant danger did not escape him.

At one point, he paused briefly to rest his eyes. It was a mistake, for he instantly started wavering and almost pitched forward until he threw out both arms to steady himself. It only just did the trick, but it was enough of a scare to focus him even more sharply. He did one final spiral, more complex than any of the others, and then, abruptly, the design had gone and he was back on safe stone flags. He collapsed on to his back, sucking in soothing breaths.

He rested for only a moment before following the corridor once more. The Spiral Path had been some kind of transition, for within a few yards the corridor had been replaced by a wall of trees, their tops lost high up in the shadows. Church had long since forgone trying to apply logic to his experiences in such areas, but the sight was still oddly disturbing. The underground wood appeared healthy enough, with full-leafed oaks and ash and hawthorn, with bracken and brambles growing beneath them. An odd green luminescence filtered amongst the trunks, but Church could not identify its source; it was enough to illuminate the way ahead, and gave the impression of first light or twilight.

The density of the forest added to the deep foreboding that had crept up on him. Anything could be hiding amongst the foliage. As if to echo his suspicions, rustling broke out in the undergrowth. A second later, two rows of sheep emerged from the forest and passed him on either side. The ones on the left were white, the others black, both lines walking in perfect step. The bizarre sight became even more unnerving when one of the white sheep bleated, for then one of the black sheep wandered over to the white queue and immediately became white. The reverse happened when a black sheep bleated. Church looked round to see where they were going, but there were none behind him. When he peered back, the last few sheep emerged from the forest and were gone.

He was sure it meant something, but he had no idea what, and the image continued to haunt him as he began his journey in the quiet, green world.

The atmosphere amongst the trees was so ethereal it was difficult to shake the notion that he was dreaming. Odd sensations began to make their way through his body—a tingling in his legs, a feeling that his hands were no longer hands—and a moment later the weightlessness that had crept up on him became palpable. It was not a hallucination, for he really was drifting a little way above the ground. He called out in surprise, only to be shocked that his voice sounded like the cry of a bird. His eyes were astonishingly sharp and his arms were wings, covered with thick, brown feathers. He was a hawk, flying up into the branches, and up and up.

There was no time to question his transformation, for he was immediately confronted by another hawk with blazing yellow eyes. "You are one with the birds of the trees," it said in an unsettlingly human voice.

It swooped down at him, talons raised in attack. Church panicked, losing all control of his form. The hawk raked claws across his back and a shower of brown feathers flew all around. He attempted to steer himself, crashed against a branch and went into a downward spiral.

The hawk didn't give up its attack, shrieking loudly as it bore down on him. Once more the talons tore through his back, and this time the pain almost made him lose consciousness. But he recovered slightly, and his mind was focused. He didn't fight against the messages that were coming from instinct, and after a slow start, where he only narrowly evaded another scarring, he found he could move swiftly amongst the trees.

He wasn't about to stand and fight—he didn't see the point of it—so he flew as swiftly as he could, before a weight pressed down hard on his shoulders and forced him to the ground. His wings gone, he hit the turf hard, tumbling athletically.

Barely able to catch his breath, he rolled to his feet, which were now grey paws. "You are one with the beasts of the field," a rough voice said. He looked round to see a large grey wolf away amongst the trees. It was watching him with the same hateful yellow eyes of the hawk.

It moved, but Church was quicker, loping through the trunks, leaping the clusters of vegetation, avoiding the pits and hollows with ease. As he ran, he moved further off the ground and his paws became hooves, while a sharp pain in his forehead signalled the sprouting of antlers like those Cernunnos sported.

The hoofbeats of his pursuer continued to thunder across the soft ground. And then Church was back on his own legs, and in his peripheral vision he could see his own hands; his lungs burned from the exertion. Church didn't know if he had truly transformed or if it had been a hallucination. He tried to look over his shoulder and awkwardly caught his foot in a root, stumbled, and slid down a slight incline.

What he saw made his blood run cold. There was no man behind him, as there had been a deer, a wolf and a hawk. At first it was a stark white glow, before he realised that what he was seeing was a pack of dogs, savage and alien, filled with their own brilliance.

He picked himself up and ran as fast as he could. The beasts' crazed howling made him sick with primal fear. They were not like the dogs of the Wild Hunt, which were fearsome enough, but were filled with an unbridled ferocity and, he was convinced, controlled by one mind. He risked another backwards glance and saw them bounding amongst the trees like spectres, there, then gone, moving on two flanks to capture him in a pincer movement.

He jumped a stream, almost skidding down the opposite bank, then hurdled a fallen log. The pack was relentless, and drawing closer; he would not be able to outrun them. Their howling became even more blood crazed as they sensed this.

He came out of the forest so fast he barely realised he had left the last of the trees behind him. The land fell away sharply, becoming hard rock again, and the roof had closed once more twenty feet above his head. In the distance he could make out a brilliant blue glow. Slipping on the rock, he tumbled, cracking his head hard, but he was up and running in one fluid movement, wiping the blood away that had started to puddle in his left eye.

He had hoped the pack would remain behind in the forest, but now their shrieks were echoing off the walls, growing more intense, more terrifying. If he looked back, he knew he would see them snapping only inches from his heels.

As he ran, he pulled out the Sword once more. Legend said it could kill anything with a single blow. Swinging it behind him without slowing his step, he felt it connect with two hard forms. A terrible howling rang up from the whole pack.

He carried on that way for a few minutes more, but his arm muscles were soon burning and his joints ached. There was no time for an alternate strategy: the path ahead of him ended abruptly at a cliff edge, and beyond was a lake of the Blue Fire, the energy rising up in coruscating bursts like the bubbling of lava.

A few feet from the edge he spun round, lashing out wildly with the sword, but the pack had already halted a few yards away. All the dogs were watching him with their sickly yellow eyes, their mouths open to reveal enormous, sharp fangs; drool ran out in rivulets to splatter on the rock where it gave a hot fat sizzle.

Breathless, he waved the Sword at them while attempting to look over his shoulder to see if there was some exit he had missed.

"There is no escape from here," the dogs said as one. "You have reached the Chapel Perilous. Your life is now over." They advanced a step in perfect, unnerving rhythm, like some drilled Roman legion.

"No," Church gasped. "It wouldn't end like this. There has to be a way out or there's no point to the trial." He looked all around quickly, but could see no exit. "I'm missing something."

"No escape," the dogs repeated. "This is your death. Behind you is the source of everything. One step and you will be swallowed up, eradicated. Here we stand, ready to tear you to pieces. To turn your meat to fibres and your bones to dust."

"I can fight," Church said.

"You can," the dogs said, "for you have already killed some of us. But do we seem any less to you?"

The pack appeared to go on forever. "Where there's life, there's hope," Church said.

The dogs advanced another step.

He wiped the blood away from his eye, his heart pounding. The Sword handle was slick with sweat.

The dogs moved four paces in rapid procession. He waved the Sword wildly. Only a couple of yards away now, the white of their coats was almost blinding. Their jaws moved in unison—*click*—their eyes rolled as one.

Perhaps this was the trial: to fight and fight and fight, until he was down to his last reserves. But against an enemy that could not be killed, or even weakened? What was the point in that? Sooner or later they would overwhelm him.

He gripped the Sword with both hands and adopted a fighting stance.

What was the meaning in that?

And then it came to him. It took only a second or two to weigh it up, and then he sheathed the Sword and spun round. The blue looked so inviting: relief after his long, arduous struggle. He closed his eyes and stepped off the cliff.

He expected burning, but there was no sensation at all for a long time, just a world of blue overwhelming everything. He also expected his consciousness—his sense of self—to be broken up within seconds of contact, then dissipated amongst the blue waves, to be returned to the source, but that didn't happen either. He remained who he had always been, since the beginning of time.

When sensation began to return, it was fitful, and quite alien. He felt the beating of mighty wings coming from his own arms; he saw with crystal-refracted vision through serpent eyes; he felt the blast of flames pass his lips, the stink of smoke in his nostrils.

"You are one," a voice from nowhere said.

He was looking at blue, but the shade was much softer. It took him a few seconds to accept the change in hue, and then a fluffy cloud drifted into his vision and he realised he was staring at the sky. He closed his eyes, smiling, enjoying the heat of the sun on his face.

Sitting up, he found himself lying on the causeway that joined St. Michael's Mount to the mainland. From the position of the sun, it must have been around noon; he had been gone barely any time at all.

Ruth's cry stirred him from memories of flying; reluctantly, he realised they were fading rapidly, but the sense of freedom didn't go. She came running along the causeway towards him, her hair lashing in the breeze. She grinned with relief and joy. He jumped up and took her in his arms, overjoyed that she was with him.

"I saw you from the top," she said. "How did you get here?"

"Look at that," he said, pointing over their heads.

A Fabulous Beast swooped on the air currents, the sun glinting brightly off its scales, reds and golds and greens. Church was overcome with a sense of wonder. The Beast was otherworldly and lithe and graceful as it gently circled the top of the Mount, but it was what it represented that truly affected him: a world where anything could happen, a world where the mundane had forever been stripped from life.

"It's the old one, from Avebury. The oldest of them all." Tom was at their side, craning his neck to peer beneath a shielding hand. "You've done it. It wouldn't have left its home if the Fiery Network hadn't been brought back to life."

"Then I really did it?" Church asked, barely believing. "I woke the sleeping land?"

"There are more of them," Ruth marvelled. "Loads of them."

Church counted ten, then gave up; they were coming from all directions to converge on the Mount. Some were smaller, some obviously younger, their colours slightly different, but they were all flying with abandon, rolling and gliding and looping the loop, so that there was an unmistakable feeling of joyous celebration.

"We did it," he said in awe.

That night they made camp on a hillside overlooking St. Michael's Mount. Tom had already located tents and sleeping bags before coming to meet them at Mousehole, and they lit a fire to keep out the autumnal chill that came down with the night. He had also found a bottle of whisky to drink to their success.

The cleric, Michael, had met them briefly after Church's return, but he was eager to get back to his parishioners to spread a message of hope. The deference he had shown Church had been almost embarrassing.

"How do you feel?" Ruth asked Church hesitantly, once Tom had gone off to build up their wood supply.

It was a question he had avoided, for he was almost afraid to examine himself. "Good," he said.

"Don't think you're going to get away with that. Do I have to kiss your hand every time I meet you? Are you going to walk on water for your party trick?"

He tapped his head. "Up here I feel pretty much the same as always. I mean, I think the same way. I'm definitely the *me* I always was, which is good because I had this feeling I'd turn out like a reformed smoker or Born-Again Christian, turned off by half the things I used to be in my old life."

Her smile showed relief; it was obvious she had felt the same way.

"But in here," he said, tapping his chest, "I feel amazing. I feel . . . I don't know, the best way to describe it is *right*. I feel at ease with everything. Positive. Confident." He thought hard. "I feel at peace."

She was looking at him with an expression that suggested she wished she felt that way too. She took his hand and gave it a squeeze.

"I expected it to be earth-shattering," he continued. "But it's so subtle. I don't feel like the man who's going to lead humanity to the next level. In fact, I cringe at the thought of it."

"Maybe that's the point. Maybe you were like a jigsaw with one piece missing. Now you've found it you can be the person you always might have been."

He shook his head, laughing quietly. "Now I know how I feel, I'm taking it all with a pinch of salt. Tom gets so wrapped up with these predictions and prophecies. They're all so vague they can mean virtually anything under any circumstance. Who knows? Maybe Veitch is the big saviour."

"But what does it mean? For us?" Her eyes shimmered brightly in the firelight.

"I'm carrying on with my life as it was. I'm not thinking about tomorrow. I'm not thinking about the big picture. I'm making the most of each minute and I'll deal with whatever's thrown at me, as and when it happens. And I'm doing it with you." He pulled her forward and kissed her tenderly.

They were interrupted by Tom's irritated muttering. "You've got time for all that spooning in the privacy of your tent," he said.

"You're only jealous because you're not getting any," Ruth replied.

The night was clear and bright and filled with a deep, abiding magic. The full moon brought silver tips to the waves, their gentle lapping a soothing symphony accompanied by the occasional breeze rustling the goldening leaves; the perfect soundtrack to Church's thoughts. Stars glistened everywhere they looked; they felt peaceful for the first time in months.

"It could be like this all over," Church said, his arm around Ruth, the two of them watching the light on the waves.

"And I thought I was the hippie," Tom said. "Don't start going soft. This is a little oasis. The real world is out there and it's thoroughly unpleasant."

"Can't we just enjoy the moment?" Ruth protested.

"You go right ahead." Tom prodded the fire with an annoyance that matched the sneer in his voice. "We'll just forget about all those bodies getting torn apart and eaten, all those lives being ruined, land being blasted, cities razed to the ground, rivers polluted. Oh, and while we're at it, let's forget the end of the world in just a few short days." He punctuated it with a tight smile.

"I didn't mean that." Ruth's eyes blazed. "But we can't do anything right here, right now, so do we have to continue flagellating ourselves? We've worked hard. We've achieved something . . . Church has achieved something. We should celebrate our victories."

"I simply wanted you to remember—"

"Of course I remember! I know what we're up against! And I know what our chances are, even with what Church has done today." Tom flinched. "Yes, I can see it in your face. Even if we win we aren't all going to make it through alive, right? So I just want to enjoy this quiet time with Church and my *friend* because it might be my last."

Tom shrugged. "Point taken." He gave a slight grin that punctured the mood.

For the next half hour, they did take it easy, enjoying their company with jokes and gossip while handing round the whisky. Even so, they found it impossible to bury the momentous events of the day and soon they were chatting animatedly once more about what had happened. Church couldn't bring himself to discuss what he had felt once he had given himself up to the Blue Fire—it had been too personal, a spiritually transcendent moment that would be devalued by being discussed. That infuriated Ruth, who was eager to understand.

"But I don't see what he *did* to bring the land alive," she said. "It wasn't as if he unblocked a channel or something."

"He gave it his life, his spirit, in honesty and openness, and the Blue Fire gave it back to him, but not before that vital surge had brought the whole of the system alive." Tom was lying on his back, watching the stars through his cloud of smoke. "It is fuelled by belief, and Church believed in a way that nobody had for centuries. Not just believed in the Fiery Network, but in himself, in humanity and the universe and hope, and childish things too, like dreams and wishing."

"So he's just one big battery."

"The only battery who could have done it."

"I don't get it," Ruth continued. "You talked about *waking the land* as if it were a big thing, but apart from the Fabulous Beasts we saw earlier, everything looks the same."

"Maybe you're not looking in the right place, or the right way. Maybe you're not *feeling*."

Ruth hurled some mild abuse at his patronising attitude. He sighed wearily and dragged himself to his feet. "Do you remember that night at Stonehenge when I gave you the first sign of the Blue Fire?" he said.

"No, I don't," Ruth said, "because I was fast asleep. You saved that demonstration for your favourite son here."

"Yes, I remember," Church said. "It was amazing. Like something I'd been looking for all my life."

"The power of Stonehenge made that easier," Tom said, "because it's a node in the network. Look around—do you see any standing stones in the vicinity?" They agreed that there weren't any.

They waited for him to continue, but all he did was smoke, and check his watch and the moon and stars, until they were convinced he'd slipped into a drugged stupor. Ruth shifted impatiently, made to speak, but Church placed a restraining hand on her forearm. She looked at him curiously; he put his finger to his lips.

After fifteen minutes, Tom said, "Now." He dropped to his haunches and placed one hand flat on the cool grass. "The time has to be right. The mood has to be right. Everything has to be right, and it's not been righter for centuries. You even need the right eyes for this—not everyone can see it—but you should be ready now. Watch carefully."

Around his hand, tiny sparks began to fly. They had a life of their own, dancing and jumping into the grass, surging towards the nearby trees. Other strands ran to Church and Ruth, infiltrating them with a prickly thrill; they both felt a sudden surge of euphoria.

"It's in everything," Ruth gasped.

"You think that's good." Tom smiled. "Watch this."

The ground erupted with Blue Fire. It shot out in lines across the land, towards the sea and under the waves, intersecting at regular points where tiny flares burned. And then it suddenly burst upwards in a tremendous, breathtaking rush, hundreds of feet high, a dazzling cathedral of lights like the one Church had seen at Stonehenge. A paler blue light shimmered between the connecting strands, turning opaque, then clear, like protective walls. Only this cathedral was not the only one. An even bigger structure covered St. Michael's Mount; and there were more beyond, stretching right across the land. It was dazzling in its potency. Caught up in the sheer wonder of it, there was no doubt the whole of the land had become infused with the vital force.

"How did you do that?" Ruth gasped.

"Sometimes when things fall into alignment it becomes more active. I simply helped you to see it."

"This is why the ancients put up the stone circles," Ruth said in awe.

"And the standing stones and cairns and other places of sacred power." Tom was now sitting cross-legged on the grass, watching the display with a beatific smile. "To channel it, to help it to live, and to reap the benefits it provides."

"It heals," Ruth said.

"It heals the body, certainly. But more importantly, it heals the spirit."

"I want to feel that." Ruth looked from Tom to Church. "You've both had experience of it. It's changed you both, I can see. I *need* to feel it."

"There'll be time," Tom said.

"Will there?" Ruth replied. The note in her voice infected them all, and gradually the astonishing display faded.

Church put his arm tightly around her shoulders. "But it's worth fighting for, isn't it?"

Veitch and Shavi escaped from the farmhouse, but only with a helping of guile and a good serving of luck. They kept to the hedgerows, hiding in ditches at the slightest sound, barely moving, barely breathing.

The Fomorii were out in force, scurrying along the roads all around the farm. Veitch and Shavi were in no doubt the Night Walkers still considered them a threat. At times when the beasts drew a little too close, Shavi used his shamanic abilities to direct various field animals to cause a distraction so they could escape. Since his return from the Grim Lands, he was even more adept at the things at which he had previously excelled.

Eventually they were faced with open countryside; as dawn began to break they were moving as fast as they could towards the west.

Over the following days, they kept as far away from any roads or centres of population as possible. They slept in trees or ditches, wrapped in dustbin bags and other items of rubbish, like two tramps. Sometimes they found a hollow where they could light a fire without being seen. Veitch cooked rabbits or birds, while Shavi satisfied himself with any autumnal berries and fruits or roots that he could scavenge.

On a day that began cold and overcast with light drizzle sweeping across the countryside in gusts, they made their way over fields towards the rendezvous point. Ahead lay a rise where they expected a good vista over the rolling valleys that led down to the Thames; the outer reaches of the London sprawl was not far away.

When they came close to the ridge, they dropped to their bellies and wriggled up the remaining few yards, their clothes already sodden and thick with mud. Peeking over the summit so they would not be silhouetted against the skyline, they witnessed a sight that made their blood run cold.

London lay beneath a thick bank of seething clouds that formed no part of the surrounding weather system. Occasional bursts of lightning punctured the oppressive gloom so they could see that, somewhere in the centre of the capital, a large black tower had been raised up. It was still incomplete, and the edges were indistinct, as if roughly constructed. It reminded Shavi of pictures he had seen of enormous termites' nests in the African veldt. Ruth had spoken of a similar tower she had seen in the Lake District, constructed from the detritus of humanity: abandoned cars, plastics, bricks and girders, old washing machines, anything that could be reclaimed and stacked. And all across the city, fires blazed, sending up thick gouts of greasy smoke to join the lowering clouds.

There were things buzzing the tower with the insistent, awkward motion of flies. The distance was too great to tell exactly what they were, but there were clouds of them, black and threatening. And from the periphery of the city, across the surrounding countryside, swarmed what at first glance appeared to be ants. The Fomorii scurried back and forth, thousands upon thousands of them, sweeping out in wider and wider arcs as they spread across the country. Their movement looked chaotic and meaningless, but that only masked the complexity of regimented actions designed to scour and destroy. It was a scene from Hell.

Veitch watched the panorama for long minutes, his face heavy with hatred and repressed anger. "How the fuck are we going to fight something like that?" he said in a cold, dead voice.

In the shadow of the M25, Laura and the Bone Inspector sheltered amongst a tangled maze of wrecked and abandoned cars. Through gaps in the vehicles they could make out waves of Fomorii fanning out across the Essex fields.

"We don't stand a chance," Laura whispered. "They're everywhere." She still felt sick from the shock of losing her arm. Pressure was building deep in her shoulder, as if her blood was about to gush out of the gaping socket, despite the stained shirt she had pressed against the wound; she still couldn't understand why she hadn't bled out.

"They're searching for us." The dismal note in the Bone Inspector's voice told her he agreed with her assessment. Their luck had run out.

"What do we do? Stay here?"

"Nowhere to run. They're all around now." He tapped a syncopated rhythm with his staff.

Laura rubbed at her shoulder joint; the pressure was growing unbearable.

"We can't stay—"

Her words were drowned out by the sudden rending of metal. Cars flew on either side, as if they were made of paper. Laura flung herself backwards in shock. The Bone Inspector raised his staff in defence, his face drained of blood. Eight or nine Fomorii ploughed through the vehicles with ease, tossing aside what they could move, rending apart what they could not.

Laura thought: *Shit. What a way to go.*

The noise of crashing metal was so loud neither of them heard the hunting horn, and so they were surprised when the first of the Fomorii dissolved in a thin, black rain. To Laura, the world appeared fractured: frozen frames, sudden temporal jumps. The Fomorii were turning as one. Red and white dogs leaped through the air, their teeth tiny yet so very sharp. Spears tipped with cruel sickles sliced into the Night Walkers, the beasts falling apart at the slightest touch. Drifting through the grey rain were men on horseback, swathed in furs and armour, their eyes hidden by shadows.

In less than two minutes the Fomorii were gone, their remains steaming amongst the shattered cars. The Wild Hunt reined in their horses and cantered around the area as the one of their number with the most fearsome face dismounted. As he walked towards Laura he began to change; antlers sprouted from his forehead, fur and leaves intermingled across his body. Cernunnos passed the Bone Inspector as if he were not there and dropped to his haunches before Laura, his wide-set, golden eyes calm and soothing.

"Daughter of the Green, I greet you."

"I thought you only came out at night in that last form," Laura gasped, not really knowing what to say.

"The world has changed. Many rules are falling like autumn leaves." Then he did turn to the Bone Inspector. "Guardian, you have moved beyond the bounds of your calling on this occasion. You sought this one out at great personal danger, and you have protected her to the best of your abilities. I look kindly on you. A reward will come your way."

The Bone Inspector bowed his head slightly. "I seek no reward."

"Nonetheless, it shall be yours." Returning his attention to Laura, he trailed his long, gnarled fingers gently through her hair. "Frail creature. *Fragile* creature, yet filled with wonder."

Laura lost herself in the swirling gold in his eyes. He held her gaze for a moment, then rose. "Come, this place is corrupted. We must find safe haven."

All Laura could remember of the journey from her seat on Cernunnos's horse—although he wore the hideous form of the Erl-King as he rode—was a blur of green fields and grey road. They came to a halt in no time at all on the fringes of Brentwood, where the Essex countryside still rolled out peacefully.

In a thickly wooded swathe of the South Weald country park, the Hunt dismounted and let their horses wander amongst the trees. The Erl-King became Cernunnos once more and led Laura off to a quiet area where he could talk to her privately.

"What's going on?" she said weakly as she lay against the foot of an enormous oak.

"Events move faster as they rush towards the point of greatest change. You are caught up in the flow, Sister of Dragons, as you were from the moment existence came calling for you. This is your time, your destiny."

"What use am I going to be?" The pressure in her shoulder made her stomach turn. "My arm—"

"Remove the rag."

Laura hesitated, afraid to see the tangled parts that remained after her arm had been torn off. He urged her once more, gently. She dropped the stained shirt and looked away. The pressure in her shoulder grew unbearable and she was forced to ram her fist into her mouth to stop herself screaming. But within a moment the pressure had broken, to be replaced by another disturbing sensation: it felt like everything inside her was rushing out of her shoulder. It was impossible not to look.

What she saw made her mind warp. The dangling tendons and skin were moving of their own accord. Before her eyes, cells multiplied and grew into long tendrils that twisted and knotted, then fused, became bone and muscle and gristle. The stump of an upper arm protruded from her shoulder. The process grew faster, reminding her of time-lapse film of sprouting plants. The tendrils lashed so quickly her face was buffeted by the air currents they made. An elbow formed perfectly. A forearm and wrist. The palm came together in a blur, and finally the fingers, the nails added with a flourish.

She couldn't take her eyes off it. Slowly, she turned it over, examining it from every angle. It was *her* arm; she knew the patterns of light and shade from the muscle structure beneath the skin. Her stomach flipped and she thought she was going to be sick, but as she brought her hand to her mouth she noticed the circle of interlocking leaves Cernunnos had branded into her flesh on the eerie island in Loch Maree. "The green blood, green skin . . . What did you do to me?" Thoughts trampled through her head. Her hands went to her stomach. "I didn't imagine it. I was ripped open when that thing came out of me. And I. Mended myself?"

Cernunnos made a strange growling noise deep in his throat that was almost sympathetic. "You are a Daughter of the Green. Within you is the potency of nature in all its fury and wonder."

"What did you do to me?"

"Your old form had reached the end of its days—"

"You killed me?" Her mind was reeling.

"There is no life or death. All things have no beginning and no end. For the immutable laws, you only have to look around you. Seasons turn. Things fall into the earth, then rise again. New forms are made, but the essence remains the same. The rules have always been laid bare for your kind to see, but in recent times you have been blinded by arrogance. You saw yourselves as special. You thought that, for you, with death there came an ending when everything around you told you otherwise. It trapped you in your forms, made you truly into frail, fragile creatures. It prevented you reaching out to existence or utilising the greatness that lies within you."

She examined her arm once more, not sure if she should feel horror or wonder. "I can grow bits of myself? Like a plant?"

"This gift is not given lightly, Sister of Dragons. You are of my essence now. You are part of the greatness of nature, you are a vibrant branch of my bountiful family."

Laura nodded; slowly it was starting to feel right. If Cernunnos hadn't changed her she would have died when Balor had been reborn into the world. But more than that, she felt something indefinable yet all-consuming, as if she had finally come to a place she was always meant to be.

"All things are open to you now, Sister of Dragons, Daughter of the Green," Cernunnos continued. "The sunlit uplands stretch before you. All is possible."

"Why me? There were others, Shavi—"

"Your heart was given to the green long ago."

He was right: in childhood, she had always been drawn to nature; as an adult, she had devoted herself to environmental activism. It had always been the most important thing in the world to her. "Ruth got the same mark from you, but she didn't get the same treatment."

"As my daughters, you each have roles to fulfil. She echoes a different aspect of my essence. The force that cannot be stopped."

"She's the sledgehammer, I'm the stiletto." She felt uncomfortable using weapons as a metaphor for abilities that were so life affirming.

"Yet there is danger for her. The gift I have given her is great. It fills her being, shifts the balance of her day and nightside. She must learn to encompass it or it will consume her." Cernunnos began to roam around her, tearing at the turf with his hooves.

"Will she be okay?"

He remained silent for a little too long. "The greatest danger lies at the place where all things converge. If her will fails her, the power will drive her down darker lanes."

Laura subconsciously flexed her new fingers. "The power's eating her up. She's losing control." She felt a pang of worry for the woman she had disliked for so long. "Can't you do something?"

"It is her gift. To intervene would make it worthless."

Laura ground her teeth; the shock of losing then regaining her arm had ebbed and she was overcome once more with urgency. "I need to get back to the others. Time's running out." She stood up shakily. "So Ruth gets all the bigshot powers. I'm just indestructible."

"You can do more. Much more. Let me show you." He smiled and held out his hand.

Church and Ruth had been intrigued by Tom's account of how he had used the lines of Blue Fire to travel vast distances, and were eager to utilise it to get closer to the rendezvous point. He refused flatly, emphasising the many dangers.

"It's not like catching a train, you know. Whatever you might think, the chance of getting lost in it is high. You need skills taught over the course of a lifetime to follow the channels and flow. I could look after one of you, but two . . . that's too many. Imagine diving into a white water river gushing through a ravine over rapids—that is what it is like. If it is a life or death matter, I will attempt it. But after coming so far, we can't afford to throw it all away by losing one of you. Time *is* short, but in my opinion the best option is to take the horses and ride them hard."

Reluctantly, they agreed, and within minutes of sunrise they were riding fast across the rugged Cornish landscape. They picked up the A30, eventually following the route on which Ruth, Laura and Shavi had been pursued by the Wild Hunt, crossing the M5 to bypass Bristol, where they joined the M4. It was still eerie to see the motorway devoid of cars. Already thick weeds and long grass had sprouted in the central reservation, and birds strutted defiantly across the lanes. At one point they disturbed rabbits gambolling lazily in the fast lane, enjoying their freedom from the tyranny of humanity.

They ransacked the motorway services for any food that had not spoiled, giving the horses water and rest, taking the opportunity to doze in the dry air of the cafeterias. But the closer they got to London, the more the atmosphere became depressive, the more they felt an unpleasant anxiety building in the pit of their stomachs. The skies were darker, filled with charred matter blowing in the wind. The stink of burning was everywhere. Their instincts told them to turn back to seek out the green fields and sunlit lands of the West Country, but they forced themselves to keep on.

With only two days to Samhain, they finally parted company just past Reading, with Tom heading on to find Veitch and Shavi, while Ruth and Church continued to the camp of the Tuatha Dé Danann. Although none of them gave voice to it, they all dreaded what the coming days would bring.

chapter sixteen
semper fidelis

Twilight was already heavy on the land when Church and Ruth wearily crested a ridge above the rendezvous point. What they saw made them rein in their horses in astonishment. After the long grey shadows, they were confronted by a sea of light filled with the noise of activity and a complex range of smells. Spread out before them was what appeared to be a mediaeval tent city, but it covered vast acres. Campfires showered columns of sparks amongst the billowing tents, some small, others of marquee size, while torches flickered with yellow-white light, marking paths and meeting areas. The air was fragrant with incense, spices and perfume, but there was also the powerful musk of horses and the aromas of cooking food. The hauntingly seductive music of the Tuatha Dé Danann rose from numerous quarters, but instead of conflicting, it came together in a symphony that made their spirits soar. For a while they were entranced by the gods walking, talking, preparing weapons, making merry.

"I don't remember this many on the ship," Ruth said.

"They must have been joined by some of the other Courts." Church tried not to be engulfed by the wonder of what he saw, but it was impossible. Whatever he might think of the gods, they were a source of remarkable magic.

They urged their exhausted mounts slowly down the slope, but they hadn't gone far when they heard a sound like wind in a mountain pass. A second later there was movement all around. Figures barely more than ghosts separated from the dark landscape to form a barrier between them and the camp. They were lower-born Golden Ones, in strange shimmering armour offset by red and white silk, with helmets that looked like enormous seashells.

"Fragile Creatures," one of them said to the others.

"We are a Brother and Sister of Dragons," Church pronounced. "We are here at the behest of the First Family."

There was sudden activity beyond the ranks. The guards fell roughly aside as another god strode through. From the more intricate designs of his armour, he looked to be of higher rank, but he had a cold, cruel face that Church instantly disliked. When he laid eyes on Church and Ruth, he gave a dark, cunning smile and did a bow that could easily have been mockery. "Greetings, Brother and Sister of Dragons. Your reputation precedes you. I am Melliflor, of the Court of the Yearning Heart. I welcome you to this place, though it lacks the charms of our home." He stepped aside and motioned to a path that had opened up between the guards. "Come, let me take you to my Queen. She will be eager to learn the latest from the world of Fragile Creatures. You will be able to rest and eat and drink your fill—"

"Hold, Melliflor." The voice was stern and a little threatening.

The guards moved to one side as another group marched up, their silver armour bearing designs based on an avian motif. Their leader's face gave nothing away, but it had none of the unpleasant qualities of his opposite number.

"Greetings, Gaelen. I was about to lead these two weary travellers to partake of the hospitality for which the Golden Ones are famed."

Gaelen barely looked at Melliflor. "I think the Brother and Sister of Dragons would rather be spared the hospitality of your Queen."

Melliflor bristled. "Step carefully, Gaelen. My Queen would not—"

"I have orders to take these two directly to the Lady Niamh. That is the desire of the First Family."

Melliflor appeared to consider challenging this, but eventually backed down. He gave another dislikeable smile to Church and Ruth and bowed once more. "Another time, then. I hope you do not regret missing the comforts on offer, nor the information my Queen could have imparted." He turned on his heel and marched away, with his guards trooping behind.

Gaelen nodded curtly before leading Church and Ruth slowly to the camp. They dismounted on the outskirts where one of the guards led their horses away for food and watering.

Within the camp their perceptions became increasingly distorted. They felt like they were drifting through a dream where everything was fluid, strong enough for them to wonder if they would remember any of it once they left. Their senses were stifled beneath the constant assault of sounds, smells and sights. As they passed, eyes turned towards them, some filled with contempt, others accompanied by a smile of greeting. They saw no one they recognised. Many of the gods were of the lower caste, but on two occasions they caught sight of burning golden lights unable to stay in one shape.

Gaelen halted at a large purple tent made of a heavy material that resembled velvet. Over it fluttered a flag showing two dragons, red and white, either in embrace or fighting. The god pulled aside the flap and bid them enter.

The inside was cosy with sumptuous cushions scattered on a richly patterned carpet. Lanterns hung from poles at intervals around the perimeter, but the flames were turned down so the light was soft and hazy. Baccharus slumped in a low chair, his legs stretched out before him, drinking from a wooden flagon studded with four rubies. He lifted it in greeting, but didn't rise.

Niamh stood next to a trestle table in the centre of the tent, poring over a large map that had previously been rolled around large brass spindles. She hurried over to Church, smiling broadly. She made to embrace him, but when she saw Ruth, her face lost its sheen and she turned away sadly.

"You completed your mission, then, Brother?" Baccharus said.

"I did," Church replied. "The land is alive again. That should at least give us something for the fight."

Baccharus sipped from his flagon. "We can feel it. It is a powerful defence. Even my kind fear the force of the Blue Fire."

Church and Ruth flopped wearily on the cushions while Niamh sent out for food and drink, "all given freely and without obligation," a statement that told Church this was a Court of the Tuatha Dé Danann in all but location.

"You've already agreed a plan?" Church asked as he ate his fill of fruit and bread.

"The Golden Ones you know as Lugh and Nuada have overseen the battle planning," Niamh said. "The Night Walkers are well established in their den and it will not be easy to unseat them. The dark ones are a foul infestation. They swarm everywhere. But a direct assault on several fronts should weaken them. We come from the North and the West. The Master will lead Wave Sweeper along the river to split their force in two."

"What about us?"

Perhaps it was a trick of the flickering lanterns, but she suddenly looked deeply sad. "Though some of my kind refuse to admit it, you are the key to defeating the Heart of Shadows. You must find a way into its lair and use the Quadrillax to wipe it from existence." She turned away, pretending to unfurl another map.

Ruth's hand fumbled for Church's and gave it a squeeze. "We'll do our part," she said.

Baccharus and Niamh left them alone to eat and doze in the warm atmosphere, but they were too tense to get much rest. Four hours later, the tent flaps were roughly thrown aside. Church automatically jumped to his feet, his hand on the Sword hilt, but he was almost bowled over by a large figure that crossed the tent in seconds and threw its arms around him tightly.

"Ey, you bastard!" Veitch lifted Church off the ground and hugged him until he felt his ribs were about to crack. "I thought you'd have done a runner by now."

"You can't get rid of me that easy." He clapped Veitch on the shoulder, more pleased to see him than he would have believed.

Shavi slipped in behind, smiling quietly, and then Tom, looking tired and irritable. Veitch turned and waved the stump of his wrist at Shavi and Ruth. "Beat you both, as bleedin' usual."

Ruth stared in horror for a while, then followed his gaze down to where the finger was missing on her hand, and over to Shavi who sported the same gap. They all burst out laughing together.

But then Veitch could control himself no longer. He marched over to pull Ruth to him tightly, burying his face in her hair to hide the emotion that rushed through him. After a few seconds, he pulled back to kiss her gently on the head. Ruth went rigid in the face of his show of feeling, knowing it wasn't the time to tell him about Church, unsure what to do, but Veitch didn't appear to notice her reticence. She flashed a glance at Church, who gave one quick shake of his head.

Veitch smiled with a mixture of affection and embarrassment. "Sorry about that." His eyes were fixed on hers, wide and childlike; there was a flush to his cheeks. "I've missed you."

Ruth smiled back awkwardly, but said nothing. The moment was deflated by Shavi who hugged Church and Ruth in turn, his emotions also close to the surface. "It feels good to be together again," he said quietly. "Now all we need is Laura."

There was a moment of uncomfortable silence before Church said, "She's dead."

"No, she's not," Veitch said, puzzled. "Shavi was the only one who was dead."

They looked from one to the other blankly.

It was hard for any of them to believe they were back together again. Each of them felt, at times, overwhelmed; and then they would simply sit and listen to the others talking, enjoying the motion of faces, the animation of limbs, the energy crackling amongst them. Elation overwhelmed them all, completely wiping out any thought of what the morning might bring. There was drinking and raucousness, jokes that made light of their hardships, and the warm glow of old friends brought together again.

Veitch held up a flagon marked with a design of a Fabulous Beast. "You seen this?"

"Isn't that the one with the pellet with the poison?" Church laughed, but Veitch completely missed the reference.

"No, no," Shavi said, grinning, "that is in the chalice with the palace. That one is the brew that is true."

"You lot haven't bleedin' changed," Veitch muttered.

Veitch was mesmerised by every movement Ruth made, as if he could barely believe she was there before him. Part of Ruth felt uncomfortable at the depth of emotion she sensed, yet she was excited by it too. That conflict made her uneasy. She knew she loved Church, so why was she responding to the attentions of someone else, in particular a man with whom she had so little in common?

When the conversation became a heated debate about Laura she was thankful for the opportunity to distract herself from her thoughts. Neither she nor Church could believe Laura was still alive; Tom and Veitch were adamant she was. It was left to Shavi to argue that they now lived in a world where anything could happen.

The conversation moved on. Ruth tried to stay out of the limelight, but Veitch brought her in at every opportunity, rapt at the tales she told.

"You hung on the outside of a ship in a storm? You're a crazy girl!"

"At least I didn't manage to lose a hand," she said wryly.

"Maybe we should get ourselves a little Amputation Club going." Veitch chortled; he was drinking too much, too fast. Beneath his upbeat exterior, they all could see the strain the loss of his hand had brought in him.

"That'd exclude me," Church said, "so in defence I'm proposing the Born Again Club."

Veitch furrowed his brow. "What's that, then?"

"Well, I died and came back." He nodded to Shavi. "So did you. And Ruth did, fleetingly, just before Laura took the seed of Balor from her."

Veitch snorted. "You're not counting me out, you tosser."

"Do not worry, Ryan," Shavi joked, "there is plenty of time for you to meet your maker and come back down to earth."

"Right. And I'll do it in style. With a choir of bleedin' angels!"

Tom muttered something indecipherable, but patently irritable. Veitch swore at him playfully, laughed when Tom bit, then broke open another amphora of wine.

"You know, I miss technology less than I thought," Ruth said, lounging back on one of the enormous cushions. "But one thing I could do with now is a CD player, or a tape deck . . . anything that gives music." She eyed Church with *faux* contempt. "As long as I don't have to listen to any Sinatra."

He laughed. "Shame. I could come up with a good soundtrack for all this." He thought for a moment. "How about 'That Old Black Magic' from *Come Swing with Me!* followed by 'It's Nice to Go Trav'ling—'"

Ruth covered her face.

"No, no, something soulful. Spiritual," Shavi said. "Curtis Mayfield. Perhaps Van Morrison—"

"Geezer music," Veitch said. "I never thought I'd say this, but I wish Laura was here. She might have been a pain in the arse most of the time, but musically she kept you music fans in your pen."

Shavi looked towards the tent flap. "I still expect her to walk in at any moment."

An outcry outside brought them all to their feet. They rushed out into the cold night to see the Tuatha Dé Danann in a state of excitement around one of the campfires.

Church grabbed one of the gods by the shoulder. "What's going on?"

The god was shocked that he had been accosted by a *Fragile Creature*, but he appeared aware of Church's reputation. "The Norta has been seen! And her sisters too!"

"What's that?"

The god struggled for the right words in his excitement. "The one your people called the Morrigan."

A hand fell on Church's shoulder and he turned to face Baccharus, equally animated. "A great portent, my friend. The Morrigan is one of our own, but she prefers her own company, or that of her sisters, Macha, Badb and Nemain. They have not been seen by the Golden Ones since the first days after the pact. But they are drawn to war . . . and . . . and bloodshed . . . and . . ."—he attempted to speak in a manner Church could understand, but he struggled with a word that was still alien to him—"death. The Dark Sisters are fearsome, both in what they represent and in their prowess. The Morrigan and her clan helped us win both battles of Magh Tuireadh. Undoubtedly, her appearance is a good omen."

"Where is she?" Church scanned the campsite, eager to see a figure of such reputation.

"The Dark Sisters will not come into the light." Baccharus raised his head to the gleaming moon. "Macha, Badb and Nemain were seen circling the camp earlier. They wore the armour of war."

"And the Morrigan?"

"There is a stream nearby. In it she was seen washing the heads of those who are to die in the forthcoming battle. The Morrigan keeps count of those who move from existence."

Church flashed back to a cold February night before he had any inkling of the terrible change that had come over the world. It was the Morrigan he had seen washing his own head in the Thames. His throat closed up when he thought how she had turned and looked at him, with a face that appeared like death itself. But another worry crept up on him: was that portent referring to his previous *death* on Skye or was she revealing what lay in store for him in the Battle of London?

"Tell me," he said, "did your people see the heads?"

Baccharus knew exactly what he was asking. "I cannot lie. There were Fragile Creatures."

Church's blood ran cold. "Who was it?"

"No!" Tom strode over, his face cold and hard. "Do not tell him! It would not help for anyone to know they are going to die. Hope is the engine of success."

Church studied his face carefully. Tom didn't meet his eyes. "You know who's going to die, don't you? You've always known."

Tom fixed an eye on Church that made his stomach turn. "Yes. Pity me for it." He turned and marched away without another word.

Church felt sick. He looked round at the others, who were talking to another of the Tuatha Dé Danann; none of them had heard the exchange. In that instant he understood exactly what Tom was going through. He couldn't tell them one of them was destined to die; it was a burden he would have to carry himself.

The sadness came up quicker and harder than he anticipated as he watched the people who had become his best friends over the last few months. He couldn't imagine being without any of them, even though that had been a constant from the moment they had banded together. Unbidden, his thoughts turned to which of them he would miss the least, and that made him feel even worse.

Dismally, he turned back to Baccharus, who deftly changed the conversation. "True Thomas is a good man. Do not blame him for being the bearer of bad news."

"We never got on at the start. I thought he was manipulating us. That he was cold and patronising and arrogant. I wish I'd been better to him."

"True Thomas has accepted his responsibility. He does not expect anything from you."

"That makes it even worse."

A whistling like an incoming missile passed overhead. Church looked up to see the terrifying form of a woman pass by, her hair as wild as winter, her black clothes streaming off her in rags, her mouth torn wide as she made the anguished noise. He shivered as her shadow passed over him.

"Badb, Queen of Crows," Baccharus said.

"I'm glad she's on our side."

He watched the other figures moving across the sky for a while, but the night was too cold to stay for long. Returning to the warmth of the tent, he found the others already in deep conversation, though Tom was nowhere to be seen. Their faces showed the mood had darkened.

"We were talking about the traitor," Ruth said as he entered.

"I don't want suspicion causing any rifts at this critical stage."

"Yeah, but we've got to be on our guard." Veitch was repeatedly unwrapping, then rewrapping the cloth around the stump of his wrist. Church knew his mind was working through numerous strategies, dismissing some, rethinking others. He was still drunk, but he was now brooding, and it was easier to see the anger that always lay just beneath the surface. "We've come through all this shit together, trusted each other. If I found out one of us had been playing the others just to sell them out, I'd kill them."

"Ryan!" Ruth said.

"I find it hard to believe one of us could be a traitor." Shavi looked around them, as honest and open as always. "We come from different backgrounds. We are all different people, with nothing, superficially, in common. Yet we have seen into each other's souls. We are good people, all of us, at heart. I trust my instinct implicitly. I cannot see anything in any of us that suggests betrayal."

"Exactly." Church sat down close to Ruth, then became aware of Veitch watching him curiously. He shuffled away an inch or two. "I can't pretend it hasn't bothered me, but we all know how much the dead love to twist things. Who knows what they really meant?"

Veitch took a knife and diced an apple into four quarters. "I'm still going to be watching my back."

The conversation drifted to lighter subjects, but they never caught the uplifting mood of celebration again. Just after one a.m., when the sounds of revelry from the camp had died down, the growing quiet was disturbed by the distant blast of a horn. It was barely audible, but it brought a chill to them all. A second or two later it sounded again, much closer to hand, followed by the fearsome baying of hounds.

"The Wild Hunt," Shavi said.

Ruth fingered the mark that had been imprinted on her hand. "Cernunnos is joining us. That's good news."

"Right. He's obviously on the side of us *Fragile Creatures*." Even so, Church couldn't shake the fear he felt at the god's Erl-King aspect. He would never forget how the Hunt had torn through the revellers leaving the pub on Dartmoor: so brutal, yet cold, like a force of nature.

They fell silent with their thoughts until they heard the sound of two pairs of footsteps approaching the tent. They waited for the flaps to be thrown back, but the visitors slipped in quietly. The tall one at the rear was the Bone Inspector, his greying hair matted with grease and filth hanging loosely around his shoulders. His cheesecloth shirt was covered with green stains.

The shorter one at the front wore a cloak with a hood pulled over her head, but Church immediately knew who it was. His stomach flipped; a shiver ran up his spine. "Laura." The word was barely more than an exhalation.

She threw back her hood with her typical flair for the dramatic. They were shocked to see Veitch was right about the tinge to her skin, but that the scars Callow had inflicted on her face were mysteriously missing shocked them more. "Church-dude. You look like you've seen a ghost. Instead of just the walking dead." She looked round at the others, who were rapt. "Well, that's the kind of wild reception I always expected from this little group."

Church jumped up, looking deeply into her eyes for a long moment, before putting his arms around her. She smelled of spring leaves and summer flowers. He didn't know what to say, so he led her to a space and sat her down.

Ruth leaned across the circle. "I want to thank you—"

"Don't. We've all made sacrifices. That's what we do." She nodded to the Bone Inspector. "He's the one you should thank. If not for him I wouldn't be here for all that mystical five symbolism baloney you need to do the big job."

"Somebody had to do it," the Bone Inspector said grumpily. He shifted around, uncomfortable with the attention. "Where's the Rhymer? I need to sort something out with him."

When they said they didn't know, he left in a bad temper to scour the camp. Their attention turned back to all the confusing emotions Laura's reappearance had raised.

"We were just saying we could not believe you were truly dead," Shavi said with a smile, reaching out to take her hand. She smiled back, sweetly, without a trace of the bitterness that had always characterised her.

"Don't get me wrong, hon. I *did* die. And now I'm back, the same, only different."

Another one, Church thought. *What does it all mean?*

"But how did you survive?" Ruth was pale and troubled. "I had Balor in me. I know what it felt like, what would have happened when it came out."

Laura lifted up her over-sized T-shirt to reveal a rapidly fading jagged white scar, running from her belly to her sternum. "Something like this?"

Ruth couldn't help gasping. "That would have killed you!"

"It would have if I wasn't already dead. This is the key." She showed the back of her right hand where she sported the mark of Cernunnos, the circle of interlocking leaves. "You know how screwed up I got about all the changes taking place in my body . . . the green blood that had a life of its own? It was such a shock at the time." She traced her finger around the mark. "I had no idea what he'd done to me . . . could never have guessed." She looked around them. "I died that day up at Loch Maree when he marked me with this."

Church shook his head in disbelief, but she silenced him with a wave of her hand.

"I died, and then he remade me in his own image. For the rest of you time was frozen. But for me . . . well, I don't know how he did it." She shook her head, barely able to summon up the words. "I'm not human, I'm a plant."

There was a hanging moment when they all tried to work out if she was joking. She laughed to herself, silently, at their expressions. "Okay, maybe that's not the right word. Physically, he turned me into something that has the characteristics of flora rather than fauna. I don't need to eat or drink or breathe, not in the same way you do. I can survive under water. I can survive where there's no air at all. And when I get hurt, I repair myself like a plant. That's what happened with Balor. I'll tell you now, I don't remember much about it, apart from the fact that it was agony. That's one thing he didn't sort out. It tore me apart. It wasn't pretty. But I put myself back together. And—" she held her arms wide "—I did it better than before." She pointed to her face. "No scars. Not on my back, either. So I've got a slight skin problem, but that's a small price to pay. At least I don't pollinate or any of that shit."

Her flippant manner made it difficult for them to assimilate what she was saying. Church's brow furrowed. "So all the time we were together—"

"That's right, Church-dude—you were having sex with a plant."

"A nature spirit." Shavi leaned forward excitedly. "He distilled the essence of what you already were, and made you an avatar."

"Well, he might have asked." Her smile was relaxed.

"Are you okay with it?" Ruth asked, concerned.

"It's better than being a nobody. And it's better than being really, truly dead. I think the same, I feel the same. I'm still the same gorgeous, wonderful, witty and charming Laura DuSantiago. Apart from the fact you have to water me twice a day."

Church leaned forward and touched her forearm. The skin felt exactly the same as it always had done. She took his hand with honest affection. "I'm okay. Really."

"You seem different," Ruth said. "I mean, as well as all that—"

"I have my flaws, but stupidity isn't one of them. When somebody shoves a big, fat, old lesson in my face, I make sure I learn from it." She looked down at her fingers as she knotted and unknotted them. "I've found peace, I guess, if that doesn't sound like some stupid, navel-gazing New Ager. It was always there, I just couldn't see it. I don't hate myself any more."

Her words were simple, but Church felt a swell of affection; he knew how deep her pain really went. If Laura had found some kind of redemption, there was hope for all of them; for everyone. The others recognised this too. As she looked round, for the first time she felt accepted.

"Then we really are all back together," Shavi said. "As it was intended."

"Yes, yes, yes, the stars are aligned, and God is looking down on you from his heaven." Tom was standing in the entrance with the Bone Inspector. "Now I suggest you get some rest. For tomorrow, as the saying goes, you may die."

Veitch slipped into a drunken sleep quickly; Shavi had a remarkable ability to nap instantly, wherever he was. Tom and the Bone Inspector sat at the table, talking quietly, their faces stern. Ruth tried to stay awake as Laura and Church chatted, but even her faint jealousy couldn't stop her eyelids from drooping.

Laura watched the regular movement of Ruth's chest for a moment or two before turning back to Church. "So I'll ask you again: have you and little Miss Frosty done the monkey dance yet?"

"Laura—"

"You still don't know me, do you?" There was a trace of sadness in her smile. "In most cultures that's known as humour."

"Are you really okay?"

"Yes, I am. For the first time in my life. So don't go giving me any pity or I might be stirred to be my old catty self." She put her fingertips on his sternum and pushed him down.

"I'm sorry I wasn't better to you. And that's not pity. What you did to save Ruth . . . that showed a side of you I never knew, and I feel bad for that. I jumped to conclusions, just like everybody else."

She rolled on to her back, her hands behind her head. "It's all in the past now. We learn, we move on, and all that shit." She looked at him from the corners of her eyes. "I'm still sorry it didn't work out between you and me, but I've finally got a good injection of reality. It wasn't the right time, maybe we weren't the right people, but I was so desperate I was trying to force it." She nodded to Ruth. "You and her, you're the real deal. She's a good person, for all her many, many problems. And you, well, you're Saint Church, aren't you? Mr. Walks On Water."

He watched Ruth's chest rising and falling and wished he was lying next to her. "Is it that obvious?"

"It was obvious to everybody right from the start. You were the only one who couldn't see it. Because, let's face it, when it comes to emotion, you're damaged goods."

"And you're okay about it? It's important to me. Really."

There was a brief pause in which he dreaded her answer, but then she said, "I'm okay with it. All I really wanted was somebody to stand by me shoulder-to-shoulder. I've never had that. But I was, like, where's the dog and the white stick? It was all around me. It's stupid. The world's falling apart and right here I've got the best friends I could ever wish for. You, the Shav-ster, even Miss Icy Knickers. We'd have got on okay if I hadn't been the Bitch From Hell from the get-go. Veitch, well, he's about as fucked-up as it gets, but if it came to the crunch I know he'd come through. I just hope I haven't learnt my big old life lesson too late."

He fumbled for her hand and gave it a squeeze. "It's a lesson we've all had to learn. When you're looking for meaning in life, don't look at the big picture, look at this. Look at your friends and your life and your loves—you need no meaning other than people."

She yawned theatrically. "You're getting up your arse again, aren't you? Just enjoy it, for Christ's sake. And don't screw up your love life this time. If she doesn't kill you, I will." She watched him for a minute, her eyes shining, and then she smiled, still a little sadly, and rolled over to sleep.

As Church shuffled down to rest his head on the cushion, his gaze fell on Veitch's still form and for a fleeting moment he thought the Londoner was still awake. The notion disturbed him, but as he slipped into sleep he couldn't quite work out why.

The cry ripped through the camp, snapping them all awake in an instant. It was the sound of a woman shrieking, filled with such desolation and horror it left them frozen in shock. The cry rose, becoming more hysterical, louder, until they thought their ears would burst, and then, just as suddenly, it snapped off. The ringing echoes of it persisted for several more seconds.

"What the bleedin' hell was that?" Veitch's face was drained of blood.

Tom pushed himself back from the table where he had been resting his head. "La Belle Dame Sans Merci."

"The Banshee, to you and me," the Bone Inspector said, bleary eyed.

"Bummer." Laura crashed back on to her cushions. "Bad omen-a-go-go."

Church looked to Tom. "Is it as bad as the legends say?"

"You don't need the Banshee to tell you it's not going to be a walk in the park tomorrow." The Bone Inspector slumped back on to the table.

"Some stories say anyone who hears it will die," Ruth said. Church wished he could comfort her, but Veitch appeared to be watching them both closely.

"You're all going to die," Tom said. "Sooner or later." He lay back down on the table.

"Thanks for the morale boost, old git," Laura said sleepily.

"It doesn't mean death for anyone who hears it," Tom said wearily. "But it does mean death. And destruction and suffering and devastation on an epic scale."

"Situation normal, then." As Veitch lay down, Church steeled himself and surreptitiously moved next to Ruth.

The others assimilated the information and after a few minutes somehow managed to go back to sleep, but Ruth was aware Church was still lying awake.

"What are you thinking?" she whispered.

His words were given greater weight by the long pause before he replied. "I'm thinking, where are they keeping the Wish-Hex? And when are they planning on using it?"

They were woken at first light by the sound of stirring across the camp. The smell of cooking drifted into the tent, teasing pangs of hunger from their sluggish forms. With an effort, they dragged themselves out into a cold, clear morning, their breath pluming; they were forced to bang their arms against their sides in a futile bid to keep warm. It was a beautiful dawn: a full-hearted swell of gold and purple before the sky slowly turned a pale blue; a day for hope and love and great things, not a day for war.

The lesser gods had gathered in the various large clearings amongst the tents, eating at long wooden tables. Church still wasn't sure that they really *needed* to eat, but they relished experience with a hunger that belied their status, as if searching for something valuable they had long since left behind. They certainly ate with gusto, shovelling down platefuls of food, swilling it down with flagonfuls of a hot, fragrant liquid.

All of the gods appeared to be in high spirits. They called Church and the others over with hearty shouts and made a space for them at the end of one table with much backslapping and camaraderie. It was so out of place that all of them felt uncomfortable. Platefuls of dried fruit and spiced meat and several loaves of bread were brought to all but Laura and Shavi, who were given an odd but tasty bouillabaise of tomatoes, mushrooms and peppers without having to ask. Laura admitted that although she didn't *have* to eat, she too, like the gods, still enjoyed the sensation.

As they ate, their spirits rose, all except Veitch who remained sullen and uncommunicative. "They look like they're eager to get off to war," Ruth noted.

"For all their many claims to a wonderful life, they lack much colour in their existence," Tom said, dipping a sausage into an egg. "Quite simply, they are bored."

"Despicable bastards, the lot of 'em," the Bone Inspector muttered as he gnawed on a chunk of bread. "Like a bunch of upper class idiots whipping themselves up before a rugby game, without a single thought for all the suffering that's going to happen. With any luck a few of 'em will meet their maker."

"That is a little harsh," Shavi said.

"Might teach 'em to appreciate life a bit more."

"I still don't get why you're helping us." Church sipped on the hot, invigorating liquid.

"That's because you're a moron." The Bone Inspector threw the remainder of his bread to a group of ravens that had ventured fearlessly into the camp.

"I can see why you and the old git get on so well," Laura said under her breath. "Both graduates of the Finishing School for Irritating, Miserable Bastards."

Shavi pushed out his chair and stretched his legs. "I would guess the Bone Inspector is simply following his office as a guardian of the land's old places. If the End of Everything happens on the morning after Samhain, there will not be many old places to guard."

"Well, aren't you the smarty-pants." The Bone Inspector was watching the ravens intently. "Ready for carrion," he mused.

"*Carry On to the End of the World*, maybe," Laura said. "With Kenneth Williams as the dark god Balor and Charles Hawtrey as the Guardian of the Old Places."

The Bone Inspector eyed her so darkly Laura realised she couldn't chide him in the same way that she toyed with Tom.

Shavi was laughing. "Oh, yes. And you would be Barbara Windsor," he said to Laura. "And Church would be Sid James—"

"Bwah hah hah," Church said flatly. "So what's going to happen after we've stuffed our faces?"

"In half an hour there will be a meeting to outline the strategy," Tom said. "As the spearhead of the attack, we must be there."

"The generals sending the disposables in first?" Veitch said sourly.

"Something like that," Tom replied. "They have their agenda and we have ours. As long as we are not swayed, who cares what their motivations are?"

"But they have the Wish-Hex." Church made the comment quietly so none of the gods could hear.

"Yes," Tom said, "which is why we shall have our own meeting first."

After the meal they wandered off separately, agreeing to meet fifteen minutes later. Ruth had not gone far when her arm was grabbed sharply enough to cause her pain. She whirled angrily. It was Veitch. She could tell instantly from his threatening expression what was on his mind.

"You couldn't wait to get off with him, could you?" There was pain in his voice beneath the anger.

"I'm sorry you're upset, Ryan, but—"

"Upset? I'm upset when my team loses on a Saturday. This is like a kick in the bollocks, and another one in the face for good luck."

She bowed her head, sorry to see him so hurt. "I didn't want you—"

"No, you didn't want me. I put my life on the line in Scotland—for you. Not for all this end of the world bollocks. I couldn't care less if the whole miserable place went belly-up tomorrow. But, you . . ." He shook his head, his long hair falling across his face. "I nearly died for you. I took risks to get down here—for you."

She was shocked to see the rage lighting in his face; there was a seething glow in his hooded eyes. "You've got so much anger in you! Were you always like this?"

Her words appeared to strike him hard. He rubbed at his temples furiously. "Stop talking about that!"

"I tried to be honest to you about how I felt, Ryan. I think you're a good man. I admire you. But there was never going to be anything between us."

"Never?" She flinched as he bunched his fist but instead he smashed it into his side. There were tears of hurt in his eyes.

She went to comfort him, but he backed away. "Ryan, don't hate Church and don't hate me. We love each other. And we both care about you, really."

"You're only saying that to keep me on the team. Afraid I'll go running off to join the other side?"

"Don't be stupid! None of us would ever think that. You said you always wanted to be a hero. Well, you are, Ryan. You are. And everyone here respects you."

He looked away towards the horizon, blinking off the tears. "Yeah . . ."

"That must mean something?"

He nodded. "But not enough. I always thought it was the most important thing. I've never had that . . . never had any respect." He jerked a thumb over his shoulder. "One of them was talking about how they'd all learned something important from all this shit. Well, I have too. I've learnt you're the most important thing to me, and if I can't have you I might as well be dead. So I can go into this with no fear 'cause I've got nothing to lose. They'll remember me as the biggest bleedin' hero of all by the end of it." The anger disappeared briefly and all she could see was the face of a hurt child, but then he turned sharply on his heel and marched away.

She called after him, but he didn't look back.

They met in their tent while the Tuatha Dé Danann were away making their preparations for battle, although Baccharus and Niamh were there, much to Veitch's suspicion. The first thing they did was distribute the Quadrillax. Church kept the Sword and took the Wayfinder lantern, while Ruth reaffirmed her hold on the Spear. Veitch agreed to carry the Stone of Fal and Shavi took the Cauldron in a pack on his back. Laura was happy to have nothing to do with any of them.

"If the Wish-Hex is here, its location has been kept from us," Niamh said when they had gathered around the table. "Those of us who believe in the destiny of mankind would never allow such a thing to be used, and certainly never in this form, adulterated by the Night Walkers."

"It would be good," Tom said, "if all your brethren felt the same way. But many believe this is too good an opportunity to pass by: two irritants wiped out in one fell swoop."

"And the prime position in the evolutionary pile secured for the Tuatha Dé Danann," Church noted. "We need you to find out where the Wish-Hex is being kept, and when it will be used," he said to Baccharus and Niamh. "We'll have to find some way to neutralise it."

"The aim would be to unleash the Wish-Hex in the core of the Night Walkers' lair, close to the Heart of Shadows," Niamh said. "The Night Walkers are more resilient than Fragile Creatures. They need to be closer to the release."

"We just get wiped out in the plague fallout," Church said bitterly.

"We will uncover the intention and pass it on to you as soon as we can," Niamh said. "We understand what is at stake."

Veitch appeared not to have been listening, and had spent the meeting carving his name into the wooden table with his knife. Then he said, "I'm worried we're spreading ourselves too thin," and Church realised the Londoner had instead been carefully weighing all the strategies. "We'll be driving forward on more than one front, and this thing will be coming up behind. We're not going to be in a position to split our attention."

"What are you saying?" Church asked.

"Sounds like a recipe for disaster to me."

Church thought for a moment. "It might help if one of us found a back way in."

"What do you mean?" Veitch said.

"I've been thinking about this . . . about a lot of things. There's been important stuff that's been there right in our face before and we missed it." He turned to Ruth. "Like Maurice Gibbons."

"The civil servant who was murdered under Albert Bridge the night we met. So?"

"We got so wrapped up in *what* he discovered, we never thought about *how*—"

"He saw one of the Fomorii changing—"

"But why was he under Albert Bridge on that particular night?"

She opened her mouth to answer him, but no words came. "Okay, smarty-pants."

"Why was that Night Walker there too?"

Her eyes narrowed. "You've already worn out your dramatic buildup, Church."

"The Fomorii were already building their base under London. And Gibbons had somehow found one of the entrances to it. He was investigating when that thing came out and killed him."

Veitch was already ahead of them. "So if we could get to it, we might be able to get straight into their base before they know it!"

"But the danger of us all going together is that it is easier to stop us with one well-timed strike," Shavi noted. "They would be able to target all their resources at us."

"Good point," Veitch mused. "All right, we split up. But we do our damnedest to get to where we're going, even if it means leaving all those golden-skinned twats behind." He nodded to Niamh and Baccharus curtly. "No offence."

"And we all know where we're going," Laura said. "That big tower they're throwing up near the City. I saw it up close. That has to be the place."

"At the ritual in Scotland, when we summoned the dead for guidance, they told us we needed to find the Luck of the Land before we could beat Balor," Shavi noted. "Do we have any more of an idea what that means?"

Tom shifted uncomfortably. "That is not a matter to concern us now."

"Why not?" Veitch asked suspiciously.

"Heed me." Tom's voice was unduly stern. "When we are closer to the confrontation."

Church noticed Ruth was deep in thought. "What's on your mind?" he asked.

She looked at him with a curious expression. "What you said about Maurice Gibbons. It made me think how much else we missed that was right in front of our eyes."

The war council took place in a heavily guarded marquee of purple silk, deep in the heart of the camp. It was at the centre of an area where all the higher-born gods had congregated, and the sense of dislocation as Church and the others entered was palpable.

Many gods were already waiting in the tent, communicating quietly, and in some cases, silently. Church recognised Nuada Airgetlámh, his almond eyes like razor blades in his golden face, and Lugh, with his long mane of black hair and his torso bearing the scars of battle; both of them exuded power. But there were many Church didn't know. Their faces shimmered and changed as his gaze passed across them. He saw famous generals, renowned political leaders at times of crisis, a bully he recalled from school, the hardened casts of terrorists and revolutionaries, but eventually their images settled down into distinctive personalities, all of them grim. Church had the unshakeable feeling the important things had already been discussed and agreed.

"I offer the greetings of the Golden Ones to the Brothers and Sisters of Dragons, who have served us so well in the past," Nuada said, seemingly unconscious of his patronising attitude. "You know me as Fragile Creatures have known me in the past: Nuada Airgetlámh, wielder of Caledfwlch, which in my wisdom I have gifted to you, Dragon Brother. Your people have also known me as Nudd, of the Night, as Llud, and Lud, founder of this place on whose doorstep we stand—Londinium. This is my place where, in the Fixed Lands, I stand supreme. This is where Fragile Creatures bowed their heads to me, made offerings of the little things that had importance in their brief lives. Where blood ran, where my heart beats."

Lugh's eyes were fixed on his Spear, which Ruth held tightly to her side. She felt uncomfortable at the attention, as if he were desperate to wrest it from her.

"You Brothers and Sisters of Dragons have proved your worth," Nuada continued, "and it has been deemed that you should wield the Quadrillax on our behalf. Only with those objects of power will the Heart of Shadows finally be wiped from all existence. But the path to it will be hard. Too hard for Fragile Creatures. And so the Golden Ones have agreed to drive a route through the shadows, to protect you from the attacks of the Night Walkers, until you are in a position to carry out the act required of you. Does this meet with your agreement?"

All eyes turned to Church. "It does."

"Then this is what is suggested. There will be three lines of attack into the city, until the Heart of Shadows' location is established. I will lead the drive from the north. My brother, whom you know as Lugh, will bring our forces from the west. And the Master will take Wave Sweeper along the river into the centre of the city."

"And that will be the most important," Church said, "because it will take us directly to one of the entrances to the Fomorii lair."

Nuada's gaze was incisive. "You have access to secrets, Brother of Dragons."

Church gave nothing away.

Tom stepped forward. "May I speak?"

"Your exalted position is recognised, True Thomas."

"Then I would suggest the Brothers and Sisters of Dragons divide into teams to ensure the best chance of success. Ruth and Ryan will join you in the attack from the north."

Ruth went cold. Surreptitiously, she glanced over at Veitch, but his gaze was fixed firmly on Nuada.

"Shavi and Laura will come from the west with Lugh," Tom continued. "And I and the Bone Inspector will accompany Church through the secret tunnels. Though he is powerful, he is also young, and we have the experience to guide him through the darkest turns."

Nuada nodded. "Your views are acceptable, True Thomas."

Laura smirked and whispered to Church behind her hand, "Fun day out with the senior citizen club for you, boy. Hope you don't get in any fights or there'll be Zimmer frames all over the place."

"Use the Quadrillax wisely," Nuada said. "You have already drawn the Sword from the stone of disbelief. Now is the time to fire it with your heart. And the others—each must be used at the right time, in the correct manner, with the full weight of your essence behind you, and even then victory is not assured. Much death and suffering lies ahead. This is a period of pain that will be remembered when the stars go out. Go well, Brothers and Sisters of Dragons. Your world turns with you."

They left the tent to prepare themselves for what lay ahead. The joy of their initial reunion had dissipated, to be replaced by an oppressive sense of foreboding. There were no jokes or smiles; they were lost to their own thoughts as they wrestled with their secret fears or searched for the depths of strength that would get them through the coming hours.

Veitch was the last to leave. Before he had gone ten paces from the tent, Nuada called him back.

"We have seen your sacrifice," the god said, motioning to Veitch's bandaged wrist. "I know only too well the pain of such a wound." He removed a glove that covered an ornately crafted silver hand that looked like it had come from some futuristic robot. "The scars go much deeper than the skin."

Nuada's eyes felt like they were going right through him. "I had to do it to bring my mate back. I'm not bitter about it."

"Not bitter, no." Nuada smiled knowingly. "Still, I understand your heart, Brother of Dragons. Listen, then: if you are to be effective, you will need a new hand. Would you like that?"

"Can you do it?"

Nuada indicated the silver hand again. "We are gods. We can do anything."

The tent was the deepest red, so that within even the air had the hint of blood. It was enormous, bigger even than the marquee where the war council had met, with numerous annexes and branching passages so it was impossible to see all of it from one view. Nuada presented Veitch to Dian Cecht, who wore robes of scarlet. He carried himself with bearing, his features as aristocratic as his manner: a high forehead above a Roman nose, sharp, grey eyes and gunmetal hair tied in a ponytail.

"We have little time," Nuada said, as Dian Cecht gently unfastened the material on Veitch's wrist stump.

"It is a simple operation on a Fragile Creature." Dian Cecht examined the burnt flesh, then shrugged and turned away, motioning for Veitch to follow.

They came to a room set with several tables. Cruel-looking silver instruments were laid out on small trays next to each table. Dian Cecht nodded for Veitch to lie down, then busied himself at a large cabinet at one end. He returned with a wooden box inlaid with gold, which he placed on the tray next to Veitch. Inside, on a velvet inlay, was a silver hand the exact replica of the one Nuada wore. "A spare," Dian Cecht said with a smile.

Veitch felt a faint flutter of excitement; the thought of being whole once more was seductive. Dian Cecht gave him a foul-tasting potion to drink, which instantly made him sleepy. After a moment he was drifting in and out of hallucinatory waking dreams, filled with strange, disturbing images, including one of a black and a white spider fighting furiously over him. He was vaguely aware of Dian Cecht working on his wrist with a long knife with three rotating blades; the smell of blood filled his nostrils with surprising potency. A glimmer of silver in the corner of his eye told him the hand was about to be fitted. He watched with the curious detachment of a drug trip as Dian Cecht placed it against his stump, now soaked with blood.

At the instant the blood touched the pristine silver, three arms snapped out of the hand and poised erect; on each one was a row of sharp silver spikes. Veitch only had a second to consider what was going to happen next before the arms suddenly sprung down, driving the spikes deep into the bone and muscle of his wrist. Even through the sedation, he screamed in agony, but there was more pain to follow: something within the hand was burrowing into his arm, wrapping its way around ligaments and tissue, bonding with nerves and veins.

Veitch's throat grew raw from screaming and a moment later he blacked out.

Church and Ruth stood behind their tent, embracing each other silently. The weight of what they wanted to say was too great, crushing them silent. Ruth blinked off tears as she pulled away. She forced a smile.

"We'll be meeting again soon," Church said gently. "In the hideous lair of the one-eyed god of death. How about that for a one-off?"

"Oh, very romantic. Every girl's dream."

"At least you'll never forget it."

Neither could bring themselves to discuss the possibility that they might not see each other again; the occasion called for sweeping optimism and hope and faith.

They pulled away, ready to meet the others, but Ruth turned and caught Church's arm. "Be careful," she said with a quiet intensity that moved him.

Tom poked his head round the corner of the tent. "For God's sake, get a move on! They're not going to hold up the end of the world for you."

The others were waiting quietly. Veitch looked pale and drained, but his new hand was a source of wonder and he appeared proud of it. The others were not so sure. "What did they demand in return for that?" Tom asked harshly. When Veitch told him nothing, he said, "I'm very disappointed in you," before walking away.

"Just be careful, Ryan," Church said to him. "They can't be trusted. And they're not known for their charity."

"'Course I'll be careful." Veitch couldn't help examining the hand in the light. "I'm whole again. That's what matters." He was patently oblivious to the foreboding that filled the rest of them.

At that time, though, they couldn't hold it against him. They hugged in turn—even Veitch and Tom. They knew each other well enough not to need to say anything more.

Once they were all on their horses, Church couldn't part without adding something. "This is what it's all been leading to, all that pain and hardship and suffering. We've been to hell and back and we've come through it. Of all the people who could have been here at this point, I'm glad it's you, all of you. You're the best there is, and I'm proud to be one of you."

Veitch looked to the horizon, his cheeks flushed. "Yeah, well, we're not going to let you down, boss. Death or glory, and all that."

"Just glory," Laura corrected.

In the moments before they departed, Church found himself turning over the wild parade of events that had led them to that place. At the start it had seemed so simple: a straight fight between good and evil for the sake of humanity. Instead, they had found themselves probing the very mysteries of existence, travelling through worlds where reality and illusion intermingled until it was impossible to tell what was real and what was not. There had been so much hardship, pain and death on every side, yet, ironically, it had been the best time of his life. He had become a better person because of it, although he knew he still had a way to go.

Now it was back to being a simple fight once more: humanity against all the alien powers that were attempting to deny its destiny. And all to be decided in two short days. He hoped they were up to the obligation that had been placed on their shoulders.

They rode over a slight rise to see a massive army spread out across the countryside in the wan October sunlight. As the call went out somewhere at the head, a charge of excitement ran through all of them. A grin jumped like wildfire from one to the other. After the weariness of all the buildup, the culmination came like a jolt of energy. Veitch gave a triumphant yell and then they spurred their horses to join the others, lost to the pump of the blood in their heads.

When they were finally in motion, it looked like a sea of gold was sweeping across the countryside towards the capital. Within it, Church and the others felt enveloped in a dreamy, yellow haze, where figures and horses faded into the background, to be replaced by an amorphous feeling of wonder.

The journey passed in a blur, faster than they could ever have galloped on normal horses. They only slowed when London hove into view, and in that instant all brightness drained from them. In the centre of the city, the monstrous black tower rose up, its summit lost in the clouds that swirled continually overhead. Greasy black smoke lapped up towards them from the fires that burned all around. There were things flying, and things moving on the ground, but Church didn't focus on any of them.

All he could think of was the prophecy of him watching a burning city that had haunted his nights since his visit to the watchtower between the worlds. It had felt like the ultimate in desolation, and as he sat there, watching the scene for real for the first time, he understood how true that feeling had been.

chapter seventeen
(don't worry) if there's a hell below

Despite all they had seen, Laura and Shavi were still overwhelmed by the incongruous sight of an army of otherworldly beings trooping along the M4, where tourist buses and cars and articulated lorries had once trundled bumper to bumper. Occasionally they passed an abandoned vehicle, windows smeared in thick dust, that only added to the sense of dislocation.

There had been a brief flurry of activity as they came into London past the now-silent Heathrow Airport. A group of Fomorii had attacked, shrieking and howling, but it had been half-hearted and directionless, and the attackers had drifted off once their casualties had started to mount. The Tuatha Dé Danann were armed with a terrifying array of weapons constructed by Goibhniu and his brothers in their secret smithies, some of which could deal death at a great distance, but it did not appear that this show of strength was the cause of the retreat. Many of the Fomorii had disappeared into the houses that lined the motorway, while the flying Night Walkers had retreated into the bank of thick clouds.

"I expected greater defiance," Baccharus said as the road wound past Osterley towards Brentford. "They will not allow us to drive directly into the heart of their nest, where their most sacred thing resides."

The atmosphere didn't help the growing apprehension. When the wind blew in the wrong direction, Shavi and Laura had to cover their mouths and noses with scarves to keep out the choking smoke filled with sickening chemical undertones. It was cold, too, the sun mostly obscured by the clouds; they were wearing several layers of borrowed clothes beneath their old jackets.

The fires blazing near to the motorway brought little warmth, but cast a hellish red glow across the empty houses, shops and business premises. Homes stood with doors torn off and windows smashed. In some the roof had caved in, while in the worst places entire streets had been demolished. Although many areas appeared relatively untouched, it was almost impossible to imagine the Fomorii occupation, and how terribly the residents must have suffered.

Shavi continually scanned the buildings on either side, until Laura said, "Can't you do something? You're supposed to be the big magician."

"Any abilities I might have are shamanic. I prefer a quiet space to meditate, something to put me into the right frame of mind."

"You set all those animals on the Bone Inspector at Rosslyn Chapel. Can't you send an army of . . . I don't know, badgers, on ahead?"

"Badgers?"

"You know what I mean. Anything."

He coughed into his scarf as a swirl of smoke engulfed them. "We would need a Ryan or a Church to offer any true resistance to a direct assault by the Fomorii. Or even a Ruth, if what I hear of her advancing abilities is true. This is not the best situation for us."

"Speak for yourself. I've learnt a few new tricks myself since I became the Chlorophyll Kid."

"Oh?" He eyed her curiously. "What can you do?"

"Mind your biz. And hope I don't have to show you." She tied her scarf tighter so she resembled a Bedouin riding into a sandstorm.

The lack of resistance was unnerving even the Tuatha Dé Dannan now. They were moving more cautiously, watching the surrounding cityscape for any sign of movement, Goibhniu's bizarre weapons levelled for a quick strike.

Baccharus rode up next to them once more. "The Night Walkers are an underhand race. We fear an attack from the side or rear, rather than an honourable face-to-face confrontation."

"An ambush makes sense," Laura mused. "Veitch made a smart suggestion for the two land teams to use the motorways to get right into the city quickly, but it does make us sitting targets."

"The Golden Ones," Baccharus said self-deprecatingly, "are too proud to hide."

Ahead of them the Hammersmith Flyover rose up as the houses and shops fell away on either side. As they passed over it, Laura could see the edges of the roundabout under the bridge way below, and the rooftop of the Hammersmith Odeon. "At least we're above the snipers now."

"Not for long," Shavi noted. "The road drops down quickly towards Earls Court."

"Thanks for wrecking my one tension-free moment of the day." Movement away to her right caught her eye. "Look at all those birds. What are they? You know, I haven't seen any pigeons yet. Do you think they've all moved out to the country?"

Shavi watched the flock swirling around one particular rooftop. "Crows," he said, and the moment the word had left his lips, he knew. Anxiously, he turned to the Tuatha Dé Danann. "Beware—!"

His warning was cut off by a deafening explosion. The ground beneath their feet rolled like water, then dropped suddenly. Shavi was still watching the birds fly into a tight formation that made the shape of a man when he realised he was falling.

Laura was yelling and fighting with her horse, which was frantically attempting to gain purchase on the crumbling road surface. They were all engulfed in noise: the panicked whinnying of the horses, the yells of the gods, the crack and rumble of the shattering flyover, the booming bursts of more supports getting blown out, a roaring cacophony that threatened to burst their eardrums.

They were lucky all the supports didn't go at once. Instead of dropping in one block, the bridge concertinaed, twisting one way, then the other, so those who were on that section slid back and forth as they moved towards the ground. Shavi and Laura were best placed. On the area where they had skidded it only fell sharply for the final ten feet, but that was enough to fling them both from their horses as they were showered in rubble.

Shavi blacked out briefly, and when he came to there was a large chunk of concrete crushing down on him. With an effort he managed to drag it off, but he could feel the blood soaking through his clothes; nothing appeared to be broken, though. He staggered to his feet, calling Laura's name. The air was so choked in dust and smoke, it was impossible to see more than a few feet, but what he could discern was bad enough. Many of the Tuatha Dé Danann had been torn apart or crushed by the falling sections of bridge. Horses lay dead or dying all around. A few of the gods staggered to their feet in one piece, and a similar number of the horses had survived.

The smoke and dust cleared enough to reveal the rest of the army in a chaotic mêlée on the remaining part of the flyover, desperately urging their mounts to move back along the motorway towards the slip road to ground level. It was exactly as Laura had foreseen: there were too many of them fighting for too little space. They were easy targets.

A sound like wind rushing through a derelict house filled the air. Mollecht was on the edge of the building, the crows that made up his body flying in ever-faster formation. The crows increased their speed until they were just a blur, and then a hole opened up in their centre. The sound of rushing wind became almost deafening. There was a flash as a fine, red spray erupted out of Mollecht's body, sweeping across the gulf to the Tuatha Dé Danann struggling to get off the bridge.

As it fell across them, the reaction was instantaneous. Black, mottling patches sprang up across any exposed skin. Foam burst from their mouths and their eyes rolled as they clawed at their throats. Those nearest to the shattered end of the bridge staggered backwards and plummeted to the ground, bursting open like sacks of jelly. Shavi had only an instant to reflect on what could have had such an effect on near-invulnerable gods before the thick smoke rolled in again to obscure the rising tide of panic on the flyover.

"Laura!" he yelled again, moving amongst the rubble.

"Here." Her voice was muffled. He found her struggling out from a thick shelter of vegetable manner that had kept the worst of the masonry from crushing her. "The wonders of green blood," she said by way of explanation.

He offered his hand to drag her out.

"Well, that didn't take long to go pear-shaped," she said bitterly.

"They were too arrogant. And we should have trusted our own judgment more."

Some of the gods staggered in a daze out of the swirling smoke. A few attempted to rein in the horses cantering around wildly. Laura watched Shavi's face grow serene; a moment later all the horses had calmed.

Baccharus came stumbling over the broken tarmac and twisted girders. "Move quickly," he yelled. He caught three horses and herded them towards Shavi and Laura. The other Tuatha Dé Danann were already mounting their own steeds.

Shavi and Laura had barely taken the reins when a gust of wind cleared the smoke and dust to reveal a sight that rooted them to the spot. All around, silent and unmoving, were the Fomorii, their monstrous faces turned towards Shavi and Laura. It was an eerie scene, as if they were robots waiting to come alive. The pile of broken masonry on which they and the Tuatha Dé Danann stood was a tiny island in a sea of black.

Shavi and Laura jumped on to their horses, casting around for a way out. A breeze rippled across the immobile sable statues. They began to move.

The shrieks and howls that rang out were deafening, the sight of the Fomorii sweeping forward in a tidal wave enough to drive all conscious thoughts from their minds.

Baccharus threw Shavi a strange sword with twin blades and a jewel embedded in the handle. "Press the jewel," the god yelled.

Shavi looked at the weapon in incomprehension.

"Press the jewel!"

The Fomorii were surging forward. One of the Tuatha Dé Danann tried to fend them off with a sword, but sheer force of numbers dragged him from his horse, and both he and the mount were swallowed up by the sickening tide.

Laura lashed out at Shavi's arm, shocking him alert. "Press the jewel, you moron!"

Shavi thumbed the gem. He felt a subtle sucking sensation deep in the heart of him as a blue spark began to crackle between the twin blades. The Fomorii appeared to recognise what was happening, and obviously feared it, for their forward motion halted and the shrieks died away with a ripple of apprehension. The Blue Fire burned a little higher up the blade.

Then, Shavi understood. He closed his eyes and focused his concentration on his heart, his spirit. The effect was remarkable. He jolted as an electric surge rushed through him, and when he opened his eyes, the Blue Fire was burning brighter than he had ever seen it. It tore up the remainder of the blades in an instant.

He thought he heard a whisper of terror rush through the Fomorii, and then the sapphire energy exploded from the sword like a summer lightning storm. The force almost knocked him from the horse; for a moment the whole world was blue. He heard Laura's exclamation of wonder, and when next he looked there was a massive blast zone around them where lay the charred remains of many Fomorii. Beyond it, the other Fomorii were backing away frantically.

Shavi felt so exhausted he could no longer sit upright. He slumped against the horse's neck as the sword slipped from his grasp. Laura caught it. "I think we'll save this for later, don't you?" She slipped it into an empty scabbard fixed on Shavi's saddle.

Baccharus was at their side, his skin so pale there was barely a hint of gold in it. "Come, we must not tarry here. The Night Walkers will not hold back for long. Although they fear like beasts of the field, their individual existence is meaningless. They will give themselves up happily for the will of the collective."

A pitched battle was raging along what remained of the flyover and the stretch of the M4 they could still see. The Fomorii were clambering over the edges of the motorway, getting torn apart by the array of Tuatha Dé Danann weapons, then coming back for more. And on the rooftops Mollecht was unleashing more of his plague-blasts.

"We won't be getting any help from them," Laura said. She looked round and pointed to a path that had been cut through the Fomorii.

They had no idea where they were going, knew there was little hope for such a small band riding ever deeper into enemy territory, but there was no chance of them going back. Even so, they refused to countenance failure, and thoughts of their deaths never entered their minds.

The only route open to them was along Hammersmith Road. They soon left behind the main mass of Fomorii, more concerned with defeating the Tuatha Dé Danann army than with hunting a few stragglers. Yet there were still random bursts of movement in the buildings on either side.

Baccharus was accompanied by nine other gods. They all looked stunned, as if they'd taken a detour into a world they never dreamed existed. Baccharus, however, had best overcome the blow and was now leading the group; they obeyed him blindly, glad that someone else was taking the responsibility.

The road led on to Kensington High Street. It was snarled with discarded cars, trucks and a burnt-out bus, forcing them to ride on the pavement. Names from another age reached out to them: Smith's, Boots, Barker's department store.

The smoke was thicker towards the eastern end of the high street. Kensington Palace was still burning, its roof collapsed, the walls blackened and broken. The huge security gates that had closed off the road leading to the palace had been torn down and lay mangled and barely recognisable in the street.

"I wonder what happened to the Royal Family," Shavi mused as they passed.

"Those sort of people always have a bolt-hole. *The Great and the Good.*" The contempt in Laura's voice was heavy. "The secret service probably spirited them off to a cushy estate in Scotland long before all this came to a head. And I bet they never told any of the *little people* that Armageddon was coming to their doorsteps."

Ahead of them the green expanse of Kensington Gardens stretched out towards Hyde Park, silent and eerie in the drifting smoke. Baccharus reined in his horse uneasily and scanned the stark trees towards the Serpentine. "Some of my people used to come here on summer evenings," he said. "They would steal children and take them back to the Far Lands. Some would stay, some would be returned."

Shavi closed his eyes, letting himself read the atmosphere. "It is a liminal zone," he said. "Green space in an open city. The boundary between here and T'ir n'a n'Og is fluid."

"I tripped here once," Laura said. "It was summer. Everything was yellow and green. Me and a friend dropped a tab up near Temple Lodge, then went out on a boat on the lake. Just drifting along. It was . . . peaceful." The memory jarred with the landscape that now lay before her. She shivered. "I don't think we should go in there."

Behind them the sound of pitched battle grew more intense. Someone was screaming, high-pitched and reedy, so despairing they all wanted to cover their ears. Another explosion sent a booming blast of pressure over them.

Shavi noticed shapes moving in the doorways across the street. Fomorii were emerging slowly. They looked wary, as if they knew of the sword even though they had had no contact with the other group.

Laura fought back another wave of nausea when she looked at them. "God, this place is disgusting! It's *infested.*" She turned to Shavi. "Are you up to using that super-cool sword again?"

He shook his head. "It is powered by the spirit. It will take a while to bring my energy levels back up."

Baccharus pointed along Kensington Road towards Knightsbridge. "The Night Walkers are attempting to cut us off. Moving across the road ahead, coming up behind us."

"Then we go across the park," Shavi said. "Perhaps lose them in the smoke. We cannot afford to move so slowly."

They spurred their horses and headed into the disquieting open space of Kensington Gardens.

The smoke was even thicker there, blowing in from the palace, and from another large fire burning somewhere nearby. They kept their scarves tied tightly across their mouths, but it was still choking them; their eyes teared so much it was often hard to see the way ahead.

It was Shavi who first recognised they were no longer alone. His ears were attuned to the shifting moods of nature and he felt the pressure drop rapidly. It was followed by rapid footsteps padding in the grass all around, moving back and forth. Although the smoke was too dense to see what was there, he had the unmistakable feeling that it was hunting.

"Be on your guard," he said quietly.

And then they all could hear the running feet, sometimes ahead, sometimes behind. They reminded Laura of a group of preschool children at play. There was no other sound; not the shrieks of Fomorii, no voices at all.

Baccharus motioned for the other Tuatha Dé Danann to bring their horses close together. They urged their steeds to step lightly, but every now and then the hooves would hit a stone with a clatter.

"What are they?" Laura whispered.

Shavi shook his head. The footsteps moved closer, as if their owners had begun to get their bearings. The Tuatha Dé Danann reined their horses to a stop and drew their swords.

The throat-rending, bloodthirsty cry behind them made Laura almost leap from her saddle. The Tuatha Dé Danann whirled ready to lash out, but it was too late. One of them was torn from his horse and thrown to the ground, where a squat figure about five feet tall stooped over it, its muscular arms rending and tearing with a frantic clawing motion. The agonised screams of the god were sickening, but the sheer brutality of the attack froze them in place.

Laura was nauseated to see the figure was wearing a hat made out of human body parts—she thought she saw half a face there—and its tangled, black hair was matted with dried blood. It turned and bellowed triumphantly. Its blood-stained teeth were large and broken, its features monstrous, but its skin was green and scaled in part. Laura felt a wash of cold.

Another launched itself from the smoke towards one of the Tuatha Dé Danann. Its huge hands were grasping with long, jagged nails as it roared ferociously. The god reacted quickly, swinging his sword down to split the beast's head open. It fell to the ground, twitching and vomiting.

"What are they?" she gasped.

"You were ill in the van when they attacked before," Shavi said. "In the Lake District. They are called Redcaps. Tom said their natural enemy is man."

"Mollecht's favourite brood," Baccharus said, with something approaching contempt.

Others emerged from the smoke—Laura counted eight of them—and these were carrying short swords that were chipped and soiled. For the first time they saw Shavi and Laura, and the transformation that came over them was terrifying to see: savage before, they were now Berserker, ignoring the Tuatha Dé Danann to drive towards the two humans.

Baccharus barked an order in his natural alien language and the Tuatha Dé Danann formed a barrier between Shavi and Laura and the attacking Redcaps. Although the gods hacked and slashed in a constant blur of weaponry it did little to repel the ferocity of their attack. While they came at the gods, they were also continually circling to find a route through the defences to the two humans. Laura's heart beat even faster when she realised the Redcaps never took their eyes off her or Shavi for an instant; the look in those eyes was ravenous hunger.

The assaults continued relentlessly for fifteen minutes until it became obvious even the Tuatha Dé Danann would soon be worn down. One of the gods eventually made a slight error in his parrying that was punished instantly. A Redcap dragged the sword from his hand, oblivious to the deep gashes it was cutting in the creature's fingers, while the one closest to it dived in and ripped out the god's neck with its talons. He had been torn savagely limb from limb before he hit the ground.

An instant later the air was filled with the fluttering of golden moths. The rest of the Tuatha Dé Danann saw them and froze, their faces registering unspeakable dread. The Redcaps sensed their moment and prepared to move.

"This is insanity," Shavi hissed, his guilt over the dead god almost painful. He turned to Laura. "Follow me." He dug his spurs sharply into his horse's flank and it shot off in the direction of the Serpentine. Laura was behind him in an instant.

Their escape stirred the Tuatha Dé Danann, who were soon following in their tracks. Shavi glanced over his shoulder and was shocked to see how fast the Redcaps were moving in pursuit. Although they were only on foot, their leg muscles were unbelievably powerful. They weaved around trees and rubbish bins without slowing their speed at all, and were soon passing the Tuatha Dé Danann, who were urging on their terrified horses even more.

Laura noticed the Redcaps approach too. "Jesus, what powers those things?"

"Hunger. And hatred."

"Any idea where we're going now?"

"We could attempt to outrun them. Or we could find a place that will offer us sanctuary, somewhere to rest and lick our wounds."

"In this place?" She laughed mockingly. "Maybe we can take in some sights while we're at it."

The smoke rolled across the surface of the Serpentine where the abandoned boats bobbed and drifted. Shavi pressed on along Rotten Row until Hyde Park Corner came into view. The roundabout was choked with dead traffic, much of it blackened and twisted in the aftermath of a flash fire that had raged through the area. It still smelled of charred oil and singed plastic.

"They're closing," Laura gasped as she sent her horse along the pavement until they found a space to get through the traffic to Constitution Hill. The high brick wall of Buckingham Palace lay to their right.

Their manoeuvres had slowed them considerably, while the Redcaps merely powered over the heaps of blackened metal.

"Shavi," Laura said, "this is the time for your big idea. You have got one, haven't you?" The jungle cat-snarling of the Redcaps was now close behind.

Shavi guided his horse in close to Laura until there were barely two inches between them as they pounded down the centre of the street. With his left hand gripping the reins, he fumbled with his right for the twin-bladed sword, then held it out for Laura.

"What am I supposed to do with that?"

"It is easy to operate."

"Get lost. You're the one with the big soul-charge. The only spirit I've got is vodka and Red Bull."

"Take it."

Uncomfortably she accepted the sword and immediately thumbed the jewel in the hilt. The Blue Fire began to build. "Now tell me how I ride while facing backwards."

"Have you never seen Hopalong Cassidy?"

"Uh, no."

"The Lone Ranger?"

"Get real."

"I am sure you will pick it up."

Laura swore at him violently, then half-spun round in her saddle. The yell erupted from her lips unbidden. Three Redcaps were so close behind they could almost touch the horse's tail. She could smell the rotting-meat reek of their breath. When they saw her face, their eyes flared hungrily with a red light.

One of them threw itself forward. The charge leapt from the sword like a missile, tearing through the Redcap's face in a blue blast. When her eyes cleared, all three creatures were headless, still twitching on the road as their bodies struggled to catch up with the news. The other Redcaps had stopped and were blinking stupidly at this strange development.

"That'll teach them to wear hats out of season," Laura said weakly. This time it was Shavi's turn to catch the sword and steady her with the other hand as she threatened to slip from the saddle. "Shit, I feel like I'm coming off a six-day bender. Is this how it was for you?"

"I feel a little better now, but it will take a while to recover completely."

Baccharus rode up and then past them, urging them on. "Come! They will be on you again in a moment!"

Laura somehow managed to get her horse moving again before resting against its neck, hoping it would find the right direction by itself. Shavi once again took the lead. But they had barely got out into the wide open space surrounding the Queen Victoria Memorial in front of Buckingham Palace when a harpoon trailing fire tore through the air to impale one of the Tuatha Dé Danann, who fell from his horse.

Fomorii were swarming over the roof of Buckingham Palace, where they had sited an odd weapon that looked like a cross between a mediaeval siege machine and a piece of WWII artillery. Five Fomorii were loading it with another harpoon that mysteriously burst into flame the moment it was in place.

"They're changing the guard at Buckingham Palace," Laura said ironically.

The harpoon rocketed into the Queen Victoria Memorial, which exploded in chunks of stone.

"They are slowly picking us off." Shavi's face had grown dark with anger. "We must not allow this."

Laura felt a tingle run down her spine when she saw the Tuatha Dé Danann were waiting on the two of them for orders. "This is about as weird as it gets," she muttered.

When she looked back, Shavi had his head bowed and his hands over his face, one of the rituals he regularly used when he was meditating.

"Quickly," Baccharus insisted. "The Redcaps will be coming."

When Shavi looked up, Laura thought she saw blue sparks leap from his eyes. "Church did a good job," he said, moving his horse on.

"What do you mean?"

"The Blue Fire is all around now. So easy to see, I barely need any concentration."

Almost the instant he said the words, Laura realised she could see it too: in some areas just thin capillaries of sapphire, in others like a raging current beneath the ground, as if the road surface was made of glass.

"Trippy! So this is what it means . . ." Her words trailed off, unable to capture the depth of what she was feeling.

"Then this city is not dead to us," Shavi said. "Church suggested the force would be a weakening power for the Fomorii. They hate it, and what it represents. And here we can see the lines leading to the most potent sources."

"Come, then." Baccharus's voice was strained, his eyes darting all around.

"What is it?" Shavi followed his gaze, but could see nothing.

"Can you not feel it?"

The moment the words were uttered, he could. Against the background of rising anxiety like a deep bass rumble, something unpleasant was stirring. The roar of the Redcaps bouncing off the buildings disturbed Shavi before he had time to analyse the sensation, and then the feral creatures surged into view with renewed vigour.

Baccharus, Shavi and Laura spurred their horses, with the other Tuatha Dé Danann following a split second later. Shavi, who had his perception fixed on the flow of the Blue Fire, took the lead.

The unbearable speed of the Redcaps was the least of their worries. They had barely broken into the once-serene environment of St. James's Park when Shavi realised what it was he had sensed. When the smoke and icy mist cleared to present a view of the sprawling city, he had the unnerving impression that it was altering its shape like a Night Walker. The edges of the stately buildings along Whitehall, of the sedate and cultured pale stone blocks of The Mall, of those further away in the West End, were continually moving, like some bad, speeded-up animation. When he realised what it was, his blood, already chilled by where he was and what he had seen, became even colder.

Thousand upon thousand of Fomorii were emerging from their hiding places, moving out into the city, across rooftops, down walls; all the sickening, alien activity of a disturbed anthill. The speed of their waking suggested some call must have gone out on a level only those hideous creatures could understand.

"They're coming for us." Laura's voice was drained of all life.

Behind them, the ferocious roaring of the Redcaps drew nearer. "No way back." Shavi spurred the horse on faster. "Only forward."

"This is what they wanted," Laura said dismally, her words almost drowned out by the thunder of the hooves. "To separate us. To get us into a place where there wasn't the slightest chance we could fight back." She gulped in a mouthful of air to stifle the rising emotion. Then: "Do you think they've got the others?"

Shavi wasn't listening. The sea of black, roiling bodies moved in rapidly on either side; soon they would be submerged in the deluge. Dread formed a lump in his throat. *Always hope*, he told himself, a calming mantra repeated over and over. *Focus on the source of the hope, not the source of the fear*. Gradually the black, oppressive world faded away into the background until all he could see were the streams of brilliant blue. And the deepest, fastest and most brilliant of them blazed a channel between the enclosing darkness. Shavi guided his horse on to it and prayed.

The scorched grass, blackened trees and thick layer of grey ash that blanketed St. James's Park passed in a blur. The jolt of hooves on hard road. Great George Street. Then the wide open space of Parliament Square, the statue of the great war leader Churchill reduced to a broken stump. Westminster Bridge shattered, ending after only a few yards in broken concrete and twisted iron girders. The Houses of Parliament seething, across the roof, through the smashed windows, bubbling out towards them. The Fomorii that had the ability to fly on leathery bat wings swarmed across the Thames like angry wasps.

"All around!" Laura yelled. "This is it!"

The Fomorii surged down Whitehall and Millbank into Parliament Square, black, gleaming bodies as far as the eye could see. Shavi guided his horse round until the dark, majestic bulk of Westminster Abbey rose up in front of them.

"There," he said.

They raced their horses to the western entrance, where Shavi saw the Blue Fire swirling into a coruscating pillar of energy, lighting up the ornate columned front with its imposing twin towers. Three of the Tuatha Dé Danann jumped down to try the handles before putting their shoulders to the heavy oaken doors without budging them in the slightest.

"Locked," one of the guards said. Panic bloomed in his face. The Square was completely obscured now; the relentless torrent was almost upon them.

"Who's there?" The voice was timorous, broken.

Shavi leapt from his horse and threw himself at the door. "Let us in! We need sanctuary!"

There was one hanging moment when they feared whoever was within had left them to die, but then came the sound of heavy bolts being drawn.

The Redcaps were ahead of the driving wall of Fomorii, jumping and leaping like crazed tigers. One of the Tuatha Dé Danann guards attempted to fend them off to give the others more time. They fell on him in a frenzy.

The door swung open and a voice shouted, "Quick!"

Shavi led them in, horses and all, and then the doors slammed shut with a sound like the tolling of a bell.

Within the Abbey there was an abiding stillness. The thick stone walls muffled the noise of the terrible force without, but all Shavi was aware of was the thunder of the blood in his brain. The entire building was filled with the iron tang of the Blue Fire, too potent, he was sure, for the Fomorii to attempt to enter. Yet as he came to terms with the amazing fact that they were safe, he gradually took in his surroundings and was overcome with surprise.

The vast body of the Abbey was filled as far as he could see with pale, silent faces. Men and women, old, middle-aged and young, babies and children, all looking up with expressions riven by fear. They stood shoulder-to-shoulder, turned towards the new arrivals, or slumped on pews or on the stone floor, at first glance barely human; sheep, he thought, even less than that.

But there was humanity behind the fear, although it was of a pathetic kind, of people desperately trying to cope with a paralysing disbelief that everything they understood had crumbled in an instant.

"Who are you?" It was the voice of the man who had spoken to them through the door. He was in his early fifties, stylishly dressed, with a sallow face, cropped grey hair and designer glasses. He appeared to notice the Tuatha Dé Danann for the first time. "Who are they? Are they—?"

"Friends." Shavi rested a calming hand on the man's shoulder. He glanced once more at the expectant mass. Around the edges of the nave were empty cans and boxes, the remains of whatever food supplies they had brought with them, but many of the faces looked hungry. "How long have you been in here?"

"From the moment it all blew up. It took everyone by surprise. We scrambled in here with what we could grab, a few provisions, not enough . . . How in heaven's name did you manage to get here? We thought everyone else must be dead by now." His voice died; there were tears in his eyes. "We can't go outside. A few tried it, to get more food." He shook his head, looked at his shoes.

Laura pulled Shavi over to one side. "This is a nightmare. They're either going to starve or go outside and get slaughtered."

"We are in the same predicament."

"Yes, but they're not like us. They're normal people. That shit is part of our job description, not theirs."

Shavi still couldn't comprehend how much she had altered. Not so long ago she would have been advocating self-preservation at all costs, and now she was urging them to accept their responsibility. Could someone really change that much? "You are right," he said, smiling. "We owe them what little hope we have, at the very least." He turned to the sallow-faced man. "Are you in charge here?"

He shook his head. "You want Professor Michell, I suppose. He's not really in charge. But he makes decisions. Any decisions that need making."

"Then," Shavi prompted, "could you take us to him?"

The nave was beautiful and awe-inspiring, with fabulous monuments on either side. An air of solemnity hung over it. As they passed through, brief hope flared in the eyes of the refugees. Some held out their hands like the Victorian poor, silently begging for food. A Nigerian woman, overweight in a too-tight coat, offered a tentative smile, her eyes flooded with tears. Children stared blankly into the shadows. A girl in a blue dress, Sunday-best smart, as if she'd been on her way to a special function when her life had been arrested, said, "Have you seen my mummy? I'm waiting for her." Babies shuddered with sobs drained of tears. Shavi and Laura tried to offer reassuring smiles to the first few, but the emotional cost was too great and they averted their eyes for the remainder of the long walk.

To distract herself, Laura nodded to a monument in the centre of the nave. "What's that?"

"The tomb of the Unknown Soldier." Shavi had stood in front of it before, but this time it was laden with meaning. "An unidentified British soldier brought back from a French battlefield during the Great War. He represents all the victims of that great tragedy, indeed, all the lowly warriors who have since given their lives in conflict."

Beyond the nave were the aisles to the choir, which was also packed with refugees. Shavi paused to examine the monuments that lined the walls. Now everything he saw was filled with so much meaning, the emotion was welling up and threatening to overflow. "This is what we are losing," he said gravely. "Not fast cars and computers and mobile phones. *This* is what truly matters." He pointed to each monument in turn. "Elgar. Purcell. John Wesley. William Wilberforce. Charles Darwin." He pointed towards the south transept. "Down there, Poets' Corner: Chaucer, Auden, Shakespeare, Shelley, Blake, Keats, Dryden, Spenser, Jonson, Milton, the Brontës, Wordsworth, Tennyson, Coleridge, Dickens, Kipling—"

"Don't get maudlin on me, Shav-ster," Laura said gloomily. She wandered off ahead.

Eventually the sallow-faced man brought them to St. Edward the Confessor's Chapel, the sacred heart of the abbey where its most precious relics lay. Here a man in his sixties, with shoulder-length, straggly grey hair, sat wearily in a Gothic, high-backed chair. He was painfully thin, his wrists protruding skeletally from the fraying arms of an old, woollen overcoat. Behind his wire-rimmed glasses, his face suggested a man burdened by the greatest of worries, but underneath it Shavi saw integrity and intelligence.

The sallow-faced man hurried over and whispered in his ear. Without looking up, the Professor gestured exhaustedly for Shavi and the others to approach. When they were in front of him, he cast a brief eye over them, but if he felt any shock at the sight of the Tuatha Dé Danann, he didn't register it. "More strays sheltering from the storm?" His voice was achingly tired.

"We are here to confront the invaders," Shavi said.

He counted them off silently. "So many of you. Did you really need to come so mob-handed?"

"We're only part of it," Laura said. "The best part, sure, but there are others. Lots of them. There's a war going on." She gestured towards the Tuatha Dé Danann. "These—"

The Professor acknowledged them with a nod. "Old gods made new again. I expected they were around, though I haven't seen any of them till now."

"Who are you?" Shavi asked.

"The wrong man in the wrong place at the wrong time." He removed his glasses and rubbed his eyes for a long period. "An academic. Just what the world needs now. Even better, one versed in anthropology." He laughed bitterly.

"So how did you get the top job?" Laura watched the sallow-faced man slope away.

"Someone had to do it. Not that there's anything to do, apart from preventing everyone from killing themselves. Though even that may be an exercise in futility."

The Tuatha Dé Danann shifted awkwardly until Baccharus silently motioned to Shavi that he was taking them back to the horses.

"So, introductions. My name is Brian Michell. And you are?"

Shavi and Laura introduced themselves before briefly outlining what was happening in the city. Michell listened thoughtfully, nodding at the correct moments. When they had finished, he said, "When I first saw those horrible things out there I knew they were the template for all the worst things in our old myths. There was something inexpressibly ancient about them, something laden with symbolism. It was only a matter of time before the ones responsible for the other archetypes appeared."

"You'd get on well with our own old git," Laura said. "Same language, same old bollocks."

"I still haven't worked out why they haven't come in here to tear us apart."

Shavi explained as best he could about the Blue Fire, but Michell picked up on the concept quickly. "Good old woolly-minded New Agers. I always knew they were on to something. The spiritual wellhead, eh? Then I suppose it's only natural this place is a potent source of it. It's been a sacred spot for as long as man's been around, so the legends say. A divine island in prehistoric times, bounded by the Thames and the two arms of the River Tyburn that's now buried in pipes. The old Isle of Thorns, sacred to the Druids. Later, sacred to Apollo, where his temple was sited. Home of numerous other now long-lost religious monuments. And still giving up all it has to our generation. Amazing." He forced a smile.

"What have you been doing for all those people?" Laura asked.

"Ensuring the little food we had was distributed fairly. Not much to do in that quarter now. In the early days, mediate in disputes. Try to keep them from taking their frustrations out on each other. They turned to me because they thought, being an educated man, I know about *things*. Now isn't that a laugh? I haven't even been able to look after my own life. The wife, God bless her, left long ago. Sick of all my cant. And the booze, I suppose. Haven't had a drink since I came in here. Now isn't that a thing? They should have examined my curriculum vitae a little more closely."

"Whatever you say, I am sure you are the right man for the job. You have held them together," Shavi said. Michell shrugged, wouldn't meet Shavi's eye. "I would like to talk to them," Shavi continued.

Michell chewed on a flayed nail, his eyes now fixed on Shavi's face. "And say what to them? I don't want you making their last days any more miserable."

"He's not going to do that." Laura grinned. "Shavi here's the preacher-boy. He's going to uplift their souls."

"I want to tell them there is still hope."

The Professor winced, shook his head. "I think we've all had enough fairy stories."

Shavi rested a hand on the Professor's thin fingers, which felt unbearably cold. "I ask you to trust me."

A tremor ran through Shavi as he ascended to the pulpit and looked down at the array of pale faces turned towards him. There was too much emotion there. It made him feel he wasn't up to the task, not even slightly. *I am just a London boy*, he wanted to say. *Not a shaman, not a hero, not a saviour.*

But after a moment, his heart took over and the words flowed to his mouth without any thought. "For centuries, this has been a place of miracles . . ."

They made their base in one of the Sir Christopher Wren-designed twin towers on the western side. Outside, night had fallen; without any lights in the city, the Abbey felt like it was suspended in space.

The Tuatha Dé Danann settled easily in one corner of the gloomy old room and rested their eyes. Shavi was still not sure if they actually slept.

"That was a good thing you did," Laura said quietly as she, Shavi and Baccharus sat around a stubby candle from the Abbey's store. "You could see it in their faces. What you did for them . . . amazing. I couldn't have done it. No one else could have done it." She gave Shavi's thigh a squeeze. "You missed your calling, preacher-boy."

"Hope is a human essential."

"Hope is essential for all things in the sweep of existence." Baccharus stared at the flickering candle flame. "It is common currency, too often in short supply." He looked up at Shavi. "And to give hope is the greatest gift of all."

"Oh, don't. His head's big enough already." Laura rested on Shavi's shoulder. After a moment she said, "So what are we going to do? We can't sit here forever."

"I fear we have been removed from the conflict," Baccharus said. "Unless my people can fight their way through to us, or one of the others achieves something remarkable that changes the situation, there is little we can do." His voice suggested he didn't expect it to happen.

"But it's so pathetic," Laura protested. "We didn't do anything! We barely got into the city!"

"No," Shavi said. "I have to ensure the cauldron is there for the final battle. Laura and I both *need* to be there. We have to find a way."

Baccharus held out his hand in equanimity. "But there is nothing we can do. We are surrounded by a city of Night Walkers where we cannot move the slightest step without being cut down. The wise one accepts when events are beyond control."

Laura looked from Baccharus to Shavi. "So we sit here waiting to die?"

"Or," Shavi said, "waiting to live."

At some point the quiet conversation became a distant drone and Laura's eyelids grew heavy, although a dim part of her was amazed that she could even consider sleeping. When she next stirred she realised the talk had stopped. Baccharus was lying next to the guttering candle, his eyes closed. Shavi was nowhere to be seen.

She stood up and stretched, although since her transformation her limbs no longer really ached. But she did feel the cold more, and her breath was clouding. She pulled her jacket tightly around her, the chill of the stone flags rising through the soles of her boots.

She found Shavi in an adjoining corridor lined with windows that looked out over the city. She might not have seen him in the pervasive gloom if not for a brief instant when the smoke and mist cleared to allow the moonlight to break through. Then he was limned in silver, like a ghost, leaning against the wall.

As Laura approached quietly, she was disturbed to see a strange cast to his face. It was heavy with dark thoughts and deep troubles, and she suddenly wondered whether his experience in the Grim Lands had affected him more than they thought. What if it had twisted a part of him, and even he didn't know?

She was considering retreating when he looked up to see her. His warm smile instantly dispelled all her doubts.

"Planning a suicide mission?" she asked.

He held out an arm so she could slide in next to him. "I was thinking about the others."

She felt warm and secure wrapped against his body. The smell of him brought back memories in a rush and she was surprised how happy they made her feel, but there was an edge of sadness to them as well. "That time we did the monkey dance in Glastonbury," she began, "I was being a little manipulator."

"I know."

"Not in a bad way. I just wanted to get close to you. I thought nobody would do that if I didn't try to play them. Anyway, I'm sorry. I should have been more honest."

"Why do you feel the need to tell me this now?"

She thought about this for a moment. "If I screw up . . . if I'm not up to what you expected of me . . . I just don't want you thinking I'm all bad. Too bad."

"I could never think badly of you, Laura."

"Yeah, well, you don't know what lies ahead. I might run off screaming at a vital moment. Or something."

"I have faith in you." He gave her a squeeze. "I wonder where the others are now. Ryan and Ruth should have realised how dense the Fomorii forces are in the city by now. I hope their regiment of the Tuatha Dé Danann had more success than ours."

"The worst thing is that we might never find out, just be stuck here while everything winds down, not knowing if the people we care about are alive or dead."

"And Church—"

"Church will be fine." She nuzzled into Shavi's shoulder. "He's got God on his side. Too damn decent to screw up."

"It must hurt you to still love him."

"Not really. Yes, I still love him. But I've got my head round the fact that we're never going to be together." She put on a fake voice. "It's just one of those terribly tragic love stories."

"It is not the end, you know."

She laughed silently. "That's a good thing to say in this predicament. But if we're just talking about our stupid personal lives, then I know you're right. For the first time I feel optimistic about me. About what I could do. Which is ludicrous when there might only be a day left, and I've got green blood running through my veins. But, you know, I feel . . . hopeful. And I never thought I'd feel that in my life."

Shavi rested his head against hers, smelling her hair, relishing the new aromas she generated since her change. Above all, he was happy for her, even if there were only hours left. "What do you want to do now?" he asked quietly.

"I just want you to hold me here like I was some pathetic child. And I want to watch the dawn come up with you."

Silence draped across them in the deep dark, with only the occasional soughing of the wind to remind them there was a world beyond their own sphere. And there was peace for both of them.

When dawn rose in intermittent bursts of gold and red through the shifting smoke, Laura was asleep on the floor in Shavi's arms. His thoughts had been too troubled to sleep himself, but the magical colour ignited in the corridor by the light through the stained glass was enough to lift his mood.

"A beautiful day." Michell was standing in the doorway. "I'm sorry—irony doesn't go down too well at this time in the morning."

Shavi slipped out from under Laura without waking her and wandered over to greet the Professor.

"I just wanted to say thank you for what you said to everyone last night," Michell continued. "It did them the world of good. I'm a little too cynical to say I was affected by it myself."

"I am glad I could be of some help." Shavi glanced out of the one window he had left open the previous night. "Has the food gone completely?"

"There's a little left. For emergencies."

"Then I suggest you divide it up amongst them this morning."

Michell searched Shavi's face and then nodded slowly, chewing on his lip. "I'll arrange it. Do you have any plans for the day? Any sights to see? I thought I'd work on a few lectures myself."

Shavi smiled. "No. No plans."

Behind them Laura stirred and yawned loudly, eventually making her way to them, still sleepy eyed. A racking shiver brought her fully awake. "When do you think the end'll start coming down?"

"It should not be too long."

"How do you know that?" Michell asked.

Shavi pointed to the open window. Laura and the Professor peered out together.

The Fomorii stood shoulder-to-shoulder everywhere they looked, packing the main drag of Victoria Street and every surrounding street to the dim distance. The entire cityscape gleamed an oily black in the wan sunlight. None of them made the slightest sound, nor did they move an inch: an army of sable statues. And all their faces were turned up to the window where Shavi, Laura and the Professor stood.

Waiting.

chapter eighteen
down to the river to pray

"Are you going to talk to me at all?" Ruth had been keeping one eye on Veitch long enough to know he was fighting to ignore her.

She instantly regretted speaking when he flashed her a glance that was so harsh it jolted her. "What do you expect? Happy smiles and blowing kisses?"

"Not from you, no."

His long hair, lashed by the cold north wind, obscured his face so she couldn't read his response, but she had watched his eyes made darker by a brooding brow ever since they had picked up the last leg of the M1. His handsome face had been transformed by the icy set of his features. Sometimes, when she saw him like that, he frightened her.

The Tuatha Dé Danann who rode in front, behind and on either side had added to her loneliness by alienating her ever since they had left the camp. They had taken to Veitch immediately, encouraging him to strip off his shirt so they could examine with delight the fantastic tattoos that covered his torso, so she knew it wasn't because she was a *Fragile Creature*. She had endured enough similar ignorance from men during her working life not to take it to heart. With what lay ahead, she could have done with a friend for support and she hated Veitch a little for not being there for her, even though she had no right to ask that of him.

At the end of the motorway they took the North Circular. It gave her a strange *frisson* to be riding a horse along deserted roads on which she had queued irritatedly in backed-up traffic so many times. At least the Tuatha Dé Danann force gave her some confidence. There were hundreds of them, maybe thousands, armed with bizarre weapons that made her blood grow cold just to look at them. They stretched as far back as she could see, and fanned out slightly on either side ahead so the force resembled an arrow driving into the contaminated heart of the city. Lugh and Nuada led the way, both of them enthused with a warrior spirit that sickened her. She didn't take any pleasure in fighting, certainly not in killing; it was a job that they had an obligation to fulfil, but that was all. And she also despised the jealousy, or contempt, she felt coming off the two gods at her possession of the Spear. The weapon rested on her back in a specially made harness Lugh had grudgingly handed over, its power warming through her clothes to invigorate her spirit.

They broke off from the North Circular, passing down North End Road until they arrived at Hampstead Heath. The expanse of greenery was looking a little washed-out in the October chill, but it had been protected from the ash falls by its lofty position above the city and the direction of the wind.

From the heights all they could see was the pall of thick smoke and mist that drifted along the Thames Valley. Occasionally, though, it shifted enough for the black tower to loom up ominously in the east.

A blast from a strange horn resembling a conch shell brought the force to an abrupt halt. Ahead, Ruth could see Lugh and Nuada in deep discussion. After a moment they beckoned to Veitch. It was noticeable that they were ignoring her, but out of bloody-mindedness she spurred her horse to keep pace behind Veitch.

Both of the gods kept their eyes fixed on Veitch's face as they spoke. "We are debating crossing this heathland," Nuada said. "It is a wide expanse that could be dangerous."

Veitch scanned the heath. "If there are any of the Bastards out there, there can't be many. There aren't that many places to hide."

"The Night Walkers are a cunning breed," Nuada said.

"I say we continue," Lugh said. "It would not do to waste the hours following the edge. And if there are Night Walkers, they will fall before the might of the Golden Ones, as they always must."

Veitch rubbed his chin. "Well, I don't know. I wouldn't like to be caught out there."

"I heard you were a mighty warrior," Lugh gibed. "That strangest of things, a Fragile Creature who is not fragile!"

Ruth willed Veitch not to be swayed, but after a moment's thought, he shrugged. "It's your call, then. Let's get to it."

Ruth sighed, but none of them looked towards her.

When they returned to their positions, Ruth said to Veitch, "Why did you give in to them? You know better than they do. You're good at what you do, Ryan. You should have more confidence in yourself."

He grunted unintelligibly, but renewed his effort to scan the heath. Clusters of trees dotted the rolling grassland, with thicker woodland to the north. They were aiming for Parliament Hill, where they could press down speedily into Kentish Town, and then on into Camden, Islington and finally the City. Ruth was dreading the final leg of the assault where the winding streets and soaring buildings would make any mass approach impossible. She expected a long, gruelling fight to their destination, and if the Fomorii could hold them off for just thirty-six hours it would end in failure. If only there were a better way, she thought.

The Tuatha Dé Danann fanned out across the heath, giving Ruth an even more impressive view of their numbers. So concentrated were they that her perception could barely cope; the gods lost their individuality, became the untarnished power that lay at the core of them, merging into one, bright glow. It reminded her of a sea of gold, licking up to an oil-stained beach. The sight was comforting and she relaxed a little. The Fomorii wouldn't stand a chance.

They moved across the heath slowly. Nuada and Lugh were leading cautiously, constantly scanning the terrain. Veitch kept his eyes on the tree line.

Briefly the sun broke through the thick cloud cover, warming Ruth's face. She closed her eyes and went with the gentle rocking of her mount, enjoying the aroma of greenery the breeze brought from the north. In her mind she pictured a perfect autumn day, walking with Church amongst a wood turning gold, red and brown somewhere peaceful, Scotland perhaps, or the New Forest. Her mind plucked a soundtrack from her memory that had been pressuring to come forward since the journey began.

"What are you thinking?"

She opened her eyes to see Veitch watching her suspiciously. "I can't get an old song out of my head. It's sort of gospelly, traditional, but it was in a George Clooney film a while back. It's called—"

In the blink of an eye, the Fomorii were there. They rose up out of the ground, not there, then there a second later, an opposing army created from thin air. By the time she had realised what was happening, chaos had erupted.

Ruth was caught in a hurricane. Her nightmares of the forthcoming confrontation had suggested it would be as sickeningly ferocious and bloody as any mediaeval battle, but what she saw around her was much, much worse. The Fomorii wielded their ugly, serrated swords like propellers, hacking and slashing in a relentless whirl. Limbs, heads and other body parts showered all around, filling the air with a blizzard of golden moths.

The Tuatha Dé Danann were just as brutal. Their weapons were unleashed in furious rounds, turning the Fomorii into a mist of black droplets or a thick sludge with only the hint of component parts. And where the fighting was too close, they resorted to their swords, jabbing and hacking as fast as their enemy. In the fury of movement and the ear-splitting din of combat, with the mud and grue covering all, Ruth could barely tell them apart.

Veitch was matching them all for ferocity. His sword whisked around with the efficiency and blurring speed of a machine, while he somehow managed to manoeuvre his horse back and forth to attack and retreat, even in close quarters. It was a staggering display of instinctive ability that left Ruth breathless. That was why he had been chosen: he wasn't just good at the role that had been presented to him, he was the ultimate warrior.

The Spear was in her right hand—she didn't recall withdrawing it—and she clutched the reins with her left. Numerous Night Walkers fell at the touch of the weapon, but she was nowhere near as good as Veitch. In fact, she felt a liability. Her own abilities were useless in that kind of situation, while the sheer senseless slaughter left her unable to think clearly.

Veitch appeared to sense this for he suddenly spurred his horse round to her side. "Let's get out of this fucking hell-hole!"

With his sword cutting down any opposition he drove the horse in as direct a line as he could to the open ground beyond the battlefield. Ruth was quick to follow in his wake, bracing the Spear against her side to take down any opposition Veitch missed. By the time they had forced their way through the final ranks, her ribs felt as if they had been beaten with metal bars.

Veitch continued until they had put a hundred yards or more between them and the fighting, then he rounded to survey the scene. "Shit. Look at that." His voice was barely more than a whisper.

From their new perspective the true horror and brutality of the fight could be seen. The Fomorii and Tuatha Dé Danann never turned from a confrontation, driving on from one fight to the next until they eventually dropped. The heath was thick with the essence of both of them—hundreds had already been slaughtered—but the Fomorii had a slight advantage in that they had no concern for their own preservation; one would sacrifice itself so another could gain a better position in a fight. The shimmer of golden moths over the scene added an incongruous touch of beauty to the horror, so that after a moment Ruth felt she was watching a strange, detached cartoon, shifting in a syrupy slow motion as golden snow fell languorously.

"Are they going to fight to the last man?" she said when she couldn't bear to look any more.

"They're not men." Veitch was seized with a cold anger. "They've forgotten the job. We're going to lose everything because they're locked up in their own stupid, bleedin' rivalry."

Before Ruth could answer, their attention was caught by frantic movement in the air down in the valley. Rising from the drifting smoke were black shapes that looked like flies from their perspective. "Fomorii," Ruth said. "Flying ones."

It was never easy to get a fix on the fluid shapes of the Fomorii, but Ruth was sure she could make out wings like a bat, but gleaming and rigid, as though they were made of metal. As the creatures fell down towards the heath, their insectile body plates shifted, folded out and slotted into place until they were covered with a hideous ridged and pitted armour. Numerous horns rimmed the skull while the eyes glowed a Satanic red from deep within Stygian orbits.

As Ruth and Veitch watched, a pair of the flying Night Walkers broke away from the formation and targeted the two of them. "Come on!" Veitch turned his horse in a bid to outrun them.

The flying Fomorii were like small jets, flattening their wings against their backs to build more speed. As their shadow fell over Ruth, she threw herself to one side. It was enough to avoid a killing blow from talons of black steel but she still felt a ringing impact on the side of her head, knocking her from the horse. She hit the ground hard, seeing stars, feeling a wetness seeping into her hair.

When she next looked up, the two creatures had zoned in on Veitch. They hovered, avoiding his blows, then diving in between his sword thrusts with the speed of hummingbirds. Even so, they'd only managed to land a couple of minor blows on him; blood trickled from a cut on his temple, another on his cheek.

As Ruth pushed herself dazedly to her feet, she saw Veitch feint and then rip his sword along one of the creature's bellies. Thick, black liquid gushed out, steaming in the cold air. It narrowly missed Veitch, splattering on the grass where it sizzled like acid. But in the Fomor's dying spasm it had knocked Veitch's sword from his hand, and the other one was preparing to sweep in for the kill.

Though her head felt like cotton wool, Ruth acted on instinct. She snatched up the Spear from where it had fallen and hurled it with all her strength. As the creature dived down, the Spear rammed through its skull, neck and out of its belly. It dropped to the ground like a stone.

Veitch snapped round towards her. At first his face was unreadable, but then a grin crept across it. "So you can be as big a nasty bastard as the rest of us."

After reclaiming the Spear and Ruth's horse, they only had a second or two to consider their options before they realised a section of the Tuatha Dé Danann force was rushing towards them. The flying Fomorii were wreaking havoc amongst the outer reaches of the Golden Ones, but hadn't yet progressed to those fighting in the thickest of the mêlée. It was obvious they had tilted the balance firmly in the direction of the Fomorii.

Lugh and Nuada patently recognised this for they were in the forefront of the retreat. The conch-like horn sounded insistently above the clash of battle and the bloodthirsty screeches of the Fomorii. The Tuatha Dé Danann attempted to extricate themselves from the thick of the fighting. Many fell in the course of the retreat.

Soon Ruth and Veitch's horses thundered across the heath. The airborne creatures continued to harry those at the rear, but away from the battle there was more room to use Goibhniu's weapons. Once a handful had plummeted from the sky the other Fomorii hung back, waiting for the right opportunity. Dropping back further, the Night Walker forces regrouped to drive the Tuatha Dé Danann eastwards; once the gods hit the built-up areas, their retreat would fragment.

Ruth could see this was not lost on Nuada. His face was drained of the arrogance that had turned his earlier smiles into a sneer; a stony cast hid his concern.

Veitch knew it too, was probably aware of it before anyone else. "We can't keep running!" he yelled above the pounding of a thousand hooves.

"Then what do you suggest?" Nuada snapped.

The thoughtful expression that crossed Veitch's face brought a smile to Ruth's lips; she recognised it instantly. "There's one route that'll take all this lot, horses and all, right into the heart of where we want to go," he said.

"Then why was it not proposed earlier?"

"Because it's probably bleedin' dangerous." Veitch turned to Ruth. "The tube."

Ruth was struggling to keep up, but Veitch's suggestion gave her added impetus. "Of course! The whole city's got tunnels running under it everywhere!"

"Not just the train tunnels. There's other shit down there. Secret passages for the Government and the army. Disused lines and everything."

Nuada reined in his mount; they had reached the eastern edge of the heath. Within a couple of minutes, the rest of the Tuatha Dé Danann would be milling around them, jammed into a bottleneck and ready for the slaughter.

"Make haste! There is little time!" Ruth thought she sensed a hint of respect in Nuada's voice.

"Okay, here's the deal. If we all head to the nearest station the Bastards'll follow us down and pick us off. But what they really want is you, Lugh and the other top dogs. Me too, probably. We're going to draw some of them off, try to lose them. Ruth's going to lead as many of your lot as she can to Archway station and then move up with some more to Highgate." He winced. "The rest are going to have to fend for themselves."

"Agreed. They can honour themselves by holding off the Night Walkers until we reach our destination." He made to go before turning back to Veitch. "You are a true champion of your kind, Brother of Dragons." And then he was away, passing on the plan to his lieutenants.

The flush of pride rose up in Veitch's cheeks and he tried to turn away before

Ruth could see. She rode up to him and placed a hand on his shoulder so she could pull him closer to whisper in his ear. "You're the hero, Ryan. Everybody knows it."

He looked deep into her face, unable to find any words that could express his thoughts. Instead he pulled her closer to kiss her just once, on the cheek; it was a kiss for old time's sake. And then he spurred his horse to round up the men he needed.

Veitch, Lugh and Nuada led a band of about thirty eastwards through the pleasant streets that bordered the heath. Within a couple of minutes they were at the place Veitch had identified from his encyclopaedic strategic memory. Highgate Cemetery brooded behind stone walls and chained iron gates, a maze of paths amongst the crumbling Victorian monuments to the dead, festooned with ivy, shadowed by clusters of dark, overhanging trees.

Lugh smashed down the main gate with one blow of his boot. They drove their horses deep into the heart of the cemetery where they dismounted. Veitch knew he had made the right choice: plenty of places to hide amongst the stones and mausoleums, the groves and hollows and mounds that gave no clear line of sight.

Yet he couldn't help a shudder when he looked round at the stones. It was the Grey Lands all over again. Images of the dead beneath his feet rose unbidden into his mind, and however much he tried he couldn't stifle the thought of them listening and shifting, gradually clawing their way up to the light.

Before he made any further move, he climbed into the low, twisted branches of an ancient yew. Through the thick greenery he could just make out the cemetery perimeter. He had been right there too: the Fomorii were milling around in the streets beyond, confused. Their hive-mind was good for any obvious confrontation, but anything involving guile and difficult choices left them at odds. It helped that he could not see any that stood out as leaders. No flapping crows, no enormous, powerful warriors like the one that had pursued them from Edinburgh.

After a moment the main body of the force set off to track Ruth through the trees, but they had hesitated long enough for her to have a good headstart. A large group turned towards the cemetery. A chill ran through Veitch as they flowed over the walls and amongst the stones like shadows at twilight. Several of the flying Fomorii joined them, swooping low over the graves, searching for any sign of their prey.

Veitch dropped from the branches to Nuada and Lugh. "You know what guerrilla warfare is? We split up into ones and twos, pick off as many as we can while we make our way across the cemetery. We meet up on the other side and head to Highgate station."

"What about the horses?" Nuada asked.

"We scatter them. They'll confuse things."

Nuada and Lugh barked something to the others in a language Veitch couldn't understand. A moment later they had slipped into the surroundings like ghosts.

A film of sweat covered Veitch's entire body despite the cold. He stepped out from behind the lichen-streaked obelisk towering over his head into plain view of three Fomorii, who moved cautiously along the path two hundred yards away. They heralded their discovery with a barrage of monkey shrieks.

The other Fomorii nearby were too distracted by the wildly galloping horses to heed the call. The mounts ran back and forth along the winding paths, in sight just long enough for their presence to be registered but disappearing before the Fomorii could see if there was a rider on their backs.

Veitch's heart thundered as the Fomorii started towards him. They moved so much quicker than their bulk suggested: efficient killing machines filled with unquenchable energy. There was something hypnotic about their power that kept him rooted and they were dangerously close by the time he had turned and was running over the lip of the hill. He knew he wouldn't be able to outrun them for long.

The strain of the last few days was beginning to tell as he darted from the path amongst the stones in the hope that it would slow down his pursuers. Exhaustion brought a dull, aching heat to his thigh muscles, his usually bountiful reserves of energy close to empty.

The Fomorii veered from the path, smashing down grave markers that had stood for a hundred years with a flex of their leg muscles or a sweep of their arms. The wind picked up the thick, unpleasant musk of them; every time Veitch smelled it he felt sick to his stomach. Now he didn't even have the strength to combat the queasiness. He hurdled a tilting cross, ripping his calf on one of the arms, then landed awkwardly back on the path. He was convinced he had broken his ankle, but after he limped a few more paces he realised it was probably only a twist, but it was enough to hamper him.

A chunk of old stone crashed against a statue of an angel, missing his head by only an inch. He rounded a bend in the path and came up on a large mausoleum covered with so much ivy it looked like a natural formation.

Gripping the ivy hard, he hauled himself on to the roof to leap to a tree branch beyond. His reactions were still sharp enough to catch the shadow falling across him. The talons of one of the flying Fomorii raked the air where his head had been. Quickly he lashed upwards with his silver hand. Nails extracted as Nuada had showed him, slicing through the creature's left leg. It lost control of its flight and he hacked again, half-severing a wing. It crashed down amongst the graves, still alive but badly wounded.

He didn't have time to catch his breath. The Fomorii were now dragging themselves up the mausoleum, but they were slowed by the ivy, which was being pulled away by their bulk; they were still managing to find enough of a foothold to progress.

Veitch leaped for the branch and swung, dropping down on to another path. Pain flared in his ankle as he landed. He stifled a yell, clutched at it and hobbled off as the path wound round into a dense thicket of trees.

A minute later the Fomorii were there. But as they turned into the shadowy grove they were confronted by Nuada and Lugh poised on either side of the path.

Veitch was leaning against a tree, taking the weight off his ankle. "Could be worse," he said with a shrug. "You could be dead."

The Fomorii were still struggling with their surprise as Lugh stepped in and gutted one, while Nuada lopped the head off another. As the third started to transform into something more offensive they both swung their swords to dismember it.

"Oh, well." Veitch eyed the steaming corpses with a confident grin.

Across the cemetery, golden shapes flitted like autumn shadows. The remnants of gleaming sable bodies hung from crosses and angels, were strewn across stone boxes or were slumped against the walls of mausoleums where the ivy flapped against their caustic cavities.

Veitch guided it all with a consummate eye for detail, and when he was convinced enough damage had been done in the limited time they had available, he directed the Tuatha Dé Danann to depart. They slipped amongst the stones to the perimeter wall, and even with Veitch limping, they were not seen once.

Ruth waited in the shadows of Highgate Station ticket office, watching the loosed horses canter along the road in the fading afternoon light. Hundreds if not thousands of the beasts were now roaming through the streets of North London, covering their tracks with great efficiency.

Barely a quarter of the Tuatha Dé Danann force had streamed down the cramped winding staircases of Archway tube station under her guidance before she had decided to move on to avoid the Fomorii. Many more now waited at the foot of the terrifyingly deep shaft at Highgate, the deepest—if her memory served correct—on the entire tube network. Without any of the lifts working, it had taken them an age to filter through the tiny station and on to the stairs, clutching makeshift torches from any wood they could find in the vicinity. And all the time her heart had been in her mouth, expecting the Fomorii to sweep down on them when they were in no position to defend themselves.

But somehow they had done it, leaving her to wait alone in painful anticipation for Veitch and the others to arrive. She clutched the Spear close to her side for comfort, feeling the warm pulse of it, the soothing heat. Strangely it appeared slightly different from when she had first received it, less rough, with more delicate inlays of brass and silver.

She hadn't given a thought to what the next twenty-four hours would bring; indeed, if she were honest with herself, she would have admitted that for several weeks she had anticipated a terrible end for all of them. It didn't frighten her anymore. When things were so likely, you made your peace with the outcome and moved on. As she stood there, she was surprised and a little disturbed to realise the worst thought that crawled around her head was that Veitch would not make it. Had his uncontrollable anger driven him to make some stupid mistake? Had his overweening bravado left him lying in a pool of blood in some Godforsaken backstreet? She was afraid of examining the subject too deeply for fear of what she would find.

She loved Church—she knew she did—but a part of her still had deep affection for Veitch; more than friendship, less than *amore*, not enough to make a song, more than enough to fill her with a consuming sadness that she might never see him again. Even her emotions had been so much simpler before the big change; now she couldn't even count on herself.

When she saw the glimmer of gold skin in the grey streets, and Veitch at the centre of them, dark hair flying in the breeze, she wiped her eyes, heaved in several deep breaths and turned towards the stairs.

"You're falling apart, Ryan. Losing a hand, now twisting an ankle." Ruth held the torch higher. The darkness receded along the walls of the stairwell like a living creature.

"We all heal quick." Veitch limped down the steps heavily, clutching on to the rail for support. Behind them Nuada, Lugh and the other Tuatha Dé Danann traipsed silently.

Veitch's mood had turned dark once more. Ruth saw it in his face the moment he had entered the tube station. Once he had passed into the gloom of the stairwell he locked himself off even further, his replies to her questions clipped and curt. There was something ineffably dangerous about him. In its milder form it was attractive, but when he got like this she was glad he was on their side.

By the time they reached the platform, Ruth's heart was pounding and her breath was short. She was surprised and disturbed by how much the claustrophobic darkness was affecting her; even with the torches, it was impossible to see more than a few feet. Although she'd been on that platform several times before, in that state it was oppressive and alien. She was acutely aware of the massive weight of earth piled up over her head. The air was stale without the circulation system working and it smelled of damp and burnt oil. It was also extremely cold. With an effort, she fought back a desperate urge to get back to the light.

"Where's the rest of them?" Veitch asked.

"I sent them down the line to rendezvous with the others at Archway." Her voice sounded strained, with incipient panic tightening its grip around her airways.

"You know it's a bleedin' maze down here. They could get lost—"

"Sorry," she snapped, sarcastically. "I foolishly thought there wasn't any time to lose."

"All right. I suppose we just have to take chances." He lowered himself down and slid off the lip of the platform on to the tracks.

Ruth hesitated a moment before following suit. She moved in close to Veitch. Lugh and a couple of the other Tuatha Dé Danann led the way cautiously, while the rest guarded the rear.

At the end of the platform, the black hole of the tunnel loomed up in the flickering torchlight; a mouth ready to swallow them, Ruth thought. Her skin grew cold as she stared into the darkness and she was overcome with a sudden premonition of a grave and none of them ever seeing the light again.

"What's that?" Her heart rattled frantically when she glimpsed a fleeting movement on the edge of the light.

Everyone froze. "Didn't see anything," Veitch whispered.

"There's definitely something there." Her voice was taut.

Lugh had found some oily rags on the tracks, which he tied into a large knot and lit with his torch. He whirled it once round his head and hurled it along the tunnel in front. The shadows rushed fearfully along the arc of the tunnel, but what was caught in the light for the briefest moment made Ruth shudder.

A sea of rats were frozen in the sudden glare, from wall to wall and as far as the light carried, their eyes glittering coldly. The sickening tableau was there only for an instant. As the burning rag fell, they retreated frantically, one brown-furred mass, rippling sinuously, until a second later the entire area was clear. The sound of scratching on metal rails faded away down the tunnel.

"Good job we have light," Veitch said. "They're fierce little bastards when they're hungry or cornered. I wouldn't fancy our chances against them in the dark."

"There were so many of them!"

"These tunnels were always infested. The whole city was. They used to say you were never more than three feet away from a rat. I expect it's worse now, with all the bodies and everything."

The image conjured by Veitch's comment made Ruth sick. "You know there's a danger some of the tunnels could be flooded," she said, changing the subject. "None of the pumps are working."

"That's the least of our worries."

"Do you think the Fomorii are down here?"

"They might use some of the tunnel system, but they'll be going about their business. They won't be looking out for us."

Ruth thought about this for a moment. "Are you sure? They've always been pretty smart in their planning. Second-guessing us, setting up all those backup plans if the main one didn't work. I know Calatin's gone, but there's always Mollecht and God knows what else—"

"Well, you be the bleedin' strategist, then."

"I'm just offering an opinion. I'm allowed to speak, you know."

"That's all you bleedin' well do."

"Get lost." She shoved him hard so he fell on to his injured ankle.

He cursed vehemently and turned, his face transformed by fury, his fists bunched. It was so terrifying she dropped the torch, which sputtered and fizzled but didn't go out.

"Give me that!"

"No!" She fended him off and snatched up the burning wood.

"If the torches go out we're screwed!"

"I know that!"

"Well, keep a hold of it then, you stupid—"

"What?" She rounded on him.

"Nothing." He realised he'd overstepped the mark.

"What were you going to say?" Her voice was edgy and shrill.

"Come on." He marched on ahead sheepishly. "Don't do this here," he said under his breath, "not in front of them."

"Who cares what they think?"

"I do."

They continued in silence for several minutes while Ruth's seething temper calmed. Finally she said, "You should see a therapist about all that repressed anger. The slightest thing and it comes bursting out."

He wasn't going to answer, but then he said quietly, "It never used to be a problem."

"You've had it as long as I've known you. And let me tell you, it's a liability. You fly off the handle at the slightest thing and you stop thinking rationally—"

"All right."

"We can't afford that—"

"I said all right!" He realised a second later that he'd done it again, but instead of apologising he speeded up his step until he caught up with Lugh and the point men.

They continued that way for half an hour, with Ruth wrapped in a shroud of loneliness, listening to the unforgiving echoes bounce crazily around, hinting at strangers nearby but never quite revealing anything. No one spoke; the atmosphere had grown more intense the further they progressed into the tunnels. Ruth couldn't shake the feeling there was some terrible threat lying in front of them, staying only a step or two ahead of the advancing torchlight.

Veitch kept his head down, but she could tell from his rigid shoulders that he was aware of her behind him. She wondered if she had been too harsh on him; the strain had been making her increasingly snappy. The niggle of guilt she felt told her it probably wasn't as one-sided as she had pretended. Veitch had performed an exemplary service; if only the stupid emotional side didn't keep getting in the way, she would be able to give him the wholehearted praise he really deserved.

As they passed through Archway station, the torchlight flared up over the tiled walls and a nagging doubt grew full-born. "Where are the others?" she asked to no one in particular.

Veitch hesitated before turning round. "Probably took a wrong turn somewhere," he replied. Ruth thought he sounded a little abashed.

"With a whole army traipsing through here, you'd expect to hear some echoes. Wouldn't you?"

They all halted to listen. There was nothing at all; the air felt dead. "Maybe they accidentally crossed over to the northbound tunnel," Veitch suggested. "Who knows? There might be a whole load of service tunnels we don't even know about. In the dark back there anyone could have taken a branching track without knowing."

Veitch could easily have been right, but the weight on their hearts grew heavier nonetheless.

Ruth lost all track of time. The only sign of the passing minutes was the growing ache in her legs and the dull parade of platforms that had once meant nothing more than a commuter liminal zone between work and home. Now they were stations on the road to Hell, their names emblazoned on her mind: Tufnell Park, Kentish

Town, Camden Town, Euston, King's Cross, Angel. She knew the next one would be Old Street and then they would be in the heart of the City. And by that time, she guessed, they would know exactly what troubles they were facing.

At one point, near King's Cross, they had heard the dim sound of clashing weapons and shouts echoing from one of the myriad tunnels converged there. They presumed it was the main Tuatha Dé Danann force encountering resistance somewhere.

Nuada was keen to reunite with his comrades to offer support if needed, but Veitch argued fiercely against this. The tunnel system was so complex the chances of locating them were slim—they could spend days wandering around down there, he stressed. And time was not on their side; at least some of them had to reach their destination.

After a heated debate, Nuada once again gave in, though Ruth could sense his patience with a *Fragile Creature* was growing thin.

Veitch came back to her side once Old Street and Moorgate stations were behind them. The air had grown several degrees colder and there was a deeply unpleasant smell that Ruth didn't want to examine too closely.

"Back in your good books now, am I?" she asked tartly and instantly hated herself, but she had been unable to resist the gibe.

This time it washed over Veitch; he had other things on his mind. "Bank next. We'll have to go up top soon." He paused. "That fighting we heard must mean there *are* Fomorii down here. We've been lucky not to meet any of them."

"Luck doesn't begin to explain it. I can't believe they've left one of the main routes into their most sacred places completely free from guards."

Lugh hurried back, hushing them into silence.

"There," Ruth hissed childishly, "tempting Fate again."

Distant sounds carried to them from ahead. It suggested many bodies on the move; the occasional foul stink caught on the air currents told them it was the Fomorii.

"They're going to push us all the way back to Moorgate before we can find somewhere to lie low," Ruth said dismally.

"Shit!" Veitch looked around like a cornered animal. "We can't waste the—"

One of the Tuatha Dé Danann was motioning to a shadowy area on the eastern wall. They hurried over to see a small tunnel wide enough for a couple of people. Veitch dived in to investigate. Less than a minute later he was back, grinning broadly. "It leads to another tunnel. We can hide in there."

"Haste, then," Nuada said. "They are almost upon us."

They bustled in as silently as possible. They had barely vacated the

Northern Line when they heard the heavy tramp of many feet drawing closer. From the noise and the time it took them to pass, Ruth guessed there must have been at least five hundred, possibly on their way to fight the Tuatha Dé Danann. She hoped that meant the Fomorii forces they were joining were doing badly.

At one point, it sounded like the Fomorii were coming down the connecting tunnel so they all hurried several hundred yards away and flattened themselves against the wall, desperately trying to shield their torches. After a couple of minutes, Ruth's pounding heart subsided a little.

The tunnel had patently not been used for a long time. Most of the tracks had been torn up, and the occasional signs appeared to date back to the earliest days of the tube system in the late nineteenth century. Ancient junction boxes rusted against bricks covered in the white salt of age and damp. Where the rails should have been there were numerous hummocks and rough piles that Ruth guessed were the dust-covered detritus of work on the other tunnel.

Once all the sounds of the Fomorii had faded away, they relaxed. "God, they smell so bad!" Ruth protested.

"They are being driven by their Caraprix." Nuada was looking back and forth along the tunnel. "When the Caraprix take an active role in direction it stimulates a powerful aroma."

"Even in you?" she said acidly.

"We, of course," he said with a smile, "smell divine."

They set off back the way they had come, but after they had been walking for five minutes it became apparent to Ruth they had gone past the connecting tunnel in the dark. "We must have missed it," she called out to the others.

"I didn't see anything," Veitch said, much to Ruth's irritation. "Let's carry on a little way."

Three minutes later their torches began to illuminate irregular shapes in the distant gloom. "Look, it's a station," Ruth sighed when they were closer. "I told you we'd gone past it."

Veitch held up his torch to read the sign over the platform. "King William Street?" he said. "Never heard of it."

"It must be one they don't use any more," Ruth said. "There are quite a few, aren't there? But you're right, I've never heard of this one."

Veitch's torch illuminated dirty, broken tiles and some torn, peeling posters. One said *Light's Out!* Another, *Loose Lips Sink Ships*.

"Looks like it was used as an air raid shelter in the Second World War," Ruth said.

"We need more wood," Lugh said. "The torches are burning through quickly."

"There might be some here," Veitch said. "Send your men in to check."

Lugh eyed him darkly; this sounded very much like an order, but then he motioned for three of the Tuatha Dé Danann to investigate.

"What time do you reckon it is?" Veitch said, leaning against the edge of the platform.

Ruth shrugged. "My body clock says eleven . . . midnight . . . Maybe later."

"We should rest."

Ruth was glad Veitch had raised it. She felt exhausted, but she was afraid to bring it up herself in case the others thought her weak. Nuada nodded in agreement and passed the information to his followers.

"We're close enough to spare a couple of hours," Veitch continued. "And we'd be no use to anyone if we turned up at the Big Bastard's door completely knackered."

"You don't have to convince me." Ruth clambered wearily on to the platform and found a spot against the wall at one end. Behind the windows of an old office she could see the torches of the Tuatha Dé Danann moving around like lazy fireflies as they searched for wood.

Nuada, Lugh and the others sat quietly at the other end of the platform, talking in low voices. Ruth was surprised when Veitch sat next to her; he didn't speak, but the fact that he was there was a loud statement. He closed his eyes and was asleep in an instant. Ruth wished she could rest just as easily, but by the time the thought had entered her head she was out.

She stirred uncomfortably, irritated by the cold surface of the hard platform floor against her behind. As her eyes flickered open when she tried to shift into a more comfortable position, she realised she couldn't have been asleep for very long at all because lights were still moving behind the office windows, beautiful, like a golden snowstorm, lulling her back to sleep.

She was so tired, enjoying the comfort of rest. Her limbs felt light and airy, after the leaden weight of the long march. Her troubled mind was cocooned in a fuzzy, yellow warmth. Yet as she tried to snuggle back into her pleasant state, she was annoyed to feel something nagging at the back of her mind. With annoyance, she tried to damp it down, but it wouldn't go away. The warmth slipped further away. Finally she realised the only way she was going to get any sleep was to examine it; something about what she had seen.

She opened her tired eyes again. The platform and track was quiet and still. The Tuatha Dé Danann sat in close conversation. Veitch was beside her asleep. Nothing out of the ordinary.

She tried again to get back to sleep, but it was lost to her now. The feelings of alarm wound up a notch. There *was* something there. What was she missing?

She looked around once more before settling on the light in the windows. She pulled herself shakily to her feet. Still half asleep, she focused hazily on the light shimmering through the panes. Earlier she had thought of it as fireflies, and now it seemed even more like that. Through her daze it was hypnotic in its dreaminess. Fireflies. No, more like butterflies. And then she had it. At first she felt shock, and then a deep iciness, before she was running along the platform to raise the alarm.

A face loomed up against the glass, hollow cheeked, contorted with terror, a sight made worse by it being the face of a god. The eyes bulged, pleading with her, with anyone, and then it snapped away as if it was on elastic.

The clouds of golden moths ebbed and flowed, fluttering against the glass, caught in the torchlight.

"No more!" Lugh was yelling. "How many Golden Ones must depart this day?" All the Tuatha Dé Danann looked on in horror, paralysed by the realisation that even away from the field of battle their kind were being wiped from existence in a manner they could never have realised in all their time.

Veitch powered past Ruth, his sword already out. "No rest for the bleedin' wicked." He levelled a flying kick at the office door. It burst from its hinges.

The three Tuatha Dé Danann lay dying on the floor, their bodies slowly breaking up. All around grey shapes flitted, although at first Ruth thought they were shadows cast by the flickering torches that lay where they had fallen.

While she was transfixed by the activity, Veitch was backpedalling along the floor where he had fallen and then propelled himself to his feet with undue haste, his sword waving in front of him. "Shit," he muttered.

"What is it?" Ruth asked.

Four figures burst from the doorway, their mouths held wide in an eerie silent scream, grey like mist, and at times just as insubstantial before there was the faintest shift and they took on a terrifying substance. They moved like light reflected off mirrors; Ruth only had an instant to take in their appearances: all women, beautiful in a haunted way, dressed in shrouds, their hair flying wildly behind them as if they had been caught in a storm. Ruth had a flash of talons like an animal's, of too-long teeth, sharp and pointed, and then they swept by her and she had only a second to throw herself out of the way.

The talons caught in her hair, ripped out a chunk, but she had avoided being caught; she had evaded those teeth.

"The Baobhan Sith!" one of the Tuatha Dé Danann said in fearful awe.

But Ruth didn't need reminding of the bloodsucking creatures that had attacked them on the lonely Cumbrian hills when Tom had betrayed them.

"They *did* have bleedin' guards posted!" Veitch threw himself out of the way of clutching hands, rolled and jumped to his feet. He lashed out with his sword, but it either passed through the creature or the Baobhan Sith avoided the blade so quickly Ruth didn't see it.

Veitch grabbed her wrist and pulled her out of the way of another of them. He chopped with his sword again. This time the spectral woman became mist as the blade cut through her, reforming as it passed.

"Christ, there's no fighting them!" He yanked Ruth hard and they both fell off the platform, landing with a bone-jolting impact on the hard stones of the track.

The Baobhan Sith moved up and down the platform wildly, twisting and turning in an imaginary wind, avoiding any attack the Tuatha Dé Danann made with any of their weapons. As Ruth watched in horror one of the creatures distended its mouth seemingly wider than its head and the razor sharp teeth folded out like kitchen knives. It flew towards one of Lugh's soldiers and clamped on his neck, the teeth snapping through the substance to suck up the god's essence; and however much he threw himself around or lashed out with his sword it could not be removed. A moment later the golden moths began to fly.

"Let's get out of here," Veitch said quietly.

"We can't leave them!"

"We stay here, we die. There's too much at stake." He could see she was still unconvinced and added, "They'll soon catch up with us."

The Tuatha Dé Danann already had formed a phalanx and were backing rapidly across the platform. One of the Baobhan Sith tore another from their midst.

"Look at that," Veitch said. "No point dragging our heels. Just bleedin' run."

He made to grab Ruth's hand again, but she had jumped up to snatch a torch from the edge of the platform where it had fallen. Then she was sprinting at his side, glancing over her shoulder. One of the Baobhan Sith had left the platform to pursue them. "They're coming!" Ruth gasped.

Their breath formed white clouds in the cold. Ruth was afraid she wouldn't have any energy left to escape. The ground was uneven, threatening to trip them, and the motion put the torch in danger of going out so that she had to shield it with her body. She didn't dare look over her shoulder any more because she couldn't go any faster if she tried.

"Which way? Where's the other tunnel?" Her thoughts fell over each other in her panic. *This is a nightmare.* The words blazed white against the background darkness of her mind.

"What's that?" Veitch was pointing into the shadows ahead; the edge in his voice turned her panic up a notch.

No more, she prayed.

There was movement on the ground ahead, not just in one spot, but in many. The soil and stone of the track floor was moving in little piles. Obliquely, Ruth realised it was the strange hummocks she had taken to be building rubble.

From one of them, a grey hand rose slowly.

Ruth couldn't restrain a brief shriek. They skidded to a halt. The hand became an arm as the stones and soil sloughed away. Across the myriad other humps the same scene was being played out as the Baobhan Sith emerged from their resting places. Earth showered from their wild hair and fell from their open mouths as they levered their shoulders up, then their torsos. Their faces turned towards Veitch and Ruth, all of them shrieking in silence, scattered from wall to wall and away into the shrouded distance. Ruth was too terrified to consider how many of them were waiting there in the tunnel.

The sheer weight of terror elicited by the Baobhan Sith emerging left Veitch and Ruth rooted for an instant. But then Veitch shoved Ruth forward and they were sprinting once more, throwing themselves into a wild dance away from grasping hands.

Behind them, the first to emerge were already on their feet, shaking off the lethargy of slumber, flitting in pursuit. Ahead, the hummocks in gradual upheaval stretched on forever.

The Baobhan Sith rose up with increasing swiftness, and however fast Veitch and Ruth ran it was obvious they would soon be surrounded. Talons bit deeply into Ruth's ankle. She yelped as Veitch's flashing sword forced the creature to become insubstantial. They continued to drive forward, knowing that if they slowed an instant they would be lost, but already the Baobhan Sith were massing ahead of them.

A few seconds later the route ahead was blocked with shimmering bodies. "Shit." Veitch ground to a halt and whirled round, his eyes feral. The Baobhan Sith swept up from all sides.

Ruth jabbed a finger excitedly. "There's the tunnel!"

To get to it would mean passing through the flickering creatures. Veitch gave Ruth a reassuring smile. "Head down. Stay right behind me. Don't let them get a hold of you."

He barrelled into the mass of them, lashing his sword in front of him. Ruth kept exactly in his step, her heart thundering as hands clutched at her clothes; some caught but were pulled free; others ripped through her hair without getting any purchase.

Just as they were about to dive into the tunnel, one of the Baobhan Sith latched on to Veitch. Ruth saw the transformation from mist to solid form as its mouth tore wide to expose the unbelievably pointed teeth. The powerful jaw muscles heaved as the head swept down to Veitch's neck.

At the last moment Ruth jabbed the Spear into the creature's mouth. The fangs smashed down on it and the thing shimmered into nothingness. Veitch dragged Ruth into the small tunnel.

Though breathless, they couldn't slow down. They could feel the presence of the Baobhan Sith at their backs like an icy shadow. In the main tunnel they headed southbound, acutely aware that they might run into more Fomorii and be trapped between the two forces.

The torch cast barely enough light to see, and it was hard running across the uneven tracks without tripping, but the Baobhan Sith drove on ceaselessly.

"They're not going to let up, are they?" Ruth gasped. "What do we do—keep running until we're face to face with Balor?" At the mention of the name the air temperature noticeably dropped several degrees and a deep, resonant rustling, like whispering voices, rose up on the edge of their hearing. Ruth resolved not to say that name again.

"We've got to lose those grey bastards before we can do anything." Veitch spotted another side tunnel, this time leading to the northbound tracks. He headed towards it. They continued southbound, both beginning to flag. A hundred yards further on they came upon a doorway leading to the conduit for power lines and fibre optics. The Baobhan Sith were almost upon them as Veitch wrenched the door open, thrust Ruth inside and slammed it shut behind him. He jammed his sword into the frame and twisted it so the handle wouldn't open.

They could sense the Baobhan Sith moving beyond the door as they collapsed against the wall and sucked in mouthfuls of air. "That should hold them until they raise the alarm." Veitch rubbed his tired eyes. "Good job they're morons with no initiative."

"We better get moving before the Fomorii turn up," Ruth said. "I tell you, I could do with a sleep."

"We'll get some downtime once we find a safe place to hole up."

"I suppose we've lost the others?"

"We can't go back for them, can we? They'll be there." A heavy pause. "At the end. You can count on it."

The conduit lay beyond another door. It was lined with cables and wires, but they could walk along it at a stoop. Every time they came to a branching conduit, they turned, right, then left. After half an hour they found another inspection door and exited into a tunnel.

"Well, I have no bleedin' idea where we are now." Veitch headed left, hoping it would lead them back towards the City.

"All we need to do is find another station." Ruth eyed the torch worryingly; the flame was burning very low.

They continued along the tunnel for a little way until their path was blocked by a large, dark object: a tube train. "Don't worry—we can squeeze by it," Veitch said.

But as they edged along the side of the train, Ruth looked up and cried out in shock. The torchlight revealed the dirty windows were streaked with blood in explosive, paint-gun patterns. Inside she could just make out the shapes of bodies. It was hard to tell from her perspective, but they didn't appear to be in one piece. The sour-apple stink of decomposition was thick in the air.

Veitch noticed it too. "The doors have been torn off," he noted.

Ruth could just make out small figures too, and frail, old ones. She fought back tears; the terrible waste still tore a hole in her heart. "The Fomorii must have moved out across the city through the network when their leader was reborn."

Veitch peered in through the ragged doorway. "Poor bastards. Didn't stand a chance."

From ahead came the tramp of many feet. Ruth and Veitch were halfway along the carriage, squeezed tight against the dirty, oily walls. They wouldn't be able to make it back to the open tunnel before the Fomorii arrived.

"In here," Veitch whispered. He crawled up through the doorway into the body of the carriage, pulling out his handkerchief and pressing it against his face. Ruth shook her head furiously in primal disgust, but she knew it was the best option. She screwed her eyes shut, covered her nose and mouth and followed Veitch in.

He guided her along the floor away from the open doors, but even with her eyes shut she had a visceral image of the scene around her. She brushed against hard and lifeless things that swung or shifted dramatically with a soft, wet sound. The floor was puddled with a thick, sticky substance; though her mouth was covered, the stench made her retch. Her stomach heaved time and again, and she didn't know how she managed to keep it silent, but then her eyes filled with tears at the thought of what had happened and somehow that helped.

Veitch took the torch, which was so low it barely cast any light, and said he'd shield it with "something he'd found"; Ruth didn't ask what that was. They'd barely ended their exchange when the carriage rocked madly as the Fomorii barged past on either side. The two of them slid backwards and forwards on the slick floor. Ruth had to jam her hands and feet against the sides of the seats to stop herself skidding back towards the doorway. She almost lost her grip when Veitch slammed his boot heel into her face, but a moment after that the violent movement subsided. They exited the carriage a little sooner than safety would have suggested, but even then they couldn't escape the stink from their fouled clothes; nor the thought of all the atrocities that had been committed.

A little further on they smelled smoke, and as they progressed they realised they could make out a faint glow tinting the tunnel walls. They moved in closer to one wall and edged forward cautiously. The smoke grew thicker, the light brighter.

Round a bend in the tunnel they glimpsed several fires burning. After so many hours of darkness it took a while for their eyes to adjust to the glare, and when they did they pulled back quickly. Several Fomorii were moving amongst piles of burning rubbish. It was obviously some kind of checkpoint or guard camp.

Veitch cursed quietly. "We're never going to get past that."

"I bet they've got camps like that all around the perimeter of their core area."

"There was a door further back. We *will* find a way past the bastards."

"I wish we could get some of that fire." Ruth examined what remained of the torch.

They retraced their steps to an unmarked door almost lost in the gloom. Veitch used his dagger to smash the lock and they slipped into a clean corridor that led on to a large thoroughfare. It had a hard Tarmac surface and there were military-style stencils on the wall pointing to locations obviously written in code.

"These must be the tunnels the Government set up in the fifties and sixties in case of a nuclear strike," Ruth said. "A good way to save all the great and good and leave the poor bastards to die. Probably a favour. Who'd want to live in a world filled with politicians, the military, businessmen and the aristocracy?"

"We're well and truly bleedin' lost now," Veitch said angrily. "Why did it have to be me who fucked up again?"

When he was like that there was no consoling him. "Pick a direction," she said dismally. "It'll take us somewhere."

His anger grew more intense as it became obvious they were moving off the beaten track. The well-tended road gave way to rough ground, the tunnel became unfinished: bare brick, then girders and scaffolding, before they came to a thick barrier of sleepers and planks.

Veitch smashed his fist against the wall, as hard as if he was punching someone in the face, but his rage wiped away any pain he might have felt. When he turned, Ruth could see his knuckles were ragged.

She cowered as he stormed around searching for something to attack. "We fucked up!" he yelled.

"We can go—"

"No! We! Can't!" His furious face thrust an inch away from hers. Suddenly she was terrified; she couldn't see any sign of the funny, gentle Veitch she had known from the quieter times they had shared.

She took a step back, but didn't show her fear. "Pull yourself together."

"What?" His eyes ranged wildly as though she wasn't there.

"I said, pull yourself together. You're the hero here—"

"Hero! I'm the bleedin' loser! Same as I always was!" He flailed his arm, obviously some sort of primal gesture to wave her away. But instead he caught the torch and knocked it from her weak grip. It smashed into pieces on the floor, the flame now a faint flicker along one of the shards.

"Ryan!" Ruth dropped to her knees desperately, but there was nothing to save.

"Oh, fuck! Now look what I've done!" He ran over and kicked the wall hard.

Ruth only saw what happened next from the corner of her eye as she bent down trying to pull the remaining pieces of wood together to keep the flame going. Weakened by his punches, the wall collapsed. Veitch plunged forward into a gulf beyond and a shower of rubble fell down reclosing the opening.

Ruth covered her head until the fall had ended, but none of the debris touched her. She looked at the faint flame and then slowly took in her surroundings.

"Oh, Ryan," she whispered. And then the tears came in force.

When she finally regained control of her emotions, Ruth wiped her eyes and resolved to find a way out of her predicament. She wasn't going to be beaten. She certainly wasn't going to die down there. Balor had to be beaten, humanity had to be saved and, more importantly—she had to laugh at that strange truth—she had to see Church again. Even if she had to crawl along pitch-black tunnels to find a way out.

The flame was barely more than a candle's height on the splinters of wood. It became trimmed briefly with blue and then began to gutter.

Here we go, she thought. *Prepare yourself*.

Then, as the flame finally began to die, she became aware of other lights in the dark. At first she dismissed it as an optical illusion caused by the sharp contrast of shadow and light on her retina. The flame became the size of her fingernail.

Almost gone now.

But the other lights remained; tiny, glittering stars sweeping across the firmament. She scanned them curiously, and then, just as the flame finally died she realised what she was seeing and her blood ran cold.

Darkness swept up around her and she heard the sharp skittering sound as the first rat moved forward.

Veitch fell fifteen feet into freezing water, slamming his head hard on the way down. The cold and wet kept him conscious, but the dark was so all-consuming he couldn't tell up from down. The water came up to his thighs and by stretching out slowly on either side he realised he was in some kind of small tunnel or gully as wide as the span of his arms. He spent ten minutes trying to find where he had fallen and attempting to climb back up, but it was impossible to see, and more rubble kept falling. Dejected and afraid he might be pinned by another collapse, he began to wade wearily forward.

He continued for what he guessed was around an hour, pausing occasionally to rest against the wall and catch minutes of microsleep. He couldn't even feel his lower legs and he wondered how long it would be before hypothermia set in. But whatever set him apart as a Brother of Dragons made him resilient, helped him to heal; he'd keep going, he thought dismally. He hated himself. He hated himself so much he considered lying down in the water and drowning himself, but it wasn't in his nature. So he had to continue with the infinitely worse burden of his guilt, thinking about what he had done to Ruth, punishing himself by images of her wandering along inky corridors until the inevitable end came. It had all been his fault; he could almost have scripted it.

The water began to rise soon after, a half-hour later it was up to chest height. He was racked by convulsive shivers, drifting in and out of a fugue state brought on by the cold. Gradually he became aware that the tunnel was becoming increasingly steep. By the time he had grasped how sharply it was falling away, his feet would no longer give him purchase and suddenly he was sliding down. He barely had time to take a breath before the water washed above his head, and then he was rattling down an incline, faster and faster, until it became a vertical drop.

The rush of water burst out into thin air. He could vaguely feel his legs bicycling as he plunged thirty feet into more water, deeper this time and rushing in a torrent. One random thought flickered through his head: Ruth's beautiful face as she told him about London's old River Fleet, now buried beneath the city as it rushed down towards the Thames. And then the impact stole his consciousness and the water closed over his head.

chapter nineteen
in the belly of the beast

Wave Sweeper was moored not far from Southend when Church came sweeping down from the northwest with the remainder of the Tuatha Dé Danann force. The journey skirting Greater London and through the green fields of rural Essex had passed in a golden blur. He was accompanied by Tom, the Bone Inspector and Niamh, but he didn't recognise any of the other gods, although he sensed many of them were not sympathetic to the cause of the *Fragile Creatures*. He wondered why his particular task force was burdened with more dissenters than the other two, but Tom wasn't too concerned when he raised the matter.

On board it felt strangely good to be back in the familiar detachment of Otherworld with its heightened sensations, away from all the suffering of the real world. There was an atmosphere of stillness that eased the anxiety coiled in his chest; even the sun was shining brighter than on the shore. He made his way to the rail where he quietly enjoyed the tang of the sea and the warmth on his skin, until Tom joined him.

"You're going to bring me down, aren't you?" Church said without looking round.

"I'm the last person to advocate an injection of reality, but—"

"I know: responsibility, obligation, and all that. Is this the standard pre-crisis pep talk?"

"Something like that." Tom leaned against the rail, facing the sun, his eyes closed. "You know, I can remember the days of my youth as clearly as if they were yesterday. Hundreds of years—although it's not really, not by Otherworld time. But it's still a long, long time and so many experiences." He took a deep breath. "I smell the blossom in the garden of my childhood, so powerful, like incense and fruit wrapped up together. I remember distinctly the way the sun-light caught the dew on a spiderweb in an old yew tree, one dawn when I had crept out of the house before anyone had awoken. The rosewater on the neck of the first woman I ever loved. The touch of her fingers on the back of my neck." He shook his head dreamily. "Amazing."

Church watched Tom curiously. He had never heard him speak so tenderly, nor talk of any of the happy times in his human life before his transformation at the hands of the Tuatha Dé Danann Queen. It was as if he had wanted to keep them secure from the horrors that had assailed him since.

"Now I begin, for the first time in many years, the memories come thick and fast." Tom's eyes glistened in the sun. "Days of tenderness, composing songs and poems. Nights watching the stars over the Eildon Hills. My mother and father, at Christmas, leading the singing before the fire. My best friend James, playing hide-and-seek in the kitchens, then later courting the girls from the village together." He turned fully to Church with no attempt to hide his tears. "Remember your own bright moments, Jack, and hold them in your heart. They will keep you warm in the coldest nights."

"Why are you telling me these things?"

"Nothing I could say would help you to comprehend right now. You will understand everything presently."

Church tried to glean some insight from Tom's face, but he was taken aback to see it was packed with complex emotions. For so long, Tom had appeared to have no feeling in him at all; as inhuman as he always believed himself to be. It felt like a sea change had come over him, even in the last hour. "What's happened to you?"

"Time has come a-calling. Finally."

Church could see he was not going to get anything out of the Rhymer; infuriatingly, his friend's unexplained words worked their way deep into his mind, where they set off a troubling resonance.

While he wrestled with his thoughts, he scanned the deck where the crew busied themselves for departure. The main Tuatha Dé Danann force had all disappeared below with their weapons. Manannan stood at the wheel, overseeing the activity. He raised a hand in greeting when he saw Church.

"I hope you're telling him what a pathetic little runt he is." The Bone Inspector's gruff voice shattered the mood in an instant. He leaned on his staff, the wind whipping his grey hair.

Tom snapped, "No—"

"I was talking to him." The Bone Inspector nodded towards Church.

"Don't start with your useless prattling." Tom eyed him murderously.

"You may have been honoured by the Culture in the times of my ancestors, but that doesn't mean I can't give you a good whupping with my staff." The Bone Inspector underlined his point by twirling the staff around his arms as if it were alive.

"Great. Two old people fighting," Church muttered. "It'll be like watching your granny barge her way into the bread queue."

"Don't forget," Tom cautioned the Bone Inspector, "the Culture dies out with you." He smiled sadistically.

"Well, that's where you're wrong. I've been making some plans—"

"Don't you think that's a little premature?" Church said.

"You shut up and concentrate on your job, you lanky-arsed weasel." The Bone Inspector returned his attention to Tom, nodding superciliously. "Yes, I've been thinking. Now the seasons have turned and all the materialistic, logic-obsessed bastards have had a rude awakening, it might be time for a reflowering of the Culture. I can see the colleges now, maybe at Glastonbury and Anglesey, like we used to have in the old, old days. Passing on the wisdom to a new generation of bright-eyed—"

"You think you'd make a good teacher?" Tom sneered. "After all that time sleeping in ditches they'll need to hose you down with industrial cleaning fluid just to get somebody in a room with you."

The Bone Inspector scowled. "At least I know my arse from my elbow."

"Yes, but do you know your arse from your mouth? I think not."

Church sighed and made to pacify them, but they turned on him so venomously he backed away. "Okay, go ahead, knock yourself out," he said tartly. "Literally, if possible."

The bickering ended when Niamh walked over. Tom gave a restrained, deferential bow, but the Bone Inspector simply looked away, as if he were alone on deck and lost in a reverie.

"The Master is preparing to sail," she said. She glanced round to ensure she could not be overheard, then added quietly, "Taranis oversaw the arrival of a container brought aboard by Nuada's personal guard. It was stowed in a section of the hold where access is restricted only to the Master and Taranis. Those faithful to Nuada stand guard without."

"I think I saw it," Church said. "Was it a large wooden chest with bands of iron around it and a gold clasp?"

"That may be how you perceived it." Niamh looked from one to the other. "I believe it to be the Wish-Hex."

"They won't even let you near it?" Church asked.

She bit her lip. "I could attempt . . . It would cost . . ." She shook her head. "No matter. There is too much at stake."

Church looked to Tom. "When do you think they'll detonate it?"

"When it's close to Balor and they're well away."

"Not on board ship?"

"Good Lord, no!" Tom looked horrified. "And lose Wave Sweeper? This isn't just a collection of timber and nails, you know!"

Church took Niamh's hand and led her to one side. "I know this is hard for you, working against your own people, but if there's anything you can do—"

"Do not feel you have to ask anything of me, Jack. I do what I do freely because I believe in the rightness of this course. And I believe in you." She looked down at where her slim, cool hand still lay in his. "You have changed my existence, Jack. And to one of the Golden Ones, who are as constant as the stars, that is a humbling and profound thing."

"I don't see how I could have, Niamh," he protested. "I'm nothing out of the ordinary."

She leaned forward to kiss him gently on the cheek. "Things are coming to a head, Jack. All will be made clear soon."

Her smile was filled with such deep love he was left floundering. She turned and drifted away amongst the frantic activity of the crew, an oasis of calm and dignity.

The ship hove to soon after and made its way into the Estuary. Though it still remained a tranquil place, the strain on all who sailed was apparent. Tom rejoined Church at the prow, looking around nervously. "Now if we can get to that pep talk without any interruptions from that old curmudgeon . . ." He pointed to the makeshift rucksack hanging from Church's shoulder. "You have the Wayfinder?"

Church removed the old lantern with the flickering blue flame that had guided him through the earliest days of the mystery to show him. "But I don't know what use it's going to be. I was thinking of leaving it here. I don't want to be carrying any more weight than necessary."

Tom shook his head furiously. "There is still one talisman to find." His smile suggested this was another long-kept secret he was relieved to be revealing. "The biggest one of all."

"Where is it?"

"Somewhere near our destination. You recall when we summoned the Celtic dead for guidance in Scotland? They said: *You must find the Luck of the Land if you are ever to unleash the true power of the people.*"

"Yes," Church said suspiciously, "and you said you had no idea what they were talking about."

"At that *exact* moment, I did not. But it came to me soon after. There was only one thing it could be."

Church bared his teeth. "And you didn't see fit to tell me until now?"

Tom shrugged dismissively. "The time was not right."

"Tom . . ."

"All right," he snapped. "I wanted only you to know. And I left it to this late stage because I did not want you to confide in any of the others, as you undoubtedly would have done with your various romantic liaisons," he added sniffily. "And then it would have been all over the place."

"All right. No need to act like my granddad."

"It is my role to be—"

"All right, all right! What is the bloody Luck of the Land?"

"The Luck of the Land is the severed head of Bran the Blessed. He was a great hero, and the closest of the Golden Ones to humanity. He knew about the destiny of the *Fragile Creatures* and he was even prepared to sacrifice himself to see us achieve it. The old stories tell how he was murdered by a poisoned arrow. On his deathbed, he told his followers to cut off his head, yet even removed, it could still eat and talk. It was brought back to London and buried beneath the Tower, where it became the source of the land's power. Of humanity's power. Another myth said King Arthur sought it out as the source of his own strength. You can see the symbolism."

"So it's linked directly to the Blue Fire? That's what all the Arthur myths mean, isn't it?"

"Correct."

Church looked out at the quiet, dead countryside that bordered the river. "But what can it *do*?"

"The Celts revered severed heads, believing them to have great magical power. In their view, the head is the source of the soul. They knew the truth at the heart of this legend. And don't forget . . ."

". . . myths and legends are the secret history of the land. I'll be happy when I don't hear that phrase again."

"The head has great power, both in real terms, and symbolically. It encompasses everything you have discovered about the Blue Fire."

"So, in the day and a half we have left, we have to avoid Balor and about a million Fomorii in the heart of their power, locate this head somewhere under the Tower of London—like it's going to be just lying around ready to be picked up—and then find some way to use it or activate it or whatever the hell you're supposed to do with it?"

"Well, you didn't expect it to be easy, did you?" Tom said curtly. "If you only had to waltz in there and chop off a head or two they could have got anyone to do it."

"I'll take that as a vote of confidence," Church said moodily.

All that remained of the Thames Barrier flood defence system were columns of concrete and twisted steel jutting out of the slow-moving water. It looked as if it had been smashed into pieces by a giant fist. The rubble just beneath the surface formed a treacherous defence that would have sunk most ships coming up the river, but Manannan's magical skill picked the only path through. It slowed them down a little, but they were still on course to be in the heart of London by noon.

As they progressed further into the eastern fringes of the capital, the mood on Wave Sweeper darkened considerably. The pleasant sunshine was soon blocked out by continually rolling black clouds whipped by the powerful winds circulating the city. It brought the temperature down several degrees while adding a permanent gloom to the cityscape. Vast swathes of southeast London were burning, bringing huge clouds of smoke rolling across the river. Church fastened a scarf across his mouth, but the foul smell of charred plastics and rubber still stung his throat.

As he saw the city up close for the first time, Church thought of all the people he knew who lived there, his old friends, like Dale, who had done so much to try to lift his spirits in the dark weeks after Marianne's death. Had they survived? Had they suffered? It was too depressing to consider, and he was almost pleased when Tom grunted, "Not as bad as the Great Fire."

"Things always were better in the good old days, weren't they?"

The ship suddenly lurched dramatically to the starboard. Church gripped the rail to avoid being thrown into the grey waters. A second later it was swinging back the other way. "What's going on?" he shouted over the wild activity that had erupted on deck. The crew struggled to restrain any item that wasn't lashed down, while Manannan fought with the wheel to keep Wave Sweeper steady.

Tom pointed into the water further upstream. A black, sinuous shape stitched white surf into boiling water.

"Their guard dog," Tom said.

"Dogs," Church corrected. Two more serpentine shapes rolled in the waves. Their attacks were throwing up so much backwash the ship was buffeted back and forth. They were tiny compared to the monster that had attempted to sink Wave Sweeper in Otherworld, but their speed and random, darting movements made them equally dangerous.

The ship sloughed towards the north bank before executing a sharp turn towards the south, rapid manoeuvres that no real-world craft would ever be able to complete. Members of the crew sprawled across the desk, clutching for handholds. Church and Tom were drenched by the eruptions of water as the serpents threw themselves against the sides, either in an attempt to hole the ship or to turn it over.

A shadow fell across them. Church knew what it was before he looked up. The serpent's head towered over them, the same terrifying features he had glimpsed in the sea off Skye: a flattened cobra head, yellowish eyes glowing with an alien intelligence, strange whiskers like a catfish tufting from its mouth, which contained several rows of lethal teeth.

It hovered for a second or two, during which time Church felt the faintest contact with an intelligence that fizzed in the back of his head. He knew what it was going to do before the head darted down towards them, jaws prised wide. Church rolled over and pulled the Sword from its scabbard, jabbing it upwards towards the descending darkness. It impaled the head as if it were slipping through crude oil. The serpent made a high-pitched mechanical whine as it thrashed madly. Church felt an electric jolt in that deep connection the serpent had made with him. An instant later it transformed into a searing scream. Caledfwlch's particular powers ensured that death always resulted from the slightest injury it inflicted.

Church tried to retreat from the bond the serpent had made with him, but it was locked in place. He felt its life force flare briefly, then dwindle down into a dark tunnel before finally winking out. Its body slipped back into the water, lifeless.

The shock of feeling the beast's final moment left Church dazed and distressed. Tom shook him roughly to bring him round, but the sensations stayed with him like a shadow in his subconscious.

Wave Sweeper continued to lurch from side to side. By then the Tuatha Dé Danann forces had made it on to the deck with several silver weapons resembling harpoons plugged into grenade launchers. Three of them manhandled one to the rail and launched it.

Lightning crackled out across the water. It headed towards the north bank, and then made an unnatural dogleg to the right to strike one of the serpents as it attempted to dive. The creature burst from the water, stinking foully as it charred. A moment later, its shrivelled form drifted downstream.

The remaining serpent was retreating as the Tuatha Dé Danann struck. It was eradicated just as quickly.

Tom saw Church eyeing the weapons cautiously. "Yes," he said. "They are too powerful to be in hands that cannot be trusted."

Manannan forged on quickly along the centre of the channel. Church watched the banks intently, but he could see no sign of any Fomorii threat. Yet the air of incipient danger grew more and more intense until deep, rhythmic vibrations began to run through Church's legs; it was accompanied by a distant noise, almost too low to be heard beneath the wind. Something about it made his stomach turn. "What is that?" he asked.

Tom stared into the water darkly. "The beating of Balor's heart." The wind whipped at him.

Soon after the smoke and river fog closed in around the ship, limiting vision to a few yards ahead. Manannan let Wave Sweeper drift slowly. The crew remained silent, listening intently for any sound of attack.

Thoom. Thoom. Thoom. The beating had grown a little louder. Church felt it in the pit of his stomach.

And then the obscuring mists parted and Church's blood ran cold. A black tower soared up from the northern bank, its top lost in the clouds above. It rested on the remnants of the Tower of London, the ancient fortress that symbolised the defence of the nation, and was constructed like a termite nest from rubble, crushed vehicles, plastics, household refuse, girders torn from other buildings and anything else that came to hand. Slowly Church looked up the structure as far as he could see. Fires blazed at various points, some inside seen through ragged windows, some on the surface where the leftovers of the twenty-first century still burned. It was a sinister mockery of the gleaming skyscrapers that rose out of the City's financial district only yards away, another source of unbridled power.

As he watched, there was movement through the windows and a second later winged Fomorii burst out in a massive swarm. They swooped up as one, then hurtled down towards Wave Sweeper.

The Tuatha Dé Danann were prepared. The harpoons that had made short shrift of the serpents were hooked upwards and unleashed. Lightning crackled across the sky, tearing holes in the Fomorii swarm before the harpoons were drawn back, reloaded and fired again.

Some of the Fomorii made it through and engaged with the Tuatha Dé Danann in fierce fighting across the deck. Church ran into the fray wielding Caledfwlch. Wherever he went the Tuatha Dé Danann stepped aside deferentially. The Fomorii he encountered shrivelled in the air like dry autumn leaves and fluttered into nothingness on the wet boards.

But the Fomorii were proving too numerous. Many of the Tuatha Dé Danann were driven over the rails into the river or carried off into the black tower to meet an undoubtedly hideous fate. Others were torn apart as the winged menace descended on them like raptors. Manannan kept the ship going at full speed, steering it as far towards the south bank as he could without running aground.

A difficult course had to be navigated through the remains of the shattered bridges—London, Southwark, Blackfriars and Waterloo—but eventually they rounded a bend in the river and the swarms of Fomorii began to fall back.

Finally, the aerial assault ended. Church slumped against the mast, exhausted. "I can't believe they've left us alone."

Tom, who had kept well out of the trouble, replied, "It is just a lull, a regrouping. They will be back in force soon."

"Then we better get to where we're going quickly."

The parade of broken bridges continued apace: Westminster, Lambeth, Vauxhall, Chelsea. But then the familiar site of the Battersea Park Peace Pagoda loomed up out of the smoke, reminding Church of Sundays spent walking there with Marianne. Finally the remains of Albert Bridge came into view, as misty as the day when it all started for Church so many months before.

He felt a brief *frisson* as the images flooded into his mind: the figure washing his head in the water, the first meeting with Ruth, the trip beneath the bridge and his first encounter with one of the Fomorii before it murdered Maurice Gibbons.

"If I'd known then what I know now . . ." he said.

"Be thankful you *don't* know what lies ahead," Tom said darkly.

As they prepared to drop anchor, Church headed below deck to find Niamh so he could say goodbye to her; he felt he owed her that at least. He searched for fifteen minutes with a number of Tuatha Dé Danann pointing him this way and that. Eventually he saw her emerging from a cabin in an area set aside for the Tuatha Dé Danann force. He called her name and was instantly surprised by what he saw on her face: unmistakable shame. She attempted to walk away as if she had not heard him, then thought better of it.

"What's wrong?" he asked, honestly concerned.

She forced a smile before leading him away from the door a few paces. "I will be allowed to accompany the small group Nuada has placed in charge of the Wish-Hex."

"To Balor? I don't think I like that. You'd be better off here."

"Why? Because you think I have not been in a dangerous situation before?"

"No, because I don't want you to get hurt." He shrugged, uncomfortable at the open way she was watching him. "The others I don't care about—"

She placed a hand on his forearm to stop him. "That makes it all worthwhile, Jack. There is no need to say any more. But I must come, for the Wish-Hex is now my responsibility, and your survival is my responsibility. If I am not there, you may die."

"Maybe—"

"That is the way it is."

The door swung open on the cabin Niamh had just exited and one of Nuada's lieutenants swaggered out. He cast a glance at Niamh, then moved lazily towards the stairs.

Church looked from him into Niamh's face, but he couldn't find the words to express the thoughts that were suddenly falling into place.

She saved him the trouble. "We all do what we can, Jack."

Deeply troubled at what he had forced upon her, Church made his way back to the deck where Tom and the Bone Inspector were waiting for him. They would be going ashore with a small group of Tuatha Dé Danann briefed by Nuada before he'd left with Lugh and Veitch. Another group would remain to guard the entrance to the tunnels so no Fomorii could come up behind them, while the remainder would stay on board Wave Sweeper to take the fight back to the enemy, as a distracting ploy more than anything.

"I want to know who's in charge," the Bone Inspector said. He patently wasn't going to accept any answer that included the Tuatha Dé Danann.

"The Brother of Dragons will lead the way," Taranis said in his usual aloof manner. "However, the Golden Ones who will be accompanying you must be free to follow their own hearts if the need arises."

Church knew what that meant—they must be free to sneak off to unleash the Wish-Hex.

While they prepared for a boat to be lowered, no one noticed the dark figure slip out from the place where he had been hiding for so long, living on the blood and meat of rats and other foul creatures. Nor did they hear the faint splash as he slipped into the cold water and swam quickly to the shore. Callow had bided his time well and now things were working out better than he could have dreamed.

The area beneath the bridge gave Church an uncomfortable feeling. Despite the fact that most of the span was missing, it was still uncommonly dark. An unpleasant atmosphere set his nerves on edge.

The Tuatha Dé Danann stood back to allow Church to search for an opening. They gathered protectively around the large chest that he knew contained the Wish-Hex. Niamh was with them, pretending to be aloof from the *Fragile Creatures*.

"I don't know how I'm going to find this," he said after five minutes wandering around the featureless area.

The Bone Inspector swore profusely. "Call yourself a leader of men?" He marched past Church and rammed his staff against a stone set into the wall on which the bridge's foundations were set. The ground fell away with a ghostly silence. "After you," he said sarcastically.

The tunnel was rough hewn, dripping with water that ran in rivulets along the edges. It was only wide enough for two people to walk side by side, though the ceiling was high enough to accommodate the Fomorii bulk. It sloped down quickly into deep shadows. Tom lit a torch they had brought with them, as did one of the Tuatha Dé Danann.

Then, when they had all steeled themselves, Church and Tom led the way, with the Bone Inspector close behind and the rest coming up at a distance as if they were barely connected.

When the tension of entering enemy territory had ebbed a little, the thought that had been troubling Church the most rose to the surface. "I've just been talking to Niamh," he whispered to Tom. "I got a hint she knows what's going to happen."

"They all do."

"I don't get it. How does that work? Even you, you're always talking darkly about what the future holds like you know it inside out."

Tom said nothing, but Church wasn't prepared to let it lie. This was fundamental.

"If everything is set in stone," he stressed to get a reaction, "what's the point?"

"It isn't like that."

"Then what is it like?"

Tom sighed. "It is beyond your perception."

"Then put it in simple terms. For a stupid old country boy." Church thought about adding a few choice words, but decided it would be unproductive.

"Those who can see the future—although that's really not the right term for it—see it as a series of snapshots, not as a movie. Sometimes there is no context. Sometimes the photos are out of order. Reading meaning in them is a dangerous business. You recall, I described it once as catching glimpses from the window of a speeding car."

"But it's still fixed."

"Nothing is fixed. Anywhere."

Church cursed quietly. "Just give it to me straight, instead of packaged around your usual—"

"Everything can be changed by the will of a strong individual. One man. Or woman. There are no rules, not at the level the great thinkers of humanity examined, anyway. Only the illusion of rules. The future runs right on like a river, but it can be turned back by someone with the right heart and drive and state of mind. What the old storybooks laughingly call a hero. The Tuatha Dé Danann pretend they know everything that's going to happen and that has happened, pretend it even to themselves, but you can see from the way they've been acting in the last few hours that in their hearts they know the truth. What they perceive might not turn out to be the way it appears, or perhaps they have missed part of the equation. Or perhaps someone like you will come along. There is a reason for free will, Jack."

Church thought about this for several minutes. It gave him a deep feeling of comfort, although he couldn't quite tell why. "Then you don't *really* know anything."

Tom remained silent for a long, uncomfortable moment. "That's not quite true. Some things are so weighed down by the monumental events around them that they might as well be set in stone."

However much Church questioned him about this, he would say no more. But Tom's words had set other thoughts in motion. Barely daring to ask, he said firmly, "Do you know who's going to betray us?"

Tom kept his eyes fixed firmly ahead.

"You do, don't you?" His anger rose quickly. After all the months of worry, Tom could have told them at any time. "Why didn't you say something? You know it could mean everything might fall apart! You've got to tell me!"

"I can't." Tom's face was unreadable.

"Even with the potential repercussions? Why not? Do you want to see us suffer?"

Tom rounded on him furiously. "Of course not! I can't tell you because there's too much that might be changed."

"How long have you known?"

"I've always known."

"Always?"

"Always. And if you'd been paying attention, you would have known too."

The words were like a slap to the face. In the space between seconds, a million memories flashed across his mind as he turned over everything he had seen and heard over the previous months. Had he missed something? Had he screwed up again? "I guess I'll know soon enough," he said with bitter resignation. "I just hope you can live with yourself when it comes out."

The tunnel followed an undulating path, the changes in the air pressure telling Church it regularly ran under the river. He had taken to holding the Wayfinder permanently aloft so the walls were painted with a sapphire wash. The tiny blue flame gave him a measure of encouragement in that dark place, and raised the spirits of Tom and the Bone Inspector too. The flame pointed dead ahead.

"Why didn't it lead us to the head before?" Church asked.

"Because it is responding to what you hold in your heart," Tom replied.

"It's alive?"

"As much as anything can be said to be alive, yes."

When they'd been walking an hour or more, the Wayfinder flame began to grow brighter. At the same time, the unnerving background beat became rapidly louder. Within ten minutes it was coming through the walls all around—BA-DOOM, BA-DOOM—a war drum marking their passage to disaster.

Two and a half hours later, the tunnel rose up, while at the same time becoming more formed, with props and stone lining the walls. The Wayfinder's flame had started to point away from the main route of the tunnel so that when they came to a large oaken door Church was prepared for it.

"Looks like we're here," he said. The door was locked, but Caledfwlch sliced through the rusty iron mechanism easily. Church looked around at the others. Tom and the Bone Inspector were grim faced, the Tuatha Dé Danann impassive, Niamh concerned and colourless; they all nodded.

He yanked open the door.

It felt like they had walked into a foundry. After the chill of the tunnel, the heat was stifling, the air suffused with the smell of acrid smoke that caught the back of their throats. The thunder of Balor's heart was almost deafening.

The stone walls and flagged floor suggested they were somewhere in the lowest level of the Tower of London. The Bone Inspector breathed deeply, despite the atmosphere. "Can you feel it? Ancient power, even though those bastards have tried to pervert it. I haven't been here for years—too many people. Should have come back sooner." He looked at Church. "This place was sacred long before they threw up this mountain of stone over the top of it. If any place can be called the heart of the country, it's here."

The Tuatha Dé Danann set the chest containing the Wish-Hex down in the middle of the room. "What *is* in that box?" Church said mockingly. Nuada's lieutenant didn't reply, didn't even acknowledge he had spoken. Church caught Niamh's eye as he turned back to the others and she gave him a secret nod. "We need to move quickly," he continued. "They might already know we're here—"

"The Wayfinder will blind Balor's perception to you, at least for a while," Tom said. "And if you hadn't brought the energy flow back to life at St. Michael's Mount you wouldn't be here at all."

Church made to follow the lantern's flame until he saw the Tuatha Dé Danann were not moving. "We shall wait here," Nuada's lieutenant said.

"I'd say we've got even less time than we thought," Church said under his breath to Tom and the Bone Inspector as they left the room.

The seething heat had them all red-faced and soaked in sweat before they had got very far along the maze of once-dank corridors. Church had visited the Tower before and had never seen any sign of that area, so he guessed it must lie beneath the zone normally open to the tourists. He had the Sword at the ready, but the entire lower level was deserted.

"They're all up top throwing rocks at the boat," the Bone Inspector said, but Church wasn't convinced.

The Wayfinder led them to a short corridor that ended in a dead end. At first sight there was nothing out of the ordinary, but then Church allowed his perceptions to shift until he could see the lines of Blue Fire running through the stone like veins, converging into the circular design of a serpent eating its own tail. He steeled himself, then placed his hand hard on the pattern. The wall ground open to reveal a shaft plunging down into the earth, the bottom lost in shadows.

The Bone Inspector leaned in to inspect it. "There are handholds cut into the stone." He tucked his staff into the back of his shirt and levered himself over the lip. "Don't know why they made these things so bloody lethal. One slip and there'll be a mess on the floor."

The Bone Inspector had disappeared from view and Tom was just about to follow when they heard the faintest sound behind them. They spun round to find the corridor filled with Fomorii. And at the head of them was a frantically fluttering mass of crows.

Church had sheathed Caledfwlch to open the doorway, but it was back in his hand in an instant. Before the first Fomorii could move, he was advancing quickly, swinging the Sword back and forth in an arc. His target was Mollecht, the leader, the most powerful. Faced with the enemy, the Sword was even more alive in his hands than he recalled. Its subtle shifts of weight forced his hand in different directions to make the most exacting of strikes, while at times he felt it squirm so hard it almost leapt from his fingers.

But before he had gone three paces, the Fomorii had closed around Mollecht to protect him. They were obviously aware of Caledfwlch's abilities, but they showed no sign of self-preservation at all. Church carved through them as they flooded forwards ceaselessly, the bodies falling then shrivelling to nothing at each cut of the blade.

Sweat rolled off him as he hacked and lunged in the sweltering heat. Eventually he began to make some headway. Soon he could see Mollecht once more, directing the Fomorii silently. It was enough to drive him to renew his efforts. He hit one high, spun round and caught another low, and then took out three with one blow. And then Mollecht stood before him once more.

But the hideous creature was prepared. As the final Fomorii fell away, Church saw the birds moving aside to open a hole that revealed the entity inside; his mind was as unable to accept it as the first time he had witnessed it at Tintagel. The energy inside the hole was already swirling and on the brink of erupting.

Tom thrust Church out of the way. The blast hit the Rhymer full on and within a second the blood was starting to seep through his pores. Church had no time to help. The Sword was tugging at his hand, as aware of the opportunity as Church himself. Mollecht had drained himself. It would be a moment or two before he had the strength to make another attack, or even to defend himself. The hole was already closing. Church drove the Sword horizontally towards the centre of it. The creature would be skewered, finally.

The dark shape exploded out of nowhere. Church only caught the briefest glimpse out of the corner of his eye before it slammed into him with force, knocking him to the hard stone floor. Caledfwlch went flying from his grip.

"Do I have to do everything round here?"

The voice stunned Church just enough to hamper his reactions, and by that time a figure had jumped on to his chest, pinning his arms over his head. He found himself looking up into the monstrous black-veined face of Callow. He was gloating in every fibre of his being.

"I want your finger, Mr. Churchill, and I want it at the knuckle. I've decided to make a necklace," Callow said gleefully.

And then the Fomorii were all around him, swamping him in darkness.

Church came round in a place that was dark and so unbearably hot he thought he was going to choke. Twisted leather bonds bound him to a splintered table fastened to an iron gear system that angled it forty-five degrees from the upright. Aches and bruises buzzed in his limbs, but beyond that he was in one piece. Scant, scarlet light was provided by a glowing brazier in one corner. As his eyes grew accustomed to the gloom, he saw with a sickening chill where he was. Cruel, sharp implements hung from a rack on one wall, reminding Church how adept the Fomorii were at torture.

The thought was knocked aside by the blunt realisation that he had failed, at the very last, after so many obstacles had been overcome; and that it wasn't even he alone who would pay the price. It was all of humanity, everyone he had ever loved.

He tore at the bonds until he was disturbed by a low groan away to his right. The figure lay like a bundle of old rags in a slowly growing pool of blood. The moonlight glow of his skin, tinged blue at his fingers, told Church he was dying. "Can you hear me?" Church asked gently.

There was no reply or movement for a second or two and then Tom tried to lever himself up on his elbow before slipping back. He made two more attempts and then managed to roll on to his back so he could look at Church. His face was covered with blood still seeping from his pores. Church felt a wash of despair.

"If there's anything you want to get off your chest, now's the time to do it," Tom said gruffly, though his voice could barely be heard above the thunderous heartbeat.

"You saved my life."

"Lot of good it did you."

"I'm sorry," Church said, "I let you down. If only I'd moved quicker."

"Nonsense." Tom coughed violently. "You have exceeded my wildest expectations. From the first time we met I could see you were the right man for the job. Oh, I know I never said it—couldn't have you getting a big head—but you were the best possible choice, Jack. The very best."

"I wish you'd said that before." Church closed his eyes, trying to deal with all the acute emotions bubbling through him. "I've still failed, though."

"You're breathing, aren't you?"

A thought sparked in Church's still awakening mind; he looked around as best he could. "Hang on. Just you and me?"

"So it seems." There was a note of caution in Tom's voice not to say any more.

Church knew how resilient the Bone Inspector was. If he had managed to evade the Fomorii, there was still a slim chance. "How long was I out?" he said with renewed enthusiasm.

"I would say it's getting on for dawn. Not long to the feast of Samhain. The gates will be opening soon. The Heart of Shadows will get all the power he needs." He coughed then added quickly, "Don't mention its name. Not here, not this close to it. The repercussions might be . . ." His voice faded.

"The Sword?"

"Behind you. And the Wayfinder. They can't touch them, you know, even with the massive advances in their power. They have to rely on Callow."

"That bastard. I was convinced he'd died on Wave Sweeper. He's like a cockroach—stamp on him and he just keeps on running."

"If you get free . . ." Tom gave a hacking wet cough ". . . you must use the Wayfinder."

"To find what? The head?"

"No. Think of the symbolism. What it *means*. It is a lantern that will light your way to the true path. It has a direct access to the source of the Blue Fire. I always told you to keep it close to you because . . ." Another cough; something splattered on the stone ". . . it's more important than you thought."

Tom fell silent; Church couldn't even hear his ragged breathing any more. "Tom?" he called out, fearing the worst.

"Yes. I'm here. It's nearly time."

"For what?"

"Remember what I said to you. On the ship. About keeping your memories close to you. They're your Wayfinder, Jack."

Tears stung Church's eyes. "Just hang on—"

"No. This is no surprise to me. I've had the chance to prepare myself."

Church forced himself to keep his voice steady. "How long have you known?"

"A long time. Longer than you've been alive."

Church couldn't begin to imagine how that could have been: to know when your death would be, to have the shadow falling over your whole life, yet still managing to keep going, to make friends, to care for people. It threw all of Tom's difficult character into a new light. Church was overwhelmed with guilt at the bad things he had thought of his friend, certainly in the early days, and all the harsh words he had ever said. There was so much he still wanted to say. Despite their prickly relationship, Tom had been an excellent teacher, and a father figure and the best of friends; he had made a deep and lasting impact on Church's life.

Tom appeared to know what Church was thinking. "I've had a long life, Jack. Too long. Too much pain and suffering. I'm looking forward to moving on."

"I'm sorry these last few months have been so hard for you."

"They have been hard, but they have also been some of the best months of my life. I've learnt a lot from all of you, Jack. You reminded me of all those things I thought I'd lost when the Queen got her hands on me. For centuries I thought I'd become less than a man. But you—all of you—showed me the truth. And now it doesn't matter what the Queen's *games* did to my body, because the thing that really counts, my humanity, comes from somewhere else. And it's still there."

Tom coughed again, and this time it sounded like the fit wasn't going to stop. When it did finally end, he was noticeably weaker. His eyelids fluttered half-closed; his skin grew ashen.

"Tom," Church pleaded futilely. He had always been so flawed and weak compared to the heroic legends of Thomas the Rhymer, but in truth his heroism was even greater; deeper and more complex than the shining, courageous myth, infinitely more worthy, because it came from the best of humanity.

"The spiderweb." The Rhymer's voice was a papery rustle. "Diamonds all along it. Little worlds." Another cough, slow and laboured. "Beautiful, little worlds."

And then there was silence and a heavy stillness.

His eyes burning, Church rested his head on the hard wood. He would miss his old friend immeasurably.

His sorrow had turned to a cold, hard anger when the door swung open and Mollecht entered, flanked by three Fomorii guards. Behind them, Callow danced a little jig. Mollecht led the Fomorii to the array of torture tools, ignoring Church completely.

"They're going to punish you, you know." Callow moved across the floor in a manner that reminded Church more of an insect; insanity burned bright in his eyes.

"I'd call you crazy if it wasn't stating the obvious," Church said. "Throwing your lot in with these bastards again, after all they've done to you. Do you think they'll give you what you want?"

Callow cast a sly, admiring glance towards the mass of flapping birds. "Oh yes, oh yes. My new best friend."

"I had some sympathy for you, Callow, but it was misplaced. You aren't how you are because you didn't get the breaks in life. There have always been too many people like you, blaming everybody and everything for their suffering because they're too weak to face up to the selfishness or the greed that drove them into bad situations. Doing the right thing is difficult, and there's always some kind of hardship, but it pays off—for yourself, for society, for humanity. You were just too lacking to go down that road. Too pathetic. You wanted things for yourself and you wanted them quick and easy. Face up to it, Callow. All your misery in your life is because of the choices *you* made."

"No!" Callow protested childishly. "Nobody looked after me! I never had what others had!"

"You said it yourself, the first time we met. Longfellow, wasn't it?" Church drove the nail home harder, enjoying every blow.

"Shut up!" Callow covered his ears.

"*In ourselves, are triumph and defeat.*"

"No!" He ran over and kicked Tom's body hard, then looked to Church for a reaction.

"He can't feel it, you know," Church said. "He's away taking a rest from this big mess. It's all of us left behind who still get to feel the pain."

Callow scuttled forward to Church's side so he could whisper in his ear, "And that's just what you'll get, old boy. Once he's finished with you"—he pointed to Mollecht—"I'll have my finger."

Mollecht completed whatever task he had been carrying out on the other side of the room and turned back. Church couldn't tell if it was his imagination, but the crows appeared to fly even faster, like a heart speeding up at the anticipation of pleasure.

"Enjoy it while it lasts," Callow whispered gleefully.

The three Fomorii guards were each carrying one of the cruel-looking implements; Church tried not to look at them, nor to think what damage they could wreak on his frail body.

Close up the sound of flapping wings was deafening, the smell of the birds potent. Church couldn't comprehend how they could fly so fast, so close together without once crashing.

Callow sloped back to the far corner of the room, obviously unnerved by Mollecht, even though he considered him an ally. The Fomorii guards roughly flipped the board back so it was horizontal, and Mollecht moved to stand at the head, where his presence was oppressive, but only partly seen. Two Fomorii positioned themselves on Church's right, one over his knee joint, the other close to his hand. The third Fomorii moved in on his left and held a rod tipped with a corkscrew over his groin; Church remembered that one well from the tunnels beneath Dartmoor.

Something was happening with Mollecht, although it was impossible to see exactly what. Church had a sense that the birds were moving their formation slightly; he could feel the air currents from their wings on his forehead. A moment later an unpleasant sucking sensation throbbed deep in his head, though he was sure it was not physical.

He writhed on the table in an attempt to shake it off; but it grew more and more intense until he felt something deep in him rushing out. There was a moment of utter darkness and then the torture room was gone, although he felt his body still lying in it. Everything was infused with intense, smoky colours, unreal, like a distorted Technicolor film from the sixties. A large, armoured insect appeared to be crawling around the inside of his head. His whole being recoiled; it was the mind of Mollecht.

Church had flashes of a nightmarish landscape where threatening creatures loomed up before receding in speeded-up motion. There was a shift and he glimpsed a building as big as a mountain made of black glass. Another shift and he was inside, in a room as dark as the deepest well despite a brazier glowing a dull red in one corner. One of the Fomorii stood hunched over the hot coals pouring some dust on to them from a glass philtre. This Fomor—whom Church knew was Mollecht—was a half-breed, just like Calatin, but while Calatin had more of the Tuatha Dé Danann in his physical appearance, Mollecht was closer to the grotesque Night Crawlers.

As the dust fell on the coals, a cloud of smoke rose up in purples and reds. Church had a sudden sense of a great Evil, greater even than Balor, lying somewhere on the edge of the universe. He felt its attention turn on him/them, and was convinced he was going to die from dread.

The smoke billowed with a life of its own. Finally it folded back and out of it flew the murder of crows, although there was something sickeningly alien about them; they were much larger, their eyes glittering red, and Church could sense in them an awful intelligence. They fell on Mollecht, pecking at his skin with blades as sharp as razor blades, tearing through flesh and bone.

As Mollecht fell to his knees, he howled in the insane monkey-gibbering way of the Fomorii, but there was nothing he could do to fend them off. At the same time as they ate him alive, they spun a chartreuse web, like spiders, that coagulated, folding within his body to make another form. As he shrank, it grew, not as large but more powerful, and when he was completely gone, it lay there, infinitely more hideous, both within and without. It was so fragile it threatened to fall apart in an instant, but the crows began to fly, faster and faster, weaving a binding spell that created a network of restraining energy. And when it opened its eyes . . .

The shock jolted Church out of the trance state; he would never, ever forget the sickness of seeing the world through Mollecht's eyes.

Mollecht retreated from his head and moved to where he could direct proceedings.

"Have you lost hope yet?" Callow jeered from the other side of the room.

"Mollecht belongs to something else," Church gasped. "He wants to challenge Balor."

All the Fomorii stopped; Callow dropped to his knees whimpering. The air pressure in the room fell; a wind rushed through it. Church was aware of a presence in the room, unbearably threatening; fear surged through him. It was only there for a second or two before moving on, but it left deep scars on his mind.

Somehow he forced himself to speak. "Where is—"

"Don't say the name!" Callow pleaded.

"Where is he?"

Church thought Callow was going to cry. He looked around in terror. "Don't you know? You are inside him."

Church had no time to ask what that meant. The crows that made up Mollecht shifted their formation; a signal. The Fomorii moved in with the torture instruments.

Before any of them could hurt him, there was another drop in air pressure, only this one felt different: Church's nerve endings tingled, warmth flooded into his limbs. The Fomorii felt it too, for they looked towards the door as one. Mollecht backed away.

The door was growing a dim blue, distinct in the darkness of the room, and it was from there that the electric atmosphere was flooding. Mollecht let out a series of barks and yelps. The Fomorii guards threw away the torture instruments and pulled out their swords, but before they reached the door, the blue glow became noticeably brighter and a resonant hum filled the room. An instant later the door exploded in thousands of shards. Church was close enough to the blast to have been torn to pieces by the flying wood, but nothing touched him at all.

When he looked back he was confronted with a miraculous sight. On the stone floor outside the door was a severed head. It was the source of the brilliant blue glow that now flooded the room. The head of Bran, the Luck of the Land; the god who had sacrificed himself for the sake of humanity. Church could make out long, flowing hair, but where the eyes and mouth should have been there were only holes out of which the blue light streamed. The most unnerving thing was that the head appeared to be still alive. Its mouth moved, the muscles on its cheeks twitched, the eyes grew wider and then narrowed.

The Fomorii guards hesitated, but another command from Mollecht drove them on. They barely had time to move. The light became a river of surging Blue Fire rushing towards them. Church was mesmerised as he watched it burn away everything down to the skeletons, and an instant later they were gone too.

In the corner, Callow was shrieking. Church's attention was drawn to the door as a tall silhouette slipped in. The Bone Inspector hurried over, his face drawn in pain. Church saw that his hands had been charred black.

"Too hot," he said in a fractured voice.

Somehow he managed to undo Church's bonds, although Church could barely look into his face at the pain he was experiencing. "You did a good job," Church said.

The Bone Inspector grunted. "I've suffered worse."

Once Church was free, he dived behind the table and snatched up the Sword. Mollecht was pressed against one wall, unable to leave the room while the head was there. Even so, the birds were shifting formation ready to unleash another of the plague attacks.

Church knew how fast they came, and this time he didn't hesitate. Bounding across the room, he began to thrash wildly with the Sword. Black feathers showered across the room. Deep puddles tinged with red formed as the crows' bodies fell heavily all around.

There was a sound that made Church's gut turn, and it was a moment or two before he realised it was Mollecht screaming. The remaining birds had to fly harder to maintain the binding pattern, but every time the Sword nicked one it plunged to the ground.

Church lost himself in a storm of black and red until there was only one bird flying frantically around the hideous shape that lay within; the thing he still couldn't bring himself to look at. He paused briefly, took a deep breath, and then struck the last crow.

The bird hit the stone flags, followed by the thing within. It thrashed and shrieked wildly for a full minute, and then slowly it began to break up, then melt away. Eventually there was only a black sludge on the floor, and soon that, too, was gone.

Church rested on the Sword, shattered from fear and exertion, and in that moment Callow broke his frozen position and darted for the door. He skirted the head, glancing back once at the threshold.

Church pointed at him. He didn't need to say a word, and he knew from the look of terror on Callow's face as he disappeared that his message had been received.

Church hurried back to the Wayfinder, lying on its side behind the table. "What do we do now?" the Bone Inspector croaked. He was resting heavily against a wall.

"I don't know. But this lantern is going to show me." He sat down and pulled it upright before him. "I hope."

Closing his eyes, he focused on the Blue Fire as Tom had taught him at the foot of Arthur's Seat in Edinburgh. The Rhymer had been a good teacher; it took him only a second or two to reach the necessary state of heightened perception.

The lantern flame surged and the energy crackled into his fingers, his hands. For the first time on his own he saw in the flames the tiny faces and minute bodies he had witnessed when Tom had introduced him to the earth power at Stonehenge. He knew what they were now. "All stars," he whispered.

Things fell into alignment.

It seemed to him that the Wayfinder had moved deep in his head, and the flame was now blazing as bright as a lighthouse. It was a direct connection with the source of the spirit fire, wherever that might be. Church felt it flare in his head, in his heart, as a doorway opened, and then the Blue Fire was streaming out of him.

Veitch awoke on a mudflat next to a grille that looked across the Thames. Next to him the River Fleet rushed out on its journey to the sea. He felt like he was dying: too cold, too exhausted, broken-spirited.

On the south bank he could see the dawn light painting the buildings in beautiful pastel shades. It was only a second or two later that he realised there was a corresponding light in the culvert in which he lay, only that illumination was a deep sapphire; and it was coming from him, from his very pores. With it came not only a tremendous sense of well-being, but also renewed vigour.

He clambered to his feet, stamping the last remaining cold from his limbs as he cracked his knuckles. "Bleedin' hell," he said in awe.

Then he was at the grille, attempting to prise it open.

The Fomorii marched back and forth at the camp in the underground tunnel, oblivious to the foul-smelling smoke rolling off the burning piles of rubbish. They were long used to the foraging rats that ventured close before scurrying back into the shadows, so they paid scant attention to the movement further along the tracks.

It was only when the activity refused to recede, indeed began to move closer than any of the rats had dared before, that they looked up, and by then it was too late.

A torrent of undulating brown bodies swept towards them from the dark, covering every square centimetre of the tunnel floor. The rats surged past the perimeter bonfires up on to the Fomorii, biting chunks out of their forms, tearing their way into any orifice they found. Their relentless speed and vast numbers belied the weakness of their size; however many the Fomorii crushed or swatted away, there were a thousand more to take their place and within seconds the Night Walkers were lost beneath the deluge.

Walking amongst them was Ruth, her eyes blazing with righteous fury. She was untouched by the scurrying creatures that moved exactly where she wanted, did just what she required. The information had been there in her mind, ready to be accessed, all part of the detailed lore she had soaked up from her familiar while imprisoned in Edinburgh. She had always thought she might be able to control one, perhaps two, maybe even three, but the extent of her abilities stunned her. She felt able to do anything.

As she passed the camp, the Blue Fire surged into her limbs, driving out the exhaustion so her physical strength could match the overwhelming confidence she had discovered. She had a sudden, deep connection with Church, and knew he had made it through to his destination. Now all she had to do was join him.

Muttering beneath her breath, the rats responded, surging on beyond the camp, with tens of thousands more coming up behind her.

"Did you feel that?" Laura's jaw sagged in cartoon style as the electric jolt jerked her limbs.

Shavi held up his hand towards the end of the corridor where the dawn light had still not penetrated. A ghostly blue aura could just be made out around his fingers. "It is Church."

Laura closed her eyes in relief. "Good job we're not all losers."

Shavi looked back out of the window at the army of silent Fomorii staring back. "We have to join him. All of us need to be there."

"That's all well and good, Shav-ster, but I'm still waiting to hear the cunning plan. Maybe the one that turns us invisible so we can waltz past the hordes of Hell."

As the sunlight slowly moved across the rooftops, the deathly silence was suddenly broken. From somewhere in the distance came the dim but instantly recognisable sound of a hunting horn, low and mournful, but drawing nearer.

And the Blue Fire rolled out across the city, joining up with the Fiery Network, and with it flowed Church's thoughts and hopes and prayers. The Wayfinder had lit the way for the very essence of his being, the part that had been transformed from base lead into gold by his experiences at St. Michael's Mount. Deep in his subconscious, encoded in his spirit, was the link he had with the vital energy that flowed into everything. He was, finally and truly, its champion, the Brother of Dragons. He was One.

When he had achieved what it became apparent that he had to do, he broke the link and put the Wayfinder aside.

"Tell me that did some good," the Bone Inspector said.

Church looked up at him with bright eyes. "The Fabulous Beasts are coming," he said.

chapter twenty
the place where all things converge

Shavi and Laura hung out of the window high up on Westminster Abbey to get a better view. At first it looked like birds moving across the rooftops, until they saw the drifting smoke and mist rolling away mysteriously before them. The occasional breaks in the cloud cover became a broad swathe, allowing sunlight to flood in across the ancient monuments and modern office blocks of London, spotlighting what they could now see were figures on horseback preceded by a pack of baying hounds.

"The Wild Hunt," Shavi said, recalling the last time he had seen them at Windsor, shortly before his death.

The unearthly red and white dogs bounded effortlessly across tiles, leaping the gulfs between buildings as if they were nothing. The Hunt thundered behind, Cernunnos in his Erl-King aspect at the head, blowing the horn, the horses galloping an inch or more above the roofs.

And the Hunt was not alone. The Dark Sisters, Macha, Badh and Nemain, swooped like ravens across the skyline, and beyond them Shavi could just make out the Morrigan, harbinger of war.

"Look." Shavi pointed to a commotion amongst the Fomorii near the Government offices off Great George Street. Black Shuck, the devil-dog that always heralded the Wild Hunt, tore through the Night Walkers with huge jaws that could rend metal.

The Hunt descended on the gathered Fomorii army, ripping back and forth until they had cleared an area where they could stand and fight. The Dark Sisters swooped from above and the Fomorii fell wherever they chose to attack. But it was the Morrigan that chilled Laura's blood the most. She walked amongst the Night Walkers as if she were strolling in the park, and whichever beast she passed crumpled to the ground, dead.

Laura and Shavi looked at each other; neither of them needed to speak—they knew the attack had given them the opportunity to break out. The Professor, who had been about to return to the detritus of humanity sheltered below, understood too. "How on earth do you propose to get out there?" he said in horror. "You'll die. Of course you'll die."

"Thanks for the pep talk, granddad. That's got me all jazzed up." Laura snickered to herself as she ran her fingers through her hair to spike it up.

"These times demand more of us," Shavi said, smiling. "From our conversation last night, I would guess you never imagined you would be a leader of men, a rock that holds a desperate community together."

"I'm not a leader." Michell looked out at the now-raucous fighting. "No, you're right. I was shaping my life to end it in the dustbin."

"And now you feel better about yourself. Now there is hope."

He nodded. "How strange that it takes a world falling apart to make us become better people."

"The life we were leading seduced us away from the things that mattered," Shavi said. "We thought society, technology, money, were offering us something better, but instead we ended up indolent, bored and depressed. This has been a terrible time, but if we find a way through it, something good will come out of it. A better life."

"There's something undeniably sad that we can't get back on the tracks without experiencing such suffering." The strain had made Michell emotional; tears flecked the corners of his eyes.

"It is the human way. But we do learn. Good does come out of bad, although at the time of suffering it is impossible to see what good there might be."

"If you two are going to keep talking, I'll just wander off and slit my throat. Jesus, analyse, analyse. Start living, for God's sake."

Shavi flashed a secret smile at Michell, who winked in return. "Come on, then," he said to Laura. "I guarantee you won't find it boring from here on in."

"Are you sure you know what you are going to do?" Shavi asked as they stood at the Abbey door with Michell ready to swing it open.

"Why don't you patronise me a bit more, you big, poncey shaman?" Laura's face was moody, with a hint of apprehension. "Offer to do somebody a favour and what do you get? Nag, nag, nag." She squatted down and bowed her head, balancing herself with one hand in front of her. "Okay, granddad. Put those creaking joints to use."

The Abbey was suddenly filled with the deafening clamour of battle. Laura knew if she looked up she would be too terrified to act; for all that Cernunnos had transformed her, she was still the frightened, unconfident woman she had been for most of her life.

She surprised herself by containing her fears; necessity was a great motivator, she thought. In her meditative state she had no problem accessing that corner of her mind she characterised as a brilliant green screen. It gave her a great sense of pride to see it, a feeling that she was doing the right thing. Environmental activism had been all she had ever truly believed in, and the thing she felt might actually balance out the weighty debit side of her life. And now, she thought, nature had paid her back by giving her a reason to live.

It started small. Hairline cracks ran out from her fingers where they touched the stone. Beyond the Abbey walls, they grew into fissures in pavements and roads; further on, a street lamp swayed, then crashed to the ground. The Fomorii nearest to her were thrown this way and that as the ground went into upheaval.

From the long-hidden soil beneath, green shoots sprouted, rapidly growing into a tumbling thicket of vegetation that moved as if it had a life of its own: bushes and vines, brambles, flowers, reeds, and then saplings that became trees, rowan, oak, yew, hawthorn.

Shavi gasped in amazement. As the abundant flora became thicker, the Fomorii were driven back and a path formed within the greenery, now stretching across Parliament Square. "Can you keep this up?"

"Not for long. It's knackering. But I can do it enough to get us through the worst of it. Then, I'm sorry to say, we'll have to run. Unless you can call up some badgers." She looked up finally and smiled with pride at her achievement. It was quickly replaced by a dark determination. "Okay," she said. "Let's go."

They glimpsed the carnage the Wild Hunt, the Dark Sisters and the Morrigan were inflicting on the Fomorii forces, but then they were across the Square and heading along the Embankment. After all the choking smoke of the city, the aromas of the vegetation were invigorating, and died away too soon, but the streets beyond were empty and Laura was already growing weak.

Shavi put an arm round her shoulders to support her as she shakily came to a halt in the middle of the road. "I'll be fine in a moment." She could already feel the Blue Fire working its wonders in her limbs. "You know what? If we get through this, I think I'm going to come back and turn the City into a garden."

Shavi gave her a hug, but he knew as well as she that the chance of them coming back were still very slim. Ahead of them lay the deep shadow cast by the ominous black tower rising out of the east. With a shiver that had less to do with the cold, they moved into it.

The journey through the tunnels to Tower Hill tube station passed in a blur. Before, Ruth had found that when she was using her new abilities she became so focused the real world was almost a distraction. Now the power was sucking her further and further from life into a place that was like a waking dream, where she could do anything; where the power defined her completely.

But as she gradually made her way up the frozen escalators, she began to slip back to how she had been. The realisation of the near-fugue state that had taken her over terrified her, as did its implications, but it was wiped away in an instant by her disgust that she was standing amidst a carpet of brown, writhing bodies that stretched as far as she could see. She closed her eyes briefly to compose herself, then continued on her way, but she couldn't help her shudders every time one brushed its cold fur against her feet.

Whatever she had done to control the rats began to diminish with her return to awareness and by the time she reached the top of the escalator they had begun to thin out. A few torches flickered in the ticket station, but Ruth was puzzled that she couldn't see any daylight. As she approached the doorway she realised the tower she had seen from Hampstead Heath had been built over the top of the tube station. The door that normally led out to the gardens overlooking the Tower of London now exited directly into a dark structure constructed out of compacted steel and melted plastic. In the walls amongst the twisted girders and building rubble, she could make out bits and pieces of the things that had been used in the building: computers, cash registers, mobile phones, cars and vans and motorcycles, part of a London bus. It was suffocatingly hot and filled with what sounded like some mining machine pounding away rhythmically nearby.

Broad steps ran up and down, with warren-like rooms on either side. She hesitated, unsure which way to go. A wave of panic flooded through her. Earlier she had sensed Church had made it, but what if he was now dead? What if she was the only one left? The responsibility was so vast she could barely comprehend it. What was she supposed to *do*?

As she agonised she caught sight of a faint blue glow above her that ignited a desperate hope. Holding the Spear before her, she took the steps two at a time. Her heart beat faster as she almost stumbled across the remains of several Fomorii, and then she rounded a corner into an intense blue light.

Church and the Bone Inspector were climbing ahead of her. She was shocked to see the illumination was streaming from what appeared to be a severed head, hanging by its hair from the same hand in which Church held the Wayfinder.

When he saw her his face broke into such an open expression of relief she had to run over and throw her arms around him. He held the head and Wayfinder away, although she didn't sense any danger from them. "Where's Ryan?" he asked.

"I don't know. Don't know if he's alive or dead."

"He'll get here if it's humanly possible," Church said confidently.

"Tom?"

Church's expression told her all she needed to know. Her spirit sagged. "I thought he'd go on forever."

"This isn't the place to stand around talking," the Bone Inspector said curtly.

They began to move cautiously back up the stairs. Occasionally one of the Fomorii would wander out of an adjoining room, only to be dispatched in an instant by Caledfwlch or by a flash of searing energy from the head.

"I presume you know where you're going," Ruth whispered.

"No. But if you stop and let yourself *feel*, you'll know you're going in the right direction."

As he spoke she realised she could sense a palpable *pressure* in the air that was slowly squeezing the life out of her chest; and it was getting stronger the more they climbed. A corresponding feeling of dread was eating away at the edges of her mind; all she could think of was the hideous thing she had seen during her spirit flight from Wave Sweeper. "What are we going to find?" Her voice suggested she hoped for some comfort, although she knew there would be none.

"I always expected it to be something like Calatin or Mollecht, only bigger. But I don't think it's going to be anything like that at all."

"Worse?"

"What do you think?"

"Hasn't Frank got a song for an occasion like this?"

"Yes, 'Get Happy.' As the lyric goes, *Get ready for the judgment day*."

"Thanks. That's dismal."

"No, no, it's positive. Really. *We're going to the Promised Land*."

There was something so naïve about him, even in the face of such terrible surroundings, Ruth felt a surge of love. "We'll get out of this," she said gently.

Her words were lost as a shadow crossed Church's face. "Did you hear that?"

She hadn't heard anything.

Church was suddenly consumed with anxiety. He dashed up a few steps and threw open a door on the outside of the tower. It was empty apart from piles of burning rubbish before irregular windows looking out over the Thames. Flying Fomorii were zipping around without, diving down on something that was below their range of vision. A tremendous shock rocked the entire tower. Liquid flame gushed past the window.

Church tried a door on the inner wall of the stairway. It was locked. "I've got to look in here," he said anxiously.

"We haven't got time," the Bone Inspector replied harshly. He was continually peering up and down the stairs for any sign of attack. "It's already morning. The gates will be opening in a few hours."

"There's time for this." Church tried to force the door.

"I told you not to be so stupid. The hour's almost here!" The Bone Inspector made to drag Church away, but Church knocked his blackened hand off. They squared up to each other.

"This isn't helping," Ruth pleaded. "Why is this room so important?"

Raw emotion flickered across his face. "Marianne's in there. I heard her."

Ruth stepped in before the Bone Inspector could began a rant. "You have to let him do it," she begged. "There'll still be time."

After a moment, the Bone Inspector relented. Overcome with apprehension, Church stepped back and levelled the Sword at the lock. It burst with a resounding crack and the door swung open.

The room was not like any they had seen before. It was spacious, about fifty feet square, with smooth walls lined with black stone. A single torch burned on the far side. The flagged floor had been marked out with an intricate pattern of lines and geometric shapes, along with bizarre symbols that suggested an alien language. The effect of the relationship of the various elements was so intensely disturbing it made Church's head spin. A large block of black stone stood in the centre of the design, and on it was a stoppered green-glass bottle.

"Be careful." The Bone Inspector held out a hand to stop Church stepping over the threshold. "Don't go blundering in."

Church scanned the room one more time. "Can't see anything that might be a problem. What makes you worried?"

"Instinct."

Church fixed his eyes on the bottle. "That's it. That's where she is." He set down the head and the Wayfinder, but held on to the Sword. "I'm going to have to chance it."

"Bloody stupid. All this at stake and you're taking risks," the Bone Inspector muttered.

"It's an obligation to someone I loved. Don't you understand that?"

There was a long pause before the Bone Inspector replied quietly, "Maybe." Then: "Get a bloody move on! Time's running out!"

In the room the temperature was inexplicably below freezing. Church's breath clouded, his body protesting with shivers after the intense heat. Church let his foot hover over the design, but couldn't think of any other way to reach the bottle. Slowly he brought it down.

"You okay?" Ruth called out.

"Fine. No problem." He took another step.

"Just keep that big head and big mouth in check," the Bone Inspector growled. "And stop dawdling."

As Church took the third step, he felt a strange tingling sensation in his extremities. Ruth noticed his surprised reaction. "What is it?"

"Nothing. Just the cold. It's like the Arctic in here."

With the next step, he lost the feeling in his fingers and toes. He shook them for warmth and was surprised to see them glisten in the torchlight.

"Tread . . . careful—" The Bone Inspector's voice was oddly distorted before disappearing completely. Church was too fixated on the bottle to be concerned about it. All he could think about was Marianne and everything she'd suffered because of his unwitting involvement in the events now being played out. He had made her a promise to free her spirit and he would not fail; his own redemption was tied up in his success.

The words of warning and encouragement from Ruth and the Bone Inspector had ended; they must have realised he was doing okay.

Several more steps passed unnoticed, so much did the bottle fill his mind. Memories of Marianne and the time they had spent together traipsed across his head until the black stone chamber almost faded from his perception. He was there with her, happy, as they always had been.

It was only when he realised he was having trouble moving forward that he jolted back to reality. What he found was so shocking it took him a few seconds to assimilate. His arms and the parts of his body he could see were strangely white. His dulled thought processes eventually told him the truth: he was covered in rime frost. It sparkled across his limbs, so thick his joints would barely work against it. Even his eyelashes were heavy with the weight of it, shimmering so that he found it hard to see past the glare.

If he had not had the Blue Fire coursing through him, he would most certainly have been dead; even now he was close to it. If he turned back there was still a chance he might actually survive. Yet the bottle was only a couple of paces away. How could he leave when he was so close? He couldn't abandon Marianne.

In his mind, there was no choice. He forced another step. Almost there. He couldn't feel any of his body now; his mind was disembodied, recalling a dream of being trapped in a person. Oddly, that helped him. With no physical sensations to distract him, his thoughts were pure and strengthened. He slipped easily into the perception where he was aware of the Blue Fire, and was surprised to see that even in that awful place the spirit energy still flowed, though much weaker.

By force of will, he drew some of it to him; a little but it was enough. He took the final step and swept the bottle off the stone with the back of his hand.

It shattered on the floor to release the gentlest breeze; he could feel it even through the thickening frost. With it came the scent of a woman he once loved, of a hot day in the Caribbean and a warm night on a boat on the Thames when they had kissed. And something else: the faintest touch of an intelligence, like a lover reaching out to reassure themselves their sleeping partner was still there in bed, still breathing. It was a small thing, but filled with so much. Church felt enormous gratitude that swelled his emotions, and admiration for him and his abilities, and forgiveness; and love, but not the love of a young couple, a spiritual thing that sent his soul soaring.

Emotions that had been held in stasis for so long finally rushed through him; it felt like someone had plunged a hand deep within him and dragged out every shadow, every shred of misery, every tear. The burden that shifted left him as light as air. Finally, an ending for something that had manacled him for so long.

She was free. And he was finally free of the burden her death had placed upon him. A tear squeezed out of the corner of his eye and burned a path through the white down his cheek.

After that the getting back was easy, despite the cold and the weight of the frost, both of which appeared to be increasing. The shock of the heat outside the room made him lose consciousness for a moment, and when he came round he was lying on the floor, his clothes soaked, with Ruth wiping his face. Her concern was unmissable, but it faded when he forced a smile.

"It was the Kiss of Frost," he said, recalling the Fomorii spell that had almost destroyed him on the Isle of Skye. "Mollecht had obviously left it there for me, knowing I'd undoubtedly attempt to free Marianne's spirit. To remind me of how I screwed up last time. His final malicious act."

"Well, you showed him, didn't you?" She brushed his hair away from his face. "How do you feel? About Marianne?"

He knew what she was saying. "It made me realise how much I love you. The relationship I had with Marianne was strong, but it's all in the past. What I felt in there was about something different."

"Care to elaborate?"

Church looked at the Bone Inspector, who appeared to be considering whether he should clout Church with his staff. "I don't think this is quite the time."

He pushed himself to his feet, pleased at the recuperative powers the Blue Fire gifted him. What lay ahead would be much, much worse.

After Veitch had torn the grille away from the stone, he stumbled out into the cold waters of the Thames. The mist and smoke that had blanketed the city for so long was drifting away, leaving a sky that was golden and pink. The rooftops of the buildings along the south bank gleamed in the early morning light. Everything hinted at a beautiful day.

The quickest way to his destination was obviously to swim; he was thankful he now felt curiously immune to the chill. He kept to the shallows where he could not be seen from the bank and let the current push him along.

The spirit energy had raised his spirits, but there was still a dark area at the back of his head where all his worst traits lay. It was there where the self-loathing multiplied at the thought that he had failed again, not just Ruth, but Church, everyone, the world, and that was such an enormous failure he couldn't keep out the seductive fantasies of suicide. And it was there, where his consuming anger generated a dull heat.

Eventually the black tower was in view. He rounded a bend in the river to see Wave Sweeper launching an attack on Balor's lair. Bizarre flashes of energy lanced out from strange weapons positioned around the deck. The flying Fomorii dived and soared like crows over food, but the Tuatha Dé Danann didn't allow them the slightest opportunity to get through.

As he drew closer, an enormous shadow passed over him. He craned his neck expecting to see another Fomorii creature, and was transfixed. A Fabulous Beast glittered like a jewelled brass robot in the sunlight, wondrous and terrible at the same time. It swooped down towards the tower to release a blast of fire that atomised a host of the flying Night Walkers. More of the serpentine creatures were approaching from all directions; Veitch had never dreamed there were so many. Columns of searing flame lanced down across the capital. As he drifted in the current, he saw the financial district engulfed in a fireball, Docklands decimated, pillars of billowing black smoke shoot up from the West End. Wherever the Fomorii had made their nests, the Fabulous Beasts sought them out.

Though he would dearly have loved to have joined in the simple battle of black and white, good versus evil, he passed unseen. He entered the Tower of London at the foot of the black tower through a riverside gate that opened on to a sandy area and a flight of stone steps where so many important men and women had trod before him.

Veitch still had his dagger, but it was little enough defence against what lay ahead. As he reached the top of the steps he came across a pile of items obviously discarded by the Fomorii as worthless. Amongst the broken doors and ripped tourist guides, jewels shimmered brilliantly. It was only when he fished out a crown bearing a remarkable diamond that he realised he was looking at the Crown Jewels. He considered—for a brief moment—prising out the diamond to slip into his pocket, but then his eyes fell on an ornate sword protruding from the bottom. He dragged out the Curtana, the Coronation Sword of Mercy. It was blunt, but it would still be a better weapon than his dagger.

As he made his way through the Tower, he was almost disappointed that he didn't meet any Fomorii. He was desperate to release some of the anger burning away inside him, an unpleasant sensation that was only getting worse.

At some point he left the historic castle and found himself in the black tower that circumscribed it. There, a pitched battle was taking place, and at the heart of it were Shavi and Laura.

Veitch was so overjoyed to see his friends, he rushed in with a whoop, whirling his sword around his head. His intervention cheered them immeasurably for they had reached a point where they feared they might be overwhelmed. Vegetation tangled everywhere, but Laura hadn't learnt enough to utilise it in close quarters. Shavi used a sword hesitantly, but his hatred of violence hampered him severely.

Once Veitch had hacked a Fomorii warrior into a pile of seeping chunks, the battle turned, although both Laura and Shavi were a little concerned at the glee with which he despatched his enemy.

Yet it was a short-lived victory. More and more Night Walkers began to stream in from outside. "They're trying to force us downstairs," Veitch said. "That means we go up."

It was easier for them to hold their ground as they fought while edging backwards up the steps. The Fomorii could stand only two abreast and as every one fell it made it harder for the others to clamber over the bodies.

"I hope we do not meet any more coming down," Shavi said.

"I'm more concerned about what happens when we get to the top," Laura replied.

Church was beginning to wonder exactly how high the tower soared above the cloud cover. It felt like they had been climbing for an hour or more, although the heat hadn't diminished at all. Increasingly, explosions rocked the construction to its very core; chunks fell from the ceiling and walls. Through the windows he occasionally caught glimpses of Fabulous Beasts laying waste to the city and was stunned by both their number and diversity. He had never seen so much grace and power in one form, so many gleaming colours. How could humanity have traded them away, and all the wild magic that came with them, for the brutal rationalism of the twenty-first century?

The Fabulous Beasts provided an uplifting counterpoint to the oppressive presence of Balor looming darkly. The rising sense of threat was putting a huge psychological strain on all of them. There was a perpetual feeling of Balor always standing one pace behind them, ready to strike.

In a sense, that was true. Church could feel Balor's essence throbbing in the very walls; it was all a part of him. The dark god of the Fomorii was an amorphous evil that pervaded everything, even the very air; Church could taste the sourness when he swallowed. The atmosphere was almost painfully pregnant; despite the power it already held, Church knew the Beast was waiting for the Doors of Samhain to open so it could claim the undreamable force it needed to destroy all life. It could afford to wait; they were insignificant beside it.

The steps opened out on a wide, flat area covering the entire floor space of the tower. It was the first time they had come across a room like it, but they could tell from the windows around the circumference that it wasn't the top. After the claustrophobic gloom, they were pleased to see the rough holes cut in the walls provided a pleasant amount of sunlight, but there was still not enough to illuminate the shadows at the centre of the room.

As they tentatively crossed the floor in search of the next flight of steps, they noticed a figure sitting hunched in that dark zone, next to a shimmering motion in the air. With weapons at the ready, they approached until they saw it was Niamh. Church laid down the head and the Wayfinder and hurried over, but she was so locked in her thoughts she didn't see him until he was almost upon her.

When she did look up, her face was filled with such a terrible grief that Church stopped short. The movement all around her were golden moths rising up to the ceiling. On the floor lay the gradually disappearing bodies of the Tuatha Dé Danann guards.

Church dropped down and put his arm around her shoulders. She rested her head against him, oddly frail for such a powerful being. "I'm sorry for your people," he said. "Did the Fomorii hurt you?"

"There were no Night Walkers."

"Then what happened?"

She raised her head to look at him deeply, her face haunted, her eyes damned. "I happened."

As her meaning gradually dawned on him, he looked around at the brutally slain bodies uneasily.

"Do not think badly of me, Jack." Every part of her was shaking. "I have committed a crime that will ensure my name is despised by my people for all time. I never thought I had it within me to commit such a monstrous act. But I did, Jack, I did."

Church tried to console her, but she would have none of it.

"I did it for you, Jack. For all Fragile Creatures. I did it for all existence. And I have lost myself in the process."

Church looked round until he saw the chest a little way away. "The Wish-Hex?"

"I attempted to prevent them unleashing it. They ignored my pleas. And so I . . . I . . ." Her face fell into her hands; her sobs were silent and racking.

"I know it's a terrible burden," Church said gently, "but you did do the right—"

"You do not understand, Jack. I failed. The Wish-Hex has been set in motion."

He stared at the chest, suddenly cold despite the heat. "In motion?"

"There is no stopping it now. Soon, very soon, it will begin."

Church fought back a wave of despair. The odds had always been incalculable, but now it truly was hopeless. He began to ask her how long it would take for the energy to drive the plague across the world, then caught himself; it didn't really matter. The Tuatha Dé Danann would get what they wanted: a universe free of competition.

He helped her to her feet. "Don't worry. You did your best." He looked across at the others, wondering whether to tell them that whatever they now did was futile.

Niamh took his hand. "There will be an ending, Jack, but it might not be how you imagine," she said as if she could read his mind.

"But what can we possibly—"

He was interrupted by the sound of violent fighting rising from the stairwell. Ruth rushed over to investigate before calling back excitedly, "It's Shavi, Ryan and Laura." The hope in her face made him feel even worse.

"We need to keep going," he shouted.

The Bone Inspector sniffed the air like an animal. "I think we're nearly there."

"Then they'll do anything they can to try to stop us."

"Time's running out," the Bone Inspector continued. He looked more worried than Church had ever seen him. "Not long left now."

"Will you stop it with the countdown!" Church snapped.

Laura and Shavi emerged at the top of the steps. Veitch was just below, holding back the Fomorii. "There's bleedin' millions of them now!" he yelled. "They're not bothering with the ship any more. They just want us!"

Ruth came running up to him. "The next flight of steps are just over there."

"Okay, shout down to Ryan. When he reaches the top of his steps, he'll just have to run for it." He turned back to Niamh, who had lifted the chest easily. "What's the point in taking that along with us? We might as well leave it here now."

"I am afraid of it falling into the hands of the Night Walkers. They created this Wish-Hex. They may know some way to ensure it destroys only Fragile Creatures."

"I appreciate what you've done, Niamh, more than you can know." Her sad smile told him how much his words meant to her.

He called Ruth over to help Niamh with the chest while he reclaimed the Wayfinder and the head; its blue glow was coming out in waves, accompanied by a dim but insistent hum. The features continued to move; Church had the unnerving feeling the head had been listening to them.

At the foot of the steps, he waited, urging the others up ahead of him. Eventually Veitch came sprinting past.

"You all right, boss?" he said with a grin.

"Fine and dandy." As he leapt on to the steps at the rear, Church threw one backwards glance and was instantly chilled. Flooding the vast room was what appeared to be a river of shadows. He knew it was the Fomorii, but it was like one entity, of one mind. It moved and spread with such speed he guessed there must be hundreds, if not thousands, of the Night Walkers pouring in.

Then the awful sight was wiped out in an instant by a blinding revelation. "What's that foul smell?" he called out.

Ruth's voice floated back. "It's the Fomorii. Nuada told me that when the Caraprix is in control it stimulates that stink."

Church felt sick and shaky as numerous troubling thoughts slotted into place. It was the same smell he recalled from the Walpurgis-induced vision of the night Marianne was murdered; and he had smelled it, too, when Tom had been driven to betray them in the Lake District. His pounding heart threatened to burst.

The traitor amongst them was being controlled by a Caraprix. That was why he couldn't imagine one of his closest friends selling them down the river; any acts of betrayal would be against type, and therefore unexpected. The Fomorii must have implanted the parasite months ago. Their scheming was unparalleled: back-up plan after back-up plan, and now this, the final defence to prevent their defeat.

He glanced up at Veitch taking the steps two at a time, thought of Ruth and Shavi and Laura. Which of them was it? It could be any one of them. And when would they be forced to make their move? He would have to watch all of them now, at a time when all his attentions should be focused on the threat without.

With a heavy heart, he pressed on, holding the head out behind him to deter the advancing Fomorii.

Gradually the circumference of the tower narrowed as they neared the top. When they finally thought they could climb no more it opened out into another large room that took up half the floor space. There were no windows to provide light, but they could just make out building debris scattered all around.

"I can't stand here holding the rest back forever," Church said impatiently. More explosions brought a shower of debris from the ceiling. As he jumped to one side to avoid it, he was struck with an idea. Directing Veitch and Shavi to collect rubble, girders and beams, and anything else they could lay their hands on, they flung it down the stairwell. It didn't take them long to jam it.

"So we won't be going down in a hurry," Laura said dismally.

"It won't take them long to get through that," the Bone Inspector said.

Veitch glared at him before venturing to the edge of the barrier. "Can't hear anything on the other side. I reckon they've fallen back."

"Now why would they do that?" Ruth laid down her edge of the chest and Niamh followed suit.

"They probably think we're a lost cause." Church almost had to shout over the echoing beat of Balor's heart.

A large stone wall bisected the floor, with an oaken door placed in the middle; it had looked unusual from the instant Church emerged from the stairwell, but up close he could see it was seeping a viscous, black liquid. The gunk oozed down into a gully and then ran through the wall and down the side of the building, adding to the tower's skin.

Church moved his ear towards the wall to see if he could hear any sound from the other side. As he neared the stone his stomach turned; radiating through it was a sensation of unbearable evil that spoke to his most primal fears.

He staggered away quickly. "In there." If it was that strong without, he thought, what would it be like when they entered?

The others must have noticed his expression when he was against the wall, for Laura said, "Are we up to this?"

"There aren't any other candidates. We'd better get the Quadrillax together."

They each gave up the artefact they had protected until the Sword, the Spear, the Cauldron and the Stone stood in front of the door. As the pieces came in proximity, a faint metallic singing rang up, melodic and strangely soothing in that awful place. Church realised that the Wayfinder and the head would be needed too. All were linked, and while they appeared as objects they all recognised, Church knew that they were not seeing their true forms at all; what they really were, he guessed they would probably never know.

During the frantic activity the futility had been put to one side, but in the lull it returned in force. He didn't know why they were there. They might as well have vacated the tower and enjoyed their final hour together, as much as they could. "How much longer with the Wish-Hex?" he asked. When there was no reply, he looked round and could tell from Niamh's face that it was almost upon them. Yet oddly he didn't see any fear there, just a deep, painful sadness; she forced a smile, and somehow that made it worse. "Then we had better get moving."

He walked up to the door. Ruth, Shavi, Laura and Veitch followed without any prompting, although the fear was obvious on all their faces. He was suddenly aware of a deeply moving feeling of gratitude that he had been allowed to spend time with them; they were the best.

A faint glow began to leak out of the Wish-Hex chest; the air pressure dropped a notch. *It's beginning*, he thought. He stooped down to pick up the Sword and something crashed against the side of his head, plunging him into unconsciousness.

The first Ruth realised was when Laura yelled and leapt back. Church was sprawled on the floor with blood seeping from a wound on the side of his head. Standing over him was Callow, his eyes baleful and filled with hatred. He was clutching a lump of rock, one end jagged and as sharp as a knife.

With a strength that belied his size, he grabbed hold of Church's jacket and began to drag him away into the shadows. Veitch dived forward, his ceremonial sword at the ready, but Callow moved as fast as a snake, yanking up Church's head and jabbing the rock against his throat.

"Anatomy lesson, little boy: the carotid artery," he said. "One slight cut and there's not a thing you can do. His beautiful heroic blood will wash across this dirty floor and it will all be over."

"You're bleedin' crazy!" Veitch raged. His temple pulsed; his expression suggested he would hack Callow to pieces at the bat of an eyelid. Callow merely smiled, which infuriated Veitch all the more.

"Please," Shavi said. "There is no—"

"There is every need. If you win, I will be lost."

"If we lose, you'll be lost, you wanker!" Veitch advanced another step.

Callow dug the rock into the pulsing artery. "Can't you understand? Humanity is weak. If we don't ally ourselves with greater powers, we are nothing. Do you think the working classes ever got anywhere on their own? This isn't a world for the powerless."

"Excuse me. Pathetic loser alarm." It was the first time Laura had seen him since he had clambered over the van seat to slash her face with a razor. Even the torments inflicted on his body didn't assuage the hatred she felt for what he had put her through.

"What lies on the other side of that wall is the greatest thing this puny little world has ever seen," Callow continued. "He will take me and give me the position I truly deserve: as a leader of men, not someone crushed by the yoke of an uncaring society. You're not going to take that away from me. This is my time that's coming. Your time is gone."

Ruth held up her hand and waggled her fingers at him so he could see where one was missing. "I was nice to you the first time we met in Salisbury. I thought you were down on your luck and maybe you just needed a helping hand. You showed me the truth when you did this. Everything I've seen over the last few months has shown me how much greatness there is in humanity. But you, you're the flip side. You're everything that drags humanity back: selfishness, and greed, and a belief that any act, however vile, is justified by your own needs."

"You seem to forget I'm the one holding your boyfriend's life in his hands."

"Yes, you are. And that's your big mistake. In Cornwall, and on the ship, I was ready to get my pound of flesh from you, Callow. And the only thing that stopped me was Church, because he's decent, and he believes in second chances and forgiveness. I don't."

Laura stepped to her side. "Who'da thought it? Me and Frosty with something in common."

"So who's going to speak up for you now, Callow?" Lightning flashed in Ruth's eyes. "Who's going to stop me?"

A shiver ran through Callow. His unblinking gaze left Ruth's face only to take in the flinty defiance in Laura's features.

A wind blew up from nowhere, rushing through the room violently. The force of it buffeted Callow a few paces backwards. "I'll kill him!" he screamed.

Ruth made a sweeping gesture with her right hand and Callow flew several feet across the floor as if he had been struck heavily. The rock went spinning away into the shadows. He jumped to his feet, looking frantically from side to side like a cornered animal. Laura squatted down, one hand on the floor. Before Callow could flee, vegetation burst up from minute seed particles buried amongst the stone flags and lashed itself around his legs, pinning him tight. He wrenched at them, screaming and cursing insanely.

Ruth was filled with an otherworldly fury, though on the surface she appeared completely calm. "Revenge does nobody any good," she said. "But sometimes you have to punish yourself."

Veitch took a step away from her, shocked by what he saw. As the tempest screamed around the room, she appeared—although he didn't know if it was an illusion—to rise a few inches above the floor.

Church came round with his head ringing and blood seeping down to his neck. When he saw Ruth, the pain was instantly replaced with a panic that slowly changed to despair. That unrecognisable cast to her face told him everything he needed to know, the one terrible fact that destroyed his life in an instant. With the route his life had taken since the gods had started to manipulate it, he could almost have forecast the traitor would be the one person who meant more to him than the world. There had been signs before, he knew, but like a child he had avoided the harsh reality of investigating them too closely. He had pretended, and in truth had known he was pretending.

The one thought that saved him was that he wouldn't have to deal with it. The light leaking from the crate was now intense; the faint hum had become an insistent throb.

Laura's head was bowed in concentration. The vegetation had bound Callow like a mummy to his neck. When she looked up, she was in two minds about whether to continue, though her anger was still clear on her face.

She looked up at Ruth for guidance and saw her friend was not going to back down. Ruth was changed; the terrifying elemental forces crackling around her appeared infinite, reaching deep into the heart of creation. Though she looked exactly the same, the others were convinced it was no longer Ruth, but what had replaced her, they were not sure.

In that instant, Laura knew it was the moment of which Cernunnos had warned. If Ruth gave in to her hatred and killed Callow she would be lost; the immense power she had been gifted would be corrupted and would consume her.

Laura had only a second to act. She threw herself at Ruth, knocking her down hard. The lightning Ruth had been calling up erupted from the ceiling and missed Callow by a hairsbreadth.

And then Ruth turned her attention on Laura. Her face was unrecognisable, her eye black and empty like space. "Mine," she hissed.

Terror washed through Laura. Ruth began to focus the power towards her.

Laura had only a slim chance to defend herself. Instead, she rolled round towards Callow and concentrated until green vegetation rippled from her fingers across the floor, lashing up Callow's body. As he ranted and raged, it twirled briefly around his neck and then jerked. The head came free and bounced away into the shadows.

Laura waited for the blow to strike her. When nothing came, she looked back to see Ruth slumped in a daze, her eyes no longer black. "Thank you," she said weakly.

Church could feel Ruth's eyes on him as he rose, desperate for comfort after her experience, but he couldn't meet her gaze. And then it was too late. The room was quickly filled with twisting flashes of yellow light. The throb became a constant drone.

They all stared at the chest blankly: they had overcome so much, over so many months, and had still failed at the last. The light washed over them, almost soothing in its way.

Before they could say their goodbyes, Niamh flicked open the chest and removed the Wish-Hex. It was so bright it hurt their eyes and they were forced to turn away.

Church was closest and only he heard Niamh say, "This is the way it must be." It was a simple statement, but it brought a shiver to his spine. She pressed the Wish-Hex to her stomach until the light began to dim. He was shocked to see that somehow it was disappearing inside her. The sight was too strange to comprehend, but he knew exactly what she was doing; she had told him, in her own way.

When the Wish-Hex was finally gone, for the briefest instant she stood exactly as he remembered her from that first, misty appearance in his childhood bedroom. Her face open and honest and filled with unconditional love.

The droning noise ended. For a second her body shimmered and distorted, as if he were watching her on an out-of-tune TV, and then she was replaced by a massive cloud of golden moths that soared up into the shadows of the ceiling, twinkling like stars before slowly fading out.

Like Tom, she had known the moment of her death, Church was sure of it. That was part of her desperation that their love affair bloom. Somehow he knew she believed that if it happened, the course of events would be changed; that she would have a happy life.

He recalled the moment he told her they would never be together. How would that have felt? Not just rejection by the one she truly loved, but the announcement of her death sentence. And she had not complained, or attempted to change his mind.

And even after all the heartache he'd dealt her, she had still sacrificed herself so alien, weak, violent, spiteful, greedy, deceitful *Fragile Creatures* could move along the road towards their destiny.

Her act was humbling, but she had shown him an important lesson: that no race should be judged by the worst elements. That however bad humanity was at times, it could always be redeemed by the best.

Ruth was at his side, her arm around his waist. "She did that for us? God, I feel so guilty!" She appeared honestly shaken by what she had witnessed.

Church looked down at Ruth in growing dismay as the repercussions of Niamh's actions slowly fell into place. They had been given another chance; now he couldn't simply let things run their course to a bitter end. He had to take whatever action was necessary to ensure their success, and that meant dealing with Ruth when she attempted to betray them. What would he do? Kill her? He had faced that terror when she had been a host to Balor, but that was before he had realised the true depth of the feelings they had for each other.

Ruth grabbed his hand. "Look at you—you're shaking," she whispered. "Don't worry, we're all scared."

"This is like Ten Little Indians," Laura said morosely. "Bags not being next." She looked round and fixed on the Bone Inspector. "Oldest first, I say."

He gave a dark, triumphant smile. "Ah, but I'm not going in there. That's your job."

In his sly way, he had pointed them back on track. They turned as one and stared at the door, then looked to Church.

"Okay," he said. "Let's do it."

As they collected the artefacts in silence, they were constantly aware of the door, like a sentient creature watching them malignantly.

"What's the plan?" Veitch asked Church.

"We have to use the talismans as soon as we get in there."

"That's a plan?"

"We might not even get a chance," Ruth said. "He's so powerful he could strike us down in a second."

"The talismans should offer us some protection." Church was aware he had to sound as positive as possible. "Individually, they're powerful. Together they'll be incredible. And with the head, the Luck of the Land . . ." He shrugged.

"So, we're winging it, right?" Laura's grin eased the mood a little.

"Just remember the legends," Church said. "He was always described as having a single eye—if he turned it on you it would cause death in an instant. I don't know if that's for real or symbolism, but there's a reason it was passed down the years. Keep it in mind."

"So what's it like in the land of the dead, Shav-ster?" Laura asked.

"It's like Jamaica, but with free drink."

"Really?"

"No."

"You could have lied, you know."

As they turned to face the door, Veitch stepped in close to Church and said quietly, "I'm glad I'm with you, boss. You've done right by us all the way down the line."

His face had the same childlike innocence that had made Church warm to him in the first place; for all his flaws, and there were many, that saved him.

"I'm okay, you know," he continued. "About you and Ruth."

Church winced.

"I feel like I've been stabbed in the gut, but that's not important. I want her to be happy. And I want you to be happy. Whatever happens here, I'm going to be a winner. For the kind of life I've had, that's the only thing that matters to me. And I've got you to thank for it, mate." He took Church's hand and shook it forcefully, hesitated a second, then stepped in and gave him a stiff hug. The others pretended not to notice.

"Will you lot get a move on." The Bone Inspector marched around anxiously. "The gates will be open any moment, and then it will all be—"

"Make sure you cheer loudly so we can hear you from way back here," Laura said acidly.

Finally, it was time. Church gripped the door handle. Before he swung it open, he cast an eye on Ruth. Her move would undoubtedly be made at the worst possible moment. But could he face up to Balor and watch for an attack from the back as well?

The answer would come soon enough. He opened the door in one swift movement and stepped over the threshold.

The room was as silent and still as night. Darkness clustered on every side, but the sapphire glow from the talismans gave them enough light to see by. The pounding of the blood in their head drowned out all thoughts and sensations for the first few seconds before everything fell into stark relief.

They each had their own idea of what monstrous form Balor would take, so they were all left floundering around when their eyes fell on a small boy, standing with his arms behind his back in the centre of the huge, empty chamber. A shock of black hair tumbled around an innocent, smiling face. His clothes were Sunday School-best, his posture polite and upright like a dutiful Victorian son.

"If I'd known we could just have spanked him, I wouldn't have got so worked up," Laura said breathlessly.

"A boy, right?" Church said. "We're all seeing a boy? You know that's only the form our own perception is putting on it."

"But why a boy?" Ruth's voice had an edge of dismay to it.

It was only then that the finer detail of what they were seeing broke through. Unimaginable dread pressed like a boulder on their chests, choking the air in their throats. A deep, primal part of their subconscious recognised what lay beyond the physical: a race memory of unbearable evil that demanded they flee or lose not only their lives, but also their souls. And then they saw his eyes were completely black, as immeasurable as the void.

The shock of the image kept them rooted for a second too long; they had already missed the opportunity to act. Something was happening to the boy. A horizontal crack opened slowly in his face. The top and bottom folded back gradually to reveal a twisting geometric shape made of brilliant red light so complex their minds couldn't make sense of it.

"The eye!"

They scattered at the sound of Church's voice; he was the head, they were the vital, component parts of the body, the reason why they worked so well together. In the instant the face opened completely they felt something as dank and chill as the grave brush past them. Church saw Shavi turn white, fight to control himself before moving off. He dabbed at his own ears and found blood on his fingers.

The thing with the body of a boy was already turning to focus on them.

"Keep moving!" Church shouted.

They scattered amongst the shadows just as death swept through them again. It whispered by a hair's-breadth away. An ache sprang up deep in Church's bones. The thing was too fast, too powerful; they wouldn't have an instant to lay out the talismans. The worst thing was that Church knew it was using only a fraction of its power. Most of it was maintaining the integrity of the tower, overseeing the Fomorii forces, preparing for the gates to open. They were a distraction, nothing more.

They ran back and forth as the boy turned this way and that. Each time the icy, whispering wind rushed out it came a little closer to them. Laura appeared to have lost the use of her left arm. Veitch was bleeding from his nose.

Yet there was a moment between attacks when the eye needed to focus, and in that time Ruth snatched up the Spear. It was the kind of smart, brave move he would have expected of her, but all he felt was panic. *This is it!* he thought.

Ruth hurled the weapon, but not at him. It shot like an arrow, much faster and stronger than she could have propelled it herself. It would have driven through the eye, but at the last instant, the boy folded like a paper figure. Instead, it rammed through his chest. White light exploded across the room like gouts of molten metal and there was a shrieking that came from everywhere at once.

Laura was already crouching, her good hand resting on the floor before her. Vegetation sprouted madly along a rapid path between her and the boy. Thorns of the hardest wood burst through its legs, vines and brambles snapping round and round like steel wire.

Church seized the moment. He turned for the talismans, but Shavi was already scrambling to lay them out. Church dived in to help him, aware of the agonies Balor was going through behind him, knowing how futile it really was. It was a shock to feel the talismans writhe and twist beneath his fingers, subtly forcing him to put them in the right place. The head sat in the centre of the array, its mouth opening and closing as if it were barking orders. Yet Church didn't feel scared by it; there was a deeply comforting warmth rolling off the objects.

Finally the five talismans they still had were laid out. Instantly they began to change. No longer were they a Sword, a Stone, a Cauldron, a Lantern or a severed head, but something that Church couldn't begin to get a fix on, yet they were undoubtedly one *thing*, unified, beating powerfully; it was like he was staring at a storm cloud through a heat haze.

One part was still missing; he could *feel* that intensely. He had to retrieve the Spear. All he needed was Veitch to launch one of his brutal attacks to keep Balor off balance and he would be able to do it.

Shavi was already moving towards the Heart of Shadows, but Church pulled him back; it was his responsibility, his risk. Secure in the knowledge that Veitch would instinctively know what to do as his exquisite strategic skills came into play, he ran towards the creature that no longer resembled a boy, now as unknowable as the talismans, growing and changing all the time.

Laura was still drawing the greenery out of nothing, swathing Balor in bark and leaf, but as his form changed he was rising above, sucking in the true power that he had dissipated throughout the tower, perhaps even throughout London. And from the corner of his eye Church saw Ruth utilising all the power Cernunnos had gifted her to attack Balor, and he wondered why, at the end, she had turned away from betraying them.

And then he was within Balor's sphere, sickened by the power and the evil, his thoughts fragmenting with the chaos that swept around him. Somehow he managed to grab the Spear; it squirmed in his fingers as he dragged it out.

White-hot pain exploded in his side. The shock snapped him away from the Spear as his mind struggled to understand what was happening.

Ruth?

He staggered backwards, blood flooding into his clothes. Scarlet flashes burst across his mind. In the madness that engulfed him, the world seesawed sharply: he saw Balor looking down on him dispassionately, its attention already moving elsewhere; and he saw Ruth, her face torn with anguish.

Somehow he found himself on the floor near the talismans, and Shavi was over him, desperately trying to staunch the wound. He tried to strain towards Ruth, but all he could see was Laura continuing her attack on Balor, her face as white as the moon. Slowly the Beast was driving her back.

Veitch drifted into his fractured frame of vision, and the maelstrom of insanity grew infinitely worse. His silver hand was dripping blood. Church's blood. Veitch stared at the prosthetic dismally as it clenched and unclenched, seemingly beyond his control. Suddenly it lashed out of its own accord, smashing with the force of a hammer into the side of Shavi's head. Shavi flew across the floor, droplets of blood trailing behind him. Blood, everywhere. More on Veitch's face, trickling from his nose, mingling with the streaming tears. The blood that did not come from an injury inflicted by Balor, as Church had thought, but was the mark of a Caraprix in action.

"Bastard!" Veitch hammered his fists against his temple, his face scarlet with the strain. "Bastard, bastard, bastard!" He bucked at the waist as the rage consumed him.

Church looked down hazily; the pool of blood around him was so large! He never dreamed he had so much blood in him. The blue light streaming off the talismans was reflected in it, as he watched those tracers in the dark he had a moment of clarity. Veitch's anger, always so close to the surface, so terrible when unleashed, was the product of his subconscious continually struggling against the subtle influence of the Caraprix. They had judged him by that anger, all of them, and they had been so wrong.

"Fight it, Ryan." Church's voice cracked; cold spread along his side. "I know they stuck one of those things in your head."

"Not one! Two!" His nails tore deep furrows in the sides of his head. A scream ripped from his throat. "I didn't know! I knew! But I didn't know!" He jackknifed at the waist again, still fighting. "Those golden bastards stuck one in first so I'd do all their dirty business to get us all together!" A sob; more tears. "I'm sorry!" He threw his head back and howled. "I'm sorry! Church, for Marianne! Oh Christ, I'm sorry! The others, Shavi, mate! Shavi!" And then he was crying uncontrollably.

Horrific images shimmered across Church's mind: Veitch bludgeoning Shavi's boyfriend to death in a South London street; Veitch murdering Laura's mother while Laura lay unconscious on the floor; Veitch gunning down Ruth's uncle in the building society rage.

And then he was back in the sequence the Walpurgis had played over and over in his head. The flat, comfortable with a woman's presence. The acid jazz CD playing. Marianne humming as she moved into the bathroom. Dread surged through Church; he didn't want to imagine anymore. But just as it had with the Walpurgis, the images came thick and fast: the gentle click of the front door that Marianne never heard. His heart boomed. The strange smell he now knew was the Caraprix at work on Veitch; the familiar shadow. Veitch slipping through the flat like a shadow, his eyes glassy. The knife glinting in his hand. Her voice, as clear as day: "Church? Is that you?" And then Veitch in like thunder. A merciful blur of limbs and steel and blood . . .

"Ryan . . ." Church felt he was swimming away from the world.

"Then those Fomorii bastards did it too! You didn't even think it through!" Veitch's voice had the shattering pain of a child who had been failed by a parent. "They dragged Tom off and stuck one in his head when we were in those cells under Dartmoor! And I was there first—why shouldn't they have done it to me?"

Church felt sick; he had never considered it for even a moment. He *had* failed him, failed them all.

Laura and Ruth fell back as Balor grew; to Church's warped perception the Beast appeared to be filling the entire room.

Veitch was sobbing now. "The Queen—that witch that screwed Tom—she kicked me out because she found out I was tainted. Useless. Just thrown away. Too much of a loser to fight back. Doing everything they made me do. Useless! A part of me always knew that shit was in my head, and I couldn't tell anybody! Couldn't even tell the part of me that did the thinking!"

There was a noise like metal sheets being torn in two. Behind Balor, a doorway had opened in the air presenting a vista on to shimmering stars hanging in the cold void. Streams of sparkling dust began to drift out of it into Balor; the final power he needed.

"Not fair." Veitch was on his knees, whimpering. "Not fair."

"The gates are open, Ryan. You can stop it." Church felt like he was calling up from the bottom of a well.

"I can't do it. I'm too weak. I've always been too weak."

"No, you're not. You've just got to see yourself. Have faith in yourself."

Veitch shook his head, blood splattering from his nose. He was still fighting it, but his heart wasn't in it; he'd already given up.

Anger flashed across his face. Against his will, he lifted the silver hand to drive it into Church's chest.

A long, low moan emanated from the glowing head of Bran the Blessed. Light flowed from it into Church's mouth, soothing, invigorating; whispers crackled across his head; the god was telling him the secrets of the infinite. A word that was not a word was branded in sapphire letters on his mind. A word of power from a language before language. A symbol that could change reality with a single utterance.

Church fumbled to one side. Caledfwlch jumped into his hand of its own accord. With a tremendous effort, he drove himself up and forward. The Sword punched through Veitch's gut, ripped upwards. For one moment they were locked together, in body and in thought.

Veitch retreated into the depths of his head. In the end he had amounted to nothing; despite all his hopes and dreams, he hadn't wished hard enough. Briefly, his eyes flickered towards Ruth, as beautiful as the first time he had seen her. He remembered them making love in a warm room, recalled the way her hair reminded him of the liquorice sticks he had as a child; the way she made him feel he was more than what he was; the deep peace she had given him in his soul for the first time in his life. Through all the violence and bitterness and despair, he could hold on to that sparkling moment of transcendence.

Life gushed from him; the room grew slowly dim. And then he was in a slow boat drifting to an island off the Welsh coast, watching a mermaid swim in the waters beneath him, seeing her wave at him and smile. And he was lying on the warm ground looking up at tiny, golden figures flitting through the trees on gossamer wings; one of them coming down to see him; to say he wasn't so bad after all.

Life filled with wonder. Moments of peace he could count on one hand.

If only . . . If only . . .

Shavi watched his friend's face grow pale. His heart broke in two. Laura stared, wishing it was her. And Ruth cried gently, tried to catch his eye to give him some affection to take with him, to say he was forgiven his sins; to say he was a good man and a hero. But he didn't see her.

Church saw the despair flare in Veitch's face, saw his dreams shatter and fall into nothing. There was one instant when life flickered in his pupils, an instant later there was nothing. He slumped to the floor, dead.

Church could barely see for his own tears. He was aware of the sucking power of the gate, and Balor rising up, ready to usher in the End of Everything. And it *was* the End; for him.

With the last of his strength, he ran forward. The word of power burst from his throat and the whole of existence turned inside out. Blue Fire leapt from the artefacts to each of the five—including the prone form of Veitch. Tom had been right; there had to be five, the final element in a spell as old as time. The energy rose up in a column in the space amongst them and then rushed towards the Heart of Shadows. For the briefest instant, Balor was drained of every shred of dark power. Church seized the moment. Caledfwlch, known as Excalibur, known as the Sword of Righteousness, drove straight into the Beast. Church saw terror etched on a boy's face, saw a sharp-suited man recoil in horror, saw a general roll his eyes in despair. And still he pressed on, driving Balor back towards the gate.

The effort was too great, but then they passed a certain point and the dreadful vertiginous pull of the beyond took over. The flesh felt like it was being ripped from Church's body. Balor went first, his form compressing as the power was sucked back out of it; and then he was folding becoming nothing, less than a child, less than the enormous black insect he resembled for a fleeting moment, and then he plunged into the gate, blocking its pull briefly.

Church had time to turn. His eyes fell on them one after the other: first Veitch for whom he grieved as if he had lost a brother, and then Shavi, and Laura, as close to his heart as he could imagine. And then Ruth, who *was* his heart.

He was dying, even if the gate didn't have him in its pull. His regrets at doubting Ruth were driven away the moment he looked into her face. All he wanted to remember was the love he saw there, mingled with the terrible pain.

"I'll love you." Ruth was shouting, her voice torn apart by an unbearable grief. "Always, Church. Always."

She loved him, she loved him, she loved him, and it wasn't fair.

She saw his face one final time, just as she remembered that first night under the bridge, filled with decency and honesty and all the best things she had ever wanted in her life. Slowly the haze that swirled at the gate's entrance folded around him. One word drifted back to her: ". . . forever . . ."

And then he was gone.

chapter twenty-one
samhain

Over London, the Fabulous Beasts swooped on heated currents rising from the raging flames that had eradicated any taint of the Fomorii. In their grace and serpentine power, in their glittering like jewels in the setting sun, they were inspirational. Hope and wonder soared with them, and on their backs rode a new age, free of the hated old ways and the tyranny of mundanity. Again, as it once had been, it was a world where anything could happen.

Of the Fomorii there was no sign. Whether they had followed their god into oblivion, or simply retreated, broken-backed, to T'ir n'a n'Og, no one knew, but no trace remained of them in the world. All the places they had made their own burned in the flames of the Fabulous Beasts: the financial district, the Palace of Westminster, Buckingham Palace; and of the black tower that had been the source of their power, nothing at all remained, not even rubble.

Ruth, Shavi, Laura and the Bone Inspector had escaped, carrying the body of Veitch, before the ultimate destructive force of the Fabulous Beasts had been unleashed on the tower; indeed, it had almost been as if the serpents had waited for them to vacate before attacking.

They made their way north through the city, skirting the areas of greatest destruction. For the main the journey passed in a blur; they were in shock, too distraught by the blows that had been inflicted on them to comprehend the scale of their victory. It was a triumph they had never imagined in their wildest dreams, but it didn't feel like one. Occasionally the Tuatha Dé Danann could be glimpsed like flitting golden ghosts, moving out across the land. Survivors, but not victors; that title belonged to humanity, thanks to the Brothers and Sisters of Dragons, and the sacrifice of people who cared.

The Bone Inspector slipped away respectfully while they buried Veitch by torchlight on the heights of Hampstead Heath overlooking the city. None of them really knew what to say; the loss was too acute, the atmosphere of broken dreams too oppressive. As they started to throw the clods of earth back into the hole, Shavi finally broke down.

"Goodbye, my good friend," he said, the tears streaming down his face.

"You brought something to all of us. And you did your best, often despite yourself, and that is more than enough. I will miss you more than you ever could have believed."

And then they were all crying, not just for Veitch, but for all the ones they had lost, and for themselves, who would have to deal with the world left behind and the lack of their friends in it; and none of them tried to hide their tears, not even Laura, who surprised herself with the weight of the emotion pouring out of her.

When all their tears were gone, and the mound of brown earth stood complete and alone in the rolling green, they turned to face the uncertain times ahead.

The night felt subtly different. The lamp of the moon cast a beautiful white light from a sable sky now devoid of storm clouds. The sourness in the air that had arrived with Balor's rebirth was gone, replaced by the aroma of green vegetation in an atmosphere slowly ridding itself of pollution; it smelled like hope.

Beneath the stars, Shavi, Ruth and Laura huddled together around a bonfire against the October chill. The Bone Inspector leaned against his staff and watched the city thoughtfully. They sensed the spirits of the Invisible World were beginning to venture abroad, as they always did on that night that had come to be known as Hallowe'en, yet the small group felt no sense of threat.

"How are you doing?" Laura said to Ruth after a long period of silence, punctuated only by the crackle of the fire. Her voice held a real tenderness that made Ruth even more emotional after their long period of rivalry.

"At the moment I feel dead." Distractedly, she prodded the grass with a stick, before releasing a juddering sigh. "And I know it's going to get worse before it gets better. I know we won . . . I know the whole world benefited . . . but the price we paid seems so high."

Laura tossed more wood on the fire, though it hardly needed it. "You can talk about Church, you know."

"Thanks. Really." Ruth wiped away a stray tear, smiled. "It seems so unfair. Personally, I mean. I'm being selfish here and I know anyone else would tell me to get some perspective—"

"That is not how grief works," Shavi interjected.

"It took us so long to get together," Ruth said, "but when we did I felt happy, truly happy, for the first time in my life. Church was always talking about searching for meaning, and for me that was where I found meaning in my life: in my love for him. Does that sound vomit-inducing?"

"Yes, but keep going. I need to make a space for dinner." Laura's gibe was gentle and Ruth couldn't help laughing.

"It would have been perfect for me if we'd stayed together into old age, and I know it's a childish thing, but sometimes you think that's reason enough for it to keep going. But life has its own plan. I think that's when you know you've grown up—when you can accept you have no control over anything. Church told me the Tuatha Dé Danann believe everything is fluid. I suppose the mind has complete control over everything, and that if you wish hard enough you can change reality. Well, I wished and I wished. And he still hasn't come back to me."

Laura fumbled for her hand and gave it a squeeze. Shavi slipped an arm round her shoulders. Overhead, a shooting star blazed across the heavens, reminding them of other times, when they had been all together.

"All I think now is what would he have wanted me to do," Ruth said. "And the answer's obvious: keep doing the right thing, make the world a better place, ignore what anybody else might tell you. Emotionally, it will be hard for me, for all of us, but that's a good reason for living. Don't you think?"

They all agreed.

"You know, I don't really want to think about this," Laura said, "but, do you reckon he suffered? I mean, he'd been stabbed and all, I know. But that gate he was sucked through—"

"I don't know. But even if he did he would probably say pain is transitory and there are better things to look forward to."

"You believe that?"

"I do. Now. I'll see him again one day, I know it."

Laura remained silent for a long moment, then said, "You know Veitch and me didn't get on. He scared me. But I think the real reason was because we were so alike. Two losers trying to escape the past that held them back. I feel bad that I'm here and he's not."

"Don't feel guilty." Ruth gave her arm a squeeze.

"No, Ryan would not want that." Shavi leaned forward into the firelight. "Ryan did the best he could, but he was a victim, and that is the great tragedy of what happened to him. Under other circumstances, he would have found his redemption, as you did."

"Those bastards took it away from him," Laura said vehemently.

"Exactly. We were all manipulated by higher powers, run ragged and forced to suffer, yet in the end we—humanity—still won. Despite everything inflicted on us. That is our great success."

Ruth watched the sparks flying high in the smoke. "When do you think the Tuatha Dé Danann first stuck that Caraprix in Veitch's head?"

"I do not know," Shavi replied, "but they were manipulating us from the moment we were born. They knew they needed the Brothers and Sisters of

Dragons together ready to free them if the Fomorii ever got the upper hand. And to achieve our destiny we all had to experience death at first hand, so they utilised Veitch to engineer that state. With the Caraprix driving him, he set off on his murderous spree. I wonder how that must have affected him? His conscious mind did not know, but it was there in his subconscious, eating away at him."

"Why Veitch?" Ruth asked. "Why didn't they get you or me to do their dirty work?"

"Because Ryan was perfect for the job. His life already contained violence. He had crossed a barrier that the rest of us would have found hard to deal with."

"So he did exactly what they wanted," Laura said bitterly, "you'd have thought they'd have left him alone after that. But they gave him that silver hand to do Church in at the end."

"That was the faction that didn't want humanity to become a threat," Ruth said. "They were scheming all the time, both the Tuatha Dé Danann and the Fomorii. Plan after plan, manipulation after manipulation. We were like kids in comparison, so trusting."

"It did not do them any good," Shavi said. "In fact, it was their arrogance that did it for them in the end. The Fomorii never saw us as a real threat. They had implanted their own Caraprix in Ryan's head, but it only came into play right at the end when it actually looked like we might stand a chance. If they had set Ryan to pick us off one by one over a period of time, they would have won. But we were just *Fragile Creatures*; beneath their notice."

"That'll teach the bastards," Laura said. "It's like the French Revolution all over again."

Ruth stretched, the aches of the past few days finally coming out. "Liberté, fraternité, égalité."

"Look. What's that?" Laura pointed to a light that suddenly flared brightly in the sea of night.

As they scanned the darkness, their breath caught in their throats, others glimmered faintly across the city. It was such a simple thing, but after so long it seemed like an act of God.

Shavi thought for a moment, then said, "An emergency generator has come on."

They were all silent for a long moment, barely daring to believe what it meant. It was Ruth who gave voice to it: "Technology is working again."

"What's left of it." With a fake dismissive shrug, Laura played up to what they expected of her. "No web, no MP3, no ER. What's the point?"

"Technology and magic, side by side," Shavi mused. "Interesting times lie ahead."

They spent the next half hour talking animatedly about what the coming months would hold as humanity crawled out from the wreckage of society and attempted to make a new life out of the devastation. Power lost, industry destroyed, food distribution ruined, transport in tatters, and how many dead—thousands? Millions? How long would it take them to get even a modicum of organisation up and running again? In the short term the hardship would be intense, but they all agreed there was hope. After all, mankind was now on a new road, one rising to a glorious future.

Eventually they decided to wander away from the fire for a while, to stretch the chill from their legs and be alone with their thoughts. Ruth found herself drawn to a dark copse; even before she had entered the trees she sensed an old magic in the air: a deep musk and the snorting of an animal that was not an animal. Antlers were silhouetted against the moon.

Cernunnos roamed through the undergrowth, his breath steaming. Beyond him, Ruth could see the woman who had haunted her during those early days after the world had changed: at first glance a wizened old hag, then a middle-aged mother, and finally a young woman, filled with vitality and sexuality.

"You called to me," Ruth said. In the branches of the trees above, her owl hooted eerily.

Cernunnos loomed up before her, his power daunting but tempered in that aspect by a subtle gentleness. "You have overcome all challenges, as I knew you would. And now you have reached your blossoming there is no longer any need for my guidance."

"I don't know who I am anymore."

"You are a daughter, not of my flesh, but of my spirit. And a daughter too, of my bright half. You are a guardian of the old ways, a champion of the moon, the sum of all the potential carried in the essence of every woman. Nature will bend before you. The grass will plead for your foot, the air for your lungs."

"Yes, but what does it *mean*? What am I supposed to do now?" Her voice was strained with emotion from the stresses tearing her apart.

Cernunnos snorted once more and prowled amongst the trees as if he was doing a strange, ritual dance. When he returned to her, he said, "You will be a light in the dark, showing the way between old days and new, between summer and winter, day and night, sun and moon, man and woman. Many trials lie ahead. But you will not walk the path alone."

"Who's going to be with me?"

"Let the seasons turn, and take them as you find them."

Ruth thought about this for a moment; she felt strangely comforted that there was some sort of direction planned for her. It would give her something to immerse herself in so she didn't have to think. "But where do I start? Where do I go from here?"

"Let the seasons turn."

"Something will turn up, I suppose. It always does." She made to go, then turned back. "Thank you. For giving me something to believe in. Something . . . more." She couldn't find the words to adequately express the depth of what she had discovered since her change, and so she simply bowed her head and left. She had no doubt she would see him again.

As Ruth walked away, Laura stepped from the shadow of the trees. "She doesn't realise exactly what she can do yet, does she?"

"Do you?" Cernunnos said.

"I have an idea."

"You will watch her? Ensure she overcomes her pain?"

"Yeah, I'll be her shadow," Laura said. "I'll be a friend, and I hope she'll be mine."

"Winter may be approaching, but this is a time for all growing things. The two of you will be needed as the heart of nature begins to beat strongly once more. Through the harsh days before the seeds that have been planted come forth, you will be needed more than ever. Existence has changed in more ways than you can comprehend. There are new rules. Old magic is loose in the land. Nothing will be the way it was." He raised his head to make a strange, throaty call to the moon. "When next you encounter the Golden Ones, they will not be how you recall."

"How will they look?"

Cernunnos ignored her question. "Unchanged for so long, my people have now had change thrust upon them. They, too, must deal with the new rules."

"There's certainly going to be a lot of bad blood amongst them. This whole business has split them in two. Will you all go back to Otherworld?"

"Some. Others will retreat to their Courts to lick their wounds. A few will remain abroad in the Fixed Lands. The success of the Fragile Creatures will have consequences even the Golden Ones cannot foresee. We will no longer see this land as our territory."

"I bet a few of you are going to hate us for what happened. There'll be trouble. And how are we going to cope with all the other crazy stuff that came out of Otherworld? That'll still hang around—the Fabulous Beasts and the Redcaps and the Baobhan Sith and all the rest of the shit."

"The Fragile Creatures are a resilient breed."

"Not so fragile, eh?" She looked up at the owl as it beat a path towards Ruth. "So Ruth and I have got our work cut out. We'll be a good team. I've got the mouth and the looks, and she . . ." Laura was surprised at how excited she was about the prospect of what lay ahead, an opportunity to do the kind of good she always dreamed of doing ". . . she'll be the best there is."

"So you're some big-shot shaman?" The Bone Inspector leaned on his staff, examining the theatre of stars. His burned hands miraculously appeared to be healing.

"So they say." Shavi was smiling in the dark at his side. He liked the Bone Inspector; all his curmudgeonly ways and his difficulty with human relationships only added to his appeal.

"I've heard lots of people say that. They couldn't do anything."

"Hmm."

"At least you haven't got a big head like some of your associates." He fiddled with his staff uncomfortably. "Do you know what you're going to be doing after this night?"

"Not yet. Travelling, I suppose. Seeing how the landscape now lies. Finding out what I can do."

"I could offer you a position."

"Oh?"

"You've heard talk of the Culture?" Shavi said he had. "The Culture were the original wise people. In society from the earliest days, from when man had just a few sticks to hack out a life, I reckon. The Egyptians sailed to these shores for guidance from us about the pyramids. The Celts revered us. We knew all the lore of the land, how animals and birds acted, trees and plants grew. We knew about the stars and the planets. The spirit fire. We knew *everything*. And then the damn Romans came. Slaughtered some, drove the rest underground where we couldn't do the job that we were meant to do. The colleges at Glastonbury and Anglesey were destroyed. It was hard to pass on the knowledge. And then, thanks to that God-awful Age of Reason, the Culture gradually died out."

"And you are the last," Shavi said.

"Now wouldn't it be a shame for all that thousands of years of knowledge to die out with me?"

"What are you suggesting?"

"The land needs the Culture. The people need the Culture—especially now when they need to learn a new way of living to cope with what it's going to be like out there." He faced Shavi, his eyes sparkling. "I want to start the colleges up again, pass on all the knowledge I've got before I'm gone. Build a new Culture."

"And you want me to help?"

"I want you to be the first to learn. And then I want you to help me pass it on. Maybe set up at Glastonbury, I don't know. What do you say?"

Shavi's face was so serious as he considered the offer that the Bone Inspector was convinced he was going to refuse. But then a warm smile crept across his face. "I think that would be an excellent idea."

When they returned to the fire, thoughts of what lay ahead were put to one side, and once more they were old friends enjoying each other's company. They remembered the ones they had lost and thought about the times they had spent together, and they cried a little. But as good friends should, they helped each other along the rocky path, and after a while they even found the strength to laugh.

Lying back beneath the sweep of stars, there was some sadness that they would soon be going their separate ways. But though they might not meet again, they would never forget all that they had shared, and everything they had learned: in the midst of hardship they had discovered the best that life had to offer, both in the world, and in themselves.

And though there were undoubtedly hard days ahead, they had been forged in the worst of times, and with hope and optimism in their hearts, the road would always rise before them.

Church woke on a hard, cold floor surrounded by the smell of wood smoke. A deep ache suffused his limbs, though slowly fading; his stomach turned queasily. Strange dreams had paraded through his head, of people in dark suits and army green, but the last vibrant thoughts he had were of the dying light in poor, tormented Veitch's eyes, of the desperate love in Ruth's face, and of plunging into nothingness in the company of a deep shadow. He was still clutching Caledfwlch tightly. His free hand moved to his side where Veitch had torn him open, but there was no blood, no wound. It made no sense.

He levered himself up to see he was in a dark, round room constructed from wood. The only light came from a fire smouldering in the centre, the smoke drifting up to disappear through a hole in the turf roof. It was undeniably primitive, filled with the aromas of animals and damp vegetation.

His thoughts careered. Where were the others? Where was Balor? As his eyes grew accustomed to the dark, he realised with a start that he was not alone.

Jumping to his feet anxiously prompted a shriek from the dark shapes huddling across the other side of the room.

Moving past the fire, he could see a woman was protecting her two children. She had long dark hair that framed a face hardened by harsh living. The children, a boy and a girl of around seven or eight, had the same dark hair and eyes. They were all terrified.

"Don't worry. I won't hurt you," he said gently, but his voice only agitated them further.

The woman jabbered in a language he didn't understand until he caught one word: *Samhain.*

As he repeated it, the woman froze, her eyes widening. "Samhain," she said again.

And then the elements began to fall into place: the house, the basic peasant clothes of the woman and children, the language. Somehow the gate had flung him into the distant past, amongst one of the tribes that modern scholars had lumped together under the catch-all title of Celts.

He closed his eyes and rested on his sword as he fought the rising panic. His first thought was that it couldn't be true, but everything he saw, heard, smelled, told him otherwise. Then the impressions came thick and fast: isolation, utter loneliness amongst people who would consider him an alien or a madman, the brutality of life in those times, of Ruth, whom he would never see again, of his friends, and his world. Slowly, he went down on to his knees, unable to bear the weight.

His torment was disturbed by the woman gradually advancing. She pointed tentatively. "Nuada?"

She was indicating the Sword. He held it up, nodding. "Nuada Aigetlámh." It was the god's sword; of course she would be familiar with it.

She suddenly pointed towards the open door and jabbered once more, excitedly this time. There was little else for him to do but follow her direction.

Outside, a wild electrical storm lit up other roundhouses clustered nearby. Frightened horses and cattle added to the deafening cannon-fire of thunder. A terrible wind tore across the landscape, though there wasn't even the faintest hint of rain; in the gale was the familiar stink of corruption that had surrounded Balor.

He looked round, overcome with the strangest impression someone familiar had only just left the vicinity. Despite the grinding sense of disconnection, he felt uncannily good, and he knew why. His deep perception showed him the Blue Fire was stronger in the land, and the buildings and the animals than he had ever seen it before. That was why the wound in his side had healed. As a Brother of Dragons he had tapped into it.

And with that realisation came another thought: he recalled Tom telling him there were no coincidences, no accidents. Then why had he been saved? There was no obvious answer, but he had the strangest feeling that somebody had wanted it to happen for him.

As he tried to decide what his next move would be, he became aware of a faint golden glow approaching across the dark, storm-torn countryside. It was Niamh. His shock was palpable until he accepted this was long before she had sacrificed herself to save them all.

She came up to him sharply, an unfamiliar contemptuous expression inscribed on her face. "Fragile Creature!" Her words were the arrogant bark of someone used to complete deference. "Is that the Sword of my brother?" As always, he understood her words in a way that transcended language.

It was intriguing to see the difference in her. Here she was more like the worst of her kind, cold and aloof with a hint of cruelty. "It was once. It's my Sword now."

Fury tinged her features. "How can a Fragile Creature dare to touch so powerful an object? How can you dare to take it from my brother, and now, when he needs it most?"

"I'm a Brother of Dragons."

This puzzled her a little. "I have not seen you amongst that dismal brood."

His spine prickled as connections began to be made. "What's happening?" he asked, listening to the noise that was almost masked by the storm.

"You do not know? It is the Second Battle of Magh Tuireadh. This night the future of the Golden Ones will be decided, when the Night Walkers are finally driven into the sea after their bitter rule."

"And the future of the Fragile Creatures," he added wryly.

She didn't deem his comment worthy of any acknowledgment.

And then everything fell into place, with a *frisson* that was so acute it shocked him. The mysterious comments that he would not find rest at the end of his struggle. The hints that he had a wider role to play in leading humanity towards the next level. Tom telling him to use his memories as a source of warmth in troubling times.

He steeled himself, letting the obligation settle into his bones. Then he said: "Take me to the battle."

"You mean to fight?"

"I intend to do what I can. And to be there when Balor is finally destroyed."

She appeared quite taken aback by his bravado; a little warmth broke into her frosty features.

"My name's Jack." His heart was already soaring as he realised the solution to his predicament. "I think we're going to become good friends."

"Friends? With a Fragile Creature?" she snorted.

After the battle he would return to the home of the gods T'ir n'a n'Og, where time could pass much slower than it did in the real world. And while he aged only slightly, the centuries would tumble by in a mad parade until he could once again step back into the world to take Ruth in his arms and meet their future together. The paradox made his head spin. For a while he would exist in two places at once: in the *real* world, where he would be born and grow to maturity; and in Otherworld, waiting for the culmination of the confrontation with Balor so he could step back into the Fixed Lands to reclaim his life. Could he sit idly by in Otherworld, knowing the suffering that would be inflicted on humanity during the Age of Misrule? Could he wait there when he might be able to save Veitch's life? Or would he cross over earlier, to meet his younger self and change the course of history? Was that at all possible, or would existence come crashing down around his ears? It was a conundrum that would have to wait.

Now he knew why Niamh had appeared in his childhood bedroom, guiding him along the path he had eventually walked, why she had been filled with such a deep love that had made no sense for the little time they had known each other. Between now and then, they *would* become friends, and he would bring humanity to her, and she would in turn convince other members of the Tuatha Dé Danann to come over to the Fragile Creatures, something that would have such great import so many years down the line. And eventually, although he would aim to prevent it, she would learn to fall in love with him.

In the meantime he had so many things to do: establishing the reputation of the Brothers and Sisters of Dragons, convincing them to prepare for the return of the Fomorii, ensuring the first steps were taken on the path to godhood.

And then one other thought came to him that filled him with warmth. In just a few brief centuries' time he would see Tom again. Tom, who had kept so many secrets, hidden his character and his emotions for the sake of those around him. They would become the best of friends and he would finally pay the Rhymer back for saving his life.

"Come on," he said to Niamh, "let's go to war."

His one hope was that the world he eventually returned to would not have been bequeathed to the worst of humanity; that the old, bad ways had simply slotted back into place. "I'm wishing," he whispered aloud, his eyes closed. "I'm wishing for a place where the good things have the upper hand: love and honesty and friendship and wonder and hope. I'm wishing enough to change the world."

In a bleak room filled with hard men, a cold wind blew. For as long as anyone could remember they had dreamed the world their way; and it was a world filled with lies and power and money, of subtle manipulation and limpid promises, where *Fragile Creatures* were held in place by a little of this and a little of that, but never anything that mattered. Yet beneath their arrogance lay fear, for sooner or later the scales might fall.

A lie was needed to cement their rule. A Big Lie. Lives were shattered in the telling of it, families torn apart, good men and women twisted out of shape. But the hard men were right to be afraid, for even in the worst of all worlds, good men and women aspire; and inspire.

With that same arrogance, the hard men believed no one could be moved by a world without money or power; dreams were for children; dreams had no power. And so they released the means to their downfall. The Lie proved more seductive than the world they had wished; it was filled with love and wonder and friendship and hope and faith; and meaning; a world where anything could happen.

A wish was all it took; because if you wish hard enough you can change the world.

The Lie became the Truth, and everything that hadn't happened, had happened. Five people quested through untold hardship; they plumbed worlds beyond imagination, rubbed shoulders with gods and beasts; and in the end brought the magic back home.

This is how it was, and is, and will be.

The cold wind blew the bad things right away. The hard men no longer existed. The hard men never existed. Their world was just a bad dream; and only bad dreams have no power.

The Blue Fire is in everything.

And the world turns slowly towards the light.

bibliography

Baigent, Michael, Richard Leigh, and Henry Lincoln. *The Messianic Legacy* (Corgi)
Bently, Peter (ed.). *The Mystic Dawn: Celtic Europe* (Time-Life)
Bord, Janet and Colin. *Mysterious Britain* (Thorsons)
Briggs, Katharine. *An Encyclopedia of Fairies* (Penguin)
Brydon, Robert. *Rosslyn—A History of the Guilds, the Masons and the Rosy Cross* (Rosslyn Chapel Trust)
Bulfinch. *Bulfinch's Mythology* (Spring)
Bushell, Rev. William Done. *Caldey: An Island of the Saints* (Lewis Printers)
Campbell, Harry. *Supernatural Scotland* (HarperCollins)
Carr-Gomm, Philip. *The Druid Way* (Element)
Celtic Mythology (Geddes & Grosset)
Coghlan, Ronan. *The Encyclopedia of Arthurian Legends* (Element)
Cope, Julian. *The Modern Antiquarian* (Thorsons)
Cotterell, Arthur. *Celtic Mythology* (Ultimate Editions)
Crisp, Roger. *Ley Lines of Wessex* (Wessex Books)
Crossing, William. *Folklore and Legends of Dartmoor* (Forest Publishing)
Davies, Margaret. *The Story of Tenby* (Tenby Museum)
Dunning, R. W. *Arthur: The King in the West* (Grange Books)
Earl of Rosslyn. *Rosslyn Chapel* (Rosslyn Chapel Trust)
Fitzpatrick, Jim. *The Book of Conquests* (Paper Tiger)
Graves, Robert. *The White Goddess* (Faber & Faber Ltd.)
Hadingham, Evan. *Circles and Standing Stones* (William Heinemann Ltd.)
Hardcastle, F. *The Chalice Well* (The Chalice Well Trust)
Hicks, Jim (ed.). *Earth Energies* (Time Life)
———. *Witches and Witchcraft* (Time Life)
Hopkins, Jerry, and Danny Sugerman. *No One Here Gets Out Alive* (Plexus)
Kindred, Glennie. *The Earth's Cycle of Celebration* (Self-published)
Knight, Christopher, and Robert Lomas. *The Hiram Key* (Century)
———. *The Second Messiah* (Arrow)
Lamont-Brown, Raymond. *Scottish Superstitions* (Chambers)
Larousse. *The Larousse Encyclopedia of Mythology*

Mann, Nicholas R. *The Isle of Avalon* (Llewellyn Publications, USA)
Matthews, John (ed.). *The Druid Source Book* (Brockhampton Press)
Matthews, John, and Michael J. Stead. *King Arthur's Britain: A Photographic Odyssey* (Brockhampton Press)
Michell, John. *New Light on the Ancient Mystery of Glastonbury* (Gothic Image)
———. *Sacred England* (Gothic Image)
Miller, Hamish, and Paul Broadhurst. *The Sun and the Serpent* (Pendragon Press)
Porter, Roy. *London: A Social History* (Hamish Hamilton)
Radford, Roy and Ursula. *West Country Folklore* (Peninsula Press)
Richards, Julian. *Beyond Stonehenge* (Trust for Wessex Archaeology)
Rutherford, Ward. *Celtic Mythology* (Thorsons)
Seafield, Lily. *Scottish Ghosts* (Lomond Books)
Siefker, Phyllis. *Santa Claus, Last of the Wild Men* (McFarland & Company, Inc.)
St. Leger-Gordon, Ruth E. *The Witchcraft and Folklore of Dartmoor* (Peninsula Press)
Stewart, Bob, and John Matthews. *Legendary Britain* (Blandford)
Stewart, R. J. *Celtic Gods, Celtic Goddesses* (Blandford)
Tabraham, Chris (ed.). *Edinburgh Castle* (Historic Scotland)
———. *Urquhart Castle* (Historic Scotland)
Various. *Folklore, Myths and Legends of Britain* (Reader's Digest)
Westhorp, Christopher (ed.). *Journeys through Dreamtime* (Time Life)
White, Richard (ed.). *King Arthur in Legend and History* (Dent)
Wilde, Lady. *Ancient Legends of Ireland* (Ward & Downey)
Zink, David D. *The Ancient Stones Speak* (Paddington Press)

Many online resources were a valuable source of reference. Since my research, some have closed, the ones remaining are:

Celtic Deities and Myth—*www.eliki.com/ancient/myth/celts/*
Kaleidoscope—Celtic Mythology—*www.softanswer.com/hans/celtic/mythology.html*
Knights Templar—*www.brjeffreys.freeserve.co.uk/knights/knights.htm*
Knights Templar Index—*http://homepages.enterprise.net/paulmagoo/index.htm*
London Underground History—*www.starfury.demon.co.uk/uground/*
The Megalith Map—*www.megalith.ukf.net/bigmap.htm*
Mythology—*www.exotique.com/fringe/mythology.htm*
Neopagan—*www.neopagan.net*
The Official Rosslyn Chapel Site—*www.rosslynchapel.org.uk*

I am indebted to all of the people behind them.

about the author

A two-time winner of the prestigious British Fantasy Award, Mark Chadbourn has published his epic, imaginative novels in many countries around the world. He grew up in the mining community of the English Midlands, and was the first person in his family to go to university. After studying Economic History at Leeds, he became a successful journalist, writing for several of the UK's renowned national newspapers as well as contributing to magazines and TV.

When his first short story won *Fear* magazine's Best New Author award, he was snapped up by an agent and subsequently published his first novel, *Underground*, a supernatural thriller set in the coalfields of his youth. Quitting journalism to become a full-time author, he has written stories which have transcended genre boundaries, but is perhaps best known in the fantasy field.

Mark has also forged a parallel career as a screenwriter with many hours of produced work for British television. He is a senior writer for BBC Drama and is also developing new shows for the UK and US.

An expert on British folklore and mythology, he has held several varied and colourful jobs, including independent record company boss, band manager, production line worker, engineer's "mate," and media consultant.

Having traveled extensively around the world, he has now settled in a rambling house in the middle of a forest not far from where he was born.

For information about the author and his work:

www.markchadbourn.net
www.jackofravens.com
www.myspace.com/markchadbourn